GUARDED SECRETS

**B.J.
DANIELS**

**MARIE
FERRARELLA**

**ELLE
JAMES**

MILLS & BOON

CONTENTS

Cold Case At Cardwell Ranch

B.J. Daniels

B.J. Daniels is a *New York Times* and *USA TODAY* bestselling author. She wrote her first book after a career as an award-winning newspaper journalist and author of thirty-seven published short stories. She lives in Montana with her husband, Parker, and three springer spaniels. When not writing, she quilts, boats and plays tennis. Contact her at bjdaniels.com, on Facebook or on Twitter, @bjdanielsauthor.

Books by B.J. Daniels

Harlequin Intrigue

Cardwell Ranch: Montana Legacy

Steel Resolve
Iron Will
Ambush Before Sunrise
Double Action Deputy
Trouble in Big Timber
Cold Case at Cardwell Ranch

Whitehorse, Montana: The Clementine Sisters

Hard Rustler
Rogue Gunslinger
Rugged Defender

Visit the Author Profile page at millsandboon.com.au.

This book is dedicated to all the cowgirls out there.

CAST OF CHARACTERS

Ella Cardwell—The cowgirl is capable of anything—even solving a murder.

Waco Johnson—The bones in the bottom of the well lead the cold-case detective straight to the Cardwell Ranch and a woman he wasn't expecting.

Stacy Cardwell—She's a woman with a lot of secrets, but is murder one of them?

Jeremiah Cardwell—He was born with a target on his back.

Marvin Hanover—The old man used money and mortal threats to rule his family until someone ended him.

Lionel Hanover—He's tried to save the family even without their father's hidden money.

Angeline Hanover—Will she live long enough to enjoy her father's money if it is ever found?

Mercy Hanover—She's never denied it. All she wants is the money.

Dana Cardwell—She just wants her family home and together.

Hud Cardwell—The marshal knows it's time to retire. Right after this case.

Chapter One

The wind whipped around him, kicking up dust and threatening to send his Stetson flying. Cold-case detective Waco Johnson cautiously approached the weatherworn boards that had blown off the opening of the old abandoned well.

The Montana landscape was riddled with places like this one, abandoned homesteads slowly disappearing along with those who had worked this land.

He hesitated a few feet from the hole, feeling a chill even on this warm Montana summer afternoon. Nearby, overgrown weeds and bushes enveloped the original homestead dwelling, choking off any light. Only one blank dusty window peered out at him from the dark gloom inside. Closer, pine trees swayed, boughs emitting a lonely moan as they cast long, jittery shadows over the century-old cemetery with its sun-bleached stone markers on the rise next to the house. A rusted metal gate creaked restlessly in the wind, a grating sound that made his teeth ache.

It added to his anxiety about what he was about to find. Or why being here nudged at a memory he couldn't quite grasp.

He glanced toward the shadowed gaping hole of the old well for a moment before pulling his flashlight from his coat pocket and edging closer.

The weathered boards that had once covered the opening had

rotted away over time. Weeds had grown up around the base. He could see where someone had trampled the growth at one edge to look inside. The anonymous caller who'd reported seeing something at the bottom of the well? That begged the question: How had the caller even seen the abandoned well's opening, given the overgrowth?

Waco knelt at the rim and peered into the blackness below. As the beam of his flashlight swept across the dust-dried well bottom, his pulse kicked up a beat. Bones. Animals, he knew, frequently fell into wells on abandoned homesteads. More often than not, it was their bones that dotted the rocky dry bottom.

Shielding his eyes from the swirling dust storm, Waco leaned farther over the opening. The wind howled around him, but he hardly heard or felt it as his flashlight's beam moved slowly over the bottom of the well—and stopped short.

A human skull.

He rocked back on his haunches, pulled out his phone and made the call. The bones were definitely human, just as the anonymous caller had said. How long had the remains been down there? No way to tell until he could get the coroner involved. He made another call, this one to the state medical examiner's office, as a dust devil whirled across the desolate landscape toward him.

He tugged the brim of his Stetson down against the blowing dirt, and Waco's gaze skimmed the wind-scoured hillside as his mind raced. That darn memory teased at him until it finally wedged its way into his thoughts.

He felt a chill as he remembered. His grandfather, an old-timey marshal, had told him a story about remains being found in an abandoned well on a homestead in the Gallatin Canyon near Big Sky. Waco couldn't remember specifics, except that it had been a murder and it had been on the Cardwell property, one of the more well-known ranches in the canyon.

While more than fifty miles from where Waco was now standing, and a good fifteen years ago, he found it interesting that another body had gone into a well. He rubbed the back of his neck. There was always something eerie about abandoned homesteads—even when there weren't human remains lying at the bottom of an old well. But right now, he felt a little spooked even as he told himself there couldn't be any connection between the two cases.

Standing, he walked back to his patrol SUV and slipped in behind the wheel and out of the wind. Taking out his phone again, he called up the Cardwell Ranch case. The story had gone national, so there was an abundance of information online. As he read through the stories, he felt a familiar prickling at the nape of his neck.

Waco didn't know how much time had passed when he looked up to see a Division of Criminal Investigation van tear up the dirt road toward him. Behind it, storm clouds blackened the horizon. This part of Montana felt as far away from civilization as he could get. But in truth, it was only a few miles north of the Gallatin Valley and the city of Bozeman, one of the fastest-growing areas of the state.

He liked that there were still places that time seemed to have forgotten in Montana. Places where a person could spend a day without seeing another person. Places developers hadn't yet discovered. Waco often found himself in those places because that was where a person could get rid of a body.

As the DCI van pulled up next to his SUV, he climbed out and felt that familiar prickling again.

His instincts told him that the person in the bottom of this particular well hadn't accidentally fallen in. If he didn't have an old murder case on his hands, then his name wasn't Waco Johnson.

Chapter Two

Ella Cardwell sat at the large kitchen table in the main house on Cardwell Ranch as she had done for almost thirty years. She tried to listen to her mother and aunt Dana discuss the ranch garden and what they would be canning over the next few weeks.

But a tomboy who preferred being outside with the critters, Ella had never been interested in what went on inside the ranch house. Since college, she'd made her living wrangling with her cousins, Brick and Angus. Until recently. Both had fallen in love and settled down, leaving her at loose ends.

She'd returned to the ranch, where there was always plenty of work to be done, and moved into one of the small cabins on the mountain overlooking the spread. This morning she was waiting for her cousin to pick her up. The two were driving south to buy a new bull—and Angus was late.

Ella noticed that her mother didn't seem to be paying any more attention to the canning plan than she was. Stacy Cardwell was staring out the kitchen window, as if a world away.

It was a look Ella had seen all her life. Her mother had secrets. Even at a young age, Ella'd sensed something dark in her mother's past. When she was older, Ella had tried to get her to talk about it. But Stacy had always brushed off her concerns and questions, denying anything had ever been wrong.

Her mother had brought her to Cardwell Ranch when she was a baby. Ella had never known her father. The ranch and her extended family were all she'd ever known. Over the years, her mother had occasional relationships with a man, but none that had led to marriage. Not that Stacy hadn't been married before. Her mother's apparent wild years weren't something the family talked about.

Just as they didn't talk about Stacy's disappearances for days at a time. No one knew where she went or why she'd left. Aunt Dana always said that Stacy just needed to get away sometimes.

"Not away from you, Ella," her aunt would say and hug her. "You're my sister's world. But we all need to escape once in a while." Except that Aunt Dana never had run away from the ranch or her children.

Ella suspected that her mother was feeling restless again. She'd always sensed it long before it happened. She knew what it meant. Stacy was about to disappear, never warning anyone or even telling Ella where she'd been once she eventually returned.

"Ella?"

She realized Aunt Dana had asked her something. "Sorry?"

Her aunt smiled. "I just heard Angus honk. He must be anxious to go pick up that bull. Didn't you say you were going with him?"

She shot up from the table, nearly tipping over her coffee cup.

"I'll take care of that. You better get going." Dana laughed. "Have fun."

Ella shot a look at her mother, wondering if she would be there when Ella got back. After a lifetime of worrying about her mother and her dark secrets, she reminded herself that Stacy had always come back. Why would this time be any different?

AT LOOSE ENDS waiting to hear something from the DCI investigators, Waco headed for Gallatin Gateway at the mouth of the canyon. "Gateway," as the locals had called it since 1917, had gotten its name from the Milwaukee Railroad when the town had become an entryway to Yellowstone Park.

The anonymous call about the bones in the well had come from a phone at the local bar in the town. It had been bothering Waco that the caller had refused to give a name. That brought up even more questions about how the person had happened to just stumble upon the bones in the well and recognized them as human remains. It made him think that maybe the caller had known the body was down there. Otherwise, why not leave a name?

Waco had listened to the recorded 9-1-1 call. The voice had been so well muffled that it had been difficult to tell if the caller had been male or female. The call had been short and to the point, a lot of bar noise in the background. "I saw some human bones in an old well on the Hanover place near Maudlow." That was the extent of it. The operator had tried to get a name but the caller'd disconnected. When she'd called back, no one seemed to know who had used the bar's landline because it was Saturday night and the place had been packed.

Waco drove into the small community originally started by the family who owned the sawmill, and parked in front of the bar. While there was a school, a bar, and at one time a service station and a place that made cheese, Gateway had never really taken off.

He entered the dimly lit tavern and talked to the bartender. He learned that there were two landline phones on the premises—one behind the bar, the other in the office at the back. No, the office wasn't normally locked during business hours. No, the bartender couldn't remember if anyone had used the phone behind the bar.

Leaving with the names of the servers who'd been working that night, Waco was driving back to Bozeman when he got the call from the state medical examiner telling him to come to the morgue.

He'd wanted the best, so he'd asked for Henrietta "Hitch" Roberts the moment he'd seen the skull at the bottom of the well. He'd worked with her before on a lot of the cold cases in rural areas that barely had a coroner, let alone a medical examiner. It just surprised him that she'd arrived so quickly—not that she'd gone right to work. That was Hitch.

As he walked into the Gallatin County morgue, she shot him a narrowed green-eyed look.

"I hope you don't mind that I asked for you," he said, holding up his hands as if in surrender. "And, yes, I did pull a few strings to get you. But I should have known, after your last rough case and what's going on with your personal life, that maybe you weren't up to this one."

Hitch laughed and shook her head. "You aren't really using reverse psychology on me, are you, Waco?"

"If that didn't work, I was not above using flattery if necessary," he answered tongue in cheek. "Seriously, Hitch, I need you on this one. But I don't want to put you in a spot with your new family." He paused briefly before getting right to the point. "DCI drop off everything from the well?"

"As soon as I got the call, I went out to the site to have a look for myself. But, yes, they delivered the obvious pieces of evidence. They are still sorting through the dirt and debris, but the main discoveries are here. Lucky for you, I've already found something that might interest you."

"Great." He nodded at the large, beautiful diamond engagement ring on her finger. "By the way, when is the wedding?" He'd heard that she was engaged to Ford Cardwell, a cousin of the Cardwell Ranch Cardwells. Soon they would be her new family.

"Christmas."

"Good for you. You seem happy."

"I am. Now, do you want to hear about what I've discovered?"

He chuckled. "Marriage isn't going to change you, is it?"

That was another thing Waco loved about working with Hitch. Once she got her teeth into a case, she didn't let go until she got answers. Waco was the same way, so it was no wonder the two of them worked well together.

He took a breath and stepped deeper into the room. With his job, he'd become familiar with a lot of morgues around the state. They all had that sterilized smell with just enough of some underlying scent to make most people queasy. Not that it seemed to bother Hitch as she motioned him over to a long metal table covered with human bones.

There was no one quite like Hitch, he thought as he watched her pick up the skull in her gloved hands and inspect it for a moment. Hitch was a petite brunette with keen green eyes. Her long curly hair was pulled into its usual bun at the base of her neck. It occurred to Waco that he'd never seen her wear her hair down on the job. Because, he knew, like always, her focus was on her work, not her physical attributes. This was a woman who loved what she did and it showed.

"You said there is something interesting about this one?" Waco asked anxiously. He needed to know if his instincts were right. If so, he had a killer to catch and enough time had already been lost. He suspected that whoever's bones these were had possibly died years ago. Not that the "when" concerned him as much as the fact that someone might have gotten away with murder all this time.

"Patience, grasshopper," Hitch said and went into medical-examiner mode. "The remains are male, midfifties," she said, carefully setting down the skull and picking up a leg bone. "Average height, six-one. Average weight, one eighty-five. Walked with a slight limp," she noted. "An old tibia break that didn't heal right, which tells me he didn't have it properly seen to by a doctor for whatever reason. He wore glasses, nearsighted." She looked up as if anticipating his surprise. "The glasses were found in the bottom of the well. Black plastic, no-nonsense frames."

"Nice job. Now just give me a cause of death."

Hitch shook her head. "You'd love a bullet hole in the skull, wouldn't you? Even better, an old pistol that had been tossed into the well after him?"

Waco admitted that he would. "So what are you telling me? This guy just stumbled into the well, died, and that was that?" he asked, wondering why she'd said there was something interesting. More to the point, why he'd been so sure it had been a homicide.

"It could have been an accident," Hitch said. "Just not in this case. If you look at the lower cranium—"

"Remember, speak English."

She smiled. "What I'm saying is that someone bashed him in the back of the head." She picked up the skull again and turned it under the overhead lamplight. "See these tiny fractures?"

Waco nodded. "Couldn't those have been caused by the fall into the well?"

Hitch was shaking her head. "If it had been any other part of the skull, maybe. But not this low, just above the spine. This man was hit with something that made a distinct pattern in the fracture."

"Something like what? A chunk of wood?"

"Something more narrow. More like a tire iron."

"Was it enough to kill him?"

Hitch gave him an impatient look.

"Wait—are you saying he didn't die right away?"

"If the blow didn't kill him eventually, then the fall into the well and being trapped down there certainly would have," she said. "But he was alive for a period of time before he succumbed to his injuries."

Waco rubbed his neck, the prickles stretching across his shoulders and down his arms. "So someone hit him with an object like a tire iron in the low part of the back of his skull, then knocked him into the well."

"It's one theory."

"Well, we know that they didn't go for help." He thought again of the Cardwell Ranch case. "Any idea how long he's been in the well?"

"I'd say just over thirty years."

"You can call it that close?" Hitch only smiled at him. "Any way to get DNA to identify the remains?" he asked.

"With bones that old, probably not. But, fortunately, we don't have to." Hitch reached into a plastic bag and pulled out something brown, dried and shriveled. For a moment, Waco thought it was a dead animal. "He had this leather wallet on him when he went into the well." The ME grinned. "Inside, I found his Montana state-issued driver's license tucked in a plastic sleeve. Luckily the well was dry. Even the money in his wallet is intact."

"You're enjoying dragging this out, aren't you," he said, understanding how Hitch had been so certain about his age and weight and the rest.

"His name is Marvin Hanover, and if the wedding ring found at the site is any indication, he was married." Hitch produced another plastic bag. "The ring's engraved. 'With all my love, Stacy.'"

"Stacy?"

Hitch gave him a look he'd come to know well. "Stacy is also the name Marvin carved into a sandstone rock at the bottom of the well before he died."

Waco was about to let out an expletive before he caught himself. *"He named his killer?"*

"Or he planned to leave her a message and didn't live long enough to write it." She handed him a photo taken at the bottom of the well by a crime-scene tech. It showed the crudely carved

Stacy followed by smaller letters that hadn't been dug as deep in the stone.

Waco stared at the photo. "It looks like *Stacy don't...* But 'Stacy don't' what?"

"'Don't forget me'?" Hitch suggested.

"Or how about 'don't leave me here'?" Waco said.

"What makes this case interesting, and also a problem as far as my being involved, is that Stacy *Cardwell* Hanover was still married to him when Marvin disappeared and—I suspect—went into the well. Coincidentally, as you know, I'm about to marry into the Cardwell family."

Waco stared at her, goose bumps rippling over his skin. "Stacy..." He could hardly speak. "So there is a connection."

"I already checked. She wasn't living on the ranch at the time her husband disappeared," Hitch said. "I looked up the date of their marriage."

"So did I," he said. "The marriage took place before the body was found in the well at Cardwell Ranch. So she would have known about that case. Three months later, Stacy reported her husband missing. She and her brothers were in a legal battle over the Cardwell Ranch at the time."

Hitch nodded. "So she would have known about the body in the well on the old Cardwell homestead." The remains of a young woman had been found at the bottom of the well. She'd been shot in the head, but apparently only wounded. She'd tried to scratch her way out after being left there to die.

Waco swore under his breath. No wonder the case had stuck in his mind after his grandfather had told him about it.

"Don't tell him those stories," his mother had chastised her father at the time. "You'll give him nightmares—or, worse, he'll grow up and want to be like you."

He hadn't gotten nightmares, but he had grown up to become a lawman. It was his grandfather's stories that he hadn't been able to forget. Waco's love of history had proved to be effective at solving cold cases. He partly put it down to his good memory skills when it came to crimes. That and his inability to give up on something once he felt that prickling on the back of his neck.

He still couldn't believe it. The cases had felt similar, but damn if there wasn't a connection between them—just not the one he'd expected. "I'm sorry for bringing you in on this case," he said to Hitch. "I figured it might be a copycat 'body dump in an old well' kind of case. I had no idea it might involve someone from your future family."

"Stacy is my fiancé's father's cousin. I've barely met her, so I'm not worried. I can notify the family for you or do anything else you need done. If it gets too close to home, I'll bow out."

He nodded. "Sorry." He could tell she'd hate to have to walk away from this one.

"It sounds like it could turn into a really interesting case."

"What can you tell me about Stacy?"

She shrugged. "She's been living on the ranch since her daughter, Ella, was born—almost twenty-seven years now," Hitch said. "She doesn't have a record, and from what I know, she babysat all the Cardwell-Savage kids. She now helps with the cooking, canning and gardening. Not really murderer material."

"You know that's not an indication," he said.

"I know, but just because there was a similar case on the family ranch doesn't mean she did this. That old case got a lot of media attention. It could have given anyone the idea."

Hitch was clutching at straws and they both knew it as he pulled out his phone and called the ranch. He couldn't wait to talk to Stacy Cardwell, the former Mrs. Marvin Hanover.

EARLY THE NEXT MORNING, Ella buttoned her jean jacket as she left her cabin on the mountainside overlooking the main ranch house. She stopped on her large porch overlooking the ranch. She and Angus had gotten back late from picking up the new bull. All the lights had been out, including her mother's, so while she hadn't been tired, she'd gone up to her cabin alone and read late into the night.

This morning she'd awakened to sunshine and the scent of pine coming in her open window. The early Montana summer day still had a bite to it this deep in the Gallatin Canyon, though, not that she noticed. She'd awakened to birds singing—but also a bad feeling that she'd had since yesterday.

She needed to check on the new foal before heading to the

main house for breakfast with Aunt Dana and her mother. The two should be busy at work canning by now. Yet she'd stopped on the porch to look out across the valley, trying to shake the anxious feeling that her mother hadn't shown up to can this morning.

As she headed for her mother's cabin through the shimmering pines, Ella caught glimpses of Big Sky in the distance. The resort town would soon be busting at the seams with tourists for the summer season. She'd noticed that traffic along Highway 191 had already picked up. Locals joked that the area had only two seasons: summer tourists and winter tourists. The only break was a few weeks in the fall before it snowed and in early spring when the snow melted and the skiing was no longer any good.

Here on Cardwell Ranch, though, only a slight hum of traffic could occasionally be heard through the trees. This morning she could hear the murmur of the river below her, the sigh of the pine boughs in the breeze and an occasional meadowlark's song. The state bird sounded quite cheerful. Normally that would have put a smile on her face.

She loved living on the ranch, working with the rest of the family. While her mother had always liked cooking in the kitchen with her sister or helping out in the garden or with the kids, from a young age, Ella had taken care of the horses and helped round up the cattle. She'd made a good living as a wrangler, traveling all over the state and beyond with her Savage cousins Angus and Brick.

But now Angus and his wife, Jinx, lived on the ranch. Brick and his fiancée, Mo, would be building a place on the spread, both of them in law enforcement rather than ranching. It had surprised Ella when her cousins had settled down so quickly. She knew it was because both had finally met women who were their equals. Love had struck them hard and fast.

She'd never had that kind of luck when it came to men and love. Not that she had been looking. With branding over, the family would soon be rounding up the cows and calves and herding them to the land high in the mountains for the summer. It was one of her favorite times of the year, now that the snow had melted enough in the peaks to let them access the grazing lands.

Ella was content here, so it was no wonder she didn't care that she hadn't met anyone who made her heart pound. But her mother had never been settled here, she thought, realizing why she'd hesitated on her porch this morning. She'd tried her mother's cell first thing this morning, but it had gone straight to voice mail. If her mother was in the kitchen busy canning with Aunt Dana, she had probably turned off her phone.

Still, Ella couldn't shake the feeling that her mother wasn't there...

Aunt Dana answered on the third ring. Ella could almost feel the warmth of the kitchen in her aunt's voice. By now, there would be canning pots boiling on the stove, as well as a cake or cookies baking in the oven. She could practically breathe in the scents.

"Is Mom there?" Ella asked, already knowing the answer deep in her chest where worry made her ache.

"No. I was going to call, but I decided to let her sleep. She's been running tired lately. Are you headed down? I've got corn cakes and bacon for you."

"In a minute." Ella disconnected as she continued across the mountain. Hers and her mother's cabins were two of a half dozen perched above the ranch.

As she neared her mother's place, she tried to understand why she'd been so worried about her mom lately. Since Ella had come back to the ranch after a wrangling job in Wyoming, her mother had been distant. Stacy swore she was fine, but Ella didn't believe it. She sensed it was something much deeper and darker. And that was what worried her. She knew her mother's mood swings better than anyone. Not that she could say she knew her mother any more than she knew the woman's well-guarded secret past.

Reaching her mother's cabin, she climbed the steps to the porch and stopped to listen. Maybe Stacy really had slept in this morning. From here, Ella could catch glimpses of the Gallatin River, the water a clear pale green rushing over granite boulders as it cut through the narrow canyon. Pines soared toward the massive blue sky overhead, broken only by granite cliffs that glistened gold in the sunlight. The smell of pine and the river wafted through the crisp, clean air.

Ella heard no movement from within the cabin. She tapped at the door. When she got no answer, she knocked harder. Still no answer.

Opening the door, she called, "Mom?"

The cabin had a hollow feel.

She stepped deeper inside, a chill moving through her. The place felt empty. She went toward her mother's bedroom. The door was ajar. "Mom?" Pushing it open, she saw that the bed had been made.

Out of the corner of her eye, she noticed the open closet doors and the empty hangers. Her stomach dropped. Even before she checked, she knew her mother's suitcases wouldn't be there. Stacy was gone.

Chapter Three

Dana Cardwell Savage had known something was wrong even before her niece walked into the kitchen. First, Stacy not showing up to help can. Then the phone call from Ella inquiring about her mother. One look at the young woman and she knew it was bad.

Ella was a lot like her mother in that she kept things to herself, minding her own counsel. Even as a young girl, Ella, with her beautiful green eyes like the river and her long blond hair like summer wheat, had always been the quiet, pensive one. Calm waters ran deep.

But it was more than that. Ella saw and felt things that others missed. Because of that, her niece had always worried about her mother—even when it appeared that Stacy had changed.

"I'm sure there is no reason for concern," Dana said, knowing she was trying to convince herself as much as Ella. "You know your mother."

When Dana had gotten up this morning, she'd noticed that one of the ranch pickups was gone. She hadn't thought much about it since anyone on the ranch could have taken it. Ella had also apparently noticed. "Stacy's probably just taking a break like she usually does."

"Haven't you ever wondered where she goes on these so-called breaks?" Ella asked with a sigh.

"Of course. I would ask all those years ago after she came back to the ranch with you, but you know Stacy... I had hoped by now..." Dana shook her head. She'd never understood her sister from the time they were little. They were so different. Stacy had always hated the ranch and couldn't wait to leave it, marrying when she was very young, divorcing, marrying again...

But when she'd come home with baby Ella and settled in, she'd seemed to be happy for a while. Dana had thought her sister had gotten all that wildness out of her system after Ella's birth. Unfortunately, now, even at the age of sixty-four, Stacy still took off without notice, returning days later and refusing to talk about it.

Dana continued slicing the early-season strawberries for jam. She'd gotten up before daylight to get the job started. Her sister had promised to help, so she'd been surprised when she hadn't shown up. Stacy was usually up before anyone.

"It's different this time," Ella said. "She took all her clothes. I don't think she's coming back."

Dana set down the knife. "That can't be true. She always comes back," she said, hoping it was true for Ella's sake. Learning that her sister had packed up everything and simply left came as a shock. But hadn't she often worried that Stacy might do something like that? Just out of the blue. Like this time. Should they be worried?

"She didn't say or do anything yesterday that seemed odd at the time?" Ella asked.

Dana frowned. "Stacy did get a phone call late in the afternoon. Not on her cell but on the ranch landline. I answered it. The man asked for Stacy Cardwell. I asked who was calling, thinking it was probably an annoying sales call." She hesitated. "He introduced himself as cold-case homicide detective Waco Johnson. I thought he was probably calling for a donation. He asked if Stacy was available and I handed over the phone."

"A cold-case homicide detective wanted to talk to her?" Ella asked, disbelieving that Dana hadn't thought that might be important.

"I honestly thought it was about the law-enforcement yearly fundraiser," Dana said in her defense. But now she wondered why she hadn't thought more of it. "I had a batch of cookies going in the oven and the timer went off, so I left your mother and returned to the kitchen."

"Did you see her after that?"

Dana shook her head. "I looked into the living room after I set the cookies to cooling and she was gone."

"So you have no idea what the detective wanted with her."

"No. But like I said—"

"What was the detective's name again?"

Dana repeated it, feeling stricken. She was surprised she even remembered his name, the way her memory had been going lately. Most calls from law enforcement were for her husband, Hud, the marshal. They were either work-related or inquiries about how he was doing after his heart attack and whether he'd retired yet.

She wanted to argue that a homicide detective wouldn't have any reason to call Stacy, let alone make her go on the run. But even as she thought it, Dana felt her heart drop. Stacy had run, taking everything but her daughter with her.

Ella had her cell phone out. "You don't remember where the detective said he was calling from, do you?"

Dana looked out the window for a moment, seeing past the pines to Lone Peak Mountain. She'd believed the call wasn't about anything important. She hadn't even mentioned it to Hud. Because while he said he was fine and had returned to being marshal part-time until his retirement date, which he kept moving farther out, she hadn't wanted to bother him.

Had Stacy been surprised? Scared? Had she reacted at all? Dana couldn't recall even a change in her sister's expression as she'd taken the phone. Dana had been busy, as usual. She hadn't thought any more about it—until now.

Strawberry juice ran down her arm. She wiped it away with a paper towel and picked up her knife to continue cutting the sweet ripe fruit. This jam needed to be canned, and right now she was thankful for the task. Not that it would keep her mind off Stacy. What was a cold-case homicide detective doing calling her sister?

Dana mentally kicked herself for not paying more attention. She should have been there when Stacy had hung up to ask what was going on.

"I'm sorry. He might have said Missoula, but I honestly can't remember. Ella…" she said, slicing the last strawberry. She then put down the knife and rinsed the sticky juice off her hands before drying them on her apron. "I'm sure your mother's fine. She's done this many times before and has always come back after a few days."

Her niece didn't look any more convinced than Dana herself was.

ELLA TRIED TO reassure her aunt that it wasn't her fault. No one could predict anything Stacy might do.

"I would say wait until your mother contacts us," Dana said, "but I can see that you're too anxious for that." As her aunt lowered herself into one of the kitchen chairs, Ella began calling around the state, trying to find cold-case homicide detective Waco Johnson. The kitchen was warm with the scent of strawberries and heavy with a worried tension.

As she placed one call after another without results, Ella looked around the kitchen. Some of her favorite memories had been made here, surrounded by family and friends over the years. This room had often echoed with laughter. Tears had also been shed here and wiped away with the corner of an apron, followed by hugs and reassurances.

Ella pulled out a chair and joined her aunt, knowing that major decisions had been made at this table and that she was about to make one. She'd tried her mother's number again and again; it had gone straight to voice mail. She'd given her mother the morning to contact them, hoping she was wrong.

Her mother had left her no choice.

She'd started with the Missoula Police Department, then the county sheriff's office, then worked her way through the state, starting with the larger cities. She was beginning to think that maybe the man who'd called wasn't even a homicide detective. That there'd been some sort of mistake. That Waco Johnson didn't exist. With a name like that…

She hit pay dirt in Butte.

"Waco?" the woman who answered at the sheriff's department said with a laugh. "He's on cold cases now and hardly ever in the office. If you leave your number—"

"I'm returning his call, but I've misplaced his cell phone number. He said it was important and to call him as soon as possible."

Silence. Then, "I'll tell you what. Give me your name and number. I'll call him to see if he still is interested in talking with you."

"Stacy Cardwell," she said automatically and gave the woman her cell phone number. If the call had been important, then Waco Johnson would get right back to her.

As she hung up, she glanced at her aunt. "If it was nothing, he won't call."

Ella was trying to sell herself on that point—and the idea that her mother had just needed a break from the ranch and wasn't in trouble—when her phone rang.

For a moment, she hoped it was Stacy. But, of course, it wasn't. It was cold-case homicide detective Waco Johnson calling her back. The moment she heard his low, deep voice, she knew he was as anxious to talk to her mother as Ella was. And that meant only one thing.

Whatever trouble her mother was in, it was serious.

Chapter Four

"Stacy Cardwell?" Waco asked, trying to keep the surprise out of his voice. The woman who answered his call wasn't the same one he'd talked to yesterday who'd promised to call him this morning—when she wasn't so busy. She'd given him her cell phone number. But when he'd tried it, it had gone straight to voice mail.

No, the voice on the other end of the line was much too young to be Stacy Cardwell.

"I'm her daughter, Ella."

That made more sense, for sure. "May I speak to Stacy?"

"I thought you spoke with her yesterday," Ella said.

He chuckled softly. "She must have accidentally disconnected after she gave me her cell phone number and promised to call me back this morning."

"So you haven't heard from her?"

"No, but if she's there, please tell her it is very important that I speak with her."

He heard the hesitation in the young woman's voice before she spoke. "I need to know why you're interested in talking to her."

He groaned inwardly. Nothing like a protective daughter. "I'm sorry, but that's between your mother and me."

"It's personal?" His slight hesitation didn't go unnoticed. "It's official police business?"

"Look, if you put your mother on the line—"

"I can't do that. She isn't here."

"When do you expect her back?" he asked, unable to shake the feeling that had his nerves on edge.

"I'm not sure."

He was wondering how Cardwell's daughter even knew about his call. "Did she tell you I had called?"

"No, I haven't seen her. My aunt Dana told me and I tracked you down."

He felt a small thrill ripple through his blood. "Are you at Cardwell Ranch now? I'd love to talk to you. And your aunt, Dana Cardwell Savage, if she's around. I can be there in thirty minutes."

"I doubt we could be of much help to you," Ella said. "Maybe if you could tell me what this is about…"

"It's about one of your mother's former husbands, Marvin Hanover. Your mother reported him missing thirty-one years ago. His remains have been found. I'll see you in thirty minutes at Cardwell Ranch."

There was a long moment of silence before the young woman said, "We'll be waiting for you."

ELLA COULDN'T BREATHE for a moment. Remains had been found. A cold-case homicide detective wanted to talk to her mother and her mother had taken off. This wasn't one of her mother's short escapes. She'd taken all of her clothes. Ella had known that this time was different. Stacy was on the run. Wherever she'd gone, she wouldn't be coming back. Except in handcuffs.

She'd heard whispered stories about what a wild woman her mother had been in her younger days. Not just quickie marriages and divorces, but missing money and devious plots. Ella had even heard that Stacy had been responsible for Dana and Hud breaking up all those years ago—before they'd gotten back together.

Everyone liked to say that Stacy had changed, that she'd put all of that behind her. Ella had hoped that was true, and maybe it was. But now she feared that her mother's past had just come back to haunt her.

"What did he say?" Aunt Dana asked, looking as worried as Ella felt.

"He said Mom's wanted for questioning in the murder of her husband Marvin Hanover." That wasn't exactly what he'd said. But she knew it was the case. "Did you know him?"

Dana shook her head. "It was her shortest marriage, I believe. Just months. She and I weren't really talking around that time."

"Evidently, he'd gone missing, but his remains have turned up," Ella said, feeling sick to her stomach. "What do you know about him?"

Dana sighed. "Marvin was a lot older than Stacy. He had grown children, two or three, I believe. One of them stopped by looking for her after Marvin went missing. I just remember that the woman was really rude. Apparently she thought that Stacy had gotten away with some of her deceased mother's jewelry and some money."

Dana lowered her head to her hands. "I had really hoped her younger, wild days were over. She'd seemed so changed when she brought you here. All these years, she's helped me here on the ranch." She raised her head. "Stacy's done a lot of things she shouldn't have, but she could never kill anyone."

Ella nodded, even though she feared there was a side to her mother that none of them wanted to acknowledge—but might be forced to face soon.

IT HAD BEEN years since Waco had been through the Gallatin Canyon. His family had taken a trip to Yellowstone Park when he was a boy and gone this way. He'd forgotten how beautiful the canyon was with the Gallatin River carving its way through the cliffs and pines, and mountains soaring up around it.

He used the patrol SUV's navigation system for directions to the Cardwell Ranch. Not that he couldn't have asked just about anyone how to get there. Everyone around here knew the Cardwells and Savages, especially with Hudson Savage still being marshal. Waco had made a point of learning everything he could after talking to Ella Cardwell.

Hud's son Brick was now a deputy, and Brick's fiancée, Maureen, had been hired on as a deputy. Rumor had it, she was a shoo-in for marshal when Hud retired. After Hud's recent heart attack, it probably wouldn't be long.

Waco figured it was just a matter of time before Hud got wind of the cold-case investigation—if he hadn't already heard. In the meantime, Waco hoped to learn as much as he could without any interference. He knew how protective families could be. As marshal, and Stacy Cardwell's brother-in-law, Hud Savage could be a problem. Hitch had told him how fierce and protective Dana Cardwell Savage could be when it came to her family. The family would quickly close ranks to protect Stacy. He'd already gathered as much from the tone of Stacy's daughter's voice on the phone.

He knew he was walking into a grizzly den. The thought made him smile. If there was one thing he loved, it was a challenge. He couldn't wait to meet this formidable family, especially the daughter, Ella. What was it he'd detected in her voice that had him intrigued? He had no doubt that she would do whatever it took to protect her mother. While he admired that, it wouldn't stop him from finding Stacy.

At the turnoff to the ranch, he slowed and pulled off onto the ranch road. He caught a glimpse of the roof of the house, and a large red barn behind it, as he crossed the bridge over the river. A dozen horses raced along the pasture fence line, the wind blowing back their manes. He put down his window and let the summer air with its scents of green grasses and pine trees rush in.

As he pulled into the yard in front of the two-story ranch house, two women stepped out. He knew at once he was looking at Dana Cardwell Savage and Ella Cardwell. Dana, in her sixties, had grayed, but there was strength in her slim body and life-etched face that he'd seen in other ranch women. She was a woman to be reckoned with.

Waco took in the younger woman and smiled to himself as he cut the engine and exited his SUV. Ella Cardwell was a surprise. Her long blond hair was plaited to one side of her beautifully carved face. She was no more than five-five, yet she had a presence that made her seem just as strong and self-assured as her aunt.

As he approached the porch steps, he felt the young woman's emerald green gaze on him and knew that he'd just met his match. He would need to tread carefully with her. If he hoped to get any help from Ella Cardwell, it was going to be a battle.

But then again, he did love a good fight.

ELLA WATCHED THE man slowly remove his Stetson and look up at her. His blue eyes seemed to nail her to the porch floor. He was much younger than she'd expected—and handsome in a way that caught her off guard. She tried not to show her surprise or react to the intensity of his gaze. When he spoke, his voice had a low, deep rumble to it that quickened her pulse at the same time it put her on alert.

"Afternoon, ladies," he said, tilting his dark head slightly as he nodded first to her aunt and then to her. His hair was longer than most lawmen she knew. He also didn't wear any kind of uniform. He was dressed in jeans and a green-checked shirt, the sleeves rolled up to expose muscled and tanned forearms.

Having always been able to pick up a sense of a person immediately, Ella found herself struggling to get a feel for this man other than the obvious. He was too handsome for his own good. His hips slim, his legs long, his shoulders broad and just as muscular as the rest of his body. There was determination in his stance and those blue eyes seemed to see clear to her soul.

"You have some kind of identification?" she asked, not letting her voice betray how off balance the man threw her.

He gave her a slow smile before reaching into his back pocket and pulling out a badge. His long legs closed the distance between them until he was standing on the lower porch step in front of her, eye to eye.

She took the badge. As she looked at it, she could feel him watching her with a concentration that would have made her nervous if she had let it. "Detective Johnson," she said and handed back the badge.

His warm, dry fingers brushed hers, making her gaze leap to his as she felt the jolt. She saw amusement and challenge in all that blue and warned herself to watch this man very carefully.

"Would you like some lemonade, Detective?" Dana asked. "I just made a fresh batch."

"I'd love some. But, please, call me Waco."

"IF YOU'D LIKE to have a seat," Dana said after she and Ella escorted the detective into the house. "I'll get the lemonade." She started toward the kitchen, but he insisted on coming with her.

"If you don't mind, I'd prefer talking in here," he said. "You have a wonderful kitchen. It reminds me of my grandmother's."

When Dana offered him a chair, he sat at the table and stretched out his long legs, reminding her of a young Hud Savage. Ella took a seat across from him, leaving the head of the table free for her. She could feel how wary her niece was of the man.

Dana poured the three of them a tall, frosty glass of lemonade each and tried to remain calm. She kept telling herself that there was nothing to worry about even as concern bloomed in her mind.

The detective looked around the kitchen, she noticed, taking it all in while also taking the measure of not just her but Ella, as well. She wondered if she should talk to him or if she should call Hud to join them.

"Can you tell us what this is about?" she asked after taking her seat at the table. Ella had filled her in earlier, but Dana wanted to hear it straight from the detective.

Waco cleared his throat. "Are you aware that one of your sister's husbands disappeared some years ago? Maybe you knew him. Marvin Hanover?"

Dana shook her head. "I know that my sister was married a couple of times. She's two years older than me. But I don't recall her ever mentioning that name."

"This marriage didn't last long. In fact, it was only for a few months. Your sister got the marriage annulled, saying that her husband had abandoned her," the detective said.

Dana glanced at Ella, wondering what she thought of the information and the detective. She'd always trusted Ella's instincts when it came to people. But nothing in her niece's expression gave her any indication of how she was feeling about the man.

"Why are you asking about this now?" Ella inquired, getting to the heart of it.

That was so like Ella, Dana thought.

"As I told you on the phone, Marvin Hanover has turned up." The detective seemed to hesitate, his gaze going from Ella to Dana and back again. "His remains have been found. The coroner has evidence suggesting that he was murdered."

"And you think this might interest my mother? As you said, it was years ago that my mother was married to him—"

"Almost thirty-one."

"—for only a few months."

Waco smiled and Dana felt her heart skip before he said to Ella, "Marvin never abandoned your mother. He never left town. His remains were recently discovered on some property once owned by his family—at the bottom of an old well—and we believe they'd been there for more than thirty years."

Dana couldn't help the gasp that escaped her lips. She felt the detective's gaze shift to her and her heart fell. Not again. Not another body in a well. She fought to keep her expression from showing the emotions suddenly roiling inside her. She'd been here before.

"I believe some remains were found in one of the old wells here at the ranch years ago," Waco said, his gaze never straying from her face. "It was back when your siblings were trying to take the ranch away from you, isn't that right?"

Dana had no doubt that he knew exactly when it was. Back when her mother, Mary Cardwell, had died and they hadn't been able to find her most recent will, leaving the ranch to Dana. Back when Hud had just returned to Big Sky to take the marshal job and steal her heart again. Back when she'd been at war with Stacy and her brothers, Jordan and Clay. They'd been determined to force her to sell Cardwell Ranch and give up the family legacy—all for money. Her siblings had only been interested in splitting up the profits. If she hadn't found her mother's will when she had…

"As it turned out, the death of the young woman in the well had nothing to do with our family," Dana said, surprised how calm she sounded.

"No," Waco said, nodding. "But the timing is interesting. Your sister, Stacy, was thirty-three. She'd married Marvin right before the remains turned up in your well here on the ranch." He hesitated for a moment. "Marvin allegedly disappeared after that—after the discovery of the body in your well. Not long after, your sister got an annulment on the grounds of abandonment."

Dana could have heard a pin drop in the kitchen. She didn't dare look at Ella, let alone speak.

"You have to admit, the timing is interesting. Now your sister's former husband's remains have been found in a similar abandoned homestead well," the detective continued. "I'm afraid, this time, it *is* connected to your family."

Chapter Five

Waco studied the two women. They both hid their reactions well. It would seem that these two didn't know where Stacy had gone or when she'd be back. He didn't think either of them would lie outright to an officer of the law—not when one of them was married to a marshal.

"You can see why I want to talk to Stacy. When did you say you expect her back?"

"We didn't. I believe we already told you that we don't know," Ella said.

He nodded. "She's taken off, hasn't she?"

"I'm sure she's just gone for a few days," Dana said and sent a silent message to her niece that she couldn't miss. Stacy had taken off after his call. That alone made her look guilty and they all knew it.

"Any idea where she might have gone?" Waco asked, guessing that, again, they didn't know. They both shook their heads and avoided his gaze. "It isn't anywhere she normally goes, I take it?" he asked when neither answered. "I see." He did see. He saw what he'd expected. They would try to protect Stacy even if she returned or called to let them know where she was. If they were telling the truth, which he thought they were, then Stacy had high-tailed it out of Dodge soon after his call without telling anyone.

He picked up his lemonade and drained half the glass. "This is very good. Thank you." He glanced around the kitchen for a moment before adding, "I'm going to be staying in the area for a few days. Can you suggest a place?"

"There are some cabins just down the road toward West Yellowstone," Dana said. "Riverside Resort. The cabins are right on the water. You might like those."

He noticed that she hadn't looked at her niece as she'd said it. Clearly, she didn't like the fact that he wasn't leaving town. Finishing off his lemonade, he put down his glass and rose.

"I would appreciate you letting me know when you hear from Stacy. It will save me from tracking her down. And I should probably warn you—I don't give up easily." He sighed. "Actually, I never give up. It's a personality flaw." He picked up his Stetson and turned the brim in his fingers for a moment. "We'll be talking again soon." Dana started to get to her feet. "Please, don't get up. I can show myself out."

He gave them each a nod and strode from the room, knowing he wouldn't be hearing from either of them. He was going to have to find Stacy Cardwell on his own.

ELLA LOOKED AT her aunt as she listened to the detective drive away. She hadn't moved from her spot at the table. She'd hardly breathed.

"It probably isn't as bad as it sounds," Dana said, but Ella had noticed the way her aunt had dropped back into her chair as if relieved to have the man gone as much as she was.

"My mother really never told you anything about Marvin Hanover?" she asked her aunt.

Dana shook her head. "Stacy and I were hardly speaking at the time, other than to argue about the ranch. She'd already been married at least one time by then…"

"I don't know what to do," Ella admitted. "It's bad enough that my mother took off the moment she heard that a detective wanted to talk to her about the man's death." She could see that even Dana was having a hard time coming up with something positive to say. With a sigh, Ella pushed herself up from the table.

"The longer she stays away, the worse it will look. I have to find her before he does."

"Why don't we talk to Hud first?"

"Are you sure you want to involve him in this?" She could tell that her aunt didn't want to involve him any more than Ella did. Otherwise, wouldn't she have mentioned that a cold-case homicide detective had called looking for Stacy?

"He'll be upset if he finds out we kept this from him," Dana said. "The detective will probably go to him anyway. But maybe not for a while."

Ella smiled at her. "That will give me some time to find Mom and get her back here, if possible. Anyway, there's nothing Uncle Hud can do," she said. "Unless he knows where my mother's gone." She studied her aunt for a moment. "Unless you do." She watched Dana swallow, eyes lowered.

"There might be one place," her aunt said as she lifted her gaze. "There's a woman Stacy knew in high school. I think they've kept in touch. The woman called her a few months ago. She lives in Gardiner. Her name is Nora Cline. I don't have any more information than that, I'm afraid. You could call her."

She shook her head. "If my mother is there, I don't want her knowing I'm on my way."

"You're assuming Stacy's running from the law."

Ella let out a bark of a laugh. "That's exactly what she's doing, and I think we can both guess why."

Her aunt shook her head adamantly. "Stacy has had her problems with men over the years, but she wouldn't..." Dana's gaze met hers. "You can't really think that she's capable of murder."

Ella figured Dana knew her sister as well as anyone. Look how Stacy had reacted to the phone call. She'd acted impulsively. It used to be her go-to reaction—especially when she was in trouble, from what Ella had heard. She gave her aunt a hug. "I'll call when I know something."

WACO DROVE DOWN the road to a pull-off where he could see anyone coming out of Cardwell Ranch. He was no fool. He'd known that Dana had been trying to get rid of him by sending him to a motel miles from the ranch.

He didn't have to wait long before a pickup came roaring out and turned north toward Bozeman. He saw a flash of blond plaited hair and grinned. Just as he'd been betting with himself, it was Ella Cardwell.

He started his truck. Unless he missed his guess, she was going after her mother.

Waco had learned early on in his career to follow his instincts. It had gotten him far. Right now, his instincts told him that the daughter would go after Stacy Cardwell. Either Ella had an idea where she might be, or, like him, she was looking for her.

He was about to find out. His cell phone rang. It was Hitch. He picked up as he started down 191, going after the pickup that had come from the ranch.

"Just checking in with you. I'm going to notify the family."

He smiled. "Great."

"I thought I'd stop by," Hitch said, making his smile grow even wider. She couldn't resist an interesting case.

"Good idea. Let me know how it goes since I'm in the process of following the suspect's daughter, hoping she'll lead me to Stacy."

"Stacy is…gone?"

"On the run, I'm betting."

Hitch sighed. "Okay. After I notify the next of kin, I'll probably step back from this case. Unless you need my help for anything." Clearly, this case had gotten under her skin, too.

He chuckled as he disconnected, keeping the pickup in sight as Ella continued down the canyon to where it opened into the Gallatin Valley. He found himself thinking about the young ranch woman in the vehicle ahead of him. He'd always been a pretty good judge of character. He'd seen intelligence in her eyes, strength and determination—all things that would make her keep whatever she learned from him. If she could, Ella would try to save her mother.

But did Stacy need saving? That was the question. Given the time frame of the Cardwell Ranch remains found in the well and Stacy's missing husband ending up in one, it looked suspicious. Add to that the fact that Stacy had taken off after his call—a telling sign. The woman had something to hide. He just had to find out if it was murder.

Chapter Six

When Mercedes "Mercy" Hanover Davis heard the news, she let out a bloodcurdling scream that set all the dogs in the neighborhood barking.

Hitch was used to dealing with a wide range of emotions when faced with delivering bad news. As coroner when she'd started, and now medical examiner, she was often the one who notified the next of kin that a loved one had died. She'd caught fainters before they hit the floor, administered to those in shock and consoled the heartbroken who'd dissolved into tears.

But Mercy's scream, followed by a string of oaths, was a new one for her. The woman beat the wall with her fists for a moment before she turned to Hitch and demanded, "What about his money? What about my father's money?"

For a moment, Hitch could only stare at her openmouthed as she tried not to judge. She'd offered to let the family know about Marvin's remains being found since Waco's number one suspect was a runner he needed to track down. At least, that was her excuse. Everything about this case was interesting and getting more so by the moment.

Now, standing in the doorway of the youngest daughter's apartment, Hitch reminded herself that everyone handled grief differently. "Your father's *money*?" That was definitely not the question she'd been expecting.

"Yes," Mercy snapped before going off again on another tirade. She was a buxom woman in her mid- to late-fifties with a tangle of brown hair and small, color-matched eyes. Right now, her mouth appeared too large for her face.

Since the door had opened, all Hitch had been able to inform Mercy of was that her father's remains had been found. Nothing else. Now she asked, "Are you interested in knowing where he was found or how long—?"

"You said *remains*. You didn't say *body*. So I assume he's been dead for a long time. Let me make a wild guess. More than thirty years. Duh. That's when he disappeared. That's when that woman killed him. We all knew she'd only married him for his money. She'd said he'd abandoned her. Ha!"

Hitch knew the woman was referring to Stacy Cardwell. She'd been disappointed to hear from Waco that Stacy had taken off after his call. She hadn't spoken to Ford yet today. She suspected not all of the family knew what was going on.

After she notified the rest of the Hanover family, she had to let this case go. It wouldn't be easy, though. Jewelry? Money? "I will be informing your brother and sister after I leave here," Hitch said.

Mercy made an impatient gesture. "Don't bother. I'll tell them. But this won't come as a surprise. What I want to know is if you found the money with his remains, or if that woman got away with not only murder—but also the rest of my father's fortune and my mother's jewelry."

WACO FOLLOWED ELLA into Bozeman. She sped through the bustling city and got on the interstate heading east. He followed at a distance far enough that he didn't think she would spot a tail and wondered where they were headed. His hope was that she would take him straight to Stacy. It would certainly save him a lot of time, and yet he didn't mind the chase. Just as long as it ended with him solving the crime and bringing justice to the dead man in the well.

His phone rang. He quickly accepted the call on the hands-free Bluetooth. "Hey, Hitch."

"Thought you'd want to hear what happened when I let Mercy Hanover Davis know."

He laughed as she told him, not surprised. "From what I've found out about the deceased, Marvin Hanover had been a loathsome, though wealthy, bastard. Someone probably would have killed him eventually anyway. But the money and jewelry issue is interesting."

Marvin had been considerably older than Stacy and wasn't known for his good looks. Waco made a mental note to find out what had happened to his estate. With Stacy annulling the marriage, he doubted she'd gotten much, if anything.

He was looking forward to talking to her, curious why anyone would settle for anything less than love. Did money really make the difference? Or had it been about security? Either way, it was a bad deal. Not that true love—if it even existed—was easy to find. He knew that firsthand.

"I'm going to notify the rest of the next of kin," Hitch said. "Can't wait to see what kind of reaction I get from them."

As he disconnected, Waco smiled. He and Ella had left the lush valley surrounded by pine-studded mountains to cross the Bozeman Pass. The highway had been cut through the mountains along a creek. As he topped out and dropped off the pass, he saw the blink of the right-hand signal on the pickup far ahead of him.

Ella was exiting the interstate at Livingston. As he followed her, he wondered if this town was where she would lead him to Stacy. But she turned right again, this time heading south through Paradise Valley toward Gardiner and Yellowstone Park.

He felt his pulse quicken at the thought of finally coming face-to-face with Stacy Cardwell. If anyone knew exactly how her husband had ended up at the bottom of that abandoned well, he had a feeling it would be her.

But then he thought of Ella. How well did she know her mother? What would it do to her if she found out that her mother was a killer? Was she ready to have her heart broken?

He couldn't help but wonder where this case was going to take not just him but Ella, as well. Not that it mattered. He was buckled in for the ride. He hoped Ella was, too, because if the prickling at the back of his neck was any indication, things were going to get ugly and soon.

MERCY STOOD AT the window, watching the medical examiner leave. She hugged herself, suddenly aware that she was shaking all over. Her father was dead. His remains had been found. And maybe the money and jewels would be found.

She felt a surge of anger and righteousness. Now Stacy Cardwell would be arrested and go to prison for her crimes.

That thought gave her little comfort. What about the money? Had Stacy taken it, spent it all? Was it gone? Or was it still wherever her father had hidden it? Was there still hope?

She pulled out her phone and called her brother.

"Lionel," she said before he could hang up. "The old man's remains have been found." For a moment, she thought she hadn't spoken quickly enough. It was unusual for her brother to even take her call, given the animosity between them. Even stranger that he seemed to still be on the line.

"Who told you that?"

"The medical examiner was just here. I'm sure she's on the way over to tell you and Angeline. Maybe you should prepare her. I wouldn't want this to kill her."

Lionel made a dismissive sound. "We've all suspected that he was dead for years. I really doubt Angeline is going to keel over at the news. Maybe it would be a blessing if she did."

Mercy cringed even though she'd never been close to her older sister. "That's pretty cold even for you, Lionel."

"You aren't taking care of her and watching her slowly die each day," he snapped.

"What happens now?" Mercy asked, cutting to the real purpose of her call.

"I have no idea. I have to go." With that, he hung up.

She stared at her phone before angrily calling her boyfriend. He answered on the third ring.

"He's really dead," she said into the phone without preamble.

"Who's dead?" Trevor didn't sound all that interested.

"My father. They found his remains. Now they will finally arrest Stacy Cardwell and we'll find out about the money before it's too late. I'm sure it's too late to find my mother's jewels."

"I thought you said Stacy Cardwell didn't have the money or the jewels."

"She hasn't lived like she has it, but maybe she's been sitting on it all this time in her cabin at the ranch." Even as she said that, Mercy knew it didn't make much sense. Who would sit on a fortune all these years?

"So have the police arrested her yet?"

"I don't know. Maybe. It should be in the news soon, I would imagine."

"How are things at the house with your brother and sister?" Trevor asked.

"Do you even have to ask? Lionel won't do anything, and Angeline is too sick to do anything. Someone in this family needs to find that money."

"I have to go," Trevor said. "Talk to you later." And, like Lionel, he, too, was gone.

Mercy felt a sense of desperation as she put her phone away. But what could they do other than wait to see what the police did about this?

She told herself that there was hope for the first time in a long time. Their father's inheritance had run out. There wasn't much to sell off anymore except the house—in spite of the fear their father's fortune was hidden somewhere inside it.

Mercy scoffed at that. They'd all searched the house, even opened some of the walls. The money hadn't been there.

She tried to hold out hope that Stacy would reveal everything she knew to save herself.

Mercy grabbed her purse, no longer worried about running up more credit-card debt. Her father had taken his secret and his money to his grave. Until now. She had a good feeling that being broke was behind her. It made her want to go shopping.

ELLA PARKED IN front of the small stone house just off the main highway into Gardiner. She'd found the address online. What had struck her was the fact that she'd never heard her mother ever mention Nora Cline. As far as she'd been able to tell, her mother had no close friends—at least, none that Ella had ever met. Stacy had seemed content on the ranch with her sister and daughter.

Now it made her wonder if her mother had a secret life—one she'd lived in the wee hours of the night. Or maybe on those mysterious days when she'd disappeared.

Ella feared that her mother's secrets were about to come out. How devastating would they be for not just her but the entire family?

Sitting in front of the small house in Gardiner, she watched the windows for a moment, waiting for the front curtain to move. It didn't. The ranch pickup her mother had taken was nowhere to be seen. But maybe it was hiding in the old garage behind the house—just as her mother was hiding inside this house.

The curtains still hadn't moved. As she got out, she could hear the sound of traffic and the squawk of a crow in a nearby pine tree. The crow watched her with glittering dark eyes as she walked up to the front door and knocked.

From inside the house, she heard movement. A moment later, the door opened. The woman standing in the doorway looked vaguely familiar, as if they had crossed paths before. About the same age as her mother, Nora Cline looked to be in her midsixties, with laugh lines around her warm brown eyes and her mouth. Her gray hair was pulled back in a ponytail. She wore a bright-colored caftan that floated around her bare feet. She looked like a person who was comfortable with the woman she'd become. Ella had to wonder if her mother would ever be.

She glanced past Nora into the small house. It was decorated in bright colors, much like the woman, from the paintings and posters on the walls to the furnishings. "Is Stacy here?"

Nora blinked. "Stacy *Cardwell*?"

"My mother," she said, meeting Nora's gaze.

"Ella! Of course. I should have recognized you. But I haven't seen you since you were a child. Come in." She stepped aside to let her enter, but Ella stayed where she was.

"I need to speak to my mother."

"I'm sorry. She isn't here." Nora was frowning, squinting into the bright summer day outside. A steady stream of tourists could be heard from one street over since the entrance to Yellowstone was just across the Gardner River. "Did she tell you she would be here?"

Ella studied the woman, wondering why it had been so many years since she'd seen her mother's friend. She couldn't remember her mother ever bringing anyone to the ranch. When Stacy disappeared for days at a time, was that when she visited her friend? Did she have other friends she kept even more secret than Nora? "When was the last time you saw her?"

Nora seemed to give that some thought. "It's been a while. Has something happened?"

Ella didn't know how much she wanted to tell her. "If she should show up here, would you give me a call? It's very important. Also, I'd appreciate it if you didn't mention the call to my mother."

Nora looked uncomfortable. "Stacy is an old friend. I wouldn't want to keep anything from her."

She liked the woman's sense of loyalty. "I'm afraid my mother is in trouble." She realized she'd have to be more honest with Nora. "Did she ever tell you anything about her past? Something she only confided in you? It's really important, or I wouldn't be here."

Nora shook her head, her expression one of sympathy. "She said she'd done some things she'd regretted, but haven't we all?"

"I was thinking along the lines of one big regret."

The woman met her gaze and hesitated. "She never told me, but... I got the feeling that there was something she didn't want to come out because of you. So I know she wouldn't want you to—"

"No." Ella shook her head. "It's too late for that. There is a homicide detective looking for her. When he called, she ran."

Nora's eyes widened. *"Homicide?"*

"Let me give you my number. She might call you, and if she does..." Ella looked up at the woman. "If you know my mother, then you know she has an impulsive side that comes out when she feels backed against a wall."

Nora nodded and pulled out her phone so they could exchange numbers. Ella did the same.

From down the street, Waco watched the interaction. He couldn't hear what was being said, but he could read a lot into the fact that Ella hadn't bothered to go inside the house. Stacy Cardwell wasn't there.

The discussion looked serious. He had no doubt that Ella was looking for her mother. To tell her the homicide cop wasn't giving up?

He was pretty sure Stacy had figured that out on her own. It was why she'd taken off. So why was Ella looking for her? To warn her. No, to help her.

He thought about what he'd glimpsed in the young woman's amazing green eyes. He knew that kind of determination well. But he'd also seen a need to protect her mother as if Ella had been covering for her for years. He wondered how much Ella knew.

While he found it admirable and even touching, he didn't see what the daughter could do to help her mother—especially if Stacy was guilty. He felt bad about that, but it was part of the job.

Ella finished her conversation and headed for her pickup, after the cell phone number exchange. What had the woman told her? Something that had Ella moving again.

Waco considered sticking around and questioning the woman in the brightly colored caftan who now stood in the doorway watching Ella drive away. But he thought he had a better chance if he stayed with Stacy's daughter.

He followed her all the way back to Bozeman. When she stopped at a grocery store along Main Street, he couldn't find a parking place and was forced to drive around the block. There seemed to be more traffic than usual even for Bozeman.

His cell phone rang while he was caught in another red light. He saw that it was one of the investigators from the crime lab and quickly picked up.

"I sent a preliminary report of our findings in the well," Bradley said. "But we just found something in the dirt taken from the well that we've been sifting through."

He held his breath, hoping whatever it was would break this case wide open.

DANA WAS TOO restless even to bake after Ella left. She'd paced the floor, debating if she should call her husband or wait until he came home for lunch to tell him. This was something she'd decided she couldn't keep from him. More than likely, the homicide detective would contact him anyway—if he hadn't already, she told herself.

Finally, unable to sit still, she'd decided to head up the mountainside to Stacy's cabin. She didn't figure that she would find anything; after all, Ella had already looked. But she knew her sister. Maybe there was a clue as to where she had gone that Ella wouldn't have recognized.

For years, Dana hadn't butted into Stacy's business. Yes, her sister took off every few months and didn't return for days without any explanation. Dana had given her room and hadn't questioned her after the first few times. All of them living on the ranch together, she knew, didn't offer a lot of privacy. And she'd wanted to give Stacy space, which she'd apparently needed. But the homicide detective's visit had changed that. If Dana could help find her sister, she had to try.

The breeze swayed the pines as she walked up the mountainside. There was nothing like summer in the canyon. The sky overhead was a robin's-egg blue, with only a few white puffs of clouds floating above the high peaks still capped with snow. She could smell the pines and the river. It was a smell that had always grounded her.

Years ago, they'd built a series of cabins on the side of the mountain above the main ranch house for guests and family. Stacy had moved into one of them when she'd returned to the ranch when Ella was but a baby. At the time, Dana had thought it was temporary. She and Hud had offered Stacy land to build her own house on, but she'd refused.

"This cabin is perfect for one person," her sister had argued. When Ella was grown, she'd moved out of her mother's cabin into one of her own for those times she was home on the ranch. So, for years, Stacy had lived alone.

"It's so small," Dana had countered.

"I don't need more room," her sister had said. "I'm fine where I am. Anyway, it makes it easier for me to just come down the mountainside in the morning to help with the cooking and baking." Before that, she'd helped with all the children, both theirs and the cousins' kids who loved spending time on the ranch.

Dana had often wanted to ask her sister if she was happy, but she'd held her tongue. Stacy was so hard to read. She'd seemed content, which had surprised Dana. Growing up, there'd been so much restlessness in her older sister. Wasn't that why Stacy had run off and gotten married the first time at such a young age?

Their mother used to say that Stacy would be the death of her. By then, Mary Cardwell had been divorced from her husband Angus. She'd done her best with Stacy, but had always felt she hadn't given her oldest daughter enough love, enough attention, enough discipline. She'd blamed herself for the way Stacy had turned out.

But when Stacy had come home years later, after their mother's death, Dana had seen a change in her. Stacy had baby Ella and had stayed on to help with Dana's four children. Their brother Jordan had also returned to the ranch, reuniting them all. Now Jordan lived with his wife, Liza, and their children in a home they'd built on the ranch.

Dana loved having her family so close. The only one who didn't live on the ranch was her brother Clay. He lived in California, where he was involved in making movies, and only got home occasionally.

As she reached Stacy's cabin, Dana slowed, reminding herself how blessed she was to have had her sister here all these years. She couldn't lose her now.

Like most doors on the ranch, this one wasn't locked. She turned the knob and let the door slowly swing open.

She heard a sound from deep inside the cabin.

"Stacy," she called, flushed with instant relief. She had returned. No doubt her sister had realized how foolish it had been to run. Stacy must have driven in along the road that ran behind the cabins, hoping no one would be the wiser about her leaving—and coming back—the way she had.

"Stacy!" Dana called out louder as she stepped inside. The shadow-filled cabin felt cool even though it was past noon on a bright sunny day. The large pines sheltered the cabins, providing privacy as well as shade.

Dana stopped in the middle of the living room as she realized that whatever she'd heard, it had stopped. Had she only imagined the sound? She stared at the normally neat-as-a-pin cabin in shock. It looked as if a whirlwind had come through. Drawers stood open, even the cushions on the couch had been flung aside, as if some-one had been searching for something.

Had Ella done this? She wouldn't have left such a mess. Dana's heart began to pound. But if Ella hadn't—

She jumped as the door she'd left wide open behind her caught the breeze and slammed shut. Startled, she tried to laugh off her sudden fear. But her laugh sounded hollow. "Stacy?"

Surely her sister had heard her. Was it possible she was in the shower? As Dana stepped toward the back bedroom where she'd heard the sound coming from, she saw that the door was partially closed. Did she just see movement behind it?

"Stacy?" She hated the way her voice broke. "Stacy!"

She was almost to the room when the door flew open. A dark figure filled the doorway an instant before rushing at her, knocking her down, as he fled.

Dana lay on the floor, dazed and gasping for air. She heard what sounded like a motorcycle start up behind the cabin. Her heart felt as if it would pound out of her chest at the sudden shock. She tried to move. It took her a moment to realize that she wasn't badly hurt—just her ego bruised and battered.

Sitting up, she pulled out her cell phone and called her husband.

Chapter Seven

On the way back from Gardiner, Ella remembered that her aunt had mentioned they were out of lemons. She stopped at the market on Main Street in Bozeman, wondering if she was still being followed by the detective as she went into the store.

When she came back out to her pickup, she couldn't see him. But there was a woman with a wild head of brown curly hair and wearing a leopard-spotted poncho leaning against her truck.

"Can I help you?" Ella asked and then realized she'd seen the woman before. An old memory nudged at her.

"You're her kid, right? Ella Cardwell. You don't look like her."

"I'm sorry?"

"I'm Mercy Hanover Davis. Your mother used to be married to my father."

Ella nodded, taking in the woman as she wondered what she wanted. It had been years since she'd seen Mercy Hanover, but the woman hadn't changed all that much. Like today, she'd been waiting by their vehicle then, too.

Only years ago, she'd been angry and much scarier. "Where's our money?" she'd demanded of Ella's mother.

"I don't know what you're talking about," her mother had answered.

"Like hell you don't, Stacy. You think we don't know what

you've done?" The woman's laugh had scared Ella more than her anger. "What did you do with him?"

"If you don't leave me alone, I'm going to call the police."

The woman had laughed harder. "Sure you are."

Stacy had shoved the woman away, and she and Ella had gotten into their pickup and driven away.

When Ella had asked who the stranger was, her mother had said she was some poor demented person who was confused. Stacy had claimed that she'd never seen Mercy Hanover before.

Ella knew better now. She decided to wait Mercy out even though she was anxious to hear what the woman had to say.

"We should have coffee." Mercy looked around, spotted a coffee shop. "You drink coffee, don't you?"

Ella was anxious to find her mother, but so far, her attempts had come to a dead end. "Why not?"

Neither of them said anything as they walked the short distance to the coffee shop.

"I'm buying," Mercy said once inside. "What do you want?"

"Just plain coffee."

The woman gave her a disbelieving look, as if buying plain coffee at a coffee shop was a total waste of money. "Whatever." She stepped up to the counter and ordered a caramel mocha latte and a plain cup of coffee.

Ella took a seat out of the way. There were only a few people in the shop this late in the day, a man and a woman, and two women. All were looking at their phones.

Mercy returned, handing her a coffee before lowering herself into the chair opposite her.

"Thanks," Ella said and took a sip. It was hot and not nearly as good as her aunt Dana's.

Given the circumstances, Ella offered her condolences to Mercy. To which Mercy grunted in response.

"You're not much of a talker, huh?" Mercy said, studying her over the rim of her cup as she took a sip and then put the latte down. "Not much like your mother."

"I suspect you have something on your mind?"

Mercy bristled. "I just thought we should get to know each other."

"Why?"

"We're almost family. Your mother was married to my father."

"That's a bit of a stretch family-wise, don't you think?"

Mercy looked surprised for a moment but then laughed. "Maybe you're more like your mother than I thought. So let's get right to it. Where's your mother?"

"Why do you care?"

The woman sighed. "You aren't going to make this easy, are you?"

Ella leaned forward. "What do you want with Stacy?" She'd called her mother Stacy when she was little because all the other kids did. Also, sometimes it was hard to think of the woman as a mother. Like right now, when she was missing and possibly wanted for murder.

"What your mother took from me. My father and his money—not in that order. She also stole my mother's jewelry before she left."

"My mother doesn't have your money or jewelry, and we know where your father is. We just don't know how he got there," Ella said. "But since your concern seems to be money and jewelry over the loss of life, I'd say my mother isn't the only suspect in his murder."

Mercy sat back with a look of almost admiration. "You're smart."

"And not easily intimidated," Ella said.

That got a smile out of the woman. "No, you're not. Look, I know your mother ran the moment my father's remains were found. What does that tell you?"

"That the law and your family would be after her—no matter her innocence."

Mercy laughed. "Honey, your mother is far from innocent. She ran because she's guilty." Ella said nothing. The woman leaned toward her. "My father was a bastard. I wouldn't blame your mother for killing him. But we need that money."

"I don't know anything about any money."

Sitting back, Mercy said, "Maybe she already spent it."

Ella shook her head. "My mother and I have never had any money. After I was born, she brought me to Cardwell Ranch and went to work with the rest of the family. Does that sound like a woman with any money?"

Mercy eyed her sharply. "How old are you?"

"Almost twenty-eight."

"That wouldn't have given her much time to spend the money." The woman sighed. "If your mother doesn't have the money, then who does?"

HITCH PARKED IN front of the huge old three-story mansion. Faded letters on the mailbox spelled out the name Hanover. In its day, this place must have been something, she thought. The massive edifice, perched above the Gallatin River, had a view of the valley.

But its age had begun to show. More modern, more expensive houses had sprung up in the valley, eclipsing the Hanover house. It now looked like a place that trick-or-treating kids would avoid.

When Mercy Davis had demanded to know what had happened to her father's fortune, Hitch had thought the woman was exaggerating. But maybe the man really had had a fortune at some point. Had Stacy gotten away with it? Maybe, since this place looked as if it was in need of repair and no one had done anything about it. Could the family no longer afford it?

Hitch walked up many steps to the wide porch with its towering stone pillars and raised the lion's-head knocker on the large wooden door. She'd barely brought it down when the door flew open and she found herself staring at a man in his early sixties. He was wearing slacks, slippers and a velvet smoking jacket. Hitch felt as if she had stepped back in time.

His hair had grayed at his temples, frown lines wrinkled his forehead, appearing to be permanent, and his mouth was set in a grim line. He looked enough like his younger sister Mercy that she knew he had to be Lionel Hanover, the eldest of Marvin's offspring.

"I'm State Medical Examiner Roberts," she said. "Lionel Hanover?" He gave her a distracted nod. He seemed to be more interested in looking down the road behind her than at her. "I'm afraid I have some bad news—"

"I know. Mercy called. Is that all?"

She was taken aback by his abruptness, as well as his complete lack of interest regarding his father's death. "Do you have any questions?" she asked almost tentatively, still standing outside with the door open. She reminded herself that he had probably let out any emotion he'd had about the news after Mercy's call. And it had been thirty years since his father had disappeared.

She quickly did the math. Lionel, the oldest, would have been in his early thirties when his father died. His sister Angeline would have been a few years younger than Lionel, and Mercy would have been in her midtwenties. Not children by any means.

That, she realized, meant Stacy had been the age of Marvin's offspring while Marvin had been the age Lionel was now.

A woman appeared from the shadows deep within the house, her wheelchair squeaking as she rolled into view. "Is this her?" asked a faint, hoarse voice.

Lionel didn't bother to turn. "I'm handling this, Angeline."

Hitch blinked as the woman wheeled herself into a shaft of light behind him. Her hair was black with a streak of white like a cartoon vamp. She was thin to the point of emaciation and, from the pallor of her skin, not in good health.

"My sister is ill," Lionel said.

"I'm not ill," Angeline snapped. "I'm dying. But I'm not dead yet." The woman turned her narrowed eyes on Hitch. "So, what are you going to do about my father's death?" she demanded, her dark gaze seeming to pin Hitch to the floor.

"Cold-case homicide detective Waco Johnson is handling the investigation," Hitch told the two of them. "I'm sure he'll be contacting you."

"Murder?" Angeline croaked and then erupted in a coughing bout.

"The medical examiner just said that a cold-case *homicide* detective would be contacting us, Angeline. So, of course it was murder." Lionel looked past Hitch to the street. A buzzing sound filled the air, growing louder and louder.

Hitch turned to see a dark-clad figure come roaring up on a motorcycle and park behind the state SUV where she'd left it. As the rider removed his helmet, she saw blond hair that dropped to the man's shoulders. He looked up the hillside toward the gaping front door and Hitch standing there. His smile was filled not with merriment but with spite.

When she turned back, Lionel's face was pinched in anger. "Thank you for letting us know, Miss…"

"Roberts," she said in the same clipped tone he'd used with her.

"Is that Trevor?" Angeline asked. "Is Mercy with him?" She didn't sound as if either's arrival was welcome.

Lionel started to close the door in Hitch's face. As he moved, he said over his shoulder, "Just Trevor, and I'm in no mood to deal with him right now."

The door slammed.

Hitch turned to look down at the road. Mercy's boyfriend? Mercy was midfifties, but the man standing by the motorcycle appeared younger—at least from this distance. As she descended the steps, she could feel his gaze on her. It wasn't until she reached his level that she saw that Trevor was quite a bit younger than Mercy. Hitch would guess a good ten years.

Trevor gave her an insolent look as he flipped his long hair back. "You the undertaker?" he asked with a smirk.

"State medical examiner."

"Isn't that the same thing?"

"I'm an investigator as well as a coroner."

His eyes widened a little. "So you cut up people? Cool."

Yes, cool. "I suppose you heard about Marvin Hanover," she said, wondering if anyone would mourn the man's death.

"Marv?" He shrugged. "Never met him. Mercy said someone snuffed him, but from what I've heard about him, he probably deserved it." His eyes gleamed. "Is it true that now they're going to be rich again?"

"I wouldn't know about that." She glanced back at the house. "They seem to be doing all right."

Trevor laughed. "Looks can be deceiving. The house is about all they have left. Pretty soon they won't even have furniture to sit on, but they still act like they're better than the rest of us." He started to turn toward the house when Lionel called down from the porch to say that Mercy wasn't there and closed the door again.

Trevor hesitated. "I had some news for them, but if they're not interested…" He grinned. "It will be nice to see Lionel eat crow." He laughed and swung a leg over his bike before starting the noisy motor and taking off.

To see Lionel eat crow? Hitch had no idea what he meant by that and, at the moment, didn't care.

Once in her SUV, she headed back to Bozeman. On the way, she'd called Waco to fill him in. Her job was done and yet she felt the pull of the case. Left with so many questions, she itched to find the answers. She likely had some time before being called in on another case and wished there was some way she could help with this one. Waco had his hands full and the DCI part of the investigation was pretty much over until he turned up more evidence—and found Stacy in the hope of getting to the truth.

Her cell phone rang. She didn't recognize the number or the name. Did she know someone named Jane Frazer?

She picked up with a simple "Hello?"

"Henrietta Roberts?"

"Yes?"

"I'm Jane Frazer. I thought you might be contacting me."

"I'm sorry," Hitch said. "What is this in regard to?"

"The death of my father, Marvin Hanover."

"*Your* father? I wasn't aware that—"

"That he had another daughter?" Jane let out a bitter snicker. "It would be just like Mercy and Angeline to completely forget me, but I would have thought Lionel might mention my name.

"I'm the product of an affair Marvin had with my mother. When my mother was killed in a hit and run, he moved me into his home. I spent time with the three of them. I knew there was no love lost for me, but it would have been nice if they'd thought to let me know about our father."

"I'm sure they're probably not thinking clearly," Hitch said, wondering why she was covering for them. "This has to have come as a shock to all of you."

Jane laughed. "You've met them. Did they appear any more shocked than I am? Nor am I surprised someone killed Marvin."

Hitch noticed that Jane hadn't immediately pointed a finger at Stacy Cardwell.

"Marvin and my mother were engaged when she died. Who knows if my mother would have actually gone through with a wedding? My father…well, he was a difficult man. But he had his…allure when it came to women, if you know what I mean."

Hitch thought she did. "Was this after Marvin's first wife died?"

"Only months after *her* tragic accident," Jane chortled cynically. "For years I was convinced that Marvin had killed his first wife as well as my mother. I still wouldn't be surprised. I expected him to kill his third wife. So I was shocked to hear that someone had killed him instead."

Hitch was trying to put all this information together, but Jane Frazer had added a whole new dimension to the family tree. "I would love to sit down and talk with you. From your area code, you live in Idaho?"

"Not far from the Montana border. If you want to know about Marvin and that family of his, then I'm your girl," Jane said.

Hitch knew she couldn't walk away. Not yet. "When would be a good time?"

MERCY HADN'T WANTED to believe Ella Cardwell, but she did after their talk in the coffee shop. The daughter didn't know where her mother was. She also didn't know anything about the money.

Her cell phone rang. She saw that it was Trevor and picked up.

"I have something you might want to see," he told her.

Since he was her boyfriend, and also her drug source, she brightened. "I'm on my way to my apartment. Am I going to like it?"

"See you in a few." He disconnected.

Fifteen minutes later she heard his motorcycle pull up out front. As he came in the door, he glanced over his shoulder as if afraid he'd been followed. Whatever he had must be good.

Mercy couldn't help her excitement. "So?" she said, holding out her hand.

He reached into his pocket and laid three photographs on her open palm.

She stared at them, trying not to be disappointed. "I thought... What are these?"

"I broke into Stacy Cardwell's cabin. I didn't find any money, but I found these in some photo albums hidden in a space in the wall behind the closet."

She glanced at the snapshots, still unimpressed. All she'd really heard was that Trevor hadn't found any money. Nor had he brought drugs.

"I think it might be a clue," he said excitedly. "I was going to show them to your family, but they weren't interested in seeing me. Their loss."

Mercy looked more closely at the photos. They were old, the clothing out of style, the shots not even that well composed. But she did recognize the much younger Stacy.

"How are these helpful?" she asked him.

"I don't know." She heard his disappointment. "I thought you might have some idea. They have to be important, right? Why else would she hide them?"

Mercy looked again at the photos. She didn't want to tell him, but breaking into Stacy's cabin had been a bonehead idea. Worse was thinking that these old photos were important. The least he could have done was taken something of value.

"I'll have to give this some thought," Mercy said, dropping the snapshots on the coffee table. "You don't have anything to smoke on you, do you?"

Trevor looked crestfallen for a moment. "I have a little weed."

She brightened, the photos forgotten as she snuggled up against him. She hoped her brother wouldn't hear about what Trevor had done. Lionel had enough problems with her young boyfriend.

Chapter Eight

Marshal Hud Savage swore as he watched his wife rub the side of her thigh she'd landed on. "Are you sure you're all right?" he asked again after she finished telling him everything that had happened.

They were sitting on the porch swing in front of Stacy's cabin. Inside, several crime-scene techs were searching for evidence that could be used to locate the person who'd not only ransacked the place, but also knocked Dana down when he'd escaped.

"I'm fine." She sounded more embarrassed than hurt. He could be glad of that. "I'll be black-and-blue tomorrow, but fortunately, nothing was broken."

Hud shook his head. "Can you describe the man?"

"There wasn't time to get a good look at him. He was wearing a hoodie. I only got a glimpse of his face. Maybe forties. Brown eyes. Long blond hair. He smelled of exhaust fumes."

Hud chuckled. She made a better witness than most detectives he'd come across.

"Oh, and there was something jingling in his pocket when he moved," Dana said. "He was just under six feet, slimly built. And he was wearing boots. I remember the sound they made on the wood floor. Biker boots, because after he left, I heard a motorcycle start up behind the cabin. That would explain the exhaust fumes I smelled on him."

Hud couldn't help but smile at his wife. "Is that all?"

"I think so. No, he also was wearing gloves."

So that meant no fingerprints. "You have no idea what he was looking for in Stacy's cabin?" The whole place had been vandalized. Full drawers dumped on the floor, containers pulled from the closet added to the pile.

"That's what's odd. If he hadn't taken the photos, I'd think he was there to steal something of value," Dana said. They'd discovered several old photo albums on the floor. Empty spaces on a few of the pages indicated that some of the photos were missing.

"I've never seen those photo albums before," Dana said. "I can't imagine the young man broke in to take photographs. Can you?"

He couldn't.

"Is it likely this has something to do with why that homicide detective is so anxious to talk to Stacy about her ex-husband's death?"

Hud wished he knew. Stacy was missing. Someone had ransacked her cabin. The intruder had knocked Dana down as he'd escaped. What bothered him most was how bad things might get before this was over.

"What do you know about this former husband of hers? Marvin Hanover?"

"Nothing, really. I never met him. He was a lot older than Stacy. She'd been married a couple of times by then. She was living in Bozeman at the time, I think. Mother and I hardly ever heard from her back then. I never really knew who she'd married or divorced," Dana said. "It wasn't like she ever brought them to the ranch. I vaguely remember her mentioning someone named Emery. That's it. She could have already been married maybe a couple of times by the time she married Marvin. That's probably why she didn't tell us about him, let alone about the marriage and annulment."

"Dana, you need to be ready for the worst. You know Stacy. She could have killed the man. She could have known about the body that had been thrown down the well on the ranch."

Dana glared at her husband. "I refuse to believe it. Everyone knew about the remains found in our well. Disposing a body in an old well would be an obvious choice to a lot of people who might have wanted to get rid of someone."

Hud had to laugh. "Remind me to stay away from old wells." Rising from the swing, he said, "You think you can walk back to the house?"

She rose, wincing but clearly trying to hide it. "Stop treating me like an old woman." Stepping past him, she started down the mountain path.

Hud followed. In his years of law enforcement, if he'd learned anything, it was that most people were capable of murder. Some people more than others, Stacy being one of those people. When backed into a corner, people did whatever they had to do to survive. Before she'd had Ella, Stacy had proved over the years that she was a survivor—even if it meant breaking the law.

"You really should have told me the minute this homicide detective called," he said to his wife's back as they descended the mountain. "Now Ella's gone looking for her?" He groaned. "What am I going to do with the women in this family?"

Dana stopped and turned to look at him. He saw the fear and worry in her expression. Family meant everything to her. He put his arms around her and pulled her close.

"Do what you always do," she said, her voice thick with emotion. "Protect us, Hudson Savage. Don't put a BOLO out on her. Not yet, please."

He wanted to argue but instead he kissed the top of her head, holding her tighter. He didn't know what he would do without Dana. She was his life. He hated to tell her that the cold-case homicide detective had probably already issued a BOLO for Stacy. If he hadn't, he would soon.

"Ella was asking me about Stacy's past," his wife said as she stepped out of his arms and they walked together the rest of the way to the house. "I didn't know what to tell her because I don't know. I've never wanted to know."

Stacy had attracted trouble much of her life. Some of it she'd brought to the ranch. It appeared she had again. "Don't worry," he told her. "Stacy will turn up." He just hoped it would be alive and not under arrest.

In the meantime, he had to find out everything he could about Stacy's past and Marvin Hanover and his murder.

WACO COULDN'T WAIT to hear what had been discovered in the bottom of the well. "What did they find?" he asked the DCI agent at the other end of the phone line. He'd worked with Bradley before and knew he was thorough.

But right now, he also had something else on his mind. Ella Cardwell. He'd followed her to the grocery store and circled the block. He'd almost circled the block for a third time when the vehicle in front of him stalled. Ella certainly seemed to be taking her time at the store, which was either a ruse or she was headed back to the ranch with a pickup full of groceries and no longer in search of her mother.

"It's a key," Bradley said.

"A key?" Waco echoed with disappointment. "A car key, safe-deposit key…?"

"Larger than a normal key. Odd shape. Definitely not a key to a car or house. Of course, we have no idea how long it's been down there or if it even belonged to the deceased. But from the look of it, the key's been down there for years."

"I'm going to want to see it," Waco said as another call came in. "Can you get it to me at General Delivery in Big Sky?" he asked before disconnecting.

"I just finished notifying the rest of Marvin's family," Hitch told him.

He listened as she described her reception at the Hanover house, her impressions of Lionel and Angeline, as well as Mercy's boyfriend, Trevor.

"The surprise was another daughter by another mother," Hitch told him. "Jane Frazer. I'm on my way to talk to her."

"Thanks. I appreciate your help on this one," Waco said as the man in the car in front of him finally got the vehicle running again.

"I'll be off this case as soon as I talk to Jane."

"Just don't stick your neck out too far. I wouldn't want you on the wrong side of your soon-to-be relatives before you even get to the altar. Or worse."

"There is one thing Jane told me on the phone that might interest you," Hitch said. "Her mother was killed when she was young. Jane ended up living with Marvin and his other children. None of them mentioned her to me."

"Interesting."

"That's not the interesting part. Marvin's wife and fiancée died in accidents. I just looked it up on my phone. Wife number one fell down the stairs, broke her neck. Almost-wife number two, Jane's mother, was killed in a hit and run."

Waco let out a low whistle.

"So it is rather amazing that Stacy Cardwell Hanover is still alive."

He grunted at that. "Maybe only because she killed him before he could kill her." Waco hadn't considered what might have happened at the edge of that well before Marvin went into it. "What if he took her out there to throw her down the well, but she pushed him instead?"

"Interesting since both the wife's and fiancée's deaths were considered suspicious," Hitch said. "Jane said when she was young, she suspected her father had killed them both. She said she thought he would kill Stacy, too, and was surprised that someone got to him first."

"Let me know what Jane has to say," Waco said as he came around the block and saw Ella pulling back onto Main. "By the way, DCI found a key in the well. I haven't seen it yet, but they're sending it to me."

"The key to Marvin Hanover's heart?"

"Hopefully, the key to this case," he said. "Oh, looks like Stacy's daughter is headed back to the ranch. I don't believe she knows where her mother is," he said with a sigh. "A dead end. At least, temporarily. Thanks for the update on the family and taking care of the notifications. You're the best. If you weren't already spoken for—"

"You'd run like the devil was chasing you if any woman seriously showed an interest in you," she said, laughing. "Save your sweet talk for someone who cares. I'd be interested to see what you make of the family. Just…be careful. I picked up on some real animosity."

"You're worried about me? I knew you had a soft spot for me, Hitch."

"Just between my ears," she said and disconnected.

ELLA DIDN'T KNOW what to make of her encounter with Mercy Hanover Davis. But apparently she and the detective weren't the only ones looking for Stacy. She couldn't help her disappointment in not finding her mother, but she wasn't going to let that stop her.

She drove home, anxious to see if Stacy might have called the ranch. At the main house, she found Dana and Hud in the kitchen. What she overheard as she walked in shocked her. An intruder had knocked down her aunt?

"You're sure you're all right?" Ella asked after hearing what had happened at her mother's cabin. She could see that her aunt was more scared about her sister than before and trying hard not to show it.

"I'm fine," Dana insisted. "You and Hud don't have to worry about me."

The marshal snorted at that and said he had to get back to the office. "Can you stay out of trouble until I get home?" he asked his wife before he kissed her goodbye.

"I'll do my best," Dana promised, smiling as she watched him leave. Then she quickly turned to Ella. "Any luck finding her?"

Ella shook her head. She hadn't learned anything from Nora Cline except that Stacy kept secrets—even from her secret friend.

After being sure that her aunt really was all right, she walked up to the cabins, going straight to her mother's. The marshal had cleared it after the forensics team had finished. Her uncle had said the intruder had apparently been wearing gloves, so he hadn't left any fingerprints.

Ella set about cleaning up the mess. Her aunt had mentioned that the intruder might have taken some photos. Dana said she had never seen the photo albums before. Ella realized that neither had she.

Taking them to a chair, she began to go through them, wondering why her mother had never shown her these albums. She'd never seen them before or any of the photos. Nor did she recognize any of the people in the snapshots—except for her mother.

When and where had these been taken? There were photographs of her mother when she was much younger, possibly in her late twenties or early thirties, with people Ella didn't know.

It felt strange, seeing her mother so young—before Ella'd been born. From the photos, it was clear that Stacy had known these people well. So where had the shots been taken? Not on the ranch or in the canyon, from what she could see.

She found her mother's magnifying glass. Stacy had been complaining that printed instructions were either getting smaller and smaller, or her eyesight was getting worse. As she studied the photos, Ella noted that they were from different years, different decades, given the clothing. Each year, each decade, there was her mother—often with the same people. The people aged the deeper she got in the album—just as her mother did.

Ella had an idea, gathered up the photo albums and took them to her cabin. Taking out her own albums from the same time period, she compared the photos of herself as a child on the ranch with her mother and family, and realized that she'd stumbled onto something.

There was a photo of her mother in a favorite summer dress that Ella remembered—and there she was in the exact same dress in one of her mother's photographs from her secret albums with the mystery people.

With a shock, she realized this had to be where her mother disappeared to for days at a time over the years—and it could be where she had gone now. Her mother had two separate lives; she'd been coexisting all these years. A secret life away from Cardwell Ranch.

Why couldn't Stacy tell them about this place, these people? Why keep it a secret when this other life obviously meant something to her? She wouldn't have kept the photos otherwise. It made no sense—just like her mother's moods.

Where was this place that her mother had gone to year after year before Ella was born? She scoured the photos again, looking for something in the background that would give her a clue as to where they'd been taken. If she could find the place, she had a feeling she would find her mother.

Her hand holding the magnifying glass stopped on what appeared to be a sign, barely distinguishable in the background. A bar? Ella looked for other similar photographs until she found one with a more legible portion of the sign. She wrote down the letters she could see and searched for more until at last she looked at what she had written. Hell and Gone Bar.

Her heart beat faster. So where was this place? Recognizing some of the license plates on cars in the background, she noted Montana plates from different years and decades. There were enough Montana tags, she thought excitedly, that the town had to be in the state.

Going to her phone, she thumbed in the words *Hell and Gone Bar*. She blinked as an older article came up on the screen. The story was about a place in Montana with a photo that made it look like a ghost town. Was anyone left? It appeared that at least a few businesses were still operating when the photo had been taken.

Removing a couple of the snapshots of Stacy and her friends from her mother's album, people who appeared to have families of their own, Ella pocketed them. If there was anything left in Hell and Gone, Montana, she thought, she would go there. Her instincts told her that it was also where she would find her mother.

But as she thought it, she realized that she wasn't the only one with photos from this other place, this other time. Whoever had broken in had taken some of the older snapshots. By now, the intruder could have also figured out where Stacy had gone.

Chapter Nine

Jane Frazer was a surprise. Hitch put the woman who answered the door somewhere around forty-five. An attractive brunette with wide gray eyes, she wore a suit and heels, explaining she had been called into her office earlier and had only just returned.

"You're a doctor of psychology," Hitch said once they were seated in her neat, modern living room.

"I blame the Hanovers for that. Spending time in that house would make anyone crazy." Jane laughed. "I shouldn't have said that. It's not polite to use the word *crazy* anymore. Unfortunately, *dysfunctional* just doesn't cover families like Marvin's. I was fourteen when my mother died. Fortunately, a maiden aunt of mine came and rescued me."

Hitch was delighted to get this kind of insight into the family dynamics and said as much to the doctor.

"Oh, my view is too biased to be clinical," the woman admitted. "So, what exactly do you want to know?"

"I'm curious. Your text with your address said that you would meet with me, but only if I didn't let anyone in the Hanover family know where you were."

Jane raised a brow. "When I tell you what I know about Marvin, I think you'll understand. I haven't been around his offspring in years, but I would suspect the apple doesn't fall far from the tree. Marvin was a very dangerous man."

"You said you thought at one point that he'd killed his first wife and your mother. Do you still feel that way?"

Jane nodded.

"Any idea who killed him?" Hitch asked.

If Jane was shocked by such a direct approach, she didn't show it. "Any number of people."

"Family members?"

"Definitely. They all hated him. The only reason they put up with him at all was because of the money."

"So I've gathered, but what kind of money are we talking?"

The doctor shrugged. "Apparently, a fortune. He'd inherited it from his father, who had made the money in shady deals back East before moving to Montana. Marvin's father is the one who built the house. Have you seen it?"

Hitch nodded.

"Like his father, Marvin didn't trust banks. At least, that was his story. I suspect the money hadn't gone into the bank because it would then be traceable and—even worse—taxable. The story was that the bulk of his fortune was hidden somewhere in that maze of a house—and Marvin was the only one who knew where. Believe me, everyone in the family tried to find it, myself included. It was this delicious mystery." She chuckled. "As far as I know, he never revealed where it was. He had this key he wore around his neck and guarded with his life."

A key? Like the one Waco said had been found in the bottom of the well? "Like to a safe-deposit box?"

Jane shook her head. "It was larger and odd-shaped. More like to a building or a steel door somewhere."

"What was your first thought when you heard about Marvin's remains being found in the old homestead's abandoned well?" Hitch asked.

"Someone found a way to get that key and now has his fortune." She smiled. "Once they start spending the dough, you'll have your killer."

"And if they didn't get the key?"

Jane frowned and seemed to give that some thought. "How disappointing. Unless, of course, the killer just wanted Marvin dead."

"Stacy Cardwell?"

"She wasn't the only woman who wanted him dead. There was another woman before Stacy, but just for a short time. Her name is Lorraine Baxter. She's in a county nursing home now. I can give you the information, but she has mild dementia. If you can catch her on a good day, she'll probably be happy to tell you why she had every reason to want to see Marvin at the bottom of a well. Or then again, she might not," Jane said with a chuckle.

Hitch thanked her and left.

Once behind the wheel, she called Waco. His phone went to voice mail. She left him a message highlighting what she'd learned and giving him Jane Frazer's phone number and address. "She's expecting your call. You might want to talk to a girlfriend he had between her mother and Stacy. Her name is Lorraine Baxter. From what I heard, she might have had reason to want Marvin dead. But so did the rest of his family members, according to Jane." She left the name of the nursing home in Livingston.

She'd gotten only a few blocks along when her cell phone rang. Seeing it was her fiancé calling, Hitch was already smiling when she picked up. "Hey," she said into the phone.

"Hey. You working?"

"Actually, I just finished."

"Good," Ford said. "Mind going to dinner at the ranch? Dana's got a giant pot roast on. I think she just needs the company tonight," he added. "I suppose you heard."

"I got called in on the case, but once I realized who the deceased was, I pretty much just notified the relatives. I'm now leaving it to the investigator, cold-case homicide detective Waco Johnson. I'm sure he'll be talking to everyone in the family." Silence filled the line for so long, she thought they'd been disconnected. "Ford?"

"Sorry, I was just closing the gate here on the ranch. I wasn't referring to a case, but maybe I was. Dana was up in Stacy's cabin earlier. There was an intruder. He knocked her down on his way out."

"Is she all right?" Hitch asked quickly.

"Just bruised. I'm sensing it's connected to this case you mentioned."

"I would imagine," she said. "What is Stacy to you?"

"My dad's cousin. Does that make her a second cousin? I don't know. Still close enough that I'm glad you aren't involved. Must be hard for you, though."

She laughed. "It is an interesting case, but like I said, I'm stepping away. Is that why you called?"

"No, actually. I just called about dinner. Dana is getting the whole family together. It's what she does when there's trouble. Can you make it?"

Hitch glanced at the time. "I probably won't make dinner, but I'll definitely make dessert. I'll meet you there."

WACO GOT HITCH'S message and decided to swing by the nursing home. He had hired a private investigator to watch Cardwell Ranch and follow Ella if she left again.

In the meantime, all he could do was keep investigating Marvin Hanover's death without Stacy. She would eventually have to show up.

Unless someone got to her before he found her.

The notion had come from out of nowhere. Could she have run because she was in danger? From Marvin's family? Or from someone else?

Lone Pine View turned out to be an assisted-living facility in Paradise Valley. It looked and felt more like a resort, he thought as he got out of his patrol SUV and entered the ultramodern facility.

Lorraine Baxter wasn't in her room. He was directed to the tennis courts, where he saw two fiftysomething women in great shape in the middle of a vigorous game of singles. Lorraine, it turned out, was the attractive redhead who tromped the other woman in the last set. She was still breathing hard when Waco walked up to her.

"Nice game," he said, recalling what Jane had told Hitch about Lorraine having mild dementia. He wondered what this place cost a month and what a person had to do to get in here. If Lorraine had gotten in because of her dementia, he had to question how bad it was. She sure hadn't had any trouble remembering the tennis score.

He introduced himself, getting no more than a serene eyebrow lift at the word *homicide*. "I'd like to ask you a few questions about Marvin Hanover."

Lorraine motioned to a patio with brightly colored umbrellas and comfortable-looking outdoor furniture. Two women appeared to be having tea at one of the far tables, but other than that, they had the place to themselves.

"I'm not sure how helpful I can be," Lorraine said.

"Because of your dementia?"

She smiled. "Because it's been so long since I dated Marvin, let alone was engaged to him—neither for very long."

"Who broke it off?" he asked.

A waiter appeared at the table. "Would you like something, Detective?" Lorraine asked. "They serve alcoholic beverages."

He wondered if she thought all cops drank. At least she hadn't suggested doughnuts. "I'm on duty, but thanks anyway."

"Then I'll take a sparkling water and a gin and tonic with lime." The waiter nodded and left. "I'm sorry. You asked who broke it off. Actually, it was mutual." She shrugged.

"You knew about his other fiancée and his wife's death?"

With a chuckle, she nodded. "Terrible accidents. Poor Marvin."

Poor Marvin? Waco stared at her until the waiter brought her drinks and left again. "From what I've heard about Mr. Hanover... well, he wasn't well-liked."

"Really? I found him delightful." Smiling, she glanced around the facility.

He took a wild guess. "Marvin is putting you up here?"

"Why, yes, he is, even in death," Lorraine said.

"I hate to even ask how much—"

"Wise not to," she said. "It's mind-boggling what they charge. But it is a nice place, wouldn't you say?"

"I'd say. But what I really want to know is how it is that Marvin is paying for it—'even in death'?"

She gave him an innocent look. "Well, when we mutually agreed to part ways, Marvin insisted on taking care of me for the rest of my life." She blinked her blue eyes and Waco got a glimpse of the young, beautiful woman who'd conned Marvin Hanover into taking care of her.

Waco let out a low whistle. "Neat trick, if you can pull it off. What did you have on him? It would have to be something big with enough evidence to put him away for life—if it ever came out." All he got from the attractive redhead was another blink of eyelashes and that knowing smile. "Does his family know?"

She chuckled. "I doubt it, since I'm still alive."

He realized she wasn't joking. "You think they would have killed you years ago if they knew how much this was costing their father?"

"In a heartbeat. So let's keep it between us. Even with my insurance, that bunch is so unstable, I wouldn't trust them to have good judgment. Anyway, that's not why you're here. You want to know who killed him. You don't have to look any farther than that house of vipers. They all hated him, desperately wanted his money and couldn't wait for him to die."

"What about you? He could have changed his mind after he met Stacy Cardwell and wanted out of the deal he made with you."

"Our deal was ironclad," Lorraine said as she touched a diamond tennis bracelet at her wrist. "There was no getting out of it. And if I die of anything but natural causes before I'm eighty… Well, he wouldn't want me to do that and besmirch the family name. Marvin worried about his legacy."

"So, just to be clear, you didn't want him dead?" Waco asked.

"I didn't care one way or the other," she said, draining her sparkling water before reaching for her gin and tonic. "But I have to admit, I haven't missed him. Not that I had any contact with him after he married Stacy. I admired her for holding out for marriage—even knowing what happened to the others."

"Maybe she thought she would make out like a bandit the same way you did," he suggested. "I understand his first wife's jewelry disappeared at some point."

Lorraine's laugh was bright as sunshine. "Really? How sad. Marvin wanted me to have it." She shrugged.

Waco shook his head. "You must have had proof that he killed his first wife and his fiancée."

Lorraine didn't admit it. But she also didn't deny it. "I got lucky. But I don't think things went as well for Stacy."

Waco didn't think so, either. So why had she married him? He watched the woman finish her drink as quickly as she had her water.

"I need to go change," Lorraine said, excusing herself. "I have a massage soon. I hope I answered all of your questions."

"You did."

HE WAS ALMOST to the Gallatin Canyon when he noticed that Hitch had left him a second message. He listened to it, hearing the worry in her voice. She passed along Jane Frazer's concerns that Lorraine might be in danger. He told himself that Lorraine was fine, but still placed the call.

When the redhead came on the line, he could hear dinner music in the background. "I thought you should know that Marvin's daughter Jane Frazer is worried that you might be in danger." He waited for a reply.

Not getting one, he continued. "She'd had a visit from the medical examiner about her father's remains being found. They discussed Marvin and his…women. Your name and your location came up. That's how I found you."

"I'm sorry—what is it you're trying to tell me?" He could hear the soft clinking of cutlery and the murmur of voices. It sounded like she was in a five-star restaurant.

"Your life could be in danger."

"Oh, Detective, that is very sweet of you to think of me, but as you noticed when you arrived here, I live in a gated community surrounded by staff and other residents. I'm not worried. Also, I still have my…insurance policy, so I'm fine."

"Marvin's dead, so that insurance policy might not be worth the paper it's printed on."

Lorraine laughed. "It wasn't just Marvin, Detective. At least one of his…offspring was also involved in helping him terminate those two relationships."

"That is the sort of evidence I'd like to see."

"You didn't hear it from me. But thank you so much for your concern." She hung up.

He sat for a moment mumbling under his breath. People often thought they were safe because a community was gated. Or because they had incriminating evidence as so-called insurance. He shook his head. Maybe Lorraine Baxter was right and there was no cause for concern.

One thing kept coming up time and again—a common denominator. The Hanover heirs. Were they as dangerous as he was being led to believe?

It was time he found out.

Chapter Ten

The last thing Ella needed right now was a family dinner. But she knew her aunt. Dana needed to get everyone together. It was her strength in times of crisis. If this wasn't a crisis, then Ella didn't know what was.

Before coming in to dinner, Ella had noticed a vehicle in the distance, the same one she'd seen there earlier. Waco Johnson or someone he'd hired to watch the ranch?

Dana had seated them all in the huge dining room. Pot roast, corn, potatoes and green beans from last year's garden were passed around the table, along with a slab of fresh sweet butter and honey to go with corn bread piping hot from the oven. There was apple pie for dessert or Dana's favorite chocolate cake. Her aunt believed food was love and that all of them seated around the table together would make whatever was happening better.

But Ella had her doubts. She wondered what Stacy was doing right now. There still hadn't been any word from her. The ranch was being watched by a homicide detective, and tomorrow Ella was headed for Hell and Gone with only a prayer's hope of finding her mother.

After helping her aunts with the dishes, Ella escaped to a corner of the living room. She heard the front door open and saw Hitch enter. Ford rushed to his fiancée. Earlier, when Ella had gone down to the barn to check on the new foal, she'd heard Ford on the phone, leaving Hitch a message. He'd said, "I know you're probably still working, but if you get a chance, give me a call. Just getting a little worried about you." Ella wondered what case Hitch was working that had him worried—surely not Marvin Hanover's murder.

She could see that Ford was relieved and happy to see his fiancée. Everyone in the family had accepted Hitch, it appeared. Ella was withholding judgment until she got to know the medical examiner better.

When Ford went to retrieve the piece of pie Dana had saved for her, Hitch approached Ella. "I was hoping you would be here," the young woman said quietly. "I heard you've gone looking for your mother."

Ella knew there was no keeping secrets in this family—unless you were Stacy Cardwell. She said nothing and waited since Hitch seemed to feel uncomfortable talking about it.

"It's gotten more dangerous," Hitch said quietly.

"My mother—"

"As far as I know, she's fine. But when I spoke with Waco—"

"You two are on a first-name basis?" Of course they were. Ella wasn't sure why that annoyed her. Lines had been drawn in the sand. Hitch was on the wrong side if she was with Waco.

"We've worked together for several years now," Hitch said.

Ella studied the woman. "Are you working on a case with him right now?"

"If you're asking about the homicide case involving your mother—"

"We don't know that it involves my mother," she interrupted.

"I just meant—"

"Waco's after my mother."

Hitch looked uneasy. "Waco is interviewing everyone who was closely associated with Marvin Hanover. He's just following standard procedure."

"Spare me the administrative lesson. My uncle is a marshal. I grew up with standard procedure," Ella snapped.

"Then you know I can't talk about it."

Ella took a breath. "But you can tell me what kind of lawman Waco is."

For a moment, Hitch looked as if she wasn't going to comment. "He's good at his job. He's thorough, but he's fair. He's…likable." Ella quirked a brow. "But he won't stop until he gets to the truth."

"I'm curious just how close the two of you are," Ella said, hating that she'd actually voiced the words out loud.

Hitch seemed surprised. "If you're asking what I think you are, Waco and I are just friends. That's all."

"You two never dated?"

The other woman smiled. "No. He's never been interested in me as anything more than a coworker."

"What about you?" Ella knew she should stop. She could see Ford headed their way.

"Sorry, not my type—not that there is anything wrong with him for someone…" Hitch's smile broadened. "More like you, maybe."

Ford walked up with a small plate and a slice of apple pie. He put his arm around his fiancée. "Dana insists you come into the kitchen. She's made you a dinner plate."

Ella felt Hitch's gaze shift to her.

"Please, just be careful," the medical examiner said, a knowing look in her eye.

Was she referring to the murder case? Or Waco?

Ella could have mentally kicked herself. She'd sounded jealous of Hitch and Waco, when that wasn't what she'd been getting at in the least. She felt a knot form in her stomach as she watched Hitch and Ford head to the kitchen. She told herself that this strange feeling had nothing to do with her and Waco, but Waco Johnson and Hitch Roberts and where—and if—the woman fit into this family.

THE HANOVER HOUSE was exactly as Hitch had described it. Waco had called and Lionel had said they would be waiting for him. After he parked and walked up to the large front door, it had opened and he'd gotten his first look at Lionel and Angeline. Like her description of the house, Hitch had done a great job sizing up two of Marvin's offspring.

He'd gone through a list of preliminary questions about Marvin and about their relationship with their father, and was just getting to Stacy Cardwell Hanover when the younger sister arrived.

Mercy burst in, the sound of her voice racing her into the room only seconds before she appeared. While Lionel and Angeline were dull as dust and about as forthcoming as rocks, Mercy was a turbocharged gust of fresh air.

The robust fiftysomething woman with her wild curly brown hair and small granitelike eyes stormed over to him. "Well?" Mercy demanded.

He pretended he didn't know what she was talking about as Lionel tried to shut his sister up and Angeline wheeled herself to the bar to pour herself some wine. Hitch had said that the woman was ill and apparently dying. Waco wondered if she was on any kind of medication and yet still drinking wine.

"What have they been telling you?" Mercy looked from Lionel to Angeline and back. "Don't believe anything they say."

Lionel groaned. "Mercy, this is not the time for—"

"They hated our father as much as I did. Maybe more."

"I'm going to do my best to find his killer and give you a little peace," Waco said.

Mercy howled at that. "You think finding his killer will give us peace? We already know who killed him. What we want is the money," the woman said, ignoring her brother's attempts to silence her.

"What money?" Waco asked, hoping he looked genuinely confused.

Mercy flung her hands in the air. "Our father's fortune. Of course, they didn't tell you. He wore a key on a chain around his neck. Tell me you have the key."

"I have the key." The room suddenly went deathly quiet. Mercy was staring at him, as was Angeline. Lionel was frowning at him.

"You have the key?" Mercy repeated. "Then give it to us."

"I'm afraid it's evidence in a murder investigation," Waco said, and the woman erupted with a string of curses. "You'll get it back when the investigation is over."

Mercy swore again. "How long is that going to take?"

"Let the man do his job," Lionel said before Waco could answer. "Have you talked to Stacy?" he asked.

"She's definitely on my list," Waco said.

Mercy shot a look at her brother. "Is he serious?" She swung her gaze back at him like a scythe. "Stacy Cardwell murdered our father. Why wouldn't you have already talked to her?"

"We haven't established that Stacy killed anyone," Waco said. "Tell me this. Why did your father marry Stacy?"

Mercy gave him a disbelieving look. "She was young, she was somewhat pretty, I suppose, and she was easier than an Easy-Bake Oven."

"He wanted another son," Angeline said in a hoarse whisper as she picked up her full glass of wine and straightened the quilt on her lap. "No offense, Lionel, but you know it's true. He would have given anything—and I mean anything—for another son."

Lionel looked down at the expensive worn rug at his feet. Waco noticed it was threadbare like the furniture. The light in this room was dim, but he began to see how outdated everything was. Was the family hurting for money? It would appear so.

"None of our father's offspring at the time met his expectations," Lionel snarled. "But I see no reason to air our dirty laundry with—"

"Our father would have married anyone he could get pregnant with a son," Mercy said, cutting him off. "Since the bitch said she was pregnant—"

"Wait!" Waco said in surprise. "Stacy was pregnant?"

"No, she *wasn't* pregnant," Mercy snapped as she shrugged off her jacket and dropped into a chair by the fire. "She lied to him so he'd give her the money he'd promised her."

"In all fairness, Stacy said she miscarried the baby after the marriage. At least, that's what she told us. Then, when our father disappeared, she got an annulment," Lionel said.

"If anything, she got rid of the baby—if she'd ever been pregnant to begin with," Mercy said. "Why keep it if it wasn't going to make her any more money?"

Waco was having trouble keeping up. "Your father paid her?"

"Ten thousand dollars to prove that she was having a son," Angeline said.

"So she was pregnant?" Waco asked, trying to fit the odd-shaped pieces together.

"He believed her, but who knows if it was even true?" Mercy said. "Stacy had an ultrasound photo in her purse that supposedly he accidentally found. But I suspect she planted it there, knowing he was so jealous and suspicious, he often searched her purse."

"What my sister is saying," Lionel added, "is that we aren't certain the photo was necessarily hers."

"But she didn't have any trouble taking the reward he gave her," Mercy piped up. "Ten thousand dollars. Apparently, that's what a son was going for back then."

"I'm sorry—I'm confused." Waco held up his hand.

"It was a boy, so Stacy's work was done," Lionel declared with obvious disgust. "Once the baby was born, he planned to divorce Stacy and raise his son himself."

Waco couldn't believe what he was hearing. "And Stacy was good with this?"

Mercy laughed. "There never was a baby. It was all a lie. You know she used someone else's ultrasound. She just wanted that ten grand he'd promised her. Once she had it, she must have realized she couldn't keep up the lie, so she killed him."

"I think she killed him because he caught her in the lie," Angeline said, her weak voice cracking as she slurred her words. "That's why we never believed that he had abandoned her. When he disappeared, we knew he had to be dead."

Mercy nodded in agreement. "*Daddy* would have wanted his money back and threatened to take it out of her hide."

Waco thought they might be right. From what he'd learned so far about Stacy Cardwell, the story might actually fit. She had used men for money before and she'd also been questioned in a police investigation about stolen money from a fundraiser event.

"She wouldn't have had to kill him," he said, realizing it was true. "She had the reward money. Why not just take off? He would have had a hard time getting his money back once he realized he'd been cheated."

"You didn't know my father," Lionel said. "He would have tracked her down to the ends of the earth. He would have gotten his money back one way or another. If he didn't kill her, he would have made her wish she was dead."

"He sounds delightful." The words slipped out before Waco could stop them. "So maybe he did find out the truth and Stacy killed him in self-defense."

Mercy groaned. "Who cares? When he disappeared, we all thought he took the money and ran. But now that we know he was murdered... If Stacy didn't get the money my father kept hidden all those years, then where is it?"

Waco didn't have an answer for her.

It was getting late. He was about to stand to leave when the boyfriend Hitch had told him about entered just in time to hear Mercy's question.

"Yeah, where is this fortune?" Trevor said in a mocking tone. "'Bout time someone produced it or I'm going to start wondering if the whole thing was just a way to keep you all in line." The cocky young man looked to Waco.

"You must be Trevor," he said.

"You've heard about me." The man smiled. "You the cop who found him at the bottom of the well?" Waco nodded. "So someone iced him, huh?" Glancing at the family, he said, "Someone in this room?" His laugh had a knife edge to it.

"Must you, Trevor?" Lionel said, shooting a displeased look at Mercy.

"You'll be notified as to when you can take possession of your father's remains," Waco told the others in the room.

"And the key," Mercy added quickly.

"That and the rest of his belongings found with him," Waco said.

"You can keep his bones," she said. "It isn't like we're going to pay for a funeral for him. Not after thirty years. Not after..." She waved her hand through the air. "As far as I'm concerned, you can keep him."

Lionel rose. "Let me see you out."

At the front door, the oldest Hanover offspring apologized for his family. "This has all come as a shock."

Waco didn't point out that they didn't seem shocked, just angry. When he'd run preliminaries on each of them, he'd found that not one of them had a job, let alone a career. Had they all been sitting around for the past thirty years, waiting for their father's money to turn up?

He'd wondered how they lived until he'd done a little investigating. He'd found ads on Craigslist where they'd been selling off their father's holdings over the years. Stocks, bonds, land. Even antique house furnishings when things had begun to turn lean. It explained the condition of the entire house.

Glancing back as he made his way to his SUV, he questioned the timing of the anonymous call. Why had the bones turned up now? He thought about the recording. Any one of the family members could have called from the Gallatin Gateway bar down the road from the house. The caller's voice had sounded hoarse. Because they'd lowered their voice to disguise it?

The big question: Had one of them made the call because they were running out of money and hoped the investigation would turn up the dough? Or the key?

Waco had felt a sick kind of desperation in that room. Marvin Hanover's children appeared to have run out of possessions to sell. If they didn't get their hands on the money soon…

What would they do? he wondered. What had one of them or more than one done thirty years ago when their father had tried to make a new family with a new wife?

Waco couldn't shake the feeling that the killer he was searching for might have been in that very room.

Chapter Eleven

It was late when Ella returned to her cabin and researched everything she could find on Waco Johnson, Henrietta "Hitch" Roberts and the Hell and Gone Bar. Not surprisingly, everything Hitch had told her about Waco seemed to be true. He had an amazing record for solving cold cases. That should have relieved her, but it didn't.

As for Hitch, she had excelled as state medical examiner, was well respected and solved a huge percentage of her cases. What Ella could find about the woman proved that Hitch was much like Waco in her dogged determination to stay on a case until the very end. Ella knew that was true from what had happened with Ford. Hitch had refused to give up. Ella wondered if that wasn't part of the reason Ford had fallen for her. That and the fact that she was beautiful and smart and had saved his life.

Researching the history of the Hell and Gone Bar turned out not to be as hard as she'd thought it would be. She found that the place was named after what had once been an old mining town in the middle of Montana, miles from anything else. Ella had never heard of it—or the bar's owner, a woman named Helen Mandeville. But the article she'd first stumbled on had painted quite a picture of the bar and what was left of the town.

"It's one of those bars that you know right away when you walk in is dangerous, with dangerous characters," the travel writer had written. "I was told that more than half of the people who frequent the bar have at least one outstanding warrant. It's a true example of how the Wild West is still alive in middle-of-nowhere Montana."

Ella was sure it was the same place in her mother's photographs. But why would Stacy go there?

"The bar had once been the true center of this small mining town, aptly named Hell and Gone, Montana," the author continued. "Now the town is little more than a wide spot on a two-lane, miles from any other community, the iron ore that had given it birth having run out long ago."

"If it wasn't for the bar, Hell and Gone would have dried up and blown away years ago," the bar owner had been quoted as saying.

What about this place had drawn Stacy all these years?

Ella had always suspected there was a secret man in her mother's life. A man so unacceptable that Stacy hadn't dared bring him to the ranch. Instead, she'd sneak off a few days here and there to be with him. Was that the case?

Early the next morning, she called Nora Cline, hoping the woman was an early riser like her mother. Nora answered on the second ring, sounding wide-awake.

"Have you ever heard of a place called Hell and Gone?" The woman's silence made Ella realize that she had. "My mother must have mentioned it."

"Jokingly, one time when we had too much to drink," Nora said. "Are you telling me it's an actual place?"

"Apparently. What did she say about it?"

"I'm trying to remember. I can't even remember what we were talking about. Life, I suppose. She said she'd been to Hell and Gone, and then laughed. Then she began to cry. We'd had way too much to drink that night. What she said after that didn't make a lot of sense. But I got the impression there was some man in her life she hadn't been able to get over."

"Is it possible he's in Hell and Gone?" Ella asked.

"If it's a real place, then that would make sense," Nora said. "But you shouldn't go alone. If your mother is in trouble, it might be dangerous."

"I won't be going alone," Ella said, thinking of Waco Johnson. "I'll have a homicide detective following me."

WACO WAS UP before the sun after a restless night. Everything he'd learned since seeing the bones in the bottom of the well and meeting the Hanover family had haunted his dreams. The PI he'd hired to watch the ranch had let him know that Ella hadn't gone anywhere. Yet. Waco didn't believe for a moment that she'd given up on finding her mother.

As soon as the post office opened, he stopped to see if his package had arrived. It had. Inside the padded manila envelope was a key in an evidence bag. The key looked old and much larger than he'd expected. He had no idea what it might belong to. He wondered if Stacy knew. But first he'd have to find her.

He still believed that Ella would take him to her. All his instincts told him that she would keep searching until she found her. So he wasn't surprised this morning, when he relieved the PI, that he didn't have to wait long before he saw the woman's pickup coming out of the ranch.

He smiled to himself as he watched her turn onto Highway 191 and head north. Where were they going today? He couldn't wait to find out. He'd sensed that she was like him. Once Ella got her teeth into something, she didn't let go.

She went straight at the Four Corners instead of turning right and heading into Bozeman. She made a beeline for I-90 and then headed west.

Waco settled in, keeping a few vehicles between them. He had a lot to mull over. Everything he'd learned about Stacy so far had led him to believe that she was quite capable of murder—especially given what he now knew about Marvin Hanover. She might even get a reduced sentence for killing the bastard.

But what about the money? *If* there really was a fortune somewhere. This key might hold the answer. If someone hadn't already gotten to it and spent every dime. From what Waco knew of Stacy Cardwell, she had left the marriage with ten thousand dollars, which had lasted only until she'd given birth to her daughter a few years later.

When she'd returned to Cardwell Ranch, she'd had a baby to raise. Was that why she'd returned to the ranch and never left? If she'd killed Marvin, then she obviously hadn't gotten the key. Why not?

The key was a puzzle. How had it ended up at the bottom of the well with Marvin if that was what the killer was after? If he'd kept it around his neck, why hadn't the killer taken it before knocking him into the well? Or had the killer tried to take it and failed. But if the killer knew the key was at the bottom of the well, wouldn't he or she have tried to climb down there to retrieve it over the years?

He had too many questions. He suspected Stacy had a lot of those answers.

Ahead, he saw Ella turn north off the interstate. With luck, it wouldn't be long now.

MARSHAL HUD SAVAGE had seen the worry in his wife's eyes. Her sister had put her through hell, but for years had been relatively stable. Except for those times when Stacy would disappear. Dana, fine with not knowing where her sister went, had begged him not to interfere.

Now he wished he had. Maybe then he'd have some clue as to how much trouble his sister-in-law was in. Stacy had had a few scrapes with the law, but nothing that landed her in jail or even resulted in a record. Her marriages, though, had been recorded, starting with her first to a man named Emery Gordon.

It didn't take long to find Emery and his home overlooking Bozeman. Hud knew he was clutching at straws interviewing Stacy's husbands. But he had to start somewhere. Stacy had been divorced from Emery for years. Still, as he stood on the man's front stoop, he could only hope that Gordon might know where she went when she disappeared.

Emery, then twenty-six, had married seventeen-year-old Stacy. On her marriage certificate it stated that she was twenty-one— no doubt she'd used a fake ID she'd picked up somewhere. Hud wondered why she'd been in such a hurry to marry—let alone to marry Emery at such a young age—except for the fact that the man must have been a way out. Also, Emery's family had money.

Hud rang the doorbell and heard the chimes echo inside the house to a classical song he couldn't quite put his finger on. He'd grown up on Western boot-scootin' music.

A woman opened the door, complete with uniform. "May I help you?"

"I'd like to speak with Emery Gordon, please," the marshal said, flashing his badge.

The woman's eyes momentarily widened before she nodded and said, "Please, come this way." She led him into a den. "Mr. Gordon will be right with you. Please have a seat."

Hud thanked her, looking around the well-appointed room without sitting. A few moments later, a man some years older than Hud came into the room and apologized for making him wait.

Like his home, Emery Gordon was dressed impeccably. While Hud doubted anyone had ever called the man handsome, he wore his age well.

"Can I offer you something to drink, Marshal?"

He declined. "I need to ask you about Stacy."

"Stacy?" Emery seemed surprised as he motioned to the set of leather chairs. "Please, have a seat, although this probably won't take long. Stacy and I were married less than a year many years ago."

They sat. The chairs were angled so that they almost faced each other. The den was warm and smelled rich with leather and the faint hint of bourbon.

"If you don't mind, why did the marriage last such a short time?" Hud asked. "I know she lied about her age when the two of you eloped." He suspected she'd lied about a whole lot more. He was uncomfortable with such personal questions and wouldn't have been surprised if the man told him it was none of his business.

But if Emery Gordon was offended, he didn't show it. "I don't mind at all. Stacy is your sister-in-law?" Hud nodded. "Do you mind telling me why you're inquiring about something that happened so long ago?"

"Stacy is missing. I'm trying to find her, which means prying into her past for answers." He didn't want to tell the man that she was wanted for questioning in the murder of one of her other husbands. He feared all that would come out soon enough—probably in the newspapers when she was arrested.

"I see. Then what I have to tell you shouldn't come as a surprise. She swept me off my feet. She had a way about her..." Emery seemed lost in the past. He shook himself back to the present. "The truth is, she married me for my money. When she found out that most of it was tied up in a trust that I couldn't touch until I was forty-five, she bailed and took what money she could. I'd like to say that I regretted the time I had with her." Emery smiled. "I can't. Even eight months with Stacy was worth the expense, the embarrassment and the painful lesson she taught me."

"I'm sorry. I hated to bring it up, but I was hoping you might know where she went next."

Emery laughed. "To whom, you mean? You're welcome to talk to him. At the time, he was my best friend. Now he's Congressman Todd Bellingham. He lives outside of Helena."

"Stacy…" Hud wasn't sure how to form the question.

"Todd didn't marry her, but it still almost cost him his marriage and our friendship. He might not want to talk about it."

Hud had taken off his Stetson and balanced it on his knee. Now he picked it up by the brim and rose. "Thank you for your candor."

"Not at all," Emery said, rising, as well. "You've brought back some interesting memories, some I actually cherish. Stacy was a wild child back then. I thought I'd heard that she'd changed. Doesn't she have a daughter?"

"Yes. Ella, who's a beautiful, smart, capable young woman with a good head on her shoulders. Nothing like her mother," Hud said, thankful for that.

"I hope you find Stacy." For a moment, Emery looked genuinely worried that something bad had happened to her.

"Me, too," Hud said, more worried than Emery Gordon could know—and not just about Stacy.

Ella had no idea what she was getting into. But he knew she was determined to track down her mother. Hud suspected that if Stacy had killed Marvin Hanover, then she'd gone to someone from her past whom she thought could help her. Someone dangerous. And Ella was headed straight for it.

HOURS LATER, ELLA looked around the wide-open, sage-covered country. She'd driven a narrow two-lane north for miles, reminding her just how large Montana really was. With each mile, the population counts had dropped considerably. Cows had given way to coyotes as the land became more inhospitable, the highways even more narrow and less traveled. What was a bar doing out here in such an isolated place?

She knew the answer to that. Want to disappear? Go to Hell and Gone Bar. That was what the writer of the article had suggested. And her mother might have done just that.

Buildings began to take shape on the edge of the horizon. The closer she got, she saw what little remained of the once-thriving mining town. Ella slowed on the edge of the community. The few remaining structures looked abandoned.

As she drove slowly through the town, she saw that the hotel still stood, its sign hanging by one hinge. Across the worn stretch of narrow pavement, she could see a neon beer sign glowing in a window and an almost-indistinguishable hand-printed faded sign that read Hell and Gone. That was the only indication that there was a bar inside. That and the four pickups parked out front. None of the trucks had the Cardwell Ranch logo on the side, although Ella couldn't be sure her mother was even still driving the ranch pickup.

A few empty building lots beyond the hotel, there was an abandoned Texaco station, its serve-yourself gas pumps rusting away. Past that, nothing but a dark ribbon of pavement forged its way through more sagebrush before disappearing in the distance.

After the town ended abruptly, she turned around and drove back through it, even more slowly. Across from the bar she noticed a tiny general store with dust-coated windows. Hand-printed signs in the window advertised sandwiches, mineral rocks and muck boots.

But Ella was more interested in the bar and its owner, Helen Mandeville. She took the first street past it and drove around the block. There were some small older houses, most in desperate need of repair and paint. But directly behind the bar on the dirt street, she spotted an attached house that appeared to have been painted in the past decade. There were flowers in the front yard. The house looked so out of place among the other buildings around it, Ella knew it had to belong to the bar's owner.

She kept driving, aware that Waco was right behind her in his SUV. Detective Waco Johnson had been following her for miles. She hadn't even bothered to try to lose him—not that she was sure she could. Now that she was here, she wasn't that sorry to see him still with her, given that this town looked like the kind of place where a person on the run would come—and disappear whether she wanted to or not.

But if Ella wanted to find her mother, she worried that no one in this town would talk to her with a cop on her tail. Getting rid of him could be a problem.

She pulled in and parked next to one of the pickups in front of the bar. Was her mother here? Because of some lost love? Or was she simply on the run from her past mistakes, especially this big one? Ella couldn't imagine her mother in this town for any reason—other than knowing she could hide here and no one would give her up, especially to the cops.

But then, that would mean Stacy had good reason to fear the law, wouldn't it?

WACO WAS AT the point that he thought Ella Cardwell was merely taking him on a long wild-goose chase when he'd spotted buildings on the horizon. Way ahead of him, he saw her brake lights. He'd thought she'd only slowed for what appeared to be some sort of dying town.

But then she'd driven through it and turned around and headed back. By the time he'd reached the edge of town, she was parking her truck next to four others in front of what appeared to be a bar.

He slowed. She hadn't tried to lose him. He watched her park and get out of her truck. By the time he pulled in, she was headed for the weathered, discolored wood door next to the neon beer sign.

She didn't seem like the sort who suddenly needed a drink. Nor did this look like the kind of place a young woman alone would choose to enter for a beverage. He could see the broken beer bottles and other garbage on each side of the front door. Everything about the place looked rough, he thought as he shut off his engine and got out. It was definitely the kind of place an officer of the law should avoid—especially one alone with little chance of getting any backup.

But all that aside, including the fact that Ella wasn't going to appreciate him being there, he couldn't let her go in there alone. The heavy weathered door groaned as he pushed it open. He was instantly hit with the smell of stale beer, old grease and floor cleaner. He caught sight of someone standing at a grill behind the bar, a spatula in his hand. He heard the sizzle of meat frying on the griddle and the clank of pool balls knocking together, followed by hard-core cussing in the back. Over all of it, country twang poured from the old jukebox.

Waco blinked in the cavern-like darkness as the door closed behind him with a solid thud. Ella was standing only a few feet inside. A half dozen men of varying ages had turned on their bar stools to stare at her. Another four were at the pool table, their game momentarily suspended as they took in the strangers who'd just walked in.

All of the men were staring at Ella, except for the ones who were leering. She'd definitely caught everyone's attention. Another song began on the jukebox to the sizzle of whatever was near burning on the grill. Otherwise, the place had now fallen drop-dead quiet as the four men in the back leaned on their pool sticks and stared.

Waco only had a few seconds to decide what to do. He stepped up behind Ella and said loud enough for the men to hear, "Honey, let's sit in a booth." There were several sorry-looking booths against the wall to their left.

At the sound of his voice, she started and half turned, making him realize that she hadn't noticed him enter behind her. He took her arm before she could resist. "What would you like to drink?"

They were here now—best to act as normal as possible. These were the kinds of bars that a fight could break out in at a moment's notice—and usually for no good reason other than the patrons were drunk and bored. Between him and Ella, Waco feared he'd given them an even better reason.

She glared at him but let him lead her over to the booth. "Bottle of beer. I don't need a glass," she said, those green eyes snapping as they telegraphed anger to cover what he suspected might be just a little relief at not being alone in this place.

"Wise decision," he said quietly. This wasn't the cleanest establishment he'd ever been in. Walking over to the bar, he nodded at the men sitting along the row of stools. They were now staring at him with way too much distrust.

The bartender, a heavyset man with an out-of-control beard,

took his time coming down the length of the bar. "You lost?" he asked quietly. The pool game had resumed with a lot of loud ball smacking followed by even louder curses.

Waco spotted several baseball bats behind the bar. He had no doubt there was probably a sawed-off shotgun back there, as well. This was the middle of Montana, miles from anything. Justice here was meted out as necessary on an individual basis.

"Two bottles of beer. Whatever you have handy." Ella hadn't stopped here because she was thirsty. Unless he missed his guess, she'd come here looking for her mother. That alone gave him pause. Why would she think Stacy would be here, of all places?

That worried him. If it were the case, then Ella wouldn't want to leave until she'd gotten what she'd come for. That fact was going to make this excursion a whole lot trickier. Because if Stacy Cardwell was here, which he had to doubt, he knew these people weren't going to give her up easily.

There would be no demanding answers here. Waco knew his badge would be useless—worse than useless. It would be a liability, and he wasn't in the mood to have the stuffing kicked out of him—let alone to end up in a shallow grave out back.

"You want these to go?" the bartender asked, glancing from Waco to Ella and back.

The open-container law aside, Waco didn't think Ella was planning on leaving that soon. "Here."

"Suit yourself." The bartender walked back down the bar to open a cooler and pull out two bottles of beer.

Waco got the feeling that not many tourists found their way here. If they did, he'd bet they sped up and kept right on going.

The men at the bar were watching him, except for the ones still leering at Ella. He cursed under his breath. Did she have any idea what she'd walked them both into?

Chapter Twelve

Stacy's second conquest attempt had a home on Canyon Ferry Lake outside Helena. Hud had tried calling Todd Bellingham's residence first, only to get a recording. He'd headed for the lake, arriving in the afternoon. The sun shimmered off the surface of the water as he pulled in, parked and exited his SUV. The day was warm, the scent of the water rising up to meet him, along with shrieks of laughter from the other side of the house.

As he rounded the front of the house overlooking the lake, he could see a group of teenagers frolicking in a cacophony of spray and high-pitched shrieks at the water's edge.

"Grandkids," a distinguished gray-haired man said from a lounge chair on the patio as the marshal approached. "I tell people they're what keeps me young, but the truth is, they wear me out." He chuckled. "Marshal Hudson Savage, right?" he asked as he started to rise from the chair.

"Please, don't get up," Hud said quickly. Clearly, Emery Gordon had called to let Todd know he was coming. "And it's Hud."

"Then join me, Hud." Todd Bellingham motioned to the chair next to him. The man glanced back through the wall of windows into the house and made a motion with his hand. "I'm having iced tea. Have a glass with me?"

"Thanks. That sounds good," Hud said as he took the lounge

chair in the shade. The view of the lake and the mountains on the other side was spectacular. Gold had been found in those mountains over a century ago, one area said to be the richest place on earth. It was no wonder that Montana had first been known as the Treasure State.

A woman appeared with a tray. "This is my wife, Nancy. Marshal Hudson Savage," Todd said by way of introduction.

The woman smiled as she left the tray. "Nice to meet you, Marshal."

"You, too," he said as she exited quickly, as if sensing this wasn't a social visit.

Below them on the mountainside, the group of teenagers had apparently exhausted themselves for the moment. The girls had plopped down to sun on the beach while the boys had climbed into a wakeboard boat and turned on the music. It blared for a moment before one of them glanced up at the house and then quickly turned it down.

"What can I do for you, Marshal?" Todd asked after they had both sipped their tea.

"I'm here about Stacy Cardwell Gordon." He didn't think it came as a surprise, given that Todd had been expecting him.

The congressman nodded slowly, his gaze on the lake. "I understand you spoke with Emery, her first husband." When Hud said nothing, Todd continued. "I was young and foolish and Stacy... Well, she was Stacy." He glanced at the marshal, then back at the lake. "Why the interest after all this time?"

"Stacy's missing and she's wanted for questioning in a homicide investigation."

Todd shook his head. "Homicide." He didn't sound surprised. "I'm sorry to hear that. I liked Stacy."

"You were married when you began seeing her," Hud said, keeping his voice down.

"I was and so was she. It almost cost me my marriage." He didn't sound sorry about that. "I almost let it." He looked over at Hud. "I was in love with her."

"What happened?"

Todd chortled. "I didn't have enough money. My future at that time didn't look great. I was working for my father at the car dealership, hating it and kind of feeling at loose ends. I would eventually inherit the business, but it wasn't quickly enough for Stacy. She wanted…more."

"More as in whom exactly?"

The man smiled over at him. "You do know Stacy, huh. His name was Marvin Hanover, a wealthy man from Gateway who apparently came from old money. She'd caught his eye and vice versa. And that was that."

Hud thought about it for a moment as below them, on the shore, the teenage boys called the girls from their towels spread on the sand into the boat. He watched them speed away, the boat's wide wake sending water droplets into the air.

"When was the last time you saw Stacy?" he asked after finishing his drink.

Todd frowned. "Just before she married Marvin. I tried to talk her out of it." He laughed. "Like I said, I was young and foolish."

"When was the last time you saw Marvin Hanover?"

"I never met the man." The congressman smiled. "If you think I killed him for her…" He chuckled at that. "A man can only be so young and foolish and survive."

"Did Stacy ask you to kill him?"

Todd Bellingham only smiled before draining his tea. "I hope you find her before…well, before anything happens to Stacy. I still think about her sometimes." His gaze took on a faraway look. "I've wondered how different my life would be if I had stopped her from leaving me." He turned to look at Hud. "Or how different hers would be now."

ELLA FELT HER skin crawl as she looked away from the leering men at the bar to check her phone. Her phone showed that she didn't have a strong connection. She should have expected it might be sketchy out here. Not that she'd thought she'd have a call from her mother. But she might have to make a call for help—and not just for her. Waco wasn't safe here; that much was clear.

She saw that she had voice messages from both her aunt and uncle. She didn't listen to them, knowing Dana and Hud were worried about her and anxious to know where she'd gone.

As the detective returned with two bottles of beer, she pocketed her phone and hoped he didn't see that her hand was trembling.

Ella had been warned that this was a rough bar. And yet, when she'd walked in, her feet had frozen to the floor just inside the door as she'd felt the suspicion, the mistrust, the menacing vibrations. She'd stared at the faces of the men, hoping to recognize at least one of them from her mother's photos. She hadn't.

Over the years as a wrangler, she'd been in dangerous situations with horses and cattle, but she'd always been in her own element, one she knew well, and had felt confident in her abilities to get herself out of trouble. Walking in here, though, when she'd looked into the faces of those men, she'd known she was out of her depth.

Waco set a beer in front of her and slid into the opposite side of the booth. He met and held her gaze as he lifted his bottle in a salute that told her he was as wary of what might happen next as she was. "The bartender wouldn't take my money. I suspect another beer will be out of the question."

She knew what he was trying to tell her. She lifted her beer to her lips but hardly tasted it. The two of them were still being watched. At the pool table, two of the players were arguing loudly.

The detective took a swig and set down his bottle, leaning toward her as he spoke. "I think we should leave."

Ella knew he was right, but she'd come here to get answers. She wasn't leaving without them. Her mother had been coming to this place for years. All her instincts told her that, now on the run, Stacy had come here again. "You know where the door is," she said with more bravado than she felt.

He chuckled. "If you think I'm leaving you here alone..." But his look said he was tempted just to show her what a fool she was.

Out of the corner of her eye, she saw a door open at the back of the bar. A woman with dyed red hair entered with an air of ownership. No one paid her any mind as she stepped behind the bar and opened a large old-fashioned cash register.

Another song came on the jukebox as a fight broke out at the pool table. The woman behind the bar picked up a glass and hurled it at the two scuffling in the back. The glass hit the wall and shattered, loud as a gunshot. The two stopped in midmotion.

"Lou, Puck, you've been warned. Outside. I've had enough

of the two of you," the woman said in a deep, gravelly voice as brash as her hair color. She turned to the bartender. "They don't leave? Throw them out and don't let them back in. Best clean up that glass before some fool cuts his leg off."

Lou and Puck were still in a brawlers hold. For a moment, they glared at each other, and then the larger of the two shoved the smaller one aside and left. The smaller man looked to the bar and the woman. "Come on, Helen," he said with a groan. "You know it weren't me that started it."

She motioned toward the back door and then turned, freezing for a moment as her gaze lit on Ella and then Waco. Her movements were slow and deliberate as she asked the bartender what they'd ordered. Then she scribbled something down and walked the length of the bar, coming around the end and heading straight for their booth.

Ella sat a little straighter. She recognized the woman even though her hair hadn't been red in the old photos. Helen had aged over the years and now had to be pushing seventy, maybe more. As she reached them, Ella swallowed the lump in her throat. This was her chance to ask about her mother.

"What are you doing here?" Helen's quiet words were directed at her. In the older woman's hand was what looked like a bill for the beers. Guess they would be charged after all.

"I need to talk to you about my mother, Stacy Cardwell," Ella said, keeping her voice low since she could feel all the attention in the room focused on the three of them.

"I don't know anyone by that name. You need to leave. Now." Helen had started to turn away when Ella grabbed her slim wrist. She looked down at the hand stopping her before looking up at Ella.

The look in the woman's eyes made her flinch inside, but Ella didn't let go. "I'm not leaving until I find my mother. I know she comes here," Ella said just as firmly as the older woman had spoken. "I suspect she's here now."

"You've made a mistake," the woman whispered. "You don't belong here."

"And my mother does?"

Helen's gaze shifted to Waco as she reached down and gently peeled Ella's fingers from her wrist. "You brought a cop?"

"He's looking for her, too," Ella said. "We're *not* together."

The woman swung her gaze back to Ella. For a moment, she thought she caught a glimpse of kindness in the woman's faded eyes. "Leave now. While you can." With that, she wadded up their bill and dropped it in front of Ella before turning and walking back to the bar.

"What are you all lookin' at?" Helen demanded of the men at the bar in a raspy bark. They all turned away from Ella and Waco as the woman took her spot behind the bar again.

Ella surreptitiously pocketed the wadded bill and got to her feet. Waco rose, as well, and reached for his wallet to leave a twenty on the table.

As they walked out, she could feel eyes on her. But only one set felt as if it was boring a hole into her back. How had she ever thought she'd seen kindness in those eyes?

"You THOUGHT YOUR mother was here?" Waco demanded once outside as he followed Ella to her pickup. She started to climb inside the truck, but he stopped her with a hand on her arm. "Why would you think that?"

She sighed and shook off his hold. "I had my reasons. I'm going home, in case you want to follow me all the way back."

"You're not leaving," he said after a split second. "I already know you better than that."

"You don't know me at all," she snapped.

"I wish you were smart enough to turn your pickup around and hightail it out of here as quickly as possible. That would be my advice—not that you'd take it. If there is one thing I know, it's that this is getting dangerous and you're just stubborn enough to think that by staying around here you're going to get some answers."

Ella mugged a face at him. "Believe what you will." She started to get into her pickup but stopped to look back at him. "I have some advice for you, Detective."

"You can call me Waco."

"You're the one who should hightail it out of here. No one's going to talk to *you*," Ella said. "You look like the law."

"I *am* the law."

"I rest my case. It's too dangerous for you here."

He laughed. "Too dangerous for *me*? Are you serious? We'll be lucky if we get out of this town alive."

"If you're trying to scare me—"

He swore and passed a hand through his hair in frustration as she climbed in and slammed the pickup door. As the motor roared to life, he swore again and stepped back before she had a chance to run over his toes. Did she really think he was going to buy her story about leaving?

But as she pulled out, she headed in the direction they'd come. He watched her go, for a moment debating what to do. Follow her? She hadn't seemed to have gotten any information from the owner of the bar and yet she was leaving? Why was he having trouble believing this? Because he thought he knew Ella after such a short length of time?

A man came out of the bar and glanced after Ella as he climbed into his pickup and started to take off in the same direction Ella had gone.

Waco let out another curse as he hurried to his SUV. Once behind the wheel and racing after Ella and the man, he glanced back at the bar's front door. Another man stood there, watching them leave before turning his gaze on Waco.

Waco floored the SUV and quickly passed the older pickup, putting himself between Ella and the male driver hunched over the wheel of the old-model truck. As he drove after Ella, he recalled the way Helen had wadded up their bill and thrown it at Ella. He'd seen the woman write something on it before coming over to them. Was it possible she had written a message on it?

Ahead of him, he could see that Ella appeared to be driving out of town—just as she'd said she was going to do. So why didn't he believe her? Just as she'd told the woman at the bar, Ella wouldn't leave until she got the information she needed.

He shook his head in both frustration and admiration. Ella reminded him of himself. Stubborn to a fault and just as crazy cagey. He just hoped she didn't get herself killed, because as capable and strong as she was, she wasn't trained for this kind of dirty business.

Glancing in his rearview mirror, he saw that the pickup from town was gaining on them. He'd known it wasn't going to be easy to get out of there alive.

Chapter Thirteen

As Ella drove, she dug the bill Helen had thrown down in front of her from her pocket. She flattened it out and read what was written on it. Just as she'd suspected, the woman had sent her a message.

She felt her pulse jump. That meant Helen had known who she was before the bar owner had come over to the booth—just as she'd suspected. Had her mother shown her photographs of Ella over the years?

She stared at the scrawled words.

Go home before you hurt your mother more than you know.

Her heart thundered against her ribs. She'd found her mother. Or at least found someone who knew her mother. But then what? How could she hurt her mother more? Stacy already had a homicide detective after her. More to the point, could Ella trust Helen, a woman she didn't know?

Her hope was that she could talk her mother into returning to the ranch—at least until she was arrested for murder. It wouldn't be easy. Worse, she had Waco Johnson dogging her every step, she thought, glancing in her rearview mirror to see his SUV not far behind. The detective wasn't giving up any more than Ella was.

She wondered how she could get rid of him so she could double back. Maybe if she could convince him that she was returning to the ranch and then somehow lose him… In the meantime, she had to act as if she really had given up.

Her cell phone rang. She figured it was Waco and let it ring a second time before she saw that it was her mother.

"Mom?" she said quickly, taking the call.

Silence, then Stacy's quiet voice. "I thought I'd better call you and let you know that I'm all right. I just need a little time to myself and I'll come home. I don't want you to worry."

For a moment, it was such a relief to hear her mother's voice, to know that she was all right, that Ella didn't respond.

"I hope everything is all right at the ranch," her mother was saying. "Tell Dana that I'll be back soon to help with the canning."

Ella was gripping the phone, trying to control a jumble of mixed emotions. Her mother was pretending that she didn't know Ella'd been in town. "Helen called you," Ella said into the phone, her words clipped. "Did she also tell you that I'm not leaving here until I see you?"

"Ella, I don't know what—"

"I found your photo albums, Mother. I know. That's why I'm here. Right now I'm trying to lose the cold-case homicide detective who is as determined to talk to you as I am. Then I'm coming back and staying as long as it takes. You can't run from this anymore. The truth has caught up to you."

"You don't understand."

"You can explain it all to me back at the bar or wherever it is that you stay when you're in Hell and Gone."

"I had my reasons for what I did." Her mother was crying now.

"For keeping the place and your life there from everyone, including me? Or for killing Marvin Hanover?"

"No, you can't believe—"

"I don't know what to believe." Ella heard the pain in her voice. She hadn't realized how hurt she was about her mother's secret life.

As she glanced again in her rearview mirror, she feared that her mother wasn't the only one who wanted to keep the past a secret. The truck from the bar was coming up fast behind the detective's SUV.

What she saw next made her let out a cry. By the time she got her truck stopped, her mother had disconnected.

WACO HAD SEEN the pickup's driver make his move. He'd known it was only a matter of time, so he'd been ready. The front of the older-model truck slammed into the back of his SUV, but not hard enough to drive him off the road. He kept going, maintaining his speed, waiting to see what the driver would do next.

Ahead of him, he saw Ella's brake lights, and he swore. The last thing he needed was for her to stop now. Worse, he realized, was for her to turn around in the middle of the road and come back. But damn if that didn't look like what she was planning.

This time, the pickup smacked the back of his SUV with more speed and force, jarring Waco and making the vehicle shudder. The pickup's driver was really starting to tick him off. He got the SUV under control and released his shotgun from the rack between the seats. This was going to get ugly, and the worst part was that it appeared Ella was determined to be in the middle of it. She was in the process of turning around and heading back this way. If he didn't do something quickly...

Hitting his brakes, he turned the wheel hard to the left. The SUV teetered for a moment, wanting to roll, just before he got it under control. The driver of the pickup hadn't anticipated the move. Waco saw the man lay on his brakes as the patrol SUV was suddenly sitting sideways on the highway in front of him.

Instinctively, the driver turned hard to the right, going off the road in a cloud of dirt. Waco grabbed his shotgun and jumped out. The pickup had come to rest wheel-well deep in the sagebrush and dirt thirty yards off the highway.

As Waco started to leave the highway, the man jumped out, fired off two wild shots with a handgun in his direction and then ran off across the expanse. Waco considered going after the guy, but only for a moment as Ella came racing up in her pickup.

ELLA GOT HER truck stopped and jumped out. Waco Johnson stood at the edge of the road, shotgun dangling from one large hand, his Stetson cocked back as he looked at her.

She'd known the man in the pickup was going to run Waco off the road. Maybe even kill him. When she'd seen the driver get out of his stuck pickup with a gun and start firing...

"Are you all right?" Ella asked as she tried to still her racing heart after watching the pickup driver repeatedly crash into the back of the detective's SUV. She'd feared that the man was going to kill Waco—even before he started shooting. That was when she'd realized he wouldn't be here if it wasn't for her. She didn't want his blood on her hands.

"I'm fine. I thought you were going home?" he asked in that deep, low voice of his. It warmed her in a way that made her feel vulnerable, which was the last thing she wanted right now. Yet her heart was still hammering from what had happened. What *could* have happened.

"You knew I wasn't leaving." She hesitated, surprised that she was about to give up the information even as she said it. "I just heard from my mother."

His gaze sharpened. "That so? She have anything interesting to say?"

"Just what you would expect. She wants me to go home and pretend that I never came here."

Waco nodded. "I would imagine that's about the same thing Helen wrote on our bar bill?"

So he'd seen that, had he? "She said that if I stayed here, I would end up hurting my mother more than I could know."

"Your mother is wanted for questioning in a murder investigation," he said. "What could you do that would hurt her worse?"

"That's what I said."

"So she's here." He didn't sound happy about that as he looked from Ella to the shotgun in his hand before heading back to his SUV. He deposited the shotgun in the rig and looked over the hood to see that she was still standing there. "I'm assuming we're going back to Hell and Gone?"

"What about the man who was trying to kill you?" she asked.

"I think I recognize him from a drug case I was working in Butte. He probably thinks I'm here to take him in." Waco shrugged. "At least he can't shoot worth sh— Worth a damn."

"I suppose there's no way I can convince you to leave?"

He seemed to give it some thought before he shook his head. "It wouldn't be chivalrous of me to leave you here alone, even if my reason for being here wasn't to take your mother back for questioning."

"She didn't kill Marvin Hanover." Ella had hoped to put more conviction into her words.

Waco shrugged. "Maybe not. But you should know that he didn't die right away. He scratched your mother's name into the rock wall at the bottom of the well. If his intent was to name his killer…well, then he did."

WACO REGRETTED HIS words as all the color drained from Ella's face. She wanted to believe the best of her mother. He hadn't wanted to take that away from her. "I'm sorry."

She quickly recovered, but he could still see fear in her green eyes. Of course, her mother would be a suspect, given that Stacy had been married to Marvin when he disappeared. But she hadn't known about the writing on the wall, the one thing that could get Stacy convicted of murder.

The sun hung low in the sky, painting them with a golden patina. He looked at Ella and felt something snap inside him. Damn, but the woman was beautiful. Not just beautiful. Smart, sexy—the whole package. The thought struck him like a crowbar upside his head. A man would have to be a fool not to have noticed.

He'd noticed, but it hadn't hit him at a primal level before. Now that it had, there was no going back, he realized.

"What?" Ella asked, frowning at him.

He stared at her, hoping he hadn't said the words out loud.

"You were saying something about the hotel?" she asked.

Hotel. "Given all the traffic backed up with my SUV sideways in the highway, I suppose we should move our rigs, huh."

She gave him a blank look since there was no traffic. "Sarcasm? Really?"

Without another word, Ella turned and walked back to her pickup. He watched her climb in behind the wheel before he climbed behind his. Starting the motor, he pulled to the side of the road and let her lead the way back into Hell and Gone. That revelation about Ella had come with an ache like nothing he'd ever felt. He wanted to protect her at the same time he wanted to ravish her.

Waco shook his head, telling himself that he needed food. It had been a long day and this case was driving him a little crazy. Worse, just the sight of the sorry excuse for a town on the horizon filled him with worry. How was he going to keep Ella safe? Worse still, he didn't know how to deal with this mix of feelings. *Nothing good will come of this*, he thought.

Yet he had no choice but to stick to Ella. Stacy Cardwell was here. Unfortunately, so were some dangerous people. He'd thought he'd recognized the man who'd left the bar earlier to watch them leave. Another fugitive from justice. This one from an assault case Waco had worked on.

The sun had sunk behind some mountains in the distance by the time he parked in front of the hotel and waited for Ella to get out of her pickup.

With nightfall coming on, both he and Ella were stuck in Hell and Gone. Just the two of them in this old hotel tonight. And that meant they were both in serious danger for a whole lot of reasons.

Chapter Fourteen

Helen Mandeville heard about what had happened outside of town. She'd known there would be trouble the moment she'd seen the two sitting in the booth at the bar. The one was obviously a cop. The other... Well, she'd recognized Ella from photos Stacy had shown her over the years.

She'd always known that Ella would show up here one day. It had just been a matter of time. She'd told Stacy, but of course Stacy hadn't listened.

"What would you have me do?" Stacy had cried.

"Tell the truth."

"You know I can't do that."

"Who are you really protecting? Stacy, did you do something back then, something that will bring the law down on us?" Helen had asked, and Stacy had assured her that there was nothing to worry about.

Except the law was here—and Ella.

After the two had left, she'd warned everyone at the bar to leave them be. "That one's a cop or my name is Sweetie Pie," one of her customers said. Everyone but Helen had laughed. "He's looking for someone."

"Just stay clear of him," Helen had told them. "He's not interested in taking any of you in."

"How do you know that?" another man demanded.

"I know. He won't be around long." She'd expected that to be the end of it as she'd taken last night's money out of the cash register and returned to her house behind the bar. But she should have known some fool would go after them.

Shaking her head, Helen hoped it wouldn't bring more cops down on them. She turned on her police scanner. It squawked a few times, then fell silent. It was quiet enough that Helen realized she wasn't alone. She turned to face the man standing in her doorway. "You heard?"

"Ray Archer never had the sense God gave a hamster," Huck said with a rueful shake of his head. He still had a thick head of blond hair, although it had started to gray at the temples. Her hair had grayed years ago. She could barely remember her natural color before that, making her aware of how many years had passed. Nor was Huck that strapping handsome young man who'd wandered in off the road too long ago to count. Not that she was the woman she'd been, either. But her pulse still quickened at just the sight of him, and he seemed genuinely fond of her.

"What are you going to do?" he asked.

They all expected Helen to keep them safe, like she was the mother hen of this chicken coop. She was getting too old for this, she thought. "Nothing." She raised her chin and straightened her back. The years had been good to her. When her ex had keeled over and left her the bar, she'd thought it was a trick or bad joke. He'd never given her anything but grief.

But the place had turned out to be a gold mine. As the only bar for miles around, she'd had no competition. Raking in the cash for years and investing it wisely, she'd known that the day would come when she'd need it. Helen had a bad feeling that day had come.

It wasn't as if she hadn't been thinking recently that it was time for a change. She'd seen too much over those years. Mostly, she was just tired of it. Well past the age of retirement, she had enough money to make the rest of her life cushy somewhere else. Maybe Arizona. Maybe Florida. Maybe some island in the middle of the ocean.

Helen brought the subject up, saying as much to Huck, only to have him roll his eyes.

"You'd go crazy within a week. You need the drama. Not to mention the fact that you'd miss us."

Helen met his gaze. "You could come with me."

He grinned, reminding her of the first time she'd laid eyes on him. He'd walked into the bar, all cocky and cute, and she'd felt her heart float like batter in hot grease. She realized that not much had changed. Except now he was one of her bartenders as well as her lover. "If you're propositioning me..." He said it in that sexy way he had, especially late at night when the two of them were curled up in her big bed.

"I'm serious, Huck."

He shook his head slowly. "You're talking leaving Montana. I'm not sure I can do that. I'm not sure you can, either. There's no place like this. You know that, don't you? Damn, woman, when's the last time you drove in traffic?"

Helen nodded, seeing that if she left, she'd be going alone. She wasn't surprised. It hurt, but she understood. Roots ran deep here. She would have a hard time pulling Huck from this place and re-planting him even in Arizona, let alone Florida. Maybe he was right. Maybe neither of them would fit anywhere but here—in the middle of nowhere with a bunch of other misfits.

"That couple who came into the bar..." He let the question hang in the air. "They're looking for Stacy, aren't they?" He didn't give her a chance to answer before he let out an oath. "I figured as much. You tell the girl where to find her?"

Helen shook her head. "You know I couldn't do that. But she's Stacy's daughter, and with what happened outside of town just now..."

"She and the cop will be hanging around for a while," he said and met her gaze. "She's going to find out. Maybe it would be better if you—"

The scanner squawked again. "It would be better if Stacy Cardwell had never come here, but she did." Helen thought of the girl who'd had a flat tire outside of town and how she'd felt sorry for her. She'd hired her to work in the bar temporarily, but then one thing had led to another.

"What are you going to do?" Huck asked.

"Deal with it like I always have until I leave. And then it will be yours, problems and all."

"I'm going to miss you," he said softly, stepping closer to take her in his arms.

She leaned into his still-strong body. Not as much as she was going to miss him, she thought.

ELLA PARKED IN front of the hotel and saw Waco do the same. It was clear that he would be doggin' her until he found her mother. She couldn't see any way around it at this point.

With a sigh, she reached over to the passenger seat for her backpack and climbed out. There was no getting away from him—at least for the moment. She hoped her mother would contact her again. On the way into town, she'd tried her mom's number. The call had gone straight to voice mail.

But as she looked around what was left of this town, she knew Stacy was here somewhere. She'd find her, somehow. Hopefully, before Waco did. After what he'd told her about the name scratched in the old well, her mom would be going in for questioning, probably handcuffed in the back of his patrol SUV.

Waco was already out of his SUV as she started toward the front of the hotel. He hurried to open the door for her. "After you," he said with a slight bow, making her roll her eyes.

The musty smell hit her first. It reminded her of antiques shops her aunt Dana had taken her to in Butte on a girls' trip. Stacy had stayed in the car, saying she didn't like old things. That had made Dana laugh and say under her breath, "Except for rich old men."

Ella thought of that now. Marvin Hanover had been one of those older men. Not so funny now, given the way that marriage had ended.

An elderly man behind the reception desk eyed them suspiciously as they approached. Ella got the feeling he'd come from the back when he'd heard them pull in. Or maybe he'd been expecting them. As few guests as she suspected this hotel registered in a month, she couldn't see him standing there all that time.

"We need a couple of rooms," Waco said and pulled out his wallet.

"I'll be paying for my own," Ella said without looking at the cop.

The elderly man behind the counter eyed them. "We only take cash. Forty dollars a room."

Forty dollars, from the looks of this place, was highway robbery. But given where they were, they had little choice. Waco threw two twenties on the counter.

The old man's watery gaze shifted to Ella.

"Do you have change?" she asked as she set down a fifty, glad she'd thought to bring cash.

Grumbling, the old man pulled out a cash box, rummaged around in it for a few moments and handed her ten worn dollar bills. Then, putting the cash box back under the counter, he turned and took keys from two of the small cubbies on the wall.

He held out two old-fashioned keys, each attached to a faded plastic orange disk. "Rooms 2 and 4 upstairs. Bathroom is down the hall. The lock's broken, so knock before entering." His gaze sparked for a moment as if he thought the two would be sharing more than the bathroom before the night was over.

Ella snatched a key from the man's hand and, with her backpack slung over her shoulder, started for the stairs. She heard Waco on the creaky steps behind her, his tread heavy and slow. She could feel his gaze warming her backside and wished she'd let him go first. Earlier, he'd looked at her...funny. She shook off the thought. The detective was too single-minded to even think about anything but finding Stacy.

The wooden landing groaned under her footfalls, making her hope the whole place didn't cave in before she could get out of town. She'd taken the number two key and now stopped to insert it into the lock. Out of the corner of her eye, she watched Waco stop at the next door down.

From what she could tell, the place was deserted. They were the only guests. She thought about the bathroom door lock that didn't work and groaned inwardly. Right now she would love a shower, but wasn't up to even seeing how awful the unlockable bathroom might be. She didn't have high hopes as she pushed open the hotel room door and saw the marred chest of drawers and the sagging double bed with its worn cover and dust-coated window behind it.

"It ain't the Ritz," Waco said with a chuckle from next door as he took in his own room. "Let's hope we aren't here long. Hey," he said to her before she could disappear into her room. "If you need me, just pound on the wall. Not too hard, though. I'm sure it's thin."

She said nothing as she entered the room and closed the door behind her. Immediately, she rushed to the window, hoping it opened. It didn't. But there was a hole in the glass where it appeared a rock might have entered and that let in some fresh air. She opened the dusty dark drapes all the way to let the night and air in and looked down on the side street.

A man stood below. His hair was dark, curling at his neck. When he looked up in her direction, she felt a start. She stepped back from the window. What was there about the man that had given her a jolt? She'd only gotten a glimpse of him, but he looked familiar. Had he been one of the men in her mother's photo albums?

Sliding the backpack off, she set it on the creaky wooden chair next to the bed, already debating how to slip out later without Waco following her.

Chapter Fifteen

Waco listened to Ella moving around in her hotel room next door. He realized that he'd been so busy trying to keep her alive—and himself, as well—that he'd forgotten his main objective. He needed to find Stacy before someone else did—especially her daughter.

Why was he convinced that Stacy Cardwell's trouble was more than just running from the law? Maybe even more than murder? He had no idea. Just a gut feeling he couldn't shake. Coming here made him all the more worried that they would find her too late.

He opened the door to his room and stepped to Ella's. Tapping, he said, "It's me." Like that would open doors for him with her. "I'm hungry."

There was nothing but silence behind the door. If he hadn't known better, he would think she'd already given him the slip. A floorboard creaked on the other side of the door a moment before it opened.

He grinned at her. "I thought food might be something we could agree on."

Grudgingly, she smiled. "I have my doubts about finding anything to eat in this town, but I'm willing to try. I'm starving."

"My kind of woman," he said with a laugh. Seeing her expression, he quickly added, "Sorry. Just an expression."

They went down the stairs and out into the twilight. Fortunately, the small shop next door hadn't closed yet. A bell jangled over the front door as he opened it and let Ella lead the way. Narrow aisles cut through tall rows of food staples, clothes and gifts. He didn't see the rocks until they made their way to the checkout counter off to one side of the store. A box of ordinary-looking rocks were marked $1.00 each.

The elderly woman standing behind the counter didn't seem at all surprised to see them. Word around town probably spread on the ceaseless wind that now rattled the front windows. Behind the counter, he spotted the milkshake machine and a microwave. On the wall was a sign that listed microwavable sandwiches.

Waco glanced over at Ella. "Name your poison." They both went for the ham-and-cheese grill and chocolate shakes.

"You can sit up there by the window or take it back to your room," the clerk said, pointing to a couple of small tables at the front of the store. "I'll bring it to you when it's ready."

"My kind of woman, huh?" Ella asked when they were seated. "What exactly is your kind of woman?"

"It's just an expression."

"Uh-huh," she said, holding his gaze with her steely green one. "So you don't have a woman in your life."

He laughed, seeing that she was enjoying giving him a hard time. He felt a spark between the two of them that should have surprised him, but didn't. He held that gaze, feeling the heat of it.

"I suppose there's a man in yours." He realized that he really wanted to know. But their sandwiches arrived straight from the microwave and the moment was lost.

Heat rose from the sandwiches, the steam making them impossible to unwrap. She seemed relieved to have the diversion. They looked at each other in terror as they peeled back the wrap and ate greedily as if neither of them had had a meal for hours.

Waco suspected it was true of Ella since she hadn't stopped for anything that he'd seen other than gas. He knew it was true for him. When the milkshakes arrived, he and Ella slowed a little on their sandwiches.

She seemed to relax, considering where she was and why. He wondered if she thought staying around here was a good idea in any way. The man who'd chased them out of town was the perfect example of how dangerous it could get. Waco figured the others back at the bar shared the man's feelings. These people didn't like strangers. Especially strangers who asked a lot of questions. In such an isolated spot in the state, these people were used to handling their own problems. He and Ella were problems.

"I suppose you wouldn't want my advice," he said and saw the glint in her green eyes. Still, he plowed ahead. "Whatever your mother might have been doing here—if she even came here—"

"She's here."

"As I was saying, people in some parts of this state don't like *anyone* asking a lot of questions. They might not even know your mother. Just on general principle, they aren't going to cooperate. So continuing to ask questions could be really bad for your health."

Ella smiled at him. "Has anyone ever taken your advice?"

He chewed at his cheek as he studied her for a moment. He couldn't help smiling. Everything about this young woman was refreshing. She intrigued him and he couldn't remember a woman who had ever interested him more. The problem was how to keep her alive. "I suspect you get your stubbornness from your—"

"Whole family. But if you're asking if my mother is stubborn…" Ella frowned and he saw a crack in her composure. "No more stubborn than me, I'd say, but then again…" She looked away, her eyes shiny. "Before you showed up, I would have said I knew my mother."

"But now?"

She shook her head. "I'm not sure I ever knew her. That's why I'm determined to find her and get some answers. No matter where it takes me. Or who I have to deal with." She narrowed her eyes at him. "Even you."

"Even if it gets you killed?" Her green eyes flared. Before she could speak, he raised both hands in surrender. "Sorry, it's an occupational hazard, trying to keep people alive."

"That and dispensing advice?"

He gave her a nod in acknowledgment of her jab. "Can I ask why you're so certain your mother is here? Did she tell you on the phone—?"

"No. She pretended that she didn't know where I was, but I'm sure Helen told her I was in town." She seemed to hesitate. He could tell something was on her mind, something she had been debating telling him.

"Someone ransacked my mother's cabin back on the ranch. My aunt stumbled onto the man. He'd been going through my mother's photographs. He took several, knocking my aunt down as he left. She's all right," Ella said before he could ask.

"All he took were *photographs*?" He was surprised at that and the fact that she'd shared this information with him. She seemed a little surprised that she had, too. "Any idea what he wanted with them?"

Ella shook her head. "I didn't even know Stacy had an album of older prints hidden in her closet."

He saw her swallow and caught the flicker of pain. How many more of Stacy's secrets would come out before this was over? Some worse than hiding a photo album of old snapshots in her closet, he figured.

Waco didn't know what to say. He had no doubt that she was strong and determined and capable. But still, she was out of her league, and he had a feeling that she knew it. Unfortunately, that wasn't going to stop her.

"Whatever the reason someone took the photos..." Again she hesitated, her eyes coming up to his and locking. "It's how I found this place. That's how I know she's here. It's...where she comes."

He stared at her. "This is where your mother comes when?"

Ella pulled her gaze away to stare out the window. With the descending night, darkness had settled among the buildings of the town, making the place look even more desolate, if that were possible. "My mother has always disappeared for a few days every few months. I never knew where she went—until I looked through the albums." Her eyes came back to his. "She came here. Apparently, she has been living a secret life for years when she comes here."

He looked out the store window at the dark, dying town. "Why?"

"That I don't know," Ella said with a shake of her head. "Evidently, she knows these people well, especially Helen, and they know her. Helen recognized me, so I would assume my mother has shown her photographs of me over the years. The thing is, whoever broke into my mother's cabin and took the photos must have realized they were important. He could come up with the same conclusion I had and show up here."

Waco had no idea what to make of this. "Do you have any relatives up this way?" She shook her head. "Helen is older than your mother." But he supposed they could be friends from way back. "You've never met her before today?" Again she shook her head.

"I think maybe my mother comes here because of a man she wanted to keep secret." He raised a brow at that. "Okay, I shared with you," Ella said. "Now you tell me about the key."

He didn't think he'd reacted, but he must have, because she smiled knowingly. "How did you hear about the key?" he asked.

"Mercy Hanover Davis. She wondered if my mother had it. It would explain why someone ransacked my mother's cabin. So?"

"Sounds like you know as much as I do."

She laughed, an enchanting sound he thought he could get used to. "Was the key in the bottom of the well?"

"It was, but I have no idea what it belongs to. Did Mercy mention—?" She was already shaking her head and looking disappointed.

"She mentioned money."

Waco nodded. "Yes—apparently, that is what is at the forefront of the entire family's minds these days."

"My mother doesn't have it, nor any of their mother's jewelry."

That he already knew from Lorraine. "She hasn't spent the money if she does have it," he said, giving her that much.

"I can't imagine the money is here. Can you?" she asked and looked away. She did have the most amazing green eyes.

"No," he said. "Only a fool would hide a fortune in a den of thieves."

"So at least we agree on that. Any idea how much money we're talking about?"

Waco shook his head. "The family said a fortune, but that's all relative, isn't it?" He could see the wheels turning as Ella looked across the street at the bar again. He hated to think what she planned to do next. "Can I ask one favor?" He rushed on before she could tell him he was owed no favors from her. "If you decide to go back to the bar, take me with you. I'll try not to look so much like the law, if that would help."

"Good luck with that," she said and took a couple of slurps of her milkshake.

The cold chocolate ice cream clung to her lips for a moment before her tongue came out to whip it away. Those lips... He dragged his gaze away, tucking just the thought of kissing those lips away, as well.

Waco had more important things to be thinking about, like keeping this cowgirl alive. They were both chasing a woman Ella wanted to believe was innocent while his gut told him Stacy Cardwell could very well be a cold-blooded killer.

They eyed each other across the table in a standoff until she sighed. "Helen won't talk with you here."

"You're assuming she'll talk to you at all. I have the option of taking her in for questioning."

"Good luck with that." Ella's gaze didn't waver. "While you're getting beat up, I can cry and get her sympathy."

He laughed as he watched her take another sip of her milkshake. "You already have mine."

She looked up sharply, and he saw that the last thing she wanted from him was sympathy. Pushing away her nearly empty glass, she rose. "Looks like neither of us is going to get the opportunity to talk to her."

He followed her glance as it shifted to the front window. Helen came out of the bar and quickly climbed into the passenger side of a Jeep. The driver took off, leaving Waco little doubt where they were headed. He wasn't sure he could catch up to them. Still, he had to try. Ella was already heading for the door.

"Let's take my SUV. It's faster," he said, knowing that if they didn't go together, she would try to catch Helen in her pickup.

As they pushed out the door, he electronically opened the doors to the patrol SUV. Ella hesitated only a second before jumping in. He swung behind the wheel, started the engine and went after the set of red taillights disappearing in the distance.

Chapter Sixteen

The sky was black except for the pinpoints of light from the vehicle ahead of them. Ella glanced at the speedometer. One hundred and ten and gaining on the Jeep in the distance.

She took in the strong angles of Waco's face in the light from the dash, questioning what had possessed her to jump into his SUV to begin with. It had all happened so fast. She'd let those moments of intimacy in the store make her think for an instant that they were on the same side. They weren't. Their reasons for finding her mom were miles apart. Now here she was. With him. Chasing after Helen and whomever was driving that Jeep.

"I don't know why I let you talk me into coming with you," she said.

He shot her a quick glance. "Because we're in this together?"

"We're not in this together."

Waco seemed to concentrate on the road ahead and the taillights way in front of them without looking at her. "But we should be," he said. "We both want the same thing."

"I highly doubt that," she said, watching him gain on the Jeep. The detective had been right about one thing, though. His patrol SUV was faster than her pickup.

Ella felt a surge of adrenaline. Earlier, she'd felt exhausted after the long day on the road. Her body ached as if she'd driven all over the very large state of Montana. The food had helped, but her conversations with Waco had affected her in other ways. Being around the man had been both intoxicating and exhausting as they'd parried. She'd felt herself sinking deeper and deeper into the quagmire that was her mother's past life, as if all Stacy's mistakes were now about to come to a head.

Now she felt the exhilaration of the chase. Helen was leading them to Stacy. It seemed too easy. What if it was a trap? Why else would Helen get into the Jeep right across the street from the hotel? Did Helen really think they wouldn't give chase? That they wouldn't be able to catch the Jeep?

"I just had a thought," she said as Waco kept the pedal to the metal. She didn't get a chance to raise her suspicions before he spoke.

"Seems too easy, right? Helen is either taking us to your mother or we're racing into a trap. Or—"

Ahead, the taillights blinked out.

Ella braced herself as Waco hit the brakes. The Jeep had disappeared into the darkness.

WACO STARED OUT at the blackness. There was no light. Not from the sky now shrouded in low clouds or from any houses in the distance, because there didn't seem to be any. He felt as if he'd driven into a black hole the moment the taillights had disappeared.

He'd thrown on his brakes, worried that the Jeep had stopped in the middle of the road, the driver turning off the lights. He didn't want to rear-end the Jeep and kill them all. Especially at the speed he'd been going.

"There!" Ella cried, pointing to her left. "I see the taillights."

He did, too, then. The Jeep had turned off onto a narrow dirt road that Waco had almost missed. As the taillights disappeared over a rise, he turned off his headlights and followed. The road was straight enough and there was just enough light to see where he was going if he kept his speed down.

Even as dark as the night was, Waco could see that they were now headed up into the mountains.

"Do you think she's going to my mother?" Ella asked, voicing the concern he'd had himself. "Or just getting us out of town so they can kill us?"

He shot her a look and shrugged. "It could be a trap, but I think Helen definitely wanted us to follow her." Now that they had, he was having his own concerns about where they were being led. He shouldn't have taken Ella. But the alternative would have meant she'd have raced out here in her pickup—alone. She was safer with him. At least, he hoped that was true.

The road left behind the sagebrush to climb into the mountains. The black skeletal shapes of pine trees on each side of the road made it easier to stay in the tracks of what was now little more than a Jeep trail. But Waco didn't dare take his eyes off the narrow dirt road for long.

Wherever they were headed, his gut told him they would find Stacy Cardwell, dead or alive.

ELLA STARED AFTER the taillights down the road. The low clouds parted for a moment. Ahead, she could barely make out the contours of the mountains, black silhouettes against a midnight blue sky.

Where were they headed? To her mother? She wondered why all the secrecy, why her mother was hiding out—possibly in the mountains ahead—and why here with these people instead of at home on the ranch.

Ella had to believe it wasn't a trap. Helen was taking her to Stacy. She was putting an end to this. For the first time, Ella wondered what she would say when she saw her mother. She had so many questions. The biggest one was why she had run after the call from the homicide detective and what a dead ex-husband had to do with any of this. But then there was the anger about her mother's secret life.

She sat back and tried not to think about it as they continued toward the mountains. Would whatever was up ahead explain why her mother had been acting strangely long before Marvin Hanover's body had turned up at the bottom of a well? If it was a man, had he been pressuring her to run away with him until her mom finally had?

The road narrowed further. The dark shape of the mountains

loomed over them as Waco turned up another path through dense pines. She saw pine trees and rocky bluffs as the patrol SUV bucked and groaned its way up the narrow rough road.

Ella's pulse pounded in her ears. Was Helen leading her to Stacy? Or did the bar owner know she was being followed and was leading them up into the mountains to finish this yet another way? Hadn't her mother always said that some secrets were better left buried?

WACO HAD BEEN forced to back way off once the Jeep began to climb up into the mountain. He caught only glimpses of the taillights through the pines as the road switchbacked upward. It was much darker in the pines, the dirt road becoming precarious.

He feared he might lose the Jeep, except he had no choice but to hang back. He had to gear down and drive slowly or use his brakes, turning on his brake lights, which he feared would alert them that they were still being followed. Unless they already knew he and Ella were behind them—as per their plan.

As the road surface worsened, his nerves grew even more taut. He finally pulled off onto one of the old logging roads and parked, killing his engine. "Stay here," he said as he heard her pop her door open. He turned to her. "Ella, don't make me lock you in the back."

She climbed out as if she hadn't heard him and started up the road. Since he wasn't going to arrest her, he grabbed what he needed and followed her up the mountain.

He hadn't gone far when he realized he could no longer hear the sound of the Jeep's engine. The driver had stopped.

Waco hoped he wouldn't need backup. Not that it could reach him in time even if he called for it. Not that it stopped him as he headed up the mountain. Ella kept pace, her expression determined. Like her, he suspected Stacy Cardwell was up here.

What worried him, though, was who might be with her and what they would do. As the two of them came around a bend in the road, he spotted the Jeep parked in front of a small rustic cabin set back in the trees. Light glowed from the front window. He caught sight of shadows inside.

But he also caught sight of a figure moving along the edge of the cabin—on the outside.

ELLA'S BREATH CAUGHT at the sight of the cabin in the woods. Her mother was in there. She felt it. She shivered in anticipation, but also from the chill. It was July in Montana, but cold up here in the mountains.

She stared at the cabin and the glow of the lamp burning inside, and took a breath as she tried to still her anger. She took a step toward it, but Waco grabbed her arm and tugged her back, out of sight of the cabin.

"Listen," he whispered as he pulled her close. "We can't just go walking in there. You understand that, right?"

She hadn't thought of anything but confronting her mother about all her lies and secrets. Every step up the mountain had made her more angry at Stacy's deception all these years. And for what? Some man?

"You have to let me handle this my way," he said, holding her gaze in the darkness. They were so close, she could smell chocolate shake on his breath. His grip on her arm tightened. "The other option is me handcuffing you to one of these trees. We do this my way."

Ella nodded, realizing that he meant it. She'd come so far to find her mother, and now that she was sure that she had, she didn't want to spend another minute handcuffed with her arms around a tree.

"There's someone outside the cabin," Waco whispered. "I need to take care of him first. Then we enter. I go in first, so you don't get shot. That means you stay behind me the whole way. Agreed?"

Ella had no choice. If she even hesitated… "Agreed." He studied her for a few more moments. "I swear," she said and got a grudging ghost of a smile out of him. "I'm behind you all the way."

They started again toward the cabin. She saw movement. A man with an ax standing next to a woodpile. The man froze for an instant as if sensing them.

But before he could raise the ax, let alone swing it, Waco had taken him down and cuffed him. When the man had tried to yell a warning to whomever was inside, Waco stuffed the man's bandanna into his mouth.

She watched him pull the man to his feet and steer him toward the steps into the cabin.

"I'd like to see my mother alone," she said behind him.

"Fat chance," he said as they ascended the steps. Reaching around the man, Waco opened the door, throwing it wide and shoving the man inside. The man stumbled and fell to the floor.

Ella was right behind the detective when she saw her mother sitting in a chair at the table. Stacy looked up. Then their gazes met and her mother's eyes quickly filled with tears.

THEY'D BARELY GOTTEN in the door when Waco barked, "Everyone stay where you are and don't move. I'm Detective Waco Johnson. So everyone just settle down."

The man sprawled on the floor was struggling to get up, but he stopped as Stacy, who'd been sitting at the table, got up, rushed to the man on the floor and dropped to her knees beside him.

Ella was so shocked that she couldn't move, couldn't speak.

As Helen came into the room, holding what appeared to be a glass of water, and stopped in the small kitchen doorway, Waco asked, "Is anyone else here?" Helen shook her head and pushed open the door to the only other room not in view—the bathroom. It was empty.

"Take off his handcuffs," Stacy demanded from the floor where she was next to the cuffed man. When the detective didn't move, she shot him a narrowed look. "Unless Jeremiah is under arrest, take off his handcuffs."

"Only if he doesn't cause any trouble," Waco said. "Otherwise, I will arrest him."

"He won't cause any trouble," Stacy said.

Ella stared at her mother, who seemed to have aged since the last time she'd seen her. She watched her comfort the man she'd called Jeremiah as Waco removed the handcuffs. Jeremiah glared at Waco as he rubbed his wrists. Ella got the impression it wasn't the first time he'd been cuffed, but her gaze quickly shifted to her mother.

She stared at her mother as if looking at a stranger. All this concern for this man? Where was Stacy's concern for her family that she was putting through all this worry?

Her mother rose and started to take a step in her direction, but Ella shook her head and Stacy froze, looking uncertain.

"What is going on?" Ella said as she found her voice. "No more lies. No more secrets. What are you doing here with these people?"

Her mother wrung her hands for a moment, tears filling her eyes again. "I'm so sorry, Ellie. It's...complicated."

She could barely look at her mother. "Sorry doesn't cut it. Not anymore. And I'm sure it's complicated or you wouldn't be here."

Stacy seemed to cringe at the look Ella was giving her.

"Don't talk to her like that," Jeremiah said, his voice sharp-edged as he stood and put an arm around Stacy's shoulders.

Ella swung her gaze to him, surprised, now that she got a good look at him, that he wasn't much older than she was. When she met his pale blue eyes, she felt a jolt. There was something strangely familiar about him. Even stronger was the feeling that she'd met him before. Had her mother brought her here when she was younger?

He appeared to be in his late twenties or early thirties, with a head of curly sandy-blond hair and blue eyes. His expression was surly. Clearly, he resented Ella's being there.

"Who are you?" she demanded. "You can't be my mother's boyfriend. She always goes for rich men twice her age." The poisoned arrow hit its mark. Stacy winced as if in pain and stumbled to the chair to sit again.

"Please, Ella," she said. "Don't take your anger out on Jeremiah. It's me you're upset with, not him."

Helen cleared her throat. "Maybe Jeremiah and I should step outside and let you—"

"No one is leaving," Waco said.

Ella felt Jeremiah's hard gaze. "Why are *you* here with a cop?" he demanded.

Ella spun on him, flipping her long blond braid over her shoulder as she tried to keep her temper in check. "I'm here to see *my* mother. The question is, who are you and why is this your business?"

Jeremiah glared at her as a tense silence filled the room. "She's my mother, too."

Chapter Seventeen

Waco turned to Ella. She looked as if the floor had dropped out
from under her. Jeremiah was her *brother*? He thought about what
he'd learned from his visit to the Hanovers. Marvin Hanover had
wanted a son. His daughter Mercy believed that Stacy had lied
about being pregnant. What if she hadn't?

His mind was whirling. He could well imagine how Ella's was
spinning. She hadn't moved. Hadn't even looked as if she had taken
a breath. Her green eyes had darkened as all the color had drained
from her face. The room had gone deathly silent.

He watched her slowly turn to look at her mother. Stacy was
crying softly as she pleaded silently with her daughter. She seemed
to be begging for Ella's understanding.

Helen went to Stacy, shooing Jeremiah away. He moved to stand
with his back against the wall, scowling at Ella in defiance.

"Is it true?" Waco asked Stacy.

She nodded distractedly, her gaze refusing to leave Ella's face.

"I'm so sorry," Stacy said. "I can explain, if you just give me
a chance."

"What is there to explain?" Jeremiah demanded. "She knows
it's true, and pretty soon the rest of the family will, too."

"It should have been done a long time ago—just as I've said so
many times before," Helen said.

Stacy could only cry and nod.

ELLA HAD TAKEN the initial shock like a blow. But she recovered quickly, because the moment Jeremiah had said he was Stacy's son, she'd known it was true. The eyes. The feeling that she knew this stranger. Still, she hadn't been able to speak for a moment as her thoughts went wild. She didn't want to believe it. It would mean that her mother hadn't just kept her son a secret. She'd hidden him from the rest of the family. She'd hidden a brother from Ella.

She realized that Jeremiah had spoken and was now staring at her.

"You know it's true, don't you?" he said.

Ella dragged her eyes from him to look again at her mother. "I don't understand."

"What's there to understand?" Helen snapped. "Your mother had a son before you were born. She had her reasons for leaving him with me."

"Her *reasons*?" Ella echoed. "What mother has her reasons for leaving her son with a stranger and never telling her family—including her daughter—about him?"

"I wasn't a stranger," Helen said. "I was a good friend."

Ella shook her head. "Such a good friend that my mother kept you a secret all these years, as well?"

Helen's cheeks flamed, anger glinting in her eyes for a moment before she lowered her regard. "Like I said, your mother had her reasons."

"It was the only way I could have him in my life," Stacy said.

"You could have brought him to the ranch," Ella declared, her voice breaking. "You didn't have to keep him a secret along with all your other secret friends. You could have let me grow up with a brother."

"I couldn't do that. You don't understand," Stacy said.

"I think I do," Waco said.

Ella had almost forgotten that he was in the room. She turned to look at him, as did everyone else.

"It was because of his father," the detective said. "You didn't want Marvin to know about his son because he planned to take him away from you once he was born."

"Not just Marvin," Stacy conceded, her voice stronger now. "His entire family. You don't know what they are capable of, but I do. When I heard about your call, I knew I had to get to Jeremiah."

Ella hated how much it hurt that her mother hadn't reached out to her after Waco's call. Instead, she'd gone running to her secret son.

"I figured Marvin was dead or you wouldn't be calling," her mother was saying. "That meant an investigation." She looked at Waco. "That's why I had to come here. I had to warn everyone, especially my son."

Jeremiah cursed under his breath. "She was just protecting me," he said, as if it needed to be said. "Now you come here with your cop friend—"

"He isn't my friend," Ella said automatically. She was still trying to make sense out of this. "So Marvin Hanover is his father?" she asked her mother.

Stacy nodded. "I'm not sure how much you know about him."

"According to the family, he paid you ten thousand dollars when you proved to him you were having a son," Waco said.

Jeremiah's jaw tightened, lips clamped.

Ella's gaze shifted to her mother.

"I'm not proud of that." Stacy looked down at her hands in her lap. "I thought I could go through with it, being married to him. But after seeing what kind of man he really was, once I found myself pregnant, I knew I couldn't turn a child over to him. Yes, he was demanding that I walk away after I gave birth. I'd done my duty, he'd said. He was kicking me out and taking my son. So... yes, I took the money. I needed it to get out of there before my son was born. I would have done anything to keep Marvin from getting his hands on my child."

"Does that anything include killing your son's father?" Waco asked and motioned Jeremiah back as he started to launch himself off the wall in defense of his mother.

"I didn't kill Marvin," Stacy said. "I swear it." She looked pleadingly at Ella and then turned to smile at her son. "I just wanted Jeremiah to be safe."

Ella followed her gaze. She'd always been the only child—at least, where her mother was concerned, she'd thought. Being raised around her cousins, she hadn't felt that way. But she'd thought there had always been a bond between her mother and herself.

Now she wondered if she would ever come to grips with this

secret of her mother's—and having a brother, let alone this one. He seemed as wild and untamed as this place where he'd grown up. Even as she thought it, she saw some of herself in him. She, too, wanted to defend her mother.

"I'm sorry, Jeremiah," she said to him, realizing that while she'd been raised on the ranch, he'd been raised here with strangers.

Her half brother shot her a withering look. "Don't feel sorry for me. I'm fine. We're not doing any brotherly-sisterly bonding, all right? You brought a *cop* here."

"She didn't *bring* me." Waco ground the words out. "I've been tailing her, knowing eventually she would lead me to Stacy, because she's one determined, strong young woman who cares about her mother."

Jeremiah actually looked chastised by the detective's words. Ella was surprised by them herself and grudgingly grateful.

Stacy said, "Please. I'll tell you everything."

Ella doubted that and wondered if Waco did, too, but she said nothing. Her body had burned hot with anger and fear, then icy cold with shock and hurt, and finally with relief that her mother was all right. At least for the moment. The day had been long, and exhaustion tugged at her.

"You're going to have to come back with me to Bozeman for questioning," Waco said to Stacy. "Jeremiah, as well."

"You don't understand," Stacy cried. "If Marvin's family finds out about my son, they will *kill* him."

"Why would they do that?" Waco demanded.

"Because Marvin knew I was pregnant. He told me he was changing his will and leaving everything to our son."

"If he really is Marvin's son."

Stacy grimaced. "So the family told you that he wanted a DNA test done even before my son was born? I'm sure they told you that's why I killed him, so it would never come out that I'd lied. Jeremiah *is* Marvin's son. At any time, he could have come forward and claimed what is rightfully his. But I couldn't let him. If they knew about him, they would never let him live. They already killed his father for the money. You have no idea what that family is like."

WACO HAD A pretty good idea after meeting them. "I can see where you would want to protect him when he was young, but why bring him here?"

"These are my friends. Helen raised Jeremiah. She kept my secret."

"All right, but now he's an adult who can take care of himself. Why not let him claim what you say is rightfully his?"

Stacy narrowed her gaze at him. "I made a lot of mistakes in my life. I suspect you're aware of that and that's why you think I killed Marvin. But since having my son and then my daughter... What do I have to do to prove to you I'm innocent of this crime?"

"Come back with me and get your statement on the record. You do realize the fact that you ran doesn't help your case."

"I had to warn my son. I knew everything was going to come out and that he would be in danger."

"You came up here to do more than warn your son or you wouldn't have brought all your clothes," Ella said, motioning to the suitcases by the door. "You were going to run again."

Stacy's cheeks flushed. "I hoped to talk Jeremiah into leaving the country. I wasn't sure I'd be able to come back."

"You know, it almost sounds as if you don't want your son's DNA tested any more than you did thirty years ago," Waco said. "Because you aren't sure if he is Marvin's son?"

"I told you—"

"Well, I can't let you run. I can't let your son run, either. To get to the bottom of this, I have to know who's lying," he told her.

"I'm not sure my son will go with you," she said quietly without looking at Jeremiah.

"I suggest you change his mind about that," Waco said. "I've already chased you all over Montana. I'm not anxious to do the same thing with him—but I will."

"Stacy, listen to them," Helen said. "You knew that one day this had to end."

Waco looked over at Jeremiah. "I think your mother's right about your life possibly being in jeopardy from Marvin's family until we get this sorted out."

"I'm not leaving my mother," Jeremiah said. "She needs me. I'm going wherever she goes."

"She has a family who'll protect her—just as we always have," Ella said, facing down her brother.

Waco figured she was wondering the same thing he was. How much did Jeremiah know about Ella and their lives on the ranch? He figured Ella still had to be bowled over by the fact that all these years she'd had a brother, one her mother had failed to mention.

"I'm part of the family whether you like it or not," Jeremiah said, his glare locking with her own.

Now THAT THE shock had passed, Ella realized what she had to say, what she had to do. "Then maybe it's time you came back to the ranch, Jeremiah. You'll be safe there. We'll make sure of it." She looked to her mother, but it was Waco who spoke.

"Ella's right. Both your daughter and your son are worried about you. The ranch seems the best place right now for all three of you."

Stacy looked from Jeremiah to Ella and back again. Helen touched her arm. "We're his family here, too, but maybe it's time for Jeremiah to take his rightful place in the Cardwell family."

Ella wondered how much of a shock this would be for the rest of the Cardwells. Dana would open her arms to her nephew. Hud would be concerned about this wild young man who might be too much like his mother—let alone his father.

If there was any good in Jeremiah, the family would bring it out. Her mother stood to hug her friend. Then, with tears in her eyes, she looked at Ella and then Jeremiah. She appeared terrified. Of going back and possibly facing prison? Or of facing the family?

Stacy straightened, lifting her chin as she said to Waco, "I've been running from the mistakes of my past for too many years. I have no choice, do I? I'm finally going to have to face not only the past but also my family."

Chapter Eighteen

It was dawn by the time they all left the cabin. Once back in Hell and Gone, Ella talked Waco into letting her take her mother in her pickup and letting Jeremiah follow in the ranch pickup. "You can follow all of us."

The detective had studied her, a smile in his blue eyes.

"I'm not going to take off with my mother and brother, if that's what you're worried about," she assured him. "Stacy's not under arrest, right?" He nodded. "They're both yours once we reach the ranch. I need this time with my mother." She saw that got to him more than any of her other arguments.

"I'll be right behind you," he said. "Don't make me chase you both down and haul you in. You don't want to be behind bars for interfering any more in my investigation."

She'd smiled, thinking how the man had grown on her. She liked the way he'd handled himself with the situation at the cabin. She liked a lot of things about him, now that she thought about it.

"I definitely don't want to be on your wrong side, Detective," she'd said with a grin.

He'd eyed her as if not quite sure he could trust her. That, too, she liked. He was a little too cocky, as if he thought he knew his way around women. Not this woman, though.

Ella wasn't joking about needing this time with her mother.

Once behind the wheel with Hell and Gone in the rearview mirror, she settled in. She was anxious to have her mother alone. She needed answers.

"I need to know the truth, Mom," she said, not looking at her mother as she drove. "It's just you and me. For once, be honest with me."

"I didn't kill Marvin. You have to believe that."

She wished she could. "Then why were you hiding out from the law?"

"It isn't just the law after me. You don't know Marvin's family like I do—and that's the way I've always wanted it. Now...well, we're all in danger. Especially Jeremiah."

"If true, why didn't you go to Hud?"

Her mother's hands were balled in her lap. Out of the corner of her eye, Ella saw her look down at them for a moment. When she raised her head, her eyes flooded with tears. "Hud can't protect me from this. I felt that if I stayed, they might come after you and the rest of the family."

"I can take care of myself," Ella snapped, angry that her mother would use her as an excuse. "Why would they threaten any of us if you had nothing to do with your ex-husband's death?"

Stacy shook her head. "Because Jeremiah is the rightful heir to Marvin's fortune."

Ella snorted. "You've seen his will?"

"I have the will, handwritten and signed and witnessed."

She shot a look at her mother. "I don't even want to know how you pulled that off. But after all these years, do you really think it's still valid? How do you know they haven't already spent the money?"

"They don't know where it is."

"And you do?"

Her mother didn't answer.

"This sounds like an urban legend to me," Ella said. "How do you even know it exists?"

"Marvin wore a key around his neck. He guarded it with his life."

"But now he's dead. Wouldn't the killer have taken it?" When her mother didn't answer, she yelled, "Stacy! Tell me you don't have the key."

"It isn't what you think. I drugged him the night before he disappeared and switched the keys." The words came out short and fast, as if even her mother knew how they would sound.

Ella rubbed a hand across her forehead. "So you have the key." Waco had told her that a key had been found in the well. Wouldn't the killer have taken the key from around Marvin's neck? Unless the killer had known it wasn't the real one.

She said as much to her mother, who seemed surprised to hear that a key had been found with the remains.

"I have no idea why his killer didn't take the key," her mother cried. "Ella, I'm telling you the truth. I didn't kill him."

"Then who did?"

Stacy was silent for a few minutes. "Any one of them could have done it. It would be hard to choose. They all hated him, and with good reason. He was horrible to his family. He was horrible to everyone. To think he wanted to take my son and raise him without me..." She turned away to look out her side window.

Ella heard the hatred and anger in her mother's voice even after all these years. She didn't want to think her capable of murder. She glanced in her rearview mirror and saw Jeremiah behind the wheel of the ranch pickup and, behind him, Waco's patrol SUV. What a caravan they were, she thought, hating to think where they might all end up.

She tried not to think about what would happen when they reached the ranch. Dana would welcome the surly Jeremiah into the family with open arms—as was her nature. But Ella wondered what kind of reception her mother would get. She had put all her siblings through so much when she was younger, and now this.

The one thing Ella knew for sure, though, was that the family would keep both Stacy and Jeremiah safe on the ranch. That was what family did, especially the Cardwell-Savage family.

"As soon as I heard about his remains being found, I had to warn Jeremiah," Stacy was saying. "For years, they've threatened me, believing I took the money."

"You took the key," Ella pointed out. "So they weren't wrong about you having access to the money. Did you dip into it?"

When Stacy spoke, her voice was flat. "I don't know where the money is, and it was hard to search for it on Hanover property under the circumstances."

She thought about the old well where Marvin's remains had been found. "Did you look for it on the old homestead?" Even though she didn't glance at her mother, she could feel her hard stare.

"You still don't believe me."

Ella couldn't deny it, so she stayed silent. Her mind was mulling over everything. Wouldn't Waco have to return the key once the investigation was over? In which case, wouldn't one of the Hanovers know what the key opened? But if they knew where the money was hidden, they wouldn't have let not having a key stop them from opening the door to the money, would they? If the money existed.

Her head hurt. Worse, she was having trouble forgiving her mother. "So when the detective called, you simply took off to warn Jeremiah, taking all your clothing with you and planning to skip the country." Her mother said nothing. "You left without a word to me, leaving me on my own. That means you really weren't that worried about me and any threats against me or the family. Did you know that Mercy accosted me on the street? I remembered the other time she did that when I was just a child."

"I'm sorry. I knew you could take care of yourself and that you had the family," her mother said.

"How could you fail to tell me that I had a half brother all these years?"

Her mother began to cry. "It was all so long ago. I was pregnant, planning my escape from Marvin, when he disappeared. It was a time in my life when I couldn't take care of Jeremiah alone. You know my history. I wasn't getting along with Dana and she had the ranch." Stacy wiped at her tears. "I wasn't welcome there under the circumstances—especially pregnant. I had only one other place to turn. I knew Helen and the family she'd made would take care of him. I would visit as often as I could."

"Yes, those days when you simply disappeared without a word," Ella said. "Is it any wonder that I've always worried about you?"

"I didn't mean to make you worry. I had to hide Jeremiah where the Hanovers wouldn't look for him. That's why I never wanted any of you to know."

Ella shook her head, realizing she, too, was close to tears. Often over the years, she'd felt like the adult and her mother the child. But no more than right now. "Stacy, swear to me on my life that you didn't kill Marvin."

Her mother looked shocked, but slowly nodded. "I swear. I couldn't go home to the ranch. I didn't want to be the one who was always in trouble. I thought I could take care of it myself. But then, when I found myself in trouble again and pregnant with you... I swallowed my pride and went home. I did that for *you*. I wish I had done it for Jeremiah, but I was too young and scared back then."

"Were you surprised when Marvin's remains were found?"

Stacy looked away. "I knew he had to be dead, but I could never take the chance that he wasn't. Or that Lionel or one of the others would learn about Jeremiah. For a while now, Jeremiah has been trying to get me to introduce him to our family. Helen, too."

Ella studied her mother for a moment, realizing that this was why her mother had been different the past year. She'd been getting pressure to tell her secret. So much pressure that she'd planned to run away instead of admit the truth.

Gripping the steering wheel tighter, Ella was silent for a few minutes. Was there anything her mother could say that she would believe? She didn't think so. "You have the key. Do you have the money?"

"No." She seemed to realize that Ella didn't believe her. "Do you really think I would have sat on millions of dollars all these years and not spent any of it?"

"Okay, you have me there."

Ella drove for a few miles before she spoke again. She knew what was at the heart of her hurt. "You should have told me. I'm your *daughter*."

"That is exactly why I didn't tell you," her mother said. "I wish I could have kept everything from my past from you. Ella, when I had you, you're what changed my life. That's why I went back to the ranch. I wanted you to have a family, a better life. It was hard going back, pregnant, the black sheep of the family. But I did it because I would do anything for you."

"Even tell the truth?"

Her mother chuckled. "Even that."

HELEN WATCHED THEM all leave Hell and Gone. Jeremiah had asked her to take care of his Jeep until he returned for it. She wondered if he would ever return. This town was all he'd known. Her and her dysfunctional family.

But she told herself that they'd had some good times. Those memories brought tears to her eyes. Jeremiah had been like a son to her. Her only child, as it had turned out. She'd done the best she could raising him in his mother's absence and in this place.

Not that it hadn't been clear who was his mother. Every time Stacy had shown up, the boy had jumped for joy. Even as a man, he'd looked forward to her visits. He'd never questioned the odd arrangement. He'd turned out fine, given the genes swimming in the soup that was him.

Helen heard Huck come out of the bar. He put his arm around her as he followed her line of sight to the vehicles disappearing on the horizon.

"They're gone?" She nodded. "Are you all right?"

She wasn't. "Yes, but I'm going to have to leave."

"I know," he said and pulled her in tighter. "It won't be easy, but you're a survivor. Arizona will never be the same once you get there."

She turned her head to look up at him. She didn't have to ask. He really wasn't going to change his mind and go with her. "You'll take care of the bar?"

"You know I will. I'll take care of everything just like you have done all these years. This place won't die."

Helen smiled, liking the idea of some things never changing—even as she didn't believe it. "I'm going to miss you," she said as he kissed her cheek.

"I'll help you pack, because something tells me you're ready to hit the road."

"You know me so well," she said as the taillights on the patrol SUV faded into the horizon and she turned toward the door into the bar.

WACO THOUGHT ABOUT Ella all the way back to the Cardwell Ranch and mulled over the case. Did he believe Stacy? Did Ella? He felt confused and was glad when Hitch called.

"I wanted to ask how you are, where you are," she said, "but I'm not supposed to be involved in this case."

He chuckled. "I've been to Hell and Gone. Yes, it's a real place in middle-of-nowhere Montana. With her daughter's help, I found Stacy Cardwell. I'm bringing her back for questioning. Heads up— she isn't coming alone, so I would imagine there will be a family meeting at the ranch, and you'll hear all about it."

"So Stacy isn't under arrest? Are you any closer to finding Marvin's murderer?"

"Not really. Once I get back, I plan to pay the Hanover family another visit. Stacy swears she didn't do it, but she has even better motives for wanting him dead than ever."

"You'll figure it out. No hint as to the topic of the Cardwell Ranch family meeting?"

"I thought you'd prefer to be surprised."

"Right. You know how I love surprises." Hitch disconnected, laughing.

Ahead, Waco saw that they were almost to the ranch.

ELLA FELT EXHAUSTED after the drive. Her mother had slept for much of it. She'd stolen glances at Stacy, trying to understand this woman who'd been such a disjointed part of her life. Even from a young age, she'd seen that there was something so different about Stacy compared to her sister, Dana. Stacy kept secrets. Stacy had a past that no one seemed to know anything about. For years, Ella had sensed something dark in that past. That was why she had always worried about her mother.

As she pulled up in front of the main ranch house, her mother stirred awake. Dana came out onto the porch, shielding her eyes from the early-morning sun as she looked first to Ella's pickup and then to the driver of the ranch pickup that had parked next to her. She saw her aunt's frown deepen as cold-case homicide detective Waco Johnson pulled up next to Ella and parked.

Her mother hadn't moved. She seemed frozen on the seat, as if facing death rather than her sister. Ella thought again how different they were. Dana faced things head-on. Stacy ran from anything distasteful.

"You might as well get out," Ella said as she looked over at her mother. "I'll be with you. And so will Jeremiah."

Stacy attempted a smile and reached for Ella's hand. "I don't know what I would have done without you all these years." She squeezed her hand and then let go as she opened the pickup's door.

DANA HAD BEEN scared out of her mind for Ella and, of course, for Stacy. She hated the thought of Ella getting involved in one of her mother's problems. Now, as she watched her sister exit Ella's pickup, she felt her heart fill with love rather than anger.

"You're going to have to help Stacy," their mother had said that night on her deathbed. "She isn't like you and me. She's fragile." Dana had silently scoffed at that but nodded. "I'm leaving you the ranch because I know it will be in good hands. That's going to hurt your sister even more than it will your brothers, but it can't be helped. Promise me you'll be there for Stacy, no matter how hard she tries to push you away. She's jealous of you, Dana, and wishes she was more like you. I'm sorry, but you're going to have to be your sister's keeper."

Dana had balked, finding herself at war with her sister over the ranch, and yet her promise had come back to haunt her time and again. Even when Stacy had returned with Ella and seemed to have settled down, she was still sometimes so exasperating, especially when she'd take off for days without a word.

But Dana knew, more than anything, she never wanted to lose her sister again and hoped with all her heart that she wasn't about to. She watched Stacy stop at the bottom of the porch steps before she started up toward her and the ranch house, a house that had withstood all kinds of trouble for more than a hundred years.

ELLA STOOD NEXT to her pickup, watching her mother climb the stairs. As if without a word, she watched Stacy step into her sister's outstretched arms. Ella couldn't help the tears that stung her eyes as she saw the two sisters hugging each other. She wiped hastily at them as Jeremiah stepped up beside her.

"You think you're not like her," he said.

"I'm not," Ella snapped. "I'm nothing like her."

"Just keep telling yourself that."

She was glad when Waco joined them.

"I thought I'd let them have their reunion before taking Stacy in to get her statement," he said.

On the porch, Stacy had stepped out of her sister's arms, and both were now looking at the three of them standing together. Ella watched her aunt's expression as she took in Jeremiah. Stacy quit talking, and for a moment, the two of them seemed suspended there on the house porch.

Dana took the first step down the stairs, then the next, making a beeline for Jeremiah. Ella looked over at him. "Brace yourself," she whispered. "She's going to hug you and welcome you into the family. She'll cry and then she'll take you in the kitchen and feed you. It's just the way Aunt Dana is, so you might as well get used to it."

He looked like a deer caught in headlights as Dana rushed at him, threw her arms around him and cried.

Chapter Nineteen

"Looks like everything is going to be all right, Ella," Waco commented as the two of them walked toward the creek. He'd noticed Stacy standing alone on the porch, watching her sister and son. There was something about the expression on Stacy's face that made him uneasy. "Did you and your mother have a nice talk on the way here?"

Ella nodded and kept walking. He followed her down to the creek, where she stopped at the edge—out of sight from the family and out of hearing range.

She didn't look at him as she said, "I need to tell you about the key you said was found in the well. My mother said she drugged Marvin and switched the keys the night before she planned to run away. If true, then the one you have is worthless."

He let out a low whistle. He knew he didn't have to tell Ella that this didn't help Stacy look any more innocent. "Your mother has the key but she's never used it?" He couldn't keep the disbelief out of his voice. A woman who would drug her husband...

"According to her, she doesn't know what it opens." Ella finally looked over at him. "But someone in that family has to know."

He caught a gleam in her eye and took a step back as he held up his hands. "Hold on. I don't think I like what you're about to suggest."

Ella looked surprised that he had read her so well. After all, they hardly knew each other. "Have you returned the key found in the well to the family yet?"

He shook his head, suspecting where this was going. "Some of the family is anxious to get the key."

"But maybe not all," she said. "Because one of them already knows the key doesn't work.

"At first," she continued, "when I heard about a key being found in the well, I thought that Marvin had taken the secret—and the key—to his grave. But I couldn't understand why the killer would have let that happen unless Marvin had refused to give up the key, which is why it was found in the bottom of the well with him. But why would the killer have let that happen? It didn't make any sense. Was the key in the well still attached to the chain Marvin Hanover wore around his neck?"

Waco shook his head, making her smile knowingly. "You think the killer took what he or she thought was the original key and tossed one that resembled it into the well so, if the body was ever found, the key would seem to be with the remains."

"I'd wager that is exactly what happened." Ella frowned. "How did you even learn about the remains in the well?"

"An anonymous caller."

There was that gleam again. "So the killer isn't going to be anxious about getting the key from you because he or she knows it is a fake," she said. "But what if the family finds out that my mother took the original?"

"By the way, where is that key?" he asked. She only smiled. "You do realize that I can have you arrested for not handing it over."

"You keep threatening to put me behind bars," she said, clearly flirting with him. "Is that a fantasy of yours?"

Waco chuckled. "Seriously, Ella. I need that key."

"I didn't have to tell you about it," she said, chewing at her lower lip for a moment. "You want to catch this killer, right?" He narrowed his eyes at her. "I have a plan."

"Forget it."

"You haven't even heard what it is," she said.

"I don't need to. I can tell it involves you putting yourself in danger and interfering with my investigation. I'm not having any of it."

Ella nodded. "My mother has the key. I'm sure she'll give it to you when you take her in for questioning." She started to turn away, but he grabbed her arm, turning her back toward him.

Waco brushed a lock of blond hair from Ella's face. He hated it when he couldn't see her eyes. All that green that seemed to change shades depending on her mood. Right now, they were a dark emerald and slightly narrowed as she took him in.

"Detective?"

"Aren't we at the point that we can use first names?"

"Waco." She seemed to move the letters around in her mouth, tasting them slowly, her tongue coming out to lick her lips. "Waco."

He smiled, loving his name on her lips as he pulled her closer. "Ella." He cupped her jaw, ran his thumb over her lips and felt her shiver.

"Was there something you wanted to ask me?" he whispered.

Her lips parted. He saw the dart of her tongue as it touched her upper lip. He felt the sensual thrill rocket through his veins.

In no hurry, he slowly dropped his mouth to Ella's. He brushed his lips over hers, felt a quiver that stirred the flames already burning inside him. He touched the tip of his tongue to hers. She let out a long sigh, leaning into him, those eyes locked with his.

It was as if all his senses came alive. He had feared that if he ever kissed Ella, there would be no turning back. He would want her. Want her for keeps.

Pulling her up, he deepened the kiss and felt her melt against him.

"Detective?"

Waco quickly let Ella go and turned to see Stacy standing on the rise over the creek above them. That one word reminded him that he had no business kissing this woman—or, worse, wanting more from her. Not now. He had an old murder to solve.

"You said you wanted a statement from me," Stacy said, looking from him to Ella and back again. "If you're interrogating my daughter...well, I do like your style."

AFTER THE KISS, Ella felt almost guilty for what she was about to do as she watched her mother leave with the detective. Her face had flushed to the roots of her hair at being caught kissing Waco.

It wasn't the "being caught" part that embarrassed her. It was the fact that she'd never felt anything like that before in just one kiss. She'd seen the way her mother had looked at her. Surprised at first, then a slow, knowing smile, as if she could see herself in Ella.

Ella tried to put that thought out of her head, along with the guilt, as she pulled out her phone and called the Hanover house. An older male answered. Lionel, she assumed.

"My name is Ella Cardwell. I think I might have something you've been looking for." Silence.

"I can't imagine what that might be," he said at last.

Yeah, right, she thought. "How about I stop by to discuss it? I'll see you in fifteen minutes."

He started to say something, but seemed to change his mind.

Ella disconnected, knowing she was taking a huge risk.

The first thing she had to find out was how badly one of the Hanovers might want the original key. It was dangerous, but not that much, she assured herself, given she wouldn't be taking the key. So, if they really wanted it, they would be smart not to harm her.

Also, she wondered about the will that left everything to Jeremiah. The will her mother swore was real. Did the family know about it—*if* it existed?

The only person in the family Ella'd ever met had been Mercy Hanover, so she was looking forward to meeting the others. Although she didn't have much time. Waco had taken her mother to the marshal's office to get her statement.

At some point, he would demand the key Stacy had taken from her former husband.

"LET'S GET RIGHT down to it," Waco said once he had the video camera set up and had entered the preliminaries. He looked directly at Stacy Cardwell. "Did you kill Marvin Hanover?"

"No, I did not. Are you leading my daughter on?"

He blinked. "This is not the time to—"

"I want to know what your intentions are toward my daughter, Detective."

Waco swore under his breath. "I'm falling in love with her. Now, can we move on? Tell me how you met Marvin Hanover."

Stacy stared at him for a long moment before she nodded and began to talk.

He'd already heard most of it, but wanted it on the record. He suspected there might have been things she hadn't told her daughter.

"Is that really important?" When he merely waited, she said, "I met him through a friend. I know what you're asking. I married him for security. He had money. We saw each other a few times and one thing led to another." She looked away. "I told him I was pregnant."

"Were you?"

"Not yet," she admitted, looking at him again. "My daughter is nothing like me."

He gave her an impatient look. "When did things go sour between you and your husband?"

She laughed. "The ink wasn't dry on the paper before he told me how things were going to be. He'd made me sign a prenuptial agreement. It promised me ten thousand in cash on the day I came home with proof that I was pregnant with a son."

"But you weren't."

"I kept putting him off, telling him it was too early to know the sex. The rest of his family were telling him that I was lying about being pregnant." She shrugged. "Actually, that worked to my benefit later when I really was pregnant, but I didn't want them to know."

"Eventually, you got pregnant with his son."

Stacy nodded. "I thought I'd gotten lucky. I brought home the sonogram and he forked over the ten thousand. That's when he told me that he was going to keep my son. That I wouldn't be allowed to ruin him, and unless I cooperated, he would divorce me without a cent."

"Sounds like motive for murder."

"Oh, I wanted to kill him, but I had a son growing inside me. *My* son. I knew I had to save my baby from this horrible man. I'd seen how he was with his other offspring. So I planned to leave him."

"Weren't you worried he would come after you?"

"I pretended to lose the baby. He bought it. The rest of the family hadn't believed I was pregnant to begin with, so it worked. I assured him I could get pregnant again with a son and I planned my escape. But before I could leave, he disappeared."

"Didn't you take something before you left?"

She looked confused for a moment. "The key. I might have drugged him and exchanged the keys." Before he could speak, she said, "Okay, I did drug him and exchange the keys."

"Where is the original key?"

She hesitated, but only for a moment before she patted her pocket. "I have it."

Why did this feel too easy? "You kept it all these years. You never used it? How do I know it is the original?"

She sighed. "I never figured out what it fit. While I lived in that house, I looked for something that a key that shape might fit into. I never found anything, and Marvin wasn't about to tell me or his family."

"How do you know he wasn't lying to keep both you and his family under his thumb?"

Stacy nodded. "That would be just like him. That way, he got the last laugh, huh."

"In that case, you would have killed him for nothing, then."

"Detective, I told you. I didn't kill him. I was planning my escape when he disappeared. I woke up one morning, his side of the bed was empty. He didn't show up the next morning or the next. No one in the family seemed that upset. They must have thought, like I did at first, that he'd gone off because he was upset about me losing the baby. Losing his son. He had been hoping to replace all of them with new children, apparently. After a week, I filed for an annulment based on abandonment. I couldn't stand another day in that house and I was worried he would show up before my annulment went through. As it was, I didn't have to worry, huh."

"You do realize that your life is on the line here, don't you?" Waco demanded.

"I didn't kill Marvin."

"We only have your word for that. His family thinks you did. Also, before he died, he scratched your name into the rock at the bottom of the well." She looked horrified. "Your name and the word *don't*."

Stacy shook her head. "I have no idea why he would do that. I swear, unless he hoped to incriminate me. It had to be one of his family who killed him. You've met them, right? That's why you have to promise me that my son will be safe."

"As long as he stays on Cardwell Ranch, he will be." Waco knew it was just a matter of time before the Hanovers heard about Jeremiah. They would do the math. Once they realized that he was Marvin's son and the heir to the fortune—

He had to find the killer before that happened. "The only way to protect him is for the two of you to remain on Cardwell Ranch until this is over. Please don't run again. I'll just have to track you down, when I need to be taking care of things at this end. Your family is safe as long as you stay on the ranch."

Stacy shook her head. "You know you won't be able to keep Ella out of this, don't you? So, basically, you will be jeopardizing the lives of both of my children."

"Ella isn't part of the investigation."

She let out a bark of a laugh. "Clearly, you don't know her. Just because you've shared a few kisses—"

He reached over and turned off the recorder. "It was just one kiss."

With a roll of her eyes, Stacy said, "I witnessed the kiss, so don't even try to downplay it to me." He started to deny the impact of the kiss on him, but she waved off any denial. "I know my Ella. You're the first man who's really turned my girl's head. I saw it right away. I should have known it would take someone like you. A *cop*."

"I thought you were going to say it was because I'm a smart, capable, relatively good-looking cowboy, cold-case detective."

"I hope you're smart and capable," she said, clearly not appreciating his attempt at humor. "Save my son and daughter. Please. Because whether you realize it or not, they're both in danger."

He nodded, thinking of Ella, thinking of the kiss. "I need the key," he reminded her and held out his hand.

Stacy reached into her pocket. He saw her feeling around, her movements becoming more frantic, her eyes widening in what could have been surprise.

"You do have it, right?"

"I *did*." She stopped searching her pocket for it.

"What?" he demanded.

"It was in my pocket. Now...it's gone."

He groaned.

"It's the truth, I swear."

"When was the last time you saw it?" he asked.

"I put my hand in my pocket on the way home. It was still there right before I fell asleep for a while. Maybe it's..." Her eyes widened again. "Maybe it's still in Ella's pickup."

"Nice try. Ella has it, doesn't she?" He thought about his and Ella's talk before the kiss. He knew how her mind worked. All the Hanovers needed was the key, because by now at least one of them must know where the money had been hidden. The killer would know that the key found in the well was worthless. But if someone offered them the original key...

Chapter Twenty

Ella had just started her pickup when the passenger-side door flew open.

"You're taking off in a hurry," Jeremiah said as he climbed in.

She cursed silently. "Get out. Please. I have somewhere I have to go."

He shook his head and buckled his seat belt. "I can't take another moment of your aunt trying to feed me. I heard her on the phone, calling people." He leaned back and closed his eyes. "I don't care if you don't like me. I'd rather be with you right now." He opened his blue eyes and turned his head in her direction, pinning them on her. "Where you're going has something to do with our mother, doesn't it?"

Ella groaned. "You can't go with me, not where I'm going." He didn't move. "Seriously, you have to get out." She was wasting time. "Fine. I'm going over to visit with the Hanovers."

His eyes widened. "Really?" He let out a laugh. "Great. High time I met them."

"They want to *kill* you."

"They don't know me. I can be quite charming when I want to be. Come on—what better way to let them know about me than to show up at their house?" Those eyes narrowed. "So why are you in such a hurry to visit them?" He grinned at her. "Baby sister, what are you up to?"

Her mother would have her head, but as Ella looked at her brother, she made up her mind. She suspected the family would be anxious to get the key. But they would be even more anxious to get it and the money once they met the heir to the fortune. That was assuming Stacy had been telling the truth and Marvin was Jeremiah's biological father and there was a will naming him heir.

"Fine." Putting the pickup in gear, she pulled out. "Maybe it's best for them to meet you, break the ice. But if they stone you to death immediately...well, remember I said this was a bad idea."

He laughed. There was something about the sound that felt familiar. Just like his smile. Ella kept seeing her mother in him. And herself, which really annoyed her.

When they reached the Hanover house, there were several vehicles parked out front, including a motorcycle. Ella cut the engine and looked at her brother. Her *brother*. She would never get used to this. "The smart thing for you to do would be to—"

He opened his door, saying over his shoulder, "I try never to do the smart thing."

"Why does that not surprise me?" she grumbled as she got out and the two of them walked up to the large front door. She braced herself. "I should probably have told you that I'm about to tell a few white lies."

He chuckled without looking at her. "I would expect nothing less."

As soon as Waco returned Stacy to the ranch, he noticed that Ella's pickup was missing. He had a bad feeling about where she might have gone—with the original key to a fortune.

Stacy headed for her cabin, saying she had a headache and needed to lie down. He watched her walk up the mountainside for a moment before he climbed the porch steps and knocked.

Dana answered the door, her usual cheery self.

"I was looking for Ella."

"She and Jeremiah left together in her pickup," she informed him, which made him even more anxious. "I'm sure she's probably just showing him around the ranch."

"I'll catch up with her later, then," Waco said and left, sure Ella wasn't just showing her brother around the ranch.

But where would she go? He felt the weight of the fake key inside the evidence bag tucked in his jacket pocket. He called Ella's cell. It went straight to voice mail.

"Ella, we need to talk. Call me. Please." He disconnected, hating where his thoughts had gone. Had he really admitted on video that he was falling in love with her? He shook his head and grinned, because, damn it, it was true. He knew he should be more upset about that. He was falling for a woman he'd just met? A woman who was almost as strong-willed, independent and determined as he was?

He actually wanted to call Hitch to tell her how wrong she'd been about him. He was capable of falling in love with a woman. He was capable of even thinking about a future with her. He wasn't commitment phobic. He had just never met a woman who made him feel like this.

As much as he wanted to share this news, Waco didn't. He was too worried about Ella because he'd come to know her. He knew where she'd gone. Worse, she'd gone there with Jeremiah.

Unfortunately, he thought he knew that, as well. Swearing, he started his patrol SUV and took off. Once he reached the highway, he turned on his emergency lights and siren and raced toward Gallatin Gateway.

A MAN IN his early sixties opened the door to Ella's knock. "You must be Lionel Hanover," she said.

Looking at her, he raised his nose in the air as if he'd smelled something that upset his finer sensibilities. Then he shifted his gaze to Jeremiah. The man's eyes widened slightly, his unpleasant expression turning even more filled with distaste.

"I'm Ella Cardwell, and, yes, we would love to come in," Ella said, even though Lionel had yet to speak. For a moment, he didn't move, and she wondered if her whole plan was about to fall apart. What if she was wrong? What if coming here, especially with Jeremiah, was the worst thing she could have done?

"Who is it, Lionel?" called a faint female voice from the darkness inside the large space. He didn't answer her.

To Ella's surprise, though, he did step back to allow them entrance. She heard the large door close behind them, afraid she would hear him lock it. She stepped into the lion's den, Jeremiah right behind her.

An elderly woman sat in a threadbare chair near the crackling fire, a lap quilt over her legs. Even though it was summer, the interior of the house felt cold. Ella wondered if the fireplace was the only heat source. Glancing around, she noticed that the entire room seemed threadbare. Was it possible they desperately needed their father's money?

"Who's this?" the woman inquired, squinting at the two of them as they moved deeper into the room and closer to the fire.

"I'm Ella Cardwell," she said. "I thought maybe your brother might have mentioned that I was coming over."

"I didn't want to upset my sister," Lionel said behind them. "Angeline isn't well."

The woman shot him a withering look. "I'm not unwell—I'm dying, you fool. But as long as I'm here, I like to know what's going on." Her gaze returned to Ella. "You're her…"

"Stacy's daughter," Lionel said as the front door slammed open again. Everyone's attention was drawn to it as Mercy came charging in. She stopped short as she saw Ella and Jeremiah. "Welcome to the party," he said sarcastically to Mercy. "I'm assuming Trevor listened in on my call and then reported to you." As if on cue, Ella heard a motorcycle start up out front and take off in a loud roar.

Lionel sighed. "You might as well join us. We were just about to find out why this…meeting has been called." He moved to a chair next to the fire and dropped into it.

Mercy stalked in to stand in front of the fire, her backside to the flames.

"Let's at least offer our guests a seat," Angeline said. "I don't know what has happened to my brother's manners. I apologize on his behalf."

"Thank you, but we won't be staying that long," Ella assured her.

The woman's gaze had shifted to Jeremiah. "And who is this?"

Ella watched Lionel and Mercy out of the corner of her eye.

Both seemed suddenly interested in the young man standing next to her. "This is Jeremiah. Your father's and my mother's son."

HUD COULDN'T BELIEVE the news when Dana called to tell him about Stacy's return—with a son in his early thirties. He left the office and drove right home to find Dana in the kitchen. Nothing unusual there.

"Where are they?" he demanded as he walked into the room.

Dana turned from whatever she had cooking on the stove, a spoon in hand. "Ella left with Jeremiah and Stacy went up to her cabin." She started to turn back to her pots, as if this was just a normal, everyday occurrence.

"Dana," he said, "what the hell is going on?"

She sighed. Turned off whatever she was cooking and put down the spoon to turn to look at him. He listened as she filled him in on Ella going to a place called Hell and Gone to find her mother and—surprise—her half brother.

"He's Marvin Hanover's son and, apparently, the heir to a fortune."

Hud shook his head. "Why does this sound like a story Stacy has made up? Do we have any proof that this young man is even her son—let alone Marvin's—and some heir to anything?"

Dana gave him an impatient look. "He's family. That's all I need to know."

"Well, I need to know a whole lot more. Where did you say he and Ella went?"

She shook her head. "Maybe she's showing him around the ranch."

Hud groaned. This man none of them had even heard about before today was with Ella and only God knew where. "I'm going to look for them. If they come back or you hear from them, call me." With that, he thrust his Stetson back on his head and stormed out. Stacy was going to be the death of them all, he thought.

He had to find Ella. He couldn't shake the bad feeling that had settled in his gut that she was in trouble.

AFTER ELLA HAD announced who Jeremiah was, the crackling of the fire was the only sound in the room. Angeline let out a curse, followed by a phlegm-filled cough. "That's not possible," Mercy cried. "Your mother lied about being pregnant. She lied about having a miscarriage. If she was pregnant, we would have known it."

Ella noted that all the color had drained from Lionel's face, but he recovered his composure the quickest.

"What kind of scam are you trying to pull here?" he demanded. "They didn't have a child."

"Sorry, but they did," Jeremiah said. "My mother has kept me a secret all these years to keep me safe. She said my father's family was nothing but a den of vipers."

Ella shot her brother a warning look. "Let's not get into all that. Instead, let's do business. I have what you need to access your father's money."

"The key?" Mercy said on an excited breath. "The detective gave it to *you*? I thought he couldn't give it to us until after the investigation was over?"

She shook her head. "We all know that the key found in the well with your father's remains wasn't the real key." The room again went deathly quiet. "My mother has been in possession of the original key all these years and now I have it."

"I would love to know how she pulled that off," Angeline said with a chuckle.

"You have it?" Lionel asked, something in his tone predatory.

"Not on me." Ella shook her head. "I wouldn't be that stupid as to bring the key with me. First, we need to negotiate a deal." Lionel laughed. "I have the key. I'm betting one of you knows where the money is hidden." She looked around the room, going from Angeline to Mercy to Lionel and back. "I provide the key and I get my cut."

Mercy swore and began to rage.

"Let's cut to the chase. How much do you want?" Lionel asked, waving off Mercy's angry response.

"It's a fortune, right?" Ella said. "Jeremiah and I want fifty percent."

The room exploded with all the Hanovers talking at once. "That's ridiculous," Lionel snapped over the top of Mercy's and Angeline's shocked responses. "Why would you think—if any of what you're saying is true—that we would give you fifty percent?"

"Because we have a copy of your father's *real* last will, leaving all the money to Jeremiah," she said. "Without the key, you have nothing. This way you have half."

"This is highway robbery," Mercy cried. "We aren't going to—"

Lionel rose, silencing his sister with a wave of his hand. "If we agree, I want to see that will."

Ella smiled. "You mean a *copy* of that will. I wasn't born yesterday."

He glared at her. "How long will it take you to get the key?"

"I'll be in touch." With that, she turned to leave, grabbing her brother's sleeve and urging him along with her.

"You just gave away half of my inheritance?" he cried once the door closed behind them.

"I didn't give away anything," she said, "and I think you know it."

He laughed as he climbed into the passenger side of her pickup and Ella slid behind the wheel. "You're running a con. And you thought we didn't have anything other than a mother in common."

Ella shook her head at him as she started the engine and pulled out. They were almost to the main highway when they spotted the flashing lights on the patrol SUV and heard the siren as Waco sped toward them.

Chapter Twenty-One

"This doesn't bode well," Jeremiah said, stating the obvious as Waco pulled them over. A moment later, Ella's uncle came roaring up, as well.

Both Waco and Hud had similar looks on their faces as they got out of their patrol SUVs and approached her pickup. Ella took a breath and put down her window. "You'd better let me do the talking."

Her brother chuckled. "Have at it, little sis," he said and crossed his arms as he leaned back as if readying himself for the show.

"Ella." Waco said her name from between gritted teeth. "Tell me you haven't been to see the Hanovers."

She said nothing for a moment as she looked from the detective's face to her uncle's next to him.

"We should discuss this back at the ranch, don't you think?" she asked, sounding more calm than she felt. Since walking into the lion's den, her heart had been pounding. But she'd succeeded in doing what she'd set out to do. "I'll tell you all about it there."

With that, she put on her turn signal and swung back onto the highway, headed up the canyon and toward home. She could feel Jeremiah's gaze on her.

"Wow. Got to hand it to you. That was smooth," he said. "Of course, I wouldn't want to be you when you get back to the ranch."

She shot him a look. "As if I put a gun to your head and made you come with me."

"Good point," he said. "Mums will have a fit."

"That's putting it mildly." Ella let out a breath. "In retrospect, maybe I shouldn't have done that."

He laughed. "Are you kidding? You were awesome back there and damn believable. Do you really have the original key?"

"I hope so. You know the woman you call Mums? She often doesn't tell the truth."

"As if that's a bad thing," he said.

Ella shook her head, afraid of how much of her mother had either rubbed off on Jeremiah or was roaring through his veins. Ahead, she spotted the exit into the ranch and slowed to make the turn. Behind her were the two patrol SUVs and two very angry lawmen.

The worst part, Ella knew, would be if they told her that she was acting like her mother. Those were fighting words.

"WHAT WERE YOU THINKING?" Hud demanded after Ella told him, and the rest of the family gathered in the large living room at the ranch, what had happened with the Hanovers. "And taking Jeremiah with you!"

"To be honest, I didn't give her a choice." Jeremiah spoke up and quickly shut up under his uncle's intense glare.

"Didn't I warn you?" Stacy demanded, pointing a finger at Waco. "I know these two."

"Everyone calm down," Dana said. "Ella and Jeremiah are safe. I'm sure they have now realized how foolish they were."

Hud groaned inwardly. He sincerely doubted that. All of this had hit him hard. It was as if his family had all lost their minds. First, Stacy taking off and then coming back with a son! A son they'd never heard about, let alone laid eyes on. Conceived before her husband had ended up murdered and found at the bottom of an old homestead well.

Dana was sure that Stacy was innocent of the crime. Of course Dana was. As much as he loved his wife, she could often be too accepting and forgiving. But then, that was what he loved about her.

But now Ella was acting like her mother, going off half-cocked.

He said as much and instantly regretted it as his niece bristled and shot to her feet.

"I most certainly wasn't half-cocked," she said, confidence in her voice. "I knew exactly what I was doing."

"She's right," Jeremiah interjected. "She was *awesome*. You should have seen her." He seemed to realize everyone was looking at him, and not in a pleased way. He shut up again. He wasn't helping her.

"I won't let you use Ella and Jeremiah as bait," Stacy cried. "Jeremiah is the rightful heir to the money—everything but the houses and businesses. Those went to the family, and they've now sold off most of it and gutted the house of all the antiques so they could continue to live the way they had without working. You can't be sure they won't kill my children, especially when they don't get the key as Ella promised."

"If I might say something—" Hud's voice was drowned out.

"Jeremiah's safe here," Ella argued.

"Easy for you to say," her brother said.

"He's right," Stacy said.

Dana added, "It's too dangerous. There has to be another way."

"I don't believe we've met," Hud said to Waco as he got to his feet. Waco shook hands with the legendary marshal.

"Detective Waco Johnson. Nice to meet you, Marshal."

"You must be Jeremiah." Hud turned to the other person he had yet to be introduced to. "I'm Marshal Hud Savage."

"Another cop," Jeremiah said under his breath.

Hud wondered how long it would take Dana's love to turn this punk around.

It was clear to Hud that no one wanted common sense right now. He looked at Waco. "Detective, what do you suggest we do now?"

The room fell silent.

"I NEED TO speak with Ella alone," Waco said as calmly as he could.

"You can use my den down the hall." Hud rose and reached for his Stetson where he'd hung it by the door. "I need some fresh air."

Waco waited for Ella to rise and follow him. She stepped into the marshal's den and he closed the door behind them.

His emotions were all over the place. Ella had scared him badly because he'd gotten to know how she thought. He'd known belatedly that she would go to the Hanover place. On top of that, her plan had been sound—it was one he would have implemented himself. In fact, he'd been considering something like it. The worst part was that the plan had a better chance of working with it coming from her—something he couldn't allow for a lot of reasons.

"I'd like to turn you over my knee."

She grinned at him. "Maybe when this is over."

"Ella, I'm serious. You scared me."

"I'm sorry." She met his gaze. "I did what I knew had to be done."

"Without telling me." This, he told himself, was why a lawman didn't get involved with anyone he was trying to protect. But it was too late for that. If anything, this had shown him just how emotionally involved he was with Ella.

Still, he couldn't believe she'd taken such a risk. Jeremiah, too.

"Do you have any idea what could have happened to the two of you if one of them turns out to be a murderer?" he asked Ella calmly.

"One of them *is* a murderer," Ella said. "This way, we find out which one."

Waco let out an oath. "That's just it. We don't know who—if any or all of them—is guilty of murder. You have taken a hell of a chance. I can't let you do this."

"You want this case over quickly?" she asked just as calmly. "It's already done. All I have to do is take them the key and a copy of the will."

He shook his head. "I can lock you up if I have to. You're interfering in an ongoing investigation, which is a criminal offense."

She didn't have to speak. He could see the determination in every curve of her amazing body—not to mention in the depths of those green eyes. "The only way you'll stop me is to arrest me." She held out her wrists. "Better pull out those cuffs, Detective. I was hoping we wouldn't use them until all of this was over, but if you insist."

Waco looked at her and shook his head as he closed the distance between them. "You think I won't?" he whispered as he stopped just a breath away from her. Their gazes locked. "I need to go back out there and assure your family that I'm not going to get you killed."

The smile reached her eyes before her lips even curved. "You can do it, Detective. I have faith in you."

He scoffed. "I don't want to lose you."

"You won't. I promise." She rose on tiptoes to brush a kiss across his lips. When she pulled back, she almost looked contrite. "I really am sorry I scared you. But I knew if I told you what I had planned, you would try to stop me."

He nodded. "You're right about that. You've put yourself in danger. You're a civilian out of your league. You have to know that."

"After that kiss by the creek, I figured you'd have my back when the time came. That's why I was waiting for the kiss."

Waco swore under his breath and closed the minimal distance between them. "You knew I was going to kiss you?"

She shrugged. "Why do you think I took you down by the creek so the others couldn't see us? I figured with means, motive and opportunity..."

He felt his blood heat under his skin. "What am I going to do with you?"

Ella grinned. "I'm sure you'll think of something."

"You aren't taking this seriously," he said, his voice hoarse with desire.

"Oh, I am." She wrapped her arms around his neck. "This is all new for me, too."

"I was talking about catching a murderer," he said.

Her grin broadened. "So was I. Waco, you and me...this? It surprises me just as much as it does you. That's why I'm just as afraid for you as you are for me."

He wondered about that, but wasn't about to argue the point. They had a lot more to argue about. But he wasn't interested in doing either right now. He lowered his mouth to hers, desperately needing to taste her again.

They held each other when the kiss was over, both breathing hard. He could feel that she knew what was at stake by the way she hugged him. The next few days might be the most dangerous of their lives. He couldn't bear the thought of losing her after only just now finding her.

She pulled her head back to look up at him. "We can do this."

He nodded, even though he wasn't sure if they were talking about the plan to catch the murderer or the two of them and where this appeared to be headed.

Chapter Twenty-Two

When Waco and Ella returned to the living room, he looked around and cleared his voice. "What we all want is Marvin Hanover's killer caught so we can put this behind us." He saw Hud come in and, having heard, raise an eyebrow. But the marshal was smart and one step ahead already. He'd figured out how this had to go down. He already knew what Waco was going to say.

"The way I see it, we need to flush out the killer and quickly," Waco continued, knowing that none of them was going to want to hear the rest of this.

"I'm not condoning Ella's actions, but the plan was a solid one." He rushed on before the marshal and everyone else in the room could object.

"The Hanovers were going to find out about Jeremiah. Maybe it's better they found out this way. We know that they know. Jeremiah should be safe as long as he stays here on the ranch. Also," he hurried on, "because of the *deal* Ella made with the Hanover family, they want her alive, as well."

"Deal?" Stacy cried. "You can't let her—"

"Let's hear the detective out," Hud interrupted. "Detective Johnson is right. The only way to keep everyone safe is to solve this case. Ella, right or wrong, has set the wheels in motion." The marshal looked to Waco.

"Thank you, Marshal," he said. "None of us likes this. We have to figure out what to do now."

"We draw out the killer and put an end to it," Ella said. "And we do our best to keep my brother alive," she added with a smile for Jeremiah.

"I feel safer already," he muttered sarcastically.

"Let's discuss this in my den," Hud said. "Just the three of us."

"Hey, you're not leaving me out of this. It's my neck on the line," Jeremiah said. "I'm part of this family now."

Waco sighed under his breath.

"Fine. The four of us in my den," Hud said. "As for you, Stacy…"

"Stacy, come into the kitchen with me." Dana quickly cut off whatever the marshal was about to say. "I think we should get dinner started. Don't you?"

Stacy looked as if she might argue, but rose with a glare at the detective as she followed her sister toward the kitchen.

Waco and the others went into the marshal's den.

"Let me say up front that I don't like any of this," Hud said as he closed the door behind them. He waved each to a seat before he looked at Waco.

"Nor do I," Waco said. "If anyone takes the key to them, it should be me."

Ella shook her head. "There is only one way my plan will work. I take the key. And I go alone. And you all know it. Uncle Hud, I know you've used civilians before to bring down crooks. So wire me up and let's do this."

"What about me?" Jeremiah asked, only to have them all glare at him.

Chapter Twenty-Three

After Hud and Jeremiah left them alone in the den, Waco pointed out to Ella all the things that could go wrong. What if someone in the family simply took the key away from her? What if she went into that house and was never seen or heard from again?

But, ultimately, Ella convinced him that the key was the one thing that would flush out the killer. "If the key my mother took from her husband really is the real one, then it will open the door to the family's alleged fortune. If that happens, then the family will more than likely kill each other over it than me. We all know they aren't going to split it with me. They don't have to kill me. They can just tell me to get lost. My mother stole the key. What recourse do I have?"

"Let's not forget that Jeremiah is the legal heir to that money," Waco pointed out.

"Allegedly, but once the money is found and dispersed, they will be the only ones who know how much was there to start with. It will be my word against theirs. Also, you know they can contest the will and drag it all out for years," she said.

"Ella, that's if they don't take the key away from you and you never see what it opens."

She smiled at Waco. "I won't let that happen. They'll be suspicious of the key. It's just that once the key works and they open the hiding place, the fireworks might start. I'll keep my head down until you get there."

He didn't like it, but he told himself he planned to be there *before* the fireworks started.

Ella pulled out her phone and made the call.

Lionel answered.

"I'll come alone but my brother will know where I went—just in case you aren't planning to let me walk away from this." She met Waco's blue eyes. "That's good to hear. See you tonight." She disconnected. "It's all set."

Waco shook his head. "I'd feel better if you were home on the ranch watching out for your brother and mother."

"They've managed just fine for years without my help," she said.

Waco held her gaze. He could see that it still hurt her, her mother's secret. But she'd get over it in time. He'd come to realize that Ella couldn't hold a grudge for long. "I'm serious. I don't want anything to happen to you. You've met these people. They're scary, and I'm afraid that at least one of them is a killer. Maybe more. Promise me you'll do just as we rehearsed."

She couldn't make that promise because she might have to improvise. She stepped up to him so quickly that she caught him off balance. Her plan was simply to kiss him so he wouldn't notice that she hadn't promised. But once her mouth was on his, she couldn't stop herself. It turned into a real kiss, so much so that even if it didn't take his mind off the nonexistent promise, it certainly did hers.

Nor did it help when he pulled her closer, prolonging the kiss. She could honestly say that her body tingled all the way to the toes of her Western boots. She felt as if she were flying. It wasn't until he lowered her to the den floor that she realized it hadn't all been the kiss that had made her feel airborne.

The door opened and Hud came into the room. He glanced at the two of them as Waco was just setting her down. Her uncle merely shook his head, mumbled something under his breath and handed Ella a copy of the written will Stacy had provided.

Ella took it, folded it carefully and shoved it into her pocket.

"Ready?" Hud said to Waco as he turned and left the den.

"I have to go," Waco said, his voice sounding rougher than

usual. "Your uncle and I have to get ready. Don't…" He must have realized that he might as well save his breath. "Just be careful. Please." He gave her a quick kiss and hurried out of the house to climb into the marshal's SUV.

Ella watched him go, wondering if she would ever see him again.

"YOU HAVE THE KEY?" Lionel demanded as he opened the door to her and looked out at the dark street anxiously. He was dressed in tan slacks, leather loafers and what appeared to be a burgundy velvet smoking jacket over a button-up shirt. It was almost as if he'd dressed for the occasion.

With a nod, Ella said, "Of course I have the key. And the will."

He studied the street a moment before he said, "You came alone?"

"Wasn't that the deal?" she asked as she patted her right-hand leather jacket pocket and stepped past him into the house.

"Good evening," she said to the others gathered by the fire. A blaze burned in the huge stone fireplace, and still the large room held a chill. Mercy had been lying on the couch, but now sat up. She wore jeans and a sweatshirt. She must not have gotten the memo from her brother about proper attire for the event. Angeline sat close to the fire in her wheelchair, a shawl around her shoulders and a lap quilt over her legs. She drained the last of her wine and put down the glass, her hand shaking. The only one missing was Mercy's boyfriend. Trevor. Her uncle Hud had told her earlier that he'd been picked up on a local drug raid and was behind bars.

"It's nice of you to make it, Mercy," Ella said. "Of course, I knew you would be here, Angeline."

Behind Ella, Lionel said with growing impatience, "Let's see the key."

"Let's see what it opens first," she said, both hands in her jacket pockets. The key was palmed in one, her cell phone in the other, with Waco listening to the conversation nearby, waiting to make his move.

Ella could feel Lionel's gaze on her. He was suspicious. But if he tried to take the key, Waco would be here in an instant. She couldn't let that happen. She needed Lionel to show her what this key opened. She needed him to show himself for the killer she suspected he was.

"You better not be lying about bringing the key. The *right* key," he said threateningly.

She wondered what would happen if she was lying, but she wasn't sure she wanted to know. "It's the key." As she moved deeper into the living room, she wasn't surprised to see Mercy looking just as anxious as Lionel now appeared.

Behind her, she heard him slam the large front door and lock it soundly. He stepped around her and, turning to face her, said, "The key, please."

Ella took the key from her pocket and held it up—out of his reach. The dim light caught on it for an instant before she repocketed it. "First, I want to see what it opens. Then I'll be happy to hand it over," Ella said. "It's only fair, don't you think? You don't trust me. I don't trust you. So why don't we do this together?"

He seemed to consider that, looking from her to his sisters. "You're assuming that I know what it opens."

Ella laughed. "What is the point of the key if you don't?"

Silence filled the room. They were all looking at Lionel, especially Mercy and Angeline. It appeared that he'd been holding out on them.

Even more interesting, no one had asked to see the will. Because it didn't matter. They were planning to take the money and run—after they killed her?

WACO COULDN'T REMEMBER the last time he'd been this nervous. Ella was doing great—just as he'd known she would. He admired the hell out of her. At the same time, he was terrified that something would go wrong. He'd used civilians before—just as most law enforcement had. Sometimes sending them in with a wire was the only way to get a conviction. While he could hear what was going on through his earbud, he had wanted to wire Ella for sound.

Surprisingly, it had been Hud who'd talked him out of it.

"They might be expecting that," the marshal had said. "If they check her and find a wire..." He didn't have to spell it out. "Supposedly she is acting on her own. Even if they find the phone, she's safer. They'll still think she's alone in this. We have to play it that way. But we'll be right outside."

"Yes," Waco had said with a groan. She'd done this on her own. It was so Ella. So much like the woman he was falling deeper and deeper in love with by the day.

Now he waited to hear Lionel's answer. He could almost feel the tension in that room as they all waited. What if Ella was wrong? What if the key wasn't that important to them because they had no idea what it opened? What if—?

ELLA FEARED FOR a moment that none of them knew what the key opened—which would blow her theory completely out of the water.

But then Lionel sighed heavily. "I think I might know what the key will open," he finally said, and she breathed again. "Come this way." He began to lead them deeper into the monstrous house. Ella realized that it might be a trap. That he'd get them all back here and—

"This is one long hallway," she said. "How large is this place, anyway?" She hated that her voice broke on the last word. The house was so large that even with the house plans from the county, how would anyone be able to find her?

She tried to concentrate. Now was not the time to have second thoughts about what she was doing. She was pretty sure they were headed to the north wing of the mansion. The other two followed, Angeline bringing up the last of the conga line in her wheelchair, wheels squeaking.

"It would be easy to get turned around in this place, huh," Ella said. "Are we headed east? No, north, right?" But no one answered her question. "North," she said more to herself. She hoped she sounded excited and not scared. But only a fool wouldn't be scared, and she was no fool.

The deeper they ventured, the less confident Ella felt. Hopefully, Waco was still on the line. That was, if there was cell phone coverage in here. That was, if he could hear her.

The place was massive. Even if he could hear her, he wouldn't be able to get to her in time. She was on her own with just her wits to guide her. But she still had the key, and so far, no one had threatened her. Yet.

JEREMIAH HAD WAITED until the two cops had left before "borrowing" one of the ranch pickups and heading for the Hanover place. He'd parked a ways down the road and worked his way cautiously to the back of the house. He didn't see Waco or Hud.

Using the glass cutter he'd picked up from the ranch shop—how wonderful that his new family had everything he needed for a break-in—he began to cut open a back window that seemed to enter a guest bedroom. Like so much of the house, it hadn't looked used.

Waco and Hud had ordered him to stay put in the cabin the family had provided for him on the side of the mountain overlooking the ranch. As if he was going to be left out of this.

He smiled to himself as the glass popped out. He caught it and gently laid it on the ground. Then, using his sweatshirt on the sill to keep from cutting himself, he slipped inside the house through the back window. He knew the Hanovers didn't have any kind of security since he'd checked that out when he and Ella had paid their earlier visit.

Jeremiah landed quietly inside what appeared to be a bedroom that hadn't been occupied in a very long time. The old iron bed had been stripped of everything but the mattress, and there was dust everywhere. He moved like a cat across the floor and opened the door to peer out into the long hallway. He had some experience with breaking and entering—but only when called for, as he would have told Helen, who'd done her best to control his criminal behavior. This was definitely called for.

This whole house felt empty. He wondered how he would be able to find Ella. He was wondering how the cops would find her when he heard a floorboard creak behind him.

Waco grabbed him by the back of his collar and hauled him into the bedroom, closing the door. "I told you to stay home," the detective whispered in his face. From the cop's grin, it was clear that he'd known all along what Jeremiah had been up to—and had followed him.

"I have to help my sister."

"The best way you can help her," Waco said as he whipped out his handcuffs, "is to stay put."

Jeremiah heard the familiar *snick* and felt the cold metal of the cuff snap around his wrist. Before he could react, the cop snapped the other end around the ornate iron headboard.

"Say a word and I will hog-tie and gag you," Waco whispered next to his ear. "You don't want to get your sister killed, right?"

Jeremiah nodded and sat on the edge of the bed, giving the cop a *you got me, all right?* look.

Waco nodded. "Stay here." With that, the detective was gone.

ELLA WAS LOSING track of all the twists and turns Lionel was taking. She couldn't keep a running commentary about each move or one of them was going to get suspicious. "It's like a maze, isn't it? I have no idea where we are." Of course, none of the Hanovers commented.

Finally, at the end of another hallway, he stopped at a large double door. As he pushed the door open wide, she felt a cold gust of stale air. Clearly, the huge room was normally kept closed.

Lionel flipped a switch and the overly ornate fixtures in the room exploded with light.

"Wow!" Ella said, unable to not exclaim at what she was seeing. She knew that a lot of older, large, expensive homes in the area had once had such a room. "A ballroom! It's huge. It makes me want to dance."

Neither Lionel nor Mercy looked in the mood to dance. "I bet you remember dances in here." She looked at Angeline since Lionel and Mercy were ahead of them and not answering.

"When I was small," Angeline said almost wistfully, her weakened voice echoing in the enormous empty space. "My grandfather loved parties and music and dancing. He used to fill this room."

"That must have been something to see." Ella took in the gold leaf, the huge faded spots on the wall—where paintings had once hung?—the heavy burgundy brocade on the walls below the ornate sconces, as Lionel led the way across the parquet floor. He stopped dead center and turned to look at them.

Ella had lagged behind a little. So had Angeline in her wheelchair. Only Mercy had been on Lionel's heels.

She could feel the anticipation in the air as Lionel ordered Mercy to help him with the huge Oriental rug. It appeared to be in better shape than any of the other rugs Ella had seen in the house.

That alone, she realized, was a clue. The rug had to be worth a lot of money and yet it hadn't been sold. It only took a moment to find out why. As Lionel and Mercy strained to roll it back, she saw the irregularity in the flooring.

Mercy stared down at the floor, then up at her brother. "How long have you known this was here?" she demanded. "How long have you been keeping this to yourself?"

He ignored her as he knelt and pushed on the side of an inlaid handhold in the flooring. It opened enough to allow him to get his fingertips under it. He lifted the trapdoor to expose a wooden staircase.

Ella stepped closer as they all crowded around the opening. The stairs were only a few feet wide and dropped deep into the ground. The air rising up at them was icy cold and smelled of damp earth, as if it had been some time since the trapdoor had been opened.

At the bottom of the dozen steps stood a hulking solid-steel vault set in the wall. She said the words out loud for Waco. "You have to be kidding. An underground vault cut into the earth below the ballroom? Those stairs down look a little…old. Your grandfather did this when he built the house?" It definitely hadn't been on the plans of the house that Hud had procured for them.

Next to her, Angeline rolled closer to stare down at the vault. But it was Mercy who let out the cry of surprise and delight. "That's got to be it!" she exclaimed. "That's got to be where he hid his fortune! You found it!" She was practically clapping.

"The key," Lionel said tersely as he spun to face Ella.

She could almost feel how close he was to the edge of control. He appeared wired, as if he'd been anticipating this moment for far too long. She wondered how long exactly. More than thirty years ago, after he'd killed his father and taken the key he'd been disappointed to find out didn't open the vault? Or long before that?

Heart in her throat, Ella reached into her pocket, her fingers locking around the key. She froze for a moment with sudden doubt. Had Waco heard everything so far? What if Marvin had fooled them all by wearing a key that didn't open the vault? What if he'd hid the real key somewhere else entirely? More to the point, what would happen to her if the key didn't open the vault?

Ella hesitated a few seconds too long.

"Give me the damn key," Lionel demanded as he pulled a gun from his jacket pocket. The look in his eyes told Ella that he would shoot her if she didn't hand it over—and quickly.

"You don't need that gun." It surprised her, how calm she sounded. She pulled the key from her pocket and handed it to him.

That was when she saw his expression darken. He advanced on her so quickly that she didn't have time to move before he grabbed her with his free hand. He opened her jacket and pulled up her shirt before spinning her around to tug at the waist of her jeans, looking for a wire. Her uncle had been right. If she'd been wired for sound, Lionel would have found it.

"Did you really think I would go to the cops?" she demanded indignantly with a laugh and a shake of her head as she stepped away to straighten her clothing.

Lionel trained the gun on her.

She saw his gaze go to her left pocket. "What?"

"Take your hand out very slowly," he ordered. "And it better be empty."

She withdrew her hand and he lunged at her, driving his free hand into her pocket and pulling out her cell phone. The copy of the will had also been in that pocket. It fluttered to the floor.

He stared at the phone for a moment. From the look on his face, he was chastising himself for being so foolish. He hadn't even considered a wire earlier—let alone thought she would have a cell phone.

Fortunately, she'd disconnected the call with Waco when Lionel had first grabbed her. Now he tossed her phone across the room, his gaze boring into her. "How foolish of you to come alone. You didn't even bring your brother with you. But you were right earlier. We should do this together. Then, if the key doesn't work... Come on," he said, motioning with the gun for her to lead the way down the stairs to the vault.

Ella had no desire to go down there, but she didn't see any other option at the moment. She moved to the edge and took a tentative step. The old wood of the first stair creaked under her boot. She took another. Behind her, Lionel's weight on the steps made the entire staircase groan and sag a little.

It was even colder down here, the odor of wet earth strong. She could smell Lionel's nervous sweat, as well, reminding her that he had a gun trained on her back. Before Ella reached the last step, he shoved her aside, and still holding the gun in one hand, he fitted the key into the vault with the other.

His hands, she saw, were shaking. She was shaking for a whole different reason. If that key didn't turn in that lock—

She heard the *click*, saw the key rotate and let out the breath she'd been holding. Relief made her knees go weak as she watched him turn the handle.

The huge steel door swung open.

Chapter Twenty-Four

As Waco quickly made his way through the maze of hallways, he had a mental image of the original house plans Hud had supplied. But the place was so large, it was taking too much time. He'd heard Lionel search Ella and was thankful he hadn't fitted her with a wire. But she'd had to disconnect the call. Now he had no idea what was happening, and that had him terrified.

All he knew for certain was that he had to get to the ballroom as quickly as possible. It didn't surprise him that it had been Lionel who'd found a trapdoor leading to stairs beneath the floor to an underground vault. Nor did it surprise him that Lionel had a gun.

He knew Ella could handle herself—as long as that key opened the vault. But even if it did, he knew that Lionel had no plan to share the fortune. Not one of them had wanted to see the will. Either because they didn't believe it was real, or because it wouldn't matter after tonight...

That meant that Waco had to reach Ella and fast. He'd suspected Lionel as the killer. It made sense. But he'd also worried that all of them might be in on it, even though Mercy seemed too scatter-brained and Angeline too frail. Not that he didn't think any one of them was capable of killing the others for the money.

Waco just hoped to have made the arrest before that happened, since Ella was at the heart of it. He tried to tell himself this was like every other case he'd ever had. He knew danger. He'd been wounded more times than he wanted to think about since he'd taken this job. That was because he caught the dangerous cases and always had.

But even as he tried not to run through the house and let them know he was coming, he couldn't pretend that this case hadn't taken a turn he'd never expected. He'd fallen in love with one of the civilians. Now she was risking her life to end this.

ELLA STARED INTO the vault. When she looked at Lionel, his eyes were as wide as her own. He must have been holding his breath, because he let out a whoosh of sound before he screamed, "It's empty!" He sounded both shocked and furious. His gaze swung to her.

She couldn't believe what she was seeing, either. Her first thought was that her mother had cleaned it out with this key years ago.

"How is this possible?" Mercy called down the stairs, sounding close to hysteria.

Angeline laughed from her wheelchair. "Why are you both so surprised that he *lied*? Our own father. The bastard lied to us our whole lives. There never was any money."

All the color had drained from Lionel's face. He seemed to be at a loss for words. Ella figured his mind was probably whirling like hers. It was only a matter of time before he came to the same conclusion she had.

Ella made a run for the stairs and got up four steps before Lionel grabbed her ankle. He jerked hard, trying to pull her back, but she locked her fingers around the edge of the wooden stairway and hung on.

The gunshot made her start. Her fingers slipped and she slid on her stomach down a couple of stairs. Overhead, she could hear screaming and the crash of Angeline's wheelchair, but all that was drowned out by a second and third gunshot.

Lionel released her ankle. Had he killed both of his sisters? She heard him moan a second before he crashed backward into the steel door of the vault. She looked behind her. His chest bloomed with blood as he slowly slid to the ground.

For a second, Ella couldn't move. She lay sprawled on the stairs, feeling disoriented and confused. She'd been so sure that she'd been hit by one of the bullets. But if Lionel hadn't fired them, who had?

Only an instant lapsed before her brain kicked in and Ella quickly started upward, desperate to get out of this hole.

But after only a couple of steps, what she saw at the top of the stairs stopped her cold. A dark shape loomed over her, the figure holding a gun. The barrel was pointed in her face.

"I'm going to need that key," Angeline said. "Fetch it for me, won't you?"

Chapter Twenty-Five

Jeremiah laughed after Waco left the room. With his free hand, he pulled the lock-pick kit from his jacket pocket. It didn't take him more than a few moments to get the handcuff off the bed frame. He worked just as quickly to unlock the one on his wrist. He couldn't have it dangling and making any noise.

The guys at Helen's bar had taught him all kinds of helpful things—even though Helen had threatened them with physical harm if they led him astray. He didn't think of it in that context. He was smart. He'd proved that at the university he'd attended with the falsified papers Helen had gotten him.

The problem was that Jeremiah wasn't sure what he wanted to do with his life. Nothing his university adviser had suggested had appealed to him. He wanted something exciting, and his degree in mechanical engineering, though helpful at times, just didn't cut it.

Once he had his hands free, he shoved the cuffs into his jacket pocket and considered what to do. Staying in the house, knowing that Waco was in here somewhere looking for Ella, now seemed like a bad idea.

But he had a thought. Rather than go through the house, he went back out the window. As he moved along the edge of the house, keeping to the dark shadows, he looked for something he'd seen earlier.

His uncle Hud was somewhere around here. He didn't want to get shot. But he wasn't about to go home, either. That was when he remembered seeing what had looked like the opening into an old root cellar. Now, as he found it, he saw the lock on the door. This time it took a little longer since he didn't want to use his flashlight he'd brought with him.

The lock finally gave and Jeremiah pulled open the door. The moment he did, he noted the stairs that dropped down. Quickly, he stepped inside and closed the door behind him before pulling out his flashlight and shining it ahead of him.

At the bottom of the stairs, he realized he was in a narrow tunnel—and that the tunnel headed in the direction of the house, just as he'd suspected.

He shone his flashlight into the tunnel, the light small and dim. He couldn't tell how far it went—or where it ended.

That was when he heard gunshots.

WACO HEARD THE GUNSHOTS—the reports echoing through the house. He realized he'd gotten turned around and had taken the wrong corridor. He rushed down the first hallway and the second. Seeing double doors at the end of the next, he pulled his weapon, rushed to it and shoved the door open at a run. Stumbling into what appeared to be the library, he swore.

There was nothing there but dusty books on miles of bookshelves. He couldn't believe this. He tried to calm himself, imagining the house plans he'd studied. The ballroom. He couldn't get to it on this floor, he realized.

Swearing, he turned around and hurried back down the hall. He wanted to run, to sprint, but he knew that the echo of his boots on the wood floorboards would warn whoever was wielding that gun that they were no longer alone.

He'd heard…three shots? Or was it four? He couldn't be sure. They'd echoed dully through the old massive house. He could feel time ticking away too quickly.

Waco wanted to scream Ella's name, needing desperately to hear her voice and to know that she was still alive. Soon Hud would be busting down the front door, backup on its way. Waco had to find Ella before that happened.

ELLA STARED AT ANGELINE. It was as if years of age and ailment had fallen off her as she'd freed herself from that wheelchair. Her hand holding the gun was steady as a rock.

"The key," Angeline repeated with that same frightening smile.

Ella realized that she couldn't hear Mercy. Earlier, she'd thought she'd heard her cry out in pain. Nor had Lionel made a sound since falling back into the vault's door. It appeared that Angeline was a very good shot.

She looked over her shoulder. She did not want to go back down those steps. She especially didn't want to have to step over Lionel to get to the key. "Why do you want—?"

The gunshot so close to her ear was deafening. She heard the bullet bury itself in the dirt next to the vault and quickly eased backward down one step, then another. When she did dare look at Angeline, she saw that the woman was still smiling. Why would she want the key? Or was that just a ruse? Was she going to slam the trapdoor and leave Ella and Lionel down there?

That was better than being shot. Not that being shot was off the table by any means. Once she handed over the key...

She carefully stepped around Lionel, trying not to look at him. His eyes were open and he seemed to be staring up at her. Reaching around the edge of the door, Ella felt for the key. It took a moment to locate it and then attempt to pull it out.

"I'm waiting," Angeline said in a singsong voice.

Finally, Ella worked the key out, stepped over Lionel again and then looked up. What was the woman going to do once she had the key? For a moment, Ella didn't know what her best chance was. But while she'd struggled to remove the key, she'd noticed that there appeared to be a dugout off to her left. How far the tunnel went under the house, she had no idea. But it was definitely deep enough to hide a person.

Ella knew she had to stall for time. Waco would be looking for her. Pretending she was moving to the steps, she pushed past them and ducked into the darkness tunneling under the house.

"What are you doing?" Angeline demanded.

Ella could tell that the older woman was leaning out over the stairs, trying to see her. "Tell me why you want the key."

Silence. Then she heard a sigh from overhead. "Because it is literally the key to the money. So don't make me come down there to get it."

Ella looked at the key in her hand. The light wasn't great down here, but she realized she'd never actually studied the key. It was large and ornate. She ran her fingers along the curved edges and felt tiny numbers stamped on the inside edge of the filigree.

"How long have you known about the vault and that it was empty?" Ella asked.

Angeline chuckled. "My father used to give me grief for always having my face in a book. I loved to read and the others left me alone. No one ever paid any attention to me, but I watched all of them."

"Clearly, you aren't dying."

"Not yet, but I was a sickly child. It was easy to continue to be sickly. Watching them was how I knew about your mother being pregnant. I knew she hadn't lost the baby. My father wasn't fooled by the miscarriage. Neither was Lionel. He knew he had to get to that money before Marvin left all his wealth to Stacy's son. We all knew that our father had already called about having his will changed. We didn't know, though, that he'd made out a handwritten will."

Ella heard the sound of paper being balled up. A moment later, the copy of the will came tumbling down the stairs to land next to Lionel.

She had to keep Angeline talking. "So, Lionel killed him, switched the keys, then found out the one around his father's neck wasn't the right one," Ella said. "How long have you known we were going to find the vault empty?"

"I wasn't sure, but it certainly made sense. My father wasn't a young man and he'd made a lot of enemies—even in his own house. He couldn't trust his wife, and he knew that once he was dead and gone, we would go through our assets unless he could protect them," Angeline said and sighed.

"Eventually you would sell the house," Ella said, seeing where she was headed with this.

The older woman laughed. "He couldn't leave the money in the vault for fear that we were so stupid we'd sell the house and never find the vault—or that one of us would take the key from around his neck when we killed him."

"How did you know the key was really the key to the money?" Ella thought Angeline might not answer.

After a moment, she said, "My father was determined the money would go to his unborn son. He wasn't about to let us get our hands on it. I was surprised when Lionel found the steel vault that he didn't try to blast it open with dynamite. Or at least try to get someone to pick the lock or make a new key."

"But then he would have had to share the wealth," Ella said.

She heard a smile in Angeline's voice. "You forced Lionel into admitting that he knew where it was. Not that he planned to share it, had the money been in there. If I hadn't shot him, my body and Mercy's would already be down there."

"So all you needed was the original key?"

Angeline chuckled. "I had no idea that your mother had taken it. I'd just assumed that when Lionel killed our father, he'd gotten the key. When that proved untrue, all I could do was wait. Then someone made an anonymous phone call from the Gateway bar about the bones in the well."

"Lionel," Ella said.

"That's when I knew for certain that he'd killed our father and somehow hadn't gotten the right key."

"But you would know the right key because it opened the empty vault," Ella said. "I suspect you're more interested in the numbers stamped on the key. Some offshore bank account number?" Ella guessed.

"I could tell you were a smart woman the first time I met you. But enough stalling. I'll make you the same deal you made with Lionel. Bring me the key."

Ella laughed and didn't move. "You must think I'm naive."

"More than naive if you think I won't come down there."

Ella jumped as another gunshot echoed in the closed space, the bullet pinging off the steel vault and thudding into Lionel's body on the ground.

WACO WAS ALREADY headed down the hall, gun drawn, when he heard the shot. He had to get to Ella and now he knew exactly where she was, he thought as he raced to the double doors at the end.

He could hear Hud breaking in somewhere else in the house. Backup would be on the way. But Waco couldn't wait for it. He had to go in. He had to try to save Ella.

As he approached, he noticed a sliver of light coming from between the double doors. He slowed and moved cautiously, his heart in his throat and a mantra playing in his head. *Let Ella be all right.*

At the sound of voices, he eased one of the doors open and peered inside. The first thing he saw was Mercy lying on the floor. She didn't move as he opened the door a little wider and noted the wheelchair lying on its side. No sign of Angeline, though.

Pushing the door even wider, he spotted her. She was standing at the edge of an opening in the floor. Who he didn't see was Ella.

Waco hadn't thought he'd made a sound, but he saw Angeline begin to turn. The gun in her hand caught the dull light an instant before he heard the shot. The bullet carved a wormhole through the wood door frame before lodging itself in the hallway wall next to him.

"Ella!" he yelled, ducking back at the sound of splintering wood off to his right. "Ella!" His voice broke. He was desperate to hear her voice and felt a lunge of relief when he heard her respond from somewhere beneath the floor opening.

He quickly peeked around the corner of the partially open door, his weapon at the ready. Angeline was gone. He did a quick survey of the huge room and, heart dropping, knew where she'd disappeared to so quickly.

JEREMIAH MOVED AS quickly as he could through the cramped tunnel. In places, the dirt had caved in and he'd had to force his way through. He could hear voices and felt he was getting closer when he heard more gunshots.

The batteries in his flashlight dimmed. Earlier, he'd been feeling pretty cocky. He had skills. But when he'd heard the gunshots, he'd hesitated for a moment. He was a small-time criminal. At least, that was what everyone in Hell and Gone had always told him. He'd resented it, but now he could see some truth in it.

Maybe the cop was right and he was out of his league and not prepared for this.

Or maybe not.

Now, as he stared ahead into the black hole in the earth, he thought of Ella. Holding his flashlight in front of him, he pushed deeper into the tunnel. His gut told him he had to get to his sister.

ELLA HEARD THE creak of the stairs after she'd called out to Waco, followed at once by the gunshot. She knew now that Angeline must have fired the shot and was coming down those stairs still armed.

She hurriedly looked back toward the vault for something to use as a weapon and spotted Lionel's gun lying next to his body. Pocketing the key, she scrambled for the weapon. She'd just wrapped her fingers around the grip when she heard Angeline's sharp bark of a laugh directly above her.

Ella spun around and pointed the gun at the older woman now halfway down the stairs.

"That gun is useless," Angeline said as she continued down the stairs. Her gun aimed at Ella's chest, she was smiling as if she knew something Ella didn't.

Taking aim, Ella pulled the trigger. *Click.* She felt her eyes widen in alarm at the dry sound. She pulled the trigger again. *Click. Click. Click.*

"I took the bullets out of Lionel's gun," the older woman said. "The fool didn't even check." Angeline was almost to her when she kicked the gun out of Ella's hand and then seemed to fly directly at her. She grabbed hold of Ella's long braid and pressed the barrel of her gun to Ella's head.

"Give me the key. Slip it into my pocket *now*."

Ella didn't hesitate. She could feel Angeline's strength in the hold she had on her hair. But it was the determination in that grip that had her turning over the key. She slipped it into the woman's pocket an instant before Angeline turned them both as Waco appeared above them.

"Throw down your weapon, Detective, or I'll kill her. I've already killed my own family. Do you really think I wouldn't shoot that tramp Stacy's daughter?"

"You're trapped," he said, sounding much calmer than Ella

felt. "You can't get away. Let her go. You don't want to make this any worse."

Angeline laughed. "How could it be any worse?"

That was when Ella heard a noise. It had come from the darkness under the house in that tunneled-in space where moments before she'd been hiding. She cut her eyes in that direction and saw something move.

Chapter Twenty-Six

Ella could feel Angeline tense. Had she heard something, as well? Or was she reacting to Waco? Either way, Ella could almost sense the woman's trigger finger getting itchy. Angeline had the key, but how did she think she would get away? Ella could hear the sound of sirens and people upstairs in the house. She knew it would be her uncle and backup.

But she feared Angeline planned to end this long before the rest of the law arrived.

Looking up at Waco, Ella knew she had to do something. *Now!*

Angeline had her gaze locked with Waco's in a standoff. Ella knew she would have only one chance. She shifted her body just enough that she could swing her arm back, leading with the elbow. She caught Angeline in the side and doubled her over.

Angeline let go of her braid, the barrel of the gun that had been at Ella's temple falling away for a moment, giving Waco a clear shot. The gun's report echoed deafeningly through the space around them. Angeline let out a cry, blood oozing from her shoulder as she shoved past Ella, dived into the darkness under the house and disappeared.

Ella didn't have a chance to move before Waco clamored down the steps. He pulled her into his arms, the gun still in his hand. "Are you all right? Ella? Look at me."

She raised her eyes to him, but all she could do was nod. She'd been so sure Angeline was going to kill him or her. Or them both.

Waco quickly released her and stepped in front of her, using his body as a human shield when they both heard movement in the darkness beyond the vault room.

To Ella's surprise, Angeline reappeared, stumbling toward them. Her clothing was covered in mud, as if she'd fallen, and she was no longer carrying her weapon. Behind her, Jeremiah came out, grinning, with her gun.

"Look who I found trying to get away," he said, his grin growing broader. "Hey, sis. Glad to see you're all right. I see the detective here saved you."

"She saved us both," Waco said. "You don't want to underestimate your sister." He put his arm around Ella and pulled her close as the rumble of footfalls could be heard on the floor above them. A few moments later, her uncle filled the opening at the top of the stairs.

She smiled up at him.

Hud shook his head and held out a hand. "Come on. It's time to go home."

Chapter Twenty-Seven

Two weeks later, Ella looked around the large living room at her family gathered there. The story about the Hanover takedown had hit all the papers, highlighting the gory details—a lot of them provided by Angeline herself. She was promising to write a book about growing up in her dysfunctional family. Said she was playing with the title *The Hanover House of Horrors*. The Hanover matriarch seemed to be enjoying her time in the spotlight, as if almost looking forward to prison.

Mercy and Lionel were dead. Ella knew she could have been, too. She'd taken a dangerous chance. Lionel had killed his father after Marvin had said he was going to replace him with another son. Ella believed more than the money had motivated Lionel, but they would never know for sure.

At least one of the Hanovers had been brought to justice. There wouldn't be a trial, though, Waco was now telling the family, since Angeline had confessed to everything and waived that right.

Jeremiah appeared instantly disappointed. Apparently, he'd hoped to get up on the stand as a witness.

He also seemed to be enjoying his moment in the sun. Even Uncle Hud had grudgingly told Jeremiah that he'd done an okay job catching Angeline before she could get away. True, backup had been waiting outside at the root-cellar opening, so she wouldn't have gotten far. But Hud left that part out.

Uncle Hud had finally retired entirely, walking away from his lifetime's calling. Ella could tell it was one of the hardest things he'd ever done. She'd looked at Waco, knowing that she would soon have the same fears her aunt Dana had had all those years. Waco loved what he did. Like Uncle Hud, he wouldn't quit until he absolutely had to.

"I think I'd like to be a cop," Jeremiah announced to everyone.

Hud groaned.

"My son can be whatever he wants," Stacy declared, daring her brother-in-law to say differently.

"I do have one question," Ella said. "The words carved into the wall at the bottom of the well…"

"Stacy don't?" Waco said.

"What do you think he was trying to tell her?"

They all looked at Stacy. "I've thought about that," she said. "I think he was trying to tell me not to get rid of his son. He wanted a part of him to live on that he could be proud of."

Ella thought that was one interpretation. She was just glad that Marvin hadn't been trying to name his killer. If true, then Marvin had been thinking of his unborn son instead of the son who'd knocked him down the well and left him for dead.

"Time to eat!" Dana announced, changing the subject. She had cooked two huge hens with dressing, garden green beans, mashed potatoes and relish she and Stacy had made last fall.

They all ate and talked, the dining room a dull roar of voices and laughter, keeping the conversation light.

Ella looked at Waco and smiled. He fit right in here as he argued with Jeremiah, teased Dana and asked for more of everything.

AFTER DINNER, she and Waco walked up to her cabin. They stopped on the porch and leaned on the railing to look out over the ranch, the river and the dark purple mountains against the starry sky.

"Jeremiah wants me to help him get into the police academy," Waco said without looking at her.

"I think he might be good at it, except for the part of following procedure, but then, you'd know more about that than I would," she said with a grin.

Waco shook his head. "It scares me that you could be more like your mother and brother than I know."

"Fear is a good thing," she joked, then sobered. "You have to admit it—my brother came through for us."

"Your brother disobeyed every order I gave him."

She smiled over at him. "So did I." She felt a chill, reminded of how close they had all come to losing their lives that night.

"I was getting to that next," he said softly, the roughness of his voice sending even more shivers over her bared skin.

"Really?" she said, tossing out the challenge as he opened the front door to her cabin. She stepped through and heard him lock the door behind her. She turned to face him.

"We're going to have to establish some rules, you and I, for the future," he said as he took a step toward her.

"For the future?" she asked innocently.

"Our future. Yours and mine."

She cocked a brow at him. "I can't wait to hear about this future."

He reached out and brushed her hair back from her eyes. "I'm going to be your husband."

"That does sound like it might be interesting."

He moved closer. "You're going to be my wife."

She met his blue-eyed gaze. "Hmm. If you say the word *obey* right now, I won't be responsible for what happens next."

He was so close now that she could breathe in his intoxicating male scent and the great outdoors in the hair curling at his neck.

"I would never waste my breath on the word *obey* anywhere near you. But we do need to discuss boundaries," he said.

Ella reached up and ran her fingertips over the scruff on his strong jaw, imagining what it would feel like on her skin. Desire shot like a flame through her veins. "Sounds serious. Where do you suggest we have this discussion?"

Waco's gaze locked with hers. Another shudder of desire rippled through her and she felt an aching need for this man that she thought could last a lifetime.

"The shower," he said in that low, sexy voice of his.

Ella tried to catch her breath. "The shower? I don't know, Detective. Anything could happen, once we get to…discussing things."

Waco grinned. "I can only hope." With that, he swung her up into his arms and headed for the bathroom before kicking the door closed behind them.

WACO HAD NEVER thought about happiness. It wasn't something he'd ever aspired to. Instead, he'd taken strength in knowing that he was capable of doing his job. But once he'd met Ella and her family…

"Everyone in the family?" he said weeks later as he pretended to be terrified as they dressed for the party involving all of the Cardwells and Savages.

Ella laughed and straightened the collar on his shirt. "You are finally going to get to meet the entire family. When my aunt Dana throws an engagement party, she throws a *party*. I just hope you're up to it." She threw that out like a challenge. She knew him so well. He *loved* a challenge.

He pulled her to him. "I've dealt with crooks and thieves and killers. I can handle one of your aunt's engagement parties."

Ella shifted her gaze from his to admire the ring he'd put on her finger. She'd told him afterward that he was making a romantic out of her. She hadn't sounded happy about that, but she had laughed.

It *had* been romantic, down by the river, the sunset making the water flash with brilliant color, the smell of the pines. He'd gotten down on one knee in the sand and looked up at her. Those green eyes… They still made his heart beat a little faster whenever he looked into them.

"Be my wife," he'd said. "Make my world."

Ella had laughed, smiling and nodding, and crying. He'd never seen her cry before, and her emotion had touched him more than she could know.

He'd gotten to his feet to wipe away her tears, and then he'd kissed her. It had been so sweet, she'd told him that her heart had taken flight, soaring over the scene and imprinting it forever in her memory.

Waco liked the idea that he might have turned her into a romantic. She'd changed him, as well. Changed him forever—the same amount of time he planned to spend with this woman.

* * * * *

Cavanaugh In Plain Sight

Marie Ferrarella

Books by Marie Ferrarella

Harlequin Romantic Suspense

The Coltons of Kansas

Exposing Colton Secrets

The Coltons of Mustang Valley

Colton Baby Conspiracy

Cavanaugh Justice

A Widow's Guilty Secret
Cavanaugh's Surrender
Cavanaugh Rules
Cavanaugh's Bodyguard
Cavanaugh Fortune
How to Seduce a Cavanaugh
Cavanaugh or Death
Cavanaugh Cold Case
Cavanaugh in the Rough
Cavanaugh on Call
Cavanaugh Encounter
Cavanaugh Vanguard
Cavanaugh Cowboy
Cavanaugh's Missing Person
Cavanaugh Stakeout
Cavanaugh in Plain Sight

Dearest Reader,

Welcome back to the world of the Cavanaughs, where the men are breathtakingly handsome, the women are feisty and beautiful, and justice always has a way of prevailing. This time around we get to meet Krystyna Kowalski, the twin sister of the heroine in *Cavanaugh Stakeout*. Krys is an investigative journalist whose spot-on articles have managed to rattle a few cages and have garnered her the angry displeasure of someone out there who seems to have marked her for retribution and death.

She brings the matter to major crimes detective Morgan Cavanaugh. At first Morgan doesn't believe her and thinks she is only exaggerating the situation until someone tries to hit her with a car while Morgan is in a parking lot with her. From there on in, Morgan appoints himself her bodyguard. Krys might have welcomed that except for the fact that the hunky detective insists on getting in the way of her pursuing her latest exclusive story. In fact, Krys's determination might be her undoing—permanently.

As always, I thank you for reading one of my books. I hope you enjoy it. And from the bottom of my heart, I wish you someone to love who loves you back.

All the best,

Marie Ferrarella

To

Korinna Rena Props-Berry,

Whose Very Kind Comment About My
Cavanaugh Justice Series

Totally Made My Day

Hope You Like This One

As Well,

With Thanks,

Marie

Prologue

She felt tired as she walked out of the office building and into the large, deserted parking lot. It felt as if she hadn't gotten any sleep since the funeral.

Maybe that was the reason Krystyna Kowalski was having trouble shaking the feeling that someone was watching her. She hadn't actually seen anyone following her when she'd turned around, but it was a feeling gnawing away at the pit of her stomach.

Krys sighed, aware just how paranoid that would have sounded if she had said it aloud. She supposed that, examined in the light of day, it probably was.

The darkness made it more real, given the nature of the work she did. As a freelance investigative reporter, she delved into dark, hidden secrets while traveling down streets where most other people wouldn't even dream of venturing.

But her work required her to burrow into and expose secrets that were thought to be completely buried. It was her job to cast light on paths that the key figures of her investigations thought were safely out of sight.

During the course of her investigations, Krys had heard herself being cursed, threatened with bodily harm and told more than once that she would be made to pay for what she had so brazenly and callously done. That kind of thing had become part of her job. She accepted it as her due and even thought of it as her badge of courage. But her safety wasn't anything she haphazardly took for granted. Krys always made sure that she took the necessary precautions. As for the rest of it, she just shrugged it off and went on her way.

But this eerie feeling had haunted her nights for the last six weeks. That was definitely something new in her life.

Even as she had sat beside her mentor's hospital bedside, holding Ian Marshall's hand as he lay dying, that uneasy feeling that she was being watched kept eating away at her. So much so that each time someone entered Ian's room—usually a hospital staff member as well as an old friend coming by to pay their last respects—something inside of Krys would tighten and instantly go on the alert. She had to mentally talk herself down each time because a great many old acquaintances came by in those few weeks to see Ian—while he was still there to be seen.

But now Ian was no longer alive to distract her. He had passed away clutching her hand. She had no regrets about being there even though she had wound up missing her only sister's wedding. She refused to leave Ian's bedside, refused to take a chance that the man with no family would wind up dying alone while she was busy celebrating Nikola's big day.

Nik had understood why she couldn't come to her wedding. They were twins, and twins intuited things about one another that no one else could begin to comprehend.

But now Ian was gone and Nik was on her honeymoon with Finn Cavanaugh. Not wanting to think about how much Ian's passing affected her, not to mention how she felt about missing Nik's wedding, Krys threw herself back into her work with a vengeance.

In the last nine months, after doggedly following a trail that led from the middle of the country to the West Coast, she had written an intensely conclusive exposé about Alan Parker, a charming, dark-haired, rakishly handsome man who, for the purposes of her article—and the nature of his crimes—she had dubbed "Bluebeard." The man with soulfully seductive blue eyes and a smile that Cary Grant would have envied made it his business to romance wealthy, lonely women and marry them.

According to the research she had done, there had been at least six of these women over the course of the last few years, although she had a hunch that there were more who hadn't come to light yet. Parker separated them from their money and eventually, he separated them from the world of the living as well.

Krys had doggedly put together all the evidence until there was enough for the police to issue a warrant and arrest the man. Everything fell into place and the man the police thought of as "Bluebeard" faced certain conviction as well as prison.

But somehow, thanks to his connections, Parker managed to escape before he could be put on trial for the murders he committed.

Right now, he was out there, free to continue his spree unimpeded.

She remembered the way Parker had looked at her when he was being arrested and taken away. For one split second, the silver-tongued smooth-talker shot her a look of sheer hatred. In that moment, her blood had run absolutely cold.

By then, she was hot on the trail of her newest investigation. Weatherly Pharmaceuticals had sunk a great deal of their money into the research, development and test trials for a new wonder drug whose properties were believed to keep cancer from metastasizing and spreading to other organs. The researchers hoped to contain the disease if not drive it totally into remission.

Fifteen years in development, the drug was highly anticipated and promised to make Weatherly's investors richer beyond their wildest dreams. The drug was, in essence, too good to be true.

For Krys, that sent up bright red flags.

Unlike her twin sister, to Krys, if something was too good to be true, she believed that it usually wasn't—and it was her job to prove that. She was currently interviewing everyone associated with this new wonder drug, both the developers and the people who had been the drug's test subjects. She was determined to get to the truth of the matter. If her hunch turned out to be true, there would be an awful lot of unhappy people at Weatherly Pharmaceuticals. People who she felt would go a long way to make sure they *weren't* unhappy.

For her part, Krys would have never become involved in investigating something of such major proportions if she didn't feel she was able to prove that the emperor had no clothes.

Possibly that was why she was letting her imagination run away with her, why she felt there were threats to her safety lurking around almost every corner.

Maybe she just needed to take a break, wind down, be a person again instead of strictly a driven investigative reporter with tunnel vision who was focused on only one thing.

Making her way to her car in the almost completely deserted parking lot, Krys shifted the pages and copious notes that she had accumulated and brought with her to this latest meeting. As she opened the driver's side door, several of the pages slipped out of the pile and unceremoniously fluttered down to her feet.

"Damn," Krys muttered, ducking her head and bending down to retrieve the errant pages.

A jolting noise just above her head, sounding like a car backfiring, screamed through the night air and effectively pierced the silence. Krys had spent enough time at gun ranges to know what that sound actually was.

And even if she hadn't recognized it, the shattered glass raining down from just above her head onto the pavement would have cleared up the mystery for her.

Her mouth went dry.

Someone had just taken a shot at her.

Chapter One

Detective Jay Fredericks was the embodiment of a man on the cusp of middle age. Balding since the age of twenty-three and paunchy, Fredericks had the unfortunate habit of shuffling his feet when he walked, and he had long given up his battle with maintaining some sort of relatively decent posture. Consequently, walking or sitting, he gave the impression of being the personification of a perpetual parenthesis. Because of this, Detective Morgan Cavanaugh had given up trying to read his partner's body language as a way of gauging whether or not the news that the man was about to deliver was good, bad or of no consequence whatsoever.

"Hey, Cavanaugh," Fredericks called out as he walked into the Major Crimes squad room and crossed over to Morgan's desk.

Looking up from his computer monitor, Morgan waited for his partner to say something further.

There was a pregnant pause on Fredericks's part, either for effect or because he couldn't find the right words to explain what was on his mind. Since Morgan was currently catching up on his paperwork, something he viewed as just a shade better than having a root canal, he had no patience for whatever Fredericks was attempting to communicate.

"Are you just trying out my name because you've forgotten

how it sounds, or do you actually want to say something?" Morgan asked.

By now Fredericks had reached the two desks that butted up against one another in the squad room. Fredericks eyed his desk, obviously tempted to take a load off, but there was apparently something stopping him.

"Umm, didn't you tell me that one of your cousins just got married?" he asked, stumbling his way into the reason he had come looking for Morgan in the first place.

The latest Cavanaugh wedding had just recently taken place. The entire police department had been invited and most of them had attended. Fredericks was one of the few who had not because his wife had insisted on picking that exact week for their annual vacation.

"You know I did," Morgan told his partner, doing his best to hold on to his patience. "Finn and Nikki. I showed you their wedding pictures," he reminded Fredericks. "Why? Where are you going with this?"

Fredericks bit his almost nonexistent lower lip. "I'm not sure," he confessed.

Morgan temporarily abandoned his paperwork and pinned the man hovering over his desk with an impatient look, waiting. Sometimes Fredericks could become exceedingly tongue-tied. That was a direct result of his wife of eighteen years never allowing him to get in a word edgewise.

"C'mon, Fredericks. Spit it out. What is it you're trying to say?" Morgan pressed.

"Would you happen to know if the newlyweds were due back early from their honeymoon?" Fredericks asked awkwardly.

"They weren't," Morgan answered without any hesitation. "Why? And for heavens' sakes, sit down and stop hovering like a seagull that's circling a garbage heap, looking for lunch," he said, exasperated.

Shifting and obviously undecided, Fredericks remained on his feet. "You think I could see that picture again?" he asked. When Morgan looked at him quizzically, his partner elaborated. "You know, the one from their wedding?"

Morgan had brought the photograph in to show one of the people he worked with who wasn't able to attend the ceremony. After he did, he shoved the photograph into a drawer and then promptly forgot about it. That was the only reason the photograph was still in the squad room rather than back at his place.

Morgan thought Fredericks's request was rather odd, but he shrugged. "All right." Opening the wrong drawer at first, he located the photograph and took it out. He passed the photograph to his partner. "Okay, again I ask, what is this all about? Or do you just have a thing for wedding pictures?"

Fredericks frowned as he studied the photograph Morgan had handed to him. "Yup, it's her all right," he murmured under his breath.

"'Her?'" Morgan questioned uncertainly. Just what was Fredericks getting at? His partner was known to be quirky on occasion, but this was downright weird.

"Your cousin's wife," Frederick answered, handing the photograph back to Morgan. "You'd better brace yourself," he warned. "I think something's wrong."

Definitely weird, Morgan decided. "You know, for a detective with the Aurora Police Force, sometimes you can be as clear as mud. What the hell are you talking about, Fredericks?" he demanded.

Fredericks pressed his lips together, making them almost disappear altogether. "She just came in asking for you."

"*Who* came in asking for me?" He was barely able to keep from shouting the question.

And then, before Fredericks could make another attempt to explain himself, Morgan suddenly had his answer. Finn's wife had just come walking into the squad room and now appeared to be heading straight for him.

He had only met Nik a handful of times, one of which was at the actual wedding. He had no idea why she would be back from her honeymoon so soon but by the expression on her face, something was definitely wrong. Not only that, but out of all the Cavanaughs who were available in this building, why would she be coming to see him? If there was some sort of a problem going on, he would have thought that Uncle Andrew, the former police chief of Aurora and the real family patriarch, would be the one the newlywed would be more inclined to turn to, especially since she had been instrumental in helping to bring Andrew's father, Seamus, around after a mugging had thrown the older man into a depressed tailspin.

Morgan rose from his chair just as his new cousin-in-law reached his desk. A dozen questions went through his head, none of which he felt were his place to ask. But still, maybe he could. After all, she had sought him out, he reasoned. He wasn't the one who had come to her.

"I take it you're Morgan Cavanaugh," the woman said to him just as she reached his desk.

Morgan gave her a bemused look. Granted, she had met a great many Cavanaughs on her wedding day, even more than she had initially met at Uncle Andrew's party on that first occasion. He knew that kind of thing could be very confusing for some people, what with trying to keep all those names straight, not to mention remembering who was married to whom. There was a time when he had gotten confused himself and he was family, although, at the time, that had been a huge revelation, finding himself related to such a huge family.

He smiled at the shapely blonde. "We met at Uncle Andrew's party," he reminded her.

She surprised him by firmly shaking her head and denying his assumption. "No, we didn't," she told him.

Morgan opened his mouth, about to tell her that she was the one who was making the mistake, but then he closed it again. He wasn't about to argue with her and get off on the wrong foot with this newest family member, so he just let her statement go.

Instead, he decided to try another approach. "Where's Finn?"

"Still with my sister would be my guess," Krys answered.

"Your sister," Morgan repeated, feeling as if he had suddenly, without any warning, somehow slipped into an alternate universe.

As far as he knew, from what Finn had told him, his new Mrs. had no family. Certainly none had come to the wedding. Having a family was part of the appeal of marrying into the Cavanaughs. They had family members to spare coming out of the woodwork in all directions, he thought with a smile.

"Yes," Krys said slowly, wondering if she had ultimately made a mistake by coming here. "My sister," she repeated.

But someone had taken a shot at her and that was a police matter, although, after that one attempt, there hadn't been any further ones made on her life.

Maybe she was overreacting, Krys thought. She usually had nerves of steel, but this had really rattled her rather badly. But rattled or not, she was used to doing things on her own. Maybe she could trace this back to the source instead of asking for help. Still, if she were being honest, she had to admit that this attempt on her life had made her feel rather vulnerable.

What had prompted her to come here, seeking Morgan's help, was that Nik had mentioned Morgan to her by name during one of their lengthy phone conversations just before the wedding. The fact that he was a detective assigned to the Major Crimes Division *was* a plus, and it was what had made her think that Morgan might be the right one to get a handle on this.

"ARE YOU SAYING that my cousin is cheating on you?" Morgan asked her, stunned. In his opinion, Finn was as straight an arrow as had ever walked the earth. His cousin was totally incapable of cheating. Morgan would have bet his life on that.

"On me?" Krys questioned, confused. "Why would he be cheating on me?" And then it suddenly hit her. She realized what Morgan had to be thinking. She had gotten so caught up in this thing that was happening to her, she had completely forgotten that other than an inch difference in height—she being the shorter one—she and Nik were totally identical.

"Oh, wait," Krys cried. "I need to explain something to you first."

Morgan could see Fredericks out of the corner of his eye. His partner was totally hanging on every single word that was being said, clearly fascinated with his cousin's wife.

"Go ahead," Morgan urged, crossing his arms before his hard, rather well-sculpted chest and waiting to hear what this extremely attractive, squirrelly woman had come here to tell him—especially since she was insisting that she and he hadn't met yet—which they definitely had.

"I'm Nik's twin sister," she told Morgan, hoping that would settle the matter.

It didn't.

He stared at her. "You're her twin sister."

This was the first he had heard of a sister, much less a *twin* sister, and he was willing to bet that he wasn't the only one in the family who had never heard about Nik's so-called twin.

Morgan found himself feeling sorry for his cousin. Finn had obviously married a beautiful but slightly delusional woman—or worse. He recalled that Finn had said something about his wife being an insurance investigator. Maybe she fancied herself a CIA agent or something along those lines.

Well, whatever the case, Morgan was willing to step up and help his cousin get help for his new wife any way he could.

"Yes," Krys confirmed patiently. She could see that he wasn't convinced. She reached into her back pocket and took out her wallet. Flipping it open to her driver's license, she held it up in front of the detective for his perusal. "Her twin sister. Krystyna Kowalski," she introduced herself. "We were born five minutes apart. I'm older," she added, anticipating his next question.

"Why weren't you at your sister's wedding?" he asked. "Or can't the two of you be in the same place at the same time?"

Very funny, she thought sarcastically.

Instead of answering Morgan's question, she opened her wallet again and looked through the different compartments. Finding what she was searching for, Krys took it out and held the photograph up to him now.

It was a picture of the two of them, Nik and herself, taken almost twenty years ago.

"See, we *can* be in the same place at the same time," she told him with a deliberately cheerful expression. "The problem is that we haven't had the occasion to be in the same place at the same time these last few years. Nik works for an insurance company while I do freelance work as an investigative journalist. My work takes me out of the state on a regular basis." Her point made, she did smile at him this time. "Different but the same," she told him. Krys's eyes met his. "So, do you need any further proof?"

"No, this'll do it for me," he told her. Morgan paused for a second, thinking, then went on to say, "I do have one more question for you."

Krys braced herself. This was for Nik, she told herself. That was also the reason she had sought Morgan out, looking for help. Because of Nik. Because what had happened to her made her afraid that whoever had done this might go after Nik by mistake.

"Go ahead," she told him patiently. "What is it you want to ask?"

"Why weren't you at your sister's wedding?" After a beat, Morgan added, "I'm just curious since according to you, the two of you are so close."

"It's not according to me," Krys corrected, taking offense at his implication. "It's a fact. And although it isn't really any of your business, I wasn't at the wedding because I was sitting at a sick friend's bedside."

Morgan raised an eyebrow. "Your significant other?"

"No," she told him almost grudgingly. "My mentor." Before Morgan could ask, she volunteered the information. "He had no family of his own and I didn't want him to have to die alone."

Morgan found himself slightly embarrassed and applauding her sentiment. "Oh."

Krys eyed him, waiting for the other shoe to drop. "Any more questions?"

"No, not right now," he replied in a voice that was totally free of any emotion. The truth of it was, he felt like an idiot for having barged into where he had no place being.

Taking in a deep breath, Morgan decided to start over. "So tell me, what brings you here—specifically to Major Crimes as well as to me?"

"I came to you," she told him, "because I thought you might be able to help me."

He felt as if he was inching his way across a thin layer of quicksand, about to sink in and go under at any second. "Help you do what?"

"Help me find whoever it is who's trying to kill me and why," she told him without any fanfare.

Morgan stared at her. It took a second for her words to sink in. There was nothing run-of-the-mill about this woman, he couldn't help thinking. "Maybe you better start from the beginning," he suggested.

"Maybe I should," Krys agreed. Aware that the man who had brought her in here was still hovering around, straining to overhear what she was saying to Morgan, she tactfully asked the detective, "Is there someplace where we can go to talk?"

Chapter Two

His curiosity officially aroused, Morgan rose to his feet. "Why don't we go to the conference room? It's bound to be quieter there than it is in here."

"That sounds good to me," Krys replied with a nod. "Lead the way."

Fredericks snapped to attention the moment he saw his partner and the woman beginning to leave.

"You need any backup, Cavanaugh?" Fredericks volunteered eagerly. He never took his eyes off Morgan's visitor. "All you need to do is ask," the man reminded his partner with a wide grin.

"No, I think I can handle this," Morgan assured the detective. He passed the older man as he went to the rear of the squad room, where both the conference and the interrogation rooms were located.

Fredericks gazed almost longingly at the blonde as she walked by.

"Well, let me know if you can't," he called after Morgan. "I'll be right here, waiting."

Krys smiled at the older man as she walked behind Morgan to the conference room. "I'll take that as a compliment."

Overhearing her, Fredericks seemed to visibly buck up at the words.

Morgan said nothing until they had reached the conference room. After waiting for Nik's look-alike to cross the threshold, he closed the door behind her, and then gestured toward the chairs surrounding the lone table in the room.

"Why don't you take a seat?" he told the woman, leaving the choice open to her.

Once she did, he took one of the chairs positioned on the opposite side of the table, facing hers. Lacing his fingers together before him, Morgan looked at her for a long moment, doing his best to read her. Was she overreacting to whatever had happened to her, or was this on the level?

Or, at the very least, did she *believe* this to be on the level?

"All right, why don't you tell me just what makes you think that someone is trying to kill you?" he asked Krys. "Were you recently threatened by someone, or did you do anything that might have gotten someone angry enough to take a permanent shot at you?"

Considering the nature of the situation, Morgan asked the question so calmly and rationally that Krys found herself laughing.

"Did I say something funny, Ms. Kowalski?" Morgan asked.

"Sorry, you had to be there," she told him, stifling another laugh.

"Unless one of us is having an out-of-body experience, I *am* there—or rather 'here,'" Morgan pointed out.

Krys took in another deep breath before explaining why she had decided that, for once, she would bring this to the police. "The first thing I want you to understand is that if it wasn't for Nik, I wouldn't be here."

Morgan nodded his head, feeling as if they were going around in circles. "You already said that. Nik was the one who told you to come to me."

"No, Nik didn't say anything of the kind," Krys corrected him. "What she did say to me was that you worked out of the Major Crimes Division. I drew my own conclusion as to whether or not you could handle this case. But that's not what I meant."

"All right," Morgan said gamely, "just what *did* you mean?"

She supposed that she wasn't being very clear. For possibly the first time in her life, her brain felt addled. She would have to spell it out for him, slowly, so she wouldn't wind up tripping over her tongue. "Nik and I look alike—"

"We've already established that," Morgan reminded her.

Something about this handsome detective rubbed her the wrong way. She would have thought that the matter would be crystal clear to a police detective, but obviously, she'd given the man too much credit.

Krys enunciated her words carefully. "I'm worried that if we don't find whoever is trying to kill me by the time Nik does come back from her honeymoon, that person might wind up shooting or even killing Nik, thinking that she's me." To her relief, Krys saw a light dawning in the detective's green eyes.

Finally!

"Now do you understand?" she asked, anticipating an affirmative response.

"Yes, I do," Morgan answered. He felt that the woman was talking down to him, but for the time being, he let that go. Technically, she was now family and as such he had to cut her a little slack—but it wasn't easy. Patience was not his long suit. "So let's go back to what I just asked you and I'll rephrase the question." Morgan used the simplest terms he could think of. "To the best of your knowledge, have you ticked anyone off recently?"

She had been so wrapped in what she was doing for so long, it was hard for her to conceive of the fact that there were people outside of the world of investigative journalism who knew nothing about her reputation.

With that in mind, Krys started from scratch.

"I'm an investigative journalist," she told Morgan. "And lately, what that seems to mean is that I—tick people off for a living."

Morgan appeared a little skeptical about what she had just said. "What is it that you 'investigate'?"

"Anything that might interest or affect the general public. My last piece was a six-part series about a man who seduced and married lonely, rich widows. All those women eventually met with untimely ends."

"He killed them?" Morgan asked, vaguely aware of reading something along those lines.

She nodded. "I gathered enough information to get him arrested." She didn't bother keeping the pride out of her voice. She had worked hard gathering that information which was used to indict Bluebeard. "He was about to be brought to trial when he managed to escape and go into hiding."

Well, if she wasn't making things up, this sounded like the most likely candidate who was trying to kill her. If that turned out to be the case, it shouldn't take him much time to bring this whole thing to a close, Morgan thought.

"And you believe that this is the person who's trying to kill you now?" he asked, expecting her to say yes.

If only it was that simple, Krys thought. "Well, he'd certainly be worth tracking down, but I'm not sure if he was the one who took a shot at me."

He would have said that this sounded pretty cut-and-dried to him. "Why? Are there more people you've gotten angry? What are you not telling me?" Morgan asked, scrutinizing her more closely.

"I'm currently working on another story."

The pregnant note in her voice had Morgan thinking that maybe he had been right. She *had* gotten more people angry at her. "And what's the story about?"

"Weatherly Pharmaceuticals has a brand-new drug that's coming out on the market next month that's been greatly anticipated," she began.

Morgan nodded. "I've heard about it," he told her. Everyone with a pulse had. The story had been on the news, growing in scope, for the last year. "What about it?"

"Once it's on the market," Krys went on, "it could stand to make everyone involved in its development a boatload of money."

So far, the woman wasn't telling him anything that was new, but the look on her face told him that she was about to.

"But...?" he asked.

"But I've done lots of research on my own and I'm not convinced that it's the miracle drug the company says it is. There are a few discrepancies that my sources say the company has gone out of its way to bury."

"And you've documented this?" he asked.

She read people for a living, but she couldn't get a handle on whether or not Morgan believed her. She had a feeling she would need to prove herself to him. So be it. Nothing she hadn't done before.

"I've been trying to locate a few of the people involved in the tests who seemed to have disappeared off the face of the earth. If I find them—and *if* I'm right—that throws a very large monkey wrench into the results," she concluded.

Morgan's expression remained unchanged. What he said next shed no light on the situation for her. He could have easily just been mocking her.

"So you think one of the company's executives is doing their dirty work and trying to eliminate you from the scene?" Morgan asked.

"I honestly don't know who's behind this or who shot at me," she admitted. "That's why I came to you. I thought with your expertise you might be able to narrow things down for me, find the person who's trying to kill me before Nik comes back from her honeymoon."

"And you're sure someone is out there, trying to kill you?" Morgan questioned again. "It couldn't just be your imagination, getting carried away?" His eyes pinned her in place as he continued to wait for her to convince him. "You know, given the stressful nature of your work, maybe you're imagining things that—"

Krys cut in. "You don't believe me." It wasn't a question.

He didn't say yes or no. Instead, he said, "Well, I do know that once an idea has found a home in a person's head, it's hard to get it out or think of alternative assumptions."

Well, that did away with any possibility that she had misunderstood him. "You don't believe that someone's out to kill me," she concluded, leaving no room for doubt.

"It's not a matter of what I believe," Morgan told her, doing his best to be diplomatic about the matter.

Now Krys was glad she had decided to drive over here instead of taking a service or having one of her friends drive her over to the police precinct.

There seemed to be only one way to convince the detective that she wasn't being paranoid. She'd brought the evidence with her.

"Would you mind coming outside with me?" she requested politely, keeping her emotion out of her voice.

Morgan thought of the reports that he still had left to fill out on his computer. Granted, he would have happily grasped at any excuse to get away from them, but at bottom, that meant only postponing the inevitable. They would be waiting for him to finish up once he got back.

Morgan had a feeling that, despite the look on Krys's face, this wouldn't turn out to be anything and he was just wasting his time by humoring the woman.

"I'm a little busy right now," he began, hoping to get out of pursuing this charade any further. But Morgan didn't get a chance to finish.

"This won't take long," she promised. "I just need you to come outside with me."

Morgan had a feeling that Nikki's sister could be very persistent. He supposed that if there was anything to her paranoia, he needed to check it out. If there wasn't, then the fastest way to settle this for both of them was to disprove her assumption.

"All right, if this isn't going to take long," he qualified, "show me what you want to show me."

Just for a moment, her eyes met his and he felt something akin to a warm shiver slithering up along his spine. Since this woman was a dead ringer for his cousin's gorgeous wife, he could see why Finn never had a chance. There was something almost hypnotic about the way the woman looked at him, and he had a hunch that it was a twin thing.

After a second, Morgan managed to shake himself free mentally—but it wasn't easy.

She smiled, anticipating both his response and his apology. She plowed ahead. "Come with me."

Said the spider to the fly, Morgan couldn't help thinking, wondering if maybe it might be a good idea to tell someone where he was going.

The next moment, he told himself he was being ridiculous. He would be right outside the police building. What could possibly happen to him in the middle of the police parking lot?

Standing up from the table, he gestured toward the door that led directly out into the hallway. "Lead the way," he told her.

Her mouth curved in what he could only think of as a seductive smile.

His mind was going to strange places, Morgan thought. This confirmed it. He was definitely in need of a vacation.

Once in the hallway, Krys strode over toward the elevator.

"Out of sheer curiosity," Morgan began, "just what are you going to show me?" he asked.

There was that smile again. "Proof," she answered.

"What kind of proof?" he asked.

Krys had learned a long time ago that people were more readily convinced of a point if there was a buildup to it rather than having everything revealed to them at once. It made for a good article and by the same token, revealing something bit by bit kept the audience.

Right now, she wanted this detective to get the full effect of what she liked to think of as "the reveal." No one would go to these kinds of lengths just to convince someone—in this case a police detective—that they weren't making something up.

The sun seemed exceptionally bright as they walked outside the rear of the building, so much so that it was almost difficult to see more than just a few feet ahead of them.

Standing on the top step, Morgan looked around. They were facing the back parking lot and nothing appeared to be out of the ordinary to him. A number of squad cars as well as police motorcycles were out at this point, patrolling the streets of Aurora in an ongoing attempt to keep its citizens safe and to continue maintaining Aurora's reputation as one of the country's safest cities of its size.

"Okay, what is it you want to show me?" Morgan asked her. He was now convinced that, in the end, this was all going to be just one big wild goose chase, aided and abetted by this woman's admittedly very creative imagination.

"It's down here," Krys said. She nodded in a general direction, beckoning for him to follow her down the steps to the parking section that was reserved for civilians coming into the police station.

Well, he had come this far, Morgan thought. He might as well see this through to the end. The sooner she showed him whatever it was that she wanted to show him, the sooner he could get back to doing actual police work.

He was surprised when she brought him over to an ordinary-looking blue sedan. It made him think of one of his sisters' dream car, the one Jacqui had religiously saved all her money for until such time as she could afford to buy the vehicle outright, rather than just pay the vehicle off in time. But that was just Jacqui. She claimed that she wouldn't feel the car was actually hers unless she was able to pay for it all at once.

"Is that your car?" Morgan asked as they walked up to it from the passenger side.

"It is," Krys answered.

"My sister would say you that you have great taste," he commented.

She recognized it for what it was, obviously a left-handed compliment. "But you wouldn't?" Krys asked, curious.

Morgan shrugged. Unlike some of his cousins, he wasn't a car guy. He never had been.

"I find that one car is as good as another," he answered. "As long as it's running, that's all that really counts."

She looked at the car that had come very close to being her coffin. "Well, it's still running," Krys replied.

He picked up on the slight note of hesitation in her voice and put his own interpretation to it. "Having car trouble?" he guessed.

Krys laughed softly under her breath. "Yeah, you might say that," she answered.

Approaching the passenger side of the vehicle, she stopped for a moment, then continued walking, circling around to the driver's side.

Seeing that she wanted him to follow her, Morgan humored Nikki's sister.

He stopped dead when he saw the shattered glass on the driver's side of the vehicle. Absorbing the total picture, his mouth dropped open.

"Wow," he said, recovering.

"That wasn't the first word that came to mind for me," Krys told him.

"When did this happen?" he asked, circling the vehicle entirely, then coming back to the driver's side for a more in-depth look.

"Last night," she answered. "Around eleven thirty or so."

She sounded almost calm, he thought, and he had to admit he

admired the fact that she wasn't being hysterical since it was obvious that someone had done this intentionally. A lot of people he knew would have been, both male and female. How far away from the window had she been standing when this happened? Morgan couldn't help wondering.

"Are you all right?" he asked, looking at Krys again, this time searching for any sign that she had been hurt or grazed.

"Other than feeling a bit shaky," she answered, "I'm okay."

"Did you tell the police?" he asked as the full impact of what he was looking at and what she had gone through sank in.

Krys turned to look at him. "That's what I'm doing right now," she answered simply.

Chapter Three

"Well, better late than never," Morgan said in response to Krys's blasé handling of the whole matter. "But you still should have called the police the minute it happened rather than waiting until the next morning. You know, that's the advantage of having your sister marry into our family. One of us would have been there in a heartbeat.

"As a matter of fact, even if you *weren't* part of the family, someone would have been there to take your statement about what happened," he told her. In his recollection, he'd never met anyone who had ever been this laid back about being the target of a shooting.

But Krys shook her head. If she had it to do all over again, under the circumstances, she still wouldn't have done anything differently.

"All I wanted to do was get out of there before whoever had taken a shot at me realized that I wasn't dead. I wasn't about to hang around waiting for them to make a second attempt. I didn't even go home," she added as an afterthought.

Morgan looked at her. She kept arousing his curiosity. "Where did you go?"

"I checked into the Aurora Hilton on Main and MacArthur," she told him. "It's the biggest hotel in the city and I thought that with all those hotel people around, I'd probably be safer there than in my own house—or at least I hoped so."

She had a point there, he thought. "But didn't they find you checking in without any luggage a bit suspect?"

"Oh, but I did have luggage," she contradicted him. When Morgan looked at her with some confusion, Krys explained, "I have a to-go bag in my trunk in case I have to take off for somewhere at a moment's notice."

Of course you do, he thought.

"Where did this shooting take place?" he asked, realizing that she still hadn't given him an exact location.

Krys sincerely doubted she would ever be able to wipe the memory of this shooting out of her mind. "In the Weatherly Laboratories parking lot. That building is adjacent to the Weatherly Pharmaceutical building," she added, although she was fairly certain he had probably already known that.

"You said this happened around eleven thirty?" he questioned as he pulled on a pair of blue latex gloves he had in the pocket of his suit jacket.

"Or thereabout," Krys answered, trying her best to be as accurate as possible. "I was in a huge hurry to get out of there. Pinning down the exact time wasn't really the first thing on my mind."

If he found her answer flippant, he gave no indication. Instead, he had other questions for her. "Did anyone follow you?"

She didn't answer him right away. Instead, she reviewed the scenario in her mind first, then said, "No, not that I could see. The streets were pretty deserted at the time, if that helps," she added.

"How about when you got to the hotel?" he asked. "Did you see anyone approaching then? Or did you notice anyone coming toward you? Think," Morgan emphasized, his eyes all but holding her prisoner as he waited for Krys to answer him.

"I am thinking. I only saw the hotel valet, and he was parking cars. He seemed really surprised when he took a look at my blown-out car window, but I guess they train hotel staff not to ask questions."

Morgan frowned as he finished carefully surveying the vehicle. For now, he didn't see anything unusual, beyond the very obvious.

"So much for hoping to find any incriminating prints," he murmured under his breath.

"The shooter didn't try to shoot me from the inside of my car and he apparently didn't leave a bomb in my car, so no, I don't think that his fingerprints could be found inside my car."

"'He'?" Morgan repeated, waiting for her to elaborate on why she was using that particular pronoun.

"Or she," Krys allowed. "I told you, I didn't see the shooter."

Rather than say anything, Morgan nodded at what she had just said, and he got on his phone.

Krys took note of the fact that whoever he was calling didn't answer immediately. When they did, she picked up on the fact that Morgan's voice took on a friendlier tone than the one he had used with her.

"Hi, Chief, it's Morgan. If I haven't caught you at a bad time, would you mind coming out here for a minute? I need to have you look at something," he told the man on the other end of the call. "In the back parking lot," he specified. "Yes, our building," he confirmed.

"Calling your superior?" Krys asked as soon as Morgan ended his call.

"No, one of my uncles," he answered.

Krys frowned slightly. "You realize that doesn't narrow things down for me," she pointed out.

"Sean. The head of the day CSI unit," Morgan clarified for her. "By the way, he might not be overjoyed that you drove away from the crime scene—*and* that you drove over in an active crime scene to boot."

The way she saw it, it couldn't really be helped. Krys shrugged. "I didn't exactly have much choice in either case. My first priority was staying alive. Sorry if that necessitated my going against the rules."

He supposed he could see why she'd gotten her back up. No one reacted well to having their mistakes pointed out. "Sorry, I didn't mean to make it sound as if I wanted you to risk your life by staying there. You did the right thing, leaving," Morgan said and then sighed. Maybe he owed her some sort of an explanation. He didn't usually see only one side of an incident, but this hadn't been a normal week for him, either. "I'm coming off a bad week," he told her.

Krys laughed shortly as she looked at what was left of her driver's side window. "Apparently there's a lot of that going around," she quipped. "Someone take a shot at you, too?"

"Only figuratively," he replied. He glanced over toward the rear double doors, but Sean hadn't come out yet.

"Okay, I'll bite," Krys said gamely. "How does someone try to shoot you 'figuratively'?"

He thought of the breakup he had just gone through, a breakup that bothered him a great deal more than he'd thought it would. There was no way he was about to get into that right now.

"Never mind," he said, waving his words away.

Krys looked at him. "I think you should know that once I'm engaged in a puzzle, I don't just back off. You were the one who started this," she reminded him. "Just what did you mean by someone shooting at you figuratively?" she asked.

He blew out a breath. "Funny you should use the word 'engaged,'" he commented.

Krys cocked her head, studying Morgan. "You were engaged and one of you broke it off?" she asked. She saw the startled expression on the detective's face and knew that she'd guessed correctly, at least in part. "I'm fairly good at reading people," she told him without any undue vanity. "Do you want to fill in the rest of it for me?"

Whether he was about to say anything further, or was just going to put her off, she wasn't about to find out at that point, because Sean Cavanaugh picked that moment to push open the rear doors. Exiting the building, he quickly came down the back steps.

His first words, however, were not directed at Morgan.

"Nikki, what are you doing back from your honeymoon so soon?" he cried, holding out his arms to her. "I thought you and Finn were going to be gone for another week. Is everything all right?" Reaching the bottom of the stairs, Sean embraced the woman in front of him before she could say a word in response.

"That's not Nikki, Uncle Sean," Morgan tactfully informed the man.

Releasing Krys, Sean stepped back and then took a closer look at the young woman. The expression on his face clearly indicated that he didn't think he had made a mistake. Looking at his nephew, he said, "You're kidding me, right, Morgan?"

Krys pulled her shoulders back and raised her head so that the man could get a better look at her, although experience had taught her that people *never* saw a difference between them because she and Nikki looked eerily exactly alike.

"Actually, Chief Cavanaugh, he's not," she told him. "I'm Nik's twin sister." She put her hand out to him. "Krys Kowalski."

Sean took the hand that was being offered to him, but he glanced rather uncertainly at his nephew as he shook it. "Really?"

"Really," Morgan told his uncle. "Why don't you show the chief the picture you showed me?" he prodded Krys. Morgan figured that was the fastest way to deal with his uncle's disbelief and dispel it.

Krys inclined her head and took out her wallet. She pulled out the photograph she had shown Morgan earlier and handed it to the older Cavanaugh.

Taking the photograph in hand, Sean studied it at length in surprised silence, then handed it back to her. He was clearly caught off guard.

"I had no idea," he confessed.

"Apparently nobody did," Morgan commented to his uncle.

"That's not entirely true," Krys contradicted him. When the two men looked at her quizzically, she told them, "Nik told Finn she had a twin. But since I wasn't going to be able to make the wedding, I told Nik to spare herself a lot of questions about why her only relative wasn't at her wedding and just not mention me to anyone else until I was finally able to come to Aurora in person, and I could meet everyone then." She glanced toward her vehicle. "It seems like my plan was pushed up a little."

Sean put his hand out again for the photograph. Krys gave it to him, and he studied it even more closely this time.

"You look completely alike," he marveled. "If you hadn't said the photograph was genuine, I would have guessed that it was a gag, something artificially put together to fool people," he said, giving the photograph back to Krys.

"No gag," she assured him and tucked the photograph back into her wallet. "And for the record," she told Sean, "I'm five minutes older and one inch shorter."

The older man nodded, taking the information in. "Well, I'm sorry you missed the wedding, but welcome to the family." His smile was warm and welcoming. She found it oddly similar to Morgan's fleeting smile, although the two men really didn't look that much alike. "Andrew is going to get a kick out of finding this out," he told her. "Now." The CSI chief turned toward Morgan. "I'm assuming that you didn't call me out here to meet this young lady. What's this all about, Morgan?"

"I've got a crime scene for you and your people to go over," Morgan answered.

The expression on Sean's face indicated that he thought this was a rather dramatic way for his nephew to proceed, but he played along. He scanned the parking lot.

"Where?" he asked.

"In part, here," Morgan answered, gesturing toward Krys's car.

Sean followed the two of them toward the vehicle. "I don't understand—oh!" He stopped talking abruptly the second he saw the shattered window. "When did this happen?" he asked, immediately reaching for his gloves.

"Last night. Around eleven thirty," Krys added, feeling like she had already repeated this information an endless amount of times.

"Where were you at the time?" Sean asked. Since she appeared to be unharmed, he assumed that Nik's twin couldn't have been too close to the vehicle.

It still seemed rather surreal to her as she repeated the information. "As a matter of fact, I had just bent down to pick up some papers I had dropped when whoever did this took a shot at me."

Sean looked at her in awed surprise. "You were that close?"

Krys nodded. "I was that close," she confirmed.

"You are one very lucky young lady," Sean told her, shaking his head as he reviewed what was left of the driver's side window.

"For now," Krys agreed tentatively. "I'm hoping that your nephew can help me find the person responsible for this so that I can stay lucky," she told the older Cavanaugh.

Sean was already taking out his cell phone to call some of his team to come out and join him.

"If there's anything to find, we'll find it," he promised Krys. "This obviously didn't happen here, though," he said, surveying the damage and leaving his sentence open for her to hopefully fill in.

But it was Morgan who spoke up. "She said it happened in the Weatherly Laboratories parking lot, across the street from their pharmaceutical building."

Sean looked intrigued. "What were you doing there at that hour?" he asked Krys.

"I was interviewing one of the research scientists who had worked on that new 'wonder' drug that's being released on the market next month," she answered.

"And someone took a shot at you out there?" Sean questioned.

"Apparently," she confirmed.

Sean nodded. "I'll send some people over there to see if they can find any shell casings, as well as broken glass. Would you have any idea how many shots were fired?" he asked Krys, knowing very well that she probably didn't. Most targets, if they were even aware of the shots being fired, usually heard just a wall of noise, but he thought it was worth a chance asking anyway.

"The shooter got off three shots. I have no idea if the shell casings are still there, or if the shooter came and picked them up. I just took off as fast as I could."

"Good thing you did," Sean agreed, "or this conversation might not even be taking place."

"All right, given how early it is," he went on to tell her, "I'm pretty sure the glass is probably still just where you left it. We'll get right on it." He stopped for a moment, wondering if this newly discovered member of the family was fully aware of what was about to happen. "You do realize that you're going to have to get a ride back to your place. For the time being, until we finish going over it, your car is regarded as an active crime scene."

It was an inconvenience, but not one she hadn't anticipated. "For how long?"

"We'll process it as quickly as possible," Sean told her. "But you have to understand that some of the tests we run take time to get the results."

She nodded, resigned. "Do whatever you have to," she told Sean. "Just get me the name of whoever did this." She saw Sean exchange looks with Morgan and knew what that probably meant. "I realize that you keep all information in-house and that I'm just the victim here, which means I get kept in the dark, but for everyone's safety, I need to know as soon as you do."

"Everyone's safety?" Sean repeated, puzzled by her phrasing.

"She's afraid that since she and Nikki look so much alike, whoever is out to get her might mistake Nik for her once Nik and Finn get back from their honeymoon," Morgan explained before Krys had the opportunity to answer Sean's question.

The older man nodded. "So the clock is really ticking on this one," he concluded.

"More than usual," Morgan agreed.

Sean saw two of his people emerging through the rear doors. "Then we'd better get right to work," he told both Morgan and Krys.

"Thank you," Krys said, smiling at Sean.

Pulling her phone out of her pocket, she was about to start dialing when Morgan asked her, "Who are you calling?"

"A car service to take me to the hotel so I can check out," she told him.

"I can take you to the hotel," he volunteered, surprising her. "It'll give me a chance to ask you more questions."

"Can't argue with that," she replied, slipping her phone back in her pocket.

He sincerely doubted that. The woman would probably find a way, Morgan thought.

Chapter Four

Krys looked over her shoulder as she watched Sean and the CSI day team diligently going over every inch of her vehicle.

Though she tried not to dwell on it, she couldn't help her eyes being drawn to the shattered driver's side window.

"The people at the insurance company aren't going to be very happy with me," she commented as she followed Morgan over toward where he had his car parked. "I doubt if they get very many claims in Aurora for windows that need to be replaced because someone had shot bullets through the glass." Circling Morgan's vehicle, she got in on the passenger side. "When was the last time someone from your police department filed a claim like that?"

"To the best of my recollection?" he asked Krys as he started up his vehicle.

"Yes," she answered.

"Never."

She laughed softly, shaking her head as she contemplated the way her claim would be viewed once the paperwork was sent in. "I guess that puts me in a class by myself."

It did that, Morgan thought as he slanted a glance at the woman on his right, but not because of a window that had been shot out by some drive-by shooter gunning for her. She didn't sound scared, but something in the way she had said it had him thinking that she was.

"Don't worry," Morgan told her. "I won't let anything happen to you."

Krys drew her shoulders back. She had temporarily let her guard down, a clear sign that she was rattled. She didn't want him knowing that. Krys pressed her lips together.

"I wasn't hinting that I needed protection," she informed him defensively.

"I didn't say you were 'hinting.' I was just stating a fact." As he drove by his uncle, Morgan lowered his window and slowed down for a moment. "Keep me in the loop, Chief. I'd appreciate it if you gave me a call when you find something."

"I always do," Sean answered without looking up. He was far too intent on what he was currently examining to look away.

"So," Morgan said, turning back to Krys as he began to drive again, "you said that when this gunman missed you, you fled to the Aurora Hilton and checked in?"

He knew this, Krys thought. Morgan Cavanaugh seemed far too sharp not to remember every single detail she had told him. But for argument's sake, she played along, "Right. On Main and MacArthur," she said. Then, in case he felt the need to continue with this charade, she told him, "That's right by the—"

"Freeway exit, yes, I know," Morgan answered. Leaving the precinct parking lot, he took a shortcut to the hotel she had stayed in. It was located six and a half miles from the police station.

Like all the buildings that had been constructed in Aurora since it had been incorporated a little more than fifty-five years ago, the building that housed the Aurora Hilton Hotel looked impressively brand-new even though in comparison to some of the other establishments in the area, it wasn't. That particular hotel had been open for business over thirty years and, like all the other establishments in the city, it prided itself on its appearance and its service.

Morgan could well understand that if Krys wanted to feel safe, this hotel, located so close to the police station, was a good place to come.

CONSIDERING HOW EARLY it was and the fact that this wasn't a weekend, the parking lot that was located closest to the hotel seemed to be rather crowded.

Not wanting to have to wait for a valet to come and park his vehicle, Morgan decided to look around for an available space that was farther away from the hotel entrance.

"Hope you don't mind walking," he said to Krys. The woman who had just broken up with him always complained if she had to walk even a small distance, but that was because she favored stilettos, which always seemed to hurt her feet. "I can pull up next to the entrance if you'd rather I let you off there. Just make sure the valet sees you."

She bit back the urge to say that she didn't need someone treating her as if she needed a sitter. Instead, she said, "Thanks, but I can walk." The last thing she needed was to be treated as if she was some sort of hothouse flower.

Picking up her on tone, Morgan merely said, "Good to know." He was only trying to be nice, not get into a verbal sparring match over it.

Driving down several rows, he saw a lone space that was facing the street on the passenger side. Morgan pulled his vehicle into it. After parking, he got out, then made his way around the front of his car and opened the passenger side door for Krys.

Well, at least he has been raised right, Krys thought. She had just swung her legs out of the car and was out of the vehicle when something—instinct?—made Morgan suddenly look over to his right just beyond his car.

There was a black van with a tinted windshield heading straight for Krys and it gave no indication that the driver was about to stop. Moving fast, Morgan managed to pull her out of the way just in time. He threw Krys to the ground and shielded her with his body as he covered her.

He could literally feel the wind that the speeding van generated. It rippled over him even as the sensation of her body beneath his shot right through him.

Damn, but that had been close, he thought. Morgan reproached himself for being caught off guard instead of being on the alert.

Other than the tinted windshield and windows, the van had looked like any other van in Aurora. It had gone by so fast, Morgan wasn't able to tell if the driver had been a man or a woman.

The van was gone in less than a heartbeat—and his heart was

pounding so hard, he found he was having trouble catching his breath. He knew that Krys had to be in the same boat if the way her heart was beating against his was any indication.

"You can get off me now," Krys told him, hoping Morgan didn't realize that the reason her heart was pounding so hard was only *half* because she had come so close to being hit by the van. The other half was because his body had been pressed against hers—and she found herself reacting to that. Really reacting. "I think the car's gone," she told Morgan, doing her best to sound gruff.

Morgan scrambled up to his knees, leaning back to look at her and quickly surveying her condition. "Are you all right?"

"I feel a lot better than if that maniac had gotten his target. I guess he's not about to give up," she said, trying not to give in to the fear pinching her stomach.

Morgan had gained his feet and extended his hand toward Krys to help her up. "He? Does that mean you got a look at him?"

"I forgot to put in my X-ray contact lenses this morning," she quipped, brushing dust off her skirt. "I couldn't see *anything* through those windows. I thought a tinted windshield was against the law around here," she said, looking at Morgan.

"It is," he confirmed. "Maybe the driver came from another city." It was his best guess. "C'mon, let's get you checked out of here," he urged. "I'm going to find out if the hotel surveillance cameras caught anything that might be useful to us." There was a glint of concern in Morgan's green eyes. "You still up to walking?"

Rather than answer him, she just began to head toward the hotel's entrance.

"I take that as a yes," Morgan murmured under his breath as he quickened his pace.

When they reached the front of the hotel, they walked passed the young, slightly balding valet who looked at them and appeared properly shaken.

"Are you two guys all right?" he asked, glancing from Krys to Morgan and then back again. He appeared genuinely concerned. "That van almost hit you! You'd think people would be more careful when they're driving, especially in a parking lot as crowded as this one is most days."

"Did you happen to catch the license plate?" Morgan asked.

The valet shook his head, his wispy hair moving back and forth. "No, I'm afraid not. I couldn't believe what I was seeing and I was too stunned to get anything but the first number. It was an 8— or maybe a 6," he amended, embarrassed. And then he shook his head, realizing that he was being no help at all. "Sorry."

Morgan had thought as much. "Thanks anyway," he said to the valet, ushering Krys into the hotel through the automatic doors.

She pulled her arm away. "I can walk," she reminded him.

"And talk, I see," Morgan quipped. "Just humor me," he requested. "My mother spent a lot of time instilling manners in me when I was a kid. I'd hate to feel I put up with all of that for no reason."

When they entered the hotel, Krys began to go straight to the front desk, but Morgan caught her arm and directed her toward the first bank of elevators. "Let's get your things first."

"Are we making a fast getaway?" she asked, only partially kidding.

"We're picking up your things before the driver-of-the-year has a chance to find your room and get yet another chance to eliminate you," he told her.

She took that to mean that he finally believed her when she said someone was out to kill her. At least that was something.

"I suppose that makes sense," she admitted.

"That's why they pay me the big bucks," Morgan deadpanned. "Making sense when everyone else around me is losing their heads."

"Is that even a thing?" she asked, getting on the elevator.

Morgan laughed, amused. "Oh, you'd be surprised."

At this point, she was beginning to doubt that anything would surprise her about this man.

When they reached the fifth floor, Krys announced, "This is me."

Getting off, she led the way to a corner room that was located just beyond the ice machine. But as she went to use her keycard to open the door, Morgan put his hand on her arm and stopped her.

"Something wrong?" she asked.

Instead of answering her, Morgan took her keycard from her, opened the door and went in ahead of her.

"Stay behind me," he told Krys as, his weapon drawn, he carefully cleared the room and then scanned all the corners to make doubly sure there was no one there.

Moving slowly, he made sure there was no one waiting for Krys inside the bathroom as well.

"Well, unless there's a child hiding under your bed, I'd say that it's safe to assume there is no one here." He looked at her. "Look around. Do you see anything out of place?" he asked, even though the room looked as if the maid had just been there ten minutes ago.

"No," she answered, and then made her way to the closet.

"Hold it," he cautioned, then slowly opened the closet door for her, exposing a shallow interior with only a small suitcase standing on the floor.

"I was just going to get my to-go bag," she told Morgan. Picking it up, she held it out to him. "You want to look inside, see if my stalker's hiding in there?"

"It's not a joke," he said.

"I know that," she said, her voice deadly serious. "My way of coping, remember?"

Actually, he thought, Krys was coping rather well, all things considered.

"You have everything?" he asked.

She paused to flip the flap on her backpack and took a look inside. The only thing she cared about was on top. Her laptop.

"Everything," she replied. Closing the backpack and taking her suitcase, she swung that off the bed. "Okay, let's go."

She was about to walk out when Morgan surprised her by taking the suitcase from her.

"Let me carry that," he told her. Then, anticipating her response, he said, "And yes, I know, you can carry your own suitcase." He nodded down at the case. "It makes me feel useful."

Krys said nothing. Instead, she walked out of the room beside the police detective and closed the door behind her.

When they came down to the first floor, this time they did cross to the registration desk.

"I'd like to check out, please," Krys told the crisp young clerk whose name tag read Jeremy. "Krystyna Kowalski," she told him so he could pull up her charges. Other than for the room, there weren't any.

Jeremy's brow furrowed. "Is there something wrong with your room?" he asked when he saw her check-in date. "You're leaving us so soon."

"No, there's nothing wrong. The room was lovely," she told him with warmth. "But I have people to meet and places to go." It was a mantra that she lived by and tended to repeat whenever she was checking out of any hotel.

"Well, I'm glad that there's nothing wrong and I hope you'll remember us the next time you're here in Aurora, Ms. Kowal—Koval—um—"

Morgan looked at her, a question in his eyes. She obviously hadn't put down her actual home address, he thought, judging by what the desk clerk had just said to her.

"Krys will do fine," she told the young man with a smile.

"Krys," he repeated a little awkwardly.

Okay, that was enough chitchat, Morgan thought. Taking out his wallet, he flashed his ID as well as his police badge.

The smile on the desk clerk's face vanished and his eyes grew huge.

"We'd like to see your surveillance tapes," Morgan told him just as Krys gave the stunned clerk her credit card.

"Is something wrong?" he asked again, this time more hoarsely as his face turned ashen.

"Ms. Kowalski was almost hit by a black van just now in your parking lot. I was hoping to be able to get the van's license plate."

"Certainly, certainly." And then the clerk paused. "Did this happen close to the hotel entrance?" he asked.

"As a matter of fact, it wasn't. Why?"

"Because the cameras located closest to the entrance are working," the clerk said, then continued, somewhat embarrassed, "but the ones that monitor the parking lots that are farther away have been down since last Saturday." His voice sped up as he continued talking. "Security promised that they'd be up and running before the weekend, but if the incident you're asking about happened in one of those lots, I'm afraid that I'm not going to be much help."

"Show me what you have anyway."

"Of course," Jeremy said almost eagerly. "I'll have copies made for you."

"That's all right. I'll take the originals," Morgan told him. "You'll get them back when I'm finished with them."

Jeremy looked hesitant. "I'll have to ask corporate," the clerk stuttered.

Listening to him, Morgan's expression never changed. He just continued eying the clerk until the latter backed off.

"I'm—I'm sure it'll be all right, seeing as how you're one of Aurora's finest," he said, his mouth moving spasmodically in a very uncomfortable, stiff smile. The young clerk's dark brown eyes shifted back and forth nervously.

"I appreciate that," Morgan told him, his voice sounding very serious. There wasn't a hint of a smile anywhere.

"We both do," Krys said, belatedly realizing that she had inadvertently made it sound as if she and Morgan were a duo that went beyond just a police detective and a near victim of a hit-and-run.

ARMED WITH THE surveillance tapes, which at first glance did not appear to have captured the black van at all, Morgan proceeded to take Krys home. He was surprised when she gave him her address and it turned out to be a house.

"You live in a house?" he asked.

"Yes, why does that surprise you?" she asked.

"I just pictured someone who's always on the go as living in an apartment or at the very most, a condo," he answered, turning in to her development.

"I like the idea of a house," she answered. "It gives me a sense of permanency. Besides, Nik lived here. That makes it seem more like home," she admitted.

The woman, Morgan thought, was less of an independent rebel than she liked to portray.

Chapter Five

As he approached Krys's front door, Morgan looked at the cacti planted amid clusters of colorful little rocks. "You know, cacti seem rather suited to you," he commented.

"Why?" she asked, unlocking her front door. "Because we're both prickly?"

"I was thinking more along the lines that cacti are independent and don't need much care and attention to survive, but prickly works, too," he added, just the slightest touch of humor evident in his voice.

While it was true that Krys certainly liked her independence, there were times when she found herself wishing for attention—the right sort of attention—from someone who mattered.

One of the last things that Ian had said to her before he had died was, "Don't be like me, Krys. Don't shut yourself off from people and just live for the job. Once in a while, you need to be vulnerable, or else you're going to wind up alone—like me. I was always sure that there would be more time to have a family, a home, the whole nine yards—right after I finished the next big story. Except that I wound up running out of time."

"Krys?"

She blinked, realizing that this wasn't the first time Morgan had said her name, trying to get her attention. She had managed to temporarily drift off. Coming to, she turned the knob and pushed open the front door.

Morgan walked in behind her. "Where did you go just then?"

"Nowhere." She could tell by the look on the detective's face that she had answered him too quickly. She didn't want to go into any explanations, especially not about something so personal as thinking about Ian's warning. "I was just trying to remember something, that's all," she said.

"About who might be trying to kill you?" Morgan asked as he closed the door behind him and flipped the lock. He tried it and it held, but he still made a mental note that she could stand to have a better lock put in in the morning.

"No, about something my friend told me just before he died," she answered.

"Oh."

Since she didn't seem as if she wanted to share whatever that was, he left it alone for now. The only thing he was really interested in was whatever detail might wind up leading him to the person or persons who were obviously out to get her and, at the very least, do her bodily harm if not kill her outright. At this point, he sincerely doubted that after two misses, whoever wanted to hurt her was just going to pick up their marbles and go home.

Morgan took a long look around her dwelling. They were standing in a spacious, open living room that led to a kitchen on one side and probably bedrooms on the other. The whole interior had the sort of orientation that allowed sunlight to reach every available corner of the house, brightening it. From what he could see, the décor appeared to be modern and modest with just enough furnishings to be functional, but not cluttered.

The word *utilitarian* sprang to mind.

"You've got a nice place here," he told her.

It didn't escape his notice that Krys had left the suitcase standing by the door where he had initially put it down. That way she could grab it at a moment's notice. He couldn't help thinking that she definitely regarded it as a "to-go bag."

"Thank you. I like it," Krys replied, not really sure if he was just being polite, or if he actually liked her house.

His eyes took inventory of every visible square inch. It seemed like a lot of space for just one person. "You live here alone?"

As a detective, she figured he had to ask that so he could get a handle on her living quarters, but somehow, the question felt almost too personal.

"Yes," she answered, looking up at Morgan. "It's just me now that Nik's married. Why?"

He shrugged carelessly. "Just trying to get the lay of the land," he told her. He made his way into the kitchen. When he didn't see a doorway leading to another part of the house, he turned in the opposite direction. "How many bedrooms?"

"Three," she answered automatically, then amended her answer. "More like two and a tiny alcove, actually. There's one bathroom and one half bath," she told him before he could ask. "Anything else?" she asked with a false note of cheerfulness.

"Only that with that attitude, I wouldn't suggest you ever think about getting into real estate to earn a living," he told her, continuing to look around. There was a sliding glass door off the small area adjacent to the kitchen. He supposed that, with a little bit of imaginative description, that might have passed as a family room. "Your back door doesn't look very secure," he said, frowning at the offending door.

Krys crossed over to it, standing on one side of the sliding door. "It has a lock on it."

He spared a disapproving glance in the door's direction. "A lock that a nine-year-old could pick, not to mention that it's a glass door, which means that it could easily be broken."

She didn't appreciate what he was doing. "Are you trying to scare me?"

Morgan frowned at the conclusion she had jumped to. "What I'm trying to do is make you aware of your surroundings."

"Oh, make no mistake about it. I am definitely aware of them," she assured him. She didn't need him pointing out the obvious. She needed him to find out who had taken a shot at her and then tried to hit her with their van.

He made a decision. "I can have a police car patrolling the area every half hour," Morgan told her, taking out his cell phone so that he could put a request in to the station.

"Every half hour," she repeated, nodding. "That'll give my killer a twenty-nine-minute window he could use to shoot me."

About to say something, Morgan paused and studied her face. "Are you afraid?"

"No." She laughed, brushing off his question. She had sounded too serious just then, she thought, upbraiding herself. The last thing she wanted was to sound like a frightened, old-fashioned damsel in distress. "Just pulling your leg."

Krys crossed back into the kitchen. "Are you hungry?" she asked. "I can fix us something to eat."

Morgan frowned impatiently. "Krys, this isn't a social call."

"I'm aware of that. That doesn't mean that you can't have something to eat. I've got some chicken soup I could warm up, or I could just get something delivered if you'd rather have that." Temporarily closing the refrigerator door, she turned around to look at Morgan. "What are you in the mood for?"

"Answers," he told her.

They were obviously not on the same wavelength right now, she thought. "What kind of answers?"

Either she was really in denial, or she had completely forgotten that he told her he wanted her to give him a list of names of the people she thought might be possible suspects in her own personal version of a murder mystery.

Giving her the benefit of the doubt, Morgan refreshed her memory. "That list of names I asked you for," he reminded her.

Krys nodded, resigned that he wouldn't eat anything until she supplied him with at least some of the people she talked to or got information about. Somewhere in that list might be a person worried enough about their future that they'd eventually decided they had it in for her.

"All right, let's get that out of the way," she agreed. She gestured around the general area. "Where do you want to sit?"

He'd always found that sitting at a desk or table made it easier for him to jot things down than sitting on a sofa. Morgan indicated her kitchen table. "How about over there?"

"Just let me get something first," she told him. She began to go toward the back of the house. He followed her, but she looked at him over her shoulder. "That's okay. I don't need an escort," she said. "I know my way around here."

Her flippant quip made him frown. "This isn't a joke, you know."

"I know," she replied tersely. "Would you be happier if I assumed a fetal position and sucked my thumb?"

"No." It was hard not to snap. "The sooner you give me what I'm asking for, the sooner I'll be out of your hair," he said, addressing the spot where she'd been.

"You know," she called out to him, "you might think about working on your technique a little."

"And you might think about taking this a little more seriously than you are, Kowalski," he told her just as she re-entered the kitchen, carrying her laptop with her.

She supposed the man needed to have this spelled out for him. "Trust me, if I take this any more seriously—if I stop moving around like this—" she spread out her hand "—I might break down altogether. I just buried a man I regarded as another father, my only relative might be in danger because of me, and some crazy person is out there, gunning for me for some reason unknown to me. So yes, I know this is serious, but I am doing everything I can not to let the weight of this whole thing crush me because then I won't be any help at all. If you don't approve of my way of handling this, I'm sorry, but I'm doing the very best I can under the circumstances."

Morgan felt for her. Maybe he had been too hard on her, he thought. "Sorry, I didn't mean to set you off like that."

Krys inclined her head, letting him slide. "Fair enough. And for my part, I'm sorry that I just went off," she apologized. She put her laptop on the table and turned it on. "I thought it might help if you took a glimpse at one of my articles, the series I did on Bluebeard."

"The pirate?" Morgan asked, thoroughly confused at this point.

"No," she explained patiently, "that was Blackbeard. Bluebeard was the nickname the news media gave the guy who was marrying those women for their money and then doing away with them, or, according to him, they 'died on him,' leaving him bereft, grieving—and, of course, exceedingly rich."

Morgan looked at the laptop screen she had pulled up and placed before him. He preferred getting his information firsthand rather than just reading about it, but since she seemed to feel that her writing was what had gotten her to this particular place, he decided to indulge Krys and review the series, at least in part. Anything to get her to give him the list of people she had come in contact with.

Morgan skimmed over several paragraphs before he looked up at Krys again. He dealt with the criminal element—and would-be criminals—all the time, but what she had in her article still took his breath away. "And this was all verified?"

"Absolutely," she answered, adding, "Every single word of it. I pride myself on my research. I interviewed everyone who came in contact with this deadly Romeo. That included the friends and families of the victims as well as people who knew him as the 'attentive spouse.'" Krys laughed dryly. "However temporary that characterization might have been."

"And according to you, this is all the same guy?" he asked.

"According to the evidence," she corrected him, "it's the same guy. With each new woman, he changed his name, his backstory, his hairstyle and the way he dressed, but it was *always* the same man."

Krys pulled up an array of photographs that, at first glance, appeared to be of different men, but on closer examination all turned out to be one and the same man.

"Look at the set of his mouth. It's the same guy," she told him. "I felt like I had just scraped the tip of the iceberg, that there were more victims I hadn't uncovered yet. I was there when they arrested him," she told Morgan. "There was something about his attitude that told me he was having the last laugh."

"And he escaped," Morgan said, remembering what she had told hum.

Krys nodded, clearly disappointed by the turn of events. "Just like Houdini," she said. "For all I know, he's vanished. That means he's gone to another state, another country—or he could be hiding right around the corner, waited to take out his revenge against the person who caused his perfect game to crumble." And it was the not knowing where and when—and *if*—he might pop up that was driving her crazy.

"But from what you made it sound like, he's not your only possible suspect, right?" Morgan asked, trying to get her to elaborate
about the heart of the matter and prodding her along.

"No, I'm afraid he's not," Krys admitted. "But the article involving Weatherly Pharmaceuticals and their 'miracle' drug hasn't
been published online yet."

"Has it been publicized?" he asked.

"I'm sure word got around," she answered. "I interviewed people, lots and lots of people," she emphasized, and then she gave
him an example of the types of people she had made a point to
talk to. "People developing the drug, people who were used as test
subjects and took this new 'miracle' drug. I wasn't working in a
vacuum and my intent wasn't a secret. Considering the number of
people involved, I'm sure someone had to have talked to someone
somewhere along the line."

"So I take it that we've got the current suspect list narrowed
down to the immediate world," Morgan said dryly. "Give or take
a few people."

"Pretty much." Unlike Morgan, she wasn't being sarcastic.

"Well, this is going to take a lot longer than I anticipated," Morgan murmured under his breath.

"Which was why I suggested making us something to eat,"
she pointed out cheerfully. "At least you'll be fortified to continue
going through the information."

Morgan shook his head. "I don't know whether to think that
you're being exceptionally brave or incredibly blasé about this
whole matter."

"Like I said, you can think of it as my coping mechanism. Now,
once again, what can I make for you? To review, your choices are
leftover homemade chicken soup or I could have something delivered. I'm on a first-name basis with several delivery services."

The first thing she had mentioned caught his attention. "Homemade?" he repeated. "Whose home?" he asked archly.

"Mine," she answered.

Morgan looked at her, trying to judge whether or not she was
just attempting to put one over on him. "You're kidding."

"Why would I kid about something like that?" she asked.

He continued to scrutinize her, trying to get a better handle on the person she was. Was she genuine, or prone to giving herself airs no matter what that involved? "You actually *made* chicken soup?"

"Yes," she answered, drawing out the single word as she tried to decide where he was going with this.

"From scratch?" he questioned.

"Is there any other way to make homemade soup?" she asked him.

"Yeah," he answered flippantly. "You can use a can opener and empty the contents of the can into a pot. Then you heat that on a burner—or the microwave if you're in a particular hurry."

There was a touch of pity in her eyes. "Well, that might be your definition of homemade, but it's not mine. This was the first thing I made when I finally came home. After burying my mentor, I felt I needed some comforting."

"So your answer was soup instead of a friend?" he asked.

"I don't like to burden people with my problems. Besides, chicken soup creates a warm, contented feeling in the pit of your stomach. It doesn't say inane things like 'he's in a better place now,' or 'he's not in pain anymore.'"

"Both true statements," he told her.

"I know, but they still don't help fill up that empty feeling you're left to try to deal with when someone you cared about is gone. Chicken soup doesn't ask you how you're doing. It just goes about its intended function to fill you up. Now, what can I make for you?"

"After that buildup? I'll take the chicken soup," he told her— and then smiled.

Chapter Six

"This is really good," Morgan declared just before he slipped another spoonful of chicken soup into his mouth.

He had agreed to let her prepare something to eat predominantly to placate her. His main goal was to eat the meal as fast as possible and move on to the real reason he was here. But after consuming several spoonfuls of the chicken soup she had placed before him, the meal, with its tempting aroma, somehow captured his attention in its entirety.

"Why do you sound so surprised?" she asked, sitting down opposite him at the table.

He debated mumbling some excuse, then decided against it. Lying at this point, especially about something so minor, would be entirely counterproductive.

To a degree, he supposed he was guilty of typecasting her. "It's just that you're an accomplished career woman. Most career women I know either don't know how to cook or they don't have the time to cook—unless their careers involve having their own cooking show," he amended with a smile.

She supposed she could accept that. "Well, I don't have my own cooking show," Krys said. "But cooking was just always something I knew how to do. I guess waiting for the pizza delivery guy got a little old after a while and I'm not really a big fan of junk food."

She gave him a rueful smile. "I eat too much of that when I'm on the road anyway." She nodded at his soup bowl. "By the way, you don't have to feel obligated to finish that. I can make you something else if you'd rather." Although she saw that he was all but finished eating it.

"Maybe next time," Morgan said, retiring his spoon beside his bowl. "But for now, I'd like a second helping of soup if you have any."

She had no idea why his request for seconds could make her feel as happy as it did. But there was no mistaking the warmth that was flooding through her as she rose to get him another helping of soup.

"You're in luck," Krys announced, picking up the ladle and using it to fill the bowl she was holding. "There's just one more serving left."

"I don't want to take your last serving," Morgan protested. "You eat it."

She turned around with the refilled bowl and brought it back to the table and Morgan. "Trust me, having you eat like this does wonders for my morale."

"I wasn't aware that your morale needed reinforcement."

She merely shrugged, not seeing anything embarrassing about the situation. "Everyone's morale could use an occasional boost."

He thought about his life over these last few months. He was finally coming around. It hadn't been easy, but life had gotten a lot better. "Mine doesn't."

"Then you are definitely the exception," she told him. Krys considered what her twin had told her about this family Nik was marrying into. "But then, being part of such a large, strong family, I guess your situation might be different than the one that we mere mortals find ourselves slogging through."

Finished with his second serving, he put his spoon in the bowl and looked at her. "What the hell is that supposed to mean?"

She spelled it out for him. "It means that there's always someone there to have your back, someone offering you emotional support even when you pretend that you don't need it."

He didn't see their situations as being different from each other. "You have your twin."

But Krys shook her head. "Not the same thing. Nik and I have taken slightly different paths. Hers wound up keeping her close by while mine has me flying around to all these different locations. Following these last two stories was the closest I've been to home—as far as this region of the country goes—in a year and a half."

There was a lot more to this woman than he had initially thought, Morgan realized. He turned back to his work. "It looks like I'm going to need a bigger notebook to document this list of suspects I asked you to give me."

"Yes, about that," Krys told him. "I've been giving this whole matter a lot of thought," she said. She could tell by the way he was sitting that he was closing himself off to what she was about to tell him. She pushed on anyway. "And, to be honest, except for Bluebeard, I really don't think that any of the people from the drug trials I interviewed could be potential suspects. I don't see them wanting to get rid of me in order to stop the articles from coming out."

She paused, taking in a deep breath before proceeding. "If anything, they might even be hoping that I'll wind up championing their cause—that is, if I could find them."

Morgan stared at her. "How's that again?" he asked. "You lost me."

"That's just the problem," she agreed. "I lost them." She realized that her comment made what she was trying to say no clearer for him. Krys backtracked. "When I started looking into this miracle drug that was scheduled to be released, I heard rumors that not all the test subjects were thrilled with the drug's result. I actually managed to talk to a couple of rather dissatisfied, or at least unhappy, test subjects.

"But when I went back to attempt to verify my initial information, those people I had talked to just seemed to have taken off. They've disappeared," she stressed, "and no one could tell me where they had gone. The two test subjects who I actually did manage to find swore up and down that I had gotten their stories all wrong. That the truth of it was they were overjoyed with the drug's results. They said they were even willing to go on record singing the new drug's praises."

He barely knew this woman, yet had gotten the impression that getting her facts right was of exceeding importance to her. Apparently, she valued the truth above all else. People like that just didn't bend the facts to suit their purposes.

"That sounds rather suspicious," Morgan commented.

"You think?" Krys asked. The fact that this man believed her meant a lot to her. It also bolstered the stand she had taken. "But they stuck by their stories. When I wanted to talk to them at length, they refused to meet with me after that. One of them actually told me that if I had anything to ask them, I could talk to their respective lawyers. Lawyers," she added, "who ironically worked for the same law firm," Krys told him in a voice that was all but dripping with sarcasm.

"It sounds like Weatherly Pharmaceuticals is the one who might be looking to ensure your silence. They might not be above using methods that are less than savory," he commented.

Taking a breather, Morgan rose from the table and took his bowl to the sink before Krys had a chance to do the same.

She turned in her chair to see what he was doing. It was a very small thing—cleaning up after himself—but she was impressed. "Someone certainly raised you right," she commented with approval.

"My mom died when I was a kid and my dad was always working. When he wasn't, I think he was a little overwhelmed, having so many kids to take care of. To show our gratitude, we all kind of pitched in. It wasn't anything we talked about, it was just something that we did."

"How many kids make up an 'all'?" she asked, picking up on the term he had used.

It suddenly occurred to him that somehow, they were no longer talking about what he had initially wanted to discuss.

"Just how did we get off topic like this?" he asked.

He found the smile that she flashed at him dazzling and it went straight to his gut.

"It's called conversation," she told him breezily, "but don't worry, we can pick up where we left off."

Morgan shook his head as he laughed. "You're definitely not your typical victim, I'll give you that."

Krys looked a little bemused. "Is that a compliment?"

She had a way of drawing things out of him that he had no intentions of volunteering. He decided to play it close to the vest. "I'm not sure yet."

"Well, at least you're honest."

"To a fault," he underscored, remembering his breakup. Joyce hated the fact that he didn't sugarcoat things. "Some people find that off-putting."

"Obviously those people haven't had to endure the disappointment of being lied to time and again until they weren't sure what to believe and what not to believe." Her eyes met his. "Honesty, even brutal honesty, is far more preferable to having to deal with a liar."

And then, for no apparent reason at all, Krys seemed to transform right before his eyes, her serious demeanor vanishing in the wake of a wide, disarming smile. "Dessert?" she asked cheerfully.

"What about it?" he asked, caught off guard.

"Would you like some?"

Okay, he needed to stop her before this went in another direction entirely. "What I'd like," he informed her, "is to continue getting as much information about those missing sources of yours and about the possible whereabouts of this Bluebeard character as you can come up with."

She realized that she had allowed the threat of a killer to temporarily make her forget something very, very important. She was obligated to protect her sources, the ones who had given her information they didn't want getting traced back to them.

"I'll tell you everything I'm free to share with you," she told him.

Morgan knew what that meant. "Wait a second. You're going to hold back?"

She should have led with that from the very beginning, Krys upbraided herself. "I can't give you the names of all my sources," she said with an apologetic note in her voice. "It was hard enough getting these people to trust me enough to talk to me. If word gets around that I just gave up their names to the police, no one will ever trust me again. And I mean *ever*. I might as well stop being a journalist right now."

Didn't she realize that one of these people she was protecting might very well be the one who was trying to kill her?

"Well, the cold hard truth of it is, if you're dead, there'll be no need to trust you, now, will there?" he asked her.

She frowned at Morgan. "You must really be an awful lot of fun at parties," she said sarcastically.

"Just rephrasing what you told me," he pointed out. "Look, thanks for the chicken soup," he told her, getting back up to his feet again. "I'll read your series on Bluebeard and see if perhaps I can get my cousin in the computer lab section to see if she can track down this guy's whereabouts. She's very good at finding people. And, until I can find whoever is behind this, I will have a patrol car drive by your house every half hour to make sure that you're safe."

He'd already told her that, but maybe he thought she needed reinforcement. At any rate, she merely nodded rather than pointing out that he was repeating himself.

"Thanks," she said, walking him to her door. Having a patrol car go by would be good, if she was going to stay home, but that wasn't feasible right now. "Maybe I overreacted," Krys told him, trying to get him to relent when it came to the patrol car going by at regular intervals.

"Someone shot at you and when they couldn't seem to kill you, they tried to run you over with a van. That is *not* overreacting. I'd say you were damn lucky that whoever is behind this missed you, but luck has a habit of running out at the most inopportune times." He turned in the doorway to look at her. For all her bravado, she suddenly seemed very vulnerable to him. "Promise me that you won't take any unnecessary chances and that you'll stay put."

"One doesn't necessarily mean the other," she said evasively.

"All right, then I opt for the second one. I want you to stay put," he told her with emphasis.

"Funny, I was leaning toward the first one myself," she cracked. Krys could see that the detective was about to tell her just what he thought of that choice. She was quick to back up her selection. "Look, I still have people to interview. I haven't finished the articles yet and I've got a deadline."

"Emphasis on the word 'dead,'" Morgan pointed out darkly.

"No," she contradicted him. "Emphasis on the fact that I haven't finished the articles yet and I gave the editor my word. I'm not about to go back on that."

Morgan sighed, clearly frustrated. But rather than walking out of her house, he went back in and closed the door again.

"Fine, have it your way," he told her. "I just need to make a phone call to my superior."

It was her turn not to understand. Why did he suddenly have to call his boss? "About what?"

He watched her for a long moment, his expression totally unreadable. "About a change in plans."

"What change?"

"I'll tell you in a few minutes." He frowned at her. "Think you can stay put for that long?"

Krys could feel her back going up. "There's no need to be sarcastic."

"Just trying to speak your language," he told her. Taking out his cell phone, Morgan put some distance between himself and Krys as he began to press the numbers on the keypad.

Krys found herself watching his back and wondering what the call was all about. She fought her natural inclination to eavesdrop, something she used in her line of work constantly. His body language wasn't much help to her but toward the end, the way he held his shoulders told her that whatever this was about, Morgan was not about to back down or change his mind.

She glanced at her watch. This was costing her the better part of the day and she was already behind in her work. Unless something earth-shattering happened, Weatherly's wonder drug would be out on the market soon. Maybe she was being overly cautious, but she still felt that she was overlooking a major issue. Maybe the drug was on the level, or maybe it wasn't. The worst that could happen was that a lot of people who were pinning all their hopes on this would be bitterly disappointed.

But the third alternative to this had presented itself to her, and that was that the drug turned out to be not just inconsequential but harmful. And that didn't even take into account that the drug would cost a fortune. People facing a spirit-crushing ordeal were already going into debt trying to handle expenses that their insurance plans—if they were lucky enough to have insurance coverage—*didn't* cover. They couldn't afford to be hoodwinked by the twenty-first century equivalent of snake oil.

Krys was about to tell Morgan that she needed to get going and that he was free to finish his phone call outside her house when she heard him say, "Thanks." He was apparently ending his conversation.

Hitting the red button, he put his phone back in his pocket as he turned around to face her.

"All right," he told Krys as if he was picking up their conversation in mid-discussion, "my boss signed off on it."

She stared at him, wondering if she had missed something. "Signed off on what?"

"From now on," he told her, "you have my undivided attention."

She had an uneasy feeling in the pit of her stomach. "What does that mean, exactly?"

"It means," he explained, "that I know all the signs of terminal stubbornness."

"English?" she prompted.

"I realize if I tell you that you need to stay home until we can find this mysterious would-be killer who's already tried to get rid of you twice, you won't listen."

"And—?" Krys knew there had to be more to this than just a declaration of knowledge on his part.

"And given the urgency of this matter, I've asked my lieutenant to let me be assigned to this case exclusively."

Krys could feel the uneasiness continue to build in her stomach. "And what does *that* mean exactly?" she asked.

"It means that where you go, I go. More simply put," he concluded with a smile that didn't quite reach his eyes, "you, Kowalski, have just acquired a shadow."

Chapter Seven

Krys's deep blue eyes grew huge as she stared at Morgan. The last thing she wanted was someone hovering at her side while she conducted an interview.

"Oh, hell, no!" she cried.

"No," Morgan corrected patiently. "Hell, yes." He grew serious. As far as he was concerned, this was nonnegotiable. "Look, by your own admission, someone has tried to use you for target practice and when that didn't work, they tried to turn you into roadkill. That kind of thing doesn't sit very well with the Aurora Police Force or the Cavanaugh clan even if you *weren't* part of the family, which you are."

He could see the resistance in her eyes. Morgan plumbed the depths of his patience in an attempt to try to reason with her.

"Now, since you obviously refuse to stay put in your house, the only way you can go about 'business as usual,' which I get the distinct impression is your goal, is if I'm going with you as your researcher or whatever it is you'll have to call me in order to pass me off as an assistant."

"No," Krys insisted, shaking her head. "That's entirely unacceptable." She could see that he still didn't seem to understand the problem. "No one is going to talk to me with you hovering around like an angel of doom. It's hard enough getting them to talk to me at all, much less talk to me with you there."

Morgan shrugged, unfazed. "Well, you'll just have to use that charm of yours and talk them into it."

She pressed her lips together to keep from screaming in frustration. Didn't he understand that what he wanted just wasn't doable? His being there would send entirely the wrong message—that talking to her was dangerous.

"What kind of a journalist would that make me in their eyes if I need to have police protection when I went out?" she asked.

"A live one," he answered matter-of-factly. He held his hand up to stop the onslaught of words that he could just tell were about to come pouring out. "End of discussion, Kowalski. I either go with you, or you don't go at all." He paused for a moment, thinking. "And, as a matter of fact, you're coming with me first."

"What?" she demanded, frustrated.

The more agitated she was, the calmer he became, she thought, something else that infuriated her.

"I think," Morgan said, "the first order of business is that we find out just where this Bluebeard character is hiding out. I have a cousin at the precinct who is nothing short of a wizard when it comes to locating people," he told her, thinking of Valri. He had already mentioned her in passing, but decided that maybe it was time for the two of them to meet.

Morgan opened the front door for a second time. "You'll like her," he promised. "She's headstrong, like you."

"I am *not* headstrong," Krys retorted defensively.

"All right," he amended amicably, "stubborn, then—like you."

"I have to be stubborn," she informed him, an edge coming into her voice. "Because if I wasn't, I would *never* be able to get the story, or people to talk to me, for that matter. The ones who are willing to talk usually have nothing to say."

He nodded, well acquainted with that particular trait. "Stubbornness also happens to be a family trait," he told her. "So there's no point in you trying to fight me on this." He thought of his sisters. "I've gone up against the best—and won." He didn't add that there were times when he lost, because that would be counterproductive to his assuring a win this time—which he both needed and wanted.

Krys sighed, knowing he was right. After slipping her laptop into its case, she slung the strap over her shoulder.

"Let's go," she told him, resigned.

Morgan was secretly relieved that she wasn't putting up a fight about this. He had actually anticipated a great deal more resistance from her because in his experience, that was what stubborn women did. They fought something at every turn when they weren't willing to go along with it. His sisters and female cousins certainly did.

Ever suspicious, Morgan made sure she was in his line of vision the entire time as they went back to his vehicle. He didn't want to take a chance that she would bolt at the last minute.

Krys didn't say anything until after she had gotten into his car and Morgan started it up. "What's this computer wizard's name?" she asked.

"Valri," he told her. "And she really is the best," he maintained. "Speaking of names, would you happen to know this Bluebeard's real name?" Morgan asked.

Krys sighed, clearly frustrated because she had to say, "No.

"I know the names he used with each of the women he married, but as for this monster's real name, I hate to admit it but that's still a mystery," she told him.

Morgan was rather surprised, given what he had learned about this woman sitting in the car next to him. "You mean with all your resources, you haven't been able to find out his actual name?"

She detected just the slightest note of sarcasm in his voice and it made her bristle.

"It's a work in progress," she informed him between clenched teeth. "His prints haven't shown up in any known database yet."

He could see that being a problem. Still, Valri had been known to work miracles with very little to go on.

"All right, do you have a list of the aliases this guy used?" he asked.

"Yes." Krys gave him the names that she knew of, reciting them in no particular order. "He's used Chris Hunter, McKinley Thompson, Duke Bradley, Alan Gaskell and Victor Marshall. There are probably more," she added, "but those are the names that I uncovered so far." She noticed that Morgan had a rather strange, surprised look on his face when she gave him the names. "What?"

Morgan spared her a penetrating glance. "You mean you don't know?"

He had lost her again. "Know what?"

"Then you're not kidding?" he questioned.

"Kidding about what?" she demanded, her voice growing progressively more and more irritated. "You're toying with my last nerve. I am really not in the mood for games so just what the hell are you talking about, Cavanaugh?"

"Those names." He rattled them off again just to make sure he hadn't heard her incorrectly. The look on her face told him he hadn't. "They're all names that belonged to movie characters."

"Movie characters?" she repeated, more confused than ever. She didn't recognize a single one of the names she had just told him, names she had practically lived with when she tracked Bluebeard down, attempting to corner the black-hearted monster and bring him to justice. "*What* movie characters? *What* movies?" she asked sharply, losing the last of her patience.

So he told her. "They are all names of characters that Clark Gable played in different movies."

"Clark Gable?" she repeated, unfamiliar with the name. And then she suddenly realized who he was talking about. "Do you mean that guy who played Rhett Butler in that old movie? *Gone With The Wind*?"

He nodded as he stopped at a red light just before the intersection. "That's the one."

That sounded pretty far-fetched to her. She still wasn't convinced, although it was the kind of egotistical thing the monster was undoubtedly capable of. "Are you sure?"

He thought of the woman he had watched these old movies with. "Oh, I'm sure," Morgan assured her.

Still, she thought that maybe Morgan was pulling her leg. He was talking about an actor who had been dead for at least sixty years, if not longer. "How would you even know that?"

A fond smile curved Morgan's mouth as he continued to drive back to the precinct. "Because I had a mother who was a big Clark Gable fan. She used to watch all his old movies whenever they would turn up on some old movie channel. She liked to share the experience with her kids, but as it turned out, I was the only one who didn't mind watching corny old movies." He laughed softly to himself. "Mainly because I liked spending time with my mother back then." A rueful note entered his voice as he confessed, "I didn't even know she was sick then. Looking back, those times spent watching those old movies were the basis of most of my childhood memories of her."

Krys was silent for a couple of minutes as she digested the scenario. And then she told him, "Count yourself lucky. At least you had a mother to make memories with."

She saw the quizzical look that came over his face as he glanced at her. About to ignore it, she reminded herself that she was the one who had brought the subject up in the first place. That meant she owed him an explanation.

"My mother took off when Nik and I were both really young. What I remember of my mother was a flurry of blond hair and really blue eyes. And a frown," she added after a long beat. "An incredibly deep, down-to-the-bone frown."

"A frown?" he questioned.

"Mother was always frowning," she told Morgan. "Like she had bitten into a really sour piece of lemon." Krys drew her shoulders back, a soldier bracing herself to go into a particularly tough battle. "How did we even get to this topic?"

There was an accusatory note in her voice. As a rule, Krys didn't like remembering her mother. Didn't like remembering how abandoned she had felt. Trying to shield her sister from that feeling was the only thing that had kept her going.

"You were pointing out how much our childhood memories differed from one another," he told her simply as he pulled into the rear police parking lot.

Without realizing it, Krys tried to distance herself from him and from the situation he had unwittingly made her unearth.

"I think that was established. You had a loving mother who didn't want to leave you. I had one who couldn't get away fast enough." She changed the subject so quickly, he nearly sustained whiplash. "Just who is this person you're bringing me to see?" she asked.

Morgan pulled up into his assigned parking spot two rows in. "You know," he told her, "it's probably easier just to show you."

After coming to a full stop, Morgan got out of his vehicle. Krys was already out on her side. It made him think of the phrase "hit the ground running." It was undoubtedly her motto.

"By the way," Krys said as they went up the stairs to the back entrance, "how long do you think they're going to have to hold on to my car?"

She saw the side of his mouth curve and thought that didn't bode well for her.

"Despite what you see on TV, it does take a bit of time to process a crime scene, especially a mobile one," Morgan told her. "But I'm sure the chief will do his best to reunite you with your car as soon as possible, although that's kind of a moot point right now," he added.

"Why would it be moot?" she asked as they entered the building.

"Because, for the time being, I'll be driving you to and from wherever it is that you have to go. I'm your shadow for now, remember?" he asked far too cheerfully.

"Then you were being serious earlier?" Krys had hoped that Cavanaugh was just exaggerating and that once they got the trace on Bluebeard underway, Morgan Cavanaugh, as handsome as he might be, would just slip into the background while she went about doing her job.

"Deadly serious," he told her as they stepped into the elevator. "You should only pardon the pun."

A few choice words came to mind, but she let them go. Seeing that he pressed the B button, she asked him about their destination. "We're going to the basement?"

"I see nothing gets past you," Morgan quipped.

"I thought all the major police departments were located above the first floor."

"Who told you that?" Not waiting for an answer, he said, "Both the computer lab and the crime scene investigative departments are located in the basement." Before she could ask why, he said, "They tend to think of themselves as being in a world apart from the other departments. And just so you know, this is also where the medical examiners do their work. The morgue was moved to the basement from an off-site area a few years ago."

That sounded positively gruesome to her. "You mean the morgue's down here as well?"

The elevator came to a halt, opening its doors to the basement. His hand on her elbow, Morgan subtly ushered her out.

"It has to be. Otherwise, the MEs wouldn't have very much to examine except for each other," he said as he led her down a winding corridor.

Coming to a swinging door, he pushed it open and then held it for her, waiting for her to follow him.

When she did, she saw that the hallway broke off into two separate directions.

"Which way?" she asked when he remained standing there, waiting for her.

Morgan smiled at her. "That way," he said, pointing to the left, where the computer lab was situated. "Unless you want to see how the investigation into your car is coming first."

She just wanted to get this over with. "We can save that for later," Krys answered. "Take me to your computer genius."

"Good word," he said with approval. "'Genius.' Valri will like that."

They went through another set of doors before they finally reached the computer lab. There were several desks in the area with computer monitors on them. The computers were all being manned by various computer techs, each with an abundance of degrees that would intimidate the average person.

The sound of keys clicking in staccato rhythm blended in with the sound of soothing instrumental music that was playing in the background.

Motioning for Krys to follow him, Morgan brought her over to an isolated area where a woman with hair the color of deep honey sat working, her fingers flying over the keyboard so quickly, Krys marveled that they didn't somehow manage to tie themselves up into knots.

It wasn't until Morgan stopped right in front of the woman's desk that Valri even became aware of his presence in the area. Whatever greeting she was going to offer Morgan faded in the wake of her obvious surprise and, belatedly, her delight.

"Nikki! I'm surprised to see you back so soon," Valri cried.

"But I tend to lose track of time when I'm working here," she confessed, then asked, "How was the honeymoon?"

The woman regarded as the reigning computer wizard looked genuinely happy to see Nikki—except that it wasn't Nikki she was looking at.

Krys sighed. She was used to being mistaken for her twin once in a while, but this was becoming a regular thing. She had the feeling that it wasn't about to change anytime soon.

"You know, I am seriously entertaining the idea of getting a badge or a name tag that says 'I'm not Nik' on it," Krys told both Morgan and the young woman he had brought her to meet.

Confusion furrowed Valri's brow. "I don't understand." She looked at her cousin for some sort of an explanation.

"It seems that the woman Finn married has a twin sister," he said, gesturing toward Krys. "Valri, meet Krystyna Kowalski."

Valri stared at the other woman, surprised and stunned. "You're kidding." Her eyes widened as she scrutinized the newcomer. "You look exactly like Nik."

"Maybe not *that* exactly," Krys told the other woman. "I'm older, Nik's taller," she volunteered, then looked at Morgan, adding, "I already told you that."

Morgan merely shrugged at the information. "If you say so," he replied vaguely. "Val, we're in need of your very special talents."

"Why? To figure out how to tell them apart?" Valri quipped.

"Not a bad idea, but maybe later. Right now we really need to be able to track down a serial killer who escaped from prison before he could be brought to trial."

"What is your particular interest in this guy, other than his pulling a disappearing act before his trial?" Valri asked.

"We suspect that he may or may not be out gunning for Krys," Morgan answered.

Before he had a chance to give Valri any details, Krys broke in. "I'm afraid that if it is him, he might wind up killing Nik, thinking that she's me. I have to find him before Nik actually does get back from her honeymoon. Morgan says that you're the best there is," she added to get on Valri's good side. "Can you help us?"

During the course of her years in the computer lab, Valri had learned never to agree to anything immediately. This time, however, was the exception. This involved family.

"Say no more," she told the woman with Nik's face. "I'm in."

Chapter Eight

"I really appreciate any help you can give me," Krys told Morgan's cousin. "Even if Bluebeard doesn't turn out to be the one who's trying to kill me, all the evidence points to him having killed at least six women if not more and at the very least, he deserves to be in jail for the rest of his life, not out there, free to prey on yet another woman."

"Believe me, it'll be my pleasure to locate the monster," Valri told her with more enthusiasm than Morgan had seen her display in a long while.

Krys pulled out her laptop from her backpack and held it up. "Tell me what you need from me. I brought the six-part online article I wrote on him, plus all the research material on him that I could get my hands on. I also have a list of all his aliases, or at least the ones I know of." She held up the piece of paper containing the various names that Bluebeard had used during his nefarious career. "There might very well be more."

Morgan leaned in toward his cousin. "Wait until you find out who this guy fancied himself to be."

The latter saw the amused grin on Morgan's face. "Go ahead," she told him. She glanced at the piles of work on her desk that she had been wading through. "I could definitely stand a laugh today."

"There seems to be a pattern," Morgan told his cousin. "The

names this guy used all seem to be characters that Clark Gable played in various movies."

Valri eyed him a bit skeptically. "You're talking about the actor who was in those old movies, *Gone with the Wind, It Happened One Night? That* guy?" she asked Morgan.

Morgan nodded. "I guess that must have fed his ego." In his day, his mother had once told him, Clark Gable was adored by millions of women. Maybe that was what the serial killer was trying for.

Valri looked at the list, then at her cousin. "You're sure about this?"

He pulled over the list that Krys had written down and glanced at it to reassure himself, and then Morgan nodded. "I'm positive." He turned the list back to Valri. "I could even tell you the names of the movies those characters were in."

Valri passed on his offer. "No, that's okay. I'll take your word for it," she said. "However, if you can think of other possible names, I could go through databases, see if anyone has turned up or been arrested using any of those aliases lately."

Krys felt guilty about putting this on the other woman's shoulders. "I know this is asking a lot," she apologized. "But there is a time crunch, and according to Morgan, you have a great many more resources available to you than I do. Or actually," Krys amended, "than anyone I know of does."

Valri waved away Krys's words. "I'll do what I can." She nodded at Krys's laptop. "Let's see what you've got."

Leaning the laptop against a corner of Valri's desk, Krys opened it, pulled up the saved data she had and scrolled down to the folders that she needed. She turned her laptop around so that it faced Valri.

"This is all the material that I managed to collect on Bluebeard," she told the lab tech.

Valri skimmed over the first few paragraphs, then looked up from the laptop. "The first thing we need to do is find out what this guy's real name is," she told the two people by her desk. She indicated the laptop. "Can I hang on to this?"

It was Morgan who answered her before Krys had a chance to. "Krys needs that for her work, Val. Can you hook her up with a printer or better yet, a thumb drive? That way she can transfer the information you need to that and she gets to hold on to her laptop so she can go on with her work."

Krys looked at Morgan in surprise, amazed that he actually remembered that.

"Sure, sounds good to me," Valri told him. She opened up her middle drawer and rummaged around until she found a thumb drive that Krys could use. "This should be all you need. It's large enough to hold the contents of two entire computers."

Accepting the small thumb drive, Krys looked around the lab. "Is there some place where I can sit?"

Valri indicated an unoccupied desk way over in the corner. "Jackson took a sick day," she said, referring to one of the junior technicians who worked in the lab. "You're free to use his desk."

Krys flashed a smile, gathering up her laptop as well as the thumb drive. "This'll only take a few minutes," she promised.

Valri gestured around at her desk. "I'll still be here."

Krys walked quickly over to the unoccupied desk. The moment she was out of earshot, Valri looked at Morgan. "You realize that you owe me, right?"

"Isn't helping to prevent murder part of your job description?" Morgan asked loftily.

"Yes, but these are *all* important cases. And my 'job' doesn't mean that I have to drop everything that's ahead of you in order to accommodate you. See this?" she asked, gesturing to the piles of papers that were all over her desk. "These are requests that are ahead of you and Nik's twin over there." She looked over toward where Krys had sat down and shook her head, silently marveling to herself. "I've seen twins before, but it's positively eerie how much Krys looks *exactly* like Finn's wife."

"I know. When I first saw Krys, I thought it was Finn's wife playing some sort of trick on me."

"And you're sure it's not a trick?" she asked him. Because if it was, then for some reason the woman copying files onto that thumb drive had gone to great lengths to fool them.

"Oh, it's not a trick. Trust me," Morgan assured his cousin. "Krys brought me her car. The driver's side window had been completely shot out and when I drove her to the hotel where she was staying so she could get her things, a black van came out of nowhere and narrowly missed running her over. It probably would have succeeded if I hadn't pulled her out of the way at the last minute."

"And she thinks that this 'Bluebeard' character she exposed is doing this now to get his revenge?" Valri guessed.

"Well, actually, he's just one of the candidates," Morgan told her.

Valri's eyes widened. "There are more?" she questioned in surprise. "This just keeps getting better and better, doesn't it?"

"Full disclosure," Morgan prefaced. "You should know that Krys is currently writing a multipart online series about a supposed miracle drug that Weatherly Pharmaceuticals is putting on the market soon. If successful, the drug stands to make the company and its investors a hell of a lot of money—that is, if it winds up living up to its hype."

"Can it?" Valri asked.

"From what I gather, that's exactly what Krys is challenging." He watched Krys as she continued transferring files. He couldn't get over how intent the blonde looked as she worked. And how totally removed from the situation she seemed. "Needless to say, there are undoubtedly people out there who are trying to get her to drop her investigation and just keep quiet."

"Permanently quiet?" Valri asked.

It was his business not to get personally involved in cases, to keep his distance and view them all impartially so he could do what needed to be done to solve them. But he found himself drawn to the crusading journalist. The idea that someone was out there trying to silence her permanently bothered him as well as worried him.

"That would be my guess," he told his cousin, trying to sound as if this was just another case he was trying to bring to a close. "All I know for sure is that someone tried to run her over and someone, most likely the same someone, took shots at her the day before that. Personally, I don't think they're going to just throw in the towel and give up."

Valri nodded, taking in the expression on her cousin's face. "You're probably right. I'll do my best to get you some answers."

Morgan smiled and brushed a quick kiss on her cheek. "You're the best."

"Talk is cheap, Morgan. If you're interested, I do accept all forms of tribute," she reminded him as Krys walked back over to them.

She had her laptop tucked back into the backpack she had used to carry it. The strap was slung over her shoulder. In her hand she had the thumb drive that Valri had given her.

"Okay," Krys announced. "Everything I have on that blood-thirsty madman is all on this drive." She surrendered the thumb drive to Valri. "If you have any questions, or something doesn't make sense to you, please call me. Anytime, day or night. Here, let me give you my cell number."

Krys paused to write the number down on a nearby notepad. After tearing the paper off the pad, she offered it to Valri.

The latter took the paper. "I'll give you a call if I find anything," she promised both Krys and Morgan.

"Like I said, I do appreciate this," Morgan told his cousin.

Valri nodded, then looked at the woman standing beside Morgan. "Nice meeting you, Not-Nik," she said with a smile. "Stay close to this guy," she advised, indicating Morgan. "If you can keep from strangling him, he *will* keep you safe."

And with that, Valri got back to work. By the time the duo had reached the first door leading out of the computer lab, Valri's mind was well immersed in her search to the exclusion of every-thing else.

"If anyone can locate this 'Bluebeard' character, it's Valri," Morgan told Krys. "She is really, really good at her job."

"I'm sure she is," Krys replied. She wasn't totally convinced that his cousin would be successful in finding out who the man was, but it had nothing to do with how capable Valri was. "It's just that 'Bluebeard' is really good at being elusive. There have been three separate police departments looking for him in three separate cities and they came up with nothing."

"Everyone's luck runs out sometime," he said as they walked to the elevator.

"I certainly hope you're right," she told him with feeling, and then added sincerely, "and that it's his luck and not mine that's run out."

Lowering his voice, he made her a promise. "I won't let any-thing happen to you."

For a split second, Krys actually felt safe. But then the feeling faded in the face of reality. He couldn't really make a promise like that. "Did I miss that big red *S* on your chest?" she asked him.

The smile he gave her created an unexpected tingle in the pit of her stomach. "As a matter fact, you did. I keep it hidden under my clothes."

"Good to know."

The elevator arrived on the first floor and its doors drew open. The moment they did, Morgan escorted Krys off the elevator. The two detectives who were waiting to get on looked at them, each murmuring a greeting just before recognition suddenly set in. The wide, welcoming smiles the two flashed were directed toward the woman beside Morgan.

"I thought you and Finn were going to be gone until next week," Detective Christian Cavanaugh O'Bannon said.

"I thought it was supposed to be longer," his brother Luke said, confused as to why something as special as a honeymoon would be cut short. He grinned at her and teased, "Did you get bored?"

Thinking that this could get uncomfortably embarrassing very quickly, Morgan spoke up. "Guys, I think you should know something."

Christian laughed at his cousin, holding the elevator door open as he looked at the woman beside Morgan. "What could you possibly have to tell us, Morgan?"

"Well, for starters," Morgan began loftily, nodding at Krys, "I could tell you that this isn't Finn's wife, Nikki Cavanaugh."

"Yeah, right," Luke responded. And then he waved away the very suggestion. "Of course this is Nikki. We know what she looks like." But Morgan's expression never changed. "Who else would it be?" Luke challenged.

The elevator doors kept shuddering, attempting to close as Krys put out her hand to Luke, the detective closest to her. "No, he's right," she said. "I'm Krystyna Kowalski, Nikki's twin sister."

The brothers exchanged looks, then laughed. "Sure you are," Luke said, dismissing Krys's attempt to set them straight.

Rather than spend any more time arguing with the two disbelievers, Krys did what she'd initially done with Morgan. She took out her wallet and held up her driver's license. "This is me," she told the detectives. "And this," she went on as she dug out the photograph depicting both herself and Nik that had been taken several years ago, "is a picture of the two of us."

Luke took the photograph first, totally stunned by what he was looking at. He raised his eyes from the photograph to look at the woman next to Morgan. And then he looked at the photograph again.

"You're right," he declared, stunned as he glanced back at Krys again. "There are two of you." He handed the photo to his brother. "Does anyone else know?"

"We're informing the family as we come across them," Morgan said, thinking that for now that was a simpler explanation than going into why Krys hadn't been at the wedding and what she was doing at the precinct now.

Christian handed back the photo and then grinned as a thought hit him. "Wait 'til Uncle Andrew finds out. Talk about having an excuse to throw a party. This'll blow him away."

"Uncle Andrew?" Krys asked Morgan as the elevator doors finally closed on Christian and Luke, taking them to their destination.

"He's the former chief of police. Uncle Andrew loves to throw parties. He's been known to use just about anything for an excuse in order to do it. And having you turn up," Morgan told her, "could very well be just about the most perfect excuse for throwing a party that he's ever had."

Krys supposed that she was going to have to meet the rest of the family sooner or later, but now wasn't the opportune time.

"Well, any party is going to have to wait until we can catch that stalker," she told Morgan. She wouldn't be able to focus on meeting the family members or having a good time while someone was out there, stalking her and attempting to kill her.

"No argument here," Morgan agreed. "Your safety is of paramount importance. Of course," he said after a beat, catching her attention, "there is that old adage about there being safety in numbers."

"That might be true, but I'm not about to take a chance on someone getting hurt because they got in the way of a stray bullet meant for me," she told him. Krys grew silent for a moment as she looked at Morgan, concerns crowding her head. "For that matter, the idea of you possibly getting hurt because you're playing my guardian angel doesn't exactly warm my heart, either."

Morgan waved away her concern. "Don't worry about it. That's what I get paid for," he reminded her.

"You get paid for being a walking target?" she asked.

His mouth curved in a lopsided smile. "I don't think of myself in terms like that," he told her as they hurried down the stairs and returned to his vehicle.

He opened the door on the passenger side and held it for her.

"Exactly what sort of terms *do* you think of yourself in?"

"I'd like to think that I can deflect those bullets," Morgan deadpanned.

Like a superhero, she thought. "Oh, so in other words, you suffer from a strong case of delusion."

"Hey," he pretended to protest, getting into his car, "I'm dedicated to keeping you safe and breathing. Maybe you should be a little nicer to me."

"If I was really being nicer to you, I'd tell you that I could take it from here and you're free to go."

Morgan surprised her by laughing.

"What's so funny?" she asked indignantly.

His lips curved as he looked at her, amusement shining in his eyes. "You."

Krys found herself struggling not to get annoyed. She didn't like to be laughed at. "You're going to have to explain that."

"You can't get rid of me that easily so you might as well stop acting tough, Krys. You're stuck with me for the duration, until whoever is trying to take you out is either dead themselves, or permanently behind bars." He looked at her just before he put his key into the ignition. "So deal with it," he told her.

Chapter Nine

"'Deal with it'?" Krys questioned, surprised that Morgan would have said something that blasé to her. It wasn't anything that she would have expected from him.

"You heard me," he told her.

Krys merely shook her head. "You Cavanaughs certainly are a pushy bunch, aren't you?"

The expression on her face made him laugh. His manner softened slightly. "You don't know the half of it."

Morgan drove his vehicle to the edge of the parking lot, just before it exited onto the street, and then he came to a temporary stop.

Pausing, he looked at Krys. "All right, where to now?" When Krys didn't immediately reply, he prodded her. "C'mon, you said you had this busy schedule and needed to meet your deadline, so where to?" he asked again, a bit more insistently this time.

"Then you were really serious about coming with me while I do the rest of my interviews?"

"Absolutely. Don't worry, I have no intentions of flashing my badge—and the gun only comes out if someone threatens you," he deadpanned.

But Krys was still hoping that, when it came right down to it, Cavanaugh was just yanking her chain. She wanted him to find whoever was trying to kill her, but that didn't mean she wanted him to physically be her bodyguard. She certainly didn't want him there during the interviews.

"You're kidding, right?" she asked, fervently hoping that he was.

For the time being, Morgan's expression remained completely unreadable. "What do you think, Kowalski?"

Krys closed her eyes, seeking inner strength. This promised to be an impossible situation if she didn't find a way to get him to back off.

And then she thought something that might be an acceptable compromise for him. "Look, how about if you stay in the car while I conduct my interviews?" she asked hopefully, mentally crossing her fingers.

Hope died a quick death as Morgan shook his head. "Unacceptable."

She frowned, still trying to come up with an alternative. "How about if I wear a wire?" she suggested. "If someone I'm questioning comes right out and threatens me, I'll get your attention by using a safe word."

But Morgan vetoed that choice as well. "No."

"It's going to have to be a different safe word than that one. 'No' is too common a word to use."

"How about this: you can introduce me as your assistant."

She gave him a long, scrutinizing look. "No offense, Cavanaugh, but you don't look like someone that I would have as an assistant."

If she was trying to put him off, she failed. "Then I'd say it's about time that you broaden your tastes. Now," he said, taking hold of the steering wheel again and releasing his brake, "where do you want me to take you?"

There was no use trying to reason with him or get him to back off, Krys thought. With a sigh, she gave him her next intended destination. "Weatherly Pharmaceuticals. I've got an appointment with Jim Peters, one of the scientists on the team researching drug number 1317."

"That's the drug's name?" he questioned, surprised. "They'll have to go with something catchier than that," he said sarcastically.

"That's the temporary working number of the 'miracle drug,'" she told him. "The drug's actual name is a secret until Weatherly finally releases it on the open market."

"They're afraid someone is going to steal the name?" he questioned, obviously amused by the thought.

"You'd be surprised." Even the code number being used had been a secret until very recently.

"You're right," Morgan said to her. "I would be. All right, then we're agreed," he said as he drove toward the Weatherly compound. "When we get to Weatherly Pharmaceuticals, you'll just introduce me as your assistant."

"Right. My assistant. Waldo Jones," she said, coming up with a name on the spur of the moment for this fictional character he had created.

Morgan winced at the name. "Waldo Jones? That's what you came up with?" he questioned incredulously.

"Hey, you can still stay in the car," she told him, making it clear that using this awful name was the only way she would go along with this charade.

Morgan sighed. "All right, Waldo Jones it is," he agreed. After all, the name, hideous as it was, didn't really matter.

"And you don't talk," she added, deciding that would probably be the best way to pull this off.

"I'm vocally impaired?" Morgan questioned, amused.

"I don't care what you label it," Krys told him. "But you're not to say anything. You open that mouth of yours to say *anything* and no one is going to mistake you for a journalist. The minute you start talking, there's no way you're going to sound like anything except a police detective."

She was definitely getting on his nerves with all these requirements. "I've got to say something," Morgan insisted. "Otherwise this Peters guy will wonder why you brought me along." *Doesn't she see that?* he wondered.

Krys opened her backpack and dug through it until she finally located her notepad. She pulled it out for Morgan.

Since he was driving, she couldn't hand it to him, but she did place it between their two seats so he could take it when they arrived at their destination. "Voilà. You can act like you're taking notes for me."

"Isn't that a little old-fashioned, considering this day and age?"

"A lot of these people don't like being recorded. This way it's more likely that they'll be at ease and talk to me—or, in this case, 'us,'" she amended. "Look, we do it my way or we don't do it at all."

Morgan knew when to back off. The intense scowl on her face made him laugh as he shook his head. "And you think *I'm* pushy?"

"Do we have a deal?" she asked.

"No." Then, reluctantly, he said, "Yes, we have a deal."

"Good, then you just stay next to me and look pretty," she instructed, letting him see that she was completely serious.

Morgan batted his eyelashes at her—lashes that, Krys noticed, were rather thick and long for a man. "I'll do my best," he promised.

WEATHERLY PHARMACEUTICALS WAS domiciled in a state-of-the-art building. It looked as if it might have been more at home sheltering an art museum than a place where cutting-edge research was conducted.

Morgan noticed that Krys grew very quiet as they drove onto the compound. It wasn't like her.

"Something wrong?" he asked.

Krys shook her head. "It's nothing."

"Nothing?" Morgan repeated, not buying it. "Your complexion just got five shades lighter. That's not 'nothing.' That is definitely 'something,'" the detective stressed.

"Aren't you supposed to be watching the road and not my complexion?" she pointed out.

"I'm good at multitasking," he protested. "Now why do you look like you've seen a ghost?"

She knew he wouldn't back off until she told him. "Because whoever shot out my window did it from somewhere over there," she told him, pointing out the adjacent parking area, which was directly in front of Weatherly Laboratories.

He'd forgotten that. "The chief and his crew already combed that entire area. They didn't find spent shells lying on the ground or any sort of evidence that you were shot at."

"Other than my shot-up window," she reminded him, tongue in cheek.

"Yeah, other than that." Pulling up in front of the pharmaceutical building, Morgan saw the wary expression in her eyes. He didn't want to lose the ground he had gained with her. "Look, just because we didn't find any evidence doesn't mean we don't believe you. All it means is that we could easily be dealing with a professional."

"Like Bluebeard," she concluded.

"Or a contract killer, someone hired for the job," he pointed out.

The very suggestion that she might be stalked by someone like that sent a cold shiver down her spine. "You do know how to make a girl feel all warm and toasty," she said sarcastically.

"Maybe not," Morgan allowed. "But I do know how to protect one. Stay put," he instructed as he shut off the engine.

"How am I supposed to do my interview if I stay put?" she asked, then sarcastically suggested a solution. "Ventriloquism?"

"No," he answered, raising his voice as he rounded the back of his car and came around to the passenger door. "I meant that you should wait until I came around to your side," he told her, opening the door for her.

She swung her legs out and noticed the way that Morgan stared at them before he forced his eyes back to her face. "Shouldn't you be looking around the parking lot, then, instead of at my legs?" she asked.

"Multitasking, remember?" Morgan reminded her good-naturedly even while he upbraided himself for getting caught up in the way Krys looked.

Meanwhile, Krys just sighed and shook her head. He seemed to have an answer for everything, even though it might come across like the wrong answer.

"Remember, no talking," she reminded Morgan.

And then she saw that he was holding the notepad she had taken out of her backpack for him. That was a good sign, she thought. She decided that it was only fair if she said as much to him.

"Oh good, you remembered to take the notepad," she commented.

Morgan's eyes crinkled a little as his smile widened. "Multi—"

"—tasking, yes, I know," she said with a long-suffering sigh, completing his sentence for him. Walking quickly, she went through the automatic doors that sprang open for her.

She braced herself, not looking forward to what lay ahead but doing her level best to be as prepared for it as she could be. After all, the next person she interviewed could very well be the person trying to kill her.

"AND YOU DO this kind of thing all the time?" Morgan asked Krys a little over two hours later as they left the building.

"Exactly what do you mean by 'this kind of thing'?" she asked, bracing herself for the worst.

"Talk to people who are in love with the sound of their own voice?" Morgan elaborated. He could see by her expression that he had struck a familiar chord. Listening to the research scientist, he could barely keep from falling asleep. "I have never heard anyone use so many words to say so little before."

Krys smiled at Morgan's description of the situation. She had run into this sort of thing more than once. Still, she was kind in her assessment. "He didn't want to give away any secrets."

Morgan laughed at the description. "Well, if you ask me, he succeeded royally. Tell me, how did you manage to stay awake?" he asked. "Because I almost fell asleep a number of times."

"By forcing myself to wait to hear that one phrase, that one sentence that would ultimately make everything crystal clear," she told Morgan.

"Did I miss it?" Morgan asked.

"No, you didn't," Krys told him. "Apparently Peters was utterly full of himself and didn't care who knew it. He's just part of the research group, not the head of the team. That's a position being held by Lawrence Jacobs," she informed the police detective.

"Jacobs," Morgan repeated. "Is he on your list of people to interview?"

"He definitely is," she confirmed with feeling.

"When's the interview?"

"I'm still working on getting an appointment to see him," she confessed. "Jacobs is not an easy man to get a hold of. He's been out of town for the last week, working on getting the final funding."

Morgan wasn't sure that he followed what she was telling him. "You mean they still haven't gotten the money for this so-called wonder drug?"

He would have thought that if this drug they had developed was really as wonderful as the company claimed it was, they would be fighting off potential investors shoving money at them, trying to get in on the ground floor.

"The company borrowed the money so they could develop it. Currently, Jacobs is trying to pay that loan off, or at least as much as he can before they launch into the last stage of production."

"So what you're saying is that it's like fraud?" he asked.

"That's not the way they choose to see it," Krys told him. "And if it winds up taking off and doing what they say it does, it'll return any money put up for it a hundredfold. It's only fraud if it fails in its actual premise."

It was growing dark by now. They had been in the building longer than he had anticipated. "You don't have another interview set up for today, do you?" Morgan asked her.

"I've got four set up for tomorrow," she told him. "The most important of which is with a potential whistleblower first thing in the morning, but no, no more interviews today." She paused for a moment, and then admitted, "Being a walking target has thrown me off my game."

He surprised her with his reaction. "Nice to know you're human."

She looked at him, confused. "What made you think I wasn't?"

Morgan grinned. Her stomach did a little flip, which surprised her. "For the sake of our working relationship, I'd better not answer that," he told her. Changing the subject, he declared, "Okay, back to your place." With that, he turned his car around and began to head toward her house. "I'm kind of hungry, anyway."

"Well, if that's the case, we're going to have to stop somewhere to pick up something to eat, or have something delivered," she told him, enumerating their two choices. When Morgan looked at her, waiting for her to elaborate further, she told him, "I suffer from the Mother Hubbard syndrome."

"How's that again?"

She put it in simpler terms. "My cupboard is bare—and so's my refrigerator—unless you're willing to consider diet soda as a new food group."

She definitely needed to meet his Uncle Andrew, Morgan thought. If a famine suddenly swept over the city, Andrew could still be able to feed the masses until such time as the famine was over.

"Okay, what are you in the mood for?" Morgan asked.

Krys shrugged. "I'm easy. Pizza's fine."

"Pizza is fine," Morgan agreed. "But you, lady, are definitely not 'easy.'"

Considering the fact that she had made him jump through hoops several times during the course of the day, Krys decided not to challenge Morgan's assessment. She did, however, have a point to raise.

"You know, if you're so worried about keeping me safe, don't you think that ordering takeout and having it delivered to my house is a bit risky?" she asked. "I mean, do you intend to pat the delivery boy down before you let him hand over the pizza?"

He grinned at the scenario she had just come up with. "Don't worry about it. I've got it covered."

Now he had her intrigued. "Care to enlighten me as to how you have this 'covered'?"

"No big secret," he informed her. "I'm going to ask one of my brothers to pick up the pizza for us. That way we won't have to deal with some stranger coming to your door."

"You have an answer for everything, don't you?" she grudgingly commented.

"There are a lot of us Cavanaughs on the police force. That amounts to several centuries of acquired knowledge among all of us," he told her.

Just how many of these people are there? she wondered. Nik had never given her a specific number. "Why do I suddenly feel hopelessly outnumbered?"

He had no answer for that, but he did have a way to view the scenario. "What you're supposed to feel is completely protected," he told her.

"Yes," Krys admitted, albeit reluctantly, "maybe that, too."

Chapter Ten

While Morgan methodically checked all the windows and doors in the house, making sure that everything was securely locked, Krys waited silently in the foyer for the pizza delivery. As she waited, she thought over what she had said to the detective in response to his question.

She did feel rather safe and protected—and it was actually the first time she had felt that way in a long, long time. Being on her own and responsible for herself was a given. It had been that way for a while now. She was forever chasing after stories and taking whatever precautions occurred to her to make sure that she was safe while she was doing it.

It almost felt strange to have someone looking out for her, however temporary that turned out to be. Krys told herself not to get used to it.

"Well," Morgan declared as he walked back into the living room, "unless someone decides to ram into your house with a tank, I'd say that you were pretty safe for the night."

Is he just being flippant or serious? she wondered. "Just 'pretty sure'?" she questioned, raising one quizzical eyebrow.

"Barring an earthquake or a wildfire, yes, I'd say I was sure," Morgan told her.

Krys knew she couldn't ask for anything better than that. "I guess those are pretty good odds," she agreed. She nodded toward the linen closet between the two bedrooms. "I'll go get some fresh bedding for you. You can have the guest room."

But Morgan shook his head, turning down her offer. "No need to do that."

Krys stopped walking toward the back. She'd heard rumors to the effect that some of the Cavanaughs were ladies' men, but until now, she hadn't thought of Morgan as being one of them. Still, she had been wrong before, she thought.

"Why?" she asked suspiciously. "Exactly where do you intend to sleep tonight?"

"I don't," he answered simply. "And besides, I can stretch out on the couch if I need to."

"But you don't think you'll need to," she guessed by the way he'd said it. "You don't plan to sleep?"

"I don't need much sleep," Morgan informed her. "And anyway, I'm a really light sleeper," he told her.

"Is that part of being a multitasker?" she asked wryly.

If Morgan thought that she was doubting him, he gave no indication of it. Instead, he left his answer deliberately vague.

"Something like that," he told Krys. "What are you staring at?" he asked, noticing the way she was looking at him.

"Your nose," she answered.

His brow furrowed. "My nose? Why?"

"To see if it grows all at once or just by small increments," she answered and then frowned at him. Just how dumb did he think she was? "*Everyone* needs to sleep."

"No argument," Morgan agreed. "But it just so happens that I don't need much. And, FYI, if there's something going on, I can stay awake around the clock without any problem."

She wasn't buying into this superhuman image he was trying to portray. "Until you collapse altogether. You won't be any good to me in that state."

His eyes swept over her almost intimately. She found herself trying not to react, but it wasn't easy. There was something about the way he looked at her that unsettled her.

"I promise you won't have any complaints," he told her, his voice low and sexy.

It was hard for her to remain detached and distant. Why did she get the feeling that he wasn't talking about being her bodyguard?

"We'll see about that," she answered, her lips feeling oddly dry as she formed the words. Added to that, her heart seemed to suddenly slam against her chest when she heard the doorbell ring.

"That must be Dugan," Morgan told her.

"Dugan?" she echoed, totally unfamiliar with the name. "Another cousin?"

"No, another brother," Morgan corrected her. "Remember? I said I'd have my brother pick up the pizza. That way I don't have to frisk a stranger," he reminded her, crossing to the door.

"Must have slipped my mind," she murmured as she watched him look through the peephole. When he flipped open the lock on the door, Krys made a natural assumption. "I take it that that's Dugan with our dinner."

He pulled open the door. "If he hasn't eaten it himself." The comment was half intended for Dugan as Morgan recalled his brother's rather fierce, endless appetite.

Dugan caught the tail end of his brother's response to the attractive woman standing just behind him. "You kidding?" he asked, referring to Morgan's assumption that he'd had some of the meal he was charged with delivering. "Toni's got dinner waiting at home," he told his brother, referring to his wife, adding, "She'd skin me alive if I filled up on pizza."

Handing the pizza box to his younger brother, Dugan smiled broadly at the woman who had asked to have the pizza delivered in the first place. "Hi, I'm Morgan's older, better looking brother," he told her, extending his hand to Krys. "And I take it you're *not*-Nik."

Shaking his hand, Krys smiled at Dugan's greeting. "I take it that Morgan warned you about mistaking me for my twin."

"No," Dugan responded, "he warned me not to *call* you Nik. I figured the rest is self-explanatory. But he was right," he said, carefully scrutinizing her, "you do look just like her."

Krys inclined her head as she flashed Dugan a smile. "Hence the word 'identical,'" she said. And then she noted as she indicated both of the brothers, "You know, you two look rather alike, too."

"She's being kind to you, Morgan," Dugan told his younger

brother, and then he turned his eyes on Krys. "He knows I'm the good-looking brother."

"Ha!" Morgan declared. "I think even Sully and Campbell might have a different opinion on that."

"When did you say you were going in for your eye exam?" Dugan asked his brother. He looked back to Krys and informed her with a straight face, "His vision is really going. You know," he said, leaning a little bit closer to Krys, "you might want to think about getting someone else to guard you while this guy's out there, stalking you."

Morgan cupped his ear. "I think I hear Toni calling you. You'd better get home before she realizes that she can really do so much better than you."

Dugan smiled broadly as he looked at Krys. "It was nice meeting you." With that, he put his hand on the doorknob, turned it and began to leave.

"Dugan, hang on," Morgan called after his brother as the latter started to cross the threshold. "What do I owe you?"

"More than you could ever possibly repay me," Dugan deadpanned.

"No, seriously," Morgan insisted as he took out his wallet and slipped out several bills. "What do I owe you for the pizza?"

Dugan glanced over at Krys and smiled. "Just keep the lady safe and we'll call it even. Remember, we've got a reputation to maintain. We don't lose people on our watch." And then he patted Morgan's shoulder. "Now I'd better go. I've got a warm meal and a hot wife waiting for me and I want to get home before either of them cools off."

Dugan went out and closed the door behind him.

Morgan flipped both locks closed and then tested the door to make sure that it remained secure. It did.

"How many brothers did you say you had?" she asked, putting out two plates for their dinner.

"Three brothers," he told her. "I've got three sisters, too," Morgan added, anticipating Krys's next question.

"Did you guys all get along when you were growing up?" she asked, wondering what a full house like that had been like.

"Define 'get along,'" Morgan told her. And then, before she

could answer, he laughed, getting her off the hook. "I guess you could say that we got along. At least we don't draw blood—anymore." An amused smile curved the corners of his generous mouth.

"You're kidding, right?" Krys asked him, taking a slice out of the pizza box and putting it on Morgan's plate, then taking one for herself.

"Sure, why don't we say that?" he agreed in a nebulous tone.

Krys shook her head. Morgan was proving to be rather hard to read. "You're not fooling me," she told him.

Morgan snapped his fingers as if to underscore and lament a lost opportunity.

"And here I was, hoping to hoodwink you," he told her. "Another hope dashed."

"You know," Krys told him as she helped herself to a second slice of the extra-large, thin crust, meat supreme pizza, "you seem to be a lot different tonight than you were this morning."

He shrugged, waiting to finish eating what he'd bitten into before he answered her. When he did, he said, "I guess I just grow on some people."

She was trying to be serious in her assessment and he was being flippant. She tried again.

"No, that's not what I meant," she told Morgan. When he raised an eyebrow, waiting for her to explain what she was trying to say, she complied. "You just seem to be nicer. Is it because you think of me as family?" she asked.

"Well, there's that," he granted, pausing before taking another bite, "but even more than that, I believe you."

"Believe me?" she repeated, slightly confused.

"Yes, that someone's trying to kill you," he told her. "You'd be surprised just how many people say something like that just to get attention, or because they have some ulterior motive. Not everyone is honest."

"Don't I know it," she murmured. "I make my living separating the liars from the people who actually have something to tell the public at large."

"How did you happen to get into this line of work anyway?" Morgan asked.

Krys shrugged, not wanting to get into it right now. But she could see that he was waiting for an answer, so she did her best to give him one. "When I was a kid, I always loved a mystery, getting to the bottom of what was going on. Solving it," she declared proudly. "Eventually, doing that just seemed to carry over into real life. Nik investigated insurance claims. And I wound up investigating things that had a bigger impact on the general public." That was just the way things had happened, she thought. She hadn't set out seeking this way of life.

Morgan nodded as he took his fourth slice. "Like a man who romances lonely, rich women, sweeps them off their feet and then winds up taking them for everything they've got."

"You're forgetting one important, damning point," she told Morgan. "He kills them so he can continue living his lifestyle, romancing women for profit."

And then she sighed, hating the fact that someone like that was still out there, doing these heinous things.

"I *really* hope your cousin is as good as you say she is and that she can track this guy down, because more than anyone I've ever exposed, he *really* deserves to be made to pay," Krys insisted with feeling.

"For trying to kill you," he assumed, nodding his head.

"And for killing those other women. All they wanted was for someone to love them and instead, they wound up dead. That isn't right on any level."

"So I take it that you're pretty convinced this Bluebeard character is the one trying to get revenge by killing you," Morgan assumed, polishing off yet another slice of pizza. So far, he had managed to eat six slices to her four.

Where was she putting all this, he couldn't help wondering. The woman was exceedingly slender.

"It does seem likely," Krys answered. "But convinced?" she questioned and then she shook her head. "No, not completely." And then she explained why. "If I can find those four drug trial subjects and discover that the reason they disappeared was because of the negative results that came up during those tests, then someone high up in the pecking order wanting to get rid of me would make a lot of sense as well."

"If you honestly believe that, then why don't you just stop looking into the drug trials—at least for the time being?"

Krys realized that the detective didn't really understand what drove her.

"Because someone has to shine a light on the truth," she told him simply. "If this drug is just some sort of a placebo that doesn't deliver what it promises, then a lot of people hoping for a miracle are going to be more than just disappointed. They were being lied to," she insisted with feeling. "This so-called miracle drug isn't supposed to be a cure, but it 'promises' to deliver a way to arrest cancer's progress. Maybe even long enough until such time as a cure is found."

Her voice grew more passionate as she got into the crux of her reasoning. "If people think they've found that drug, then perforce researchers will stop looking for it because they feel that it's been found. That is a horrible, gross lie on every single possible level."

Morgan found her passion arousing. Krys seemed nothing short of deadly serious as she made her point. More than that, she made him think of a modern-day crusader.

A crusader who could very easily lose her life if she was onto something that someone was dead set against her exposing and bringing to the public's attention.

Morgan studied her for a moment. He found himself more worried about her than he should have been. His concern went beyond his role as a detective. That was when he realized that he was having feelings for this woman. Even so, he couldn't make himself back off. "Did you ever consider doing something that's, oh, I don't know, a little bit simpler and a hell of a lot less dangerous for a living?"

Her mouth curved as amusement slipped into her eyes. "You mean like hang gliding over the Grand Canyon?" she asked. "I've thought about it. But that's still pretty dangerous," she told him.

"Right," he agreed sarcastically. "And antagonizing a cold-blooded killer as well as an entire pharmaceutical company isn't?" Morgan questioned.

"Well, when you put it that way..." Krys's voice trailed off—and then, inexplicably, she laughed. "I think that it was Sammy Davis Jr. who used to sing a song entitled 'I've Gotta Be Me,'"

Krys told her sister's cousin-in-law, looking at him intently as she made her point.

"Granted," he allowed. "But in order for you to do it 'your way,' you're forgetting one thing. You have to be alive to do it."

"Well, that's where you come in, isn't it?" she questioned. "You're the one who's supposed to *keep* me alive, remember?"

He shook his head. She was a Cavanaugh all right, if only by marriage.

"It would be a lot easier on me if you weren't standing on the tips of your toes, balancing on a narrow ledge, waving your arms and acting as if you didn't realize that you're calling attention to yourself and behaving like a perfect target," he told her.

"Good point. I will definitely try to refrain from waving my arms," she told him, all the while keeping a straight face.

He didn't believe her for a minute. She was going to continue doing what she was doing, but short of tying the woman up, he knew there was nothing he could do about it—except be there for her when the need and the situation arose.

Chapter Eleven

"Well," Krys said, pushing herself away from the table, "that was great, but I've got work to do. Be sure to thank your brother for the less-than-nutritious dinner," she said with a grin as she closed the lid on the practically empty pizza box.

Morgan nodded, getting up from the table as well. He picked up her plate, placed it on top of his and took both of them to the sink. "This work isn't going to take you out of the house, is it?" he asked as he rinsed off the two plates.

She watched as he took a sponge and applied it to each of the plates. "Not tonight," she answered, then raised her eyes to his face. "Why?"

"Because I'd be going with you if that was the case," he told her. Leaving the plates on the rack, he dried off his hands with the dish towel.

"Well, you can stay put for now. Tonight I'm going over the notes I took while Peters was pontificating to me and see what, if anything, I can use for my article."

"What about the notes I took?" he asked, folding the dish towel into thirds and slipping it over the handle on the oven.

She didn't understand. "Your notes?" she asked.

"Yes, the ones I took," he reminded her. There was still no sign of comprehension on her face. "I was supposed to be your assistant, remember?"

"I remember." But she didn't act as if she was enlightened. "You really took notes?" Krys asked him, surprised.

Morgan still didn't see what the big mystery was. "I thought you wanted me to be believable."

"I did," she agreed, "but I just thought you were writing gibberish on the pad, you know, to sell the part of my assistant."

"No, not gibberish," he said, then explained why he'd written down actual thoughts. "On the slim chance that Peters might be involved in some sort of conspiracy to get you out of the picture, I listened to what he had to say and took notes. That was just in case he wound up accidentally letting something useful slip— although, from the sound of it, it was far more likely that he just enjoyed hearing himself talk."

She sorted through what Morgan had just told her and decided that it wouldn't hurt to go through whatever he felt was important enough to jot down.

"Now that I think about it, sure," she told him. "I would be interested in seeing your notes."

Morgan looked around the area for the legal pad he had brought in with him. Seeing it lying on the sofa, he crossed over to the light gray piece of furniture, picked it up and brought it over to her.

"Here," he said, holding the pad out to Krys.

Taking it from him, she quickly skimmed over the more than two pages of writing. It did make sense, she realized.

"Thanks," she murmured. "I'll be sure to read it more carefully." She raised her eyes to his. "What are you going to do?"

"Don't worry about me," he told her. "I've got ways to stay busy."

Krys was definitely curious about exactly what he intended to do, but since Morgan didn't seem like he wanted to elaborate, for now she just kept her questions to herself.

Taking her laptop over to the corner desk that she had set up as her work area, Krys started writing. Within moments, she was completely immersed in her work. She carefully waded through this latest interview and compared it to the content within her other interviews.

What she was looking for was not a narrative but to see if what the various researchers had said wound up contradicting one another or confirming the details.

For the most part, Krys was focused on her work, but she did find it difficult to concentrate because her mind kept insisting on returning to the striking, handsome man who had set himself up at the kitchen counter with a tall glass of sparkling water. Whenever she slanted a glance in his direction, he appeared to be sitting at ease and nonchalantly taking everything in.

C'mon, Krys, stop letting your mind drift. This damn thing isn't going to write itself and you're not getting paid for procrastinating like this. Eyes on the prize, Kowalski, she silently lectured herself.

FINALLY, IT HAD somehow gotten to be three hours later. Her bright blue eyes were a little less bright. They were also burning and threatening to shut at any moment. With a weary sigh, she saved her work and then shut down her laptop.

"Problem?"

Krys nearly jumped at the sound of his voice. She hadn't realized that he was standing right over her.

"You sighed," he explained when she looked at him as if he were some sort of a ghost, hovering over her.

Taking a breath, she willed her heart to calm down. "I feel like I'm missing something," she explained, nodding at the closed laptop. "Something that's right out there in plain sight, mocking me."

In his opinion, she was pushing herself too hard. "Could be that you just wore yourself out and you're exhausted."

"Could be," she agreed, but she wasn't really convinced that was the case as she added, "But it's probably not likely."

Now that her laptop was shut down for the night, she put her hands on the desk and pushed herself up into a standing position. "I guess I'll call it a night." Her eyes swept over him. "Some of us don't run on batteries."

He smiled, playing along with her comment. "Not even rechargeable ones?"

"Nope." She shook her head. "Not even those." Krys glanced toward the end of the corridor, where the bedrooms were located. "Sure I can't interest you in a bed?"

The second she asked the question, she immediately realized how that had to sound to a man, especially one as good-looking as Morgan Cavanaugh. Her complexion immediately turned a bright red.

"I mean to sleep in. By yourself." The more she attempted to correct the impression she had inadvertently created, the worse her words sounded to her ears.

Morgan laughed. Taking pity on her, he came to her rescue. "I know what you mean and I'm sure," he told her. "I'll be fine right here," he said, nodding down at the chair he'd been sitting in.

"The recliner?" Krys asked in disbelief, clearly skeptical about the choice he had made. "That can't be a very comfortable way to spend the rest of the night," she observed.

"Hey," he protested, attempting to sound as if he was challenging her dismissive tone, "some of my best sleep has been gotten standing up." She would have believed him except for the way his eyes seemed to twinkle as he said it. "But I don't intend to do any real sleeping."

She cast a disapproving glance at the recliner. "Doesn't look all that comfortable for fake sleeping, either."

His smile came easily, and he got the definite impression that she was predisposed to argue with him about everything.

"Like I said, don't worry about it," he told her.

Surrendering for the moment, Krys shrugged. If the man was determined not to sleep, that was his choice. "Suit yourself. But all I know is that it'll reflect rather badly on me as a brand-new member of the family if I wind up wearing out one of the Cavanaughs less than a week after I turn up."

He laughed at the image she had wound up projecting. "Don't worry about it. We're a hardy breed," Morgan assured her. "We don't wear out that easy."

"Good to know," Krys replied. Morgan got the feeling that she wasn't all that convinced.

"Don't forget to lock your bedroom door," he called after her as she left the room and walked toward the rear of the house.

Krys stopped and turned around. "Why, are you planning on breaking in?"

Instead of answering her, Morgan grinned in response. "I make it a rule never to mix business with pleasure."

What is that supposed to mean? she wondered. Krys also had a strong urge to ask him just which category she ultimately fell into, business or pleasure? But she already had enough trouble swirling around her without openly inviting more, and even though he was supposed to be her protector, this man was definitely trouble with a capital *T*.

"Good night, Cavanaugh," she said as she resumed walking down the hallway.

"Good night, Kowalski," he called after her.

Smiling to himself, Morgan settled in on the recliner, prepared to keep watch for the night.

KRYS SPENT A restless night trying to sleep.

Rather than being comforted by the knowledge that Morgan was out there, keeping vigil over her, she found that it agitated her. Although the thought didn't keep her awake, it *did* keep waking her every forty-five minutes to an hour or so with a fair amount of regularity.

The fifth time she opened her eyes, fully alert, Krys gave up trying to stitch together a decent night's sleep. This was even worse than the time she had been overseas, researching a story on the doings of a reluctant hero who had captured the public's attention—at least for that month. She had relentlessly pursued him until he had surrendered his entire story to her. She remembered being very proud of her work at the time. And also exhausted.

This wasn't quite as bad as that, she reminded herself. But it was definitely close.

Telling herself that she might as well get on with her day, Krys took a quick shower and felt incredibly vulnerable for the six minutes that she was undressed and in the shower. Thanks to her stint overseas, she had learned how to take what amounted to the world's quickest showers: in and out at what seemed like the speed of light.

Drying her hair took longer, but only because she had gotten dressed first. That way she was confident she could make a really quick getaway if that turned out to be necessary. The condition of her hair wouldn't have slowed her down, although it might have wound up attracting attention.

Showered and dressed in less time than it took to think about it, she found the world was finally coming into focus for her and hurried down the stairs. She crossed into the living room—where she found Morgan wide awake and looking a great deal better than she felt he decently should have.

The man definitely didn't look as if he had spent the night in a recliner.

"Why do you look as if you slept all night?" she accused the moment he turned around. The man looked absolutely refreshed. "You didn't sleep all night, did you?" she questioned.

"No," Morgan answered matter-of-factly. "I took a catnap from around two fifteen to two thirty-five," he told her. He added with a smile, "That seemed to do the trick for me."

She stared at him. He was kidding, right? "How is that even possible?" she asked, telling him, "That's not normal."

"I didn't say it was normal," Morgan pointed out. "I just said I took a catnap. About the best way that I can explain it is that when I'm not on duty this way, I manage to store up a fair amount of sleep. I seem to be able to tap into that storage whenever I need to."

He had to be making this up. There was no other explanation for this uncanny juggling act of his that he was boasting about. "I don't believe you," she told him.

"That is your prerogative," Morgan replied magnanimously. "So, now that you're up, what's on tap for today?"

Discounting what he had just said to her about his unbelievable sleeping pattern, she focused on answering his question. "I've got four interviews set up for today. One of them is with a test subject who abruptly took back the story she had told me. I want to find out if she was lying to me then, or if she is currently lying now."

He thought of what he'd had to go through himself on those occasions when he was forced to dig down until he finally got to the truth. Sympathizing with her, Morgan shook his head.

"Something wrong?" she asked him. She could feel herself growing defensive even though she didn't have a clue as to why.

"Doesn't it sometimes get to you?" Morgan asked her.

"Doesn't *what* sometimes get to me?" Krys asked.

"Always having to lock horns with people, dealing with them as if lying was a given, or that they thought of you as the enemy," he said.

"I tell myself that I'm ultimately looking for the truth and that's really enough to placate me," she told Morgan.

He didn't look convinced. "What if you don't find the truth?"

That meant giving up and it just didn't happen, she thought. "Then I just keep digging until I do," she told him.

Morgan had no doubts that she was telling the truth. She didn't give up until she had her answers no matter how long it took—and that apparently was what was putting her life in danger, he thought.

He supposed that sort of dedication was to be admired, but he wasn't here to admire her. He was here to make sure that she didn't get killed because of her "noble" dedication.

But who would take over after he accomplished his job? After he kept her safe until her stalker was apprehended—or permanently stopped. He had no doubt that she would continue operating this way when she undertook her search for the next story, the next truth.

The next dangerous subject matter that could get her killed.

Not his problem, Morgan told himself. He just had to get her through this.

Even as he thought it, he didn't completely believe it.

"Since you don't have anything to eat, how do you feel about getting breakfast at your local fast food place?" he asked her.

"I feel fine about it," she answered. "As a matter of fact, my system would probably go into some kind of shock if I actually ate breakfast in a real kitchen," she confessed.

He looked at her thoughtfully. "That sounds like a challenge," he told her.

"No, no challenge. Just a simply fact," she replied. At this point in her life, she'd had more breakfasts on the go than she had consumed sitting down in an actual kitchen.

He nodded, getting ready to leave with her. "Remind me to stop at a grocery store on our way home tonight so I can pick up some things and make you a real breakfast tomorrow morning."

"Do you actually *want* to cook?" she asked him, saying the verb as if it was tantamount to running naked through a town square.

"Do I really want to?" he repeated, rolling the question over in his mind. "No," he answered honestly. "But it's one of those necessary evils that you learn to live with," he told her. "Right along with paying taxes—and obeying the law."

Does he really equate the two? she wondered. "You're kidding me now, aren't you?"

He grinned. "I guess I must be doing a decent enough job at it since you're obviously not really sure *what* I'm doing."

No, she thought, and that went double for her because instead of concentrating on the story, the way she should have been, she found herself thinking things about Morgan Cavanaugh that had absolutely nothing to do with her story, or leads or what she did for a living.

Focus, damn it. Stop thinking about how he makes your skin tingle, she upbraided herself. You don't get paid for that.

"Let's just say I'm good at guessing," she finally told him. "Now I've got less than an hour before my first appointment, so let's hope that fast food place lives up to its name."

"Count on it," he told her as they walked out of her house.

He paused in order to make sure that her door was securely locked. Satisfied, he nodded and gestured for her to keep walking.

Chapter Twelve

Krys shifted in her seat.

"I feel like I'm growing roots," Morgan said. His eyes never left the entrance leading into the Mexican restaurant. He and Krys had been sitting in the parking lot for almost an hour and a half waiting for her contact to arrive. "I've certainly consumed enough ice tea to sufficiently water a tree. You sure that woman you're supposed to be meeting got the name of the restaurant right?" he asked Krys.

"She was the one who picked it," she told Morgan.

So far, Claire Williams, the woman who had already changed her story once, was turning out to be a no-show. The meeting for the interview had been set up to take place in this restaurant, which was clear across the city, far away from Weatherly Pharmaceuticals, solely for the reason that the woman was afraid of being accidentally overheard by someone from the company. But apparently Claire Williams had decided that this wasn't safe enough, and she had either changed her mind about the meeting or even possibly lost her nerve.

They had been sitting out here all this time waiting for her to show, but it was looking as if she wasn't going to.

Krys had been checking her phone every few minutes for a call or text, expecting to be on the receiving end of at least an excuse if not an outright apology, but so far, neither appeared to be forthcoming. After ninety minutes had gone by, she was beginning to lose hope.

Morgan had been watching Krys grow progressively more agitated. "I think it's safe to say that this woman isn't coming," he finally told her. "Why don't we just move on to your next appointment? Maybe something came up and for some reason this Williams woman wasn't able to make it to the restaurant."

Krys sighed. "I suppose you're right." Having the woman be a no-show just didn't sit well with her. Claire hadn't seemed like the type to do that without so much as an explanation. "But I just can't get over Claire standing me up like this. She just seemed so genuinely sincere."

Morgan had seen this sort of behavior countless times before. "It happens," he told her. "Maybe she had time to think this over and decided that it just wasn't worth the risk and was too embarrassed to admit it. Or she might even have been threatened—or bribed," Morgan told her, citing a couple of reasons why the woman was a no-show. "Believe me, there are a lot of ways to get someone to change their story."

"I know," she replied. She wasn't born yesterday, Krys thought defensively. "But I would have bet anything that Claire wasn't like that. When she first came to me, it wasn't easy piecing everything together. I had to practically *drag* the information out of her word for word," she told Morgan. "She didn't relish being a whistleblower or telling me that the tests conducted on her hadn't yielded the desired results."

"But didn't she first tell you that they did? That her cancer had appeared to have gone into remission?" he asked her.

"That was what she was first told, but then she found out her data had been manipulated so that the resulting figures made it *seem* as if her condition had gone into remission," she told Morgan. "Claire was adamant about that, not to mention upset. Someone like that doesn't just do an about-face at the last minute, claiming she had been mistaken after all. That's why her disappearing act now looks so suspicious."

The journalist seemed so passionate about the stand she was taking, Morgan was inclined to believe her. Something *could* have happened to Claire. Maybe whoever had tried to eliminate Krys had gotten to Claire as well.

"Why don't you give me all the information you have on this woman," he told Krys. "I can send someone to check her out, find out where she's currently staying."

"You don't think that something's happened to her, do you?" Krys asked. She really didn't want to face that possibility.

He could see that beneath her bravado, Krys was sincerely worried. She did not harbor a Pollyanna view regarding the nature of some of the people she was dealing with. Morgan couldn't help wondering just how far one or more of the key people at the company would be willing to go to squelch any damning testimonials about this so-called miracle drug Weatherly Pharmaceutical was backing.

Rather than answer her question outright, he said, "I've found that expecting the worst and hoping for the best have always worked for me. Where are you supposed to meet the next person you're going to be interviewing?"

Krys didn't have to look at the appointment log she had on her phone. She knew all the entries on it by heart and answered Morgan's question. "I assumed that Claire's interview was going to last until eleven, so we have some time to get to Gerry's."

"Gerry's?" he repeated.

Thinking he was unfamiliar with the restaurant, she wrote down the address for him. "Gerry's," she declared, turning the piece of paper around so that he could look at it.

He took in the location. "That's clear on the other side of the city," he said. Why was she chasing around from one end of Aurora to the other? "Were you trying to qualify for frequent flier miles with these interviews?" he quipped.

"I was dealing with paranoid people," she told him. "I didn't want to risk one person seeing the other or overhearing their testimony," she told him. "That could cause all four subjects to just clam up."

Morgan nodded. He could see that. "That makes sense," he agreed.

"Glad you approve," she said tersely.

He realized she was disappointed, but he didn't care for her tone. "Hey, in case you missed this point, I'm on your side, remember?"

She flushed. He was right and she wasn't being fair. "Sorry," she apologized. "I guess my disappointment got the better of me," she explained, although that really wasn't an excuse. "Not to mention that I *am* worried about Claire."

Morgan let the incident slide. "My mother used to have a saying: don't borrow trouble. It'll find you soon enough if it wants to. There's no point in worrying about it until then."

Krys managed what passed for half a smile as she acknowledged the late woman's comment. "Your mother sounded like a nice, levelheaded woman."

He heard the wistful note in Krys's voice. "She was," he agreed. He'd been thinking about his mother these last couple of days. He normally didn't unless he was at a family gathering, and even then it was only once in a while. And Krys was the kind of person his mother would have liked. "That's why her advice to you would be not to take unnecessary risks pursuing your stories."

Krys laughed at the directive. "Everything about being an investigative reporter involves taking so-called 'unnecessary' risks." She didn't want to argue about it. Instead, she turned his 'advise' back on the detective. "And what about you?"

He wasn't sure what she was getting at. "What about me?"

"You're a police detective. Isn't that all about having to take risks?"

He assumed that Krys was still talking about his mother's advice. "She was the wife of a policeman. She knew all about that. She just wanted to make sure all of us were careful when we chose our battles," he said matter-of-factly.

She could see that they could wind up debating over this all day—and she didn't have all day, so she deliberately changed the subject.

"Didn't you say something about having someone on the police force check into Claire's whereabouts, make sure she's all right?" she reminded him.

"Yes, my partner," he told her. "I'm on it," he said, taking out his cell phone before he got into his vehicle. He nodded toward her ever-present laptop. "Give me whatever particulars you have on this woman so I can pass it on to Fredericks."

Krys obliged, flipping open her laptop. She tucked the cover under the keyboard so that Morgan could read any information he needed as if it was written on a regular pad.

As Morgan read aloud to his partner, Krys continued scanning the area in the hopes that Claire was just running late and would turn up at the last possible moment.

Morgan had barely finished giving Fredericks the most pertinent information about the absent whistleblower when he heard his partner mutter something inaudible under his breath.

Straining to hear, Morgan asked, "Anything wrong, Fredericks?" He thought his partner was about to beg off looking into Claire's whereabouts, saying that he was currently swamped.

There was a pregnant sigh on the other end. "Well, about that person you said you wanted tracked down—" Fredericks began, then paused.

"Yes?" Morgan coaxed, waiting.

"I've got some good news and some bad news," Fredericks said. "Which do you want first?"

Morgan frowned to himself. "That was fast," he couldn't help commenting, still keeping his back toward Krys. "I'll take the good news."

"We found her."

"You found her?" Morgan questioned. "You mean Claire Williams?" he asked, confused. "You found Claire Williams?"

"Yes," his partner confirmed.

It didn't seem possible. "But I just asked you to look for her less than a minute ago," Morgan protested suspiciously. "How could you have found her?"

"That's the bad news," Fredericks told him. "She's dead. A couple of hikers found her body in the park earlier this morning."

"Are you sure?" Morgan asked as he glanced over toward Krys.

"I'm sure," Fredericks answered. "She had her ID card on her."

The moment he had looked in her direction, Krys became alert. She instantly cut the distance between them, her heart slamming against her chest. She'd seen that look before. It reeked of apprehension.

"It's Claire, isn't it?" she asked. Then, before he could say anything, she filled in the crucial piece of information herself. "She's dead, isn't she?"

Knowing what that would mean to her, not to mention that this was about another human being, he would have given anything to be able to deny her assumption. But he couldn't.

"Yes."

"When?" she asked, struggling to get past the sick feeling in her stomach.

He told her what Fredericks had told him. "This morning. I don't have a time of death yet, but her body was found this morning in the park."

Guilt pierced her like the business end of a saber. "Because she was coming to give me the specific details about her doctored test results. She's dead because of me," she cried. "This is my fault."

"No, it's not," he insisted. "This is the fault of whoever killed her—and whoever ordered that she be killed, not you."

But she wasn't buying his excuse to whitewash what she had brought about. "None of which would have happened if I hadn't pushed this," she insisted, angry tears filling her eyes.

Fredericks was saying something to him. He couldn't listen to two people talking to him at the same time. "I'll be there as soon as I can," Morgan told his partner, then ended his call. He shoved his phone into his pocket. "C'mon," he told Krys. "I'll feel a lot better getting you to the police station so I can have a squad of cops guarding you."

She wasn't about to get sidetracked, or allow fear to stop her. "This article is more important than ever now. I have to make sure it gets out," she insisted. "I owe it to Claire."

"Nobody is telling you not to write it," Morgan told her. "But it won't hurt to be cautious. A few more days isn't going to make a difference."

She didn't agree. "The drug is due to be out on the open market in a week. There's a huge demand for it. Who knows what kind of damage it might do if what Claire had told me was right? And, for that matter, who knows what sort of desperate measures someone in the company is willing to go to in order to ensure that it *won't* be taken off the market?" she asked him.

Guilt was mounting up within her, making her feel sick. She had never dealt with anything like this before and it was hard to keep from breaking down.

"Right now, my main concern is keeping another person from getting killed, namely you," Morgan told her. "Now stop arguing with me and get into the car." He held the door open for her.

Krys took in a deep, shaky breath and did as he asked. She desperately tried to see an upside to this. She could only think of one. "I guess this rules out Bluebeard trying to kill me."

Morgan didn't totally agree. "Maybe yes, maybe no." His response surprised her. "This could all be a coincidence," he told her.

She stared at him, confused. "You're going to have to be clearer than that."

"Maybe this Bluebeard does want revenge because you're responsible for ruining his perfect scheme. Meanwhile, someone killed Claire because she was about to blow the whistle on the drug trials and that could wind up costing the company a fortune."

This was just getting worse and worse, she thought. "All I know is that I feel like Typhoid Mary, spreading death in my path without even realizing it."

He had to stop her before she got too carried away blaming herself. "Don't be too hasty donning that hair shirt just yet."

"Are you telling me you think I'm being some sort of a martyr?" Her voice rose sharply.

"No. I'm saying that you're *anticipating* being a martyr. Let's not get ahead of ourselves, okay?" he advised.

"Ahead of myself? Maybe someone should tell that to Claire," she snapped. She was struggling, but she was on the verge of breaking down. The guilt was all but suffocating her now. She had never cost anyone their life before and the very thought was overwhelming her.

Consumed with guilt, Krys didn't realize that he was pulling over until Morgan had stopped the car and turned off the engine. Blinking back tears, she looked around. They weren't anywhere near the police station. She saw that he had pulled his car into a parking lot.

"What are we doing here?" she asked. "For that matter, where *is* here?" she asked, her voice breaking.

"I thought maybe you needed a moment to pull yourself together before we drive to the police station," he told her.

"I don't need a moment," she insisted angrily. "I'm fine. I'm fine," she repeated. And then her voice cracked completely and she began to sob.

"Yeah," he agreed, placating her. "You're fine all right." Slipping his arm around her in an effort to comfort her, he held her close to him. "You just need a couple of minutes until that 'fine' gets under control."

She wanted to protest what he was saying, to tell him not to treat her like some fragile little doll that was about to shatter. But she couldn't say a word.

The tears welling up in her throat kept intelligible words from forming. Unable to speak, she gave in to the helpless, awful feeling that lay siege to her soul. She turned her face in against his shoulder and just sobbed uncontrollably.

"That's it," Morgan told her soothingly, holding her and stroking her hair. "Sometimes all you can do is just cry and let it all out. There's no shame in that. Go ahead. Cry," he coaxed her. "There's no one around to see you. No one to try to act tough for."

"You're here." She finally managed to sob the words out.

"I don't count," he told her, holding her to him.

She struggled to regain control over herself, but all she could do was sob. Krys cried for at least a full five minutes and then she drew her head back, determined to stop.

Morgan dug into his pocket and pulled out a handkerchief. "Here."

She accepted the handkerchief, wiping her eyes, then handing it back to him. "I'm sorry," she apologized.

"For what? Being human?" he asked. "Hate to tell you but it happens to the best of us." He closed his hand over hers, pushing the handkerchief back to her. "Hold on to that. Tears have a nasty habit of popping back up just when you think you've finished crying. I'm pretty sure I won't be needing it right now."

She sniffed, crumpling up his handkerchief in her hand. "You're not supposed to be this nice."

"I'll work on it and see what I can do," he promised with a wink.

A ghost of a smile emerged on her lips in response to that. And then something else happened as well.

Before she could think better of it, or stop herself, Krys found herself expressing her gratitude to him in another way.

She kissed Morgan.

Surprised, he didn't want to seem as if he was taking advantage of her or the situation and began to pull back. But then, before he realized he was doing it, he framed her face with his hands and kissed her back.

With feeling.

Chapter Thirteen

All sorts of emotions flashed through Krys at what felt like the speed of light. At once drawn to Morgan and stunned by what she was experiencing at this very moment, she definitely wasn't reacting to him on any sort of a professional level.

Pulling back, Krys began to say that this wasn't like her, but then Morgan managed to disarm her by asking her if she was all right. He sounded as if he was concerned about her emotional state.

Her heart was pounding like a drum and her pulse was racing at what felt like ninety miles an hour.

"No," she answered truthfully, trying her best to will herself to calm down. "I'm not all right. But I'm getting there." She took a deep breath, blowing it out again slowly. A wave of self-consciousness washed over her. "I promise I won't embarrass you in front of your friends."

"I wasn't concerned about that," he told her. "And besides, you have nothing to be embarrassed about."

They had a slight difference of opinion about that, but she wasn't about to continue protesting. She focused on moving forward. And most of all, she was determined to find whoever had killed the woman who had been brave enough to step forward and bring attention to this so-called miracle drug's shortcomings.

"We can go to the police station now," she told Morgan, pulling herself together. She wanted to do whatever she could, help any way possible, to get this investigation on solid ground.

"Are you sure?" he asked her, starting up his vehicle again. "We can hold off going there for a bit longer if you want more time to get yourself together."

"What I want," she emphasized, "is to get the bastard who's responsible for killing Claire." Aside from feeling that she owed this to the young woman, it was the only way for her to be able to deal with this overwhelming guilt she was feeling.

"Then that's what we'll do," Morgan declared. "We'll get him." As he drove to the precinct, he told her what his plan was. "I'm going to drop you off in the squad room while I go and talk to the medical examiner about her autopsy findings." While he could talk to any of the medical examiners who worked with Aurora's police department, he could usually get more answers out of his cousin-in-law. As luck would have it, she was on call today. Trying to make Krys feel better, he shared this piece of information with her. "I think Toni is on tap today."

"Tony?" Krys questioned.

"That's 'Toni' with an *i*, not a *y*," Morgan said, filling her in. He added the crucial point. "She's my sister-in-law."

"Of course she is." Krys shook her head. This family seemed to be everywhere. Did her sister know what she was getting herself into? "Is everyone associated with the police department a Cavanaugh?"

"No, not everyone," Morgan said. "But there are a lot of us."

ARRIVING IN THE police parking lot, Morgan pulled his vehicle up into his usual parking spot. As he got out of his car, he debated just bringing Krys into the first-floor lobby to wait for him rather than up to the squad room. "I won't be long," he promised.

She caught his arm. "You won't be long at all," she corrected him. "I intend to come with you."

"To the morgue?" he questioned. He had no desire to witness her suddenly get sick to her stomach. "I don't think you should go," he told her, emphasizing, "You're already upset enough."

"No, I *was* upset," she said, going up the stairs and to the front door quickly. "But I've gotten all that under control now," she stressed. "Look." She went through the automatic doors as they parted for her. "I'm never going to get to the bottom of this awful thing by burying my face in my hands and hiding from reality."

Like his sisters and his cousins, this woman seemed to thrive on arguing. He didn't have time for this. "I admire your resolve, but it's not your job to get to the bottom of this. It's mine."

She realized that he thought he was being kind to her, but he wasn't going to get her to back off. And he was wasting precious time because arguing with her was futile. The man meant well and he had a great set of lips on him, but he was *not* going to get her to change her mind or back off. She was determined to find out who had done this awful thing.

Morgan must have recognized stubbornness when he saw it. "All right, how about this? Why don't we just compromise and agree that finding the truth behind this is *both* our jobs? We'll work together."

The way he saw it, this was the best way he could think of to keep an eye on her and not have her taking off on him.

She saw Morgan grin encouragingly at her. She wasn't sure what to think, but she was braced for anything. He surprised her by saying, "You would really get along well with my sisters."

She raised an eyebrow as she regarded him suspiciously. "Are your sisters just as stubborn as you?"

He grinned. "Oh, they're much more so."

That would be taking stubbornness to an incredible level. The very idea almost had her laughing at him. "Oh, I find that really hard to believe."

"You wouldn't if you knew them. I guarantee it." As Morgan followed her into the elevator and took it down to the basement, a thought came to him. "As a matter of fact, that isn't a bad idea."

"What isn't a bad idea?" she asked.

"Getting to know my sisters. Getting to know everybody."

Morgan made a mental note to talk to his Uncle Andrew. Andrew enjoyed nothing more than having an excuse to gather the entire family together. Initially, Andrew had served on the police force, working his way up until he became the chief of police. He would have remained one until he retired if it hadn't been for his wife's sudden disappearance. Rose went missing for eleven years, leaving him with five children to raise. He had no choice but to take an early retirement. But he never gave up hope that Rose was out there somewhere. He moved heaven and earth to find her, but it was far from easy.

After being on the force, he found that he needed something to help occupy his time when his kids were grown and had joined the force themselves. He decided to split his time between searching for Rose and bringing the rest of the family together every chance he got. A twist of fate helped him locate his wife who, because of an accident that caused her car to go off the road and into the lake, had her suffering from amnesia. Andrew devoted himself to helping her regain her memory. When she finally did, it felt as if he had been suddenly granted a "do-over." From then on, he lived his life like a man on borrowed time, never taking even a moment for granted.

He threw parties for the family every chance he got. And when he wasn't throwing parties, Andrew was still rustling up meals for family and friends whenever someone happened to just drop by.

Morgan decided that Krys could really use one of his uncle's famous parties. In his opinion, it would be just what the doctor ordered and it would serve as her formal introduction to the family as well as their introduction to her.

He was going to call Andrew the first chance he got, Morgan promised himself. He knew that the family patriarch would undoubtedly welcome the chance to meet Nikki's twin sister and, Morgan was sure, Krys could certainly use a good dose of Cavanaugh closeness and affection if only to raise her spirits.

This sort of thing would be right up his uncle's alley, he thought with a smile.

But Krys didn't look as if she was entirely convinced that this would be a good time to meet all the members of the family. "Why don't we at least wait until we find out who killed Claire?" she suggested. "I'm not going to be able to enjoy anything until I'm sure that this killer isn't lurking somewhere out there, waiting to ambush my sister—or me."

Even as she said it, she couldn't keep from shivering over the mere suggestion of that possibility taking place.

"Don't worry," Morgan said, trying to comfort her. "I guarantee that within the hour, everyone at the precinct—not just the family—will be on this."

"No offense," she told him. "But I won't be happy until this is finally over."

He laughed shortly. "You're not the only one," he assured her. "But allow me to point out that Aurora has the best low crime rate for a city of its size in the entire country."

He wasn't telling her anything that she didn't already know. Aurora's exceptionally low crime rate was well-known. "I know," she told him. "But low isn't the same as nonexistent."

And all it took was one killing if it involved her—or Nikki, she thought.

"No," he agreed, getting off the elevator as it opened on the lower level, "it isn't. But you have to focus on your odds," Morgan advised. "And they are damn good."

They continued walking until they reached the morgue. Morgan looked at the bulletin board. He had been right about his cousin Toni being the ME who was on duty.

They came in. Before he could make the introductions, Toni looked up from the autopsy she had just completed. The moment she did, she appeared surprised.

"Nikki?" Dugan's wife cried, stripping off her rubber gloves. "What are you doing back so soon? And why are you here of all places?"

Shaking her head, Krys offered the woman a tight, patient smile. "No, I'm not Nik. Nikki is hopefully still on her honeymoon with Finn and completely oblivious of this whole thing."

Toni drew a little closer, taking another look at the woman that Morgan had brought into the morgue with him. "Then Dugan wasn't kidding," she remarked, properly impressed as she circled around Krys. "He mentioned seeing you when he'd delivered that pizza last night. You do look *exactly* like her."

Krys tried not to sigh. This was getting old. She and Nik didn't usually travel in the same circles. "I get that a lot."

She really had to be tired of saying that, Morgan thought. He was *definitely* going to have Andrew throw that get-together. That way everyone could meet Krys once and for all and finally stop remarking how much she looked just like her twin. He knew that Krys would appreciate that.

"I bet you do," Toni said, agreeing with Krys.

"What about the dead woman?" Morgan prompted, trying to move this along.

"She doesn't look a thing like Nikki—or—Krys, is it?" Toni asked, looking at Krys.

"Yes, it's Krys," Morgan confirmed, "and I realize that she doesn't look a thing like the body those hikers found today," he said patiently. "What I want to know is if you have any information about the victim's time of death or the way she was killed?"

"That I can give you," Toni said, becoming all business. "The time of death was early this morning, between six and seven," she told Morgan. "From the looks of it and what she was wearing at the time, I'd say that the victim was jogging."

"How did she die?" Krys asked quietly.

Toni raised her eyes to look at the other woman. "She was shot," she answered simply. Slipping on another pair of gloves, she turned the dead woman's head to display the wound at the back of her neck. "Most likely by a sniper."

"A sniper?" Morgan repeated, somewhat surprised. "What makes you say it was a sniper?"

"There was just one shot," Toni told him. "Taken at an impressive distance," she pointed out. "To me that definitely says sniper."

The fact that this was the work of a sniper made Morgan feel that Krys was in even more danger and was more vulnerable than he had initially thought. He was *not* about to take any more chances with her life.

"That settles it," Morgan declared abruptly. "I'm keeping you under lock and key."

Krys was instantly up in arms. "I can't live that way."

"Well, you might not be able to live any other way," he pointed out. "Did you think of that?"

"He has a point, you know," Toni told her.

"I'll be all right," Krys assured Morgan as well as the medical examiner. "I've got sources I can count on to warn me. People on the street who could put the word out," she elaborated, "and see who might have made use of a sniper in order to get rid of Claire."

Morgan looked as if he was very close to losing his temper. "Kowalski, you can't—"

But she immediately cut in before he could complete his thought. "I can and I will," she informed Morgan. "Look, don't you see? The sooner we find out who did this, the sooner we can find out the name of the person who paid to have this hit carried out. I am *not* going to live in fear," she insisted, incensed. "I can't," Krys underscored.

For a moment, it was as if they had both forgotten that they were not the only ones in the room. "I'm not telling you to live in fear," Morgan said, his voice growing louder. "I'm telling you to let me do my job—and I can't do my job if I'm worried about you."

He suddenly realized that Toni was in the room when he saw the stunned look on her face. He had obviously said too much. But no one had ever managed to push his buttons the way this woman did, and he couldn't even begin to explain why, not even to himself.

"You know, Morgan, we do have a lot of resources available to the police department that can be put to good use," Toni reminded her brother-in-law.

"I know that," he said.

"Then why don't you use them?" Krys asked. "Between the two of us, maybe we can come up with some answers," she said hopefully. With the prospect of possibly regaining some semblance of control over the situation, Krys was beginning to feel better.

Morgan frowned slightly. "I liked it better when you were being vulnerable," he told her.

Krys shot him a less-than-pleased look. "I didn't," she told him. "Vulnerable people get taken advantage of. That isn't my style."

Time to wrap this up, Morgan thought. "Anything else?" he asked the medical examiner.

Toni shook her head. "Not right now. I'll let you know if I find anything else," she promised, "but to be honest, I'm not expecting any more surprises."

"I'd say that we've had just about enough surprises for one day," he told Toni. And then he looked at Krys. "You have anything you want to ask?"

Krys paused for a moment, as if thinking. And then she answered, "I've got just one question for you," she told the examiner.

"Go ahead," Toni encouraged.

Krys took in a breath, as if to steel herself. "Was it quick?"

The medical examiner looked at her sympathetically, impressed that Krys should care this much about a woman who was, from what she had gathered, in essence a virtual stranger to her.

"I'd say she never knew what hit her," the other woman told her.

Krys blew out the breath she had taken in. "I guess at least that's something," she said. "Thank you for answering my question."

Toni offered her a quick smile. "Don't mention it." She glanced toward Morgan. "It's nice meeting someone who cares and doesn't view this whole thing impersonally." As Krys began to leave with Morgan, Toni called after her, "Nice meeting you, Krys. I just wish it was under better circumstances."

"That makes two of us," Krys replied.

"Do you want to go somewhere for coffee?" Morgan asked Krys the moment they walked out of the morgue and into the corridor.

Krys shook her head. "Not unless that coffee comes with a side order of answers," she told the detective.

"In my business," Morgan replied, "those take time." He paused for a moment as a thought occurred to him. "Since we're down here, why don't we stop by the computer lab?" he suggested.

She thought of the puzzle they had dropped in Valri's lap the last time they had stopped there. She doubted if the woman had come up with any answers, but since Morgan had suggested it, she thought they should check. She had already called ahead to reschedule her appointment at Gerry's.

"Sure," Krys agreed gamely. "Might as well get all my disappointments over with at once," she told Morgan.

"I didn't peg you for someone who just gave up," he commented as they went down the opposite direction in the hall.

"I'm not giving up," Krys protested. "I'm just taking your advice and preparing myself for the worst."

"I also said, hope for the best," he reminded her as they went toward the lab.

"Sorry, right now my optimism is in rather low supply." And then she realized how that had to have sounded to him. "But don't worry, I'll rally soon," she promised. "It's just that at the moment,

I feel a little beaten down—although not nearly as badly beaten down as Claire is—was," she corrected herself.

Morgan thought it was safer not to comment on what she'd just said.

However, as he walked into the computer lab, he looked at Valri. He found it impossible to gauge her mood. This could be good or bad.

"Listen," he told his cousin, "if you have anything hopeful to tell us, now would be the time to do it."

"All right," she agreed. "But this might be one of those things that qualifies as a bad news/good news situation," Valri told him.

"We've already had one of those today, but go ahead," he encouraged. "Tell us."

"You said you wanted me to find out who Bluebeard was," she reminded the two people at her desk.

"We did," Morgan confirmed. His breath felt as if it was sticking in his throat as he never took his eyes off her face, waiting to hear what he was almost certain that he was going to hear.

Valri smiled. "Well, I did."

Chapter Fourteen

Krys stared at the police department's main computer expert. "You actually found out Bluebeard's real name?" she asked Valri, hardly able to believe what she was hearing.

Valri was obviously pleased with this unexpected development. "It took a bit of doing," she admitted to the two people standing at her desk, "but yes, I managed to track down his identity."

"How?" Morgan asked, stunned. "I mean, I know you're good, Valri," he freely admitted, "but this is way beyond good since no one else was ever able to find out just who this diabolical killer is. Ever since he first surfaced, this guy's been like an ever-changing chameleon."

Valri merely smiled. She was obviously proud of herself. "Well, it seems that very early in his career, before he began killing his blushing brides, 'Bluebeard' *was* arrested and fingerprinted because his extremely unhappy 'lady love' had him brought up on charges. Your guy did manage to give the arresting officers the slip, but not before they got his fingerprints on file," Valri informed them. "See, here he is almost a dozen years ago, just when he was starting out."

Valri scrolled down to show them the only mug shot, an early one, that she was able to find on file. He looked almost like an innocent teenager, except for his eyes. His age listed him as being older than he looked.

"So, what is his name?" Morgan asked, looking over Valri's shoulder.

She scrolled down further. "Well, the name 'Bluebeard' gave the arresting officer at the time was Chris Hunter, but as you can guess, that wasn't his real name," Valri said.

Krys frowned. "Big surprise," she murmured to Morgan.

"After he escaped, the arresting detectives were incensed, and they took it upon themselves to try to track him. They eventually found out that his real name was—get this—" she prefaced because the name was so anticlimactically mundane "—Elmer Smith."

Somehow, the name seemed almost like a letdown. Krys looked at the computer tech. "You're kidding."

Valri shook her head as she smiled. "No, I'm very, very serious."

Krys nodded her head. This was an important step forward. "I guess we go looking for this Elmer Smith," she said, glancing at Morgan. And then her mouth curved. "I can't even say that with a straight face."

"Spoiler alert. You don't have to go looking for Elmer Smith," Valri told them when they stared at her in confusion.

Morgan didn't understand. "Why not?" he asked. "Did he do another disappearing act? Because if he did," he began to say, anticipating her answer, "he's not—"

"No, he didn't disappear," Valri told them, looking from one to the other. "It turns out that the infamous Bluebeard is dead."

Krys blew out a disgusted breath. "That's what he wants everyone to think, but he's done this sort of thing before. He's—"

"That's what I told the police chief," Valri said, cutting into what Krys was about to tell her. "Which is why the CSI unit chief is having the body flown out here from Arizona," she told the duo. "'Elmer Smith' should be here sometime tomorrow morning with all the proper papers of identification."

Morgan saw the stunned, disappointed look on Krys's face. "How long has he been dead?"

"According to the report, he was killed a week and a half ago," Valri said.

"How did it happen?" Krys asked, still trying to come to grips with the information.

"According to the detectives who were pursuing him, Elmer was in a car accident. And there was a woman with him," Valri added. "He was fleeing the police and going over a hundred miles an hour. I guess Bluebeard bought into his own legend and thought he had a charmed life. According to the official report, he lost control of his car, and that's when he flipped it over an embankment. When the police finally managed to reach them and pull them out, they were both hurt," Valri said.

Right now, heaven help her, Krys's attention was only focused on Bluebeard. "He could have faked being hurt," was her first thought.

"He could have," Valri agreed, "but he didn't. Someone caught the whole accident on video. They're sending it to me and I'm going to use facial recognition on it to make sure we're dealing with the genuine article and that no one's trying to put one over on us," she told the duo. "But it does look like he's dead." She could see how frustrated Krys was by this latest development.

"I'll let you know as soon as the body gets here." Valri looked from one face to another. "But you realize what this means, don't you?" she asked, waiting for the information to sink in.

Krys said the first thing that occurred to her. "That no more wealthy widows will be bilked out of their money and then killed for it in order to seal the deal."

"Well yes, there is that," Valri granted. "But it also—"

"It also means that if he was killed a week and a half ago, he wasn't the one who tried to kill you recently. And in case there's any doubt, he also wasn't the one who shot Claire," Morgan pointed out.

"What about the woman with him?" Krys asked. "Did she die too as a result of the accident?"

"That hasn't been determined yet. She was alive when the ambulance took her to the hospital, but they confessed that they lost track of her after Bluebeard was declared dead," Valri said.

"So she just disappeared?" Morgan asked, trying to get the story straight.

"Apparently," Valri told him. "The hospital and the police are trying to sort all that out."

"Meanwhile," Morgan said, "We're losing sight of the big picture." When Krys looked at him quizzically, he said, "We still have someone out there who seems to want you dead."

Krys merely shrugged as if that was of no consequence to her.

Valri looked at the other woman in surprise. "Why don't you look more upset?" she asked. Maybe the full import of this development hadn't sunk in yet, she thought. "This means the killer is still out there, waiting to take you down."

"I know what it means," Krys answered. "But it also means that we're not any worse off than we were before, and at least now a lot of families out there finally get to have closure," she pointed out.

Morgan shook his head. "You either have nerves of steel, or you haven't grasped the full seriousness of the situation yet," he told Krys.

"Oh, I grasp it all right," Krys assured him. "But I choose to make the best of it."

Morgan glanced over toward his cousin, and shook his head. "You are one strange, strange lady, Kowalski." And then he told Valri, "Call me the minute the body gets here."

"You might want to relay that message to Toni and Uncle Sean," Valri told Morgan. "They're the ones who are going to be handling the autopsy as well as the body in general."

"What about the missing woman?" Krys asked. "Is anyone trying to find out what happened to her?"

"So far, no one seems to know," Valri admitted.

"Maybe he kidnapped her and when she saw her chance, she wound up killing him," Morgan said.

"That would definitely be poetic justice," Krys agreed.

Morgan looked at Krys. "You know you, when the body gets here, you don't have to—"

She didn't let him get any further. "The hell I don't," Krys declared, anticipating what he was about to say. "All those families of those pitiful, unfortunate 'brides' aren't the only ones who want closure. I've been waiting for this day for a long time," she told Morgan. "I chased after these stories until I felt as if I was a member of all those dead women's families and that this was being done to me, too."

Morgan had been in that same position as well, having gotten so caught up in a case that he needed resolution as much as the victim's families did. He knew all about that edict of not allowing a case to get personal, but being human, he couldn't always keep things at a distance.

So he wasn't about to waste words to try to talk Krys out of feeling that way. Krys was a big girl and knew her own mind.

"I guess we'd better go back and give Toni the 'good' news," he said to Krys.

"I already took care of that for you," Valri told her cousin.

He should have known, Morgan thought. "You notify Uncle Sean, too?" he asked.

She surprised him by saying, "No, I left that for you. I've got to get back to my own work sometime," she said, nodding at the papers spread out on her desk.

"And here I thought you thrived on multitasking," Morgan told her with a grin.

"Thank you for everything," Krys told her, stopping short of hugging the computer expert.

"Don't thank me until we get whoever's after you off the street and put away," Valri replied.

The next moment the woman was completely immersed in her work.

"You look a little shell-shocked," Morgan said to Krys as they left the computer lab.

She didn't hear him at first, not until she realized he was talking to her and played back his words in her head. "I am," she admitted.

"You want to talk about it?" he suggested.

"Not really." Then, because he was including her in this investigation and she felt she owed him an explanation, Krys said, "You know how you feel when you've spent such a long time waiting for something to happen and when it finally does, it doesn't seem as if it's actually real?"

"Yes?" Morgan acknowledged, waiting for her to continue.

"Well, that's how I feel right now. I've been waiting for that guy to pay for what he's done and now that he's gone, somehow it doesn't feel like it's real." She pressed her lips together and then suddenly, she shook her head as if to shed the thought. "I don't have the luxury of trying to dwell and wallow in the feeling. Nik is going to be back in less than a week and there's still this killer out there who has to be found and put away before she gets back."

She wasn't worried about herself. She was worried about her sister, he thought. That put her in a class by herself.

"Like I said, don't worry," he told her. "Everyone's on this."

She realized that he had gotten into the elevator. This wasn't where he'd said they were going. "Shouldn't we be going to see your uncle to tell him that Valri located Bluebeard's body and it would be arriving here by tomorrow morning?" she asked.

"I decided that notifying him and his team would amount to overkill," Morgan told her. "You'd be surprised at how fast word travels here. Incredibly fast."

"But Valri said you should tell him," she reminded Morgan. "So don't you think—?"

He knew what she was going to ask and he shook his head. "I know Valri. She said that purely for your benefit." He knew that his cousin probably viewed it as reinforcement, to make Krys feel as if the situation was proceeding the way it should.

For her part, Krys wasn't sure that she understood. "My benefit?"

He nodded. "So you wouldn't think that we were dropping the ball now that Bluebeard was dead," he told her. Pausing, he added, "You did come across as being rather antsy."

She supposed that he had a point. "Because until I see that monster's body buried, I'm not going to relax for a second," she confessed. Krys paused for a moment, then made a decision. "I know you're going to think I'm pushing too hard, but—"

"You want to go and officially tell Sean about the body coming," Morgan guessed.

"Yes," she said with feeling.

He took a breath and then said, "All right. Far be it from me to deny you a simple request," he told her. "You want to notify Sean, we'll go notify Sean."

"Thank you," she told him.

"Don't mention it," he told her.

Dutifully, Morgan went to where the crime scene investigation unit was housed, in the basement next to the computer lab. He notified Sean about the body that would be arriving at the morgue the next morning.

Sean, who for all the world resembled a younger version of Brian, the Chief of Detectives, looked properly impressed. "So they finally have an identity?" he marveled.

"That's what Valri said," Morgan told him.

"This is fast, even for us," Sean couldn't help commenting. He looked at Krys. "You know, I think that the stars just aligned themselves for our benefit this time." Sean smiled at the journalist who had been relentlessly pursuing this story from the beginning. "Maybe you turned out to be lucky for all of us." And then Sean turned toward his nephew. "When's the body due in?" he asked.

It was Krys who answered his question. "The plane will land first thing tomorrow morning. Valri said someone would call us when it finally arrived."

Sean nodded. "That would be my department," he said. "Once the body is delivered, I'll notify the ME on duty."

"Toni?" Krys guessed.

Sean nodded. "Toni, or whoever will be on duty tomorrow."

"Could I make a request that it be Toni?" Krys asked.

Morgan glanced at Krys. "Any special reason you would want her?" he asked.

"Actually, yes," she answered. "I already know her and I won't have any qualms about asking Toni questions. If there's another ME on duty, that ME might have a problem with answering my questions. After all, I'm not part of the department."

"Getting Toni shouldn't be a problem," Sean assured her. "But if it makes you feel better, I'll put in an official request for Toni to be on duty."

Her smile, Morgan caught himself thinking as she flashed it at his uncle, was positively sunny.

"I'd really appreciate that," she told the CSI unit head.

"My pleasure," Sean said with sincerity.

"Okay," Morgan declared, slipping his hand against her waist and beginning to guide Krys toward the hallway. "I think we've made enough progress for one day," he told her as well as his uncle. "Time for you to go home."

Krys began to protest Morgan's decision, but her body was worn out and completely exhausted. All this had taken a lot out of her.

"You might want to listen to him," Sean advised her, reading her expression. "Morgan is easygoing, but he's been known to browbeat people on occasion," he said, his mouth curving in amusement. "It's not a pretty sight, trust me."

"I'll keep that in mind," she told the man, taking her leave. As soon as they were alone and heading toward the elevator, she told Morgan, "I like your uncle."

"Which one?" Morgan asked innocently.

Krys began to protest that there was only one man she could be referring to, but then she stopped. "I forgot you had a whole slew of uncles," she confessed. "I'm talking about the one I first met when this whole thing got started. Your Uncle Sean."

Morgan's smile was genuine. "I'll be sure to let him know."

"I didn't say that so you could flatter him," she pointed out. "I just wanted to say that I thought he was a really nice guy."

"He is," Morgan told her. "Especially given what he's gone through when he was younger."

That immediately piqued her curiosity. "Why?" she asked. "What did he go through when he was younger?"

Morgan remembered hearing the story when he was a lot younger. "Uncle Sean was the one who the hospital had gotten mixed up at birth."

They were on the first floor now and she stared at Morgan as they got off the elevator. "Come again?"

"When Uncle Sean's mother, my grandmother, gave birth to him, there was another baby born in the hospital at the exact same time. Somehow, because of their same coloring and size, not to mention that the parents' last names were similar, Uncle Sean and the other baby were mixed up at birth."

"So what happened?" Krys asked. "How did the mix-up finally come to light?" She couldn't begin to imagine how that had all gotten untangled.

"Well, it didn't, not for a long time, actually. As it turned out, the other baby, the one the family all *thought* was Uncle Sean, died before his first birthday. The funny thing was, Grandpa's wife always swore there was a mix-up, that the baby the hospital handed to her wasn't hers.

"Eventually, thanks to DNA tests, the mistake finally came to light, although not before Grandma died. As for Uncle Sean, he always claimed that he felt as if he was 'different' from the family he was supposedly 'born' into. Eventually," he told her, "mistakes surface, even if it does take a long time."

She laughed, shaking her head. "Certainly can't say that you people aren't interesting," Krys commented.

He thought of the phone call he was planning to make later on in the evening, once Krys finally went to bed. Uncle Andrew was really going to enjoy meeting this one. "No, you certainly can't say that."

She gave him a look. "I know what you're trying to do."

The first thing he thought of was that she had guessed he was going to ask his Uncle Andrew to throw a party introducing her to everyone despite her protests, but he decided not to admit as much until she confronted him with it.

"And what am I planning to do?" he asked as he drove Krys to her home.

She answered him seriously. "You're trying to divert me with these bits and pieces of family history so I'm not focusing on the fact that the person I thought was trying to kill me turned out to be dead and we're back to square one."

Morgan was about to deny it, then thought better of it. "I guess you caught me," he told her. "Seems like this is one time a Kowalski is smarter that a Cavanaugh."

"I don't know about smarter, but at least I know when I'm being snowed," she told him.

"I guess I won't try to do that again," he said innocently. "Want to pick up something to eat on the way home?"

"Are you in the mood for Chinese?" Krys asked.

"I'm in the mood for food," he answered. "It doesn't matter what kind."

"Okay," she agreed with a grin, appreciating what he was trying to do, "mystery food it is."

Chapter Fifteen

Morgan looked over toward Krys's desk. She had been sitting there for most of the evening. She'd even eaten most of her take-out Chinese dinner there while working on her laptop. So far, he had noticed her head drooping at least three separate times. At least one of those times he had been certain that she had fallen asleep, but then her head had popped up because she had managed to wake herself.

"Maybe you should think about packing it in and going to bed," Morgan suggested when he saw her subtly trying to smother a yawn.

Krys looked as if he'd just insulted her. "I'm a little too old to need someone telling me to go to bed," she informed him. "And I wish you'd stop doing it." It was not the first time he had told her that she should go to bed. She was particularly irritated because deep down, part of her agreed with him, but she'd be damned if she was going to come right out and say as much. "But hey, if you're so obsessed about being tired, maybe you're the one who should go to bed."

Morgan merely smiled at her. After all the time he had put in on stakeouts, he was well versed in the fine art of catching a few winks whenever they were available.

"Don't worry about me," he said to Krys. "I can always grab a catnap or two whenever I feel the need for one."

Krys squared her shoulders. "Well, the same goes for me," she informed him, struggling to stifle another yawn. "As a matter of fact, I'm as fresh as a daisy."

Right, he thought. *If that daisy was about to fold up and wilt.* However, wanting to avoid an argument, he kept his opinion to himself.

Five minutes later, Krys gave up the ghost and had closed her eyes again. This time, though, they remained closed. The sound of the dedicated journalist's even breathing told him that she had lost her battle against Morpheus.

While she had been busy trying *not* to fall asleep, Morgan had been busy with his own work. He had been reviewing all the available surveillance footage that had been gathered from the nearby area where Claire had gone for her morning jog. When he finally spotted something that looked like it might provide a clue as to what had gone down, he enlarged it.

Staring at the photo from every possible angle and trying to get a clearer view, he started to think that he was going cross-eyed.

"Hey, Kowalski," Morgan said, not looking in her direction. "What does this look like to you?"

When she made no response, Morgan raised his voice and asked her the same question again. Still not receiving an answer, he looked over toward her. Apparently, she had fallen asleep and continued to remain that way rather than jolting awake.

"How about that?" he murmured under his breath in surprise. "I guess you really were tired this time."

Krys had folded her arms in front of her to lay down her head just for a moment and had, apparently, instantly fallen asleep.

Morgan rose to his feet and crossed over to her desk to check her out before he made the logical assumption.

Circling her from both sides to make sure he wasn't making a mistake, he grinned to himself. She continued sleeping.

He debated between waking her up so she could finally go to bed and just leaving her where she was. But from where he stood, neither solution was acceptable. If he did wake her up, since she was so incredibly stubborn, for all he knew she just might deliberately force herself to remain awake. And if he left her where she was, sleeping with her head on the desk, she could very well wind up having one hell of a crick in her neck when she woke up in the morning.

There was a third alternative.

"Looks like I'm going to have to put you to bed whether you like it or not," he told her softly. He sighed, shaking his head. "You know, Kowalski, this would be a whole lot easier if you weren't so damn stubborn."

Moving very carefully so he wouldn't wake her, Morgan bent down and slipped one arm just beneath her legs, another around her shoulders. And then, very slowly, he picked her up.

"C'mon, Sleeping Beauty," he quietly whispered. "Your bed-chamber awaits."

With that, moving at an extremely slow pace so as not to wake her up, Morgan carried Krys to her bedroom. Halfway there, he froze as she murmured something under her breath and then curled up against his chest.

He had just started walking again when she tucked her arm around his neck and sighed.

Morgan couldn't help reacting to the feel of her body up against his, to the scent of her hair as it seemed to curl its way through his senses. Most of all, he had a hard time resisting the very strong pull of desire that insisted on telegraphing itself throughout his entire body.

"You do know how to make this hard on a guy, Kowalski," he whispered softly to the woman he was holding in his arms.

Making certain not to jostle her as he walked, Morgan very carefully made his way into her bedroom and then, bending over in a painfully slow manner, he laid Krys down on her bed.

Once he had her on her bed, Morgan didn't even attempt to take off her shoes, much less any other article of clothing. He just spread a blanket over her because the nights were still getting chilly this time of year and he didn't want Krys getting cold.

Morgan withdrew from the room very quietly, eased the door and then managed to tiptoe away.

He returned to the sofa in the living room where he had been keeping vigil at night.

Time to get back to his post.

But first, before he made himself comfortable for the night,

Morgan had one more thing that he wanted to take care of. Taking out his cell phone, he pressed buttons on the keypad that he was so familiar with he could do it in his sleep. Having completed the sequence, he waited while the phone rang on the other end.

When it finally did, he heard it quickly being answered.

"Morgan," the deep, resonant voice on the other end of the phone said. "Is anything wrong? You don't usually call at this time of night. Or, for that matter, you don't really call at all," Andrew noted. "What can I do for you?"

"No, nothing's wrong," Morgan quickly told the former chief of police. He paused, looking for the right words. All of this had seemed so much clearer in his head, but now that he had the man on the phone, he found himself slightly at a loss for words. He decided the best course of action was to dive right in. "Um, I don't know how much you've heard through our family grapevine, but it turns out that Finn's new wife, Nikki, has a twin sister."

He heard Andrew's deep laugh resonate against his ear. "Yes, I've heard," Andrew replied. "I'm retired from the police force, Morgan. I'm not dead. I doubt if there's anything you can tell me about this young woman that I don't already know. I have my sources."

The thing of it was, Morgan thought, his uncle was probably right. The man did have his finger on the pulse of events concerning things that had to do with the police department and all the people connected to it, *especially* his family.

"Sorry, I didn't mean to insult you," Morgan apologized. "The truth of it is, I didn't want to take anything for granted."

Andrew chuckled again. "No need to apologize, Morgan. You were just being thorough. That's what makes you a good cop. Now, is that the main reason you called, to let me know about Krys, or is there something else?"

"There's something else," Morgan admitted.

"Ah. Well, let's have it. The night's not getting any younger," he prompted, "and neither am I."

"How would you like to have an excuse to throw one of those famous family get-togethers of yours?" Morgan asked, then quickly began to explain, "I don't usually like to impose like this, but—"

"Morgan?" Andrew said, raising his voice and cutting through his nephew's rhetoric before he could get carried away.

Morgan abruptly stopped. "Yes, sir?"

"How hard have your superiors been working you lately?" Andrew asked.

The question caught him up short. "I don't understand, sir."

"I figure they had to be working you hard in order to make you forget how much I enjoy having everyone over to the house for a party," Andrew explained. Then he got down to the crux of the matter. "Since when do you feel the need to tiptoe around asking me to have a family party? This is me, boy. I neither need nor want an excuse. Just a simple 'go-ahead' is more than sufficient.

"Now, is there a specific reason we're having this gathering, or is it just because you suddenly have an overwhelming craving for one of my dishes?"

There was no conceit involved in the question, just genuine curiosity.

"Nikki's twin sister is being stalked," Morgan began, then stopped. "I know you already know that."

Rather than confirm the assumption or remind him about what he had just said earlier, Andrew merely told his nephew, "Go on."

"I thought it might make Krys feel less alone right now if she met some more of the family and felt their support. And since you put on the best spread in town, I thought that might just be an added bonus for her."

"Not that I needed an excuse," Andrew told his nephew, "but it's always nice to know the reason behind why something is being requested. So, any particular time you'd like me to throw this little shindig?" he asked.

He felt that he had already made enough requests of his uncle. "Whatever works for you, Uncle Andrew, is fine."

"All right then, we'll make it the same time as always. Any time after eleven in the morning," Andrew told him. "So, anything else?"

"Yes. How do you do it, Uncle Andrew?" Morgan asked the man, curious.

"How do I do what?" Andrew asked.

"Feed the masses the way you do. There always seems to be

enough food put out to feed everyone no matter how many of us show up and how many servings we take."

"Number one, I like to cook and number two, everyone always chips in whatever amount they can whenever they can. They do it out of courtesy. Otherwise—" Andrew laughed "—I would have had to sell the house a long time ago." Morgan could have sworn he heard the grin in his uncle's voice. "You people do tend to eat like piranhas."

"Sell the house, eh?" Morgan repeated. "Ever consider not putting out such a huge spread anymore?" he questioned.

"Nope, never once," Andrew answered. "I enjoy cooking, enjoy feeding my family and really enjoy their company. As far as I'm concerned, for me this is a win-win situation," Andrew admitted. "So, this Sunday all right with you?"

"This Sunday is perfect for me," Morgan said with enthusiasm. "Thanks for doing this, Uncle Andrew."

"Thanks for asking me to do it," Andrew responded. "Nothing I like better than having an excuse to get everyone together."

Morgan thought of something. "You planning on throwing another one of these parties when Nik and Finn get back?"

Tickled, Andrew laughed heartily. "You'd better believe I am," he told Morgan. And then he paused for a moment as he listened to a melodic voice calling him in the background. "That sounds like my better half calling me. I'd better go—unless there's something else you need to tell me."

"No, that's it for now, sir. As long as you tell me if you need anything from me for this thing," Morgan thought to add.

"I will," Andrew promised. "All right, then," he said, "Sunday." Just before he hung up, Andrew told his nephew, "Keep her safe, Morgan."

"I am doing my best," Morgan told him.

"Can't ask for more than that," Andrew said as he ended the call.

You can if your best isn't good enough, Morgan thought for no apparent reason, putting his cell phone back in his pocket.

They were making progress. They had a name, and presumably a body to go along with that name, for the man who had been known as Bluebeard. But that still didn't help them find whoever had attempted to kill Krys not once but twice.

"Who were you just talking to?" Krys asked, suddenly walking into the living room. Her appearance caught Morgan off guard. After all, she'd been sound asleep a few minutes ago.

Surprised, Morgan asked, "What are you doing up?"

"The question is," Krys corrected him, "what was I doing down in the first place? I woke up to find myself in bed. The last thing I remember, I was sitting at my desk, working on the latest installment of my article about Weatherly's so-called miracle drug. I'm planning on dedicating it to Claire," she told him as an aside. "Now, how did I get into bed?" she asked.

He grinned. "Well, you fell asleep. I tried to wake you up. When you didn't, I carried you to bed."

Her mouth fell open. "You did not," she argued.

"Sure I did," Morgan insisted. "You found yourself in bed, didn't you?" he pointed out.

"No, I mean you didn't try to wake me up," she told him.

"You're just a hardier sleeper than you think you are," Morgan told her. Krys went on staring at him. "Okay, okay, I said your name but I didn't really try to wake you up. The way I saw it, if you actually wound up falling asleep, you were too exhausted to be staying up. Any work you did would have to be redone." He could see he hadn't convinced her. "What's the harm in letting you sleep? It's not like you were goofing off. You put in more than a full day and headway was made today. Things were discovered."

"I still have to get this article done," she pointed out. "The time to get this in is running out."

"You put too much pressure on yourself," Morgan insisted. "You can't do your best work if you're tired," he told her.

"Said the man who doesn't sleep."

"I sleep," he told her. "I just ration it out and do it during lulls."

"Yeah, yeah, I'll believe it when I see it," she told Morgan.

"Well, since you're up," he said, attempting to change the subject, "I do have something to run past you."

"What?" she asked suspiciously.

"An invitation."

Instant wariness telegraphed itself throughout her body and she froze. Krys realized that she was growing more and more attracted to Morgan, but that attraction created a whole new set of problems as far as she could see. Problems that could undoubtedly only get worse. And that was a minefield that she wanted to avoid walking through, at least for the time being.

"Look, Cavanaugh, I'm very flattered," she told him, trying very hard to be kind about this, "but I think in view of family harmony, I'm going to have to turn you down, at least for now."

He stared at her, confused. "Turn me down?"

"Yes. Turn you down. For that date you're asking me out on," she said, clarifying what she meant by increments.

"Well, I guess that's rather fortunate for both of us." Morgan said.

"How so?" Krys questioned.

Morgan smiled at her. This was a definite mix-up. "Well, because for one thing, I'm not asking you to go out with me."

Her eyebrows drew together. She tried not to pay attention to the wave of embarrassment. "Then what was this invitation all about?"

"Remember I mentioned my Uncle Andrew's parties? Well, he's having one this Sunday and he wanted me to extend an invitation to you."

He was grinning now. Broadly.

Chapter Sixteen

Krys could feel warning signals going off in her head.

"Did he specifically ask that I be there?" she asked. "Or did you *suggest* that I be there?"

Morgan didn't believe in lying, but he didn't want to make it sound as if he'd had to talk his uncle into including her. She definitely wouldn't go then.

"What does it matter which came first, the chicken or the egg?" he asked her. "The main thing is that Uncle Andrew is going to be throwing a party this coming Sunday and he would really like to have you attend so that he can finally get to meet you. By the way, Uncle Andrew has a high opinion of your sister," he threw in for good measure.

"Well, that's nice to hear, but it seems like a lot of trouble for him to go to in order just to meet me," she countered. "If it's all the same to him, why don't I just swing by wherever he lives tomorrow before I go to my interview?"

Morgan stopped her before she was off and verbally running.

"First of all, Uncle Andrew doesn't see it as a lot of trouble—he likes nothing more than 'cooking for the masses.' And second of all, when were you going to tell me about this interview that you're conducting tomorrow? Who is it that you're planning on interviewing?" he asked.

She could feel her back going up, but she told herself that Morgan was just focused on doing his job, even though she didn't like being held accountable by someone, even Morgan.

"I didn't realize that I was supposed to ask your permission before I did something. I said that I was going to be talking to more people in connection with this article and after what happened to Claire, the other interviews had to be postponed." She sighed, doing her best to get her temper under control. "But since you asked, specifically I've got an appointment to speak with Lawrence Jacobs, the head of the drug research team at Weatherly Pharmaceuticals. The appointment is at two o'clock tomorrow. He's granting me a fifteen-minute window. According to him," she said, less than pleased about the way things were playing themselves out, "it's all he can spare. There. Now you know everything."

He sincerely doubted that, but he kept the observation to himself. Instead, he asked a far more practical question. "And you think that fifteen minutes is enough time for this interview?"

"It's going to have to be," she told him with a sigh. "Besides, I can talk very fast."

He could testify to that, he thought. But there was one other small problem. "He might not answer fast."

"I can also tell if someone is stonewalling me," she told the detective, adding, "I can be very direct and I intend to ask Jacobs if he knew that Claire intended to change her statement about the accuracy of the test results."

Now there was a bomb waiting to go off, Morgan thought. "In other words, you're planning on poking at Jacobs with a stick."

"I'm planning on poking him with whatever I need to use in order to find out if he had any part in eliminating Claire because she posed a threat to the success of his miracle drug." It was all about the bottom line, she thought. With any luck, she'd get a few answers tomorrow.

He frowned, shaking his head. "I don't think that's a good idea," Morgan told her. "But I know you won't listen to me."

"Glad we understand each other," she said with finality because, come hell or high water, she intended to see Jacobs and get him talking. Who knew where that might lead?

"I really doubt that, but I know enough to pick my battles," Morgan told her. "However, I am coming with you so at least Jacobs realizes that the police department is committed to protecting you."

She shook her head. "No, you're not," she declared. "I let you come with me to the other interviews, but this is the head honcho we're talking about, the guy who makes things happen. I'm lucky to get him to agree to see me at all." She was walking a tightrope with this. "He certainly won't talk to me if you're there."

But Morgan wasn't about to budge on this point. "Too bad," he said in a deceptively mild voice. "He's going to have to learn."

The man was infuriating. Didn't he see what was at stake here? She tried to bargain with Morgan. "Okay, I'll go with you to this family gathering of yours if you back off about the interview. I *need* to do this."

His expression never changed, but Morgan continued to hold fast. "Sorry, nonnegotiable, Kowalski. I go with you on that interview, or you don't go."

Her eyes flashed. "I don't need a mother hen hovering over me," Krys all but shouted at him.

"No, you need a keeper," he informed her in an easygoing voice. "End of story."

She curled her hands into fists, frustrated beyond words. "But—!"

He rose, towering over her, the immovable object confronting the irresistible force. "Look, I am *not* explaining to your sister when she comes back from her honeymoon how you happened to wind up dead even though there were enough warning signs for even a simpleton to realize that you were playing with fire. Now, I either come with you when you talk to Jacobs, or you don't go. It's as simple as that.

"Don't forget," he pointed out in a voice that was so low-key it made her want to scream, "Claire was killed—murdered—in Aurora. That makes this the police department's case. *My* case, since you all but dropped it in my lap."

She blew out a ragged breath. "I'm not going to win this, am I?"

The smile he gave her just managed to further incense her. "There will be arguments in the future that you will win," he told her in a tolerant voice. "Probably a lot of them, given how stubborn you are, but you're not winning this one, no," he confirmed her suspicion. "I'll even pretend to be your assistant again if that helps to make my presence more acceptable to this CEO."

She uttered a totally exasperated sound, then said, "Okay, you win. I surrender," Krys said. She pressed her lips together, making a decision. "Now I guess I'll get some rest or I'll wind up falling asleep in the middle of the interview tomorrow."

"Good idea," Morgan said, nodding. "Good night," he told her, saying the words to her back as she walked away, heading to her bedroom.

He was surprised when she remained there.

KRYS STAYED IN her bedroom until a few minutes past five in the morning. At that point, she was fairly confident that Morgan had probably fallen asleep, taking one of his "catnaps." The house had been still for a while now. There was no sound coming from anywhere, other than the intermittent hum of the refrigerator in the kitchen whenever it turned over for a few minutes.

Rising out of bed in slow motion, Krys got dressed even slower and quieter. She took care not to disturb anything that might create a noise that would alert her infuriating bodyguard. She knew Morgan had a job to do, but she had a job to do as well.

She supposed that in an odd sort of way, those jobs overlapped. Someone had killed Claire just because the woman chose to tell the truth and Claire had chosen to tell that truth to *her*.

If she hadn't prodded, Claire would be alive. She was still having trouble containing her guilt over that. At the very least, she owed the woman something for what had happened to her. She intended to get to the bottom of this, never mind that the same person who killed Claire might also be trying to kill her.

All because almighty *profits* were being threatened.

She was the first to admit that she liked money as much as anyone, but certainly not at the expense of someone's life. That just couldn't be allowed to happen, Krys silently swore.

Lord, she had never gotten dressed this slowly, she thought. Even as a kid, she would hurry into her clothes, whether she was going out to play, or to school, or just to run errands for her father. Moving this slowly was killing her. Her arms practically ached as she slipped on her two-piece suit, shoes and dark-colored pantyhose. She wanted to look conservative and presentable for this interview.

At the last minute, she decided to carry her shoes rather than wear them so her heels wouldn't make noise on the tile that lined the entranceway.

Carrying her shoes in one hand, her laptop slung over her shoulder and held fast with the other, Krys held her breath as she almost silently tiptoed past Morgan.

She had her hand on the doorknob and was about to open the front door when she heard Morgan's resonant voice calmly ask, "Going somewhere?"

Her heart slammed against her chest and she froze, then slowly turned around, fury in her eyes as she glared at Morgan.

"How long have you been awake?" she demanded.

"The entire time that you were engineering your great escape." She found his smile irritating beyond words. "I was never asleep."

Her initial surprise gave way to anger. "Then why didn't you say something?"

"I just wanted to see how far you were going to carry out this little pantomime of yours. I'm impressed," he said as he rose and crossed to her. "I didn't know you could move that quietly, or that slowly. Although, if you had made it out the door, the surveillance detail I have posted would have stopped you."

Damn it. She'd been so focused on getting out without waking him, she'd forgotten all about the protective detail he had told her about.

"I'm glad you find me so entertaining, Cavanaugh," she retorted.

Standing beside her now, he looked down into her face. "Oh, trust me, Kowalski, I find you a lot of things."

For a moment, she could have sworn he was going to kiss her, the way he had when she had broken down about Claire. But then that moment was gone and her eyes were boring holes into him.

"Now what?" she asked.

"Well, that's up to you. But since you're all dressed, I'd suggest that we go out and have breakfast and then begin our day. You did mention that there were some other people you wanted to talk to before you interviewed that mucky-muck who walks on pharmaceutical water."

He wasn't calling Jacobs anything that she hadn't already thought of in her head, but for the time being, she was holding her animosity in check. She didn't know if he could do the same—and it was important for her article that he could. "I think you'll have to put a lid on your attitude if this is going to work. Otherwise, you'll wind up getting us kicked out of the building."

"Don't worry," he reassured her. "I can be charming if I have to be."

Something warm undulated through her as her eyes met his. "Yes, I know."

Morgan's smile drifted up into his eyes. "I'll take that as a compliment."

She was going to have to watch that, Krys warned herself. This wasn't the first time he had caused her guard to slip.

Drawing her shoulders back, she told him, "Take that any way you want to."

Morgan merely continued smiling at her.

Krys was extremely glad they were about to get out of the house. The way she was feeling right now, it wasn't safe remaining here with him. She was completely aware that there were police officers in the vicinity, watching her house—watching her—but that didn't help her situation right now, not when Morgan was right here, up close and personal and practically in her very shadow.

A few minutes later they were all ready to leave to grab a quick breakfast before she got started going to her interviews when Morgan's cell phone rang.

"Cavanaugh," Morgan said as he swiped opened his phone.

Morgan saw that the incoming call was from the CSI unit head. He didn't know whether to relax or brace himself.

"You asked me to call you when Bluebeard's body arrived," Sean told his nephew.

Krys saw Morgan glance in her direction. She was instantly alert.

"What is it?" she asked.

Morgan didn't bother to cover the microphone. "It's the CSI unit chief," he told her, then said, "The body just arrived."

Everything except for her two o'clock interview was immediately put on hold in her brain. She could reschedule the other interviews. This was more important.

"Let's go," she urged, then headed for the front door.

"You guessed it. She definitely wants to see the body. Right," he confirmed. "We're on our way."

Krys waited for him to open up his vehicle. "He didn't think I'd want to come?" she asked, getting in on the passenger side. She'd thought she'd made that clear the other day.

"It's not that," Morgan told her, getting in on the driver's side. "He just didn't think you were going to almost break your neck getting to view the dead body."

She looked at Morgan as he started up his vehicle. "I want to be sure it's him, and I want to be sure he's dead," she told him. "Now let's go."

Morgan gave her a little salute as he pulled out of her driveway. "Your wish, Kowalski, is my command."

Settling back in the passenger seat, she blew out a deep breath.

"Something wrong?" Morgan asked her.

"No, nothing," she said. "I just still can't believe he's dead."

"Well, someone in that coffin certainly is," he told her drolly.

Krys stared straight ahead, different thoughts going through her head. "I spent more than nine months chasing after that man's story, putting the pieces together, making sure that all those different men were actually one and the same person. And now I've got the final proof. It's hard to believe it's really finally over," she said in a dazed voice. She turned to look at Morgan. "They're sure it's him, right?"

"They're sure," he told her. "The fingerprints match. It's him."

She shook her head as realization sank in. "So many families are going to be relieved. I feel like I should give Valri something for all the hard work she did," she told Morgan suddenly.

"Valri won't accept it," he told her. "She'd be the first one to tell you that she was just doing her job and that seventy-five percent of this kind of thing is pure luck."

"Uh-huh." Krys slanted a look at him. "There's no need to be so modest. There're no points off if you or Valri *don't* take a huge bite of humble pie." She firmly believed that people needed to take credit where credit was due.

"No humble pie," Morgan assured her. "It's just the way we were raised."

They arrived quickly. Morgan paused after he got out of his car, and he looked at Krys intently. "Are you ready for this?"

"I've been ready for this for a long time," she assured him.

But as she got off the elevator, walking beside Morgan, her hand dropped to her side as her breath backed up in her throat.

She felt Morgan take her hand, slipping his fingers through hers and tightening them. He didn't say anything, but the simple action spoke volumes to her.

Taking a deep breath, she nodded her head slightly and then began to walk down the corridor, straight to the morgue.

Sean and Toni were waiting for them when they came into the room. Krys's eyes were immediately drawn toward the body that was on the table.

"Is that him?" she asked in a whisper.

"That's what the paperwork that came with him said," Toni told her. "They did an autopsy on him, but there were some things that were left unaddressed. I want to conduct my own autopsy on the man, but I thought you'd want to see him first."

Krys said nothing as she approached the body of the man who had caused so much grief and pain.

"Doesn't look like the kind of man who could sweet talk women out of their life savings and their common sense, does he?" Krys asked in a hushed voice.

"Most con artists don't," Sean told her.

"What about the woman?" Krys asked suddenly. Looking up, she turned toward Sean. "The report said that he had a woman with him. Do we have any details at all about her? Do you think she was his next victim?"

"We don't know that yet," Sean told them honestly. "Nothing's been determined. Speculation is that he had kidnapped her and was fleeing with her when the police caught up to him. Most likely, he was planning on using her as a shield or perhaps as leverage to get the police to let him go."

That sounded likely, Morgan thought. "So where is she?" he asked.

"Well, that's the other thing," Sean told them. "When the police came to get her statement at the hospital, they couldn't find her. Apparently, she was gone. Nobody saw her leave and so far, nobody has been able to find her."

"But they are looking, right?" Krys asked.

"They're looking," Sean confirmed. "But the problem is that everyone was so focused on bringing Bluebeard here in, nobody really got a good look at his hostage. Consequently, they don't have a viable description of her and aren't really sure just who they're looking for."

"So this still isn't over," Krys said as she turned toward Morgan. "But at least he didn't get a chance to kill her. That is something." She saw that as a victory. Krys said the words more to herself than to anyone else in the room.

Chapter Seventeen

Myriad questions raced through her brain, jockeying for position. She hardly knew what to ask first.

"Do we have an exact cause of death yet?" she finally asked the medical examiner.

"That much we have," Toni told them, glancing at the autopsy report. "Apparently Bluebeard broke his neck when his car went over the hill. What I'm really surprised about, I have to admit, is that the woman wasn't killed along with him."

Krys shook her head. "That we know of," she pointed out. "For all we know, the woman might have died later, after she took off from the hospital," she commented. "As for Bluebeard's fate, if you ask me, it couldn't have happened to a more deserving person."

Pausing, she looked at Toni. "So you're not satisfied with the autopsy report that was done on Bluebeard?" she questioned. She was glad that Toni was performing a second autopsy, but she was curious about the medical examiner's reasons.

"Well, I hate pointing fingers," Toni said. "But to be honest, the autopsy that was done appears to have been rather slapdash, and since two of the man's victims were Aurora citizens, I think it might be a good idea for the department to perform an autopsy of their own. What do you think?" she asked Sean, turning toward the CSI unit leader.

"Seeing how many women were killed by this man, if there are *any* unanswered questions about this killer, I vote 'go ahead,'" Sean told the medical examiner.

Toni nodded. "That's what I'd hoped you'd say." Her eyes shifted toward the other two people in the room. "I'll let you know if I come up with anything new," she promised.

"All right then," Morgan told the medical examiner, "we'll leave you to your work."

"I've got a question," Krys said as they walked out of the morgue.

"Only one?" Morgan asked wryly.

"Oh, I've got more," Krys assured him. "But I'll just ask this one for now."

He stopped at the elevator, pressing the Up button. "Go ahead."

"Who's looking for the woman that scum had with him in the car and supposedly abducted?" she asked.

Morgan had wondered when she'd get around to that. "It's what we're looking into," he told her. "But right now, your guess is as good as mine." He could tell by the expression on her face that this was really bothering Krys. It bothered him as well because of all the questions it raised, but for the moment, there was nothing he could do about that.

The elevator arrived and they got on. Wanting to distract Krys, Morgan asked, "Don't you have those interviews you wanted to conduct?"

He was right. She couldn't allow herself to lose sight of her objective. Bluebeard's story was all but over. She had an obligation to focus on Weatherly Pharmaceutical's "miracle" drug.

One foot in front of the other, Krys told herself. Nodding her head in response to Morgan's question, she said, "I guess I should put this in the 'win' column."

Morgan was in complete agreement with her conclusion. "Considering how many unresolved cases there are each year, this is more than just a win. It's a really big deal."

Arriving on the first floor, she got out of the elevator ahead of him. "I know, I know. But I just can't help wondering about that woman who was with him. What's her story? I can't make sense out of her running off." She turned toward Morgan. "What would make her run away from the hospital like that? For all intents and purposes, she was finally safe."

He had no pat answer for her. "Who knows? Maybe she was totally spooked. Being abducted and then in a car accident, maybe it affected her thinking and she didn't know who to trust." He thought of his Aunt Rose, Uncle Andrew's wife. "Maybe she even got amnesia and everything around her just contributed to her being spooked."

He could see by the look on Krys's face that she was skeptical about his explanation. "Something like that happened to my Uncle Andrew's wife," he told her as they left the building. He headed toward the rear parking lot and his car. "Years ago, she accidentally drove her car over an embankment and plunged right into the lake."

Krys looked at him in horror. "My lord, what happened to her?"

"Well, from what was eventually pieced together, someone saw the accident and managed to save her. But the accident took place far from where she lived and she had no ID on her. Upshot is Aunt Rose was missing for years. But Uncle Andrew never gave up looking for her, never gave up hope of finding her." Every time he heard the story, it just seemed so incredibly remarkable to him. "He followed up every lead he could. Eventually," he concluded, opening his vehicle and getting in, "he managed to stumble across Aunt Rose—totally by accident."

Krys got in on her side. Listening to Morgan tell the story, she came to what she thought was a logical conclusion. "And she recognized him?"

"No," Morgan said. "It took Uncle Andrew a while longer before he could convince Rose that he wasn't trying to take advantage of her, that he really *was* her husband and moreover, that they had five children. In the end, it was getting sprayed in the face by a malfunctioning showerhead that triggered her memory."

That must have really been one hell of a surprise for the woman, Krys thought. "Wow."

Morgan couldn't help smiling. "That was what everyone else in the family said once they heard the story. But fortunately it all ended well."

It was the kind of story that made people believe in happy endings, Krys couldn't help thinking. "You do have a pretty remarkable family."

"It's your family, too, now," Morgan reminded her.

But Krys lifted her shoulders in what amounted to a noncommittal shrug. "That's going to take some getting use to."

"Well, that's what Uncle Andrew's party is for," Morgan told her. And then he changed the subject. "What do you say we get those interviews over with while you're in an upbeat frame of mind," he encouraged.

He wasn't about to get any argument from her, Krys thought.

"NOT EXACTLY WHAT you hoped for, was it?" Morgan asked Krys as they left the last interview site. They had spent what amounted to a totally fruitless day talking to the remaining three out of four test subjects she had managed to unearth.

Krys sighed, shaking her head. "No, but to be honest, it was kind of what I expected."

They walked back to his vehicle. Morgan wasn't quite sure he was following her. "How so?" he asked.

Her smile was weary. "It was as if they were all reading words that were written by the same person from the same script. Oh, they were all slightly different—" she pointed out "—just different enough to make it seem as if they had slightly different things to say," she said. "But all three test subjects who agreed to talk with me made it sound as if they really believed—or were made to believe—that they were part of some groundbreaking process."

Her face clouded over. "If you ask me, they were afraid to say anything different because none of them wanted to wind up like Claire. Dead."

Morgan couldn't argue with her conclusion. "You're right. The department did its best to keep what happened to Claire Williams out of the news, but we failed. One of your journalist buddies broke the story the second that someone leaked it and he was able to get his hands on it."

She frowned, thinking how hearing about Claire's murder must have influenced the people she had talked to today. Fear had obviously been their motivating force. "He wasn't *my* buddy," she corrected him sharply.

"Just a figure of speech," he told her. He didn't mean to insinuate that the person who had broken the story had been someone associated with her inner circle. "At least the people you talked to today seemed like regular people. Frightened," he emphasized, "but real. That Jacobs guy," he said, thinking of the CEO who had been her last interview today, "was like some character who was sent here straight out of Central Casting."

There hadn't been a single genuine thing about the man, Morgan couldn't help thinking. How could someone come across that phony, that caricature-like, and still be breathing?

Krys laughed, but there was no humor in the sound. "You got that feeling, too?" she asked him. "It was as if Jacobs had been programmed to sound like an earnest, hardworking CEO who had nothing but the best of intentions motivating him when it came to the drug his company is working on."

"Not working on," Morgan reminded her. "They're just about ready to launch that thing on the open market. If there's even a *hint* of impropriety with that drug's production, not to mention with Jacobs himself, the company could stand to lose a fortune. That's the only reason Jacobs gave you that fifteen-minute interview instead of telling you to go take a hike. He wants to make it look as if he's cooperating with you, answering your questions and being totally affable so that you walk away from the interview completely satisfied and thinking that cancer drug they're putting out is the just the best thing short of the Second Coming."

"I know," she said with a frustrated sigh. "I totally agree with you. The only problem is that we don't have a shred of evidence to back us up."

He thought of one thing they did have. "You have Claire's original interview."

"Yes, which supposedly she was in the process of rescinding," she reminded him. At least, that was what the woman had initially said to her—just before Claire had called her again and hinted that she had been forced to say that. Krys had the impression that the woman was about to go back on that, but she was never going to know for sure.

Morgan remained where he was, in the Weatherly Pharmaceutical parking lot, thinking about what had just transpired. "Well, we're not going to change anything tonight," he told her. "Right now, what you need is to relax a little, blow off some steam. What do you usually do?"

Her answer was automatic. "I work."

He shook his head, refusing to accept that. "You can't work *all* the time."

"Yes I can," she told him. Then, when he continued looking at her as if he knew better, Krys threw up her hands. "All right, you win. I *don't* work all the time. Sometimes, when I really need a break, I curl up on the sofa with a bowl of popcorn and watch *Casablanca*."

He waited for her to tell him what she really did. When she didn't change her statement, he said, "You're kidding, right?"

Krys frowned. "You asked," she said, slightly insulted by his attitude.

Maybe, as illogical as it seemed to him, that *was* her go-to move.

"No, you're right," he conceded. "I asked. Tell you what, you deserve a break no matter how strange that break seems to me. We'll pick up some popcorn at the grocery store, go home, and I'll download the movie from that internet app I've got. Then you can go to town and knock off some steam by watching—" he took a breath as if saying it was actually painful "—*Casablanca*."

"That's all right," she told him. "You don't have to do that. I'll just work on my article tonight, try to put it in the best light—"

"No," he contradicted her, "I said we're going to do something to help you unwind and a Cavanaugh always lives up to his word. You want *Casablanca*, you'll get *Casablanca*," Morgan told her. "Although why is beyond me."

His determination managed to coax a smile out of Krys. "Don't forget the popcorn," she reminded him.

"Heaven forbid," he said, turning his car toward the closest grocery store.

"So THIS REALLY does it for you?" Morgan asked in amazement. They had returned home and true to his word, he had provided her with popcorn and the classic movie. They had finished almost all of the former and the better part of the latter.

She had settled in against him and was rabidly watching the black-and-white movie.

"Each and every time," Krys answered, never taking her eyes off the wide-screen TV.

"Each and every time, huh?" Morgan repeated. "Just how many times have you watched this movie?" he asked, curious. He couldn't conceive of watching this even once, much less more than that. At least, not willingly.

"Probably ten, maybe eleven times," she told him, making a calculated guess. Her eyes never left the characters on the screen.

"You're kidding," he said, stunned.

"No." She continued watching. "How many times have you seen it?"

"Counting this time?" Morgan asked.

Krys spared him a quick glance before answering, "Yes."

"That's easy," he told her, then answered, "Once."

Her hand stopped mid-dip into the tiny remaining handful of popcorn. Turning toward him, she stared at Morgan as if he had just informed her that he was an alien life form.

"You've never seen *Casablanca*?" she asked him in disbelief.

"Well, I have now," he reminded her. "Or at least most of it."

"But it's a classic," she cried.

Morgan shrugged. "My education has some gaps."

"Apparently," she concluded, looking back at the screen.

Morgan decided that it was better if he just kept silent until she had finished watching the movie. That was why he'd downloaded *Casablanca* for her in the first place, so she could watch it and gather whatever benefits she could from watching what to him was a rather predictable movie—except for the small fact that the hero didn't end up with the heroine when the credits finally rolled by.

After what seemed to him like a long time, the final words, about this being the beginning of a beautiful friendship between Bogart and the policeman, Claude Rains—the only words he was familiar with—were finally uttered.

Thank Heaven! Morgan thought with relief.

Krys, he noticed, had sat riveted through the end, and then through the credits. Wondering how much longer she intended to watch, he turned toward her—which was when Morgan realized that the woman sitting there had wet cheeks. Both of them.

"Are you crying?" he asked in amazement.

"No," she answered in a voice that was close to cracking. "It's raining and I forgot to wear my hat."

"Okay, wise guy," he said, approaching the situation from another angle. "*Why* are you crying? I thought you said that you like this movie."

"I did, I do." Sniffling, she went on to explain, "He did something noble and beautiful for her—he gave her up—because he loved her." Krys let out a long, shaky breath. "Things like that don't happen in real life," she said sadly.

He felt for her. More than that, he could feel himself being drawn to her. "Sometimes they do.".

Her tears were still flowing as she shook her head. "No, they don't," she told him.

Morgan could feel something stirring inside of him no matter how hard he tried to block it. Oh damn, maybe he was going to regret this. But she seemed so unhappy and he really hated seeing her like this.

He had sat through this movie because he wanted her to shake off the frustration she had experienced today, wanted her to be happy, at least for a little while even if it was vicariously.

But that obviously hadn't worked.

In an effort to comfort her, Morgan put his arm around Krys's shoulders.

That was all it was supposed to be at first, just a simple act of comfort. Human contact between two people who had spent a rather frustrating day that had one thing after another piling on top of each other until she was all but buried underneath it.

But that human contact led to something more. Before he was fully aware of it, holding Krys against him had her turning her face up to his. He knew he should have just left it at that, or, if he felt he had to do something, he should have simply brushed his lips against her cheek.

But then she had turned her cheek toward his chest and he wound up kissing her lips. Before he fully realized it, he was full-on kissing her.

Rather than just stopping there, the kiss blossomed into a deeper one.

And an even deeper kiss after that.

Morgan's pulse quickened. He kissed her over and over again until he finally pulled her onto his lap, enfolding her in his arms. He deepened the kiss between them until it felt as if her very soul was touching his and everything that had come before this moment was just a prelude to what was happening between them right now.

No, damn it, he was getting ahead of himself, Morgan's mind all but shouted. He couldn't let this happen even though every part of his soul was begging him not to stop.

He wanted her.

But it didn't matter what he wanted, Morgan silently insisted. He wasn't the one hurting here. He wasn't the one in need of something to raise his spirits and bolster his very soul. He wasn't the one who mattered here. She was and he couldn't allow himself to take advantage of this situation, not if he felt that she was swept away without being given a chance to think.

And he did.

So, as hard as it was, Morgan forced himself to draw back from Krys even as every ounce of his body begged him to stay, to take this to its very logical, very fulfilling conclusion.

And when he did pull away, Krys could only stare at him, utterly stunned.

Chapter Eighteen

Morgan took the surprised look on Krys's face as a clear indication that he had overstepped his boundaries. He hadn't meant to do that, despite the fact that he was really attracted to her, really wanting her.

"I am sorry," he apologized. "I shouldn't have done that. It wasn't very professional of me," he admitted.

"No," she agreed, "it wasn't." Then in a softer voice, she told him, "But it was very nice."

That just added to his confusion. "Then you *didn't* mind?" he asked, trying to understand what was going on in her brain and to reconcile that with what was happening in his. He wanted Krys more than he had ever thought he could want a woman, but he was afraid she might feel as if he was trying to force himself on her or to take advantage of the situation.

Krys smiled at him. "Not everything has to be taken up for a vote," she told him.

Morgan was being incredibly sweet. Far sweeter than she had thought he could be and she really appreciated that.

Apparently his outward persona hid a completely different man on the inside.

"I know," Morgan replied, "but I didn't want you to feel that I was trying to take advantage of the situation or of—"

Krys bracketed his face between her hands. "Cavanaugh, the lady is throwing herself at you. The least you can do is have the decency to catch her."

That was when Morgan grinned at her, his smile traveling straight up into her bloodstream. Shining in his eyes, it seemed to leave her all but breathless.

"Well, if you put it that way," he told her, taking her words into account as his voice trailed off.

Oh lord, but she wanted him.

"I do," Krys whispered, her heart pounding so hard against her rib cage, it threatened to break a few of those ribs.

Morgan pulled Krys closer to him and kissed her.

Again.

Kissed her with all the powerful emotion he had been so vainly trying to deny or at least suppress.

This time, however, he allowed the fire that was igniting to consume him. Allowed himself to let go of the restraints he had been trying so unsuccessfully to impose on himself.

Rather than hold back, he was suddenly set free. Free to make love with Krys, free to savor every warm, willing inch of the woman he was holding in his arms in anticipation of the final consummation.

Anticipation grew stronger and stronger within him as his lips traveled along her face, her neck, her shoulders. Each kiss he pressed against her soft, supple, willing skin just continued to fuel the fire that he felt burning within his own loins.

It was as if he had unleashed an overwhelming desire the likes of which he had never experienced before. The more Morgan kissed her, the more he touched her, the greater this incredible desire to possess her grew within him.

All she had wanted to do tonight was to ride out this sadness within her she was dealing with. She had wanted to forget, for a few hours, all the frustration, all the fear that insisted on haunting her thoughts, shadowing her path.

But right now she had managed to get so much more than she had bargained for. When she had returned his kiss, she hadn't realized that she would wind up getting so caught up in this incredibly exhilarating feeling of desire.

It was, she thought, like dancing on air. She was giving herself up to the swirling, heated feelings that were growing ever stronger, increasingly more demanding as they stole her very breath away.

Krys felt weak and her head was swirling. The eagerness palpitating within her was almost impossible to contain.

A part of her wanted nothing more than just to consummate what was happening between them, to feel the sweet euphoria that lovemaking wound up generating. Another part of her wanted nothing more than to savor what was happening, to feel that sensation building ever stronger and more powerful as she waited for that absolutely delicious explosion to ricochet throughout every single hungry inch of her body.

She went with the second part.

That feeling only heightened as she felt him undressing her, running his strong, capable hands all along her throbbing body.

Wanting desperately to reciprocate, to make him feel what she was feeling, Krys began undressing Morgan, pulling his clothing away from his taut, hard body with all its tempting muscles.

She couldn't hold herself back, eagerly pressing her lips against his bare skin.

Gratified, she could feel Morgan reacting to her and it just added to her ever-growing excitement, heightening it.

Morgan moaned in response to what he felt was going on within him. Who would have ever thought she was like this? That this work-obsessed woman could also be wild once her inhibitions were subdued and she was unleashed?

With her lips pressing themselves everywhere along his damp body, she created ripples of passion within him and he struggled to hold himself in check. Morgan was determined to pleasure Krys first before his own final release occurred.

She had become that important to him.

Capturing her hands to keep them still so that she wouldn't interrupt his concentration and he could focus it exclusively on her, Morgan slowly laid a wreath of soft, openmouthed kisses along her body.

He worked his way down, moving ever lower along her trembling body until he heard her gasp in delighted surprise. Her fingers delved into his hair, pressing his head to her as she twisted and turned beneath him. More than anything, she savored the sensations Morgan had managed to create within her.

She wanted more.

Krys arched and bucked against him as she desperately tried to absorb the tantalizing feelings that were growing ever stronger, ever more gratifying throughout her exceedingly tantalized body.

She climaxed once, twice, all but collapsing in extreme gratification from the experience. The wonderful sensations created by the climaxes echoed throughout her body and all but vibrated, leaving their imprint on her.

She wasn't prepared for Morgan to slowly slide up along her loins, wasn't ready for the urgent, throbbing demands that suddenly surfaced, all but begging her for more.

And then, just like that, he was there, seemingly suspended directly above her, so close that their breaths mingled, forming a single entity.

Capturing her hands in his, Morgan laced their fingers together. And then, his eyes holding hers, he parted her legs with his knee. Moving almost achingly slowly, he entered her.

Krys drew in her breath quickly, her heart beginning to pound in anticipation. Morgan slowly began to move within her.

The rhythm was timeless and eternal, managing to grow stronger and stronger with each movement, each forceful thrust.

As every second passed, she felt the rhythm between them grow more and more forceful, increasing in its demands. Her hips moved more urgently, matching his, which then in turn matched hers.

It built like this, one movement surpassing the other, until they could barely keep up with one another. Barely keep from gasping for breath.

And then, their lips sealed to each other's, Morgan and Krys raced for that one final culmination, that final joyous, all-encompassing explosion that wound up raining over both of them.

When that final moment came, there was nothing else but that, nothing else but them and the wild, erratic pounding of their hearts that beat so hard, it felt as if they had become one.

Her chest was moving so fast, she could barely catch her breath. She was convinced that she never would, but eventually, Krys felt herself freefalling to earth in slow motion as euphoria slipped away through her fingers.

Reality with the world in tow came back into the room.

It took Krys a few moments before she was able to form any coherent words. When she finally could, she murmured, "This was better."

Morgan shifted his weight off her, moving as best he could into what little space was available beside her on the sofa.

"Did you say something?" he asked, not certain if he had imagined her voice or if she had actually said something to him.

Krys took in a deep breath and repeated herself. "I said 'This was better.'"

Morgan still didn't understand. Was she trying to compare their lovemaking to something? "Better?" he questioned. "Better than what?"

Shifting her head, she looked up at him and smiled. "This was definitely better than *Casablanca*."

He didn't know why that would strike him as funny, but it did and he started to laugh. Once he began, he couldn't stop himself. Delighted at her assessment, laughing at her innocent observation, Morgan tightened his arms around her and kissed Krys again.

Any residual tension disappeared like a sprinkling of dust left in the spring rain.

Settling in and turning his face toward hers, Morgan deadpanned, "All right, so what do you want to do next?"

Her eyes sparkled as she suggested, "How about more of the same?"

"Lord, yes," he wholeheartedly agreed, enthusiasm ringing in his voice. "But you're going to have to give me at least thirty minutes to regroup."

"Thirty minutes, huh?" she asked, rolling the directive over in her head and then raising her head to press a kiss to his neck.

He could feel the effect of her mouth against his skin, creating a warm ripple that grew in magnitude and desire. He could feel himself wanting her more quickly than he thought he was capable of.

"Well, okay," he amended. "Maybe twenty."

Krys shifted, raising her body so that she could reach the other side of his neck and then kissed that.

"Maybe make that ten," Morgan corrected himself, finding that he was having some trouble trying to catch his breath.

"Ten?" she asked teasingly, feathering her fingers slowly down along his torso until she finally brushed just the very tips of her fingers along a swiftly growing part of him.

Morgan groaned again, then caught her hand with his, keeping her fingers still. She had definitely aroused him.

"You realize that you could definitely wake up the dead," he told her.

The smile that curved her mouth was nothing short of pure mischief, and her eyes dipped down again to take note of the havoc she had just created with her lightly moving fingers.

"That, Cavanaugh," she told him with pride, "is definitely not 'dead.'"

With a gleeful laugh, Morgan shifted their positions and proceeded to make love with her for the second time that night, this time deliberately going so slowly that every single precious moment that followed burned itself into her memory.

WHEN KRYS WOKE up the next morning, she found herself alone on the sofa with only a light blanket thrown over her.

Startled, not knowing what to think, she sat upright, clutching the blanket to her. When it began to slip, she realized that she was still very nude beneath it. She grabbed the blanket and held it against herself. Then she did her best to wrap it around her like a less than fashionable-looking sarong.

Rather than calling out Morgan's name, she decided to try to find him first.

Moving from one room to another, she refrained from giving in to the very strong urge to demand to know just where the hell he was. He couldn't have run out on her during the night, could he?

No, he might have wanted to, she argued, but the man was all about duty and he had made it clear to her that he wasn't about to leave her on her own unguarded.

So where was he?

At the end of her patience as well as growing slightly panicky at this point, Krys finally found him in the back bedroom.

He was on the phone.

Morgan looked up when she entered. "Gotta go now," he told the person on the other end of the call. "Something just came up."

With that, Morgan ended his call and put his phone away.

Unlike her, Krys noted, Morgan was completely dressed. "Going somewhere?" she asked him, hiking up her drooping blanket and holding it closer to her.

"Eventually," Morgan answered, never taking his eyes off her. How did she make a simple blanket look so sensuous? He took a few steps closer to her. "I like what you're not wearing."

In the light of day, Krys felt somewhat insecure about what she had allowed to happen between them. Hell, she had not only allowed it to happen, she was the one who had *pushed* for it to happen.

Well, no time like the present to talk about the elephant in the room and get it out of the way.

"About last night," Krys began.

But she got no further, stopped cold by the very wide, happy grin on Morgan's face.

"That was pretty spectacular, wasn't it?" he asked her.

She frowned a little, pulled up short. "That wasn't what I was going to say."

"It wasn't?" he questioned innocently. "Well, I was—and I just did," he added. Morgan looked at her more closely. "Didn't you enjoy yourself?"

Even though she wanted to deny that she had, she couldn't very well lie about it. He'd see right through her. "Well, yes, I did." Then, annoyed, she told him, "But that isn't the point."

"It's not?" he asked. "I certainly thought it was. A very pertinent point," he added. "But I'm interrupting," he told her. His eyes captured hers, delving into them. "What was it that you were going to say about last night?"

She took a deep breath, as if to fortify herself, and then said, "That it shouldn't have happened."

"Oh. But it did," he pointed out. "That means the cat's out of the bag and there's no putting it back in," he told her, his grin only growing wider with each word. And then, just like that, it vanished. "Are you having regrets?"

"Yes," she said quickly, then amended, "No, I'm not." Finally, she said, "Not exactly."

"I didn't realize I was asking a multiple choice question," he told her, his grin returning.

Krys frowned slightly. It was a frustrated frown. "I shouldn't have done it."

"Can we vote on that?" he asked her. "Because if we can, then I vote yes—that you *should* have done it."

"I'm getting a headache," she said, running her hand along her forehead as if that could somehow wipe it away out of existence.

"I happen to have an old family remedy for that," Morgan told her. He cocked an eyebrow and asked, "Interested?"

It made her laugh. *He* made her laugh. But the remedy had to be made up, she thought. "I think I'll pass," she told him.

"Too bad. It really is a great remedy," he confided.

She chose to ignore him.

Chapter Nineteen

Krys had just slipped into her bedroom after telling him she was going to get ready for his uncle's party. She closed the door behind her.

Morgan resisted the temptation to follow her. While it was true that over the last few days, he had gotten to intimately know every inch of her body and she his, it still wouldn't be right to have her think that he was taking things for granted. After all, she did deserve her privacy.

Trying to keep his mind occupied, he decided that this would be a good time to check in with his partner to see how things were going. The last he had heard, as of yesterday, his team was still following up every available lead to find out just *who* had killed Claire Williams. He knew that Krys was hoping they could trace the person back to Jacobs, the CEO in charge of production at Weatherly Pharmaceuticals, but right now, all they had was her gut feeling, or what passed as a gut feeling.

As he listened, the number at the other end of his cell rang a total of five times. He was about to hang up and call again when he heard the cell on the other end being picked up.

Finally!

"I was beginning to think that you had gone on vacation," Morgan quipped to his partner. "Your phone must have rung at least ten times, if not more."

"You're exaggerating, Cavanaugh," Fredericks told him. "And besides, I've got better things to do than just to sit around, waiting for your call."

"Right. You know, for a change of pace, you could try calling me," Morgan pointed out.

"If I wanted to be nagged about a litany of imaginary shortcomings, I would have stayed home today," Fredericks told him.

"Okay, truce," Morgan said, shifting his phone to his other hand. He didn't want the sound of his voice to carry and alert Krys until he knew what, if anything, he was going to hear. Now was not the time to upset her in any way. "I'm calling to find out if there's been any headway made in finding out who was responsible for the Claire Williams shooting."

He heard Fredericks chuckle and knew the man did have something to tell him. "Well, as a matter of fact, I've got some good news and some bad news about that." His partner paused, possibly for dramatic effect, and then said, "Oddly enough, it's the same news."

"Since when did 'gibberish' become a second language for you, Fredericks?"

"Look, you want to hear this or not?" his partner asked. "Because I can just as easily hang up right now and leave you and that hot little journalist friend of yours hanging."

Morgan rolled his eyes. He had forgotten how touchy his partner could be at times. It was the result of feeling as if he was on the outside, looking in when it came to the Cavanaughs. "Sorry, what's this dual news of yours?"

Fredericks paused in order to give the moment its due, then declared, "We found the person who killed that woman in the park."

Morgan came to attention. Just like that? This seemed too easy. "You're sure it's the killer?"

"No, I'm making this up because I want to leave the precinct early. Yes, I'm sure," he snapped, stressing the point.

"Why didn't you call me as soon as you found this out?"

"I just did," Fredericks informed him. "I just literally found this out and finished verifying the information."

Morgan assumed that this was the good news. "So, what's the bad news?" he asked.

"The bad news is that it turns out this execution, so to speak, has nothing to do with the attempts on the journalist's life," Fredericks told him.

Rather than ask Fredericks a bunch of questions that would either make his partner irritable or wind up sending Fredericks off track, he let his partner explain, at his own pace, how he had come to that conclusion.

"Go on," Morgan urged.

"Age-old story," Fredericks told him. Then, after a pregnant pause, he said, "Her boyfriend killed her. That is, her *ex*-boyfriend," Fredericks clarified. "According to the story, they were having some problems and she was looking to leave him three months ago. According to a restraining order she filed, he was controlling and had become abusive. Anyway, she got her chance to get away from him when she became part of that miracle drug test group. She used that to have some time away from him and then, when the testing was over, she found the courage she needed to tell him that she'd decided to move on."

This was all new information, Morgan thought. Krys had given him no indication that she'd even known the murder victim had a boyfriend. "I'm assuming that he didn't take it very well."

"You can say that again," his partner told him with a mirthless laugh. "It turns out that this was a classic case of 'if I can't have her, nobody can.' Thompson gave her one last chance to come back to him, said that all would be forgiven if she did. When she refused, he decided to just bide his time and when the opportunity presented itself, he killed her."

Morgan thought there was just one flaw in the narrative. "CSI said it was the work of a sniper."

"It was," Fredericks agreed.

"But I thought you just said—"

Fredericks talked right over him. "With a renewed purpose in his life, Thompson put in an inordinate amount of time at the rifle range learning how to become a marksman. According to the guy who runs the place," Fredericks told him, "he became pretty damn good. In typical stalker fashion, he knew her routine, so it was no big deal for him to lie in wait and pick her off that morning."

Morgan thought of the surveillance videos he had reviewed. "You have proof of this?"

"Proof?" Fredericks echoed. "When we confronted Thompson about his actions, he bragged about it. Said he'd been waiting for someone to put the pieces together." Morgan's partner paused, then said, "So, while we now have our killer in custody, we still don't have a viable suspect for whoever is trying to kill your journalist."

"She's not *my* journalist," Morgan corrected him. There was no point in getting ahead of himself until he knew how Krys felt about what had happened between them. "And her name is Krys," he told Fredericks.

The man went along with the correction. "Yeah, her." Fredericks sighed. "The fact of the matter is that I don't know if I should put this in the 'win' column or if I should apologize because this solution now puts you back at square one."

That made two of them. "Well, thanks for the update," he told Fredericks. "Let me know if you find out anything else." With that, he hung up.

He really didn't look forward to telling Krys that it now looked as if Jacobs might be innocent, at least of hiring someone to eliminate Claire. It also might mean that the CEO wasn't guilty of paying someone to attempt to do the same thing to her.

So who the hell was out there, trying to kill her?

For the moment, he was extremely grateful for his uncle's party. At least that would get her mind off all of this for the space of a day.

"You look as if you've got something on your mind," Krys said the minute she walked out of her bedroom and looked at his face. "Let me guess," she declared. "The party's been called off."

He shook his head. "No."

Glancing down at her outfit, Krys said, "You don't like the dress."

She was wearing a soft, light gray-blue dress that clung to her body like an old friend—the way he wanted to. "No, I love the dress," he told her, his eyes taking in every square inch of her. "Although I have to admit that I'd also like the chance to peel it off you—slowly."

"You would, huh?" And then she completely threw him by asking, "Does your thinking that way make us a thing, a couple?"

He congratulated himself on his quick recovery. "It makes us anything you want us to be," he told her.

She sighed. "That is a typical vague male response, you realize that, don't you?"

"Well, in my defense," he told her, "it's only vague because I don't want to spook you or have you running for the hills."

Her eyes gave nothing away. "And if I want to?"

He didn't know if she was baiting him, or if she was giving him her honest reaction. "That is your right," he told her, although it cost him. "And we'll talk about it," he had to add, "but only after we go to Uncle Andrew's get-together and *after* we find that killer who is out there, roaming the streets of Aurora, waiting to get another crack at you."

That was rather a long to-do list, she thought. Once it was out of the way, that just left the two of them with nothing more to deal with than each other.

"I must say, you do come up with a compelling argument." Krys paused for a moment, raising her eyes to his. She changed the subject by going back to her initial one. "So you don't want me to change?"

"Not so much as a hair," he told her, amusement curving his mouth.

She scrutinized Morgan, trying to unravel what he was telling her. "Are we still talking about the dress?"

His smile seemed to wiggle into every available crevice in her body. "I'll leave that up to you to decide," he told her. "Meanwhile," he glanced at his watch, "we'd better get going."

"I thought you said that we didn't have to be there at any specific time," she reminded Morgan.

"We don't," he agreed. "However, the later we get there, the harder it is to find someplace to park—unless you don't mind taking a tour of Uncle Andrew's development—from the other end of it—and it is a very *long* development."

Krys nodded. "Okay, you've talked me into it," she told him. Glancing down at herself one final time, she said, "I guess I'm ready."

He gestured for her to walk ahead of him.

Krys did, then turned around to lock her front door. Getting into his car, she said, "By the way, who were you talking to?"

The question came out of the blue and caught him off guard for a moment. He had already made up his mind to put off telling her about the person who killed Claire until they got back from the party. "When?"

"Just now, before I came out of my room," she told him.

"I didn't think you heard me. You must have ears like a bat," Morgan commented.

Krys laughed. "One of the requirements of being a freelance journalist is to be able to hear people talking to one another practically a mile away."

Morgan nodded. "Apparently." Okay, here went nothing. "Well, I was going to wait until today was over to tell you because I wasn't sure how you were going to take this."

That definitely aroused her curiosity, not to mention that it sent a chill down her spine. "Okay, now you have to tell me," she said, repeating and stressing the word "now." She looked at him expectantly, waiting.

"Claire Williams wasn't killed by someone that Lawrence Jacobs hired to do her in," Morgan told her.

"How do you know that?"

"Simple," he said. "Because it turns out she was killed by her jealous, possessive ex-boyfriend."

Stunned, she stared at Morgan. She hadn't even known that there was a jealous ex-boyfriend in the picture. Claire hadn't said anything to lead her to believe that, but now that she thought about it, it would explain the very faint purple bruise on the woman's neck. Claire had almost succeeded in covering it up with makeup.

Still, Krys pressed, "Are you sure?" She was having trouble wrapping her head around the scenario. Claire had seemed so calm, so self-possessed. "Who told you there was a jealous boyfriend?"

"My partner, Fredericks, of all people, and yes, he's sure," he told her before she could ask. "Turns out the guy, Jason Thompson, didn't even try to hide it. According to Fredericks, he confessed. He even boasted about the fact." Morgan slanted a glance in Krys's direction as he turned down another street. "You do know what this means, don't you?"

Krys's shoulders all but slumped. She knew damn well what this meant. It blew up her theory as well as her hard work. "That Jacobs didn't have her killed. And, extrapolating on that, in all probability he might not be the one trying to have me killed." She sighed, then looked at Morgan. "But someone certainly is," she insisted, adding, "I didn't just imagine those attempts."

"You don't have to convince me," Morgan told her, even though initially he had had to be convinced. "I was there to witness the second attempt on your life and before that, I saw what someone did to your car window."

She rolled the events over in her mind. "You know, suddenly I don't feel very festive." She shifted in her seat, looking at Morgan. "I won't be any good at your family's gathering. Why don't you just drop me off somewhere and I'll get a ride home?"

Was she kidding? "Right, like that's going to happen," Morgan scoffed. "And you're wrong about not fitting in at the family gathering. This is exactly the right time for you to be there. Trust me, my family is perfect when it comes to getting your mind off this whole thing. In addition to that, you will be totally surrounded by your very own blue wall," he pointed out. "More than half the people at Uncle Andrew's gathering are on the Aurora police force—and absolutely *none* of the people attending would allow anything to happen to you, I guarantee it," he told her. "You would be safer there than you would probably be any other place in the entire universe."

Krys shook her head, surrendering. Her wide, grateful smile was a sight to see. "I bet you were on the debate team when you were in high school."

Morgan shook his head. "No." When she seemed surprised by his answer, he said, "College."

She laughed. "You also have a very perverse sense of humor."

"Guilty as charged," he acknowledged. "So," he looked at her for a moment, "did I manage to talk you into attending?"

"If I said no, you'd probably handcuff me to the inside of your car and take me over there anyway."

Morgan merely smiled, but didn't say anything one way or another.

She dropped the subject. Instead, she had another question she wanted answered. "So, did Fredericks give you any more details? Tell me everything."

He told her what he knew. "The ex-boyfriend took lessons on the rifle range. From what I gathered, he wanted to be letter-perfect because he didn't want to miss his 'target' and take a chance on her running away. I guess that when he gave her one last chance to get back with him and she turned him down, she wound up signing her own death warrant."

Krys sighed as she shook her head. "Dating certainly has gotten much more complicated in this supposedly 'enlightened' age," she murmured under her breath.

Morgan laughed. "Yes, it was so much simpler when fathers got to hold out for horses, trading their eligible daughters for fine specimens of horse flesh."

Krys looked at him. "What's so funny?"

"My dad could have gotten rich on my sisters," Morgan answered her.

"I'm sure that they would love to hear that," she told him. She gave him an innocent smile. "You'll be sure to point them out to me when we get there, won't you?"

Morgan momentarily glanced in her direction. "Don't think I don't know what you're doing."

She became the soul of innocence as she said, "I have no idea what you're talking about."

"You're trying to get me to skip my uncle's party and take you back to your house." The smile on his lips was deliberately pasted on. "I wouldn't hold my breath if I were you," he told her. "Besides," he announced as he pulled into the development and made a right turn, "We're here."

She leaned forward, looking all around the well-manicured area.

"This is nice," Krys commented as Morgan wove his way through the well-cared-for streets lined with majestic trees that were bowing their heads toward one another, forming impressive arches.

"This development is one of the oldest ones in Aurora," he told her. There was no mistaking the pride in his voice. He thought a moment. "It was built almost fifty-three years ago."

"You're kidding," she said in surprise. "Everything looks so new and clean."

The development she lived in was only seven years old. At that age, she expected the area to look as new as it did, but hearing how old this one was really surprised her.

"The people in Aurora as a whole know how to take care of things." He was proud of the fact that there wasn't a single part of Aurora that could be singled out as needing a lot of work or upkeep. "There's a lot of pride in the community around here."

"Apparently," Krys acknowledged. She continued taking the scenery in. "I can see why my sister wanted to live here."

"You live here, too," Morgan reminded her.

"Only because she settled here," she confessed. They didn't see each other much because of her own work, but just knowing that Nik was close by was enough for her peace of mind. "Besides, we are each other's only family."

Not anymore, Morgan thought.

"We're here," he announced out loud. He had managed to find a space that was near the front.

"We certainly are," Krys murmured, seeing all the cars that lined both sides of the street and seemed to bleed even further into the development.

The number of cars overwhelmed her.

Chapter Twenty

Krys was standing just half a step behind him at former chief of police Andrew Cavanaugh's front door. Morgan heard her take in a deep breath just as he rang the doorbell.

Glancing at her over his shoulder, Morgan saw that she had drawn back her shoulders as well, making him think of a soldier who was getting ready to encounter the opposing side.

Leaning his head in toward her, Morgan whispered into Krys's ear, "Remember, they don't bite," just as the front door opened.

With everything in the kitchen either cooking, grilling or having already been prepared, the meal Andrew intended to serve to his family was completely under control. The chief had taken the opportunity to step away from his oversized kitchen, a kitchen that had already been remodeled and expanded three times since he had retired and begun to indulge in his latest passion.

The very surprised look on the family patriarch's face when he opened the front door dissipated almost immediately.

"You're right," Andrew declared, sparing a quick glance toward his nephew. "She really does look like her sister." Giving Krys a quick embrace, the family patriarch told the young woman, "Welcome to my home, Krystyna."

Krys smiled. There was something about Andrew Cavanaugh that had made her feel instantly at ease.

"Everyone calls me Krys," she told him, then added with whimsical humor, "Sometimes they call me Nik."

Andrew laughed. "I bet that gets old," he sympathized.

"It does," she agreed, "but only sometimes."

"Well please, come in, come in," Andrew invited, stepping back and clearing the threshold for the latest arrivals. "Half the family's already here," he told Morgan, then turned toward Krys. "I don't suppose you've heard from your sister yet."

"Actually, I did get a postcard from Hawaii the day before yesterday," Krys told the chief. "It said, quote, '*Don't* wish you were here.'" There was a wide grin on her face.

Delighted, Andrew laughed. "I would have been surprised if she had left out the word 'don't.'"

A noise from the kitchen caught his attention and the chief glanced in that direction. "Well, I should be getting back to my kitchen. Contrary to what some of the younger generation seem to think, food does *not* cook itself. But I'll leave you in Morgan's capable hands," Andrew told her. "He'll be your guide. That means he'll show you where all the entrées, appetizers and desserts are around here, plus he can introduce you to everyone." Andrew smiled as he looked at his nephew. "You *have* finally learned everyone's names, haven't you, Morgan?"

"Just about," Morgan said with a straight face. He glanced toward Krys, who was looking at him with a quizzical expression on her face. "It's not as easy as you might think."

They had moved into the expanded family room now, and Krys looked around at all the various relatives, large, medium and small, who were already there. And from all indications, she assumed that there were more of them coming.

"Oh, trust me, I don't think it's easy at all," she assured Morgan, then asked, "Shouldn't you people come with name tags or something?"

Morgan laughed. She hadn't given voice to a sentiment that hadn't been shared by a lot of other people the first time they found themselves encountering the family en masse.

"Oh, we've thought about it, but where's the challenge in that?" he asked with a wink.

"I don't want to be challenged," she told him quite honestly. "I want to be right."

And that, Morgan thought, was the key to Krys's personality. "We'll work on that," he promised. "In the meantime, let's get you something to eat. After that, the introductions will begin. Don't worry," Morgan assured her as he brought Krys over to the patio, "it's painless."

Painless, huh? "Is that before or after my head explodes?"

It occurred to Krys that she hadn't seen this many people milling about outside of a convention center since she had traveled through some areas in Indonesia when she had been gathering background data for a series she was doing at the time on human trafficking.

"It won't explode," he assured Krys. "It'll only *feel* like it's exploding."

She gave him a skeptical look. "You don't have this comforting thing down pat yet, do you?" she asked him. Making her way to one of the side tables, she picked up a paper plate that resembled a plate made out of actual china. Holding it in her hand, she placed a couple of appetizers on it.

"I'm a work in progress," Morgan confided in reference to her observation. He nodded at her plate. "And you do know that you can take more than that, right?" He assumed that she was being polite and trying not to deplete his uncle's supply. "You wouldn't believe how much food Uncle Andrew makes for one of these gatherings."

She shook her head as he started to offer her another appetizer. "That's okay. I'm not sure I can hold anything down yet." When he looked at her in confusion, she explained, "My stomach's been in a knot ever since you told me that we lost my likeliest stalker suspect when you found out that it was Claire's former boyfriend who murdered her."

Morgan moved in closer and lowered his voice. He felt fairly confident that Krys wouldn't appreciate his sharing this piece of information with the people in the immediate area, at least, not until she felt comfortable with all the members of his family. He was well aware that as much as he loved them, they did take some getting use to.

"I promise I'm not going to leave you until we get this stalker and permanently lock him up in prison." Morgan looked into her eyes, hoping to erase the anxiety he saw there. "Feel better?"

"Oddly enough, I do," she told him. She was not the type to play the damsel in distress, nor the type to take solace in promises. Not usually. She was usually the type who insisted on tilting at her own windmills and fighting her own battles.

But something had changed for her since she had lost her mentor and, in a way, lost her sister as well, even though Nik had just gotten married and not left her permanently. But even so, it felt as if the parameters of her world had shifted, making her feel vulnerable. It wasn't a feeling that she relished.

Vulnerable. The same could be said for the way she had responded to Morgan.

This certainly hadn't been her first experience in making love. But somehow, this experience had been different. It had left her with a very different feeling. One she wasn't used to.

"Earth to Krys."

Krys blinked as Morgan's voice penetrated her consciousness. She realized that for a moment, she had gotten lost in her own thoughts and hadn't heard what he had said to her.

"I'm sorry," she apologized. "I didn't mean to zone out like that."

"That's okay. I just want to make sure you're all right," Morgan told her. He motioned toward a gazebo that was set apart from the tables scattered around the rather large backyard and patio area. "We can sit over there," he told her, thinking she might want some time to get used to having all these family members around.

"No," she said, turning down his offer. "If it's all the same to you, I think it's time I started meeting more of these people here," she told him, indicating the various clusters of family members in the immediate area.

Morgan grinned, happy to act as a tour guide. "Sure, it'll be my pleasure," he told her, and she felt that he really meant that.

KRYS APPROACHED THE next few hours as if she were on assignment, or at least she did initially. When she was on assignment, she carefully put her own feelings and thoughts on the back burner and concentrated on learning about the people she was meeting for the first time and interacting with. That was her own way of making the people she was writing about come alive for her readers as well as for the editor who would eventually be reviewing her work.

But somewhere along the line in that first hour and a half, Krys unconsciously stopped being a reporter, stopped working the groups of people as if they were her assignment and started seeing them for what they were. Morgan's family.

A family that, despite his teasing comments to the contrary, he was very much attached to—and, she discovered, with good reason. Because the love that radiated from these people and between these people was simply impossible to miss.

It made her realize how stark her own upbringing had been in comparison. And how much worse it would have been if it hadn't been for her sister and her father, even though her father had to be absent from her life a great deal out of necessity.

Over the course of those few hours, Morgan saw the slow, subtle shift in Krys, saw the transformation in her demeanor as it was happening.

Even so, Morgan held his breath for a little bit, worried that she might be overwhelmed by the sheer number of people in the house. But gradually, he realized that he was worrying for no reason. Krys seemed every bit up to this challenge of holding her own in the company of his cousins and siblings.

Not that he felt they might run right over her, but he knew they expected and wanted the best for one of their own—just as he would if the tables had been turned and he was judging a companion who had come with one of his sisters.

Cavanaughs were nothing if not protective, he thought. But they were also fair and prone to giving someone another chance if they felt that person was deserving and had accidentally made a misstep they were eager to rectify.

OVER THE COURSE of the day, Morgan never left Krys's side, even after he felt that she was more than capable of holding her own and growing very comfortable in the company of the people around her.

As the afternoon wound its way into evening, it was like watching a rare flower bloom and open up in the night air.

Finally, he felt she had put in enough time for one day. "Ready to go home?"

She had just finished talking to Brian, Andrew's younger brother and the chief of detectives. Morgan's question had caught her by surprise. "Is it time to leave already?" she asked him, stunned.

Morgan found the word "already" very telling. "No, not really. We don't *have* to leave," he assured her. "But I just thought that you'd want to. I mean, after having put in your time and all…" His voice trailed off, allowing her to fill in the implied meaning.

"You make it sound like penance," she remarked. She didn't see it that way at all and implied as much. "If it's all the same to you, I'd like to stay a little longer."

"Sure," he agreed, doing his best not to let her see how pleased her decision had made him. While he couldn't see *anyone* not warming up to his family, there was always the outside chance that harmony wouldn't be the end result here. "We can definitely stay," he assured her. "Uncle Andrew has had people who stayed for an entire weekend—and longer—after one of his parties. He has only one ground rule for his guests."

"What's that?" Krys asked.

"That the person or persons honestly enjoy themselves."

Krys grinned. "Then I guess I meet the criterion. Maybe I shouldn't admit this to you," she confided, "but this is really like living out a fantasy for me."

"You're going to have to give me more than that," Morgan said.

This wasn't something she talked about often, or for that matter, at all. But she had been the one to start this, so she said, "After my mother ran off, my dad, sister and I moved around a lot when I was a kid. Looking back on it now, I think the reason we did was that my father was trying to find my mother without actually admitting as much to us. I think he didn't want to disappoint us if he couldn't locate her—which, as it turned out, he didn't.

"Because we moved around so much, Nik and I were always on the outside looking in when it came to school. This," she nodded around at her surroundings, "was the way I always imagined it would be like to belong to a large, loving family." She smiled at him, her eyes twinkling. "Thanks for letting me live out my fantasy for the space of a night."

He wanted to tell her that the fantasy didn't have to end tonight, or for that matter, soon, but he didn't want to risk scaring Krys off. A woman who had been as independent as Krys had been for as long as she had been could very well balk at having someone rein her in or appear to give her boundaries, even if he did it for the best of reasons. She might feel that she had to insist on being free. He definitely didn't want her feeling that she had to back off.

But Morgan really wanted her to get used to having these boundaries around her. So for now he said nothing. He only savored the small victories he had made, savored the tiny steps forward that he had managed to gain.

And he promised himself that there would be more coming soon.

AS IT TURNED OUT, Morgan and Krys wound up being very close to the last people to leave the family gathering that night.

Krys's eyes were all but closing by the time they said their goodbyes and made their way to the front door.

Even so, she wouldn't just slip away the way Morgan had suggested when he saw how her eyes were drooping. Krys wanted to be sure to take proper leave of the people who had thrown this gathering as well as the ones who were still left in attendance.

"I can't thank you enough for inviting me, Mr. Cavanaugh."

"Oh please," Andrew told her, "Call me Chief. My wife does," he added with a mischievous wink.

Standing beside her husband as she did at the end of each of these gatherings, Rose Cavanaugh slipped her arm around her husband's waist.

"You wish," she said with an old, familiar laugh. "You can call him Chief, or Uncle Andrew, the way everyone else here does. But you can't call him 'honey,'" she told Krys. "That label belongs strictly just to me."

"As do I," Andrew assured Rose, pressing a kiss to his wife's temple.

The simple, sweet gesture spoke volumes, Krys thought.

Andrew turned toward Krys. "And thank you for coming and for putting up with all of us. I know, despite everything, that it couldn't have been easy for you, seeing what you're going through."

Krys nodded, acknowledging his words. She should have guessed he would know all about the fact that she was being stalked as well as how the likeliest candidate had just been eliminated.

"Morgan told me that you have your finger on the pulse of everything that goes on in Aurora."

"Morgan exaggerates," Andrew told her. "But I am very protective of my family," he readily admitted. Then, in case there was any lingering doubt in her mind, the patriarch added, "And you *are* part of the family." Andrew turned toward Morgan and shook his nephew's hand heartily, bidding the young man goodbye. "Now see that you get home safely."

Andrew's words were directed toward both of them.

Chapter Twenty-One

Feeling beyond exhausted, Krys was really relieved to see her house coming into view some twenty minutes later.

"You know," she said as she breathed a major sigh of relief, "I really like your family."

"Yeah, I think they wound up tolerating you pretty well, too," Morgan deadpanned, pulling his car into her driveway.

"Very funny," she answered. Growing serious, Krys said honestly, "My sister is very lucky to have all of you. I guess I can finally stop worrying about her."

"You were worried about her?" This was news to him, Morgan thought as he got out of the vehicle on the driver's side.

"Well yes, sure." From her point of view, that only made sense. "I'd be gone for months at a time and she was back here, by herself. I mean, she had friends she could turn to if something was wrong, but that's just not the same thing as having family to depend on," Krys stressed. She was very protective of her twin sister. She always had been.

He thought about that for a moment. "True," Morgan agreed as he opened her door for her. "But," he went on to point out, "not all families are the kind you can depend on."

"I guess it's lucky for my sister that yours turned out to be the kind that is." She walked up to her front door.

She thought she noticed the patrolman Morgan had posted sitting across the street in his vehicle. She was still being watched even though Morgan was acting like her own personal bodyguard. It made her realize that he really did think she was still in danger.

"Well, like it or not, you're part of that family now, too," Morgan told her.

Her brows drew together over the bridge of her nose. "You mentioned that before," she recalled, "but I thought that really only happened if you married a member of the family."

He did his best to keep a straight face as he told her, "I'll have to look at the bylaws about that, but I think there is some leeway in the rules."

Krys's frown deepened as she put her key into the door and unlocked it. "You're laughing at me," she accused Morgan.

"No, I'm laughing with you," he told Krys, unable to keep a wide grin from curving the corners of his mouth.

"There's only one problem with your defense—I'm not laughing," she pointed out.

Morgan turned the doorknob and pushed the door open for her, then stepped to the side to allow her to enter first. "Let's go inside and I'll remedy that."

Suddenly, Krys thought as she went inside and felt Morgan's arms slip around her, she wasn't nearly as sleepy as she thought she was.

"I DON'T BELIEVE IT," Krys cried as she got off the phone with the online editor who had been overseeing this latest controversial project of hers. The editor had initially okayed the assignment even when everyone else had been inclined to shut it down or advised her to walk away from it.

Krys had gone into the precinct with Morgan today so that he could continue working with his team. They were still searching for what had happened to the mystery woman who had apparently vanished from the hospital after the infamous killer had been pronounced dead. So far, no one in the police department had been able to locate her.

Working her own sources, Krys had just terminated her call and was looking far from pleased, although Morgan thought he picked up a note of momentary victory in her voice—but he just might have been reading into it.

Looking up from what he was doing, Morgan asked, "What don't you believe?"

She was still shaking her head, stunned. "After all the time I put in, all the people I interviewed, trying to get enough evidence to get Weatherly Pharmaceuticals to pull that so-called 'miracle' drug of theirs off the market because it just seemed to be too good to be true, Jacobs *himself*," she emphasized, "just issued a statement that said, due to certain abnormalities that came to light in this very last round of testing—*completed late yesterday, mind you*—the company has decided to pull the drug off the market until such time as they can determine whether or not this drug is actually as beneficial to the patients as it was originally thought to be." Her brows narrowed. "In other words, they're willing to admit that the drug was misrepresented."

Morgan looked at her. Why did she look so angry? He didn't understand.

"Well, that's good, isn't it?" he asked. "That was what you wanted, right? It was what your gut had you believing all along, right?" he pressed. He would have thought it was a win-win situation in her eyes, not something to be upset about, which she clearly seemed to be.

"Right," she answered, snapping out the word.

Okay, something was definitely wrong, Morgan thought. He had gotten to know her well enough to be able to pick up on that.

"But?" he asked when she didn't continue. She raised a brow in his direction. "I hear a 'but' in your voice."

She didn't know if she felt like kicking something, or ultimately celebrating. "Jacobs just issued the statement ten minutes ago," she informed the detective grudgingly.

Morgan shook his head, at a loss. "I still don't hear the problem."

Right now, she was angry enough to spit. "If that CEO was the one who issued the statement—voluntarily—and apparently he did—then he *couldn't* have been the one who tried to have me killed so that he could stop me from bringing this thing to the public's attention." She all but spit the words out.

Shifting in his seat, he considered the basic reasons that would make a man call off something that he had pinned all his hopes on—not to mention the company's projected skyrocketing profits.

"Maybe he had no choice. It's one thing to try to silence one annoyingly pushy journalist—his thoughts undoubtedly, not mine," Morgan told her with a wink. "It's an entirely other thing when it involves other board members bringing it to his attention and worrying about how this would affect the company stock, not to mention the company's portfolio and reputation if it really did fail to deliver."

She looked at Morgan, feeling frustration all but throbbing through her. She knew she didn't have to say this. He knew this just as well as she did. It was just taking all the wind out of her sails.

"Nobody profits if the company is backing a bad drug, or a drug that fails to deliver on its promise," she stated flatly.

"However," Morgan pointed out, "if that particular shortcoming wasn't brought to light, it would take a while, possibly even a *long* while, before people would find out that the drug wasn't everything that it was saying it was, that it didn't deliver or help maintain the status quo the company had led everyone to believe that it did. In other words, that it didn't keep the cancer from progressing the way the company had initially promised that it would. They were undoubtedly hoping for enough of a gray area to make people believe that the drug was helping them."

She nodded her head, stating the bottom line here. "What you're saying is that Jacobs could have still been trying to get rid of me, but when other people raised the same point, he realized that he just couldn't silence everyone and so instead, to look innocent of any wrongdoing, he came up to the podium and issued a statement saying that the company was holding off further production until such time as they could be satisfied that the drug was doing what it claimed it could do."

That was it in a nutshell, Morgan thought. "Exactly."

While she was glad that the company had backed off rather than capitalizing on selling false hope to the public, this still left her wondering if her initial premise had been wrong or had been abandoned out of necessity.

"Okay," she said gamely, "so now what?"

He thought for a moment before answering. "Now I have Valri

or one of her minions check Jacobs's financials to see if there have been any unusual withdrawals made recently—just in case he did try to have you killed. Plus we also pay Jacobs another visit."

Morgan looked at Krys as he rose from his desk. "And this time, I plan to go to his office as a police detective and not as your faithful assistant," he informed her. "*That* should rattle the CEO's cage a little—although I'd say that of the two of us, you probably are the one who's more capable of striking fear into his heart," he speculated.

Fredericks, who had been eavesdropping, took this break in the conversation to ask Morgan, "You want me to do anything?"

"Yes, I want you to go on looking for that so-called mystery woman who disappeared from the hospital," Morgan instructed.

Fredericks looked rather disappointed. "Can't we close that case yet? The guy's dead and from all indications, he worked alone. This 'mystery woman' didn't have anything to do with those deaths." It was obvious that Morgan's partner thought pursuing the case seemed like a lost cause, especially since the serial killer was dead.

"Maybe not," Morgan agreed. "But something about this just doesn't feel right."

Fredericks sighed and shook his head. "You Cavanaughs and your 'gut' feelings," he complained. The fact that some cases were solved strictly because of a Cavanaugh's gut feeling was practically legendary in some circles. But that didn't mean Fredericks had to like it.

Morgan looked at his partner. "Humor me."

The other man frowned, but it was clear he wasn't going to be the one who raised a protest. "Do I have a choice?" Fredericks asked his partner.

Morgan grinned. "Knew I'd get you to see things my way," he said as he headed for the doorway. "Okay, let's go and talk to your favorite person, Kowalski," he said to Krys.

"I thought you'd never ask," she said, pasting a tolerant smile on her face.

LAWRENCE JACOBS APPEARED far from happy to see her when she and Morgan entered his office.

"If you're here to hound me, Ms. Kowalski, you're too late," he informed her. "I just made my statement to the press."

Ivy, his secretary, entered breathlessly right on their heels. The woman looked distressed. "I'm so sorry, Mr. Jacobs. I told these people that you weren't to be disturbed." She looked obviously afraid of her boss's reaction because his office had been invaded this way. "I'm calling security immediately," the petite woman told Morgan and Krys, hoping that this would make them back off.

"Don't bother," Morgan told her as he held up his badge and ID. "I'm a police detective with the Aurora Police Force."

"Moonlighting?" Jacobs asked with a smirk. It was obvious that the CEO didn't believe Morgan was what he claimed to be. Jacobs picked up his phone, his manner indicating that he was going to place the call to security himself.

"No, that was undercover work previously," Morgan informed the CEO. "And if this turns out the way I think it will, you'll be entitled to one phone call. You really want to use it up checking out my identification?" he asked the older man.

Jacobs looked at the two people in his plush office with belittling disgust, but it was also obvious that he believed Morgan. Or, at the very least, he didn't want to take a chance that he had made a mistake.

So instead of calling security, he replaced the telephone receiver in the cradle and glared accusingly at Krys.

"Why are you here?" he demanded angrily. "I said what you wanted me to say. We're holding off putting the drug on the market until further testing can be done. That should have you dancing in the aisle," he told her with contempt. "As for that woman you were so sure was going to lead you to the promised land—and didn't—" he underscored "—her death wasn't my fault, either. Her crazy ex-boyfriend confessed to killing her."

The expression on his face turned positively ugly in Krys's opinion.

"The way I see it, you've got nothing except egg on your face, so get out of my office before I have *you* arrested on harassment charges," he threatened Krys, his complexion turning red.

"I'd watch my threats if I were you," Morgan informed the CEO.

"Someone who came within inches of hoodwinking a vulnerable public and making a profit on their very real fears is in no position to threaten someone who has just been doing her job by trying to keep a very vulnerable group of people safe."

Jacobs's small brown eyes grew into dark slits as he focused them on Morgan. "Careful, Detective. I pay your salary." The threat he was issuing was more than just implied.

But Morgan was not about to back down and he refused to be intimidated by a man he considered to be a weasel.

"So do all those people you did your very best to deceive," Morgan pointed out, curbing his anger. But it was coming very dangerously close to the surface—and erupting.

Jacobs looked as if his head was about to explode. "I believe we're done here," the CEO informed the duo standing in his office, his voice growing hoarse with fury. "Ivy, see these people out of my office!" he cried, his voice cracking.

"I LIKED SEEING his face turn colors," Krys confessed. "I've never seen anyone turn red and then white all within a few minutes. What do you call that color anyway?" she asked Morgan as they left the spacious office. "I believe that's what they mean by a lighter shade of pale, isn't it?"

Morgan laughed as they headed toward the elevator. "Something like that."

"So that's that?" Krys asked, disappointment clearly in her voice. "Are you letting him off the hook?"

"I'm not 'letting' him off anything, not until Valri finishes checking out his financials," he answered her, pushing for the Down button. "If there have been any unexplained large checks paid out in the last month, Jacobs is going to have a hell of a lot of explaining to do," he promised Krys.

Krys mentally crossed her fingers, hoping that Valri was successful.

"If Valri can actually find something, that would be terrific. It would really be worth a lot to me to be able to watch that man be put in the position to sweat bullets," she told Morgan. "But what if it turns out that there *is* no paper trail?" she asked. "What if there are no checks written for large amounts—or a whole bunch of little checks, all written out to the same person? What then?"

"Then it looks as if Jacobs wasn't the one who has been trying to kill you, which is all I care about," Morgan concluded.

"Then what?" she asked.

"Well, then it'll be back to the drawing board—*again*," Morgan emphasized. "But it's nothing that either one of us hasn't been through before," Morgan reminded her.

If they weren't out in public, he would have given in to the urge to put his arm around her and comfort Krys. But they *were* out in public, and he knew that she wouldn't appreciate any public displays of affection.

She slanted a glance in his direction as they came out of the elevator. "Granted, but all those other times, nobody was out to kill me the way they obviously are now," she said, searching her mind for answers.

That started Morgan thinking. He stopped just before they left the building. "Could it all possibly be a mistake?"

She wasn't following him. "What do you mean?"

"Could it all be an awful coincidence?" he asked. "A terrible, terrible coincidence where on one day you were the victim of a senseless drive-by shooting and then the next day, you just turned out to be the wrong person in the wrong place and someone almost sideswiped you with their car?"

She stared at him. "Do you honestly believe that?" Krys asked.

"No, not really," Morgan admitted. "But I did want to run it past you and give you some food for thought," he told her.

"That 'food' isn't even palatable and ever since I was knee-high to a grasshopper, I was taught to believe that there were no such things as coincidences," she told him.

He nodded. "Well, when it comes to that, I do tend to believe you're right."

She smiled. "Thank heaven for small miracles," she told him. "Now, let's go talk to Valri and see if she can find something for us to sink our teeth into. Otherwise, we still have a killer out there who wants to have my head on a platter and at this point, we don't even have the slightest idea who it is or why they feel this way," she said with just the slightest touch of despondent hopelessness.

He nodded, leading the way to the elevator. "Next stop, the basement," he announced.

And hopefully, some answers, Krys thought.

Chapter Twenty-Two

That night Krys curled up against Morgan in her bed, loving the way his warmth felt as it radiated along her bare skin. She hated the fact that practical thoughts insisted on interfering with the happy glow she felt. But try as she might, she couldn't seem to be able to shut down her mind.

If anything, it was going ninety miles an hour.

"You know, we're running out of time," she said to the man who seemed to be able to make her heart sing so easily.

She felt his chuckle in his chest, rippling along her body.

"Oh, I don't know. I could go again," Morgan told her, pressing a kiss to her forehead. "Just give me a few moments to catch my breath."

Balling up her fist, Krys punched his shoulder. "I'm not talking about that, wise guy," she laughed.

"All right, what *are* you talking about?" he asked. He became fully engaged with anointing her shoulder, spreading a wreath of kisses along the length from one side to the other.

It was hard for her to think when he was doing something like that, but she gave it her best.

"Nik and Finn are…coming back from their…honeymoon soon and…we still haven't—haven't found…out who wants to eliminate…me and…perhaps…by accident…her." Because she was quickly losing her train of thought, Krys had to put her hand up against his mouth and stop Morgan from continuing to play havoc with her thought process.

Morgan raised his head and looked at her. "Well, there haven't been any more attempts on your life for almost two weeks, right?"

"Right," she was forced to agree.

"Maybe whoever it was has given up. Or," he said, "maybe I was right when I said that those two attempts were actually just terrible coincidences."

It was a possibility, but she felt that they were taking too much of a chance going with that. "If you don't mind, I'd rather not bet my sister's life on that theory."

Morgan propped himself up on his elbow and looked into her face. "Well, neither would I, which is why I've arranged for Nik to have a protective detail the second she gets off the plane."

She knew Morgan meant well, but she viewed his solution from a woman's point of view. "Just what Nik needs, a squadron of police officers around her and Finn. Perfect way to start off her married life." Before he could say anything more, another thought occurred to Krys. "Besides, isn't there some sort of a time limit on this?" She saw him raising a puzzled brow so she explained, "Someone within the department must be balking at what this is all costing the city of Aurora."

"There isn't any cost limit," he told her.

That just didn't make any sense. "What are you talking about?" she asked. "*Everything* costs these days. I imagine police protection has to cost a fortune in overtime pay."

"It would," Morgan agreed. "But not when it's all off hours."

She didn't understand. "Off hours?" she questioned. What was he talking about?

"That's right. This is family business," Morgan explained, "not police business." He smiled broadly. "That's one of the benefits of being a Cavanaugh," he told her. And then he drew her closer to him. "Now, don't you have anything better for your mouth to be doing than talking?" he asked her. "Because if you don't," he said, lowering his voice, "I can think of at least one thing—possibly two," he added as he returned to lacing a wreath of kisses along her neck.

He was doing it again, Krys thought. He was pulling her back into the enticing vortex of heat and dizzying passion that he was so very capable of creating for her.

Krys gave up voicing her concerns and just allowed herself to become totally wrapped up in the heady, mind-blowing reality that was Morgan.

COME MORNING, KRYS was once again acutely aware of the lack of time she was currently dealing with. She wished she could buy into the theory that Morgan had voiced, that whoever had been out to kill her, for whatever reason had first prompted him, had given up or just called it a day. She tried to believe that she, and consequently Nik, were in no more danger now than they normally were.

But something in Krys's gut made her feel that this wasn't over yet. That there was another verse of this melody that still needed to be played out. Moreover, she didn't have any idea of where or when the melody would start up again. Or just how intense it would wind up being.

A deep dive into not just Lawrence Jacobs's financials but the financial dealings of anyone close to Jacobs turned up nothing.

"If the guy was paying off a hired killer, he found a new source of currency to do it, or he had someone else paying for it." Morgan leaned back in his chair, staring at the information he had waded through that was on his screen.

So much information and he had gotten nowhere.

"If you ask me, if Jacobs *was* paying someone to eliminate you, he lost faith in the assassin and decided to call the whole thing off." He waved at the screen. "There's no paper trail and, don't forget, no more evidence of any further attempts on your life."

"Then what? You've decided to call off the protective detail?" Krys asked. She wasn't worried about herself, but she *was* worried about her sister.

"No, not yet," Morgan told her, not wanting her to worry. "We'll give it a few more days once Nik comes back to Aurora." He thought for a moment. "Say a week after Nik and Finn get back. If at that point there are no indications that she—or you—are in any danger, then maybe we'll think about packing up our tents and slipping off into the night."

He looked at Krys to see how she felt about this latest school of thought.

Krys felt that she had to agree with him. Morgan was right and she was undoubtedly just being paranoid.

She forced herself to say as much. "You're right." But even as she said the words, she could feel her gut tightening—for more than one reason.

"Does this mean you won't be camping out in my house anymore?" she asked. She did her best to sound blasé about it, but the truth was that the thought of his not being with her was upsetting. She had gotten very used to having him around.

"Why don't we just take this one step at a time?" he suggested. "There's no sense in rushing anything, right?"

There was a smile she couldn't begin to fathom or untangle playing on his lips. A smile that nonetheless made her stomach flutter.

Krys inclined her head. "I bow to your superior wisdom."

"Well, I think I can safely say that's probably the last time I'll *ever* hear anything even remotely like *that* again," Morgan told her with a genuine laugh.

They were in the squad room, which meant that this really wasn't the time to let herself react to Morgan and that sexy laugh of his. It was a lot safer if she just changed the subject—which she did.

"Since you haven't said anything, I assume there's been no progress in locating that woman who Bluebeard had taken hostage and was in the car when he had that accident?" Krys asked.

From the information that had been available, they had come to the final conclusion that the woman had to have been the serial killer's next intended victim. There was nothing to point to any other reason she had been in the vehicle with him.

"None whatsoever," Morgan answered. He was nothing if not persistent and said as much to her. "But we haven't given up trying to find her. It's just looking pretty slim at the moment." He saw the frustration in her eyes and tried to get her to redirect her focus on something else. "How about you? Have you been given any new assignments or is your editor letting you relax for the time being?" he asked.

The word "relax" was not as appealing to her as he might have thought. "A writer needs to write," she told him. "As a matter of fact, my editor said she would be interested in seeing an article from me about what it feels like to be stalked by someone I know is looking to kill me."

His smile faded. "I think that's a bad idea," he told her flatly. "That's like waving a red flag in front of a charging bull."

"Well, right now, according to you, there might not actually be a charging bull, remember?"

"That's just one theory," he told her. "And all things considered, I don't think it's all that smart to tempt fate."

He could see that stubborn look in her eyes. "Are you telling me that you don't want me to write the article?" Krys asked him.

Morgan knew if he said he didn't want her doing it, that would accomplish the exact opposite. So, although it killed him, he said, "No, I'm just asking you to be careful and to think about what you're doing—before you do it."

"All right," she said, "I'll think about it." She said the right words, but he doubted that she really meant them. He knew her well enough by now to realize that when she wanted to do something, she went right ahead and did it. He had to find some way to get her to refrain from doing this insane piece.

"Look, since Walker is out on medical leave," he said, referring to one of the members of his team, "why don't you stay here and use his desk to write that article—once you think over the pros and cons?"

Morgan made it sound as if she was actually going to consider whether or not to write the article, even though they both knew that in the end, she was going to do it.

She looked at the empty desk. "Wouldn't someone frown on me doing that now that it looks like the case might be wrapped up? Like maybe the head of the Major Crimes Division?" she suggested. Having her here had been acceptable while the case was ongoing, but now that Jacobs's supposed reason for killing her had been eliminated and the other major suspect was dead, there was no longer a reason to keep such a close eye on her.

"Don't worry about it. The lieutenant is a pretty easygoing guy. He'll be okay with it," Morgan told her. "You just sit there and do your thing."

Krys cocked an eyebrow and looked at him. "My 'thing,' huh?"

He caught the inflection in her voice. "You know, I get the feeling that you're spoiling for a fight."

Krys realized that maybe she *had* sounded a bit defensive. "I'm just frustrated, that's all," she told him. Every theory so far had fallen through, and every path had wound up being a dead end. "I don't like not getting answers."

"You get used to that," he said philosophically, thinking of his own work. "A lot of life doesn't have answers."

That might be true, but she had never allowed it to stop her. "I usually keep after something until I can find some sort of an answer—or wind up wrapping that 'something' up."

Just then the phone on Morgan's desk rang. He looked as if he was going to ignore it and continue to try to talk some sense into her.

"Better get that," she told him. "It might be another case. One with an actual resolution going for it," she said, waving her hand at the phone as it rang again.

Morgan shot her a dubious look. He would have preferred making her his primary—and only—focus until he either actually resolved the case once and for all, or was convinced that there was no longer anything to resolve. But he knew he didn't have that luxury. He had to get back to his job, and his job was solving cases, sometimes juggling several open ones at a time.

"Cavanaugh," he announced into the receiver, then turned his chair away from Krys so he could talk to whoever was calling privately.

She needed to get back to work, Krys thought. Maybe she could focus on another article for the time being. Agonizing over the unresolved details of these two previous cases was going to drive her crazy. There was something else she had been meaning to write about, she remembered—now that there was no one actively trying to run her over with their car or shoot her.

She just needed to focus—

Krys felt her cell phone vibrating in her pocket. Glancing toward Morgan, she saw that he was still busy talking to whoever had called him. Covertly, she pulled the cell phone out of her pocket and glanced down at the screen. There was a name and number on it she didn't recognize.

Miranda Wilson.

Most likely it was a robocall. When it rang for a third time, she decided to take it. But not here in the squad room. The noise level would necessitate that she raise her voice, and that would direct Morgan's attention over to her.

Krys slowly rose from her desk. She saw that the simple movement had caught Fredericks's eye, but Morgan still had his back to her.

An ounce of prevention, she thought. "If he asks," she said to Morgan's partner, "tell him I went to the ladies' room."

Hiding her cell phone, Krys moved swiftly and left the squad room.

The second she was in the hall, she took out her cell phone and held it up to her ear. "Are you still there?" she asked the caller.

A quiet woman's voice answered her. "Yes, I'm still here."

"Hold on a second longer while I find somewhere quiet where we can talk," Krys requested.

Not waiting for an answer, she quickly marched down the hall to the ladies' room.

Once inside, Krys carefully looked around. The stalls were all empty. She had her privacy, she thought, hoping that all this effort turned out to be worth it.

"Hello, are you still there?" she asked the party on the other end again, afraid the person had hung up.

"Yes, I'm still here," the woman told her a little impatiently.

Krys thought she detected a slight accent, but she couldn't place it. Moving ahead, she asked, "So, what can I do for you?"

Many of her conversations with her sources started this way, she thought. With any luck, this would be another one of those.

"I hear you're looking for me."

A little electric shock traveled through her, but she wasn't going to get carried away. Not yet.

"That all depends," Krys replied in a calm voice. "Who are you?"

"I thought you would have figured that out already. I'm the woman who was in the car with the man you called 'Bluebeard.'"

Every fiber of Krys's body came to attention as she replayed the words she had just heard. Still, she was well aware that this could all just turn out to be a hoax. There were a lot of strange people out there and it never ceased to amaze her just what some people were capable of, the kind of lies certain people could tell in hopes of being able to secure their fleeting moment in the sun.

"The woman who was taken to the hospital after the accident," Krys guessed.

"Yes, that was me," the woman acknowledged.

"They said it was a miracle that you survived the accident," Krys said, still wondering if this was a hoax, or if the woman who had been in the car was actually calling her.

"I guess I've always been lucky like that in my own way," the woman on the other end of the call told her.

"Why are you calling me?" Krys asked. She knew she could very well be chasing the woman away, but in order to make sure the woman was who she said she was, she needed to have this question answered.

"Because my story needs to be heard," the woman said simply.

"All right." For the time being, she was willing to go along with this. She could get more proof later. "Tell me this. If you were hurt, why did you flee from the hospital?"

"Because I was afraid," the woman admitted.

"Afraid?" She didn't understand. "Of who? The police? The doctors?" If this woman was telling the truth and she was who she claimed she was, it didn't make any sense to Krys why she would suddenly vanish the way she had. Why didn't she remain to be treated properly?

"I was afraid of Alan," the woman answered, her voice sounding almost breathless.

"Of Alan?" Krys repeated. The name rang a bell. It had been one of aliases that Bluebeard had used. "You mean Bluebeard?"

She heard the woman make a dismissive noise. "That really is such an awful name," she said with feeling. "Yes, I was afraid of him. Of Alan," she repeated.

"But why were you afraid of him? He was killed in the accident," Krys told her. "You must have known that. The police had to have told you he was dead."

There was a long pause on the other end of the call, and then the woman said, "Yes, they told me. But I didn't believe them. I thought he made them lie to me. He was capable of something like that, of getting people to do what he wanted them to do. You have no idea how charming Alan could be when he wanted to."

"So you took off," Krys concluded, prodding the woman to go on talking.

"I had to," the woman told her.

Krys felt her head filling up with questions she wanted to ask. She needed to meet with this woman face-to-face, to look into the woman's eyes as Bluebeard's last victim told her story.

"Look, is there anywhere that we could meet?" Krys asked. "I've got a lot of questions I want to ask you."

She heard the woman hesitating, and then she said, "I don't know if I can trust you."

"You called me, so some part of you has to feel that you can trust me," Krys pointed out, trying not to push, but to make the woman feel secure enough to tell her things.

She heard the woman sigh. *Gotcha*, Krys thought.

"All right," the woman on the other end agreed reluctantly. "I'll meet you right inside William Mason Park," the woman said, then added, "Come alone. If I see you bringing someone—if I even *think* that you've got someone with you—this is over and I'm out of there. Do you understand?"

Krys thought of Morgan. He was going to want to be there with her. There was no way he would let her do this on her own, but she had to if she wanted this interview.

This was going to take some work on her part. Therein lay the challenge, she thought, anticipation growing within her.

She wanted this interview so badly, she could taste it.

"I understand," Krys answered.

Chapter Twenty-Three

Hurrying out of the ladies' room, Krys narrowly avoided colliding with Morgan.

He caught hold of her shoulders to steady her as he scrutinized her face. "Are you all right?" he asked. "You were in there a long time. I was just about to get one of the female officers to go in there and look for you."

Maybe another time she might have even been touched by his display of concern, but right now it was interfering with her escape plan. "What did you think happened to me?" she asked. "That I slid down the drain?"

"No, I thought that maybe you weren't feeling well," he answered.

She was embarrassed by her flippant retort, and upset that she had to lie to Morgan. But she knew that there was no way he was going to let her go off to meet with this Miranda person by herself and she *knew* that the woman wasn't going to say a single word to her if Morgan came with her. She might not even stick around at all.

No, to get this story, she needed to slip away.

She had no choice but to lie to him and hope that he would understand why and eventually forgive her.

"Actually, that's very perceptive of you," Krys said. "I hate admitting it because it makes me sound like some sort of a weakling, but I'm really not feeling all that well," she told him.

Instantly concerned, Morgan asked, "Why, what's the matter?" Then, before she could answer him, Morgan prompted, "Why don't we go back into the squad room so that you can sit down while you describe your symptoms."

She shrugged, afraid that she might have oversold this. She didn't want him taking her to see a doctor.

"I'm just feeling a little under the weather," she told him, dialing it back a little as she sat down at the desk opposite his.

For his part, Morgan put his hand to her forehead, checking for a fever.

"It's nothing serious," she insisted, pulling her head back. "I just thought maybe I should go home and lie down for a bit. I'll probably be better in the morning."

Still looking concerned, Morgan glanced around the squad room as if searching for something. "Let me see if I can get someone to take over what I'm working on today and then—"

"No," Krys said firmly. He looked at her, confused. "I can't let you do that. I don't want to keep disrupting your life like this," she told him. "And I don't need to be coddled, either. All I need is a few hours of rest and I'll be good as new, I promise." Her tone softened a little. "You've already done more than enough for me, Morgan."

"You still need a ride home," he pointed out. Then, just in case she was planning on arguing with him about that, he reminded her, "Since you came in with me."

"No, I know that," she responded. "But you don't have to go through all this trouble. I could call a ride service and have one of their drivers take me back to my house."

Morgan made no comment about her suggestion, but she felt that the expression on his face said it all. She was not going to be calling a ride service.

Seeing one of the police officers assigned to running errands for his lieutenant, Morgan gestured the man over to his desk.

"Riley, I need you to take Ms. Kowalski here to her home. And once you get her there, I want you to stay and keep an eye on her for me. She's still under protective custody," Morgan pointed out.

"You can count on me, Detective," the police officer said with enthusiasm.

"Good. The department doesn't want anything happening to her," Morgan added. "Brigham and Malcolm are already in the area, keeping watch, but a little overkill in this case wouldn't hurt."

Riley's dark, slightly shaggy head nodded. "Yes, sir."

Turning toward Krys, Morgan told her, "I'll be there as soon as I can."

"You really don't have to rush on my account," she told him. "Most likely I'll probably just fall asleep for a while."

Morgan nodded as they parted company. "That's probably the best thing for you," he agreed. He watched her as she put her laptop into its case. His parting words to her were, "Remember to stay put."

She gave Morgan an innocent smile. "Where would I go?" she asked him as she walked out in front of the police officer.

RILEY WAS EAGER to be of service and he wasn't nearly as hard to get rid of as she'd thought he would be. Once the rookie officer brought her to her door and she had assured him that she would be fine, he retreated into his patrol car, where he proceeded to sit watching over her front door.

The other two officers Morgan had doing stakeout work were still posted in the area, but she already knew where they were. Eluding them as well as Riley should be relatively simple, Krys decided. All three policemen were on the lookout for someone bent on breaking into her house. They weren't looking for her to break out.

She knew that she couldn't use her own car, but she wouldn't have to. Ian's old car was housed in a nearby storage unit. He had left it to her, among other things, in his will. Since the whole situation with Ian was all so fresh, she hadn't had an opportunity to figure out what she wanted to do with it yet. It appeared that this would be the perfect time to take the car out for a spin, she thought. Ian would have approved of the use she was putting his car to.

Krys gave her newest bodyguard ten minutes to settle into place. Then she quickly changed her clothes.

Moving quietly, she slipped out of her back door. Then, utilizing a hole in the fence, she cut across a neighbor's yard. Once on the other side of that yard, she walked to the storage unit where she kept Ian's car. Excited, she wanted to run all the way there, but she forced herself to move at a normal pace. She didn't want to attract any undue attention to herself.

When she finally got to the storage unit and slid behind the steering wheel, Ian's car didn't start up immediately. It took her several attempts to try to start it before the engine finally rolled over and kicked in.

Letting out a deep breath, Krys glanced at her watch. She was cutting this close, she thought. She had told "Miranda" that she would meet the woman at the park at two thirty. It was already a few minutes after two.

Travel was light at this time of day, so she would probably be able to get there with a few minutes to spare, she told herself. That would give her enough time to scope out the area. The local park was predominantly designed for families who wanted to enjoy having picnics with their children.

She assumed that Miranda had picked that particular location to ensure her own safety. The woman had sounded genuinely spooked when she had talked about "Bluebeard" to her.

Her pulse hammering, Krys arrived at the park in minutes. She pulled into the park via its only entrance and then drove into the general area that was reserved for people who wanted to enjoy the family park.

Given that it was the middle of the week, there weren't all that many people in the park. In Krys's estimation, the park attendants probably outnumbered the people who had actually come to the park to enjoy a picnic with their small children.

Ian's car had turned out to handle a lot better than she had thought it would. It had started out a little sluggish, but once it kicked into gear, it drove very smoothly.

Thank heaven for small favors.

After parking the car in a designated spot for vehicles, Krys went to the appointed area that she'd agreed to meet the woman—by the picnic tables.

Every step she took seemed to vibrate through her.

She looked around, and at first she didn't see a lone woman who resembled the general description Miranda had given her. She was afraid that the woman had had a change of heart.

And then a movement by one of the tall shade trees along the perimeter caught her eye. She saw a flash of yellow. Looking, she saw that it turned out to be blond hair.

Krys wanted to call out to the woman, then decided against it. During their brief conversation earlier, Miranda had struck her as being definitely skittish. Krys didn't want to risk scaring her or say anything that would make Miranda take off before she had a chance to talk to her.

So Krys picked her way carefully over to the woman's location, keeping her stride even and never taking her eyes off her.

She didn't say a single word until she was practically right on top of her quarry.

"Miranda?"

Startled, the tall, thin woman swung around. Krys couldn't tell if Miranda was going to bolt or take a swing at her. Prepared for anything, Krys took a precautionary step back and caught the woman by the arm.

"Miranda, it's me. Krys," she told the woman in a calming voice meant to reassure her. "You called me earlier, remember?"

Myriad emotions filtered across the attractive face. Krys couldn't even begin to guess what was going through Miranda's head.

"You're here," Miranda finally said in an almost surprised, breathless voice.

"Yes, I told you that I would be," Krys said. "And I'm sorry. I didn't mean to startle you," she apologized. She saw the woman's eyes darting about. It made her think of a deer that had been caught in the headlights and didn't know which way to run. She guessed at what Miranda was afraid of. "Don't worry, I didn't bring anyone with me. I'm alone. Completely alone," Krys emphasized.

"Just like me," she thought she heard Miranda murmur coldly

under her breath. And then a strange look came into the woman's sad eyes. "How do I know that you came alone?" Miranda asked. "You could have people planted all around here," she accused in a nasty voice. "Listening."

"I wouldn't do that," Krys insisted. "You told me not to."

But Miranda's eyes continued darting around the immediate area. "I don't want to stand out in the open like this," she insisted. "Anyone can see us."

Krys looked around, then pointed over in the distance. "There's a more secluded area a little ways from here. There're some benches there overlooking the lake." She smiled, recalling something she had once read. "I think it's a romantic spot for teenagers. They go there at night thinking that they were the first ones to ever invent giving in to their romantic urges." She was hoping to put the other woman at ease. "We could go there if you like. Nobody will bother us in the daytime," she speculated.

Miranda nodded. "That sounds good," she agreed. She gestured ahead of her. "Why don't you lead the way?"

Something cautioned Krys not to move ahead. Instead she said, "The terrain is a little bit rocky around here. I think we'd be better off going over there together. That way, if one of us happens to slip, the other one can grab her arm and hold on to her."

Miranda's expression told Krys she didn't really like this suggestion, but finally the woman pressed her lips together, sighed and reluctantly nodded. "All right, we'll do it your way. Where're these benches again?"

"They're right this way," Krys answered.

She began to slip her arm through Miranda's. She intended on guiding her to the benches, but the woman abruptly jerked her arm away, acting as if she had just been burned.

"What's the matter?" Krys asked, surprised by the other woman's reaction.

"You touched me!" Miranda cried, her voice cracking. And then she seemed to get herself under control. "I don't like being touched."

Being touched probably reminded Miranda of what Bluebeard

had done to her, or perhaps even what he might have tried to do to her, Krys thought. She should have realized that.

"I'm sorry," she apologized to Miranda. "I wasn't thinking."

"No, you weren't thinking, were you?" Miranda accused, raising her voice again, glaring at Krys. "You weren't thinking at all."

Krys stared at the woman. Miranda was beginning to look more and more wild-eyed and incensed.

She had dealt with crazy people before and this was beginning to feel like that, Krys thought. "Excuse me?"

"No, I can't," Miranda shouted at her. Before Krys was able to say anything or realized what was happening, Miranda seemed to be having a meltdown right in front of her.

The woman pushed her hard. Krys stumbled, hitting her back against one of the trees that were spread out in the immediate area. They offered seclusion for those who wanted it.

She should have given this more thought, Krys realized, before she agreed to this location. She stepped away before Miranda was able to slam her against the tree again.

Miranda looked absolutely furious as she spit, "I can't excuse you at all."

She needed to get this woman to calm down. "Miranda, I think you'd better—"

"I'd better what?" Miranda shouted viciously. "Not kill you for taking the only person I ever loved away from me? Is that what you want?"

Krys stared at the woman. "What are you talking about?"

"Oh don't play dumb with me. I know what you did. You hounded that wonderful man with those awful, prejudiced newspaper articles of yours until he had nowhere to turn. You were actually going to have him facing a death penalty. But I saved him," she boasted. "I managed to help him escape. And he promised to take me with him. Promised that we were going to start a whole new life together," Miranda said happily. And then fury creased her brow. "But you wouldn't give up, would you? You had the police looking for him, hounding him," she shouted, her face turning ugly.

How could the woman even think that? "Miranda, he killed a

lot of women for their money," she said, trying to somehow reason with the woman.

"He had a right to live, too!" Miranda cried. "Until you took that away from him." She was all but shrieking now. "Well, I can't bring him back, but I can sure as hell make you pay for taking him away from me!"

The second she saw the woman reaching into her purse, Krys knew what was going to happen next.

Her heart slammed into her chest, beating madly. She knew if she tried to grab the woman's hand there was a very good chance that she would wind up getting shot point-blank. But the odds seemed to be equally against her if she stood there and did nothing because then she would wind up getting shot, too.

"You don't want to do that," Krys told her, doing her very best not to let Miranda see just how very frightened she was.

"Oh, but I do. I really do," Miranda answered. "You act like you're so smart, but you don't know anything. You didn't even have a clue that I was the one who's been trying to kill you."

"That was you?" she cried, widening her eyes as if she was stunned. From the moment that Miranda had begun ranting, she had started to suspect as much. But right now, Krys was playing it for all it was worth, stalling and pretending to be impressed by the woman's deviousness. "Really?"

"Yes, it was me," Miranda bragged, throwing back her head, her hair flying over her shoulder. "And when I missed, I bet you thought that you had some kind of a charmed life, didn't you? Well, you don't!" she shouted into Krys's face. "You were just lucky. You ducked to pick up something when I shot at you and then the next day, the guy pulled you out of the way just as I was about to hit you with the van. But your luck couldn't last forever and it just ran out," she declared gleefully. "I'll be kinder to you than you were to Alan. I'll let you make your peace with your maker."

"You'll let me pray?" Krys asked, scanning the immediate area and desperately trying to find something she could use as a weapon.

"Yeah, I'll let you pray. But pray fast," Miranda ordered, cocking her weapon.

"I'd rethink my next move if I were you," Morgan warned the would-be killer as he stepped forward.

His weapon was drawn and aimed right at the woman.

Miranda shrieked a curse as she swung around and pointed her gun at Morgan.

Chapter Twenty-Four

Krys didn't even remember thinking, just reacting. It all happened at lightning speed. Realizing that, because of her, Morgan would be dead in less than a moment, she grabbed Miranda's wrists and pushed them high overhead with all her strength as she struggled to gain possession of the weapon that Miranda was pointing right at Morgan, about to discharge it.

Krys was aware of being utterly terrified. She could literally *see* the scenario playing itself out in her head and she couldn't let that happen.

She and Miranda were instantly locked in a deadly battle, shifting from one position to another.

Morgan tried to get off a clear shot. But he couldn't, not without risking the possibility of hitting Krys.

Struggling, Krys succeeded in getting Miranda off balance by kicking the taller woman's legs out from under her. Miranda's weapon went flying just as Krys threw her full weight right on top of the furious woman. The latter was cursing a blue streak.

That was the moment Morgan finally managed to get a clear shot at the stalker. "This ends right here!" he ordered.

The sound of the detective's weapon being cocked punctuated his warning. The gun in his hand was pointed at Miranda, who was still on the ground.

"You can get off her now, Krys," he said. "And as for you," he told the stalker, "you can stand up!"

Staggering to her feet, Miranda let loose with a wild, guttural screech as she lunged at Morgan. She looked as if she wanted to kill him with her bare hands.

The screech had warned Morgan and he met the head-on attack with a right cross, aimed at Miranda's chin. She fell to the ground, knocked out cold. Morgan lost no time in whipping out his handcuffs and cuffing Krys's crazed, unconscious assailant's hands behind her back.

Shaken, hardly believing it was finally over, Krys blew out a breath. "Lord, I am *so* glad to see you," she cried, throwing her arms around the man who had just saved her.

Krys's words didn't quite get the response she had expected.

With her stalker out cold and safely handcuffed, all the fear that Morgan had experienced in the last half hour came pouring out and he shouted at Krys.

"Why the hell would you come out here by yourself like this?" he demanded angrily. "Do you have some kind of a death wish?"

Krys stared at him, her mouth falling open. All the gratitude she had felt a second ago instantly transformed into anger. That was when it suddenly occurred to her that Morgan had come to her rescue far too conveniently.

She dismissed his question, hitting him with one of her own. "Never mind that. How did you know where to find me?"

In view of what had just happened, he saw no reason to hide the truth. If he hadn't done what he did, she would have been dead by now.

"I had a tracker put on you and it's a damn lucky thing that I did or this nutcase," he gestured down at Miranda, who was still unconscious, "would have killed you."

Krys was speechless, but only for a moment. "You had a tracker put on me?" she asked, stunned. "When? How? *Why?*" She emphasized the last question.

"I did it while you were asleep that first night," he told her. "With the stalker out there after you, I slipped the tracking device into your cell phone just under the battery. I did it just in case you were kidnapped."

"No, you didn't. You did it in case I eluded you, which I did," she pointed out.

He wasn't about to argue the point with her. Instead, he shrugged and said, "Pota-to, po-tah-to. In either case, it turned out to be damn useful. I wouldn't have known where to start looking for you without it." Realizing that she was missing had encompassed the most terrifying ten minutes of his life.

Krys looked down at the prone figure on the ground. Unconscious, the woman didn't appear so frightening as she had been.

"She was the one, you know," Krys said to Morgan, her voice losing some of its animation. It had all suddenly really hit her hard. She was lucky to be alive. "The one who was trying to kill me."

"Her?" It all sounded almost too fantastic to be true. As far as he knew, the unknown woman had never even been considered a suspect. "Do you have any idea why she was trying to kill you?"

A hollow laugh escaped Krys's lips. "She wanted to get back at me. In her demented mind, I was the reason Bluebeard lost his life. From what I pieced together, as strange as it sounds, she seemed to be in love with the man."

It was finally beginning to make some kind of sense, Morgan thought. "Then she was the woman in the car with him."

Krys nodded her head. "She was."

Morgan looked down at the woman he had been forced to knock out to protect himself and Krys. "I take it he didn't have to kidnap her."

"I don't know the backstory to this little sick romance yet," Krys admitted. Handcuffed or not, she was keeping her distance from the woman, just in case. "All I know is that according to her, Miranda here was the one who wound up springing Bluebeard out of his prison cell. She did because she was planning to live 'happily ever after' with that maniac."

Morgan shook his head. It really did take all kinds, the detective thought. "Didn't she know the kind of insane killer this guy was? What he would undoubtedly eventually do to her?"

"If she knew, she really didn't seem to care. Or maybe she thought he'd never hurt her," Krys speculated with a shrug. "Whatever it was, she's obviously proof that love really is blind."

"And deaf," Morgan said. "Don't forget deaf," he told her, thinking of all the news stories that had been broadcast about the serial killer when he was captured the first time.

"Speaking of deaf," Krys said, cocking her head as she listened to the sound in the distance that was growing progressively louder, "are those sirens I hear in the distance?"

Morgan nodded. "They are. That would be the sound of the rest of my team finally getting here," he told her. "I thought, given the situation, that I might need some backup."

Krys thought about what had just happened. Just for a moment, she allowed herself to take a deep breath and willed herself to relax—or at least try to.

"Turns out," she told Morgan as she faced him, "that all I needed was you."

Krys had certainly held her own against that insane woman, he thought. Anyone else in the same situation would have just gone to pieces.

"You didn't exactly do so badly yourself," he said. And then Morgan relived that one awful moment when he saw Krys throw herself at her stalker, wrestling with the woman for possession of the gun. "But don't you ever, *ever* scare the hell out of me like that again."

Krys couldn't help wondering if that was just a throwaway comment on Morgan's part or if he was subtly telling her that this wasn't the end of the line for them, at least not yet.

But she couldn't ask him that without sounding needy, so she said nothing, keeping the question to herself as the area was suddenly filled with police cruisers as well as CSI personnel.

Morgan put his arm around her, drawing Krys over to the side.

"We'd better get out of everyone's way right now," he told her.

They both watched Miranda, still handcuffed and unconscious, being placed on a gurney and wheeled into an emergency vehicle.

"Looks like your nightmare is over," Morgan said to Krys.

Krys sighed. It was hard for her to really believe that this was all finally over.

Despite her hope to the contrary, the word "over" seemed to almost ominously echo in her head as she slanted a glance at Morgan.

THERE WERE REPORTS to be made and paperwork to be filed, not to mention loose ends that needed to be cleared up. None of it was shirked and finally, after what felt like an eternity, everything was completed to everyone's satisfaction. This included the department heads and the chief of detectives.

By the time Morgan brought Krys back to her house, it was nearly ten o'clock at night.

The house felt somehow lonelier than she'd thought it would as she unlocked the front door. Morgan's footsteps echoed her own as he walked in with her. In her heart, she couldn't help thinking that this might very well be for the last time. After all, the case was over and he had accomplished what he had set out to do. He'd caught the person who had been trying to kill her—with her inadvertent help of course, she thought with a sad smile.

Krys was trying to find the right way to word what was on her mind when Morgan's voice broke into her unformed thoughts. "Just what the hell were you thinking?"

She stared at him, completely thrown by his question coming out of left field the way it was. "Excuse me?"

"When you threw yourself at that woman, just what were you thinking?" he demanded. He had relived the whole thing again on the way home and it brought a chill to his heart. "I had the drop on her."

"What I was thinking was that if I didn't push her weapon up, out of the way, that crazy witch was going to kill you."

"With you throwing yourself at her like that, she was more likely to shoot you than me—right in that beautiful face of yours," he emphasized. "What the hell were you thinking?" he repeated. "And where did you learn to move like that?" he asked, referring to some of the self-defense movements she had executed.

"The kind of solo work I do makes self-defense a vital part of my survival," she said matter-of-factly. "And all I could think of was that she was going to shoot *you*—and I couldn't let that happen." Even as she relived the event, her heart was in her throat all over again. "If you died saving me, I couldn't live with myself."

"Instead, you were willing to die to save me," he pointed out. Did she really think that was a better solution?

"You were willing to do that, too," Krys insisted angrily, her eyes blazing.

Morgan blew out a breath. "I guess this is what they call a stalemate."

"I guess so." She paused, pressing her lips together. She could tell by his body language that he was just about to walk out. She had to say something to stop him. "You know, you don't have to leave tonight," she said, despite the fact she had promised herself on the ride home that she wasn't going to say anything to him on the subject.

But she just couldn't bear the idea of seeing Morgan walk out the door.

When he raised one eyebrow, she started talking fast. "I mean, it is late and all and we've both had a really draining day. You could always clear out your things tomorrow."

Morgan examined the words she had just used. Was she really saying what it sounded like she was saying? He just didn't know.

"Then you want me to go?" he questioned.

"I didn't say that," she answered defensively and much too quickly to her own ear. Krys cleared her throat, doing her best to sound calmer. "I mean I just thought you'd want to, what with the case finally being over and all."

His eyes never left hers. "I didn't say that."

So much had happened today, her head was throbbing as her disjointed thoughts became even more jumbled. She knew what she wanted—she wanted him to stay, but she wasn't about to sound as if she was begging. He had to be the one to make the all-important decision and make it clear that he wanted it to be this way.

She let out a breath, struggling not to allow it to sound shaky. "What *are* you saying?" she asked.

He didn't want to be taking anything for granted. "That I don't want to be underfoot."

She stared at him. He had to be kidding, right? "What made you think that I thought you were underfoot?" she asked him, confused.

"Well, for one thing, you are fiercely and incredibly independent," he pointed out. "I practically had to sit on you to get you to accept any sort of protection—and," he went on to remind her, "when you thought you'd lose out on what you were sure was going to be an exclusive story, you deliberately disregarded every shred of common sense, eluded everyone who was determined to protect you and bolted. And then—"

"I was wrong," she told him.

Morgan came to a skidding halt midsentence. He stared at her, dumbfounded. He hadn't expected this from her. "What did you say?"

"I was wrong," Krys repeated, sounding repentant. "I'm sorry."

"Do you have *any* idea what I went through when I realized you were missing? Do you *know* the kind of awful thoughts that went through my head, torturing me?" he demanded.

She hadn't even stopped to think of what he might have gone through. Now that she did, she felt guilty. "I shouldn't have done that to you."

"No," he agreed with passion, "you definitely shouldn't have."

"How can I make it up to you?" she asked him, looking, in his opinion, extremely contrite as well as sincere.

Was he being a total fool, taken in by the look on her face? But when he thought of the way he'd felt, afraid that she was in trouble, none of the rest of it mattered. He didn't want to win this argument, because it wasn't about winning. It was about having her. Loving her.

All he wanted was her.

And all it had taken was a crazy woman to bring that home to him.

"Well," he said slowly, "if you're serious abut making it up to me…"

"I am," she answered with enthusiasm.

"Then I can think of several ways you could do that," he said, the makings of a wicked smile on his face.

The smile that slipped over her lips was the first smile he had seen on her since they had had breakfast this morning. Looking back, it felt like that had been a hundred years ago.

"Does one of those 'ways' involve you staying the night?" she asked him.

He pretended to consider her question. "It might involve staying even longer than that," he told her, then asked, "How would you feel about that?"

Maybe it was the lighting, but he could have sworn it looked as if her eyes were shining.

"Guess," she breathed.

"I might need a hint to do that," he told her, keeping a straight face.

"All right," she agreed gamely, suddenly feeling that everything was going to work out just as she had hoped. "One hint coming up," she declared, wrapping her arms around his neck as she stood up on her toes and brought her mouth up to his.

She sank into the kiss, feeling herself quickly catching on fire. Krys put her entire soul into it, kissing him for all she was worth.

And then she drew her head back. "Well?" she asked, waiting for his reaction.

"Sorry," he told her after a prolonged minute, "I'm afraid that I'm going to need more of a hint than that."

Krys's smile filtered into her eyes. "You do drive a hard bargain."

"Giving up?" he asked innocently.

"Oh no, not by a long shot," she promised. "Brace yourself, Cavanaugh. The hinting has just begun—" she promised "—if you're up to it."

"Oh, I'm up to it all right," he assured her. "I've been waiting to be 'up to it' for what feels like my entire life."

"Well, then, I'm happy to tell you that your wish has just come true," she informed Morgan with a delighted laugh.

"You talk too much, Kowalski," he told her, tightening his arms around her as he drew her even closer to him.

Krys raised her chin, her invitation very clear. "Then why don't you go ahead and make me stop?" she challenged him.

"Gladly," he said, his mouth covering hers.

And then there was no more talking after that for a very long, long time.

Epilogue

"You know, I don't remember the last time I ever saw Krys looking *this* happy," Nik confided to her husband as the church where they had gotten married six months ago was now filling up with family and friends, gathering there to witness yet another Cavanaugh wedding take place.

"And I didn't realize that when you told me you had an identical twin, she was *this* identical." Finn laughed, shaking his head. "Looking at the two of you is like really seeing double."

"Well, when we stand next to each other, I'm an inch taller," Nik reminded him.

"That really doesn't help if you're standing in different parts of the room," Finn pointed out.

Nik grinned. "All you need to remember is that Krys is the one in the wedding dress, marrying your cousin," she said. "And you're married to me."

Finn laughed. "Like I could forget the greatest thing that ever happened to me."

Andrew's wife, Rose, came out from the rear of the church. Seeing Nik, she hurried over to the younger woman, her light gray dress rustling as she moved.

"Your sister's looking for you, Nikki," she said. "The ceremony's about to begin, so I'd move fast if I were you."

Nik nodded, knowing how important it was to Krys to have her there for this. She had really missed her twin at her own wedding, but she knew that it couldn't have been helped. She had always known that Krys was nothing if not loyal to a fault.

"On my way," Nik told Rose, hurrying to get to the vestibule before Krys began to think that she had been abandoned.

"I'm here, Krys," she announced, making her way into the tiny room. Seeing her twin, Nik nodded in approval. "That's a nice look on you."

Krys glanced down at the form-fitting full-length gown. "It's the wedding dress. It would make anyone look good."

"The dress is really very pretty," Nik agreed. "But I was referring to the smile on your face. It makes you look radiant."

Krys laughed with pleasure. "That is all Morgan's doing. Oh Nik, I've never been so happy," she said with enthusiasm.

"I can tell," Nik said. And then she cocked her head, listening. "I think that's our cue, Krys. Time to get this show on the road." She paused just for a moment to give her sister a heartfelt big hug. "Prepare to be even happier," she predicted.

"I'm not sure I can do that without exploding," Krys confessed.

Nik winked at her. "Try."

Clutching her flowers in her hand and trying to calm down the wild, fluttering butterflies in her stomach, Krys left the shelter of the vestibule.

Preceded by her five bridesmaids, all either Morgan's sisters or cousins except for Nik, her matron of honor, she focused on making her way down the aisle and to the altar. She really hoped she could do it without tripping on the edge of her satin-and-lace bridal gown.

Krys stopped thinking about tripping the moment she saw Morgan standing next to his best man, waiting for her at the altar.

"I was afraid you got wind of another story you just had to pursue," Morgan whispered to her when she reached him.

Krys shook her head. "This is the story I've been waiting to pursue my whole life," she told him. "There was no way in the world I was going to wind up missing it."

"I'm really glad to hear that you feel that way," he said, smiling at her. "Because I do too."

And then, as they turned together in unison to take their vows and pledge their undying, everlasting love to one another, Krys felt that, after all this time, she had finally managed to come home.

* * * * *

Marine Force Recon

Elle James

Elle James, a *New York Times* bestselling author, started writing when her sister challenged her to write a romance novel. She has managed a full-time job and raised three wonderful children, and she and her husband even tried ranching exotic birds (ostriches, emus and rheas). Ask her, and she'll tell you what it's like to go toe-to-toe with an angry 350-pound bird! Elle loves to hear from fans at ellejames@earthlink.net or ellejames.com.

Books by Elle James

Harlequin Intrigue

Declan's Defenders

Marine Force Recon

Mission: Six

One Intrepid SEAL
Two Dauntless Hearts
Three Courageous Words
Four Relentless Days
Five Ways to Surrender
Six Minutes to Midnight

Ballistic Cowboys

Hot Combat
Hot Target
Hot Zone
Hot Velocity

SEAL of My Own

Navy SEAL Survival
Navy SEAL Captive
Navy SEAL to Die For
Navy SEAL Six Pack

Visit the Author Profile page at millsandboon.com.au.

This book is dedicated to my father, who will always be my number one hero. He spent twenty years on active duty defending our country, and he has spent a lifetime caring for and protecting his family. He's what heroes are made of, and I love him so very much.

Love you, Dad!

CAST OF CHARACTERS

Declan O'Neill—Highly trained Force Recon marine who made a decision that cost him his career in the Marine Corps. Dishonorably discharged from the military, he's forging his own path with the help of a wealthy benefactor.

Grace Lawrence—Divorced and trying to make a new life in DC with the help of her roommate...until her roommate goes missing.

Charlotte "Charlie" Halverson—Rich widow of a highly prominent billionaire philanthropist. Leading the fight for right by funding Declan's Defenders.

Mack Balkman—Former Force Recon marine, assistant team leader and Declan's right-hand man. Grew up on a farm and knows hard work won't kill you—guns will.

Frank "Mustang" Ford—Former Force Recon marine, point man. First into dangerous situations, making him the eyes and ears of the team.

Augustus "Gus" Walsh—Former Force Recon marine radio operator; good with weapons, electronics and technical equipment.

Cole McCastlain—Former Force Recon marine assistant radio operator. Good with computers.

Jack Snow—Former Force Recon marine slack man, youngest on the team, takes all the heavy stuff. Not afraid of hard, physical work.

Riley Lansing—Engineer on special projects at Quest Aerospace Alliance.

Alen Moretti—Riley's supervisor of special projects at Quest Aerospace Alliance.

Chapter One

Declan O'Neill hiked his rucksack higher on his shoulders and trudged down the sidewalk in downtown Washington, DC. The last time he'd seen so many people in one place, he'd been a fresh recruit at US Marine Corps Basic Training in San Diego, California, standing among a bunch of teenagers, just like him, being processed into the military.

He shouldered his way through the throngs of sightseers, businessmen and career women hurrying to the next building along the road. The sun shone on a bright spring day. Cherry blossoms exploded in fluffy, pinkish-white dripping petals onto the lawns and sidewalks in an optimistic display of hope.

Hope.

Declan snorted. Here he was, eleven years after joining the US Marine Corps…eleven years of knowing what was expected of him…of not having to decide what to wear each day. Eleven years of a steady paycheck, no matter how small, in an honorable profession, making a difference in the world.

Now he was faced with the daunting task of job hunting with a huge strike on his record.

But not today.

Why he'd decided to take the train from Bethesda, Maryland, to the political hub of the entire country was beyond his own comprehension. But with nowhere else to go and nothing holding him back—no job, no family, no home—he'd thought *why not?*

He'd never been to the White House, never stopped to admire the Declaration of Independence, drafted by the forefathers of his country, and he'd never stood at the foot of the Lincoln Memorial, in the shadow of the likeness of Abraham Lincoln, a leader who'd set the United States on a revolutionary course. He'd never been to the Vietnam War Memorial or any other memorial in DC.

Yeah. And so what?

Sightseeing wouldn't pay the bills. Out of the military, out of money and sporting a dishonorable discharge, Declan would be hard-pressed to find a decent job. Who would hire a man whose only skills were superb marksmanship that allowed him to kill a man from four hundred yards away, expertise in hand-to-hand combat and the ability to navigate himself out of a paper bag with nothing more than the stars and his wits?

In the age of the internet, desk jobs and background checks, he was doomed to end up in a homeless shelter. With his last ninety-eight dollars and fifty-five cents burning a hole in the pocket of his rucksack, he'd decided to see the country's capital before he couldn't afford to. As for a place to sleep? He could duke it out with the other homeless people for a back alley or a park bench. Maybe he'd get lucky and someone would slit his throat and put him out of his misery.

He paused at a corner, waiting for the light to change and the little walking man to blink on in bright white.

As he waited, he noticed a couple of dark SUVs sandwiching a long, sleek white limousine. Not that he hadn't seen at least half a dozen limousines pass in the last twenty minutes he'd been walking. But he was standing still now and had nothing else but the backs of people's heads to stare at.

The lead SUV turned on the street in front of Declan.

Before the limousine could follow suit, a white van erupted from a side street, tires screaming, and plowed through the people traversing a crosswalk to cut off the white limousine before it could make the turn.

Another white van followed the first and raced to block the rear of the limousine, effectively bracketing the big vehicle.

Men dressed in dark suits and ties jumped out of each of the dark SUVs, weapons drawn. They'd only taken two steps when the sliding doors on the vans slashed open and men in dark clothes and ski masks leaped out, carrying submachine guns.

"Get down!" Declan yelled. He grabbed the blond-haired woman in the fancy skirt suit beside him and shoved her to the ground as bullets sprayed into the men in suits from the SUV. Declan threw his body over the woman's, shielding her from the rain of bullets.

The men and women surrounding him dropped to the pavement out of fear or injury. Ladies screamed, children cried and chaos reigned.

While the gunmen from the white van continued to fire toward the pedestrians, more men piled out of the vans and raced for the white limousine. They yanked at the vehicles' doors, but the handles didn't budge.

One of the attackers aimed at the handle and pulled the trigger on his handgun.

The limousine door burst open. A black-suited bodyguard poked a gun out and fired.

The man who'd shot the door handle edged out of range, jammed his handgun through the door and pulled the trigger.

Over the top of the other side of the vehicle, another man in a dark suit emerged from inside the limousine and aimed at the man who'd just shot one of the limousine passengers.

From his prone position, Declan watched as it all went down. Whoever the security detail was guarding must have been important enough for trained gunmen to stage such a daring operation in the middle of the day, on a crowded street.

Unable to stand by while people were being attacked, Declan shrugged out of his rucksack and shoved it toward the woman he'd pushed to the ground. "Watch this," he commanded. "I'll be back in a minute."

The woman lay with her cheek to the ground, her eyes wide, a frown marring her pretty features. "Where are you going?"

"I can't just stand by and do nothing." He bunched his legs beneath himself and pushed to a low crouch.

A hand reached up to capture his arm. "Don't. They'll kill you."

"If nobody does anything, they'll kill everyone in that limousine and the security detail that was supposed to protect them."

"But you're only one man." She stared up at him with soft gray eyes.

"Just watch my ruck. Everything I own is in that bag. And stay down." He didn't wait for her response. Instead, he ran to the side of a Lincoln Town Car that had stopped short of the vans and SUVs caught in the crossfire.

The driver lay sideways in his seat, the front windshield having been peppered with bullet holes. He wasn't moving, his eyes open, unseeing.

Declan moved on, keeping the body of the sedan between him and the men wielding submachine guns. He waited for the shooter closest to him to turn away before he pounced, throwing the man off-balance and pushing him to the ground. With a combination of surprise and strength, he took the man down and jerked his head back with a decided snap.

The man hadn't even fired another round. He lay still, unmoving at Declan's feet.

Declan retrieved the attacker's submachine gun and moved to the next man closest to him. Again, his attention focused on the limousine and the crowd lying crouched against the concrete sidewalks.

Moving silently, Declan eased up behind the next guy.

A scuffle with another security guard in the limousine generated more shouting and an eruption of gunfire.

Under the resulting confusion, Declan made his move and took out the next attacker, bringing him to the road surface with barely a whimper before he snapped his neck.

Sirens wailed in the distance.

One of the attackers yanked a dead security guard out of the back seat of the limousine and reached in to grab someone.

"Let go!" a voice inside yelled.

The attacker yanked a woman out of the limousine. She had gray hair and wore a dark gray suit and sensible pumps. "Don't hurt anyone else. I'll go with you. Just don't hurt anyone else."

He pulled her against him and pointed the handgun against her temple.

Declan cursed silently beneath his breath. A hostage meant the attackers had more than the upper hand. No matter how many bad guys he took out, he couldn't get to the one who held the bargaining chip. Unless...

He'd worked his way closer to the white van blocking the front of the limousine. A couple of bad guys stood at the front of the vehicle and one guarded the rear.

Declan rolled beneath a long black sedan parked several feet away from the van. If he could just make it to the van the kidnapper was edging toward, he might be able to...

A police car rounded the corner two blocks away, lights flashing, siren screaming. It ground to a halt. The two officers inside flung open their doors and leaped out, using the doors as shields.

"Time to go," the kidnapper shouted. Holding his victim with the gun to her head, he hurried toward the van closest to Declan.

If the kidnapper made it inside, the police would not be able to stop him without potential injury to the woman.

The van door slid open. A man inside grabbed the kidnapper's arm and the woman's and yanked them both inside.

The rest of the attackers backed toward the other van, still providing cover but unaware of Declan standing near the rear of the kidnapper's vehicle.

As the sliding door started to close, Declan reached for the back door of the van. The handle turned, the door swung open and Declan leaped in as the sliding side door slammed shut.

Four bad guys filled the interior. The kidnapper had released his charge and was in the process of shoving the woman to the floor of the van.

When she collapsed to her knees, Declan had a clear shot.

He braced himself and pulled the trigger on the submachine gun as the driver shifted the gear into Reverse.

The kidnapper and the man who'd helped him into the vehicle dropped on top of the woman and lay still.

"Stop the vehicle," Declan yelled. "Or I'll shoot."

The man in the passenger seat swiveled, a handgun in the palm of his hand.

Declan didn't hesitate—he fired several shots at the man, the bullets hitting him in the arm and penetrating the back of the seat. The man slumped forward, the pistol falling from his hand.

The driver hit the accelerator, with the vehicle still in reverse, and he pulled hard on the steering wheel.

Centrifugal force flung Declan across the bed of the van. He hit the other side with his right shoulder, losing his hold on the submachine gun. The weapon clattered to the floor and skittered beyond his fingertips, out of Declan's reach.

As he righted himself, the driver shifted into Drive and gunned the engine.

Barely reclaiming his equilibrium, Declan staggered backward, caught himself and lunged for the driver, ready to end the rodeo. He grabbed the back of the driver's seat to brace himself and then wrapped his arm around the driver's throat and pulled up hard. "Park it. Now!" he yelled.

The driver clutched at the arm with one hand and steered with the other, directing the van toward a heavily populated sidewalk and the corner of a brick building beyond.

With a quick twist, Declan snapped the man's neck, shoved him to the side, leaned over the back of the seat and steered the van away from the crowded sidewalk and back into the street crowded with other vehicles.

Though dead, the driver's foot remained on the accelerator.

Declan held on tightly as the vehicle plowed into a delivery truck, rocking it on its wheels. The van crunched to a full stop, slinging Declan forward.

Because he held on to the back of the driver's seat, he wasn't thrown through the window; instead he flipped over the back of the seat, hit his head on the steering wheel and landed headfirst into the driver's seat.

He lay stunned for a moment, a dull pain throbbing in his head where he'd hit the steering wheel, but he was alive. He pushed backward over the seat, sat down hard on the floor of the van and surveyed the carnage.

A moan sounded from beneath the two men who'd hauled the woman inside.

Declan shook the gray haze from his head and crawled toward the groan. "Ma'am, are you okay?"

For a moment, nothing but silence came from beneath the two men.

"Ma'am?" Declan repeated. "Are you all right?"

"Can't breathe," her voice sounded.

Declan dragged the top man out of the way and then the other. Blood soaked the woman's gray suit, though she showed no signs of open wounds or ripped clothing. Declan assumed the blood wasn't hers. When she tried to sit up, he touched her shoulder. "You might want to lie still. You could have an injury from being handled so roughly."

"I'm all right…no broken bones… I just need to…sit up." She pushed to an upright position, her hands covered in the blood of her captors.

Declan glanced through the front windows.

Police vehicles surrounded the van, and men in SWAT uniforms rushed toward them, rifles aimed at the van.

"The police have arrived," he said.

"Thank God." The older woman wiped her hands on her skirt, leaving bright red streaks. Then she pushed the gray hair back from her face and squared her shoulders, a frown pulling her brow downward. "Do you think they know these terrorists have been stopped?"

"We can't bank on it. They might take one look at me and shoot."

Her eyebrows shot upward. "But they can't. You saved my life."

"You in the van, come out with your hands up!" said a voice amplified by a bullhorn outside.

"Coming out," Declan said. "Don't shoot!" He reached for the door handle.

The gray-haired woman touched his arm. "Let me go first. Surely they won't shoot me, and I can let them know you're one of the good guys."

Declan shook his head. "You never know when one of them might get trigger-happy. I'll go first…with my hands up."

"At least let me open the door so they will see your hands up." The woman grabbed the handle and pulled back, opening the door slowly. "Don't shoot," she called out. "We're unarmed."

When Declan stepped out of the van, he held his hands high.

"On your knees!" a voice boomed.

Declan dropped to his knees.

"Hands behind your head."

Declan laced his hands behind his neck.

The man with the bullhorn called out, "Anyone else in the van, get out now, hands in the air."

Out of the corner of his eye, Declan could see the gray-haired woman step out of the van, her hands held high, her hair disheveled and blood smears on her gray suit.

"On your knees. Hands in the air," boomed the man with the bullhorn again.

"I will not go down on my knees in this skirt. Never mind, my knees can't take that kind of brutality." She started to drop her hands, but must have thought better of it and held them higher. "My kidnappers have been disabled and are in the van behind me." She nodded toward Declan. "This young man saved my life. I expect you to treat him well."

"Ma'am, you need to get on your knees," a SWAT officer said from behind the door of his vehicle.

Declan glared at the man. "She's not the problem."

"Silence," the SWAT guy said. "On your knees."

"Oh, for the love of Pete." The woman dropped her arms and eased herself to the ground, on her knees.

"Hands in the air," the SWAT team leader commanded.

"Pushy bastard, aren't you?" the woman said.

A chuckle rose up Declan's throat. He swallowed hard to keep from emitting the sound.

The SWAT leader motioned for his men to close in on the van. Once they ascertained the other men inside the vehicle weren't a threat, they dragged them out on the ground and laid them out in a line.

The other van had been stopped before it had gone two blocks. The men who'd been inside were lined up on their knees, being handcuffed.

Several SWAT team members approached Declan with their rifles pointing at Declan's chest.

He didn't dare move or breathe wrong. With a vanload of dead men, they would assume the worst first and check the facts later. Declan couldn't blame them. Not with the woman bathed in blood.

"I told you, this man saved my life," she was saying. "Treat him well, or I'll have your jobs."

"It's okay," Declan said quietly. "I'll be all right."

"You'd better be," she said with a frown. "I haven't had a chance to thank you properly."

A man grabbed his wrist and pulled his arm down behind his back. Then he pulled the other one down and bound them with a thin strand of plastic. Once they had him zip-tied, they yanked him to his feet and patted him down thoroughly, removing his wallet and dog tags. "Declan O'Neill, you'll have to come with us."

"Aren't you going to tell me why I'm being detained, and read me my Miranda rights?" Declan asked.

"We will. On the way to the station," the man closest to him said.

"I left my backpack with a bystander. I'd like to get it before we leave for the station."

Before Declan finished speaking, the SWAT team leader was shaking his head. "I'm sorry. But you'll have to come with us now."

"You don't understand." Declan stood still, resisting the pressure on his arm. "That backpack is all I have in this world." Geez, he sounded like a pathetic homeless character. Then again, he was homeless.

The SWAT team leader nodded to one of his guys. "Find the man's backpack."

One of his men peeled out of the group and walked toward the bystanders on the sidewalk.

Forcibly dragged, Declan had no other choice but to go with the officers. He was shoved into the back seat of a police service vehicle, and then the door was shut in his face.

Without his backpack, he had nothing. Absolutely nothing. It contained his last bit of cash, a couple changes of clothing and photographs of him and his Force Recon team before they'd either been killed or split asunder. His phone was also in his backpack. It contained the numbers for his friends. He couldn't remember any of them off the top of his head. He'd never needed to commit the numbers to memory. They'd always been in his phone directory. Now he wished he had taken the time to learn the numbers.

His heart hurt as the vehicle pulled away. He twisted in the seat and stared back at the crowd, searching for the blond-haired woman. He didn't see her or his rucksack. The man who'd gone looking for it was on his way back to the rest of the SWAT team… empty-handed.

His only hope was if they gave him at least one call. He hoped the woman he'd left the rucksack with would answer the cell phone inside one of the pockets. And he prayed it had enough battery power left for her to answer. Considering he hadn't had a chance to charge the cell phone, he doubted it would ring.

Just when he'd thought he'd sunk as low as life could take him, he'd once again been proven wrong.

Chapter Two

Grace Lawrence had been on her way to interview for a job when the attack began and she'd been dragged to the ground and covered by the hulking hunk of a man. Too stunned to resist, she'd lain still, listening to the popping sound of shots being fired and the screams and shouts of women and men as they dove for cover.

All too soon, the man on top of her shifted and shoved his backpack at her, telling her to keep it safe. Left unprotected, she lay as flat to the ground as she could. Afraid of getting shot, Grace remained still for a few seconds after the man had left her with his camouflage rucksack. Gunfire seemed to blast from all around her. Some women continued to scream or sob, while other people fled.

She lifted her head high enough to see an older woman being hauled out of the limousine and shoved toward a white van.

Her gaze scanned the area, searching for the stranger who'd left the rucksack with her. She'd seen him dart toward a vehicle and roll beneath the chassis. Then she'd lost sight of him.

Her heart raced as she considered what could be happening. The man could have left her with a bag full of explosives. She could be holding on to a bomb that was about to blow her and the entire block to hell and back.

She shoved the rucksack away from her, knowing it wouldn't be far enough. And she couldn't get up and move…not with bullets flying through the air. Then she spied Mr. Rucksack running from the front of one vehicle to the back of another, edging his way toward one of the men holding a submachine gun. What man would leave a bag full of explosives and then go after an armed shooter, barehanded?

As she watched, the hunky rucksack owner took down the gunman without being noticed, and then dragged the guy out of sight. The next moment, her guy's feet appeared beneath the carriage of another vehicle, heading toward the white van.

Was he out of his mind? There had to be a dozen gunmen scattered around the vans, limousine and security vehicles. How could one man stop all of those attackers?

Grace pulled the rucksack toward her and clutched it close to her chest. He'd asked her to watch his bag. Hell, he could end up dead before the attack was over. She might hold the only clue to his identity and be called upon to help identify his body.

A shiver ran through her. Grace sent a silent prayer to the heavens that the crazy man trying to stop a deadly attack didn't die that day. She didn't want to visit a morgue, and he was too good-looking to leave the world just yet. He deserved to live long enough to grow old and gray and develop a gut and wrinkles. Which would probably look good on him, as well.

When the sirens sounded in the distance, the group of attackers fired off rounds and backed toward the white vans. One of the men held the gray-haired woman at gunpoint, shoving her ahead of him. When they reached the van, the side door slid open and the man and woman were yanked inside.

Remaining attackers fired again and ran toward the second white van at the rear of the limousine.

The van with the woman inside backed away from the limousine and spun around.

At the same time as the side door slammed shut, the back door of the van swung closed. But not before Grace saw who had climbed into the rear of the van.

Her breath caught and held. The man who'd saved her from being mowed down by the gunmen had entered the back of the van.

Had she been wrong? Was he with the bad guys after all? She glanced at the rucksack, afraid to move in case it would explode.

Then the white van veered erratically and gunfire sounded from inside.

"Get up and move!" someone yelled. A hand reached down and dragged Grace to her feet.

Despite her misgivings, she grabbed the rucksack and ran, stumbling away from the commotion.

Police cars and SUVs converged on the street, blocking the other white van. The one her guy was in drove up on a sidewalk.

People scattered.

The van swerved back out onto the road and crashed into a delivery truck, bringing it to a stop.

A police car arrived beside Grace and officers leaped out. One pulled his weapon and aimed at the white van, while the other waved his arms. "Move back. The show's not over."

Herded like cattle, Grace and the others caught in the attack were urged to run until they were a full two blocks away from the scene.

The crowd thinned enough that Grace was finally able to stop and turn around.

She waited with the rucksack clutched to her chest, the weight of the bag making her arms ache.

"Lady, move along," a police officer advised. "You don't want to get hit by stray bullets."

Beyond the police officers now blocking the sidewalk and street, Grace could see the white vans had been stopped. The men inside the one farthest away dropped to the ground, hands high in the air.

The other was still for what seemed like a very long time before the door slid open and Mr. Rucksack stepped out and dropped to the ground on his knees. Shortly afterward, the gray-haired woman stepped out with her hands up.

That was him, her rucksack guy. Grace recognized his faded gray sweat jacket and short dark hair.

Grace took a step forward.

A police officer blocked her path. "Sorry, ma'am, I can't let you go in there."

"But, that man…"

The officer shook his head. "You'll have to stay back."

The SWAT team secured her guy's hands behind his back and led him to a waiting squad car. A moment later, it sped away.

Grace stared down at the rucksack. Now what was she supposed to do with it?

She found a bench and sat. Holding the bag between her feet, Grace waited for most of the people passing by to clear the area before she opened the bag. Then she drew in a deep breath and unzipped one of the sections. She told herself that if it exploded, she wouldn't know what happened. It would kill her instantly. Still, she couldn't help closing her eyes. When nothing happened, she opened them and searched through the interior of one compartment after another. Inside, she found a pair of worn jeans, a couple of T-shirts, several pairs of boxer shorts and a shaving kit. No plastic explosives, sticks of dynamite or detonators were hiding inside the bag.

She pulled out an envelope filled with photographs of men in marine uniforms, fully outfitted with weapons, helmets, rifles and ammunition. They stood in what appeared to be a camp in the desert.

The man who'd entrusted his rucksack with her was military or prior-military. No wonder he'd taken on the attackers like he knew what he was doing.

Her heart squeezed hard in her chest. And the police had treated him like one of the terrorists who'd gunned down innocent men and women.

Grace found a cell phone in a side pouch and touched the power button. Nothing happened. The screen wasn't cracked, but the battery might be dead. On the outside of the bag, embroidered on a strip of camouflage, was the name O'Neill in bold green letters.

Grace would call the local police station and see what she could find out about the mysterious Mr. O'Neill. For now, all she could do was head home. She'd have to call and reschedule her interview when she wasn't bruised and dirty from having lain on the ground, crushed beneath a man who'd proven to be a hero.

Slipping one of the rucksack's straps over her shoulder, she headed for the metro station and caught the train out of the city to Alexandria where she shared an apartment with her roommate from college. Once on the train, she pulled her cell phone out of her pocket and searched through the recent calls for the one she'd taken to schedule the interview.

Once she found it, she dialed, lifted the device to her ear and covered her other ear.

"Halverson Enterprises, Margaret speaking," a woman's voice came on the line.

"This is Grace Lawrence. I was supposed to interview with Mrs. Halverson today."

"Oh, yes. I was just about to call and advise you Mrs. Halverson will not be available today. She has been regrettably detained."

"Oh," Grace said. "Okay."

"I've been asked to reschedule your interview for tomorrow morning at 8:30 a.m. Mrs. Halverson will see you then."

"Thank you. I look forward to meeting her."

"Wait," Margaret laughed. "You called me. Was there something I could help you with?"

"Oh, thank you but... I was just calling to confirm the interview," Grace said. Margaret didn't need to know Grace had called to say she couldn't make her scheduled appointment.

Grace ended the call and released a sigh. At least she hadn't blown her chances by being a no-show.

By the time Grace stepped off the train at her stop, the shock of the day had set in. Her knees shook as she walked the few blocks to her apartment complex, and she fumbled with her keys before she could open the front door.

Once inside, she set the rucksack on the floor, kicked off her heels, collapsed on the couch in the living room and dug her cell phone out of her purse.

A text message displayed across the screen.

Leaving work on time tonight. What's for supper?

The message was from early that morning. Grace had just noticed it. She snorted out a laugh, the sound catching on a sob. What a day. Her roommate, Riley Lansing, wouldn't believe what had happened to her. Grace would have to wait until Riley arrived at the apartment before she could tell her about it.

In the meantime, Grace needed to find out where O'Neill was and arrange to get his rucksack back to him.

She spent the next hour calling police stations, trying to locate the man, but with no luck. After hitting one brick wall after the other, she set her cell phone aside and wandered into the kitchen, looking for something to eat.

A glance at the clock on the stove made her frown.

Riley had said she'd be leaving work on time, which would have been over an hour ago.

Grace abandoned the refrigerator and retrieved her cell phone from the coffee table in the living room. She texted Riley.

Did you stop at the store?

She waited for Riley's response. When it didn't come, she tried again.

Hello? I thought you'd be home by now.

Grace shrugged and headed for the kitchen again. Perhaps Riley *had* stopped at a store with lousy reception, or her cell phone was buried at the bottom of her purse, or she'd turned off the sound. Riley wasn't one to say she'd be home on time and then take a lot longer, without calling.

A bad feeling washed over Grace. She tried to shrug it off as residual nerves from the earlier attack in DC. But the longer she waited for Riley, the more worried she became.

Since Grace had moved in, she and Riley were the other's support system. Grace's parents had been an older couple when Grace was born and had since passed away. Riley's folks were on a world cruise and not scheduled to be back for another twenty days.

Grace called Riley's number and listened to it ring six times before it went to her voice mail. She called again and the voice mail picked up immediately.

She left a message. "Riley, call me. I'm worried about you."

By midnight she was past being worried and beginning to become frantic. She called the police and reported her roommate as missing.

"How long has she been missing?" the dispatcher asked.

"At least five hours. She's never late. She texted me this morning, saying she'd leave work on time tonight. Leaving work on time means she would have left more than five and a half hours ago."

"Could she have stopped at a friend's house?" the dispatcher asked.

"Not without calling to tell me," Grace said.

"Where is her last known location?" the woman on the other end of the line asked.

"She was leaving work at Quest Aerospace Alliance." Grace gave the address and waited.

"We'll have a unit check it out. If you hear from her, please let us know to call off the search."

"Thank you."

The dispatcher ended the call.

The simple act of reporting her friend as missing did nothing to allay Grace's fears. She couldn't stay in the apartment, waiting. She had to go out and look for herself. If the police found her in the meantime, they would contact her on her cell phone. She'd have it with her.

Grace scribbled a note to Riley and left it on the counter. If Riley came home while Grace was out, she was to call her immediately.

Grace shrugged into her jacket, grabbed her purse, slipped the Taser Riley had gifted her at Christmas inside the front pocket and left the apartment, heading...

Hell, she didn't even know which way to go.

Squaring her shoulders, she walked through the dark streets to the train station, her gaze searching the shadows for potential threats. When she reached the metro stop, she climbed aboard the train headed toward Quest Aerospace Alliance. She'd start there and work her way backward, praying she'd find Riley at a bar or hanging out with a friend.

Deep down, Grace knew she wouldn't. She was Riley's friend and they didn't have anyone else they hung out with.

Grace tucked her hand into the pocket of her purse, curling her fingers around the Taser it concealed. Riley had an identical device. She'd been the one who'd often insisted that they needed some kind of protection in the big city.

Grace didn't feel any safer, but a Taser was better than nothing. She just had to be prepared to use it. Perhaps Riley hadn't been as prepared. When she found Riley, she'd be sure to ask. Because she *would* find Riley. *Alive.*

DECLAN SPENT TWO hours in a holding room, where he was repeatedly grilled about his part in the attack in downtown DC. Thankfully, he'd had his wallet on him, but the majority of his money was in his rucksack. If...no...*when* he was released, he only had a five-dollar bill to get something to eat, but no money to get around. He might as well stay the night in the jail. At least he'd get a free meal and a bed to sleep on, out of the cold, rain or whatever the weather was doing outside.

The police had allowed him to make one phone call. When he'd dialed his number, the phone service indicated his phone was not online at that time. Meaning the battery was dead and the woman he'd entrusted all of his worldly goods to had yet to find or charge it.

His one call wasted, he was escorted back to the holding room, where he was questioned all over again by yet another detective.

"What organization are you with?" the detective asked.

"I'm not with any organization," Declan responded.

"Witnesses reported you were armed with a submachine gun. One like the other attackers carried."

"I was in the right place at the wrong time. I watched those men kill the security detail surrounding a limousine, and then they kidnapped that woman. While others stood around gawking, I took it upon myself to do something."

"So, you just waltzed in with your submachine gun and jumped into the back of a van?" The man snorted. "Highly unlikely."

"I was unarmed. However, I was able to disarm one of the attackers and confiscate his weapon."

"Convenient." The detective's lips pressed into a thin line. "By all accounts, the attackers were highly trained. How is it you were able to relieve one of them of his weapon?"

Declan shrugged. "You obviously aren't buying anything I have to say. Why should I bother talking to you?" He looked past the detective. "I want to talk to a lawyer."

The detective glared. "You'll be talking soon enough."

Though his hackles rose on the back of Declan's neck, he stared back at the detective, wiping all emotion from his face. "I'll talk when I have a lawyer."

The detective smirked. "You got one?"

"I will as soon as you let me make a call."

"You had your chance to make a call."

Declan sat back in his chair and crossed his arms over his chest.

The detective leaned forward, his lip curling back in a snarl. "Look here, jerk, I have ten dead tourists, nineteen injured, and the DC mayor and the President of the United States breathing down my neck for answers."

Declan clamped his lips tight. He was done talking.

The door opened behind the detective and an older man in uniform stuck his head in the door. "Solomon, a word with you."

The detective gave Declan a narrow-eyed glance. "We're not through here."

As far as Declan was concerned, they were.

Detective Solomon left the room. A moment later, a different officer entered. "Mr. O'Neill, please come with me."

Declan rose, fully expecting to be led to the rear of the building and stuck in a cell. His stomach rumbled. He was all for being incarcerated if it meant getting a meal out of it.

Instead, the man led him out of the holding area and back to the front of the building.

A group of men in dark suits stood in a cluster around a woman. She waved them aside and strode toward him, her head held high, her blood-stained clothes worn like a suit of armor.

She was the woman he'd saved from the kidnappers.

"Declan O'Neill?" she asked.

"Yes, ma'am. That's me."

"You have been cleared of any charges. These kind officers are releasing you." She raised her eyebrows and stared around at the policemen standing by, as if challenging them to say anything different.

"I don't understand," he said.

"What do you not understand about your being released?" she asked. "I told them that you saved my life and fought valiantly against my attackers, risking your own life to save mine." She frowned. "I'm appalled they took you into custody to begin with. Thankfully, I wasn't the only one who witnessed your heroism. Between my account and those of others who were nearby, you've been cleared of any wrongdoing."

"Thank you, ma'am."

"Please don't call me ma'am. Makes me sound like your grandmother." She sniffed. "As well I could be. But that's neither here nor there. My name is Charlotte, but my friends call me Charlie. I prefer Charlie. And if you don't have a ride, I would gladly take you anywhere you want to go. And the sooner, the better. It's almost midnight, and I've had a hell of a day."

"Thank you, Charlie." Declan squared his shoulders. "I don't need a ride," he lied, unwilling to admit he was homeless, possessionless and broke.

"Then we'll wait until your ride arrives." The woman looked around, found a chair and promptly sat.

"You don't have to wait," Declan said. Appalled that he would be caught out in his lie.

"I want to make sure the police don't decide to reacquire their prisoner." She glared at the nearest officer. "He's not one of the terrorists who attacked me," she reiterated.

The officer held up his hands in surrender. "I'm not saying he is, but we can't have a crowd in the building. We have work to do."

The older woman harrumphed and rose to her feet. "Fine, we'll wait outside for Mr. O'Neill's transportation to arrive." She nodded toward the four men in suits. "Come along."

Charlie led the way to the exit. Before she could open the door, Declan stepped in front of her. "Let me," he said.

Charlie smiled. "Such a gentleman."

"No, ma'am." He stepped through the door and closed it in her face. After scanning the area around them, he turned and opened the door for her to come out.

She stood with her arms crossed over her chest, a frown wrinkling her brow. She leveled her glare at the men in suits. "You should have gone out first and checked for potential attackers. Instead, you let this young man do it for you." She flicked her fingers. "You're all fired."

The men in suits frowned. One of them stepped forward. "But—"

Charlie held up her hand. "Uh, uh, uh," she said. "No excuses. You may go home. I won't be needing your services." She dug in her purse and pulled out a one-hundred-dollar bill and handed it to the man who appeared to be in charge. "To get you back to your own transportation."

The man took the bill and left with the other three to find a taxi back to wherever they'd parked their vehicles.

Charlie sighed. "Now what am I supposed to do?" She gave Declan a bright smile. "I don't suppose you would like to come to work for me, providing my protection?"

A job? Declan didn't want to appear too needy, but hell, he'd just been offered a job.

"What exactly would it entail?"

"Oh, I don't necessarily want you to be a bodyguard. However, I'd want you to be in charge of hiring a bodyguard for me, or four or five. I lost three good men today. And two more are in the hospital, fighting for their lives. I'm tired of terrorists getting away with murder, and the authorities are doing so very little about it.

"And after I'm situated with personal protection, I might want you to do a lot more."

"More what?"

"More making things right where they've gone completely wrong."

He held up his hands. "I'm not into being a vigilante."

"And I'm not into spending years on red tape and bureaucratic nonsense while good, honest people are taking the fall, literally. Like today. Not that I'm all that good or honest, but what happened shouldn't have."

"Why did it happen? What did they want with you?"

"I'm sure they were going to hold me for ransom or some such nonsense. I'm loaded. Everyone always wants to get their hands on my money. Hell, if they asked for it nicely, I'd probably give it to them." Charlie waved her hand. "You haven't answered my question. Do you want a job or not?"

He wanted one, even if it was with a slightly deranged older woman. But she had to know the truth about him. "Don't you want to see my résumé, do a background check, see if I have a criminal record?"

She ran her gaze from his head to his toes. "I've seen all I need to see."

He bristled at her perusal. "I'm not a gigolo."

She laughed out loud. "Now, that conjures way too many tempting thoughts." Her smile faded. "Not that you're hard to look at. But I loved my dearly departed husband completely, despite what the tabloids might have said. I don't anticipate any man filling his shoes anytime soon, if at all."

With the possibility of being hired as a sex toy cleared up, Declan still had one more obstacle. "I was dishonorably discharged from the US Marine Corps." There, he said it flat out. It still hurt to say the words. He'd put his entire life into his career as a Force Recon marine.

Charlie slipped her purse over her shoulder. "I know."

Declan stared at the woman, shocked. "You know?"

"You don't think I'd offer you a job if I didn't know what I was getting into, do you?" She looked at him with raised eyebrows.

"No, ma'am."

"Charlotte or Charlie. Not ma'am." She held out her hand. "You're coming to work for me?"

He hesitated only a moment longer before taking her hand. "Yes, ma'—" he took her hand "—Charlie."

"How soon can you start?" she asked.

"As soon as you want me," he said. "Preferably sooner than later. I don't have a ride and the five dollars in my wallet is going toward a hamburger."

"Dear Lord, why didn't you say so?" She nodded toward the parking lot. "I'm hungry, too. I haven't had a decent hamburger since I hired a French chef. It's well past time to indulge." She held out her arm.

Declan gripped her elbow and glanced at the parking lot, where a long black limousine stood, blocking police cruisers into their parking spaces. He chuckled. "I'm surprised you don't have a handful of tickets on that boat."

"I left my driver in the driver's seat for just such an occasion." She waited for him to open the door before slipping inside. Charlie patted the seat beside her. "I'd feel better if you rode back here with me. Although, you might not want to. My other bodyguards—God rest their souls—didn't fare well earlier today." Her smile dipped into a frown. "Those bastards deserve to die for killing my men and all of those innocent bystanders."

Declan slid into the back seat, next to Charlie.

She captured his gaze with a shadowed gray one of her own. "Don't you see? Those are the kinds of wrongs I want to right. I have more money than I could ever spend. I want to do something to help others. If it means going around the law to see it's done right...so be it."

"I'm not in the habit of breaking the law, despite my lousy military record," he warned her.

"I'm not asking you to break the law. Maybe bend a few rules, but not exactly break the law." She reached for his hand. "Sometimes the authorities get in the way of justice or let people off who we know good and well are as guilty as sin. I've seen it happen more often than I'd care to admit. Someone like me, with more money than sense, buys his way out of jail or buys his son or daughter's way out of serving time. No one should get away with murder." Her hand clutched his tightly.

"Why are you so passionate about this?" he asked.

For a moment, she stared down at his hand. Then she released it and stared out the window. "My husband was murdered. The police got nowhere. No matter how much money I threw at private investigators, they couldn't tell me who pulled the trigger. I know how I felt, losing my husband, who should have been around to grow older with me. I don't want others to have to go through what I did."

"I'll work for you and do what I can," Declan said. "But I won't break the law."

"Unless you have to in order to save a life," Charlie said. "I had to pay a big bribe to get you out of hot water for using that submachine gun."

Declan hadn't considered the fact he might have been breaking the law when he took up the gun.

Charlie nodded with a smug smile. "That's right. Possessing that kind of weapon isn't legal in DC."

Declan cursed beneath his breath. "I didn't know. All I was worried about was saving you."

"I know that, and you know that." She sighed. "But the law is clear. If you're caught in possession of a submachine gun, you can be thrown in jail. Again, some rules are meant to be bent. You wouldn't have saved my life if you hadn't snagged that man's weapon and used it on his cohorts."

Declan had once again backed himself into a corner of his own doing. If not for Charlie's ability to sway the police force with a sizable contribution, he wouldn't be free. He'd be sitting on a hard cot in a cell. "How much do I owe you? All I can do is work it off."

Charlie touched his arm. "No, dear. I owe you my life. The least I could do was make sure you weren't blamed for something you didn't do." She pressed a button on the armrest and the window between the driver and the rear of the vehicle slid downward.

"Carl, could you stop at the next corner? I believe there's a hamburger establishment there."

"Excuse me?" Carl glanced back at them through the rearview mirror, his expression incredulous. "Hamburger?"

"You heard me. And not one word to Francois, my chef. He would be appalled to know I had eaten something as banal as a hamburger with extra onions and pickles."

Declan sat back against the seat, wondering just who this woman was and why she'd decided to hire him on the spur of the moment.

He was grateful for the opportunity to work and earn an honest paycheck, but he wondered if there was more to Charlie than met the eye.

Time would tell. For now, Declan was grateful for the wealthy woman and the hamburgers they ordered at the drive-through window. Or rather, the hamburgers the driver ordered, paid for and received on their behalf.

Declan leaned across the seats to grab the bag of burgers and fries, the scent nearly crippling him, he was so hungry.

The next few minutes were spent in silence as Charlotte, Declan and the driver consumed the food, washing it down with iced tea.

When Charlie asked where Declan lived, he knew it was useless to lie. "I'm new in town," he said, avoiding an answer rather than attempting a lie.

"Oh, so you haven't had time to check into a hotel?"

"No, ma'am...er... Charlie. But I'll be fine."

"Getting a hotel at this late hour can be hit and miss." She talked to the driver by using the intercom. "Carl, take us home." Charlie patted Declan's arm. "You'll stay at my house until you can get a place of your own. I'll start you out with funds to set you up in an apartment as part of your pay."

Declan stiffened. "I can't accept your charity."

"Oh, I wouldn't call it charity." She sat back on the leather seat. "You will be earning your pay in my employ." She patted her belly. "And that was perhaps the best hamburger I've had in a very long time."

"Charlie, I can't do this. I've never in my life taken advantage of a woman's generosity."

She lifted her chin and stared down her nose at him. "Oh, believe me, I have plans for you. You'll earn every dime working for Halverson Enterprises."

With no other choices to fall back on, Declan squared his shoulders and faced his future.

Chapter Three

Grace stood outside of the Halverson Enterprises building near K Street at 8:20 a.m., feeling like she'd been hit by a truck, and probably looking like it. She'd spent the majority of the night retracing what she would have thought would be Riley's route on her way home the evening before.

The guard at the gate to Riley's office complex had refused to let her in, insisting that the building was closed for the night. She'd have to return in the morning and talk with the security supervisor. He didn't seem to understand that the morning might be too late. The train held no clues as to Riley's whereabouts, and the path between the office complex and the train was clean of any traces of Grace's roommate.

The police had done a perfunctory investigation, running into the same issues as Grace and coming up as empty-handed as she had, and they hadn't contacted her in the past three hours.

She'd even tried calling Riley's supervisor. But all she had was his work number. The connection went straight to his voice mail.

Riley was missing, and Grace had an interview for a job she could care less about as long as her friend and roommate remained missing. Still, she could have stayed at her apartment and hoped Riley would stroll through the door, announcing she'd spent the night with a hot guy she met at a bar. But the waiting would have killed Grace.

Instead, she'd showered, blow-dried her hair and applied a minimal amount of makeup. Dressed in a tailored skirt suit, she'd tucked her cell phone in her purse and left the ringtone on high in case Riley actually called. Grace didn't care if she was in an interview or a meeting with the President of the United States—she'd answer the phone.

After taking a deep breath, she strode through the glass doors and stepped up to the reception desk.

The woman took her driver's license and handed her a visitor's pass. "Mrs. Halverson is expecting you."

Tears welled in Grace's eyes and she almost turned around and ran.

"It's okay," the woman at the reception desk whispered. "Mrs. Halverson is a really nice lady. You'll do fine."

Blinking to clear her vision, Grace nodded.

"Twelfth floor, straight out of the elevator. Her secretary will greet you."

"Thank you." Grace choked on her words and turned toward the elevator.

The receptionist held out a tissue. "You might want this." She gave her a warm smile. "Really, she's nice."

Grace nearly lost her composure there, but held it together long enough to make it into the elevator, where she waited until the door closed before she let the tears fall. But only a few. She was afraid she wouldn't be able to read the screen on her cell phone if she cried too much.

For the hundredth time, she checked for text messages from Riley.

Nothing.

The floor numbers flashed green on the display panel as the elevator car rose to the top of the office building.

Grace dabbed at her eyes, sure her mascara was running by now. What a great impression she'd make on Mrs. Halverson, a sobbing, hot mess of a woman in a wrinkled suit, with red-rimmed eyes and a runny nose.

Grace didn't care. Riley was still missing.

The elevator stopped.

As the doors opened, Grace jabbed at the buttons to go back down, but it was too late. Mrs. Halverson's secretary spotted her and smiled. "Miss Lawrence, I'm so glad you could make it after we stood you up yesterday. I'm Margaret Berkman." She rounded to the front of her desk and held out her hand.

Short of being completely rude, Grace was forced to step out of the elevator, cross to the secretary's desk and shake the woman's hand. "You didn't stand me up. I was caught up in the shooting yesterday. I didn't even make it to this building."

The woman's eyes widened. "Oh, dear. You will have so much to share with Mrs. Halverson. She was there, too." The secretary turned toward the door behind her. "Come with me."

"If she was there yesterday, perhaps now isn't a good time to conduct this interview." The timing was terrible for Grace. She felt as if she would break down at any moment.

"Mrs. Halverson was looking forward to meeting you. I'm sure she will be fine."

Mrs. Halverson might be fine, but Grace certainly wasn't.

She squared her shoulders, glanced at her cell-phone screen again and followed Margaret into a spacious office with a wide solid-mahogany desk. A gray-haired woman sat with her back to the door, staring out at the buildings making up the skyline of Washington, DC.

When Mrs. Halverson turned, she smiled and pushed to her feet. "Miss Lawrence, so very nice to meet you."

Grace gasped. The woman was the same one who'd been yanked out of the limousine the day before and hauled into the kidnapper's van. "You...you were the one."

Mrs. Halverson frowned. "Pardon me?"

Grace shook her head slowly. "You were the woman at the shooting yesterday. The one they tried to kidnap."

Mrs. Halverson clasped Grace's hand in hers and nodded, her lips pressing into a thin line. "Yes, that was me. But that was yesterday, and I prefer to push it out of my thoughts. Horrible event. Just horrible." She drew in a deep breath and let it out on a sigh. "You're here to interview for the position of personal assistant, am I right?"

Grace didn't move from where she stood, her mind spinning with the frightening memories of the day before. "Are you all right?" she asked.

"I'm fine," she said, a shadow crossing her face. "But I lost some good men in that disaster. Fine men with families."

"They didn't hurt you?" Grace asked.

Mrs. Halverson smiled. "Thankfully, a nice young man rescued me from the kidnappers before they could take me to parts unknown." She frowned and stared at Grace. "You were there?"

Grace nodded. "I was. I think the man who rescued you saved me before he went after you."

Mrs. Halverson's lips twitched upward. "Sounds like what he would do. That young man doesn't think about his own safety. He's too busy saving everyone else. And the police had the nerve to arrest him."

So, that's what had happened to him after he'd left his backpack in Grace's care.

"But enough about me. Tell me about you," Mrs. Halverson said. She waved a hand toward several leather chairs arranged around a low coffee table.

Grace shook her head. "I… I can't do this."

"Do what? Have a conversation with me?" Mrs. Halverson took Grace's arm. "I tell you, I'm okay. I really need a personal assistant. Otherwise I'd reschedule."

"You don't understand." Grace pulled her arm free of Mrs. Halverson's grip. "Yesterday was bad on more levels than just the attack downtown." She shook her head, her heart pinching hard inside her chest. "My roommate didn't come home last night. I've been worried sick and combing the streets, looking for her." The tears welled again and some spilled over, sliding down her cheek. "Mrs. Halverson, I'm afraid I can't do this interview."

Mrs. Halverson drew Grace into her arms and led her to a sofa. She settled her there and held her at arm's length. "Tell me what happened. When did she go missing?"

Grace told her what she knew, where she'd gone and how she'd contacted the police. Tears slipped from her eyes and trailed down her cheeks.

The older woman shook her head. "I'm sorry about your friend.

I'd be worried, too." She lifted Grace's chin and stared into her eyes. "But you've come to the right place. I think I might be able to help."

Grace laughed, her voice choking on a sob. "How can you help? The police couldn't do anything. I couldn't find her." She sucked in a shaky breath and let it out. "I don't know what else to do."

Mrs. Halverson patted her hand. "I know someone who might be of assistance. And this is just the kind of thing I hired him for."

"You do?" Using the tissue the receptionist had given her, Grace scrubbed the tears from her eyes. "Who?"

Mrs. Halverson stood. "You stay right there." She walked to the door, poked her head out and said, "Send in my new hire. I have a job for him."

Mrs. Halverson returned to the couch and drew Grace to her feet. "I'm sure he'll be able to help you. He's a trained warrior and quite good at it."

"A warrior?" Grace shook her head. "I need a tracking dog."

"I'm sure he can do that. He's pretty versatile." She smiled and looked past Grace. "Ah, there you are." Mrs. Halverson turned toward the door. "Declan, meet Grace Lawrence."

Grace turned and her jaw dropped. She knew this man.

Mrs. Halverson continued. "Grace, this is Declan—"

"O'Neill," Grace finished.

The older woman frowned. "You know each other?"

Declan nodded while Grace shook her head.

"I have your rucksack," Grace said. "I didn't know how to find you."

"I tried to call my cell phone, but the battery must have died." He held out his hand. "What were the chances we'd find each other here?"

Mrs. Halverson shrugged. "Since you two know each other, I'll leave you both to the task of finding Miss Lawrence's roommate. I have a lot to do." She drew in a deep breath and let it out slowly, a shadow passing over her face. "Arranging for the funerals of my bodyguards." She stared at Grace. "As for the job—are you still interested?"

Grace nodded. "I am, but I need to find my roommate before I can get my head on straight."

Mrs. Halverson shook her head. "You need to get your head on straight to *find* your roommate. Once you do, come back for that interview. I still need an assistant, but I can wait." She nodded to Declan O'Neill. "Now that you've located your rucksack and phone, you can contact your friends. I'm sure they'll make fine additions and can assist you in our new venture. Remind me, we need to come up with a name for your team."

"Yes, ma'am—" O'Neill caught himself and smiled. "Thank you, Charlie. I'll do my best to help Miss Lawrence."

"Now, if you'll clear out of my office," Mrs. Halverson said, "I have some calls to make. Keep me up to date on your discoveries."

"We will," O'Neill said. He hooked Grace's arm and led her out of the office.

Mrs. Halverson's secretary stood as they closed the door behind them. "How did the interview go?" Margaret asked with a smile.

"It didn't," Grace responded.

Margaret's smile fell. "I'm sorry to hear it. I'm sure she has her reasons, but I was hoping she'd find an assistant. She really needs one."

Grace gave her a gentle smile. "The interview has been postponed. I'll be back soon." She glanced up at the man Mrs. Halverson had called Declan O'Neill. "In the meantime, Mr. O'Neill and I have work to do."

She didn't know this man from Adam, but having witnessed his military prowess under the stress of being fired upon, she had no doubt he'd be of some assistance. And knowing she had someone to help her find Riley made her more optimistic than she'd been since her roommate had gone missing.

The secondary fact that O'Neill was muscular, ruggedly handsome and skilled with his hands made Grace quiver inside. Not that he'd use those hands on her. Preferably, he'd use them to take down whoever had snatched Riley and make him pay for any harm that might have come to her friend.

"Where do you want to start?" he asked.

"Where she works," Grace said. "They wouldn't let me in last night."

"We can do a preliminary call to her supervisor and ask what time she actually walked out of the building," O'Neill said.

Grace nodded. "And if that doesn't help, we can ask the people at the front desk when she came through," Grace suggested.

"After that?" he asked.

"I don't know what else to do other than canvass the train station at the time she would have been there. I have a recent photograph of her on my cell phone. We can ask people getting on and off the train if they saw her last night."

O'Neill led the way to the elevator, punched the down button and then turned to face her. "We can also check with the train service to see if they have video cameras and historical data we can go through."

"Good thinking," Grace said.

The elevator door slid open and Grace stepped inside.

Her newly assigned private investigator stepped in beside her.

O'Neill's broad shoulders made the elevator feel so much smaller and seemed to suck the air right out of her lungs.

She focused on what was important, her missing roommate. But that didn't keep the heat from rising beneath the starched collar of her shirt.

Sure, a man like O'Neill could turn any woman's head. But Grace had been divorced for three years, and her husband had been hot. Maybe not muscular, he-man hot like O'Neill, but he'd turned his share of heads and ruffled a few female skirts before he'd asked Grace to marry him.

She'd been flattered and fancied herself in love with him. And then he'd changed. Perhaps *changed* wasn't exactly right. His true colors came through. Mitchell had been full of himself and wrapped up in his business as a high-powered financial planner. He'd wanted everything his way, never considering Grace's needs and desires. She'd gone along with his plans at first, but no more. She wouldn't be cowed by any man ever again.

Grace could admire the beauty of nature in a handsome man, but she didn't have to pluck the flower or sip the nectar. She performed an internal eye-roll. As she'd told Mrs. Halverson, she had to get her head on straight. What was important was finding Riley.

The elevator door opened and Grace practically jumped out. As she did, her cell phone rang. Her heart racing, she dug in her purse, her hands shaking so much that she couldn't get them to work.

"Good grief," Declan said. "Give it to me." He took the purse, dug his hand in, found the phone and hit the answer key. Then he handed it to Grace.

She shot a glance at the screen but didn't recognize the number. Grace pressed the phone to her ear, praying whoever it was would have news of her friend. "Hello?"

"Grace Lawrence?"

"That's me."

"This is Sergeant Kronkski with the DC Metropolitan Police Department."

Grace's heart stopped beating. "Go on," she whispered, her breath lodging like a knot in her throat.

"We just wanted to keep you up to date on your missing person's report."

"Have you found Riley?" she asked, her hand gripping the cell phone tightly.

"No, ma'am. We haven't. You said the last place you had contact with her was from her place of employment yesterday?"

"That's right. I told the officer on duty that last night."

"We sent a unit by her office complex this morning. They have no record of her being at work yesterday. She didn't clock in."

Grace frowned, her gaze going to Declan.

He took the phone and punched the speaker key before handing it back to her.

"What do you mean, she never clocked in? She texted me from work yesterday morning. Riley never missed a day of work, even when she was sick."

"That's what we were told. Her supervisor confirmed she never arrived at the office yesterday."

"That can't be right," Grace said, shaking her head, though the sergeant wouldn't see the effect. "She went to work like always and texted me that she would be leaving on time."

"Some people live secret lives," the sergeant said. "Perhaps she has another job you don't know about?"

"No way. Riley doesn't keep secrets from me. We're friends from our first year in college."

"I can only tell you what we learned," the sergeant said. "Is there anywhere else she might have gone? To see family? A friend? A boyfriend?"

Grace's lips pressed together. "She said she was coming home. She has no other family in the country but me, her roommate. Her parents are on a world cruise, out of touch most of the time. She's not married and, as far as I know, she doesn't have a boyfriend."

"Okay, I get it," the sergeant said. "But these are the questions I have to ask. More often than not, missing people haven't been abducted. They've ducked out of sight, either running from the law or needing some space."

"I know my roommate," Grace said. "She wouldn't have told me she was coming home and then not shown up without calling to say why. She's conscientious and considerate like that. If she'd been detained or changed her mind, she would have called or texted me to let me know she was all right."

"I'm sorry we don't have more news, but I wanted to let you know where we stood. We have her picture out to all the street units now. If they see her, you'll be notified."

Grace let go of the breath she'd been holding. Getting mad at the cops wasn't conducive to securing their help in finding Riley. Grace sucked it up and thanked the sergeant. "I appreciate the update and look forward to hearing from you soon." Really soon. Riley's life could depend on it.

Chapter Four

Declan stood in front of Grace throughout the cell-phone conversation. When she hung up, he took the phone from her and captured her hand in his. He was surprised at how much he liked the feel of her long, slender fingers. "We'll find her."

She stared down at where their hands interlocked. "I don't know how you can say that with such assurance when even the police can't find her." Her chin lifted and she stared into his eyes. "Riley's all I have. She's more than a friend. She's like family."

"All the more reason for us to get on this right away." He pulled her hand through the crook of his elbow and walked with her toward the exit. "Do you have a vehicle, or are we going to take the train?"

"I have an SUV, but where are we going?" Grace's hand curled around Declan's elbow and she skipped to keep up with his pace.

"To Riley's workplace." Declan had to get a feel for the street and the path to the train station to better understand how Riley could have disappeared.

"They're a secure facility," Grace said. "They won't just let us walk in without an appointment."

"Do you know Riley's supervisor?" He stopped at the curb and looked around.

"I know his name." Grace pointed toward the parking lot. "I'm parked over there. The charcoal SUV."

He held out his hand. "Mind if I drive?"

She frowned. "And if I do?"

Declan shrugged. "It might be hard for you to drive and call Riley's supervisor at the same time."

"I'm calling her supervisor?" Grace dug in her purse for her keys.

"Yes, you are. On the way to her workplace, call him and see if he will let us in to talk to him about Riley."

Grace handed him the keys. "I tried calling him earlier, but he was out of the office or hadn't come to work yet. The call went straight to his voice mail."

"Try again." He stepped off the curb and strode toward the parking lot.

Grace steered him toward her vehicle.

Before they reached it, Declan clicked the remote to pop the locks open. He held the passenger door for Grace and waited while she settled in the seat. Then he closed the door and rounded the front of the SUV. It was smaller than the vehicle he'd sold before his last deployment, but it was roomy enough to accommodate his six-foot-three frame without bumping his head.

He slid into the driver's seat, adjusted it for his height and started the engine. Before he shifted into gear, he turned to Grace. "GPS directions?"

She tapped the screen on her cell phone.

With the cell-phone voice calling out the route, Declan backed out of the parking space and shifted into Drive.

Grace called Riley's supervisor and waited while the line rang. She shifted the call from her phone to the car speaker so that Declan could hear the conversation.

"Quest Aerospace Alliance. Alan Moretti speaking."

"Mr. Moretti? This is Grace Lawrence, Riley's roommate."

Declan turned onto the road leading to one of the main arteries through town.

A long pause greeted Grace's announcement.

"Miss Lawrence, I'll tell you what I told the police. Miss Lansing never showed up for work yesterday. I don't know where she is."

Declan touched Grace's arm and whispered, "Appointment."

"I have nothing more to add to my statement," Moretti said. "I'm sorry your friend is missing, but I had nothing to do with it."

"I understand, Mr. Moretti. But could you spare a few minutes to meet me in person? I have a few questions I'd like to ask for myself."

"I'm sorry, but no," he said. "I repeat, I have nothing to add." A click ended the call.

Grace stared down at the phone. "Now what?"

"We go to Quest Aerospace Alliance and figure this out." Declan frowned. He hadn't liked Mr. Moretti's answers. "You say Riley texted you from work yesterday?"

"That's right," Grace said. She touched the screen on her cell phone and brought up her text messages. "She specifically said she was leaving work on time that night."

Declan glanced at the cell-phone display screen as he paused at a red traffic light. Grace had repeated Riley's message verbatim.

"Why would she say she was leaving work on time if she was somewhere else?" Grace asked.

"Would she ever have played hooky from work?" Declan asked.

"No. She's a very conscientious person. She wouldn't lie, and she's a rule follower."

"Was she involved in a relationship with someone?" Declan asked.

Grace shook her head. "No. She said she didn't have time. She lived her job."

"How long has she been your roommate?"

"This time or in college?" she asked as they crossed the Potomac and drove into Arlington, Virginia.

"Anytime. Tell me everything. You never know what little bit of information is important. What is your relationship with Riley? What does she do at Quest Aerospace?"

Grace drew in a deep breath. "Riley and I were roommates in college. We were assigned the same dorm room as freshmen and stayed friends throughout. While I went into political science, she studied engineering." Grace smiled. "She was much better at math than I was." She glanced his way. "Then we went in different directions after college. I worked on Capitol Hill for the previous administration, met a guy and got married. My career went on hold for him. He wanted a trophy wife, someone to stay home, cook, clean and entertain for him." She shook her head. "Archaic, right?"

Declan's chest tightened and he shot a glance at Grace's bare ring finger. "You're not wearing a ring now."

Grace snorted softly. "Yeah, I wasn't very good at being a second-class citizen, and my brain was getting mushy from too many sitcoms on television."

Declan knew there was little chance Grace's marriage had anything to do with Riley's disappearance, but he couldn't help asking, "So, you left your husband?"

Grace nodded. "I consider my marriage as one of my greatest failures and learning experiences. Failure in my ability to recognize a person's true character, and learning how to rebuild my life." She sucked in a deep breath and let it out slowly. "I'd kept up with Riley all through the past few years, calling every three or four months to see how she was doing in her career. I envied her ability to focus and go for what she wanted. Since my parents are gone, she was the first person I called when my divorce was final. She insisted I move in with her until I get on my feet. I put it off for a couple of years and finally gave in a few months ago."

"Is that why you were interviewing for the job with Mrs. Halverson? Are you new in the area?"

With a smile, Grace shook her head. "No, I took other odd jobs, working for a temp agency, but I wanted something more full-time and as permanent as can be expected in this day and age."

Declan twisted his lips. "Something along the lines of your political science major?"

"I really don't know what I want. To feel needed, perhaps. As a personal assistant to a high-powered woman, I was sure to be needed." She cringed. "Sounds pathetic, but there you have it."

"And Riley? Was she ever married?"

"No." Grace stared straight ahead. "At least she got that right. She focused on her career."

"Did she date? Have a boyfriend?"

"She did see a guy for a while after she graduated college, but he was heading for the military. She wasn't ready to follow him to parts unknown and give up her opportunity to gain experience in her own field of aerospace engineering."

"Any harsh feelings between them at their parting?" Declan asked.

"From what Riley told me back then, they left on mutual agreement and good terms."

"No brokenhearted, lovesick ex who could have come back to claim what he thought was his?"

"No." Grace twisted her hands in her lap. "That's what has me worried. As far as I know, she didn't have an enemy in this world."

Declan glanced toward her briefly. Grace seemed to be a person who would trust a friend completely. "Are you sure you know all there is to know about your friend Riley?"

"She worked. Sometimes to excess, and that left her with little time for a life outside of the office. Some nights she'd go for a beer at a local pub. I went with her on occasion. She always wanted to stay longer than I did. But she always came home."

"A lone woman in this city? Isn't that dangerous?" Declan asked.

"Lots of women get around this city all by themselves." Grace drew in a deep breath and let it out. "She knows how to defend herself. She showed me some of her moves. Riley is quite capable of fighting off an attacker."

"If she was, she might not be missing."

Grace's brow dipped low. "Unless it was someone she knew."

"Since she worked so much, most of the people she knew—"

"—were the people she worked with." Grace stared across the console at Declan. "We need to get inside Quest and ask some questions."

In Crystal City, Declan pulled into a parking lot across from the high-rise building that was Quest Aerospace Alliance and parked in a slot facing the building.

"Why did you stop here? Shouldn't we try to get inside?" Grace asked.

"We need to study the building and look for weaknesses. Since we can't get in without an appointment, we need to find another way to gain access. When I was with the Marine Force Recon teams, we did a lot of reconnaissance missions prior to conducting an operation. It gave us the intel we needed to make the effort go smoothly."

"Force Recon? What's that?"

"We're part of the Marine Special Operations Command."

"Are you like the army's Special Forces and the Navy SEALs?"

"Yes. Only Force Reconnaissance teams focus on marine expeditionary and amphibious operations."

"Reconnaissance, huh?"

"And direct-action operations, usually based on the reconnaissance and intel gathered."

Grace's eyes narrowed. "I thought you military types threw in hand grenades and lobbed mortars prior to going in. You know, the whole shock-and-awe thing."

Declan's lips twitched upward. "We have a little more finesse most of the time. But we do have occasions when we use the noise and big bangs."

Grace nodded, mockingly. "Teach me, oh wise one. Frankly, I don't care if you were a member of the Navy SEALs, Army Rangers or the local VFW, as long as we find Riley."

His lips twitched again. "The fact Quest is claiming she never showed up for work makes me suspicious. I think it merits getting inside and snooping around."

"If they're lying about Riley never showing up—" Grace tapped a finger to her chin "—it makes me wonder what they're trying to hide. Riley wouldn't have lied to me about leaving the office if she hadn't been there at all."

"How long have you been roommates this time with Riley?" Declan asked.

"Four months."

"And how long had you been living apart?"

Grace tipped her head to the side and used her fingers to count silently. "Seven years."

Declan glanced her way. "A lot could change in seven years."

"I know, but Riley is still the same Riley. She's smart."

"How long has she been with Quest?"

"Two years. She took a demotion to go to work for Quest. She said she wanted to get back into more project design and Quest was doing some innovative things."

"Like?"

"I'm not quite sure. Riley couldn't talk about it. She said it was all hush-hush to keep others from stealing their ideas and data."

"Which would be a good reason to restrict entry into the facility," Declan said. "How did Riley get in?"

"She had a badge she used to get in and out of the building. I had to take it to her once when she forgot it."

Grace rested her fingers on the door handle. "Now that we're here, what's next?"

Declan reached across and rested his hand on hers. "We watch the people coming and going from the building."

Grace's eyebrows lowered. "How is that going to help us find Riley?"

"Be patient," he said. "You'll see. It'll be lunchtime soon." He watched the gate. Several delivery trucks arrived and were allowed to enter the gate after the guard checked his computer tablet and shined a light into the rear of the truck. If he could get into the back of one of the delivery vehicles, he might make it past the guard and onto the compound.

People parked in the lot beside the building, and they entered and exited the gate on foot. As the hour approached noon, a rush of people left the building and walked a couple blocks to a row of food trucks and cafés.

"How are you at flirting?" Declan asked as he pushed the door open on the SUV.

"Flirting?" Grace stared at him as if he'd lost his mind.

"You know, batting your eyes and saying things you know will make a guy want to talk to you." He winked. The woman was beautiful. She'd have no trouble getting attention. "Really all you have to do is smile and you'll have a guy's complete attention."

Her cheeks blossomed with color.

Declan couldn't help but think Grace's husband must have been a jerk. This woman was beautiful and cared about the people she loved. All she needed was a little attention and she seemed to come alive.

Declan rounded the vehicle and held the door for Grace. She dropped to the ground and placed a hand on his arm to steady herself. "Who do I need to flirt with, and what am I trying to gain by it?"

"We can gain information, maybe even borrow an employee badge."

"Borrow?" She shook her head. "I told you I didn't want to do anything illegal."

"I said borrow. We'll give it back, or leave it at the front desk."

Grace chewed on her bottom lip, the movement distracting Declan more than he cared to admit. "I've never deceived anyone in order to break into a place."

"Neither have I." He took her hand and turned her to face him. "Do you want to get inside Quest and find out the truth about your friend Riley?"

Grace's eyes narrowed. "I do." She squared her shoulders and met his gaze. "Whatever it takes…short of committing a major crime, of course."

His lips twitched. "A minor crime is okay then?"

"We'll borrow the badge, with the full intention of returning it once we're done with it." She squeezed his hand and let go. "We'd better hurry before lunch is over."

As they neared the first café, Declan studied the people sitting at different bistro tables on the sidewalk. "It might be better to split up. Are you okay working on your own? I'll be nearby if you need me."

Grace nodded, her gaze on the people settling in to enjoy their meals. "I'll be okay."

Declan slowed to look at a menu affixed to a stand out front of one of the cafés. He wasn't hungry, but he pretended to peruse the menu while Grace searched for a spot in the open seating area outside the packed restaurant. The crowd worked in her favor. She was able to find a place at a table with a man who sat alone. A man who had a Quest badge clipped to his pocket.

Fighting the urge to smile, Declan weaved through the tables and stopped at the one behind Grace. Two middle-aged women occupied the table with a couple of spare seats. "Do you mind if I share your table?" he asked.

The two women smiled up at him.

One with auburn hair said, "We'd love the company."

The other with faded blond hair nodded. "What woman wouldn't want a handsome guy to share her table?"

"Thank you." Declan held out his hand. "I'm Dan."

The auburn-haired woman held out her hand. "Rachel and this is Joanne."

"Nice to meet you." He tipped his head toward the high-rise building. "Do you two ladies work at Quest?"

"We do. How about you?" Rachel stared across the table at Declan. "Do you work at Quest?"

"No, but I've thought about applying." He looked at the menu. "I hear it's a good place to work."

"It's work." Rachel grimaced. "But some days I find myself counting the days to retirement."

He glanced up. "Is it that hard?"

Rachel shrugged. "Not so much hard."

"It's just some managers are better than others," Joanne said.

"You get that just about anywhere you work," Declan commented.

Rachel sighed. "I know. I've outlasted three managers over the fifteen years I've worked at Quest. Some were good. One was bad. I've learned to keep my head down and my mouth shut, and eventually the bad manager will move on."

"Some take longer to move on than others," Joanne muttered and stuffed a bite of her salad into her mouth.

Rachel reached out to pat her friend's hand. "Just do like I said and keep a low profile. You'll be there fifteen years before you realize they've passed."

Joanne snorted. "Or disappear into oblivion."

Declan's attention zeroed in on Joanne's last comment. "Disappear?"

"Yeah, disappear." Joanne leaned forward. "I heard one of the engineers in special projects didn't show up for work this morning. People are speculating that she was let go." Joanne shook her head. "They don't—" she made quote marks with her fingers "—let go of people out of the special projects area. They know too much."

Declan leaned forward, his brows dipping, giving Joanne his full attention. "What do you mean? They don't let people leave their jobs?"

The dingy blonde's eyes narrowed and her voice dropped to just above a whisper. "It's like a mob. Once you're in the secret circle, you can never get out."

"Joanne, you don't know that." Declan raised his eyebrows, feigning shock. "That woman could have been canned for sharing those deep, dark secrets to someone outside the company. If the project died, they could have laid her off."

Joanne stared into Declan's gaze. "Whatever. She hasn't come back to work and the police have been asking about her. Everyone's talking about it."

Rachel touched Joanne's arm. "Shh. You're going to scare Dan."

He laughed. "Don't worry about me. It takes a lot to scare me. Besides, it's a great story."

Rachel's brow furrowed. "Are you a reporter?"

Declan held up a hand. "Good Lord, no." He spied a delivery truck that was parked along the street. A man in a dark uniform stepped out. "I'm a delivery-truck driver," he said. And if he wasn't mistaken, that delivery truck could be heading in the direction of the Quest building. He leaned forward and smiled at the women. "I just remembered something I forgot to deliver." He stood. "Please excuse me. I hope I didn't disrupt your meal too much."

"Oh, please." Rachel's lips twisted into a wry grin. "Having you at our table was a delight. Maybe you can come by at lunch every day."

"Thank you for sharing your table." Declan leaned forward and held out his hand to Rachel. As he did, he swept his other hand over her employee badge lying on top of her wallet. He did this, blocking Joanne's view of what he was doing. Then he closed this hand completely around the badge and shook Joanne's hand. "You two ladies made my day. It would be an honor to have lunch with you again." He winked and walked by Grace's table, pretending to accidentally bump into her. When he did, he dropped the badge into her open purse and walked away.

Once he was away from the café, he ducked between two buildings and circled around to emerge in the parking lot, where he'd seen the delivery van. The driver was stepping out of the van, carrying a large package.

When he entered a building, Declan slipped into the side door of the delivery van. A quick scan of the packages on the metal shelves indicated that many of them were destined for Quest. The back of the van contained larger packages that appeared to have been picked up along the man's delivery route.

Declan dropped low behind several larger boxes and stacked one of them even higher to keep the driver from spotting him.

Next to him, hanging from a metal shelf, were a couple of uniforms like the one the driver wore. On the lapel was a name tag with Rodney written in bold black letters.

The delivery van dipped slightly as the driver stepped aboard, engaged the engine and took off down the street.

While the vehicle was in motion, Declan texted Grace.

Found a ride in the back of a delivery van headed for Quest. Dropped ID badge in your purse. Get to Quest before the ladies I sat with leave the café. I'll find you inside.

Chapter Five

Grace had no trouble getting the man at the café table to talk to her. Hell, she couldn't get Jordan to shut up. When the text came through from Declan, she'd been hard-pressed to read it without appearing rude.

His message set her heart racing.

Declan had swiped a badge from one of the women he'd been sitting with and placed it in her purse?

Her breath caught in her throat and her pulse pounded so hard against her eardrums, she could barely hear the man talking to her across the table. "I'm sorry," she interrupted him. "I'm not feeling very well. Please, excuse me for a moment."

Jordan leaned forward, his brow furrowing. "Do you need me to go with you?"

"No, really. I don't think you'd want to go to the ladies' bathroom." She gave him a weak smile and patted her flat belly. "Stomach issues."

The waitress chose that moment to arrive with their food and set it on the table.

Grace pushed to her feet. "I need to go."

"What about your meal?" Jordan asked.

She dug in her purse for her wallet, feeling the hard plastic of the employee badge against her fingers. After tossing a bill on the table, she gave her tablemate another smile. "Thank you for the company and sharing your table. I'm sorry, but I think I'd better leave now."

As she passed the two women Declan had been with, one of them was looking at the table, a frown denting her forehead. "I know I brought it with me." She opened her wallet and looked inside, shaking her head. "It's not here."

A wave of guilt washed over Grace, making her stomach roil. She wasn't cut out to be a spy or secret agent. She could barely function with the guilt of knowing she possessed someone else's property. Especially when that someone was clearly disturbed by the loss. She almost went back to her and handed over the badge.

But she didn't. She was doing this to find Riley. The woman would get her badge back eventually; it was just a piece of plastic. Riley's life was more important.

With that in mind, she entered the café, weaved her way through the tables to the rear, where the bathrooms were and the back door.

Once outside, she walked down the alley, passing several buildings before emerging on the sidewalk leading to Quest. She fell in step behind a group of women walking the same direction. All of them had Quest employee badges clipped to their clothes or on lanyards around their necks. When they reached the gate, they swiped their cards at a reader before a turnstile. When the light on the reader turned green, they entered the campus.

Her hand shaking, Grace swiped her stolen badge and held her breath. The light turned green. She pushed against the turnstile, but it didn't move. Her pulse pounded and she thought she might pass out.

"Push a little harder. It can be a little stubborn at times," a woman said from behind her.

Grace pushed harder. The turnstile moved, allowing her to enter. Once through, Grace drew in a deep breath, bringing a rush of air into her oxygen-starved lungs. She'd made it.

The woman who'd been behind her smiled and passed her. "See? Just needs a little more oomph." She winked as she walked by.

Grace followed without catching up and blended in with others returning from lunch. Once inside the building, she headed for the elevators like everyone else. Riley had said she worked on the eighteenth floor. Before she reached the elevator, a man in a delivery uniform stepped out of a hallway and approached her from the side.

"Excuse me, miss." He carried a large box that covered half of his face. "Could you hold the elevator for me?"

Grace entered the elevator, scooted to the side and pressed the button to hold the door open.

The delivery guy stepped in next to her, a little closer than she would have liked, but because of the crowd returning from lunch, she couldn't move over.

She pressed the button for the eighteenth floor. "What floor are you going to?" she asked.

"It's already lit up," he said, sounding vaguely familiar.

Afraid someone would say something about not recognizing her, Grace kept her head down and waited as they stopped on what seemed like every floor in between the ground and the eighteenth.

At the sixteenth floor, everyone but the delivery guy had exited.

When the doors closed, Grace noticed the only button lit was for the eighteenth floor.

"I thought we would never be alone," the delivery man said, his voice so familiar, Grace shot a glance to his face.

"Declan."

He shook his head and tipped it toward a corner of the elevator car and whispered, "Security camera."

Her heart pounding, Grace had to focus on not looking toward the corners of the car. "Do you have a plan?" she whispered.

He chuckled and said equally softly, "I was hoping you did." Then he added, "Actually, my plan is simple. Gather info. Let's find her office. Ask some questions. Make observations."

Great. They were inside a building they had no business being in, headed for the floor Riley had worked on. They had no guarantee they'd get any farther on the employee badge Declan had swiped. Riley had been working in Special Projects and she'd been adamant about the level of secrecy for the project. To the point she didn't share any details with her closest friend, Grace.

The elevator tone sounded and the door slid open.

Fear gripped Grace, freezing her feet to the floor.

"We've got this. What's the worst they can do?" Declan whispered. "Kick us out?"

"Throw us in jail? Shoot us? Make us disappear like Riley?" Grace listed in a voice so low, she doubted Declan heard her.

His soft chuckle assured her he had heard and wasn't too worried.

Having him there bolstered her confidence enough so that she was able to move, placing her foot outside the elevator door, onto the smooth marble tile of the eighteenth floor.

The stark white walls and the white marble made her feel as if she were walking into a futuristic science-fiction movie. At any moment she expected an alien to appear in front of her and lead her to a special room where humans were dissected or probed.

A hysterical giggle rose up her throat. Grace swallowed hard to keep from letting it escape.

"Which way?" Declan asked.

"This is as much as I ever got from Riley. Eighteenth floor. That's it." Grace turned right. "She worked in Special Projects."

Declan pointed to a sign on the wall to the right. "This must be the place." The sign read SPECIAL PROJECTS.

At that moment, a man stepped through the door.

Grace caught a glance at his name tag.

Moretti.

She had to catch herself to keep from grabbing the man and shaking the truth out of him.

"Sir, could you hold the door? I have a delivery for Special Projects."

The man seemed distracted and in a hurry. He paused for a moment and backed into the room to hold the door.

"Thanks. I'll hold it for him," Grace offered.

"Good. I have work to do," Moretti said and then quickly left them in the open doorway.

Grace breathed a sigh as she walked past the ID-card scanner beside the door. Had she tried to use her stolen card, it might have set off alarms.

As it was, Moretti had probably just broken a rule by allowing them to enter without scanning a badge. He'd practically sprinted down the hallway to the elevator.

Grace let the door close between them in case he decided he'd made a mistake and came back to demand identification.

The room they'd stepped into was a huge bank of cubicles with five-foot-high walls.

Declan leaned toward her ear. "Was that Moretti, your room-mate's supervisor?"

She nodded.

His eyes narrowed. "Let's start in his office."

"Would be good to know where that is." Grace glanced around.

"Follow an outside wall," Declan said. "He's bound to have a door."

Grace turned right and walked along the outskirts of the cube farm, careful not to make eye contact with anyone in the aisles between the cubicles. She passed an office with a woman's name on a placard beside the door. The door was open, but no one was at the desk inside.

The next office had a sign indicating it was the duplication room. Inside were a couple of copiers, plus a large printer like those used to generate engineering or architectural drawings. It, too, was empty.

The next door was to a break room. The smell of coffee wafted out. A woman stood at a coffee maker, pouring a mug full of the dark brew.

At the corner of the large room was a larger office with a plac-ard on the side of the door that read Director of Special Projects Alan Moretti.

The door was closed.

Grace reached out and twisted the handle, fully expecting it to be locked. It pushed open as if Moretti had left in such a hurry, he hadn't pulled it completely closed.

A quick glance around assured her there weren't any people close enough to notice her and Declan slipping into the office. And if they did, Grace would tell them that they were delivering a package for Mr. Moretti.

She entered, held the door for Declan and closed it as soon as he stepped through.

Once inside, Declan set the box on the floor and crossed to the desk.

"What exactly are we looking for?" Grace asked.

"Anything that might give us a clue as to what happened to

Riley. A file, computer records, something belonging to Riley herself. Just look."

Grace twisted the lock on the door in case someone happened to hear them rummaging around inside the office.

Moretti had a fairly large office, with bookshelves on one side, a massive desk in the middle and a mini-bar with decanters filled with amber liquid. Huge windows stretched from floor to ceiling, with a view across the river of downtown Washington, DC, and some of the government buildings.

Declan sat behind the desk and tapped the keyboard.

Grace crossed to a door on the left. It led to a small closet. Inside was an umbrella and a freshly laundered suit and starched shirt still wrapped in the thin plastic from the dry cleaner's. An extra pair of patent-leather dress shoes rested on the floor of the closet. On the shelf above was a flashlight and a hard hat. Nothing that would indicate Riley's whereabouts.

Grace backed out of the closet and attempted to open a dark mahogany file cabinet, but it wouldn't budge. "Know how to pick a lock?" she asked.

"Know how to hack a computer?" Declan responded.

"As much as I know about picking a lock."

"Switch for a minute. Maybe you'll have more luck." He rose and passed her, touching her hand as he went. "It'll be okay. We'll find her."

"I hope you're right. The longer she's missing, the harder it will be."

"True. But we have to keep positive. For Riley." He pulled up his uniform pant leg and slipped a knife out of a scabbard strapped to his calf. He glided the knife between the lock and the drawer of the cabinet and popped the cabinet open.

"Show off." Grace shook her head, wishing she could slip a knife into the computer and pop the screen up.

She sat at Moretti's desk and wiggled the mouse. Most people couldn't remember the myriad of passwords required to function in the modern-day technical environment. Moretti couldn't be any different. He had to have a place he kept his passwords to include the one that got him onto the system.

Grace opened the top drawer on Moretti's desk. Nothing but

pens, paper clips and business cards. She checked the drawers on either side and found a golf ball, a tee and golf gloves. In the drawer on the other side, she found a stack of magazines about airplanes, the space program and country living.

The man had a strange mix of reading material, but no bits of paper with computer passwords written on them. She ducked her head and checked the bottom of the desk. As she came up, she noticed something yellow beneath the keyboard.

When she lifted the keyboard, nothing was there. Turning the keyboard over, she found a yellow sticky note with the word *trinity* written followed by what appeared to be a date. Maybe a birthdate? She studied the name and the date.

"I can't see anything of interest in these files. It's mostly evaluation and training records of employees."

"Is Riley in there?"

"Yes, but all her folder has are some outstanding annual evaluations."

Grace set the yellow sticky note next to the computer keyboard and brought the screen to life by wiggling the mouse. The log-on popped up. She keyed in *trinity* and the date and waited.

Username or password failed

Grace tried again without the dashes in the date.

She waited for the computer to churn.

Seconds later, the same failure notice popped up.

Afraid to push the limit and lock out the log-on, she abandoned the computer and rose from the desk. On a cabinet behind her was a printer and supplies. The printer had a single sheet of paper lying in the output tray.

She lifted the sheet, turned it over and read.

Declan walked up behind Grace and looked over her shoulder. "What is it?"

A ripple of awareness washed over her. When Declan stood so near, Grace couldn't think straight. "Looks like the location of something," she said. "Let me plug it into my phone and see where it is."

Declan read off the number and street, while Grace keyed it into the map application on her cell phone.

"It's the Blue Gill Bar & Grill, about thirty minutes from here."

Voices sounded outside the door.

The metallic rasp of a key being pushed into the door lock alerted Grace and Declan.

"The closet." Declan grabbed Grace's hand and bolted for the only other door in the office. They had just ducked into the closet when the office door burst open.

Grace eased the closet door closed, leaving just enough of a crack to allow her to peer into the room.

Moretti hurried in, walking past the large box Declan had left in the middle of the room.

Grace held her breath, waiting for the man to say something about the box. If he'd expected the door to be locked, surely he would wonder how the box made it into the room.

But he didn't stop. Again, he appeared to be preoccupied. He walked across to the printer, snatched the paper with the address out of the tray and folded it to fit in his pocket.

He stopped at his desk and stared down at the screen, a frown furrowing his brow. He tapped the keyboard and shook his head. "Who am I kidding? I don't have time to go through my email." He turned toward the closet.

Grace shrank back against Declan, pressing into him, trying to fade into the farthest corner of the tiny space.

Declan's arm circled her waist, the solid muscles like a band of steel around her, making her feel a little safer.

A cell phone rang in the office. Moretti answered, "Yeah. I got the message. I'll be there. Seven thirty, tonight." His voice sounded as if he were coming close to where Grace and Declan hid.

The closet door burst open and an arm reached in and snagged the bag of dry-cleaned clothes.

Grace froze. All Moretti had to do was look to the right and he'd see her as plain as day.

His arm retracted without him having leaned in far enough to see the two people hiding inside.

Still, Grace didn't move. She leaned against Declan, her body melting into his. She had no desire to move—*desire* being the key word in the scenario. Being this close to the man made her body come alive, as if it was waking up from a long sleep. Her skin tingled where he touched her, and her core coiled and heated, sending warmth throughout her body.

"I think he's gone," Declan whispered against her ear. His breath stirred the loose tendrils of hair brushing across her neck and made her shiver with the strength of her awareness.

"It's okay," he said softly, his deep voice resonating in his chest.

Grace wasn't so sure she was okay. She'd never felt quite so viscerally attracted to a man before. Not even her husband when they were together at the honeymoon phase of their marriage.

What was it about Declan that made her forget she was hiding in a closet in a building she'd entered illegally? Her gut told her to turn in his arms and see what happened next.

"Grace?" As if reading Grace's thoughts, Declan turned her in the circle of his embrace. "Are you okay?"

She stared up at him in the limited light from the open door of the closet. "I d-don't know."

"You're scared." Declan swept a strand of her hair out of her face and tucked it behind her ear.

Electricity fired across her nerves where his fingers brushed against her skin. She drew in a sharp breath, her gaze going to his lips.

"We'll get through this together," he whispered and bent to kiss her forehead.

"We will?" she said, her voice gravelly.

He smiled. "We will." Then he touched his lips to hers. "I promise."

Grace's knees turned to liquid. If Declan hadn't been holding her around her middle, she would have melted to the ground in a puddle of goo.

Never in her life had she been this incapacitated by a simple, meaningless kiss. And it scared the stuffing out of her.

She couldn't let a man have that kind of effect on her. Marriage to Mitchell had been hell. Divorce had been her only option to get away from his mental and physical abuse. She would never let a man control her again. Ever. No matter how tempting.

Grace straightened and pushed away from Declan. "We need to go."

"Were you able to get into the computer?"

"Sorry. I couldn't figure out his password."

"No worries. Let me try one more thing." He gripped her arms and gently moved her to the side.

Grace inhaled deeply, her breasts rubbing against his fingers around her arms, setting off sparks of fire.

What was wrong with her? Her friend was missing, they were basically breaking and entering, and she was lusting after a man she'd met less than twenty-four hours ago.

Declan left the confines of the closet, hefted the big box up from the floor and headed toward the exit. "Go to the elevator and press the down button."

"But—" Grace didn't like being separated from Declan. They were a team. At least she felt like they were a team. And she also felt safer when he was around.

"I'll be okay. If I'm not there by the time the car arrives on the floor, go down, leave the building and campus. I'll meet you back at the parking lot." He handed her the keys to her SUV. "Wait for me there."

When she hesitated, he gave her a gentle smile. "What I do next is better done without worrying about what's happening to you. If you're out of the building, I can move more freely. I can run for an exit, if I have to. Now, please. Go."

He didn't wait for her to agree or disagree. He left the office and strode into the bank of cubicles. "Is there a Riley Lansing on this floor?" he called out.

Grace wasn't sure what he was up to, drawing attention to himself. But she didn't want to get in the way of his plan. She left the office, exited the Special Operations area and headed for the elevator.

Her heart raced and she strained to hear any sounds coming from the offices she'd just left. She braced herself for the blare of an alarm going off, indicating the building had been invaded and all exits should be closed off.

With that thought in her head, she punched the down key for the elevator and waited, her breath caught in her throat.

As soon as the elevator doors opened, she gave one last glance down the hall, willing Declan to come running from the Special Operations area. When he didn't, she was forced to enter the elevator alone.

She prayed Declan would be okay. His boss, Mrs. Halverson, was a very wealthy woman. Even so, Grace wasn't sure Mrs. Halverson would be able to bail him out of jail for unlawful entry into a secure facility.

Chapter Six

Declan strode down one aisle of cubicles, calling out, "Delivery for Miss Riley Lansing."

"She's not in," a female voice said. A woman with bleached-blond hair leaned out of her cubicle, took one look at him and smiled. "Maybe I can help you?"

"I have a delivery for Miss Lansing. Do you know when she'll be back?"

The woman shook her head. "Not a clue. She lit out of here yesterday like her hair was on fire, and I haven't seen her since."

"Yesterday?" Declan glanced at the box. "She has to sign off on the delivery. I don't suppose you know where I can find her?"

The woman shook her head. "No, but maybe I'll schedule another delivery. Will you be the one to bring it?" She winked at him.

Declan gave her a hint of a smile. "I doubt it. They switch up the drivers," he said, making it up as he went along.

A man in a polo shirt and dress slacks stepped out of his cubicle. "Are you looking for Riley?" he asked.

"Riley Lansing," Declan said. "Can you point to where she sits? This box is getting heavy." It wasn't, but it was as good an excuse as any to get someone to show him where Riley's office was.

"She has the office near the back." The man in the polo shirt pointed to the wall behind him.

Declan strode past the man as if he belonged in the Special Projects area. He'd made it to a cubicle by the back wall with a placard bearing Riley Lansing's name when the polo shirt guy commented.

"I didn't know they allowed external deliverymen to bring boxes up here. I thought all packages came from our internal mail-room staff." He'd followed Declan to Riley's office.

"They were slammed down there and asked me to bring this up. It was marked urgent on dispatch."

"I guess it won't be as urgent, considering she hasn't bothered to show up today."

"But she was here yesterday? What, is she out sick or something?" Declan asked casually, setting the box on the floor. He took his time, his gaze scanning Riley's desktop for clues.

"I didn't see her, but she was here. Sometimes senior engineers work in the lab. She could have been in there."

"Are you sure she isn't in there now?" Declan asked. "Could you check to make sure? I can't leave the box without her signature."

Polo-shirt guy frowned. "I'm almost 100 percent sure she's not in there."

"Seriously, man. I can't leave the box without her signature." Declan raised his eyebrows. "Would you please go check?" *And get the heck out of here so I can look through Riley's desk.*

"Okay. I'll be right back." The man left.

Declan waited in the aisles until he turned down another corridor and disappeared out of sight.

Making certain no one else was watching, Declan searched Riley's desktop. He wasn't sure what he was looking for, but anything could be a clue. Papers were scattered around the surface as if she'd been working and left in a hurry. A notepad sat by the telephone. The top page was empty, but it had indentations from the person writing the previous note. He took the top page and shoved it into his pocket.

As he straightened, he noticed a shiny silver object on the floor. He bent to retrieve a charm bracelet. This, too, he shoved into his pocket.

"Like I thought, she wasn't there," a male voice called out.

Declan hefted the box up off the floor and smiled. "Thanks

for checking. I'll take this back to the mail room. They can deal with it there."

"I could sign for it, if you like." The man in the polo shirt held out his hands.

"Sorry, it's supposed to go to Miss Lansing." Declan stepped past the man and strode the length of the cubicles, past the woman with the bleached-blond hair and out of the Special Projects area.

As he left the restricted area, two police officers and a security guard stepped off the elevator.

Declan lifted the box higher, blocking his face from view. He passed the group and was stepping onto the elevator when the security guard said, "Hey! You're not supposed to be up here."

Declan punched the button for the first floor and the button to close the elevator doors.

The security guard performed an about-face and started toward the elevator, but the doors closed before he could reach it.

Figuring the guard might call his buddies, Declan stopped the elevator on the third floor, punched the second-floor button and then exited. He found a bathroom, where he ditched the box and shucked the uniform shirt. He left the bathroom wearing the button-down cotton shirt he'd had on beneath the uniform.

He strode to the stairwell and walked the last two flights to the ground floor.

Several security guards stood in front of the elevator bank as the door to the elevator Declan had been on opened and a woman stepped out, a frown marring her face as she walked around the guards.

One of the security guards stepped into the elevator as if he might find someone hiding in it.

Declan swallowed a chuckle and walked out of the building and through the gate. No one stopped him or yelled at him to slow down.

He walked slowly, though he wanted to sprint to the parking lot to make certain Grace was safe. As he neared where he'd parked the SUV, his stomach sank. The vehicle was gone.

Before he could react, a dark SUV pulled up beside him and a window rolled down.

"Get in," a female voice called out.

He turned to find Grace in the driver's seat of her SUV. He hopped into the vehicle and closed the door. "Why did you move the car?" he asked.

"I thought you might need me to be ready to make a run for it. Backing out slows one down."

He laughed. "You're getting good at this."

She shook her head. "I don't *want* to get good at this." She left the parking lot and drove away from the Quest building. "What did you find?"

He dug the bracelet out of his pocket. "Do you recognize this?"

Grace frowned. "That's Riley's. She wore it to work yesterday morning."

"Are you sure?"

"I'm sure. I helped her put it on. She was in a hurry and the clasp can be tricky." She shifted her gaze back to the traffic in front of her. "Where did you find it?"

"Under her desk."

"So, she was at work yesterday." Her eyes narrowed. "Why would her supervisor lie?"

"I don't know, but he should have gotten his story straight with the people she worked with. One woman said she left in a hurry yesterday." He pulled the sheet of paper from his pocket. "I don't suppose you have a pencil?"

"In my purse. I keep a mechanical pencil."

"Not sure that will work, but I'll try."

"Try what?"

"I found this paper on her notepad. I thought she might have scribbled a note before she left."

Grace nodded toward her purse. "Check in the side pocket. The pencil is in there."

Declan dug around in her purse, found the pencil and rubbed it over the note. At first, he couldn't see anything, but as he continued across the page, two words appeared.

GET OUT

Grace swerved and righted the vehicle. "Does that say what I think it says?"

"Get out," Declan said.

Grace's fingers tightened on the steering wheel until her knuckles turned white. "What's happened to you, Riley?" she whispered.

"One thing we know for certain, Riley was at the office yesterday and her supervisor didn't want the police to know it."

Grace's lips tightened. "Why?"

"I don't know. But we know where he'll be at seven thirty, tonight."

Grace shot a glance at Declan. "We're going there?"

"You bet we are. Or at least I am." He tilted his head. "It might be better if you don't go."

Grace slammed her foot on the brake and glared across the console at Declan. "Why the hell not?"

Declan was glad he'd fastened his seat belt or he'd have been halfway through the windshield. "I get the feeling this might get dangerous."

"Riley's out there somewhere. If she's in danger, I'll do anything to help."

"Including putting yourself in danger?"

"Damn right, I would." Grace's eyes welled. "She's my friend. Practically family."

A horn honked behind them.

"The light's green," Declan said softly. "You want me to drive?"

"No," Grace said. Then she wiped her eyes and hit the accelerator a little too hard. The SUV leaped into the intersection. "I'm okay. I just want Riley to be okay."

"I get that."

"We have several hours until the meeting this evening. Where should we look next?"

Declan glanced around. "We could retrace Riley's route she would have taken to the apartment and see if we can find any clues to her whereabouts."

"I did that last night into this morning."

"And?"

Her lips thinned into a straight line. "Found nothing."

"Does she have any places she hangs out when she doesn't want to go the apartment? Maybe she's afraid to go to the apartment. If she left on her own yesterday, she might be running from someone."

Grace concentrated on driving for a few moments before answering. "There's a coffee shop a couple of blocks from our apartment. They have Wi-Fi. She goes there occasionally because she likes their coffee."

Declan folded the note and tucked it into his pocket. "Then let's hit all her normal haunts, get a late lunch/early dinner and be ready when Moretti goes to his meeting."

GRACE DROVE THROUGH the congested traffic to the coffee shop near their apartment. By the time they arrived, she needed the coffee to steady her nerves. "There's a reason I take the train as much as possible. Traffic is awful. We usually walk from the apartment to the coffee shop."

"Let me drive from here."

She handed him the keys. "You're on."

"When did you move in?"

"Four months ago, I had a hard time finding steady work paying enough to afford an apartment on my own. Riley offered to let me live with her until I got something that paid enough. I've been working for temp agencies, but I need to find a full-time job with benefits."

"Thus the interview with Mrs. Halverson?"

Grace nodded and climbed out of the SUV. "What about you? I don't know anything about you. When did you start to work for Mrs. Halverson?"

"Last night."

Grace frowned. "After the kidnapping incident?"

"Yup," he said and walked with her into the coffee shop.

At the counter, he waited for her to order, then he got a coffee for himself.

"Black. No sugar or cream. Just plain black coffee," he said.

Grace laughed. "Most people come for the fancy coffee."

"Unlike them, I like coffee just the way it is." He took the cups from the barista and nodded toward a table in the corner. "It's from years in the military, grabbing coffee when you can get it. It wasn't always available. You took it any way you could. And that was usually black."

He set the cups on the table and held a chair out for Grace.

She wasn't used to someone holding her chair for her. Her ex-husband hadn't been as concerned about her well-being. This made Grace like Declan even more. So far he was nothing like Mitchell. That was a huge plus in his favor. She lifted her cup and sipped the steaming brew. "How many years were you in the military?"

Declan took his seat and lifted his cup before answering. "Eleven years."

"Eleven?" She tipped her head. "I would think you'd have stayed for the full twenty before getting out."

His jaw hardened and his eyes grew dark. "It wasn't my choice."

"Oh." She could tell he didn't want to talk about it, but she couldn't stop the questions. "How does that work? Did they not let you reenlist?"

"I was discharged," he said, his tone implying she'd asked enough questions. "You said you have a picture of Riley on your phone. Could you bring it up? I'll take it to the barista and ask if she's seen your friend."

"Yeah." More questions burned to be asked, but Grace could tell she'd pushed too hard already. She found a picture of Riley she'd taken three days ago. She had been sitting at the dining table in their little apartment, her laptop open, staring at the wall, a bit of a wrinkle in her brow. Grace had snapped the picture and then asked her what she'd been thinking about.

"Nothing," she'd said. Then she'd captured Grace's gaze. "When someone asks you to do something you know is right but will cause you a lot of grief, do yourself a favor and tell them to go to hell."

At the time, Grace thought the comment was odd and out of left field. "What do you mean?" she'd asked.

Riley had heaved a big sigh and then redirected her focus on the laptop screen in front of her. "Nothing. Never mind."

Grace had gone to bed thinking her friend had had a bad day at the office and that she'd be her usually cheerful self the next day.

Then she'd gotten up early and gone into work before all the traffic became too congested. Grace had gotten up to use the bathroom only to find Riley struggling to get her lucky bracelet on.

"Here." Grace handed the phone to Declan.

When his fingers touched hers, the jolt of electricity passing from him to her made her drop the phone before he had it firmly in his hands. It clattered to the tabletop.

Declan captured her shaking hands in his. "Are you okay?"

Grace nodded. "I'm fine—just a little unnerved by all that's happened." She would have pulled her fingers free of his big hands, but she liked how warm and rough his skin was against hers. She didn't want him to let go.

But he did. And he lifted the cell phone. "This is Riley?" he said, staring down at her roommate's image.

"Yes. She's pretty, isn't she?"

"If you like redheads with green eyes," Declan said. "I've always liked blondes with blue eyes."

Heat rushed into Grace's cheeks and warmth filled her chest. She was a blonde. The warmth faded. "I have gray eyes."

"Did I say blue?" He glanced up, his eyes wide, innocent. "I meant gray." Then he winked.

Grace laughed, albeit a little forced. "I used to go for the guys with black hair and brown eyes. They were so mysterious."

"Used to?" Declan asked.

"Until I married Mitchell."

"Mitchell's your ex, right? Not a new husband?" His look was one of horror. "Are you on marriage number two?"

This time Grace laughed, humor bubbling up inside. She hadn't laughed like that in a long time. "No. I'm not married. I'm very divorced."

Declan let out a relieved sigh. "Thank goodness. I'd hate to think I'd kissed a married woman."

That heat returned to Grace's cheeks. "Speaking of which... Why did you kiss me?"

He rose from the table, phone in hand. "Time to get back to work. We have a missing person to find." He walked to the counter and turned the full wattage of his smile on the barista.

He had the woman blushing as much as Grace was sure she had been over his statement that he preferred blondes.

Grace tried not to stare, but she couldn't look away.

Declan had broad shoulders, narrow hips and thick thighs. When he walked, he had a natural swagger that couldn't be hidden, and it made Grace's heartbeat go from zero to 122 in two seconds flat.

He showed the woman the phone. The barista tilted her head to the screen, brushed her hair over her shoulder, smiled and nodded.

Grace leaned forward.

Did the barista's nod mean she'd seen Riley? Or was it more flirting with the former marine? Not that Grace could fault the woman's taste in men. Declan had it all. Good looks, a killer smile and a body that would haunt any woman's daydreams and night-time fantasies.

When Declan returned, he walked toward her with the grace of a tomcat on the prowl.

Grace's mouth went dry and her pulse pounded through her veins. She wet her lips, her gaze going to his naturally.

"She thinks she saw her last night."

"Thinks?"

"She knows Riley as a repeat customer. A woman who looked a lot like Riley—same height, build and hair color—came in last evening, wearing a baseball cap pulled low over her eyes. She ordered the same drink Riley orders and sat in the seat she usually occupies when she comes to the coffee shop to work on her laptop."

"Why isn't she sure it was her?"

"She didn't wait on Riley and she had another customer. She only saw Riley out of the corner of her eye."

"What about the barista who waited on the woman in the ball cap? Where is she?"

"*He* doesn't work again until the weekend. He was training last night and wouldn't know Riley from anyone else. He's new."

Grace inhaled and let her breath out slowly. "Riley might have been here last night." She shook her head. "Then why didn't she come home? And where did she stay?"

"She might not want to involve you in whatever made her leave her office in a hurry," Declan said. "She could be on the run."

"From who? What?" Grace stared into Declan's eyes. "She's an engineer, not a secret agent."

Declan took her hands in his and squeezed gently. "We might not know until we find Riley."

"She's got some explaining to do." Grace pressed her lips together and then softened, her gaze on the man's hands holding hers. "She must be really scared." She glanced at the pocket Declan had slipped the notepad paper into. "Why would she write the words *GET OUT* and then disappear? So far, I haven't heard of any others from Quest Aerospace Alliance being threatened or having gone missing. There hasn't been anything in the news. Riley's disappearance seems to be unique. No one else has vanished, as far as we know, from Quest."

"Could she have been working on a project someone wanted more details about?"

"Someone willing to kidnap her to get it?" Grace shivered. "She could have been. Again, she didn't talk about work. She has a top secret clearance. Not many people get one of those in the private sector. She could have been working on something important. I wish she'd told me more."

"What is interesting is that Riley was here yesterday. And the barista said she was alone."

"Not kidnapped or held at gunpoint," Grace said. "Which means she disappeared intentionally." Her gaze met his. "I hope our efforts to find her aren't putting her into more danger."

"Me, too."

Grace tightened her grip on Declan's hands, glad he was with her. Thankful Mrs. Halverson had assigned him to assist her in her search for her roommate. "Riley's on the run, hiding from someone. But who?"

"Maybe Moretti will lead us to the ones Riley is hiding from."

Grace glanced at the clock on the wall behind the counter. "We have a couple of hours to blow. Want to come to my place? I have your rucksack there and I have some leftover lasagna in the refrigerator."

"Sounds good to me. But I don't want to take your food."

"Nonsense. I always cook too much. I'm a firm believer in leftovers. That way I don't have to cook as much during the week."

"Good thinking. I grew up in a house where there was no such thing as leftovers. I was one of three brothers and a sister. My mother, to this day, says she doesn't know how she kept enough food on the table for all of us during our teen years." Declan smiled. "We tended to wipe out the refrigerator every third day.

All of us were very active in sports. We burned a lot of calories. My mother was a saint. We were the sinners. I never knew how much she did for us until I had to do everything for myself when I joined the US Marine Corps."

"Your mother sounds amazing. Is she still with you?"

"She and my father live out west. In Wyoming."

"That's a long way from DC."

He shrugged and released her hands. "I haven't been back home since I left the military."

"Why?"

"I'm not quite sure how to tell them I've been discharged from the US Marine Corps." He shook his head. "My father was so proud the day I graduated basic training. And when I was accepted into the Force Recon training, you'd have thought I'd hung the moon. Dad couldn't have been prouder."

"I'm sure your folks would understand that whatever got you discharged from your unit, you had to have good reasons."

"We thought so at the time," he said softly.

"We?" Grace searched his gaze for emotion. What had he experienced? What had been bad enough he was kicked out of the military? "Who else was involved?" When he let go of her hands, she reached out this time to comfort him and refused to let go.

He stared down where their hands intertwined, without speaking for a full minute. Then his lips twisted. "Five of my Force Recon team and I were processed out. Dishonorable discharges, all of us. For doing what we knew was right." His words came out tight, and his fingers squeezed hers to the point they were hurting her.

But she didn't utter a word, figuring the pain of his grip was nothing compared to the pain of losing the career he'd obviously loved and watching his fellow marines going down with him.

"I'm sorry," she said.

"Why? You didn't do anything wrong. We did. We knew what we were doing and that it was against orders. But we did it anyway. We also understood the consequences." He pushed to his feet. "Now, if you're serious about those leftovers, we should get going. We want to be at the meeting location before Moretti arrives."

Grace rose and left the coffee shop with Declan. The more

questions she asked of him, the more she wanted to know. But all in good time. Declan obviously didn't feel comfortable talking about the incident that had gotten him kicked out of the US Marine Corps.

She could wait. But it didn't stop her from wondering. The man seemed to be a straight shooter, one who would do anything for someone else. She couldn't picture him as a traitor to his country. What else would have constituted a dishonorable discharge from the military? Unfamiliar with military law, she didn't know. Soon, she would find out.

Chapter Seven

After a fully satisfying meal of lasagna and garlic toast, Declan thanked Grace and then drove them across town.

They stopped at a convenience store for some disguises—two baseball caps—and moved on to the Blue Gill Bar & Grill, where Moretti was scheduled to meet with someone for something. Who and what? He had no idea.

They settled into a booth at the far corner of the barroom, in full view of the entrance and exit, in case Moretti came from either direction.

The waitress took their orders and returned with two glasses of fizzy ginger ale. When she'd left, Declan cast a glance toward Grace. She'd grilled him about his prior service, and he found himself wanting to know more about this woman who'd taken on the task of finding her missing roommate with fervor and undaunted determination.

"You and Riley were roommates in college?"

Grace smiled. "For four years. We never knew our first semester together would start a life-long friendship. Even after we went our separate ways after college, we kept in touch. We led completely different lives. Like I said, I married and focused on my husband and his life. Riley focused on her career." Grace laughed, the sound flat and strained. "Perhaps I would have been better off if I had stuck to my career."

"How long were you married?"

"Five years."

"And how long have you been divorced?" Declan shook his head. "You don't have to answer. I'm just killing time until Moretti arrives."

Though Declan gave her the out, she didn't take it; instead, she answered, "A few years."

"I'm sure you had good reasons."

She snorted. "Some might not think so."

"Try me."

She hesitated a moment and then said softly, "I forgot who *I* was."

"One of those *I found myself* situations?"

"Kind of." She swirled the ice in her drink, staring at it as it circled inside her glass. "My husband always made sure I knew who he was and how important his life was to him. I spent all my time living up to his expectations of what a proper wife was supposed to be—an extension of her husband. She shouldn't have a thought of her own—one that was not put there from her husband's mouth."

His lips twitched. He could imagine Grace standing up to her husband. "Let me guess…you had a thought and it pissed him off."

"Once I remembered I was a living, breathing human being with a brain of my own, I had many thoughts. Not all reflecting him and his ideals. When we weren't in the company of others, he would punish me for speaking out." Grace touched the tiny scar on her cheekbone. Until that moment, Declan hadn't noticed it.

His fists clenched. Any man who hit a woman wasn't a man at all. He was a coward with control issues.

The scar did nothing to detract from her natural beauty. But he was certain it caused her more pain through her memories than it did when the injury had been inflicted.

"He made me feel like I deserved it," she said. "I embarrassed him in front of his colleagues."

Declan reached across the table and brushed his thumb along her cheek. "No man has the right to hit a woman. If you were mine, I would never raise a hand to you." He dragged his knuckles across

her jaw and down the side of her neck. "I'd treat you with the re-
spect you deserve."

Grace leaned her cheek into his open palm and stared into his
eyes. "A girl could get used to hearing words like that, but what
would it buy her? Maybe a few years of happiness, then more
years of pain."

"Not all men are the same. Not all of them cause pain." He
wanted to reassure her that his words were truth, but he wasn't in
a position in his life to guarantee that assurance. He was, more or
less, a marked man. On any job application or background check,
his dishonorable discharge would come up. If not for Mrs. Halverson, he'd be homeless and jobless. Out of the goodness of one
wealthy woman's heart, he wasn't completely destitute. For now.
"And now you know who you are and what you want out of life."

"I'm me. For better or worse. And I know I want to be in control
of my own destiny. I never want any man to control me ever again.
Beyond that, I'm still trying to figure out what it is I'm going to
do in this life. I seemed to have missed the career opportunities
of a fresh college graduate. But I'm not going to let that stop me."
She gave him a tight smile. "Enough about me. What was so bad
that the military thought you couldn't be given a second chance?"

She'd come out of left field with the question. He'd been so
engrossed in her story, he wasn't ready with a canned answer.
How did a man tell a beautiful woman he'd practically committed mutiny?

GRACE FIGURED SHE'D pushed again. But after baring her soul to
the man, he should reveal a little more about himself to her.

Declan opened his mouth and then shut it, his gaze going past
her, his jaw tightening. "Moretti just walked through the door,"
he said, his voice low but intense.

Grace fought to keep from spinning around to stare at Riley's
supervisor, the man who'd lied to the police and to them. Why was
the man hiding the fact Riley had been to the office that morning? Did he think he'd get away with it? Already someone from
his own office had refuted his story.

Willing herself to remain facing Declan, Grace pleated the napkin in her lap and waited for Moretti to pass their table so she could watch his every move.

Her curiosity wouldn't let her just wait. She had to know. "What's he doing?"

Declan smiled at her, though his gaze angled over her shoulder to the man at the entrance. "He stopped at the door to look at his phone. Apparently, he just received a text message."

"Do you think he'll recognize us as the people he met at his office?" Grace asked.

Declan's lips twitched. "Not with the ball cap. It shadows your face nicely."

"As does yours." Grace smiled. He really was nice to look at. And reassuring, just being there. She couldn't imagine finding Riley on her own. "Thank goodness there's something for everyone in today's convenience stores."

Moretti strode by and took a seat in the farthest, darkest corner of the barroom. He lifted a menu and propped it up so that all that could be seen of his face were his eyes. And they were wide and watching everyone who came into the Blue Gill.

"He's awfully nervous." Grace lifted her glass to her lips and took a sip.

"Yeah?" Declan's eyes narrowed. "What's he doing now?"

She chuckled. "Hiding behind his menu and watching the door. Anyone interesting coming from that direction?"

"Nothing so far." Declan took her hand and rubbed his thumb across her knuckles like a man who was showing affection to his date.

Grace sucked in a breath and held it. Declan's fingers were doing crazy things to her insides. And they were only touching her hand. She could imagine how sensuous they'd feel on other parts of her body. With considerable effort, she dragged her attention back to Moretti, afraid to look away for too long should he get up and leave without her knowing.

He was still there. Still looking over the top of his menu.

"Hmm." Declan's fingers tightened on hers. "My gut says the people who just walked in are interesting."

"Should I look?"

"No, keep your eyes on Moretti. Any reaction from him over the newest arrivals?"

"He just ducked behind his menu completely. All you can see are his hands."

"Like I said…interesting."

"How many?"

"Three. And they look like Mafia thugs."

"Holy hell," Grace said. "I need to see this." She swiveled in her seat and raised her hand, as if summoning the waitress.

Three big guys stood just inside the door. Each had dark hair, ruggedly angular faces and fists like ham hocks.

The waitress nodded at Grace and raised one finger. "I'll be with you in just a minute." She walked to the men at the door and offered to seat them.

They shoved her aside and stalked through the barroom, the leader's dark brow low on his forehead.

At that moment, Grace's cell phone jingled with the tone she'd assigned to incoming texts. Giving only a perfunctory glance at the screen, Grace didn't want to take her attention away from the drama about to unfold. But the words on the screen made her do a double take.

GET OUT!

The hairs on the back of Grace's neck stood at attention. The text had come from an unknown number. She stared at it for a moment and then passed the phone to Declan. "What do you make of this? It's the same message Riley had written on her notepad."

The jingle sounded again and another text came through.

Declan held the cell phone in his hand this time.

GET OUT NOW!

The three big guys chose that minute to pass their table, heading for the corner where Moretti hunkered low behind his menu.

Declan pushed to his feet, grabbed Grace's hand and yanked her out of her chair.

"What are you doing?" she said softly.

"I'm getting you out of here so that I can ravish your body," he said and waggled his brows. "The sooner the better." He didn't wait for her response, but tossed cash on the table and then half led, half dragged her out of the bar and into the street.

As soon as they cleared the door, gunshots rang out behind them.

Declan pulled Grace to the side of the door and pressed his body over hers, sandwiching her between himself and a brick wall.

With her face pressed to his muscular chest, Grace couldn't see anything. Her heart raced and her hands circled his waist, holding him close. Whoever was shooting hadn't run out of ammunition yet.

Declan lifted his head and glanced around. Shielding her body with his, he walked her to the entrance of an apartment building, opened the door and shoved her inside. He pointed at her. "Stay."

Grace grabbed his finger and glared at him. "I'm not a dog. You can't tell me to stay."

"Please stay," he amended. "I don't want you to be caught in the crossfire."

When he turned and started to walk out of the apartment entrance, she grabbed his arm. "Where do you think you're going?"

"Back to see if I can help."

"Help who?" Grace said. "Moretti? The Mafia? You're not even armed, are you?"

He pulled a handgun from beneath his jacket. "Charlie loaned me this."

Grace reeled backward, shocked that he'd been carrying the weapon throughout the day and she hadn't known he had it. "Are you even licensed to carry?"

"I am...was...before I was discharged from the army."

"Do they revoke licenses to carry from people who are discharged from the army?"

"I don't know," Declan said. "But I have it if I need it." He replaced it in the holster beneath his jacket. "I'm going back in. There are other people in there who might need help."

"Then I'm going with you," Grace insisted.

Declan shook his head. "It's too dangerous. You're not a trained soldier. I am."

"And don't most trained soldiers have buddies to cover their sixes?" She lifted her chin. "I've watched all those special-forces movies. I know you're supposed to have someone cover your back. Well, I'm your buddy. I'll cover your back."

"And you're armed?" Declan challenged.

Grace dug around in her purse and pulled out a Taser. "This is my weapon. And I'm not afraid to use it."

Declan frowned and glanced over his shoulder. "I need to go back in there. But I don't trust that you'll stay out of harm's way."

"Damn right I won't." She pushed past him. "Come on. The longer we wait, the more chance someone is getting hurt."

Declan snatched her hand and pulled her behind him. "You can't cover my back if you're not behind me. At least stay low and well to my rear until I figure out what's going on. Promise?"

He held on to her hand, refusing to let her move until she agreed.

"Okay," she said. "I promise to stay back behind you."

After another second, Declan moved, jogging back to the entrance of the bar. The sound of sirens wailed in the distance. "I'm going in. Stay out here and let me know if any other bad guys show up. And when the police get here, let them know there are innocent people inside."

"But I'm your backup. I should go in with you."

"Seriously, I need to go in first and make sure it's safe."

"And if it's not, and they shoot you, how am I to know?"

"Hell, Grace, if I'm worried about you, I'll get myself killed."

She clamped her lips shut on the words she was about to say. He had a good point. "Okay. I get it. I don't want to distract you from doing what you do best." She flung her arms around his neck and pressed her lips to his in a brief, hard kiss. "Concentrate on staying alive."

He nodded. "I will, if I can have more of that."

"Incentive, man. There's more where that came from, but you have to come out alive to collect." She winked and stood to the side of the door into the bar that had gone eerily quiet. "Be careful."

"I will." Declan dove into the bar.

Grace counted to ten, feeling like a child playing a dangerous game of hide-and-seek. At ten, she still hadn't heard anything from inside, and she could barely breathe.

Letting the air out of her lungs slowly, she pushed back her shoulders, ducked low and slipped through the entrance. Using the techniques she'd learned from cop movies and reality television, she moved quickly to one side and crouched in the shadows.

Soft sobbing sounded from behind the bar. Two men lay on the floor behind an overturned table, peering out from the sides of the tabletop.

Grace's gaze went to the far corner, where Moretti had been hiding behind his menu. The corner was empty, and Moretti, the Mafia thugs and Declan were gone.

The bartender rose up from behind the counter, a full bottle of unopened white wine held in his hand like a hammer.

The waitress crawled out from under an overturned chair, her mascara running in dark lines down her cheeks, her eyes red-rimmed from crying. She sniffed and looked around. When she spotted Grace, she whispered, "Is it safe to come out?"

"I don't know. Where did the big guys go?" Grace asked.

The waitress pointed. "Through the back door."

Grace hurried toward the rear of the building, her pulse thumping through her veins, her knees wobbling. Where was Declan? Surely he hadn't chased after the bad guys. They outnumbered and outgunned him three to one.

The rear emergency exit stood open. Grace eased up to the door and stuck her head around slowly.

The alley behind the bar stood empty, but for the big trash bin.

Her heart fluttered. Grace saw no sign of the Mafia brothers or Declan. It was as if they'd disappeared entirely. Had Declan surprised them as they got into their escape vehicle? Would they have knocked him unconscious and taken him with them? If so, would they kill him and dump his body in the Potomac?

She stepped out of the building and walked toward the corner. As she passed the trash bin, a faint sound caught her attention. She stopped and strained to hear it again. A groan sounded from inside the bin.

Grace leaned over the top and peered inside. The smell of rotting food and moldy trash hit her first. Then something moved among the boxes, bottles, cans and leftover food.

She pulled her cell phone out of her purse, hit the flashlight icon on the screen and shined the light down into the refuse.

Moretti lay among the trash, his body covered in blood.

The shock of her discovery made her stomach roil and bile rise up her throat. She stepped away from the bin and glanced down at her cell phone, her hand shaking so badly, she could barely function. Then she dialed 911 and gave her location. "There's a man with multiple gunshot wounds in the trash bin behind the building."

The dispatcher told her to seek safety until the police arrived. They already had an ambulance on the way.

By the time she finished the call, police officers emerged through the back door of the bar, weapons drawn.

Grace raised her hands. "I'm not armed. But there's a man in the bin. I think he's still alive."

An officer pulled her aside and frisked her. When they were certain she wasn't carrying a weapon, they made her go back through the bar and stand out on the street, in the midst of several squad cars. Still Declan hadn't returned.

The ambulance came and the EMTs loaded Moretti onto a gurney and carried him away to a hospital. Grace had about given up on Declan when she spotted him standing on the periphery of the small crowd gathering around the crime scene.

Her joy at seeing him surprised even herself. Afraid the police would pull Declan in for questioning and discover he had a weapon on him, Grace didn't rush over to see him. She asked the officer in charge if they needed her anymore. They had her information and knew how to get in touch with her.

The officer told her she could leave as long as she remained in town in case they needed to ask her more questions.

Finally, Grace left the center of the investigation and walked away from the bar to where they'd left her SUV a couple of blocks away, in a paid parking lot.

Declan was there, waiting for her.

Grace walked straight into his arms.

He engulfed her in his embrace and held her for a long moment.

She inhaled the warm, musky scent of his aftershave and ran her fingers across the hard plains of his chest. He really was there. He hadn't abandoned her.

"I told you to stay out front." He smoothed the hair back from her forehead and pressed a kiss there.

"It was so quiet. I couldn't stand outside, not knowing what was happening."

"I see they found Moretti. Where was he?" Declan asked.

"In the trash bin behind the building." She leaned back and stared up at him. "Where were you?"

"When I went into the bar, I saw that Moretti and the thugs were gone. Since we came out the front and they didn't, I figured they'd exited out the back. I ran through and got to the back door as a dark SUV pulled away. I thought they might have taken Moretti. I wanted to get a license plate number so we could trace the vehicle, so I ran after it."

"You ran after their getaway vehicle?" Grace laughed and shook her head. "Are you crazy?"

He ran a hand through his hair, retaining his hold around her waist with the other hand. "Yeah. I am a little crazy." He drew in a deep breath and let it out. "They weaved through the streets. I knew I couldn't catch up with them by running behind them, so I cut through some alleys and side streets. I almost caught up when they got onto a main road and sped up." He sighed. "I lost them."

"Did you get the license number?" Grace asked.

His lips twisted. "No." He nodded in the direction the ambulance had gone. "What about Moretti?"

"The EMTs got him out of that trash bin and took him in the ambulance, but I don't know how he is. He was a bloody mess, with multiple gunshot wounds. I'll be surprised if he lives."

"Think we can get into the hospital to ask him some questions?"

"The man is possibly dying."

Declan raised his hands, palms up. "Haven't you heard? Dying men tell no lies."

Grace shook her head. "That's dead men tell no lies. I asked the ambulance driver which hospital they were taking him to. We could at least get a status on the man."

"And if we play our cards right, I can slip past security and ask him about Riley." He brushed her arm with the back of his knuckles.

His touch set off a flock of butterflies in Grace's belly. She swallowed hard and lectured herself on falling for a stranger. Declan was making it entirely too easy. "You don't give up, do you?"

His smile slipped. "Not when it's important."

Grace nodded. "We'd better get going. Moretti might not live long enough for us to get any information out of him."

"Now you're talking." He lifted her hand and pressed a kiss into her palm. "Let's go." Then he opened the passenger door and held it while she slipped in. He rounded the front of the vehicle and slid behind the steering wheel.

Grace keyed the name of the hospital into her cell phone's map application and brought up the directions.

They arrived several minutes later and pulled into the parking lot of the emergency room. Grace and Declan got out and walked to where the ambulances unloaded patients.

Two police cars were parked nearby. An ambulance had just left the dock when another pulled in.

"Might be difficult getting in to see Moretti if he's still in Emergency," Declan said.

"I have an idea. I'll create a distraction, and you slip in." Grace hurried toward the ER entrance where they were wheeling an old woman through the sliding doors. "Excuse me, excuse me," she called out as if attempting to get the attention of the paramedics already inside the hospital.

Her real goal was the ambulance driver, a guy the size of a refrigerator, who stepped in front of her, his arms crossed. "I'm sorry, ma'am, you can't enter the ER through the ambulance entrance, you'll have to go through the ER reception."

"But that's my grandmother. I have to stay with her."

"Lady—" the man shook his head, his lips pressing together briefly "—you have to go through the other entrance. The receptionist will help you once you check in."

"But she raised me when my mother abandoned me. She's all I have!" She stood on her toes in an attempt to see past him to the woman on the gurney headed down the hall. "I promised I'd stay with her. She'll be scared."

"She's unconscious," the ambulance driver said. "You'll have time to check in with reception."

"Oh, my God. Grannie!" Grace dodged to one side.

The driver clotheslined her with a beefy arm, catching her in the throat.

Grace played it and dropped to the ground, clutching at her neck. She held her breath and pointed at her throat, mouthing the words *can't breathe.*

"Oh, come on," the ambulance driver said. "I didn't hit you. You ran into my arm." He bent and held out his hand. "Take my hand. I'll help you up."

Out of the corner of her eye, Grace could see the EMTs with the gurney had made it down the hallway with the old lady and Declan had circled wide, coming around the other side of the ambulance. He was about to step through the doors when the ambulance driver straightened and started to turn to where his teammates had gone.

Grace had to do something, or the man would see Declan slipping through the door. She reached out and grabbed the driver's hand, bringing his focus back to her.

He pulled her to her feet, his brow dipping low. "Are you all right?" he asked.

She would be as soon as Declan made it inside. Grace swallowed hard.

And Declan was inside, the door closing behind him.

Letting go of the breath she'd held, she nodded. "I think I'll be okay." She gave the driver a weak smile. "I'll just go in through the main ER entrance, like you said. I'm sorry I caused such a commotion."

"Don't worry." He patted her arm. "They'll take good care of your grandmother. I'm sorry I had to be so stern with you, but it's against policy to let unauthorized personnel in through the back door."

"I understand. You were just doing your job." Grace brushed the dirt off her clothes, turned toward the main entrance to the ER and left the ambulance driver to close up the ambulance and wait for his team to return.

Now all she could do was wait for Declan to resurface, hopefully with some clues or information from Moretti.

She fished her cell phone from her pocket and stared down at the messages she'd received prior to the shoot-out between the three Mafia guys and Moretti.

GET OUT

GET OUT NOW!

Who had sent the messages? Could it have been Riley? Had she been somewhere close by and seen the three men coming in? Or was it the people who'd warned Riley to get out of her office?

The more Grace learned, the more she realized she didn't know.

She prayed Declan would find out something from Moretti. If not, they had very little to go on and still had no idea where Riley was. One thing was clear: if what had happened to Moretti was any indication, Riley was in danger.

Chapter Eight

Declan slipped into the emergency room behind the men pushing the gurney with the old woman. As soon as he could, he ducked into what appeared to be a supply closet filled with medical kits, gauze and surgical paraphernalia. Hanging on a hook were two white doctor smocks. He grabbed one and slipped it over his clothes. Then he found some blue shoe booties and a face mask and pulled them on. His disguise complete, he stepped out of the closet and almost ran into the EMTs on their way out, pushing an empty gurney.

One of them gave him a chin-lift greeting.

Declan gave one in return and kept walking toward the exam rooms. He lifted the chart from the bin hanging on the wall outside the first door he came to and flipped it open. The name on the chart was Archie Cooper. He replaced the chart and moved on to the next door and chart. Rita Davis. The scent of antiseptic stung his nose and reminded him of the times he'd been laid up in a hospital with shrapnel or gunshot wounds. He hadn't liked being in a hospital. He'd done his darnedest to get the heck out and back to his unit as quickly as possible. He had an unfounded view that hospitals were places where people went to die. It didn't make sense, because he'd been in one and hadn't died. Many of his teammates had been in them and come out alive. The ones who'd died had left an indelible impression on him.

As he approached the next door, a doctor and nurse emerged. The doctor was giving orders to the nurse. The patient was to be moved to the OR as soon as the surgeon on call arrived. In the meantime, they were to give him blood and do their best to stabilize him prior to moving.

Before they could look up and see him clearly, he entered the door beside him and let it close.

When he turned, he found the old woman who'd been brought into the hospital when he and Grace had arrived. She had been put on oxygen and an IV. Her skin was pale and waxy and her breath shallow.

Memories flooded in on Declan. Until then, he hadn't thought much about when he'd come as a teenager to watch his grandmother die in a hospital. He'd loved his grandmother and had spent many days on his grandparents' ranch in Wyoming, riding horses, swimming in the creek and running wild. He'd never thought about death or dying until his grandmother had fallen, broken her hip and succumbed to pneumonia. She'd wasted away, going in and out of the hospital until her frail body couldn't take it anymore and she'd passed away.

He went to the woman and lifted her hand. "I hope you get better. Someone out there loves you and wants you to come home."

A loud beeping sounded from the next room. Over the intercom system, a woman's voice said, "Code blue. Code blue in room seventeen."

Footsteps sounded outside the room where Declan stood. He walked to the door and pushed it open enough to see the doctor and several nurses rushing into the room next to the one he was in.

Declan dared to step out. Everyone else was focused on the code blue and didn't notice him hovering outside the room.

The nurses and doctor worked over the man, desperately trying to save him. With so much blood spilled on the floor, the medical staff slipped in it.

After several minutes, the doctor shook his head. "It's no use. He's bleeding internally. He won't make it until the surgeon can get in there and plug all the holes."

The pulse monitor showed an irregular heartbeat and low blood pressure. As Declan watched, the man's heartbeat flatlined.

"Call it," the doctor said after a few moments passed.

One of the nurses recited the time of death. Another noted it on the chart. The nurses and doctor stood back as a man's life ended.

Declan turned and ran into a woman in scrubs.

She frowned, her gaze searching his person. "I'm sorry, do I know you?"

"No," Declan replied automatically. "I'm new here."

"And you would be?" The woman's brows rose.

"Leaving. I think I'm in the wrong department." He nodded and dodged her, heading for what he hoped was the exit into the ER reception area.

"Someone call security," the woman said behind him. "Stat!"

Declan picked up his pace, taking long strides without running. He reached a door marked Exit, hit the button on the wall and waited while the door swung open.

A security officer hurried toward him.

Declan met him head-on. "Oh, good. There's a guy back there causing problems. They need your help with him." He stepped aside and let the security guard enter the restricted area. As soon as the door closed behind him, Declan scanned the waiting area for Grace and he removed the mask from his face.

Her brow furrowed and then smoothed.

A shout from inside the restricted area spurred Declan to move. He tossed the mask into a trash receptacle, pulled off the booties on his shoes and shucked the white jacket. By then Grace had reached him.

"Time to go." Declan took her hand in his and walked toward the glass double doors. The sensor set them in motion. As the restricted door started to open, Declan and Grace stepped out into the open air.

"What happened in there?" she asked beneath her breath.

"I'll tell you when we get out of the parking lot." He pulled her hand through the crook of his arm and hustled her along. They had climbed into Grace's SUV by the time the security guard emerged from the hospital.

"Duck," Declan said.

Grace leaned forward, below the windows.

Declan followed suit, raising his head only enough so he could track the progress of the security guard.

The man he'd passed on his way out of the restricted area was joined by another man in a security uniform. They walked through the parking lot.

As they neared the SUV, Declan's hand hovered over the ignition switch. He was ready to start the engine and pull out of the lot.

"Anything?" the guard one aisle over called out, his voice muffled through the window of the SUV.

The man near the back of the SUV responded, "Nothing."

They both turned and headed back to the building.

Declan let go of a sigh of relief. He waited until the guards were inside before he started the engine and shifted into Reverse.

"What was that all about?" Grace asked, straightening in her seat.

"A sharp nurse figured out I didn't belong in the back and turned the guards loose on me." He pulled out onto the street and hit the accelerator.

She touched his arm. "What about Moretti? Were you able to get in to him?"

He liked how her hand felt against his skin. For a moment, it derailed his thoughts...but then he was back. "I was close. But he wasn't talking."

"No?"

"No." Declan's jaw hardened. "The emergency room staff were working on him."

"And?" Grace's eyes widened.

Declan shook his head. "He didn't make it."

Grace slumped against her seat. "Damn."

"Yeah." Declan's lips twisted. "We're back to square one." He scratched his chin. "Does Riley have a computer she uses at your apartment?"

"She has one she uses for social media, but she was never allowed to bring her work home, because it was top secret."

"Let's find that computer and see if it will shed any light on where she might be."

"I checked it out when she went missing, but I could have missed something you might see. I hate to think Riley is out there, running for her life." Grace chewed on her bottom lip. "She must be terrified."

Declan nodded. "Especially after what happened to her boss."

"Do you think she knows about Moretti?"

"Not only do I think she knows, I think she's the one who sent that text at the bar. I don't think we would have gotten out unscathed if it hadn't been for whoever sent that text."

Grace snorted softly. "It had to be Riley. She's like that—thinking of others when she's in hot water."

"Let's look through her room and see if anything will give us a clue. Maybe she has a secret hiding place for stuff she doesn't want anyone else to find."

Grace frowned. "I'll feel awful going through her things. She values her privacy."

Declan reached out to take her hand and squeezed it. "I think she would forgive you if it means saving her life."

ALL THE WAY back to the apartment, Grace tried to think of anything Riley had said that could clue her into what was going on. For the past couple of months, Riley had gotten quieter about her work at Quest. When Grace asked how her day had gone, Riley had always responded vaguely. Nothing she'd said seemed to stand out.

On occasion, she'd received calls at night and rushed to take them in her bedroom, saying it was something to do with work and she didn't want to disturb Grace. Who had she been talking to?

As Declan pulled into the apartment complex's parking lot, Grace glanced up at the window she knew to be the one into their living room. A shadow passed by the open blinds. "Look," she said, pointing to the window. "There's someone in my apartment." Her heart sped and she threw open the door of the SUV. "Riley's back." She ran for the stairs and up to the apartment.

"Grace, wait," Declan called out, his footsteps pounding on the steps behind her.

"It's Riley," Grace said, the joy of finding her friend making a smile spill across her face.

"Wait," Declan said again as Grace reached for the door handle. She hesitated when she noticed the door ajar.

Declan caught up with her in time to grab her around the waist and pull her back. "What if it's not Riley?" he whispered.

"Not Riley?" Grace asked, her brain unable to comprehend. Who else could possibly be in her apartment? She and Riley were the only ones with keys, besides the landlord.

Then it dawned on her—the part of the doorframe right beside the lock was splintered and broken.

Her pulse hammering for an entirely different reason, Grace backed into the strength of Declan's body.

He shoved her behind him, pulled his handgun from the holster beneath his jacket and nudged the door wider with the barrel.

The sound of something crashing to the floor made Grace jump. She clamped a hand over her mouth to keep from gasping aloud.

"Call 911," he said softly. "And stay here. Do. Not. Follow. Me. Do you understand?" He caught her gaze and held it until she nodded in compliance.

Then he was inside the apartment, ducking into the shadows.

Grace pressed her back to the wall and focused on the gap between the door and the doorframe. She hated the thought of Declan in the apartment with a potential killer. The burglar could surprise, injure or kill the former Force Recon marine. But she had a job to do. She dialed 911 on her cell phone and pressed it to her ear.

When the dispatcher came on, she spoke in a quiet voice. "I have an intruder in my apartment." She gave the address.

"Are you in the apartment now?" the dispatcher asked.

"No, I'm outside the door. Please," Grace begged, "send someone quickly."

"Miss, I need you to stay out of the apartment."

"I will," Grace said. Though, if she heard a commotion and thought Declan was hurt, she might have to revisit that promise.

"I have units on the way. Stay on the phone."

A shot rang out and a loud crash sounded inside the apartment.

"Sorry, I can't stay on the line. Shots have been fired." Grace leaned hard against the exterior wall, her knees shaking. "Get the police here, now!" She ended the call and braved a glance around the doorframe and into the living room.

Two men were silhouetted against the moonlight shining in through the windows, locked in what appeared to be a wrestling match for the handgun in one man's hand that was pointed at the ceiling.

The hand shook, and shook again. The gun fell from his grasp and clattered against the coffee table before hitting the carpet with a dull thud.

Then one man threw a punch into the other man's face.

Grace gasped, praying the man throwing the punch was Declan, not the other way around.

The men fell over the armchair and crashed to the floor.

Grunts and bone-crunching pummeling sounds rose from the floor.

Her view blocked by the couch, Grace eased into the apartment. She snatched a lamp from a table in the hallway, yanked the cord out of the wall and advanced on the pair rolling on the floor.

Sirens screamed outside the apartment.

Her courage bolstered by the arrival of the cops, Grace held the lamp over her head, ready to slam it down onto the intruder's skull.

The men rolled again, and this time, the man on top was unmistakably Declan.

Unable to help, Grace stood back, praying for the chance to take out some of her anger, frustration and fear on the burglar.

Then the man bucked, shoved Declan to the side and lunged to his feet. Instead of running for the door, he grabbed one of the metal-framed barstools and used it like a bat, swinging at the living room picture window.

As footsteps pounded up the stairs, the chair crashed through the glass.

With a desperate lunge, the burglar dove through the window and fell two stories to the concrete sidewalk.

Declan and Grace ran to the shattered window and stared down at the ground below.

The man lay for a moment, unmoving. Then he drew his knees beneath himself and pushed to his feet.

Two policemen burst through the door, weapons drawn.

"Hands in the air!" one of them called out.

Declan and Grace raised their hands.

"The intruder went out the window. He's on the ground outside now." Grace stepped to the side and pointed at the window with one of her raised hands. "If you don't get someone on him now, he'll be gone."

The officer spoke into the radio mic clipped to his collar, asking for his backup to go around the end of the building.

"He's armed and dangerous," Grace added. "He tried to kill my…boyfriend," she added, stumbling over the word.

"Are you two all right?" the officer asked.

"I am," Grace said. She glanced toward Declan, running her gaze over him.

"Can we lower our arms?" Declan asked.

"I guess," the officer said.

Declan lowered his but then held them out.

Grace walked into them and he closed them around her.

"I'm glad he didn't hurt you." Declan pressed his lips against her hair.

"Are you kidding?" She laughed. "You appeared to have bitten off a little more than you could chew."

"I wouldn't say that. I'm fine." Declan squared his shoulders.

"Yeah, you're fine." Grace grabbed tissue from the bar and dabbed at the blood on his brow. "You might need stitches."

"I'll be fine." He turned and pressed a kiss to her palm. "You were pretty fierce with the lamp."

"I was going to clobber him—" Grace nodded toward the lamp she'd set on an end table "—but he went out the window before I could."

The officer took their statements, making notes on a pad. "Anything missing?"

The intruder had gone through the apartment like a mini tornado, tossing cushions from the couch. Drawers in the kitchen were dumped on the floor, and flatware and cooking utensils lay scattered across the tile.

"I don't know," Grace said.

"When you get a chance," the officer said, "make a list of anything damaged, destroyed or missing and give that to the detective in charge of the case." An electronic crackle sounded from the man's radio. The officer in charge spoke into the mic. "Status on the perp?"

"We got him," a staticky voice came over the radio.

Grace's pulse increased. "They did? They caught him?"

The officer held up his hand and spoke into the radio again. "Take him to the station. They'll question him there."

"Can we question him?" Declan asked.

The policeman shook his head. "I'm sorry, but you'll have to leave it to the detective."

"But he might know something about my missing roommate," Grace said. "Why else would he be in our apartment? Why now?"

"I can't answer that, lady, but you can come to the station and ask the detective all these questions. I'm sure he'll be of more assistance." He scribbled something on a piece of his notebook paper, ripped it off and handed it to Grace. "Detective Romsburg will help you at the station at that address."

The EMT checked out the intruder and declared him fit to go to jail. The police officers loaded him into a squad car, finished documenting the incident, took pictures and left.

Grace and Declan closed the door behind them and turned the dead bolt. It didn't hold since the doorframe had been damaged.

Tears stung Grace's eyes. "What has Riley gotten herself into?"

Declan pulled her into his arms and held her for several minutes, stroking her hair. "We'll find her. I'm sure she'll clear everything up."

When Grace had more control over her emotions, she squared her shoulders and leaned away from the strength of his broad chest. She wished she could remain in the comfort of his arms, but they had to find Riley.

"Based on the way we found everything, the intruder was looking for something. But what?" Grace walked around the apartment, setting it to rights, looking at things from a completely different perspective.

Declan helped her set the cushions back on the couch and stand a chair upright. They straightened the kitchen, tossing the flatware and cooking utensils into the dishwasher. Then they moved into Riley's bedroom.

"He must have just gotten started when we arrived," Grace said. "It doesn't appear as if he made it in here."

Grace walked around Riley's room, her gaze skimming across everything personal to Riley. She rummaged through Riley's dresser drawers, searching for anything that might provide a clue to what was going on. All she found were sexy underwear, yoga clothes and T-shirts.

Declan turned the mattress on her bed upside down.

"What are we looking for?" Grace muttered, running her hand inside the drawer and the underside of the dresser top, thinking maybe there was a secret pocket or lever.

"Documents, a key to a safe-deposit box, flash drives or any other objects Riley might have hidden."

As Grace turned away from the dresser, Declan settled the mattress in place and smoothed the sheets and blankets, giving them military-tight corners.

Grace smiled. "You can take the man out of the military, but you can't take the military discipline out of the man."

He shrugged. "You do something often enough, and it becomes a habit."

She nodded. "Find anything?"

"Nothing." Declan pulled open the drawer on the nightstand and dumped its contents onto the bed. Riley had everything from hand lotion, paperback novels and phone-charging cords to an optimistic package of condoms.

Heat flooded Grace's core, rose up her torso, into her neck and filled her cheeks. She spun away, pressing her palms to her cheeks.

Not that she had thoughts of making love with the rugged marine. No. They'd just met. Their focus was on finding her roommate. The roommate who kept a stash of condoms in her nightstand when she hadn't been dating in the months Grace had been in the apartment. But it was like Riley to always be prepared.

"If I was Riley," Grace murmured, "where would I hide something that no one else could find?"

With a chuckle, Declan stood next to Grace as she surveyed the room with narrowed eyes.

"Did she have a favorite jacket, a box of collectibles—" he looked up "—a journal?"

Grace frowned. Each night, Riley had sat in the living room, jotting notes into a brown notebook. "Yes!" She hurried to the adjoining bathroom. They'd searched the living room, kitchen and bedroom. After a particularly stressful day at the office, Riley liked soaking in the tub. She kept magazines and novels on a stand near the bathtub, within easy reach.

Under an engineering trade magazine, Grace found the leather-bound book. "Got it!" she called out and carried it into the bedroom. Grace sat on the bed and settled the journal on her lap.

Declan sat next to her.

"I feel guilty looking into her personal journal."

"If it helps us help her," Declan said, "I'm betting she'll be okay with it."

"Agreed." Grace opened the journal, praying she'd find something in Riley's notes that would help her locate her roommate, or at least understand what was happening with Moretti and the project Riley had been working on at Quest.

The first few pages dated back almost a year and rambled on about a shopping trip Riley had taken to New York City.

Grace flipped a few pages, bringing the dates to eight months ago and Riley's assignment in the Special Projects area. She'd been excited that she'd been given the opportunity to work on a top secret project. She'd already been through the extensive background check in order to attain her clearance to work in the area.

Grace skimmed the pages going forward. Riley wrote about her excitement with the work she was doing without actually divulging just what the project was all about. She wrote about Grace moving in with her and how she loved having her friend back in her life.

Tears welled in Grace's eyes. She'd felt the same. Riley was the sister she'd never had. Having grown up the only child of older parents, she'd led a pretty solitary life up until she'd roomed with Riley. The four years they'd spent together had been some of the happiest of Grace's life. Based on Riley's notes, she'd felt the same.

Two months ago, her entries changed, became more stilted and her satisfaction not as complete.

"Look at this," Grace pointed to a passage.

Had an interesting lunch meeting today outside the office. Not sure what's going on, but I can tell it's not good. The people involved mean business.

"What do you make of this?" Grace asked.

Declan shook his head. "Could you tell she acted any differently at that time?"

"I don't remember. But she did start keeping to herself more about that time. I thought it was because she was working so hard at the office, she didn't have time to spend with me. I didn't push it, giving her space to get the job done."

Grace kept reading.

I don't know how long I can keep going like this. Someone is going to figure it out and come knocking. I don't feel safe anymore.

"Figure out what?" Grace asked. "What were you doing?" She couldn't believe her friend had been worried and suffering all this time and she hadn't known a thing about it.

I'm going to tell them I want out. I can't do this anymore. Living this lie is making me jittery. I can't sleep. I'm looking over my shoulder all the time. I don't have anyone to talk to about it. It's getting more dangerous with each passing day. But I still don't know who is behind it. Until I do, I'm stuck in this mess. Why did I let myself get into this situation?

Grace gripped the book. "Why didn't she talk to me? I've been here."

"Maybe her problem was with the project she was working on. You said she couldn't talk about the project because it was secret."

"That's what she said." Grace pressed her lips together. "I should have dug for more information. I was so caught up in trying to find a full-time job, I didn't consider Riley might have problems. I thought she was just pushing to finish her project and gave her room to think and work."

Declan slipped an arm around Grace's shoulders. "You thought you were doing right by staying out of her way so that she could concentrate."

Grace flipped to the next page.

I hate that I'm scared all the time. I wish whoever he is would show himself so they can do something about the situation. I can't take this much longer. I told them I wanted to quit and they said I couldn't.

A shiver rippled along Grace's spine. "She was scared. Oh, Riley. I wish I had known."

Chapter Nine

Declan hated seeing the tears in Grace's eyes. She cared deeply about her roommate. That she would do anything to help her friend said a lot about Grace. She was a human being with a heart as big as the Wyoming skies.

He stared at the writing on the page of the book. "Who was the *he*—the one she wanted to show himself?" he asked, drawing attention back to the problem they both needed to solve.

Grace curled her fingers into a fist. "And who were the *they* who wouldn't let her quit?"

"Anything else in that book?" Declan asked.

Grace rifled through the rest of it, but the pages were blank and nothing shook loose. "That's all." She flipped to the back and stopped. "No, wait." On the last page was a number and the initials *SBOA*. She held the page up for Declan. "What do you think this might be? Anything?"

He studied it for a moment. "Could it be an account number and the initials of the business?"

Grace studied the initials and shook her head. "I have no idea."

Declan tapped his chin, trying to think what the numbers and letters meant. "Does she have any paperwork here in the apartment? A file of some sort?"

Grace nodded. "She has a small fireproof lockbox, where she keeps all her bills and legal documents."

"Where?" Declan asked.

"In the bottom of her closet." Grace leaped up from the bed and ran to the closet. She dove into the back, hauled out a laundry basket and some shoes, and then dragged out a heavy metal storage container the size of a one-drawer file cabinet. She sat on the floor beside it. "This is what she uses to hold all her legal documents and account information."

Declan tried to open the box, but it was locked tightly. "Any idea where she might keep the key?"

Grace's lips twisted. "On her key chain. The one she probably had with her when she disappeared."

"Does she have a spare set?" Declan asked.

Her eyes narrowing, Grace tilted her head. "I think so. Now, where did she keep them?" She glanced around Riley's bedroom and shook her head. Then her eyes widened. "The kitchen. She keeps a spare set of keys hanging on a hook in the pantry." Grace hurried past Declan and out into the living room.

Declan followed close behind.

When Grace reached the kitchen, she pulled open the door to the small pantry. On the inside panel of the door was a set of hooks. One had a key chain with a bright red plastic heart and several keys on it.

Grace snatched the chain from the hook, spun around and walked straight into Declan's chest.

Declan wrapped his arms around Grace's waist to steady her.

She rested her hands, keys and all, on his chest, her eyes rounded, her breathing ragged. "Oh, I'm sorry... I didn't know you were there."

"It's okay." He stared into her beautiful eyes, captured with how clear and gray they were. For a long moment, he stood with Grace in his arms, unwilling to move and break the spell she held him under.

Then she swallowed and raised the hand with the keys. "I found it." Her voice was no more than a breathy whisper, drawing attention to her mouth and her pale, rose-colored lips.

Before he could think about what he was doing, Declan bent

and brushed his mouth across hers. When he realized what he'd done, he reached for the key ring and set her to arm's length. "My apologies. I don't know what got into me. No, that's wrong. I do know what got into me. But it doesn't make it right." He turned and walked back into the bedroom, surprised Grace hadn't accused him of taking advantage of her with that unexpected kiss. He wouldn't be surprised if she told him to leave and never come back. He'd overstepped the boundaries of his position more than once.

For that matter, what was his position when it came to Grace? He was there to help her find her roommate. But she wasn't his boss. Charlie was his boss. What did that make Grace? His partner? What did it matter? He had a job to do. Find Riley. Nowhere in that job description was the task of seducing Grace.

But he wanted to.

Boy, did he want to. When his arms circled her body, he had to fight his natural urge to tighten his hold. And he'd lost that struggle when he'd kissed her.

Hell, he had to remember he was damaged goods. Nothing he could do would erase the black mark on his military record. It would follow him around for the rest of his life. Anything he did would be tainted with that mark. And he'd been so very proud of his job, his connection with the US Marines and, most of all, his position on Force Recon.

He had nothing to offer a woman like Grace. Not a home, nor a bankroll. She deserved someone with a clean record and an unsoiled past.

He selected the bright silver key on the key ring, slipped it into the lock on the box and twisted it with a little more force than necessary, angry at himself, the situation and the injustices of the world.

The lock opened, but he hesitated, his breathing ragged, his heart pounding. The one little kiss reminded him of all he'd given up when he'd made the decision he had back in Afghanistan.

Would he do it again?

Hell, yeah.

Then he had to accept it and move on. Without Grace.

A hand on his shoulder brought him back to the task before him. "Are you all right?" Grace asked.

"I'm fine," he said through gritted teeth. He swung open the door and pulled out a drawer with neatly arranged files in alphabetical order. He thumbed through to the *s* tab, where he found several receipts from businesses starting with the letter *s*. He kept moving through the file until he reached a folder marked Signature Bank of America.

He checked the number on the account against the number on the page in Riley's journal. They didn't match.

"Apparently she banks there, based on the statements," Grace said. "But why would she have a different account number?"

Then it struck Declan. "Could it be the number on a safe-deposit box?"

Grace frowned. "Why would she have a safe-deposit box?"

"Most people put things of value in a safe-deposit box. Something they don't want lost or stolen," Declan said.

"Do you think whoever broke into the apartment might be looking for that something?" Grace asked.

"Maybe." Declan dug into the SBOA file and located a sealed envelope. "I'd ask if she'd be mad if I was going through her things, but I think we're way past that now." He ripped open the envelope and found a sheet of paper and a strange heavy key with a number engraved on the side. The number matched the one written in the back of Riley's journal. "Bingo."

Grace drew in a deep breath. "Doesn't Riley have to be the one to get into her own safe-deposit box?"

"Yes. Unless you have permission to enter the box." Declan held up the sheet of paper.

Grace leaned over his shoulder, her long blond hair brushing against his cheek. "She created a power of attorney for me? How did I not know this? Why wouldn't she tell me?"

"Maybe she figured you didn't need to know," Declan guessed.

"Until I needed to know." Grace folded the paper and tucked it into the journal. She hugged the book to her chest and stared up into Declan's eyes. "What's next?"

"We go to the police station and see if we can get any information out of our burglar," Declan said.

"Well, we did come here for the laptop." Grace pointed to a shelf by Riley's bed. "It's there."

Declan grabbed the laptop from the shelf. "You said there's nothing on it, but we'll take it with us if we don't get the answers we're looking for."

Grace nodded. "Too bad it's too late to go to the bank."

Declan gave her arm a gentle squeeze. "We can go there tomorrow."

GRACE WAS MORE than willing to let Declan do the driving. Declan found a piece of plywood near the apartment trash bin. He borrowed some wood screws and an electric drill from Mr. Miller, the neighbor in the apartment two doors down. In a few short minutes, he had the doorjamb fixed enough that they could lock the door and leave, feeling moderately sure no one would be able to get in easily. Not that there was anything else of any great value inside to be stolen, other than the television.

Nothing in the apartment was irreplaceable, except Riley.

A knot formed in Grace's throat as she sat beside Declan. She had no idea what she would have done without his assistance and support. She'd have been waiting by her telephone for the police to call. She would probably have been home when the intruder had entered her apartment.

Her hands shook as she held her purse with the journal and the key to the safe-deposit box inside. What would she have done if the intruder had caught her alone? Sure, she'd have fought tooth and nail to protect herself, but would it have been enough?

And what was Riley having to deal with? Was she being held somewhere? Or had it been Riley who'd texted her to get out of that bar when the three thugs had come in to get Moretti?

Hope had been fleeting when she'd thought Riley might be trying to protect them. Since that text, she'd heard nothing more. She'd even sent a text back to the same number, but received no response. Minutes later, the text had shown up as undeliverable.

In one day, her seemingly insignificant worries about finding a full-time job had morphed into life-or-death concern for her roommate and now herself. Whatever had frightened Riley into hiding might have put Grace into just as much danger. The people after Riley had killed her boss. If Grace had been home alone when the intruder broke in, she too might be dead. She had Declan to thank for sneaking into Riley's office with her, being with her at the bar and scaring off the intruder from her apartment.

She stared across the console of her SUV at the man driving. "I know so little about you," she admitted.

His lips twisted. "You've only known me a day. And vice versa."

Grace snorted. "Do we ever really know other people?" Her fingers tightened around her purse, which contained the journal that had revealed so much more about her friend than Riley had ever shared.

"What do you want to know about me?" Declan asked, his attention on the road ahead.

"Other than why you were booted out of the Marine Corps?" When he turned with a frown, she held up her hand. "You don't have to say unless you're ready. How about we start with something less damning, like what were you like growing up? Are you the youngest or oldest of your siblings, and what's your favorite song? We have at least five minutes at this stoplight, based on the line of traffic in front of us." She gave him a wry smile. "Go."

He sighed. "Like I said, I grew up outside Cheyenne, Wyoming. We lived on a small ranch with cattle, horses and wide-open ranges to run around on. I have one sister, Susan, and two brothers, Patrick and Daniel. Our parents are still alive and, like I'd already told you, they are probably wondering why I haven't contacted them since I got back from deployment."

"I can't believe you haven't let them know you're safely back from Afghanistan."

Declan's lips pressed together. "My father is a retired army infantryman. One of my brothers is an Air Force pilot and the other brother is army infantry like our father. My sister joined the navy as a nurse. Call me a coward, but I don't know how to tell them I was kicked out of the Marine Corps. I didn't want to go home with my tail between my legs." His hands tightened on the steering wheel, his knuckles turning white with the strength of his grip. "I had to find my way back."

"Based on Mrs. Charlotte Halverson, you have a job now. Isn't that enough?"

He shook his head. "I haven't proven myself yet." He shot a

glance her way. "I haven't found Riley. As Charlie would say, I haven't made a difference."

"Charlie?"

He gave her a tight smile. "Charlie doesn't like me calling her ma'am."

Grace had met the woman and figured she was a force to be reckoned with. "After we find Riley, will you talk with your parents and let them know what happened?"

He nodded. "I love my folks. I just don't want to disappoint them."

And Grace could bet that Declan couldn't stand to see what he would expect to be the disappointment in their faces. If they truly loved him, which she suspected they did, they would not judge him and find him wanting. They would be ecstatic to have him home. They would understand whatever decisions he'd made and support him all the way.

But Declan had something to prove to them. No...to himself. He had to find his own worth and new path in life before he could go back home.

The light changed, and Declan drove on. Soon he pulled into the police station, where the officer in charge had indicated they'd taken the intruder.

Dusk settled over the city and streetlights flickered on.

Inside the station was a hub of activity. Men in uniform led lawbreakers past the front desk and into interrogation rooms and holding cells. Grace really had no idea how it all worked. She clutched her purse to her side and followed Declan inside, where he asked for the detective working the breaking-and-entering case at her apartment complex.

The desk sergeant scanned his computer, clicked the keyboard and frowned. "Are you sure they brought the suspect here?"

"That's what the officer in charge of the investigation at my apartment told me." Grace fumbled in her purse, her pulse beginning to race. "He said I could speak with the detective on the case, if I wanted more information." She gave up on her purse when she remembered where she'd placed the sheet of paper. Grace pulled the note the officer had given her out of her back pocket and handed it to the sergeant. "This is the address he gave me and the name of the detective. Detective Romsburg."

The desk sergeant stared at the paper and shook his head. "That's this address, but we don't have a Detective Romsburg."

Grace blinked. "No? Not now? How about in the past?"

The sergeant shook his head. "Not now or ever—that I know of. Not at this station or in this precinct, at least not for the past twenty years I've been here." He handed the paper back to her. "I'm sorry, miss, I don't have record of the break-in. We can't help you."

"But I placed a 911 call. You have to have record of that," Grace said.

"Address?"

Grace gave it, along with her phone number.

The sergeant frowned and clicked his computer keyboard. His frown deepened. "I have record of the call and then another call to cancel the request, saying the caller was mistaken."

"That can't be right. I didn't call back." Grace's head spun and she felt the blood drain from her face.

"Sorry, ma'am. That's all I have," the sergeant said.

Declan gripped her elbow and held her steady until the dizziness passed. "Thank you for your assistance, officer." He turned Grace and marched her out of the building.

"What's going on?" Grace asked as soon as they cleared the exit. "Why would that sergeant lie about the break-in?"

"He might not have been lying. The officer in charge at your apartment might have given you the wrong address. Let me get on the phone and see what I can find out. In the meantime, we're going to get you some food and take you back to your apartment for rest." He hooked her elbow and led her toward the SUV.

Grace dug her heels into the pavement. "But we haven't found Riley. We can't give up now." She knew she was being unreasonable, but her frustration level had maxed out. "I can't give up on her. She's all I have."

"Tell me about her on the way back to your place. Maybe we'll get lucky and she'll be there, waiting to fill you in on her latest adventure."

Grace frowned at Declan but let him lead her to the vehicle and help her inside. "You don't really think she'll be there, do you?" she said as he fastened her seat belt around her waist.

He smiled and pressed a brief kiss to her lips. "We can always hope."

The brief kiss had her head spinning even more. How could she think straight when the man kissed her? And not for the first time. The first time had taken her completely by surprise.

What did it mean?

Nothing. Don't read anything into that kiss. He's just being nice.

And the kiss *was* really nice. His lips were soft but firm, warm and dry. And sexy as hell.

Declan slid into the driver's seat and paused before starting the engine. "I did it again. I'd say I was sorry, but I'm not. I can't help it. Every time I'm near you, I can't help kissing you. Tell me to stop, and I will." He finally glanced her way, his eyes a light blue. But it was his mouth Grace couldn't lose focus on. That mouth that made her lips tingle and her insides coil for more.

Grace touched her lips, pressing her fingers against them to stop the tingling. But the sensation wouldn't go away. "It's okay."

"No," he said and started the engine. "It's not okay. I shouldn't kiss you. I'm supposed to be working for you to find your roommate. This isn't the time or place. Maybe I'm the wrong person for this job."

She touched his arm. "That kiss was more than okay. For that brief second, I felt safe and hopeful. Maybe it wasn't the right time, but I needed it." Grace dropped her hand to her lap. "I needed it," she whispered.

And she *had* needed that human contact. More than that, she'd needed a reminder that she wasn't alone.

Chapter Ten

Back at Grace's apartment, Declan made a few calls. First to the local police headquarters, describing what had happened and how they had been misdirected.

The police headquarters said they'd look into the incident and get back to them.

Not holding out much hope, Declan placed a call to his new boss, Charlie.

He still struggled with calling the older woman by her first name. But the more he did, the better she liked it.

"Have you found Grace's roommate?" Charlie asked.

"No, ma'am. I was wondering if you had any connections on the police force."

"As a matter of fact, my late husband was a big proponent of the local Fraternal Order of Police. We donated a lot of money to the survivors of police officers lost in the line of duty." She paused. "Why?"

Declan told her what had happened up to that point. "If you have any pull on the local police force, I could use a contact."

"I'll get one for you. I refuse to believe they lost the perp. There has to be a perfectly good explanation."

"Let me know when you find it," Declan said.

"What are you going to do next?" Charlie asked.

"I don't like that an intruder made it into Grace and Riley's apartment."

"You aren't going to leave Grace alone, are you?" Charlie asked.

"No. I'm staying with her tonight."

"Do you want to stay at my place? I have an excellent and very expensive security system."

Declan smiled. "I know. If things get even more dangerous for Grace, I might take you up on that offer."

"Please do. I hate the idea of another innocent person being hurt."

"Speaking of innocents, how are you?"

She snorted. "Like I'm an innocent. I'm staying put inside my wonderful security system until your guys arrive," she said. "I did venture out long enough to express my condolences to the families of my bodyguards killed in the skirmish yesterday."

"I'm sorry you had to go through that."

"I'm sorrier it happened to such good people. Their families shouldn't have had to suffer their loss. Those were good men, doing their jobs."

"Any word on what they had in mind by kidnapping you?" Declan asked.

"The FBI questioned the guys they captured. They're still not talking." She sighed. "I'm a rich woman. They probably hoped for a sizable ransom."

"Are you sure you don't want me there?" Declan asked. Not that he wanted to abandon Grace and Riley. Not now that he had so much effort invested in their welfare. But Charlie had been attacked and her welfare was important to him as well. He could take Grace to her place and keep them all secure.

"No. I'm safe behind my walls," Charlie said. "Your guys are on their way. They'll arrive tomorrow."

"Again, Charlie, thank you for having faith in me and my team."

"I wouldn't have offered to set up Declan's Defenders if I didn't believe you and your men were the ones to make it happen. Based on what you told me, you all made the right decision. Your commanders had to make the decisions they made, right or wrong. I'm sorry you had to leave the Marine Corps." She laughed. "I'm sorry for you. I can't say I'm sorry for me. If you hadn't been released from the marines at the time you were, and if you hadn't been on the street you were at the time you happened along, I might not be here today." She paused. "I believe some things are meant to happen for a reason. Call it divine intervention, fate or dumb luck. I don't care. I'm just glad you found me."

Declan's heart swelled. "And I'm glad you found me." He pushed back his shoulders. "Thanks for taking a chance on me. I'll do my best to prove I'm worthy of your trust."

The older woman chuckled. "Sweetie, you already have. But wait… What do you think about the name I've coined for your group?"

"What was that?"

"Declan's Defenders," Charlie said. "I'm all for alliteration."

"You should have named the organization after you. It was your idea."

She chuckled. "And I might have, but I couldn't come up with something satisfying that went with Charlie, other than Charlie's Angels…and well…that wouldn't do. So, unless you have an objection to it, Declan's Defenders it is."

"Thank you, Charlie. You're an amazing woman."

"I know. Now, bring Riley home safely."

"Will do, ma'am—Charlie." Declan ended the call and went in search of Grace.

The door to her bedroom was open, but she wasn't there. He heard the sound of the shower through the bathroom door.

His groin tightened.

When he'd held Grace in his arms earlier, he'd felt something special. Yeah, he'd held women in his arms before, but Grace was different. She was strong, yet vulnerable. And her body fit perfectly against his. She wasn't painfully thin like some women liked to be. The woman had curves and valleys and hips his mother would have called good for breeding.

As his thoughts turned to breeding, he let his imagination go down that path with Grace in mind.

Grace would bear beautiful children. Blond-haired, gray-eyed girls like their mother. They'd be kind, courageous and beautiful, just like Grace.

He didn't realize he'd been standing, staring at the bathroom door until the water shut off and he heard the sound of the shower curtain rings sliding across the curtain rod.

Declan left her bedroom door and hurried back into the living room. Grace didn't need to know he'd been having crazy daydreams about her babies. Babies whose lives he'd never be a part of.

When he'd been younger, before he'd joined Force Recon, he'd always thought he'd marry someday and have three or four children like his parents had. He liked kids and they liked him.

After so many deployments in which he'd gone into villages where innocent women and children were used as shields or forced to be weapons of war, he wasn't as certain. After all he'd seen, all he'd done, how could he feel right about bringing children into a world so broken?

Yet he'd stood in Grace's bedroom and thought about what it would be like to hold her baby in his arms. To make her pregnant with his child.

Declan groaned at the image conjured up of Grace naked in her bed, him driving deep inside her body, filling her with his seed.

*And if wishes were horses…*his mother would have said. Wishing got him nowhere. Action was what was needed. Inaction made him crazy. He stood in front of the boarded window overlooking the back side of her apartment complex. The drapes were drawn and a board stood in the way of his view, but he closed his eyes and imagined the trees he had seen earlier that day.

A soft hand touched his arm. "Hey. What are you thinking about?"

Declan flinched and took a step away. "Nothing."

"Sorry. I didn't mean to startle you." She wrapped the tie of a silky powder-blue robe around her middle and cinched it. "You were frowning. I thought maybe you were in pain."

He couldn't tell her he was in pain because he was thinking about making love to her. Hell, if she looked down, she'd see the evidence in the swell beneath the fly of his jeans.

"Were you thinking about your team?" she asked.

"No." At that moment, he was thinking about untying the blue robe and sweeping Grace up into his arms. He wanted to make mad, passionate love to the woman as he pressed her to the wall—the bed being too far away.

Declan took another step away.

Grace frowned and closed the gap. "Seriously, were you in pain?" She raised her hand to cup his cheek.

He grabbed her wrist and held it. "The only pain I'm in is when I touch you. Go to bed, Grace." He let go of her hand and again moved a step away.

Her eyes flared and her cheeks grew pink. "You were thinking of me?"

"Yes. Now, do us both a favor. Go to your room alone, close the door and sleep."

She shook her head. "I can't."

"What part can't you do?"

Grace inhaled a deep breath and released it before she spoke. "After all that's happened today, I can't go into that room alone. We don't know if the intruder escaped the police. He could come back. Logic tells me he wouldn't dare try again. But deep down, I don't trust that he'll stay away."

He started to reach for her, to pull her into his arms. He raised his hand halfway to her arm, stopped and let it fall back to his side. "I'm here. I won't let anything happen to you."

"You'll be in here, but I'll be in the other room. What if he hurts you? I'd never know until it was too late." She took another step closer. "It seems to me, we could protect each other. You know... I'll have your back and you'll have mine."

Declan closed his eyes, his hands all over her naked back in his mind. "No can do," he said.

She ran her tongue across her lips, making him exponentially hotter. "What if I leave the door open? Then at least I could hear if someone comes in." Grace went to him and laid her hand on his chest. "I could help you."

"I'm supposed to be helping you, not the other way around." Placing his hands on her hips was his first mistake. Getting lost in the depths of her pretty gray eyes was his second. "Don't you understand? I'm trying hard to keep my hands off you. And I'm failing miserably."

She curled her fingers into his shirt and inhaled deeply, her breasts brushing against his chest. "Then quit trying so hard."

She leaned up on her toes and pressed her lips to his in a feather-soft kiss.

Declan groaned and his arms tightened around her middle. "Now you've gone and done it," he said against her mouth. Then he claimed her in a breath-stealing kiss that started out hard, almost punishing. He wanted to chastise her for making him lose control. But as the kiss deepened, she opened to him, letting his tongue slide past her teeth to take her in a long, silky caress.

She raised her hands to clasp the back of his neck, pulling him closer. Her hips pressed against his, the evidence of his desire nudging against her belly.

A moan rose up her throat and warmed his mouth. She wrapped her calf around his and rubbed the apex of her thighs across his thigh.

Past any kind of restraint, and hopelessly in danger of losing complete control, Declan swept Grace up in his arms and held her against him. "Now's the time to back out. Say the word and this ends here." How he'd stop, he wasn't sure. But he had to give her an out.

She cupped his cheek, her lips hovering over his. "I want you to hold me," she said. "All night long."

"Let's be clear. Hold you only?" He shook his head. "Can't promise you that."

"Then let me make myself crystal clear." She bracketed his face between her palms and stared into his eyes. "I want you to make love to me all night long."

Still he hesitated. "You're not concerned that we only just met?"

"I've never been more certain in my life." Then she kissed him and pressed her body closer.

Clutching her to him, he strode into her room and stood beside her bed without breaking the connection. When at last they separated for air, he lowered her legs and let her slide down his body until her feet touched the ground.

Grace reached for the tie on her robe.

Declan brushed her hands away and loosened the knot.

She shrugged the silky robe from her shoulders and let it slide down her back and arms. It slipped over her body to land on the floor at her feet.

Beneath the robe, she wore a matching blue baby-doll night-gown that teased the tops of her thighs and left her legs completely exposed.

He groaned. "Do you even know what you're doing to me?"

Her chuckle warmed his insides. "I have an idea." She reached low and cupped the bulge of his straining erection through the denim of his jeans. Then she grasped the button and paused. "I should feel guilty for wanting this when Riley is on the run, but I can't help it."

"*You* can't help it. I thought resisting kissing you was hard enough. This goes far beyond that."

She pushed the button loose and slid the zipper downward in an agonizingly slow movement. Finally, his stiff erection sprang free of the confines of his jeans.

Grace's mouth curved upward as she circled him with her warm, supple fingers. "We can't do any more for Riley tonight, and I don't want to be alone." Her fingers tightened around him and slid to the base of his shaft. "Make love to me. Make me forget, if only for now. Tomorrow we'll find Riley."

Chapter Eleven

Grace leaned her head back as Declan brushed his lips across hers and then blazed a path along her cheek and down the long line of her neck to the base.

Her pulse beat hard and fast as he flicked his tongue across her collarbone, sweeping the straps of her nightgown over her shoulders and down her arms.

She shrugged, letting the slippery fabric slide farther downward, stopping as it caught on the swells of her breasts. She wanted to be free of the gown, free of all clothing, exposed to his tongue, fingers and any other part of his body that might come into contact with hers.

Her core tightened and a rush of hot liquid slicked her channel in anticipation of what would come.

She leaned into him, wrapped her arms around his neck and guided his mouth lower, toward her aching breasts. She wanted him to take them, to roll the nipples between his teeth, to tongue their tight little buds until she squirmed.

He didn't disappoint. As he trailed his lips lower, she inhaled, raising her chest, offering him more in the movement.

He covered one taut nipple with his mouth through the fabric and tongued the tip.

Grace moaned and circled his leg with her thigh. Pressing her belly to the thick, straining shaft between them.

One coarse hand tugged on the nightgown, dragging it over first one swell and then the other. Free of the speed bumps, the gown drifted to the floor, pooling around her ankles.

Declan cupped her breasts as if weighing them in the palms of his hands. Then he took one into his mouth and sucked, pulling hard, drawing a gasp from her lips.

He let go and lifted his head, a frown descending across his brow. "Did I hurt you?"

She shook her head, barely able to draw air into her lungs. "No," she said. "Don't stop." Grace guided his head back to where he'd been, desperate to again feel the sensations he'd elicited. Her blood hummed through her veins, and heat spread from her center all the way out to her fingertips. She wanted this stranger more than she wanted to breathe.

Declan took the other breast between his lips and tongued, sucked and flicked the nipple until Grace writhed beneath his touch. How could something feel so good but not be enough? She wanted more.

When he raised his head, Declan's gaze bore into hers. "I want you, Grace. All of you."

"Nothing's stopping you," she said, her voice barely above a whisper, her lungs unable to fill with air when he touched her like he did.

He cupped her butt cheeks and lifted her onto the bed, letting her legs dangle over the side.

Grace reached for his jeans, pushing them over his hips.

He grabbed her hands and stayed her action. "Not yet. First I want you to be as crazy as you're making me."

"Trust me," she said. "I already am."

"Sweetheart, you aren't nearly there. I have a lot more I want to do before I come inside you."

Her breath caught and held in her chest and her channel creamed. He had her so turned on, for the moment, she was able to think about him and not Riley.

Declan ran his hands along the insides of her thighs, gripped her knees and spread her legs wide.

Grace's heart raced and her breathing grew ragged.

She reached for his hips, wanting him inside her. Now.

He captured her hands and turned them palms upward, placing a kiss into each palm before letting go. "I want to take you there first."

"I'm already on fire," she assured him.

"Then we'll take it up a notch to incendiary." His lips quirked as he dropped to his knees between her legs.

"Oh, sweet heaven," Grace whispered.

Declan parted her folds with his thumbs and chuckled. His warm breath against her nubbin of desire nearly sent her over the edge. Nearly. Not quite.

A flick of his tongue made her gasp. Another flick got the blood raging, hot like molten lava, pushing through her veins.

Grace threaded her hands through his hair and held him there. "Please," she keened.

"Please what?" he asked and then flicked the nubbin with the tip of his tongue.

"That!" she said, her breathing compromised by the assault on her control.

"This?" he asked and flicked her again, followed by a long sweep and twirl of that incredible tongue.

"Oh, yes," she cried. "That. Do it. Do it again." She let go of his hair and leaned back on her hands, spreading her legs wider. He couldn't get close enough. She had to have so much more of what he was doing to her.

As he flicked that strip of nerve-packed flesh, Declan also thumbed her entrance and dipped into the drenched channel.

Grace shot over the edge, rocketing out to the stratosphere. Her hips rocked and she clutched his head like a lifeline to keep her grounded.

Declan milked her release until her rocking slowed, then he rose between her legs, pressed his shaft to her opening and paused.

"What are you waiting for?" Grace pushed up on her elbows. "Don't you want to make love to me?"

"More than you can imagine. But we need what we found in Riley's nightstand."

Reason returned in a flash. Grace reached beneath her bed pillow and extracted the condom she'd placed there before walking out of her bedroom, dressed in her sexiest nightgown. She hadn't been completely convinced Declan would make a move on her, but she'd wanted to be prepared if he had.

And thank the stars, he had made that move. Never before had she had such a complete and utterly satisfying reaction as she had at Declan's hands...and tongue. Even her ex-husband hadn't been able to elicit such a response. Far from satiated, she wasn't done. She knew he could bring her even more pleasure.

She held up the condom for a moment and then tore it open, rolled it down over his straining shaft and clutched his buttocks. "Please don't make me wait any longer."

He pressed the tip of his shaft against her entrance, barely dipping in and out.

Her control slipping, Grace tightened her hold on his cheeks and slammed him home.

Declan drove deep, filling her, stretching her channel deliciously.

Grace lifted her knees, dug her heels into the mattress and raised her hips, meeting Declan thrust for thrust.

He powered in and out of her, settling into a fast, smooth rhythm, increasing the speed and intensity with each pass.

Again, Grace felt the tingling begin at her center and flood outward, vibrating through her body to the very tips of her fingers and toes. She dug her fingernails into his flesh, urging him to join her in her release.

His body tensed and his thrusts became more powerful until he finally buried himself inside her as deeply as he could go and held steady, his shaft pulsing inside her.

When at last she could breathe again, Grace slowly drifted back to earth and the mattress.

Declan dropped down on top of her, his body limp, his erection still thick and hard inside of her. He rolled them both onto their sides, without losing that intimate connection. For a long moment, he held her in his arms, the silence between them comforting, not awkward.

Grace closed her eyes and snuggled her cheek against his chest.

She inhaled the musky scent of his aftershave and sighed. This was what she'd been missing in her marriage.

Pure, unchecked passion.

Declan had it in spades.

Grace realized, from that day forward, she would refuse to accept anything less. She wanted more than just doing it every Friday night on schedule.

Declan had seen to her needs and desires before he'd slaked his own. He gave a damn whether she was satisfied. Her ex-husband hadn't cared enough about her sexual preferences.

She lay in the comfort of Declan's arms and wished she could be there for much more than just the one night.

The truth was that once they found Riley, Declan would be on to his next assignment. After only one day with the man, Grace knew he'd be leaving a new and gaping hole in her love life. More of a hole than the five years with her ex-husband had created.

She must have fallen asleep because the next thing she realized was that something was buzzing and she couldn't seem to wake enough to figure out how to make it stop. She pushed against a solid wall of muscles and sat up in bed, blinking her eyes to clear the sleep from them. At last, she was able to locate the source of the buzzing and lifted her cell phone.

She didn't recognize the number, but figured anyone who called her that late at night might be in an emergency situation.

Or it could be Riley.

She hit the talk button and held the phone to her ear. "Hello?"

"Did he find my file?" Riley's voice came over the cell phone.

"Riley." Grace clutched the phone like a lifeline. "Where are you? Are you all right?"

"I'm okay. But I can't talk long. Did the guy who broke into our apartment find my file box?"

"How did you know about the break-in?" Grace asked.

"It doesn't matter," Riley said. "Did he find my file box?"

"No. Declan scared him off before he got to your bedroom. We found a key in your bank file."

"Oh, sweet heaven. Good. Take that key to the bank tomorrow and remove the contents of my safe-deposit box. I'll contact you tomorrow. Don't tell anyone what you have. If possible, disguise yourself before going into the bank. They're probably already watching you."

"They? They who?" Grace wanted to know.

"I don't know. That's the problem. Get to the bank, retrieve the envelope in my safe-deposit box and hang on to it until I contact you. It's important. The sooner I get it to the right people, the sooner I can come home."

"Riley, what's happening?" Grace asked.

"Sweetie, I'm sorry you got dragged into this. Please stay safe."

"Where are you?" Grace asked. "Let me come get you."

The line was dead…and the call ended. Riley was gone.

Tears welled in Grace's eyes and slipped down her cheeks. "Oh, Riley, what's happening?"

Declan's arms circled her and pulled her back against his rock-solid chest. He held her while the tears fell, comforting her in the darkness.

When her tears were spent, she turned in his arms and rested her palm against his cheek. "Thank you for being here. I don't know what I'd have done without you."

He kissed her forehead and the tip of her nose. "You'd have been just fine."

"Maybe so, but I don't have to be alone. Not when you're here." She pressed her lips to his in a gentle kiss.

He cupped the back of her head and deepened the kiss, his tongue thrusting past her teeth to caress the length of hers.

When the kiss ended, he continued to hold her, demanding nothing but giving all the comfort she needed.

If only Riley was safe and back in her home, where she belonged, perhaps life could return to normal.

Who was she trying to kid?

Nothing would be the same again, not after having experienced a night in Declan's arms.

DECLAN HELD RILEY close as she slipped into a deep sleep, her breathing steady, her body relaxed against his. If he were any kind of a gentleman, he'd leave the bed, tuck Grace in and go sleep on the couch. But he wasn't, and he didn't want to leave her alone for a second. Not only for her sake, but because of his own desires. He was a selfish bastard.

How, in less than two days, had he fallen completely under this woman's spell?

He'd been homeless, jobless and pretty hopeless before he'd met Grace and Charlie. Now he had an amazing woman in his arms and a problem he had to solve before he could prove to this woman, his family, his new boss and mostly himself that he was worthy of all that had fallen into his lap.

Getting to the bank and removing whatever it was Riley had in her safe-deposit box would be easy enough, as long as the people who'd been after Riley and whatever it was she wanted them to get weren't lying in wait to snatch the item, Riley or Grace. He was pretty sure he could handle one or two attackers, but any more than that would be risky. And he didn't want to risk the lives of Grace or Riley.

His arm tightened around Grace's naked body and his shaft hardened instantly. Though he wanted to make love to her again, he knew how much she needed her sleep.

Smoothing a hand across her brow, Declan tucked a strand of her golden-blond hair back behind her ear. Then he brushed his lips across hers. They were so soft and kissable. He fought to control the rise of passion, which was threatening to overwhelm him.

With all the strength he could muster, Declan settled back in the bed, closed his eyes and willed himself to sleep.

Dreams came to him of that small village in Afghanistan.

CHILDREN PLAYED IN the dirt in front of their mud-and-stick homes.

He and his team had been to the village earlier that day on a mission to build goodwill between the tribal elders and the American troops that were stationed nearby. They'd also been in the village, scouting for potential infiltrators. The intel community had sent word that the village was harboring a high-powered Taliban leader in their midst.

On that day, Declan and his team hadn't seen any sign of the Taliban, only poor villagers, consisting of women, old men and children. They'd even given the children packets of MREs and a handful of candy.

The mothers had looked on with tentative smiles and softly spoken words of thanks in Dari, one of the official languages of the country.

Later that evening, back at Camp Shorab, the team played cards and joked around before turning in.

Bored of cards, Declan had risen and started for his quarters when word had come from a runner.

"The CO wants you in the ops center ASAP," the young private said.

"Just me?" Declan had asked.

"You and your team," the private had said.

"Coming," Declan said. He hurried back to the card game. "We've been summoned."

The team split, heading to their respective quarters, where they jumped into their uniform trousers and shrugged on jackets. In less than five minutes, they were on their way to the operations center for a briefing on their next assignment.

As he entered the tactical operations center, Declan frowned. His commander stood at the front of the room, along with a brigadier general and four other men. Three of the four men were wearing dark clothes, radio headsets and shoulder holsters with SIG Sauer handguns; they also carried M4A1 rifles with military-grade SOPMOD upgrades. The man speaking with the brigadier general wore a pair of trousers from a business suit, a white button-down shirt, a loosened tie and a bulletproof vest over all of it.

Declan got a bad feeling about the meeting. He shot a glance toward Mack Balkman, his assistant team leader.

Mack shrugged and turned to Frank "Mustang" Ford, their point man who'd arrived ahead of them. "What's going on?"

Mustang shook his head. "I got here a minute before you. They haven't spoken a word to me. I think they're waiting for all six of us to assemble."

Gus Walsh, their radio operator, had arrived at the same time as Declan and Mack. "Who's the dude in the suit?"

Cole McCastlain stepped through the door in time to catch Gus's question. He stared at the man in the bulletproof vest. "I don't know, but he's bound to be important if he comes with his own bodyguards."

Jack Snow, their slack man and the most junior member of the team, entered, buttoning his jacket. "What did I miss?" He stared at the man in the suit and his jaw dropped. "Damn, that's Congressman Patrick Ryan. What's he doing here?"

Declan and the other four members of the Force Recon team stared at Snow.

"How do you know that's Patrick Ryan?" Declan asked.

"Haven't you been following the news? He's been over here for the past couple of days, visiting troops and taking stock of the continued operations in this country." Snow frowned. "Midterm elections are coming." He tipped his head toward the man. "He's probably trying to boost his ratings."

At that moment, the congressman, brigadier general and their commander stopped talking and turned to face the team.

Their commander nodded. "Good. You're all here. Take a seat, gentlemen."

Declan didn't like how formal the CO was. They usually stood around the map and discussed the missions. Apparently, this one would be different. They'd sit and the commander would give them their marching orders. With a brigadier general and a congressman in attendance, their input might not be appreciated.

"Intel had a confirmed sighting of Abdul Kareem Rasul, a high-powered leader of the Taliban's secret organization, the Quetta Shura. He's responsible for the recent attacks on four government outposts in Northern and Eastern Afghanistan, killing thirty-five Afghan security-force guards and four American soldiers. He directed the attack on the hotel in Kabul that killed twenty-two people, including four Americans. He's also behind the bombing of the girls' high school in Logar Province near Kabul. We've been looking for him for three years, but he's been slippery, hiding in the hills and crossing into Pakistan."

General Thomas stepped forward. "Our intelligence operatives tell us he's in the village of Bawshi."

"We were there today and didn't see any sign of him," Declan said.

The general nodded. "Our sources say he's very careful to keep a low profile when he enters a village. They also say he has relatives in the village, which led them to look for him there."

"The point is," Colonel Felton said, "he's there now. Your team is to take him out, using whatever means of force you have available. He's considered dangerous and has already been the cause of many deaths, both Afghani and American."

"We need you to take this man out," General Thomas echoed. "No matter the cost. We cannot let him escape us this time."

Declan nodded. "We'll do our best."

"Do better than your best," Congressman Ryan said. "We've got a lot riding on this operation."

"We'll leave you to the details," General Thomas said and left the room with Ryan and the congressman's entourage.

Colonel Felton waited until the door closed behind them. "You will be equipped with helmet cameras. We'll be monitoring the events as they unfold."

"Great. So, we need to keep our noses clean and kill this guy at the same time." Declan knew the stakes. With the general and the congressman involved, they would be expecting footage to take back to the States to prove their worth on the other side of the ocean. All while he and his men were supposed to go into hostile situations with their hands basically tied. Collateral damage got more airtime than Taliban takedowns.

"Just do your job and don't let Rasul get away," Colonel Felton said.

The team studied the map the intelligence guys had provided with a building identified as Rasul's last known location in the village. They were to go in under the cover of night and take him out with the cameras on to record the event.

Declan had known in his gut that the mission would be difficult. A small village full of women, children and old men would be hard to navigate without civilian casualties. Images of the small children they'd met that day came back to him.

He hardened his heart and got down to the task of planning where they would enter the village, what weapons they would carry and the communications equipment they would need.

That night, the 160th Night Stalkers transported them in a US Army Black Hawk helicopter to within two miles of the village. From there, they hiked the rest of the way, carrying what they needed on their backs, strapped to their chests or in their arms.

As team leader, Declan sported the helmet camcorder.

Mustang, on point, slipped into the village first, keeping them abreast of what he was seeing as he entered. Declan followed, providing cover for Mustang.

At the corner of the next building, Mustang paused.

Declan held up his fist, motioning for the others to hold in place.

"Light ahead. Some kind of gathering. The buildings to my right and left appear empty. Going in."

Declan hurried to the corner where Mustang crouched.

When he reached it, he peered around, his rifle pointed toward the center of the village. As Mustang had indicated, light illuminated the village center, where a gathering had amassed.

"Going to get closer," Mustang said. He leapfrogged to the next mud-and-stick building and stopped.

Declan aimed at the village center, his gaze panning the surrounding buildings and rooftops for any sign of snipers or Taliban gunmen.

At the center of the village, it appeared as though every villager, and possibly more individuals who weren't from the village, were in attendance of some kind of celebration.

Torches had been lit at the village center, casting light and shadows over the men in the headdresses, women cloaked in scarves and children scrambling in and out of the crowd, chasing each other when it was well past their bedtimes.

"I see Rasul," Mustang said excitedly. "He's at the center of the crowd."

Gus, the radio operator, slid in beside Declan. "What have we got?"

"Some kind of celebration," Declan said. "I'm moving forward, cover me."

Gus leaned around the corner of the building, his rifle at the ready. "Go."

Declan hunkered low and ran toward the position where Mustang crouched.

"I don't know, boss," he said. "Doesn't look like a Taliban indoctrination session. Too many women and children in attendance."

Declan studied the crowd. About that time, the people moved, opening a gap so that they could see into the center.

Like Mustang had said, Rasul was there, his bearded face and black turban undeniably distinct. Others around him wore white turbans and next to him stood a young man with a white turban. A woman stood beside the man in white, covered from head to toe in white. Her face could not be seen, but she carried a bouquet of bright red and pink flowers.

"Hell, it's a wedding," Declan declared. "They're having a wedding."

"The general told us to use whatever means we had to in order to take out Rasul," Mustang reminded him.

"Yeah, but storming a wedding would be political suicide," Mack, Declan's assistant leader, said.

"What should we do?" Gus asked into Declan's headset.

Declan shook his head. What could they do? If they didn't take out Rasul, he would live on to kill again. If they raided the wedding party, there would be too many civilian casualties...women, children, maybe even the bride and groom. Despite his commanding officers' orders, he chose to err on caution. "We wait and see if we can pick off Rasul without taking out the wedding party."

He positioned his men around the village, hoping at least one of them would get a clear shot of the Taliban leader. In the process, they located the vehicles the Taliban had arrived in, parked beneath a crude lean-to with a grass-thatched roof. If they tried to make a run for it, they'd head in that direction.

The celebration went on for another hour, the Taliban leader in the thick of the crowd, too close to innocent women, the bride and groom, and small children. At one point, he even lifted a child into his arms and held her long enough for her to fall asleep on his shoulder.

He was surrounded by other men dressed in white garments, with black turbans. They carried AK-47 rifles and remained close to the Taliban leader throughout the ceremony.

An hour and a half of waiting came to a close when the bride and groom stood and moved toward the Taliban leader. He rose, but was surrounded immediately by women, children and his bodyguards.

"Mack, can you get a clear shot?" Declan asked.

Mack was the best shot among the team. He had logged the highest number of enemy kills in the eight months they'd been in the country. If anyone could take out the Taliban leader, he was the guy.

Mack swore into his mic. "Can't without taking out the bride or groom."

Declan lifted his rifle to his shoulder and aimed at the Taliban leader.

A woman carrying an infant blocked his direct shot to Rasul.

"Anyone else got a direct line of fire?" Declan asked.

One by one, each member of his team reported. "No."

"We have to make a move. If it means breaking up the party, so be it."

"The commander and general both said to use whatever means necessary. You heard them. Rasul has to go," Mack repeated.

"Then let's get this party started." Declan shifted his rifle in his arms. "Be ready. If you get the shot, take it. Do your best to limit collateral damage."

Declan didn't wait for his team to respond; he stepped out in the open and fired his rifle into the air, sure to aim with enough trajectory to take the bullets far from the village. As soon as he fired the burst of rounds, he ducked back behind the cover of the building.

Screams sounded from the crowd and people scattered in all directions. Declan couldn't reemerge from the same building. The enemy would have spotted him and be aiming for him.

Mustang had climbed to the top of the building with his rifle. "I got a bead on Rasul."

"Take him out," Declan said.

"Damn," Mustang said.

"What?"

"He grabbed the bride. He's using her as a human shield." Mustang cursed again. "I can't get a clean shot."

The commander had been clear. He'd authorized using whatever means necessary. In Declan's world, that meant the needs of the many outweighed the needs of the one. One bride.

He could end the terror and destruction of many more by taking the shot...through the bride to the Taliban leader.

"This mission is headed for the crapper," Mack said.

Declan peered around the corner of the building.

The Taliban men had gathered around their leader, holding

women and children in front of them. Over the heads of their hostages, they fired their weapons in Declan's direction.

Chunks of hard-packed earth and sticks splintered off the building beside Declan's head. He slipped back out of range.

He rounded the other side of the building and ran to the next. If he was correct, the Taliban leader and his bodyguards would be heading for their vehicles, which were parked at the north end of the village. They'd have to let go of their hostages long enough to climb into their trucks and SUVs. "Cut them off where they parked," he said.

"On it," Gus responded.

"Getting there," Mack said.

"Almost there," Cole chimed in.

"Right behind you," Snow said.

"Gotcha covered," Mustang added.

Weaving through the narrow streets of the village, Declan came out at the north end, within twenty yards of the Taliban vehicles.

At that moment, it seemed the entire village spilled out of the alleys between the buildings, flowing like a river, carrying the Taliban leader toward the waiting vehicles. He still had the bride clutched against him.

The bodyguards hadn't emerged from the town, which made Declan pause. "Rasul is still surrounded. Where are his bodyguards?"

"Got one coming up from behind you," Mustang said. Shots were fired in the darkness. "One down. Five more to go."

"I'm going for Rasul," Declan said. He started out of the cover of the building he'd been hunkered down behind.

"Hold on," Mustang's voice came across. "We've got a big problem headed our way."

"What?" Declan didn't want to wait too long, or else Rasul would escape, but he ducked between two huts.

"The other five bodyguards are converging on your location. They have babies strapped to their chests and they're herding small children and women through the streets wearing vests full of explosives."

"Holy sh—" Declan cursed beneath his breath. He knew how badly their CO and the general wanted this kill, but to do it would mean taking out the entire village. The face of the child he'd played with earlier swam before his eyes. And then he saw that child emerge in front of the parade of villagers destined to die if the Americans didn't back off.

"Abort," Declan said.

"Abort?" Mack asked. "But we haven't taken out Rasul."

"And if we do, his bodyguards will kill every last person in this village." Declan couldn't live with that on his conscience. If that wasn't bad enough, the press would get hold of the story and blame the Americans. They'd be labeled baby killers, and the corpses of the bride and groom would be paraded in front of the cameras for the entire world to see and know the US Marines were no better than the jihadist suicide bombers who killed indiscriminately.

"You heard me," Declan said. "Abort."

"What about our orders?"

"To hell with our orders. Those people aren't collateral damage," Declan said. "They're people who didn't ask to be used as human shields."

"We're following your lead. If you say we're out of here, we're out of here," Mack said.

The team pulled back, slipping out of the village and into the night to meet up with their ride home aboard the Black Hawk helicopter, their mission a failure.

The next day, Rasul went on to bomb a convoy containing members of the US State Department and a high-powered member of the EU in front of a school filled with Afghan children. Twenty-seven people died that day.

Those in Washington who had authorized the mission to assassinate Rasul were blamed. Heads rolled and the buck stopped with the Force Recon team. Declan and his team didn't know that night they decided not to kill Rasul was the end of their careers as Force Recon marines.

Chapter Twelve

Grace woke to a repeated buzzing. She rolled over and snuggled into the hard, muscular chest beside her and reveled in how safe and warm she felt. She'd never been more content…if not for that annoying buzzing sound.

The man beside her stretched to the side and ended the buzzing, but started talking, pulling her more completely from the deep sleep she'd needed so badly.

"They are?" Declan said. "Yes, ma'am… Charlie. We'll be there in thirty minutes."

Grace opened her eyes, memories of making love to this stranger rushing back to warm her all over. That's when she realized she was still naked beneath the sheets, with her body pressed against his equally naked form.

A different kind of heat rushed into her cheeks. How did she extricate herself from this man gracefully? A man as ruggedly handsome as Declan had to have been with beautiful women in his past. Surely he'd forget her as soon as he completed his assignment and moved on.

Declan started to toss the bedsheet aside, but Grace held on tightly to her corner.

"You go ahead. I'm not quite awake yet," she said, her cheeks so hot she feared she might ignite the sheets. She looked away as he shifted in the bed.

A warm hand caressed her cheek. "Hey, you're not having regrets, are you?" He turned her to face him. Declan leaned up on his elbow and stared down into her eyes. "Because I don't regret a single moment with you. Except..."

Grace braced herself.

"Except that I didn't make love to you sooner." He bent and pressed a kiss to her lips. "You're amazing."

She let go of the breath she held and laughed nervously. "Yeah, but we barely know each other and we're...we're..."

"Perfect in bed together? Fit like we belong together?"

"We're naked," she gushed out.

Declan chuckled. "Yes, we are." He traced a finger along her jaw. "And I'd make love to you all over again, but I don't have enough time to do it right."

"Like you did last night?" Her heart beat like a snare drum, because damn, he'd rocked her world the night before. So much so, she was completely out of her depth and slightly off-kilter. Waking up in this man's arms would be all too easy to get used to. Something she couldn't risk.

Declan wasn't going to be around for long. The man had a job. She and Riley were that job. When he resolved the problem, he wouldn't have an excuse to hang around. He'd be off to his next assignment.

Would it be a beautiful woman? Would he find her more attractive and a better lover?

Grace bunched her hands into fists, her fingernails digging into her palms, the sting of jealousy burning in her chest. How could she be jealous of a woman who might not even exist? All over a man she'd met the day before.

Again, he cupped her cheek and smiled down at her. "No use being shy. It shouldn't matter after what we shared last night."

"Maybe it doesn't matter to you," she argued, pulling the sheet up over her chest as she propped herself up on her knees. "But it does to me."

He kissed her full on the lips and gave her naked bottom a playful smack. "Then I'll get a quick shower, while you're dressing." He nibbled behind her ear. "Although, I'd rather see your naked body."

He rose from the bed and crossed to the bathroom, magnificently nude, his hips narrow and his buttocks tight and rounded.

Grace couldn't look away. The man was too gloriously good-looking, like a buffed-up Greek god. He shot a wicked smile over his shoulder. "Caught ya looking."

Again, her cheeks heated. She grabbed a pillow and threw it at his head, the sheet she'd held to her front slipping to expose a breast. She quickly covered herself. "You're way too full of yourself, Declan O'Neill."

He smiled and winked. "Maybe, but you still looked." Declan entered the bathroom and soon the sound of water hitting the shower curtain came through the paneled door.

Grace sprang from the bed and pulled on her robe, knotting its tie securely. She was grabbing her clothing and shoes when Declan emerged from the bathroom, a towel slung low around his hips. He wore nothing else.

Grace's jaw dropped and she ran her tongue across her suddenly dry lips. "Uh, my turn in the bathroom?"

He nodded. "Yes. And I would have dressed first, but my bag is out here."

She started around him, but he hooked her arm as she passed and slid his hand up to hers, where she clutched her clothes to her chest as if they were armor.

"Do I make you nervous?" he asked, a frown drawing his eyebrows together. Declan lifted her hand to his lips and pressed a kiss to her palm.

She stared at his mouth, rather than his eyes. "I'm not ready for this," she whispered.

"For what?"

"You know…" She should have pulled her hand free, but she couldn't. His fingers on hers, his lips on her skin… "I'm not ready to jump back into the morning-after routine. I don't know how to date. I don't remember how to act after…well…after…"

He gathered her in his arms and held her. "Maybe we shouldn't have gone so fast, but I can't regret what happened last night. My only regret is that you're uncomfortable now." He leaned back, tipped her chin up with his finger. "Would it make you feel better if we can pretend it didn't happen and go back to friends working to find Riley?"

As much as she'd like their connection to be more, she really wasn't ready for it. Her heart beat too fast and her knees wobbled. Both symptoms could be attributed to the fact she was pressed against his naked body, the electricity generated scrambling her brain.

"Yes," she said.

He brushed his lips across hers in barely a kiss, then he straightened and stepped away.

Grace dove for the bathroom, shut the door, threw her clothes on its hook and leaned against the wall. She didn't want to go back to being friends, not after experiencing the magic of a night in Declan's arms. But she wasn't ready for the pain and disillusionment of being discarded once the magic wore off. Three years after her divorce, she had just begun to feel right in her own skin. Her ex-husband had been so controlling and critical of everything she did, she had to fight her way back to any level of confidence. She couldn't afford to lose that.

She pushed away from the wall, leaned over the sink, splashed water onto her face and then brushed her teeth. She noticed a red mark on her neck where Declan's stubble had rubbed against her skin as he'd kissed his way down to her breasts. Her nipples puckered and tingled at the memory of his tongue flicking the tips.

With a groan, she splashed cold water on her face again and patted it dry, refusing to acknowledge the red marks or pointed beads of her nipples making little tents against her robe. No, she couldn't go there. Riley was her focus.

Hoping it would calm her down, she took a fast shower, toweled off and ran a brush through her still-damp hair. She pulled on her clothes—just jeans and a soft blouse—ready to face the day…and Declan.

When she exited the bathroom, she entered the empty bedroom. Through the open bedroom door, she could see Declan standing in the living room, at the boarded-up window.

He turned when she approached. "My team has arrived at Mrs. Halverson's. The bank doesn't open until nine o'clock. I'd like to swing by Charlie's place and connect with them before we hit the safe-deposit box. I think they will be useful in providing backup when we retrieve whatever Riley stashed there."

"I'm all for additional protection. I'm afraid whatever we're getting from that safe-deposit box would either hurt who she's running from or is something they want."

"Exactly." Declan's brow dipped low on his forehead. "Which puts you in just as much danger as Riley's in now."

A shiver rippled down the back of Grace's neck.

"Are you okay with this? You could hand the key over to the FBI and give them permission to enter that box."

Grace shook her head. "I can do this. Once I have it, she'll contact me for the handoff. She said not to trust anyone."

"Not even me?" He gave her a gentle smile that made butterflies take flight in her belly.

"I trust you," she said. "You saved Mrs. Halverson from kidnappers. You went after the intruder in our apartment. I'm convinced you would have done both those things regardless of who Mrs. Halverson was."

He shrugged. "I did what any decent human would have done."

Grace chuckled. "Most people would have saved themselves and never considered going after the bad guys." She stared up into his eyes. "You're real hero material."

"Not according to the US Army." His lips thinned into a straight line. "If you're ready, let's go."

She hoped Declan would loosen up enough to tell her what he'd done that got him discharged from the military.

A few moments later, she settled into her SUV, stealing a glance over to where Declan sat with his hand curled around the steering wheel. Trusting him was not an issue. Grace trusted the man with her life. She just wasn't sure she could trust him with her heart.

DECLAN PULLED THROUGH the gate at Mrs. Halverson's estate in Kalorama twenty minutes later. A dark SUV stood in the circular drive.

His pulse quickened and his heart grew lighter as he climbed out of the vehicle and rounded to the passenger door.

Grace had the door open and was swinging her legs out.

He extended a hand and helped her to her feet, then tucked her arm through his elbow and led her up the stone staircase to the front double-door entrance.

Before he could reach for the bell, the door burst open and five men spilled out.

"O'Neill," Mack greeted him first with an outstretched hand.

Declan grabbed his assistant team leader's hand and tugged hard, pulling him into a tight hug and then clapping him on the back.

"You're a sight for sore eyes," Mack said.

"Good to see you, man." Declan's eyes stung. He knew he'd missed his team, but hadn't realized just how much. Now that they were in front of him, he felt as if he'd come home.

Mustang nudged Mack aside and moved in for a bone-crunching bear hug that left Declan chuckling and breathless. "Missed you, old man." Mustang stepped back and let Cole, Gus and Jack have their turns at greeting their old team leader.

"Who do you have with you?" Jack held out his hand. "I'm Jack Snow, slack man on the team."

"Grace Lawrence." Grace's brow wrinkled. "What's a slack man?"

"He's the newest man on the team," Gus said.

"Which makes him the pack mule," Cole added. "He carries everything the rest of us don't want to carry." He backhanded Snow in the belly. "Speaking of which, where'd you put my duffel bag?"

"Bite me," Snow said. "We're not on active duty anymore. You carried your own bag. Find it yourself."

"We're a team, aren't we?" Cole said. "Every Force Recon team needs its slack man. If you're not our slack man, what are you?"

"Excuse these two jokers." Mack pushed Cole and Snow aside. "I'm Mack Balkman, assistant team leader, second only to our man O'Neill." He held out his hand to Grace.

Cole and Gus introduced themselves to Grace, each holding her hand a little longer than the last.

Finally, Declan had enough and walked between Gus and Grace, forcing Gus to let go. "When did you get in?" Declan asked.

Gus grinned and stepped back.

"I got in around two in the morning," Mack said. "Snow came in shortly after me."

"Gus, Mustang and I came in around two in the morning, too. We drove in from Virginia Beach," Cole said.

"Becoming professional beach bums?" Declan asked. "You haven't gone soft on me, have you? I sold you to Charlie as the best of the best."

"Yeah, but you didn't tell her the best of what, did you?" Mustang winked.

"We're ready and more than willing to do whatever you have in mind," Cole said. "A couple of months of hanging out at the beach and going to the bar was getting old." He cracked his knuckles. "I'm ready to get back into the action."

"You mentioned using our skills," Mack said. "What exactly do you and Charlie have in mind?"

Declan waved toward the door. "Let's go inside and I'll brief you and Charlie on what's going on."

AN HOUR LATER, Declan's team had been briefed and had come up with a plan to support Grace on her trip to the safe-deposit box at the bank.

"It might be overkill," Mack said.

"But better overkill than mission failure or Miss Lawrence getting hurt," Charlie said. "I'm glad you're all going with her. I'd go myself, but that might add more complications to the operation. Especially after what happened the other day."

"True." Declan wouldn't want to worry about two women at the same time, especially one who'd proven to be a target for kidnappers. He didn't like the idea of Grace putting herself into danger, but she insisted she had to do this for Riley.

"I'm leaning toward overkill," Grace said. "I'll feel a whole lot better with a few more able-bodied men watching my back. With your help, I'm going to walk into that bank, get whatever is in that safe-deposit box and walk back out." She wiped her hands together. "That's it. No problem."

A knot formed in Declan's gut. His instinct told him it wasn't going to be that easy. Someone had killed Moretti. If the killer wanted what Riley had stashed in that box, he might be willing to kill Grace to get it.

"If you don't mind, I like the redundancy of having my team as backup. I'm hoping it's as easy as you seem to think it will be. If it is, great. If it isn't, we have skilled operatives who know how to take the bad guys down."

Grace gave Declan a twitch of a smile. "I'm okay with your way of thinking. It's almost time for the bank to open," Grace said with a glance at her watch. "Let's go."

"Wait." Declan held out his hand. "Give me your cell phone."

Grace's eyes narrowed. "Why?" she asked as she handed it over to him.

"Just in case, for some unexplainable reason, we get separated, I want to be able to find you." His gaze captured hers. "Do you mind if I put a tracker on your phone?"

She shook her head; her heart was warming to the idea. He cared enough to want to find her should they be parted. Sure, it was all because of the task he'd been assigned, but she liked that he would go to the trouble to set it up.

He brought up the applications store and selected a tracking application. When it had downloaded, he added information that would allow his cell phone to track hers. He handed the phone back to her and she put it into her pocket.

"I'd rather tag you with a smaller tracking device, but for now, this is what we have to work with."

Charlie stepped up beside them. "Declan, you and I need to work on what our new organization might need in the way of communications equipment and weapons."

He nodded. "And we will. But for now, we have to get moving."

Declan insisted on leading the way out to Grace's SUV. He helped her into the passenger side and slipped in behind the steering wheel.

Mrs. Halverson had loaned the men two of her estate's black Cadillac Escalades. The men split up, two in one vehicle, three in the other. They could all have fit into one, but this way they had multiple vehicles if they needed to chase the bad guys.

Charlie stood beside the lead vehicle as the men climbed in. "I took the liberty of loading the rear of these with some of the weapons my husband collected in his own personal armory. Hopefully you won't need them. But I also included ammunition, should things get sticky. If this weaponry gets you in hot water, call me. I know people who will make sure authorities know you're okayed to use these things."

Declan bent and kissed the older woman's cheek. "Thank you. It's nice to know you're looking out for us."

The drive to the bank took fifteen minutes. Declan pulled the SUV into the parking lot beside the one-story, gray stucco building.

Grace didn't say a word on the way. She sat with her gaze on the road ahead, her purse clutched so tightly to her chest, her knuckles turned white.

Declan reached over and touched her hand. "You'll be all right."

She gave a shaky laugh. "I don't know how you and your team could walk into enemy territory and not be scared out of your minds."

"Don't let my team tell you differently," Declan said. "We were pretty scared at times. We just didn't let it slow us down. We had a job to do, and got busy doing it. The end usually justified the means, and we did our best to make our efforts count."

Declan slowed at an intersection and then turned right. "Until we didn't follow orders," he added softly, his lips pressing together.

"You must have had a good reason." Grace tilted her head and stared into Declan's eyes. "If you had it all to do over again, would you have made the same decision?"

An image of the babies strapped to the Taliban's chests and the bride and groom being used as human shields flashed before Declan's mind. "Yes."

"Then you did the right thing." Grace smiled. "Now, let's get this over with. I want my roommate back in one piece. Preferably alive." She faced forward, her head held high.

Declan's lips twitched.

Grace was scared, but she would do whatever she had to in order to help her friend.

Declan parked as close to the front entrance as possible.

When Grace started to get out, he put up a hand. "Wait for me. I can't protect you if you're standing out in the open, alone."

She stared at him. "As long as you don't intend to use yourself as a shield to catch bullets aimed at me."

He shrugged. "I'll do what I have to. Hopefully it won't come to that."

Grace frowned. "It better not. I like you just the way you are. Not peppered with lead." She chuckled. "I never thought I'd utter that phrase. Sounds like something out of an old Western movie."

The other members of his team arrived shortly after Declan and Grace, parking at opposite ends of the lot, probably trying to look like they weren't arriving together.

When they got out of the SUVs, they were so much alike in build and bearing, only an idiot wouldn't put the five of them together.

Declan preferred that they act as a visual deterrent to anyone who might try to attack Grace. He glanced around the lot. Several cars were parked and two more pulled in as he helped Grace down from the vehicle. He slipped an arm around her, pulling her as near to his body as possible.

She didn't resist; instead, she leaned into him, holding her purse in front of her. "You think anyone will try to attack me?"

"I don't know. But I don't want to take any chances." He smiled down at her. "I think I like you, and would hate for anything to happen to you so early in our potential relationship."

She shot a quick glance up at him. "You like me?"

He nodded with a gentle smile. "Yes, I do. So, let's get this over with so we can have coffee and get to know each other in a little-less-volatile environment."

"I'm game." She smiled up at him and walked with him to the door.

Once inside, Declan loosened his hold but didn't relax his vigilance.

Grace asked to access the safe-deposit box, showed her identification, along with the power-of-attorney papers, and presented the key. The receptionist asked them to take a seat and left her desk to find a manager. She was gone for at least five minutes when finally a dark-haired man appeared with a smile, wearing a name tag with Branch Manager engraved on the gold-colored metal. He introduced himself as Alan Jordan. He checked the computer, presumably looking up the box information. After he verified Grace was who she said she was, he finally showed her into the vault where the boxes were located.

When Declan went to follow, Jordan held up his hand. "I'm sorry, sir, only the key owner is allowed into the safe."

Declan was forced to remain outside the safe until Grace returned. He didn't like it, but he couldn't argue against the rules.

The entire time he waited, he studied the people coming in and out of the bank.

An old woman walked in with a cane, her body hunched over, her gait slow and steady.

A man wearing jeans and a polo shirt came in, carrying a money bag for deposit. He nodded toward Declan and headed straight for the tellers' counter.

Mack and Gus entered without giving Declan so much as a nod. They made brief eye contact and stopped at the receptionist's desk to inquire about opening accounts.

A woman carrying a small baby came through the doors and stood in line at the tellers' counter, bouncing the baby on her hip as she waited.

None of the people in the bank appeared to pose a threat to Grace.

Declan checked his watch. Grace had been inside for three minutes. How long did it take to open a safe-deposit box? He paced the floor in front of the receptionist's desk. The woman had yet to return to her post. Had she gone on break?

He looked around at the different offices, all with glass fronts and people working with customers. The receptionist had gone down a hallway to an office that didn't have glass walls.

Declan assumed the office belonged to the branch manager. Until that moment, he hadn't thought about why the receptionist hadn't come out of the branch manager's office with him, assuming she might have gone on break in the back of the building.

Not wanting to leave his position in front of the vault, Declan nodded toward Mack, who was waiting in a chair for an account representative to call him to open an account.

Declan caught Mack's gaze and tipped his head in the direction the receptionist had gone.

Mack rose from his chair and walked toward the hallway.

One of the loan officers chose that moment to enter the hallway ahead of Mack and knocked on the closed door.

When she didn't get a response, she opened the door and leaned in. The scream she emitted echoed throughout the bank lobby, generating more screams from the tellers and account representatives.

The loan officer raced back toward the lobby and ran into Mack. When he caught her shoulders, she screamed again and struggled to get free. "They're dead. Oh, my God. Laura and Mr. Jordan are dead!" She collapsed against Mack.

Declan leaped over the counter and ran toward the safe, his heart pounding hard against his ribs.

If the receptionist and Mr. Jordan were dead, who was the man in the vault with Grace?

Chapter Thirteen

Grace walked into the vault with the branch manager, clutching the key to the safe-deposit box in her hand. This was the day of reckoning. Riley must have stored something very important in the box. In Grace's way of thinking, it could be a life-or-death revelation.

Her mouth dry and her heart racing, Grace followed Mr. Jordan into the room with the safe-deposit boxes. He searched the numbers until he found the one that matched the key she held. "This is the one. You'll need to use the key to open the box."

"Could I have a moment alone?" Grace asked. She didn't want the bank manager to see whatever it was she was supposed to retrieve from the box. Not knowing what it was, she wasn't sure anyone else should know.

The man's smiled slipped. "I'm sorry, Miss Lawrence, a bank employee has to witness the removal of anything from the safe-deposit boxes. If you don't mind, I have work to do. Could you hurry it along?"

Grace frowned at the man's rudeness, but she got on with the reason she'd come to the bank in the first place. Riley wanted her to get something out of the box. If she was that concerned about retrieving the item, it had to be important.

Her hand shaking, Grace slipped the key into the lock and turned it.

Mr. Jordan stepped up beside her. "Here, let me help you."

"That won't be necessary. I can manage on my own." She gripped the handle and pulled the drawer out of the wall of boxes far enough so she could reach inside.

The box was high up the wall, so Grace couldn't look down into it. She pulled it out and set it on a table in the center of the room for this purpose. Nothing was inside the drawer except an envelope, which she quickly retrieved.

Clutching the envelope in her hand, Grace slid the drawer back into the wall of safe-deposit boxes and removed her key. "I'm finished here. I'm ready to go." She turned to leave.

A hand wrapped around her face, covering her mouth.

Grace tried to scream, but the hand clamped tighter, muffling her attempt.

"Give me the envelope," Mr. Jordan said, his voice hard and steely, not at all like the accommodating manager who'd shown her into the vault.

An icy shiver ran from the base of Grace's skull all the way down her back. Using one of her self-defense moves, she twisted free of Mr. Jordan's hold and turned to face the bank manager, a frown pulling her eyebrows together.

"You heard me." He held a wicked-looking knife in his right hand and motioned with the left. "Hand it over."

Grace shook her head, her fingers curling around the envelope. "But it's just a piece of paper." With something small and square inside. And Riley needed it. "Why would you want something so personal?"

"Your roommate has been duping us for the past few months. It's time she gave us what we paid good money to acquire."

"I don't know what you're talking about."

"You don't need to know. Just hand over the envelope." He grabbed her wrist in a vise-like hold.

Using the self-defense techniques she'd learned from a police officer at the local YMCA, Grace twisted her arm and thrust it downward and out, breaking the man's hold.

He swung the knife at her, catching her sleeve, the tip nicking her upper arm.

Grace eased backward toward the vault door. "You're not the

branch manager, are you?" One step at a time, she edged toward the exit, still holding the envelope in her hand.

"Give me the damn envelope," he demanded and lunged.

Grace screamed and dove for the door, and she would have made it out, but the man with the knife was fast and had longer legs. He threw himself at her, tackling her like a pro football player.

Grace hit the marble-tiled floor hard, the air knocked from her lungs.

"Give me the envelope," he said, his voice low and dangerous. "Or I'll slice into your jugular."

"It's mine," Grace cried and kicked at the man's hold on her ankle.

He let go long enough for Grace to jerk her leg free and scramble to her feet.

She made it all the way to the threshold of the vault before he caught her by the hair and yanked her back against him.

He pressed a knife to her throat and growled into her ear. "Make any stupid moves, and you won't see your precious roommate ever again." He pressed the tip of the knife into her skin.

Sharp pain made Grace freeze. She didn't dare scream again for fear the man would carry through on his promise. "Take the envelope," she said, lifting it up for him to grab.

"I will," he said. "But you're coming with me as collateral. I know your boyfriend has this place surrounded with his buddies. They won't let me out of here unless I take out a little insurance policy." He let go of her hair and wrapped his arm around her middle, still pressing the knife to her throat. A warm, wet trickle dribbled down Grace's neck.

With her heart racing and her knees shaking, she struggled to keep her wits about her, searching for any opportunity that might present itself to make an escape. If her abductor would just not press the tip of the knife so hard into her skin.

From behind, he walked her through the vault door and nearly ran into Declan.

"Get back!" the man behind her yelled. "Get back or I kill the girl."

Declan raised his hands. "Okay, okay. Don't hurt the woman."

He eased backward. "Let her go and I promise you won't be harmed."

The man snorted. "I'm not letting go of my little insurance policy. She's coming with me. Now, move out of my way or I stick it to her." He increased the pressure on the knife and more blood trickled down Grace's neck.

"All right. Calm down." Declan's nostrils flared and he stepped to the side. "Just don't hurt her. We'll give you whatever you want."

"That's more like it." Grace's captor half lifted, half shoved her forward. "Tell your men to stand down." He kept moving forward. "Now!"

Declan raised his voice, "Mack, Gus, stand down."

Grace couldn't turn her head left or right to see Declan's guys, but no one came running to help her. And she was glad they didn't. If the hand at her throat tightened any more, that knife would slice right through her jugular vein and she'd bleed out before they could call 911.

She kind of liked her jugular vein intact. "I'll be okay," she tried to assure Declan, though she had no idea how she could possibly be fine. The man would have no more use for her once he got away from the bank and claimed whatever was in the envelope Riley had asked Grace to retrieve.

"That's right," her abductor said. "Play your cards right and I'll let your girlfriend go when I'm well away from here." He squeezed his arm hard around her middle. "Call the police, and I'll take her apart, one piece at a time."

Declan's fists clenched and he took a step forward.

Her captor faced him with Grace between the two of them. "Don't think I will?" His voice deepened to a low, dangerous growl. "Try me. Maybe I'll take her pretty ear first." He trailed the knife up to her ear.

Grace closed her eyes and gritted her teeth, prepared for the pain sure to come.

"No need. I believe you," Declan said.

Grace opened her eyes and stared into Declan's.

"I'll get you out of this," he promised.

She gave him a weak smile. "I'm counting on it." Her eyes stung with unshed tears. She couldn't see how he would be able to help her. Until the man holding the knife put down his arm, she was his to toy with, to threaten and use as a shield.

"I'll need a car and a fifteen-minute head start." Her captor returned the knife to the base of Grace's neck, where her pulse beat a thousand times a minute. "If all goes well, you'll see your girl again. If not, well, it's on you. Make sure I get out of here, and I'll go easy on her."

Grace doubted the man would keep his word, but she didn't have much of a choice. She'd have to go with him unless she found an opportunity to run before he got her into his car. She braced herself, ready to react at the slightest chance she might get away.

DECLAN COULD HAVE kicked himself. How had the man gotten into the bank before Declan and his guys? The only way he could have done it was if he'd had prior knowledge that Grace had found the key and was going to the bank. Perhaps he had tapped Grace's apartment or had some way of listening in on her conversations with Riley or Declan. However he'd done it, the fact was he had Grace and would use her to extricate himself from the bank and from any confrontation with the police.

Declan had failed Grace and now had to find a way to get her out of the danger she faced. He'd been on fire with worry when he'd heard her scream for help earlier.

"Let me go ahead of you to let my guys know you're coming out." Declan hurried to the lobby doors and stepped outside. He spotted Snow and Mustang standing at the corners of the building and Cole leaning against an SUV, pretending to talk on his cell phone.

When they saw Declan, all three men straightened.

"Grace is coming out. She's not alone, but don't make any sudden moves." He stood back and held the door. "My guys won't get in your way," he assured the man holding Grace.

The man led Grace through the door, his eyes narrowed, the wickedly sharp, military-grade knife firmly pressed to Grace's throat.

If Declan dove for the man's arm, he might be able to knock the knife loose. Or he might bump the man's hand and be responsible for the knife slicing into Grace's jugular vein. He couldn't take that risk. The thought of anyone slicing into Grace's long beautiful neck made his stomach roil.

He couldn't take a shot at the man for fear of hitting Grace, or missing and the man following through on his promise to slice her throat.

Declan couldn't do a damned thing but let the man go...with Grace.

The abductor walked with Grace into the parking lot, turning again and again, his gaze on Declan's men, his lip pulled back in a feral snarl, daring them to make a move.

Each time Grace faced Declan, he died a little more. The man was getting away with the woman Declan felt could change his life for the better. She was everything he could have wanted in a woman and more. So beautiful, inside and out. He couldn't let it end here. He wouldn't.

A car whipped around the end of a row of parked vehicles and drove up beside Grace and her captor. The passenger door was flung open from the inside.

Still holding the knife to Grace's throat, the man backed into the seat, forcing Grace to sit on his lap, blocking any chance for anyone else to get a bead on him and blow him away.

A moment later, the car burned rubber, speeding out of the parking lot.

And Declan's heart slipped like a bag of rocks to the pit of his belly.

Grace was gone.

His men gathered around him.

"We can't just let him get away with her," Mack said.

"If we go after them, he'll know and kill her," Cole reasoned.

"Now that he's gotten away, what's to keep him from killing her anyway and tossing her body out in a ditch?" Mustang said.

Declan shot a murderous glare in his teammate's direction. "He's not going to kill her. And we don't have to follow closely. I have her phone on a tracker."

"What if he finds her phone on her and he tosses it out of the vehicle?" Gus asked.

"Then we're sunk." Declan punched the code into his phone to find Grace. When the screen came up, he could see that the phone was still moving. "For now, she still has it." He ran toward Grace's SUV. "Let's move."

Before they could get out of the parking lot, a plain silver sedan pulled in and blocked the exit. A woman with auburn hair leaped out and waved them down. "Any of you Declan O'Neill?" she asked.

Declan shifted into Park and flung open his door. "I am."

"I'm Riley." She glanced around. "Where's Grace? Did she get the envelope out of my safe-deposit box?"

"She did." Declan's jaw tightened. "And someone got her and the envelope."

Riley swore beneath her breath. "I should have gotten it myself." She glanced around. "I can't stay out in the open. Where can we go to talk?"

"Get in the car. We were about to follow the tracker on Grace's phone."

"Thank God." Riley pulled her car to the side and jumped in with Declan.

He handed her the phone with the tracker. "Navigate. We have to catch up before they discover her phone on her."

Riley shook her head. "They're not going to be happy with the memory card they have."

"That's what was in the box?" Declan asked. "A memory card?"

"A very small memory card, packed with the data they wanted all along."

"What the hell's going on? Why have you been on the run? And why do they want this card?" Declan wanted all the information he could get. Grace's life was on the line, and the more he knew about his adversaries, the better equipped he'd be to face them.

"I'm working on a secret project. I can't tell you exactly what it's about, but I can tell you that I was approached by the FBI to help them find out who was stealing secrets from Quest about this particular work. I didn't know how to do it other than to create two sets of data. One good set and one bad set. I presented the bad set. It was the one that was being sold to whoever was buying. I figured I'd keep putting out the bad data until we found the culprit." She stared out the window. "I didn't think it would take so long for the seller to surface. And I never considered it would put Grace in danger. I thought I was the only one committing to the undercover sting."

"Did you figure out who was selling the data?"

She glanced his way. "I think Moretti was in on it. But I didn't think he was smart enough to orchestrate the deals. Someone with a better understanding of what this idea is worth has to be behind it. Someone with connections to foreign buyers." She shook her head. "Moretti isn't that guy. He doesn't like traveling outside the region, much less the country. Oh, he was involved, but I think he was just a middle man. He took the fall for someone else."

"Any idea who?" Declan asked.

Again, Riley shook her head. "I was getting close to finishing the project with the good data and knew I wouldn't be able to hold out much longer. The program team was at the point they needed my work to complete the project. It was key to making it all work."

"I take it whoever was buying the bad data figured out it was bad."

Riley nodded. "I got a text just as I got to my office two days ago. The message said to get out." She pressed a hand to her chest. "I've never been so scared in my life. I got up from my chair, grabbed my purse and walked out of the office, out of the building and kept walking. Another text told me to lie low, find a hotel, but pay cash. In other words, I had to disappear. I couldn't even call Grace to let her know what was happening." Riley sighed. "Until I bought a burner phone."

"Were you the one who warned us to get out of the bar?"

She nodded. "I didn't know if they'd come looking for me at my apartment. If they did, they'd find Grace. So I've been shadowing her since this all began, staying far enough away to remain in hiding, but close enough to warn or help out, if I could. I was meeting with my FBI handler this morning when you and Grace were on your way to the bank. I left that meeting as soon as I could. I never thought anyone would dare to cause trouble at a bank. Outside the bank, maybe, but not inside a bank." Riley banged her fist against her palm. "I should have gotten the key from Grace and gone into the vault myself. I didn't even tell the FBI handler about the spare memory card. I was afraid a double agent might be working against me."

The road they followed led toward Baltimore. Soon they were passing through a warehouse district and shipyards where cargo and containers were stacked neatly on the shore.

"Is the memory card Grace retrieved encrypted?" Declan asked.

"Yes," Riley said. "They won't be able to break into the data. We don't have to worry about them getting into the information."

"You might want to revisit that idea. If they can't get into that information, they might kill Grace out of anger."

Riley shot a fierce frown in his direction. "Damn." She glanced at the screen, her eyes widening. "The cell phone locator blinked off." She looked up.

"Damn," Declan echoed. "Without the locator, it will be impossible to find her. She could end up anywhere."

Chapter Fourteen

Grace sat stiffly in her captor's lap all the way through the city, scared as much by the knife at her throat as by the DC traffic and her lack of a seat belt. Darkened windows kept anyone from seeing her inside during snarled traffic. There was no way she could signal someone for help.

She braced a hand on the dash and prayed they didn't hit anyone in front of them or were hit from behind, thus throwing her through the windshield.

Eventually, they broke out of DC proper and headed toward the warehouses and docks near Baltimore, MD.

All the while, Grace prayed Declan and his guys would catch up and do something to help her out of the situation.

At the very least, she hoped the police would stop them for having two people in the passenger seat, neither in a seat belt—if they could see in. What happened to stopping people for not wearing seat belts? Why did stuff like that never happen when you needed it to?

Neither Declan nor the police caught up to them. And if they had, Grace was sure the driver would have made a run for it, thus initiating a high-speed chase that would have ended badly for more than just the people in the car she was in. Others on the highways would have suffered. Her only saving grace was that they hadn't found the cell phone she'd tucked into her jacket pocket.

She waited patiently for the car to stop and her captor to get tired of holding her and put down his knife.

When they'd come to a long line of container yards at a shipping port, her captor finally lowered his knife.

Grace inched her hand toward the door handle, waited until they slowed at a corner and then yanked, shoved the door open with her foot and tried to dive out.

The arm around her middle caught her before she could clear the door, and dragged her back inside the vehicle.

After bringing the car to a screeching halt, the driver grabbed her hair and pulled hard enough to bring tears to her eyes. He held her by her hair until her abductor could close the door again.

The man holding her around her waist shifted her around, settling her back in his lap. In the process, he must have felt the phone in her pocket. He swore and dug it out. He rolled the window down, cocked his arm and almost threw it out. But he must have thought better of it, pulled the back off and removed the battery instead. He dropped it into his pocket and retrieved his knife, pressing it to her throat again.

The driver released her hair, returning his hands to the steering wheel.

Grace's heart sank to her knees. She'd hoped Declan could track her phone, but with the battery removed, he wouldn't be able to.

Resuming his course, the driver continued past several yards before he pulled into one. He weaved his way through to a small office nestled in the middle of rows and rows of stacked containers in all colors and markings.

Once the vehicle stopped, several men in dark clothes stepped out of the little office building, carrying semiautomatic weapons or handguns.

One of them approached the passenger door and opened it.

Her captor shoved her off his lap and into the arms of the man who'd opened the door.

Grace ducked her head and plowed into the man's belly, hitting him as hard as she could.

He grunted and doubled over.

Grace used that opportunity to slip past him.

She didn't get far before he snatched her wrist and yanked her backward. He spun her around, twisted her arm up behind her back and applied enough pressure that Grace was forced to stand on her toes to keep the pain at bay.

The man who'd kidnapped her got out of the vehicle and stretched.

Grace still held the envelope she'd retrieved from the bank. She tried to slip it beneath her shirt, but her captor caught her wrist before she could and ripped it from her fingers.

"The boss has been waiting for this." He turned and walked toward the office building.

"What do you want me to do with her?" the man holding her arm up between her shoulder blades asked.

"Throw her in one of the containers or kill her," her captor said. "I don't care."

Grace's heart leaped into her throat and her pulse hammered against her eardrums. She couldn't let them kill her. She had too much to live for. Riley would be beside herself, and Declan...

Grace wanted to get to know the marine better. She knew in her bones the man was special and that he would be worth the effort to live, if only to see him once again. He'd given her hope that not all men were like her ex-husband.

Her original captor paused in front of the structure. "No, wait. Don't kill her. We might need her again. But go ahead and lock her in one of the containers."

The man holding her grunted his acknowledgment and shoved her toward a row of the long, rectangular boxes.

He opened one with his free hand and swung the door just wide enough for a person to fit through. Then he ratcheted her arm up a little higher in the middle of her back.

Grace couldn't get any higher on her toes to relieve the pressure. Tears burned the backs of her eyelids. She bit down hard on her tongue to keep from crying out or showing any fear.

The man shoved her hard from behind, sending her flying into the container.

She fell, landing on her hands and knees. Before she could

scramble to her feet, the door slammed shut behind her, leaving her in the dark, dank, steel space.

She felt her way along the sides to the door and ran her hand all along the interior, searching for a lever or latch that would allow her to open her cell. She couldn't find one.

Knowing the containers sometimes had doors on both ends, she felt her way along the side to the other end and again searched for a handle, lever or latch.

Hope leached from her system when she realized she was trapped inside the metal box, with no way to get herself out. She leaned against a wall and slid down until she sat. She couldn't lose her confidence now. Declan would find her. She had to believe that. He'd promised she'd be all right. All she had to do was wait and reflect on all that had happened in the past forty-eight hours.

She'd gone from worrying about finding a full-time job to worrying about living to see another day.

If she lived, she hoped and prayed her roommate was alive and well and found a way out of the danger she was in. On a more selfish note, Grace hoped she'd get to spend more time with the hunky marine. He was a man worth getting to know. A man a girl could count on when times were tough. A man of integrity and honor.

What couldn't have been fifteen minutes later, the metal-on-metal sound of the latch being moved on the door made Grace lurch to her feet. The door to the container swung open.

Her captor stood outside with a gun pointed at her chest. "Come with me."

Unless she wanted to risk having a massive hole blown through her, Grace had no other choice. She marched at gunpoint into the little office a few yards away, grateful to be out of the metal box.

Inside the office, several men gathered around a computer monitor. One sat in a dilapidated office chair, his fingers flying feverishly over the computer keyboard. He cursed and slammed his hand on the metal desk. "She's got it encrypted and password protected. It could take me days to hack in."

"We don't have days. We have to know that we can access the data. The boss is already angry he doesn't have the correct information. He will not be pleased if we leave here without what we promised. We might not live long enough to hack in." The man who was speaking turned to Grace.

She studied his face with all the intention of picking him out of a lineup, if the need arose.

He had short, dark hair and brown-black eyes. Thick eyebrows practically grew together over the bridge of his nose. He wore black trousers and a black jacket. His eyes narrowed as he studied her. "You will enter the password for this memory card."

Grace shook her head. "I don't know it."

He pressed a handgun to her temple. "Enter the password or die."

Grace had been through a lot that day. Having another weapon pointed at her should have made her shake in fear, but somehow she was beginning to get used to it, or she was numbing to the danger. She shrugged. "I guess you'll have to shoot me. The only person who knows how to get into that memory card isn't in this room." She lifted her chin and focused on not flinching if the man pulled the trigger. If she was going to die, she'd die fearless. On the outside, if not inside.

She waited, fully expecting the gun to go off and her life to end.

When it didn't, she flashed a glance at the man. He lowered his handgun and turned to the man who'd disguised himself as the bank manager. "You said she had a cell phone. Give it to me." He held out his hand.

Grace's original captor dug the phone from his pocket and handed it to the dark-haired, dark-eyed man, who quickly reassembled the battery and replaced the back. When the phone had booted, he handed it to Grace. "Call Miss Riley Lansing."

Grace shook her head. "You won't get the code to get in. I know my roommate. She would never betray her country by selling secrets."

The man snorted. "Let's test that theory. Call her."

"No," Grace said.

Red flooded the man's ruddy cheeks and his eyes narrowed even more to a squint. He grabbed Grace's hand and bent her thumb back so hard, she was convinced it would break. The pain had her twisting and writhing.

"Are you going to call your roommate? Or am I going to break each of your fingers, one at a time?"

Grace gasped. "I'll do it." Feeling as if she was failing her friend, she placed the call, praying Declan and his buddies had some way of finding her soon. She didn't want to put her friend in danger, but calling her might buy Grace time for the men to get to her first.

She pressed the last number with which she'd had contact with her roommate.

I'm sorry, Riley.

AS THEY NEARED the location where the cell phone had stopped moving, Riley's burner phone rang.

Declan nearly drove off the road in an attempt to reach for it. He righted the vehicle and focused on staying between the ditches.

Riley punched the button and held the phone to her ear, her gaze on Declan's. She listened for a moment and nodded. "Don't hurt my friend. I'll do whatever you want. Just don't hurt her."

Declan's chest tightened. He wanted to reach through Riley's phone and choke the person on the other end of the conversation. If anything happened to Grace, he'd personally hunt down anyone who harmed her, and kill them with his bare hands.

Riley's frown deepened. "If you hurt her in any way, you can forget about getting into that data. I'm the only one who knows the password for that file. Look, I'll make a deal with you. You trade her, unharmed, for me. When I see she's well away and safe, I'll give you the password and you can have it all. Just tell me where to meet you." She paused. "I'll arrive unarmed and alone." She paused again and then continued, "How do I know you'll release my friend? I'm not just going to walk into a trap and give you all the cards to hold."

It was making Declan crazy to hear only one side of the conversation. Sitting back and listening wasn't the action he needed to unleash his pent-up energy.

When Riley ended the call, she stared down at the handheld device. "At least they're willing to make a trade." She sighed. "I knew I shouldn't have agreed to work with the FBI. None of this would be happening. I'd be blissfully ignorant that I was aiding the sale of secrets to foreign spies. And Grace wouldn't be held hostage by ruthless thugs."

"You did what you thought was right," Declan said softly. Doing the right thing didn't always work out well in the end. Much like what had happened to himself and his team. The corners of his lips twitched. "No good deed goes unpunished. We will get Grace out of this alive, if it's the last thing I do."

"We might get that opportunity to rescue her. Only I have to go in alone." Riley's lips thinned and she stared at the road ahead. "Though I have to go in alone, it doesn't mean you and your men have to wait for Grace to come out. You can be infiltrating the area all around our rendezvous site. You just can't let them see you." She turned to face him. "We need to nail these bastards. Not only are they threatening my best friend, they're stealing secrets from our country."

His fingers tightened on the steering wheel as he pictured Grace being led off by the man with the knife to her throat. She had to still be alive. He wanted so much more time with the woman, having only scratched the surface of her personality and desires. "Grace was willing to do anything to find you. She's amazingly loyal and determined."

Riley's brow dented in the middle as she studied him. "You like her, don't you?"

Heat rose in his cheeks. "She's an amazing woman," he said, refusing to look toward his passenger lest she see how deeply his feelings were entangled in the pretty blonde's life.

Riley's brows rose. "Oh my God, you two had sex?"

His foot jerked off the accelerator for a moment. "Who said we had sex?" Making love to Grace after such a short amount of time together sounded insane. But they had. And it had been incredible, soul-lifting, life-affirming and Declan wanted to do it again. But he didn't want the world to know. Not yet. He didn't want anything or anyone intruding on his campaign to win over the sexy divorcee.

Riley frowned. "You didn't take advantage of her, did you?"

"No. I would never take advantage of Grace. She deserves nothing but happiness."

"I agree. But what are your intentions toward her?" Riley insisted.

"I have to state them now, even though we only met a little over a day ago?"

"Hell, yeah. Grace is my best friend. We look out for each other."

"Even though you keep secrets from her?" Declan asked.

"You know the government rules," Riley said. "Top secret means you don't even tell the ones you love. I love Grace like the sister I never had. She is my sister in my heart. She deserves to live and be happy."

Declan didn't know what the secrets were that Riley couldn't reveal, but he knew enough about Grace to know she could be the one for him. He needed more time with her. Maybe the remainder of his life. In the few hours he'd known her, he'd come to care for the woman. He'd wade through a field full of enemy snipers to free her from the bad guys.

"I agree. Grace deserves to be happy and live a long life."

"I'm glad you feel that way." Riley gave him a lopsided smile. "Her ex-husband didn't give a damn if Grace was happy as long as she made his life more comfortable and entertained his guests exactly the way he liked."

Declan's jaw hardened. "Sounds like a winner."

"He's a real jerk, and he did a number on my friend. I'm glad Grace got away from him. She's come a long way in regaining her confidence." Riley poked a finger at Declan. "Don't screw it up."

Raising his right hand, Declan nodded solemnly. "I'll do my best to make it right for Grace."

"Good. Because if you don't, you'll have to contend with me."

He nodded. "Understood." Hauling in a deep breath, he let it out slowly and then clapped his hands. "Let's go get Grace," Declan said. "But first we need a plan." He motioned for his team to pull into an empty parking lot. They all exited their vehicles and gathered around their team leader.

Declan briefed them on how they would let Riley drive into the meeting alone, but not until the team had infiltrated the location and were ready to take action.

"We have only a few minutes' lead on Riley's expected arrival.

We have to make good use of that time." Declan went to the rear of one of the Escalades and opened the back. Inside was a large plastic box containing military-grade rifles with high-powered scopes.

"It's a shame Charlie's husband is dead." Mack lifted one of the rifles out of the box and held it in his hands. "I think I would have liked him."

"He had good taste in weaponry." Gus selected an AR-15 rifle with a scope and grabbed a magazine full of rounds. He slammed the magazine into the weapon and slipped the strap over his shoulder.

Cole did the same and selected a nine-millimeter handgun, as well.

While his men armed themselves, Declan looked up the meeting location on a map application on his smartphone. They were less than a mile away. After each of Declan's team members secured a weapon and loaded it with ammunition, they synchronized their watches and took off on foot to the site. Riley would wait for fifteen minutes and then take Grace's SUV to the rendezvous location.

By the time she arrived, Declan would have his men in place.

As they reached the edge of the container yard, clouds moved in, darkening the sky and signaling a storm. Declan had the men fan out and move in, keeping a close watch out for Tangos in sniper positions atop the containers. They moved from shadow to shadow on silent feet, their urban-operations training coming back to them.

Though they didn't have the high-tech communication devices they were used to as Force Recon marines, they had their cell phones and Bluetooth earbuds to keep in touch while moving through the container yard. Before they'd entered the yard, Declan set up a conference call with all of his team, Riley included. They left the call up as they moved in.

When he and Charlie had time, he'd make sure his team had the best communications equipment and weapons. If they were going to take on tasks like the one that had presented itself in Grace and Riley, he would make sure they had the tools to be successful no matter what the assignment.

"I'm headed your way," Riley said into his earbud at the fifteen-minute mark. "ETA three minutes."

"We'll be ready," he said softly.

Mustang had point, moving through the containers ahead of the rest of the team. "I see a small office building in the middle of these building blocks," he reported.

"Any Tangos?" Declan asked.

"None so far." Mustang paused. "No, wait. I see one on top of a container near the office structure."

"Don't take him out until the rest of us get in place. We can't spook them until the exchange of hostages is underway."

"Roger," Mustang said. "I'll be ready. In the meantime, you can move forward. The other guards are on foot on the ground, near the office. I count five." He gave their locations. "Going silent. Getting too close for chatter."

Declan and the other four members of his team slipped between containers, hugging the shadows.

Gus, Cole and Snow circled around to where Mustang had indicated three of the guards were standing at the corners of the metal shipping containers.

"Bear in mind, if bullets start flying, it's possible some will ricochet off the metal," Mack warned.

Declan heard the words, but his attention was now on the office building he was almost certain held the woman he'd come to save.

No sooner did he have it in sight than Grace's SUV appeared from around a corner of containers stacked three-deep.

"Everyone in place?" Declan asked.

One by one his men checked in, careful to be quiet and not walk on each other's transmissions.

When all had reported in, Declan slipped through the increasing darkness of the murky sky, edging toward the office.

Riley pulled in, stopping short fifty yards away from the building. She sat in the SUV for a long time without opening the door.

Declan could imagine the woman working up the nerve to get out and expose herself to being shot at or nabbed before they let Grace go free.

The office door opened and four men surrounded a tall man with black hair and dark eyes. He held Grace in front of him with a handgun pressed to her temple.

His rifle tucked into his shoulder, Declan stared through the scope at the men surrounding Grace. He didn't have a clear shot yet. They were standing too close to her.

He turned his scope to Grace and his heart skipped several beats.

She walked with her shoulders back and her chin held high. The woman was not going to show those men fear.

Declan's chest swelled with pride at the same time as fear squeezed his gut. Anything could go sideways. Grace was in grave danger.

"Should I get out now?" Riley asked, pulling Declan back to the task at hand.

"No," he said. "Stay until they get far enough away from the building that they can't run back in."

"Did you forget?" Snow mentioned. "I have a grenade launcher. All I need is a clear shot."

"Hold on to that thought," Declan said. "Hopefully we won't need to destroy the office and everyone in it."

"But if we do, I'm your man," Snow said. "I have the most recent experience with this weapon."

Declan chuckled. "Okay, I'll keep that in mind. Just a reminder, our goal here isn't to blow up buildings. We're here to rescue two women. We are not in the Middle East, and explaining a grenade launcher to local authorities could get sticky."

"Roger," Snow responded. "Although I do miss blowing up stuff. Do you think we'll ever get the chance to level any buildings ever again?"

"Not anytime soon," Declan said.

Snow sighed. "Then I'll just have to make do with my rifle."

"Are you with us, Mustang?" Declan asked into his mic.

"Raring to go," Mustang responded. "What's the first order of business?"

"Be ready to take out the sniper up top," Declan answered. "Make it as quiet as you can."

"I have him in my scope," Mustang whispered.

"Okay, Riley," Declan said. "You can open your door and lean out. Tell them to let Grace go and you'll come to them."

Riley did as Declan said. She opened her door and leaned out. "Let Grace go, and I'll come willingly."

"Get out of the SUV now, or we will shoot your friend."

"If you shoot my friend, I'll run you over with my car. And don't think shooting me will help you. You still need me to open that memory card. So let her go." Riley spoke with iron-hard firmness.

"I think I'm in love," Mack said.

Declan ignored his assistant team leader's comment, his focus on the men standing near Grace. One of them led her forward and slightly in front of him, a handgun pressed to her temple, her arm twisted up behind her back. He stopped in front of the SUV where Riley sat. "Get out of the car," he said. "You won't run me over as long as I have your friend. And if you don't get out, I'll shoot her."

"What do I do?" Riley asked quietly.

"Again, tell them to let her go." Declan couldn't quite get the shot on the man holding Grace close to his chest. "Whatever you do, don't get out of the vehicle."

The man holding Grace moved the gun away from her head and fired a round into the ground. "Get out, now! Or she dies."

Declan jumped. Grace's captor appeared to be losing his patience. If he'd just move an inch more to his left...

Declan controlled his breathing though his heart raced. He didn't dare open fire until he had a very clear shot. One that didn't involve shooting Grace in the process.

Chapter Fifteen

Grace knew she had only one shot at escape. When the guy holding her shifted his weapon away from her temple, she took her chance. Ignoring the pain in the arm he had jacked up between her shoulder blades, Grace cocked her free arm and slammed her elbow into the man's gut.

He jerked his hand up, firing another round that pierced the front fender of Grace's SUV.

She twisted around, broke free of his grip and dove for the ground, rolling beneath the carriage of her SUV.

Gunfire sounded in the container yard, with the ping of bullets bouncing off metal storage boxes.

Grace lay low with her hands over the back of her neck. She couldn't tell if the gunfire was all from the men who'd held her captive, or if there were more men in the yard. Based on the number of shots fired, she suspected there were more people firing than just the men responsible for her abduction. She prayed the others were Declan and his team of defenders.

The sound of bullets hitting her car made her afraid for Riley. Her roommate needed to be down lower, out of the line of fire.

Grace inched her way beneath the chassis of the SUV to the driver's side and she poked her head out into the open. The driver's door was open. Riley lay over the seat.

For a moment, Grace was afraid Riley had been hit. "Riley! Sweetie, are you all right?"

"Grace?" Riley started to raise her head.

"Keep low, Riley. Can you get out and onto the ground beneath the SUV? It's probably safer down here."

"I don't know."

More gunfire sounded, making it feel like a war zone.

Grace wasn't giving up. She'd finally found her roommate. She sure as hell wasn't going to let her die from a gunshot wound.

Shouts sounded and footsteps pounded across the pavement.

Grace rolled over and glanced toward the front of the vehicle. The man who'd most recently pointed a gun to her temple lay on the ground in front of the vehicle, a pool of blood forming beside his head.

Usually very forgiving of transgressions, Grace couldn't find it in her heart to forgive any of the men who'd held her hostage that day, or who had broken into her apartment. She hoped they burned in hell.

Again, she turned her attention to Riley. "Come on, Riley, we need to get to somewhere safe. You have to come down here."

Staying as low as possible, Riley turned in her seat behind the steering wheel and glanced down at Grace. "You don't know how glad I am to see you."

Grace smiled. "I could say the same, but we can't waste time. Come down here and slide under the SUV."

Riley grabbed the keys from the ignition and tossed them to Grace.

Grace caught them and tucked them into her pocket. Then she eased Riley's feet onto the running boards as she slid out of the SUV and to the ground. Once there, Riley dropped all the way down until she lay flat against the pavement. She tucked her arms beneath her and rolled under the chassis.

Grace rolled in beside her roommate and waited for the opportunity to run for the shelter of one of the containers. She low-crawled to the rear of the vehicle and gauged the distance between the SUV and the nearest metal storage box. It might as well have been the span from one wall of the Grand Canyon to the other. To cross it would put them out in the open long enough for a bullet to catch at least one of them.

She turned back to Riley and gasped.

Her roommate slid backward out from beneath the SUV, her fingernails digging into the pavement but finding no purchase.

The man Grace had thought was lying dead in his own pool of blood had a hold of Riley's ankle and he was pulling her out from beneath the SUV.

Grace tucked and rolled toward Riley, determined to get to her before the gunman had a chance to pull her all the way out from beneath the vehicle.

By the time she spiraled out from beneath the car, Grace was too late.

Her captor had Riley in a choke hold around her throat. "Make a move, and I'll kill her."

Grace didn't hesitate; she swept her leg to the side as hard as she could, catching the man in the shin. His legs buckled and he flailed his arms, releasing his hold on Riley.

Riley dove forward, out of the man's reach.

The dark-haired, dark-eyed man hit the ground hard.

Grace scooted back to where Riley sat against the side of the SUV. She gathered her friend in her arms and held her close as the battle raged around her. "I was wrong. Get back into the SUV."

"I can't." Riley shook so hard, her teeth rattled.

"Climb into the vehicle," Grace ordered. "I'm getting you out of here."

Riley rallied, pulled herself up into the SUV and over the console to the passenger side.

Grace had to wait for her to get all the way across before she could climb up. She'd placed her foot on the running board when she heard a shout in the distance and another voice sounded behind her.

"I should have killed you from the start."

Tired to her bones, Grace turned to face the barrel of a handgun.

The man she'd just kicked in the shins held the weapon, standing a little too far away for her to knock it out of his hands or slam the door on his arm. This was it. Her number was up.

What she needed now was a miracle.

DECLAN WAS TOO far away from the action to help Grace when she made her move. As soon as she dove for the ground, Declan fired on the man who'd been holding her. Declan had to trust Grace had gotten out of the line of fire, because as soon as he took the shot, all hell broke loose.

"Get the sniper," he called out to Mustang.

Gunfire rang out.

A man dropped from the corner of a stack that was three containers high. With the sniper out of the game, they were on a more level playing field. But there were plenty of places to take cover with the heavy metal container boxes to hide behind. The trouble with the boxes was that they didn't absorb all bullets. Some of the rounds ricocheted off the metal sides and continued on to strike other things.

Declan hoped those other things weren't his teammates or the women.

He aimed his weapon at the men near the small office building. They took up covered positions behind other cars in the parking lot and it became an all-out war. Instead of hiding in trenches, they took cover behind vehicles and slung bullets back and forth.

These men weren't regular Joes off the street. They were highly skilled killers with weapons as impressive as Mr. Halverson's collection. "Take your time," he cautioned his team. "Conserve your ammunition. You'll get the chance to take them out when they start making mistakes."

Declan's team knew how to tease them into expending ammunition. They fired enough to keep the enemy firing until the numbers of bullets dwindled.

A shadow moved by the office building.

Declan lined it up in his scope and discovered a man hiding behind a pillar. He kept his sights on the target and waited.

The man held up a rifle and aimed at Declan.

Declan pulled the trigger first. The man fell and lay still against the ground.

That's when he saw Riley being held by the man he thought he'd already killed.

His heart seized in his chest and he shifted his aim. But he couldn't shoot without taking out Riley. Then the man toppled sideways, and Riley dove beneath Grace's SUV.

Declan shifted his attention to the ground where Grace lay on her side, with her leg outstretched.

He chuckled.

She'd taken the man down with a sweep of her leg.

Grace and Riley huddled together for a moment on the ground and then Riley climbed into the vehicle.

Good. They could get in and drive away, out of range of any gunmen.

Then he noticed the man Grace had knocked down reach for the handgun he'd dropped.

"Grace, watch out!" he cried. He raised his rifle to his shoulder and stared through the scope, praying his aim would be true and swift.

The man stood with his handgun pointed at Grace.

Declan held his breath and squeezed the trigger.

The sound of his rifle firing seemed to be echoed by the blast of another weapon.

For a long moment, the man holding the gun and Grace remained exactly as they'd been before Declan pulled the trigger.

Then the gunman crumpled to the pavement. A half second later, Grace slipped to the ground, as well.

Declan's heart stopped beating.

"That was the last one down. All bogeys have been accounted for," Mack said into Declan's Bluetooth earbud.

Declan couldn't understand the words over the buzzing in his ears. He staggered to his feet and ran toward the SUV.

"Grace!" he called out, his eyes burning, his heart breaking into a million pieces. He couldn't see her face, couldn't tell if her eyes were open. Had she been injured? Or killed?

He ran as fast as his feet would carry him, sliding down on his knees when he came to a halt in front of Grace.

Her eyes were open. By all that was good in the world, her eyes were open.

Tears stung the backs of his eyelids when he realized she wasn't dead.

"Grace," he said and pulled her into his arms. "Are you hurt?

Were you shot? Tell me you're all right. I think I died a thousand deaths in the past thirty seconds." He pushed her to arm's length, his gaze raking over her. "Talk to me."

She laughed and shook her head. "I would, but you wouldn't shut up long enough." Grace smiled up at him. "I'm okay. But after all we'd been through today, and then nearly being shot in the chest, I just couldn't stand anymore." She cupped his cheek. "I'm sorry I scared you, but I was a little scared myself for a while there."

He bracketed her face between his palms and stared into her eyes. "You are the most amazing woman I've ever known. I want to hold you, kiss you and shake you for scaring years off my life." He laughed and pulled her close again. "Promise me something, will ya?" he said against her ear.

She shivered at the way his breath on her neck made her all hot and aware of him as a perfect male specimen. "Promise you what?" she said, her voice ragged, breathy with desire.

"Promise me you won't get cornered by a gunman ever again. I don't think I can handle it."

She smiled and pressed her lips to his. "I'll do my best to keep that kind of promise. Trust me, I don't ever want to be at the business end of a handgun anytime in the rest of my life."

"And promise me, now that we found your friend, you aren't going to disappear out of my life. I think I could fall for a girl who can defend herself and her friend. You're my hero." He kissed the tip of her nose and then brushed her lips with his.

"Are you kidding? I'd be dead right now if you hadn't taken out that guy. At that precise moment, I was in the market for a miracle, and you came through with it." She wrapped her arms around his neck and pulled him down for a toe-curling, heart-stopping kiss that rocked him to his very core.

When the kiss ended, Declan laughed. "Yes, I think I could very easily fall in love with you."

"Good," she said against his mouth, "because I'm well on my way there myself."

He leaned back, a frown tugging his brow downward. "You'd want to be with a guy who has a dishonorable discharge on his record?"

"Only if it was you. What I've learned about you so far is that you're a straight shooter and you believe in fighting for what's right. Whatever you did to get kicked out had to have been for all the right reasons. I know that in my heart."

"For the record, I didn't follow orders. It meant taking a shot through a bride and a groom on their wedding day and through babies strapped to Taliban cowards." He shook his head. "I refused to shoot through the innocents. A particularly bad terrorist got away because my teammates and I refused a direct order to take out the target no matter what. That refusal, plus a politician's agenda, got us released from military service."

"I'm sure if you had appealed the decision, they would have overturned it," she said.

He shook his head. "It's a done deal. Besides, the guys and I have jobs we can stand behind. We're going to help Charlie fight for truth and what's right."

"And maybe find time to see me?" Grace added. "I'd really like to see you again, even if your assignment is over."

"You can count on that. I might even take you out to dinner and dancing."

"You really know how to sweep a woman off her feet."

Declan pulled her into his arms. "I think you've proven you can sweep a man off his feet. You've blown me away in the short amount of time we've known each other. I look forward to more time with you."

"Do you think you two could break it up long enough to explain to the local police why there are dead men lying around a container yard?" Mack stood over them, shaking his head.

Declan pushed to his feet and reached down to take Grace's hand. "Time to call Charlie. Let's wrap this up. I have a date with a beautiful woman."

He pulled Grace up and into his arms. "I'm glad I found you on that sidewalk in the middle of an attack."

"Me, too," Grace said. "I can't even imagine what might have happened had you not been there that day. If I didn't believe in fate before, I do so now."

Epilogue

Charlie sat at her desk in her Washington, DC, mansion, staring at the men sitting and standing in the massive office. "Now that you have located Miss Lansing, and the people responsible for abducting my new assistant Grace from the bank have all been accounted for and jailed, what should we work on next?"

"We need to ramp up with communications equipment, first thing," Declan said. "And I don't think it's over for Riley Lansing. She seems to think the guy behind the sales won't stop with the death of her supervisor, Moretti."

"Any guesses as to who is behind the sale?" Charlie asked.

Declan shook his head. "No. And since Riley is the only one who can decode the memory card, they will continue to target Miss Lansing until they get what they paid for, regardless of her FBI handlers."

Charlie nodded. "Sounds like we still have a task. We need to provide protection for Miss Lansing." Charlie looked around at the six men in her office. "Anyone here want to take on the responsibility of being a bodyguard to a highly intelligent young engineer?"

Mack stepped forward. "I'll do it."

Declan clapped his friend and second in command on his shoulder. "You've got this. And we'll have your back, should you need us," Declan said. "And my gut tells me you're going to need us."

Mack snorted. "And I thought fighting the Taliban was difficult. I have a feeling Miss Lansing will give me a run for my money."

* * * * *

Chapter One

It was surreal, staring at a photo of himself and feeling as if he were looking at a stranger. No, that wasn't exactly right, Jarrett Ross amended, studying the framed rodeo picture on the wall of his father's home office. The word *stranger* implied he didn't know the dark-haired cowboy, that he had no feelings about him one way or the other.

A wave of contempt hit him as he studied the cocky smile and silvery, carefree gaze. *Selfish SOB.* Six months ago, his only concerns had been which events to ride and which appreciative buckle-bunny to celebrate with after he won. A lot had changed since then.

Six months ago, Vicki wasn't in a wheelchair.

"Jarrett?"

He turned as Anne Ross entered the room. He'd been so mired in regret he'd almost forgotten he was waiting for his mother. Dread welled as she closed the door behind her. Did they need the privacy because there was more bad news to discuss? He wanted to sink into the leather chair behind the desk and bury his face in his hands. But he remained standing, braced for whatever life threw at them next.

"How did Dad's appointment go?" Jarrett hadn't been able to accompany his parents to the hospital this afternoon. There was too much to do at the Twisted R now that he was the only one working the ranch. But even without the countless tasks necessary to keep the place running, he would have stayed behind in case Vicki needed him—not that his sister voluntarily sought out his company these days.

"You know your father. He's a terrible patient." Anne rolled her eyes, but her attempt to lighten the situation didn't mask her concern. "Overall, the doctor says we're lucky. He's recovering as well as can be expected from the heart attack and the surgery. The thing is…"

Jarrett gripped the back of the chair, waiting for the other boot to drop.

His mother came forward and sat down in the chair across from him, the stress of the past few months plain on her face. Even more telling was the slump of her shoulders. She'd always had a ramrod-straight posture, whether sitting in a saddle or waltzing across a dance floor with her husband.

"I have to get your father off this ranch," she said bluntly. "I've been after him for years to slow down, to get away for a few days. I even tried to talk him into selling the place."

That revelation stunned Jarrett. He'd never realized his mom's complaints about the demands of ranch life were serious. He'd thought her occasional grumbling was generic and innocuous, like jokes about hating Mondays. People griped about it all the time, but no one actually suggested removing Monday from the calendar. It was impossible to imagine Gavin Ross anywhere but at the Twisted R. Not sure how to respond, he paced restlessly around the office. Despite the many hours he'd spent here over the past month, it still felt like trespassing. As if his father should be the one sitting behind the desk making the decisions that would affect the family.

"Your dad refuses to accept that he's not in his twenties anymore," his mom continued. "At the rate he's going, he'll work himself to death! And after the added stress of Vicki's accident…"

Guilt sliced through him. Was his dad's heart attack one more thing to trace back to that night in July? His mind echoed with the metallic jangling of the keys he'd tossed to his younger sister. He hadn't gone with her because a blonde named Tammy—or Taylor?—had been whispering in his ear, saying that as impressive as he'd been in eight seconds, she couldn't wait to see what magic he could work in an hour's time.

Jarrett pushed away the shameful memory. "So you and Dad want to take a few days of vacation?" he asked, leaning against the corner of the desk closest to her.

"A few weeks, actually. I haven't discussed it with him yet, but Dr. Wayne agrees that it's a good idea. My cousin has a very nice cabin near Lake Tahoe that she's been offering to let us use for years, and Dr. Wayne said he could give us the name of a good cardiologist in the area. Just in case."

When you were recovering from open-heart surgery, "just in case" wasn't nearly as casual as it sounded.

"Your father is mule-headed. Now that he's starting to feel a little better, he'll try to return to his usual workload. I can't let him do that. He may seem larger than life, but he's not invincible." Her gaze shifted downward. "And…without us as a buffer, Vicki would naturally turn to you for company and assistance."

The soft words were like a pitchfork to the gut. His sister, younger than him by almost seven years, had grown up idolizing Jarrett. Now his parents had to evacuate Texas just to force her to speak to him again.

"She's going to forgive you." Anne reached over to clasp his hand. "The drunk driver who plowed into the truck is to blame, not you."

He wanted to believe her, but it was his fault Vicki had been on the road. They'd had plans to grab a late dinner. Between his travel on the rodeo circuit and her being away for her freshman year of college, they'd barely seen each other since Christmas. But instead of catching up with his kid sister as promised, he'd ditched her in favor of getting laid. Vicki had been trapped amid twisted metal and broken glass when she should have been sitting in some restaurant booth, debating between chicken-fried steak and a rack of ribs. She'd always had a Texas-sized appetite, but her athletic hobbies kept her trim and fit.

Past tense. She no longer had much of an appetite. And although the doctors assured her that, with physical therapy, she would walk again, it would be a long damn time before she played softball or went to a dance club with her sorority sisters. She hadn't even been able to return to campus for the start of the new semester in August, another consequence that ate at him. Unlike Jarrett, who'd earned a degree with a combination of community-college courses and online classes, Vicki had been accepted into one of the best universities in the state. How much academic momentum was she losing?

Anne blamed Gavin's heart attack on years of working too hard and his stubborn insistence that "deep-fried" was a valid food group. But it was no coincidence that the man had collapsed during one of Vicki's multiple surgeries. The stress of his daughter's ordeal had nearly killed him.

"Jarrett." Anne's scolding tone was one he knew well from childhood. "I see you beating yourself up. You have to stop. If not for yourself, then for me."

"I'm fine," he lied. She was shouldering enough burden already without fretting over his well-being, too. "I was just processing the logistics of running the Twisted R while taking care of Vicki. I'll figure it out. You and Dad should definitely go."

"Thank you. Be sure to voice your support when he objects to the idea." She pursed her lips, considering. "We probably have a better shot at convincing him if you're *not* handling Vicki and the ranch by yourself. What if we found a part-time housekeeper who could act as her companion? Or, ideally, even someone with medical experience. My friend Pam's a retired nurse. I can ask her about home health care."

"Are we sure that's in the budget?" The mountain of medical bills was already high enough that Gavin had recently let

go of their sole ranch hand after helping him find a job on another spread. Gavin insisted the Twisted R could function as
a father-and-son operation if Jarrett was available to help full-
time. No more rodeos for the foreseeable future.

Or ever. He hadn't competed since the night of Vicki's accident, and it was hard to imagine enjoying it again. Everything
he'd loved—the adrenaline, the admiration of the spectators—
seemed shallow in light of what his sister and dad had suffered.

"I'm not suggesting we hire a long-term employee," she said.
"Just some help for a month or less. We have plenty of space.
Maybe with Pam's help we can find someone temporarily willing to accept low pay in exchange for room and board. There
could be someone young who needs the experience and a rec-
ommendation."

His mother made it sound almost reasonable, as if there were
lots of people who would work practically for free and wanted
to move in with a surly nineteen-year-old and a rodeo cowboy
who'd taken early retirement. *What are the odds?*

Then again, they had to be due for some good luck.

"Okay," he agreed. "Call Pam and see what she says."

Meanwhile, he'd cross his fingers that his mom's friend knew
someone who was truly desperate for a job.

"WHAT THE HELL do you mean I'm out of a job?" In her head,
Sierra Bailey heard the familiar refrain of her mother's voice
chiding her. Unladylike language was one of Muriel Bailey's
pet peeves. *I just got fired. Screw "ladylike."*

Eileen Pearce, seated at the head of the conference table,
sucked in a breath at Sierra's outburst. It was too bad Eileen
and Muriel didn't live in the same city—the two women could
get together for weekly coffee and commiserate about Sierra's
behavior. "The board takes inappropriate relationships with patients very seriously, Ms. Bailey."

"There was no relationship!" Except, apparently, in Lloyd
Carson's mind. Bodily contact between patient and physical

therapist was a necessity, not an attempt at seduction. Sierra had never once thought of Lloyd in a sexual manner, but he'd apparently missed that memo. The man had unexpectedly kissed her during their last session. Which, in turn, led to his wife angrily demanding Sierra's head on a platter.

Taking a deep breath, Sierra battled her temper. "Patients become infatuated with medical professionals all the time. It's a form of misplaced gratitude and—"

"Yes, but in the year you've been with us, we've had multiple complaints about you. Granted, not of this nature, but your track record is flawed. Perhaps if you'd listened on previous occasions when I tried to impress upon you the importance of professional decorum…" Eileen paused with an expression of mock sympathy.

Comprehension dawned. This wasn't about Lloyd Carson and his romantic delusions. The board of directors had been looking for an excuse to get rid of Sierra. She felt foolish, not having seen the dismissal coming, but she truly believed she was good at her job.

Was she mouthy and abrasive? Occasionally.

All right, regularly. One might even argue, frequently. But sometimes PT patients needed a well-intentioned kick to the rear more than they needed to be coddled. *Lord knows I did.*

At twelve years old, Sierra had been a pampered rich girl whose parents treated her with a much different standard than her three rough-and-tumble brothers, as if she were fragile. Dr. Frederick Bailey and his wife, Muriel, had raised their sons with aspirations of global domination; they'd raised their daughter with the promise that she'd be a beautiful Houston debutante someday. No one had challenged her until the gruff physiotherapist who'd helped her after she'd been thrown from a horse.

He'd taught her to challenge herself, a lesson she still appreciated fifteen years later. The side effect was that she also tended to challenge authority, a habit the hospital's board of directors resented.

Given the barely concealed hostility in Eileen's icy blue gaze, it was a miracle Sierra had lasted this long. *You're partially to blame here, Bailey.* While she'd deny with every breath in her body that her conduct with Lloyd Carson had ever been flirtatious or unprofessional, Sierra could have been more of a team player. She could have made an effort to care about occupational politics.

As Eileen went over the legal details of the termination, Sierra's mind wandered to the future. Her savings account was skimpier than she'd like, but she was a trained specialist. She'd land on her feet. It was a point of pride that she'd been making her way for years, without asking her parents for money.

You'll find a new position. And when you do? Stay under the radar instead of racking up a file of grievances. In the interests of her career, Sierra could be detached and diplomatic.

Probably.

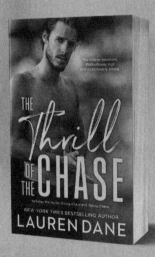 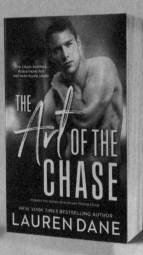

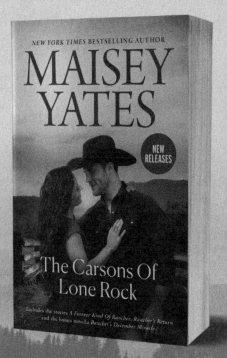

Subscribe and fall in love with a Mills & Boon series today!

You'll be among the first to read stories delivered to your door monthly and enjoy great savings.